I0748459

CHINA TIDAL WAVE

People's Republic of China (PRC): Administrative Divisions
RUSSIA
RUSSIA
MONGOLIA
Urumqi
XINJIANG UYGHUR A. R.
INNER MONGOLIA A. R.
HEILONGJIANG
Harbin
Vladivostok
JILIN
Changchun
Shenyang
LIAONING
BEIJING
KOREA
Seoul
Tokyo
JAPAN
GANSU
NINGXIA
HUI A. R.
Yinchuan
Hohhot
HEBEI
Shijiazhuang
TIANJIN
Aksai Chin is claimed by India.
QINGHAI
Xining
Lanzhou
Taiyuan
SHANXI
Jinan
SHAN-DONG
Xi'an
SHAANXI
Zhengzhou
HENAN
JIANG-SU
TIBET A. R.
Lhasa
SICHUAN
Chengdu
CHONGQING
HUBEI
Wuhan
Hefei
ANHUI
Nanjing
SHANGHAI
Hangzhou
ZHE-JIANG
INDIA
Most of the area of the Indian state of Arunachal Pradesh is claimed by China.
Changsha
HUNAN
Nanchang
JIANGXI
GUIZHOU
Guiyang
Fuzhou
FUJIAN
Taipei
TAIWAN
Kunming
YUNNAN
BURMA
GUANGXI
ZHUANG A. R.
Nanning
GUANGDONG
Guangzhou
HONG KONG
MACAU
HAINAN
Haikou
Province
Autonomous Region
Municipality
Special Administrative Region
The People's Republic of China and the Republic of China both claim the Paracel and Spratly Islands, not shown on this map. The PRC controls the Paracels (also claimed by Vietnam), while the Spratlys are disputed among several neighbouring countries.

CHINA
TIDAL WAVE

— A NOVEL —

ᘛ

Wang Lixiong

Translated from the Chinese by

ANTON PLATERO

GLOBAL
ORIENTAL

CHINA TIDAL WAVE
Wang Lixiong

Translated from the Chinese by Anton Platero

First published 2008 by
GLOBAL ORIENTAL LTD
PO Box 219
Folkestone
Kent CT20 2WP
UK

www.globaloriental.co.uk

ISBN 978-1-901903-50-2

British Library Cataloguing in Publication Data
A CIP catalogue entry for this book is available from the British Library

Set in Bembo 11 on 12.5pt by Mark Heslington, Scarborough, North Yorks
Printed and bound in England by Athenaeum Press, Gateshead, Tyne & Wear

Preface to the English Edition

ଔ

This novel presents a new view of China quite different from that of the world today. It describes the collapse of the Chinese state and society and the flight from China of several hundred million refugees that becomes a disaster for the whole world.

Fifteen years ago, when *Yellow Peril*★ was first written, I expected that the events I visualized then would happen quite soon. Yet today, everyone is talking about the 'rise of China', and the state is exceptionally stable. Yet it is precisely because of this stability that I continually have a sense of impending crisis.

In China today, apart from the state, there is no organized force that has the power to create an integrated society. The normal constituents of civil society: ideology, opposition groups, the national army – which in many ways can have this function – if they have not already died a natural death, have been banned, or have been so oppressed that they could not survive. In the absence of any challenge or opposition, stability is hardly surprising.

The crucial question is: what will happen if this stable political power does, in fact, collapse? Without it, all the crises are likely to explode at once. Without an integrating force, this will be the beginning of the break-up of China.

The description in this book is of course fictional. It may happen differently. But the collapse of an autocratic regime will happen sooner or later and is often unexpected (as in the case of the break-up of the Soviet Union). Therefore, I consider the 'Yellow Peril' not far distant and may occur at any moment.

This book has long been known to a large number of Chinese in the world and it is being continually reprinted and distributed, including in the mainland of China where it is still banned. I have always hoped that Western readers would be able to read it, not only because other countries apart from China are bound up with the events I have described. But also the people of the whole world can help prevent the catastrophe for China and the world from happening.

WANG LIXIONG

[★ The Chinese title is *Huang Huo*, meaning 'Yellow Peril']

THE CHARACTERS

(In alphabetical order)

ଓ

Bai Ling: Huang Shi-ke's secretary.

Big Ox: protégé of Ouyang Zhong-hua, & commander of the 'Green Guard.'

Chen Pan: A biologist. Ouyang Zhong-hua's secretary and lover.

Commander Bai ('The Fox'): Commander of the Nanjing Area Military Command.

Ding Da-hai: submarine commander.

Gui-zhi: a peasant woman fom Shanxi Province, an old friend and lover of Shi Ge.

Huang Shi-ke: Deputy Governor of Fujian Province.

Li Ke-ming: deputy chief of security at the Three Gorges Dam construction site.

Li Liang: Li Ke-ming's cousin.

Liu Ya-ji: a rich merchant of Fuzhou.

Long-kou: Former member of the Special Training Brigade. Electronic engineer.

Lu Hao-ran: Premier of the State Council (Prime Minister), later General Secretary of the Central Committee of the Chinese Communist Party.

Major-General Su: Deputy Chief of Staff of the Nanjing Area Military Command.

Ouyang Zhong-hua: leader of Chinese environmentalists, writer.

Shasha: Chen Pan's 'child'.

Shen Di: Colonel. Confidential agent of Wang Feng.

Shi Ge: Head of Unit Sixteen.

The Actress: Zhou Chi's disciple and assistant.

The Chairman: veteran of the revolution, former Vice-Chairman of Military Commission of the Chinese Communist Party.

The Leftist: Nickname of the Chief of Political Security.

The Major: Japanese hit man.

The Sage: member of the Green movement and Director of Taibaishan Base

The Secretary General: of the Central Committee of the Chinese Communist Party (not named), also President of China.

Wang Feng: Lieutenant-General, Deputy Secretary General of the Military Commission

Xing Tuo-yu: a leader of the People's Front

Ying-ying: 'the Chairman's' daughter

Zhou Chi: Master of *qigong*. Director of National *Qigong* Association. Chairman of the All-China Qigong Association

1

Beijing: Tiananmen Square – Tokyo – The Yellow River – Beijing – Western Hills – Shandong Peninsular: Naval Base 201 – Beijing – A conference room in Zhongnanhai – Yellow River flooded area – Beijing: Zhonghan Park

ᴓ

Beijing: Tiananmen Square

A vibrant, twanging sound filled the air in the semi-darkness of the street, like a background musical to a scene of horror. It came from a taut steel wire strung across the road at a calculated height. Like a scythe, it had cut off the heads of the people standing in the back of a truck as it raced past.

In the headlights of the truck that had managed to stop a few yards behind, Shi Ge could see the blood spurting out at different heights. Though he had never experienced war at first hand, he had often seen dead bodies, but never had he witnessed such a blood-curdling spectacle; not even here on Tiananmen Square during the massacre of June Fourth in 1989. The street between the two trucks was scattered with severed heads. One of them had hit the front wheel of his bicycle. The head of someone with long hair, clenched teeth. Two Chinese characters meaning 'reverse the verdict', written in black ink on his forehead, looking like two eyes. There was a smell of blood.

As soon as he could move—still feeling that he was living in a nightmare—Shi Ge began to direct those who had rushed up to help. Both trucks had been full of supporters of the People's Front on their way to reinforce their comrades in the square. The survivors were so shocked that Shi Ge had to shout at them before they would react.

The television relay van arrived much sooner than the police. It was fifteen minutes past midnight, but a crowd soon gathered, lights went on in houses along the street and heads appeared at windows. As TV and press floodlights were switched on, Shi Ge backed away and prepared to leave discreetly. There was blood on his hands and his heart was pounding.

The crowd buzzed with noisy speculation. Many people said that it must have been the Democracy Front who put up the wire to prevent the rival group from bringing up reinforcements. At that time, the two hostile factions were both trying to take possession of the Monument in Memory of the Heroes of the Revolution which stood in the square, in order to become the symbol of the movement to 'reverse the verdict' on June Fourth. The television journalists excitedly transmitted this rumour to the public and searched for people to confirm it.

When he became an involuntary witness to this drama, Shi Ge had been on his way home after stopping at Tiananmen Square to check on the situation there before going abroad. Now his bicycle had been trampled on and he could no longer ride it.

'This old man was the nearest.' Several bare-chested young men pointed to Shi Ge, and the lights and cameras turned on him. Dressed as he was, they took him for a worker. 'Tell us what you saw.'

The reporters all stared at him. Shi Ge turned his face away. This was the kind of awkward situation he dreaded. He could do no more than gesticulate vaguely and try to move away.

'Hey! Where are you off to?' He was now surrounded by a crowd of people, and someone took hold of him. The hot thundery weather intensified the smell of blood and sweat. Short and stocky, he was hidden in the middle of the crowd. There were beads of sweat on his face. He kept turning his head to avoid the lights and cameras.

The press fired questions at him like fire-crackers. They seemed to be neutral questions, but he could easily detect the provocation behind them. He was 'on the inside' and knew that the media had received their orders, and were already slanting their coverage accordingly. When this bloody scene appeared on the television screens a few hints would be enough to convince people that it was the work of the Democracy Front. In the present stalemate between the two factions this would be pouring oil on the flames, and add to people's hatred for the pro-democracy movement. There was nothing he could do about that, but if he was shown on television with blood on his hands, it would be much more difficult for him to explain his presence.

A tall young man with a self-confident 'rebel-and-proud-of-it' air about him quickly snatched a hard-cover pass from the small bag Shi Ge was carrying, catching him unawares, and held it up at arm's length so that Shi Ge could not reach it.

'Hm, a staff pass…' A pause while he examined it in the TV lights. 'to the Office of the Central Committee of the Communist Party.'

Everyone was astounded. What could such an insignificant looking man have to do with the Central Committee? The TV reporters immediately stopped questioning him and the cameras and lights moved away. Shi Ge knew that he need not worry about them any more, but other problems were going to be much more difficult to deal with. The TV stations were tools of the Party and would not dare tangle with him. Not so the people around him. Anyone connected with the Centre would be sure to arouse their suspicion and hostility. He could no longer prevaricate. In such a situation the slightest mistake could turn their hatred into violence. More and more pointed questions were thrown at him as he explained that he was merely passing by and had stopped to adjust his bicycle. He had a pass to the Central Committee but was dressed like a worker on night-shift. He had a bicycle rather than a car, and even the bicycle was in a pitiful state. Anyone with the slightest imagination would take him for some sort of secret agent, a plain-clothes policeman or someone with a secret assignment...perhaps to stretch a steel wire across the street?

'I work in the kitchens,' he said finally. 'There are cooks in the Central Committee building as well, you know.' They did not believe him. How could he explain why he did not look like 'an official?' He had to play for time and hope the police would soon arrive. Hardly anyone got away without cuts and bruises from these 'citizens' interrogations,' very common in Beijing these days.

The police were a long time coming, but a vehicle belonging to the People's Front drove up like the wind. The first thing Shi Ge had done just after the bloody scene had been to send someone to phone the police, but there was still no sound of sirens. This surely meant that the steel wire had been no ordinary steel wire. It must have been connected with someone who could give orders to the police, and even to the media. The TV relay van had arrived very rapidly. If the police had come first the whole area would have been sealed off and the TV teams would have had difficulty getting close enough to begin their insidious coverage. Nor would the car carrying the People's Front leaders have been able to get through and react to this murderous provocation by calling for immediate revenge and the blood of their rivals.

The interrogators pushed Shi Ge to one side and everyone went to see what the new commotion was about. A youngish man was shouting to the People's Front supporters to keep calm, and warning the TV teams and the reporters against using this incident to frighten people: 'This is a plot to make the two Fronts fight each other and destroy the democratic movement.'

This man, whose name was Xing Tuo-yu, was the chief commander of the People's Front and a well-known figure in the democratic movement. Many reports, including confidential government reports that Shi Ge had seen, described him as a hothead, but the reality was more complex. After listening for a while, Shi Ge decided that this was the moment to get away. But first he must retrieve his pass. It gave him access to the nerve centre of government and to lose it would be very serious. It was not going to be easy, and might get him into more trouble. The man who had taken the pass now seized him as well and handed both over to a People's Front picket saying 'This is a very suspicious character.'

A whole convoy of police cars finally arrived while Shi Ge and a sack were being put into a jeep, which accelerated away, ignoring the police loudspeaker ordering everyone to remain where they were for questioning.

The headquarters of the People's Front was in a large building with light showing in all the windows. Posters covered the facade and hung from the roof, flapping in the wind. Inside someone was making an impassioned speech. As soon as the jeep drew up it started to pour with rain and all the people outside pushed their way into the building for shelter. There was paper everywhere, a choking cloud of cigarette smoke and the smell of sweat and neglected toilets. Everyone spoke very loudly. The chaos was unimaginable. Shi Ge's escorts did not even know where to take him and made him squat with several others in the corridor with his hands on his head.

At his feet he noticed an out-of-date copy of *Taodafen*, which had become the most popular magazine in the capital, after a compromising photograph, taken abroad, of the leader of the Democracy Front in the company of a prostitute had been published in the first issue. The magazine's title and purpose was 'muck-raking.' At first it had targeted high officials and the power aristocracy, but recently it had become involved in the struggle between the two factions. The majority of popular political organizations were divided along the same lines: the pro-democracy movement which had revived not long ago, was already splitting into hostile factions.

Shi Ge considered that the Tiananmen massacre on June Fourth 1989 had created an impasse from which Chinese politics had never since escaped. Some people regarded it as a national dishonour that could never be wiped out. For others perhaps, a long-awaited opportunity, or else a sharp double-edged sword. Sooner or later there would have to be a reckoning. As the old generation of leaders gradually disappeared, the demand for 'reversing the verdict' would become even more insistent. Already the authorities were more tolerant. Although there had been no public announcement of a change of policy, the government did little to curb illegal organizations, demonstrations and publications, which had previously been considered as a great threat. People who not long ago had been called 'the June Fourth thugs' had been released from prison, and those who had fled abroad and founded the Democracy Front had been allowed to return. These were unprecedented concessions.

With some pressure from abroad, a movement for 'reversing the verdict' had grown, but already it was divided. Most of the leaders of the People's Front had been arrested and sentenced after June Fourth. Many of them had spent years in prison and suffered a lot. They believed that even before June Fourth, the leaders of the Democracy Front had planned to back out, appropriate the funds of the movement and become residents of the USA, where they could enjoy the publicity and a comfortable life and bask in the wave of international sympathy. Now they were hurrying back to China to pick up the fruit. They tended to be arrogant and ambitious, and regarded themselves as natural leaders; but were really a new aristocracy, cut off from Chinese reality, opportunists who adopted Western ways in order to impress. China did not need such opportunists, Shi Ge reflected.

The People's Front on the other hand, had considerable support among the workers and the urban population. Yet it was the rival Democracy Front, active for seven years abroad that had become the symbol of the pro-democracy movement. It accused the People's Front of lacking theory and a long-term view, of not understanding world trends and—more important—being incapable of reforming China since they had no direct experience of a democratic system. Disagreements of this kind rapidly degenerated into personal attacks. When *Taodafen* published defamatory photographs the Democracy Front replied by publishing all the evidence and 'confessions' of their rivals after their arrest, and a list of people they had implicated.

The hubbub in the entrance hall increased and mingled with the sound of someone being beaten and cries of pain. A member of the Workers' Patrols that were active during the curfew which followed June Fourth, now head of a Residents' Committee, had been seized and brought here. It was several years since those he had reported to the police had been executed, but the hatred of their relatives was as strong as ever. A widow wanted to rip his tongue out and his daughter was on her knees pleading for his life. A common scene these days. Today's government bulletin had reported that thirteen people had been executed that afternoon in similar circumstances. Shi Ge could not see what was going on, but in the tumult of hatred he heard the soft yet firm voice of a woman trying to calm people and save the man's life. She must be beautiful, he thought, or at least attractive to many men. Having got them to listen to her she turned away and asked,

'What about these people?' pointing to those squatting in the passageway. She Ge felt that the voice was somehow familiar. There was a faint, pleasant fragrance in the air.

'Citizens' arrests,' said the guard respectfully. 'There has not been time to interrogate them yet.'

'Have you set up a court?'

'No, we don't want to damp down people's enthusiasm.'

'I think you should lead, not just follow the masses.'

The guard did not reply.

'At least you should not allow this to happen: the man's covered with blood!'

She Ge, who had squatted for far too long, struggled to his feet, and the woman stretched out to support him. Yes, she was beautiful, and not that faultless beauty that sometimes goes with a proud and domineering character.

She cannot have been more than thirty, and had slightly curly hair, large eyes and a rather sad expression. She was simply and unpretentiously dressed as one who is indifferent to the opinion of others, and she wore flat shoes. Her appearance, as well as her voice, seemed familiar.

She looked him up and down. 'If you were not here and not covered with blood I would take you for another man called Shi Ge.'

'There is no other man called Shi Ge, I have got blood on me and I am here.'

'My name is Chen Pan,' said the woman. Shi Ge could still not place her. 'I went to Cangzhou to call on you, because Ouyang Zhong-hua had been arrested.'

Of course. She was Ouyang's secretary. She had been working under cover as a nurse in Nuclear Protection and most of her face had been concealed by a mask. At the time he had hardly noticed her. Security had arranged for her to be Ouyang Zhong-hua's secretary—and also his lover. Much as he disliked such mixing of roles Shi Ge had agreed to get Ouyang released. In any case, the accident at the nuclear power station had caused immense damage and to lead a protest of local people was no crime.

Ouyang Zhong-hua was famous and had written several books which had caused something of a sensation in the country; he was also a leading figure in the Chinese Association for the Protection of the Environment. After June Fourth, when political control was very tight, the Association was the only source of opinions different from those of the government. Its only concern was to prevent the government from 'tearing off its Green mask'. Even insincere concern for the environment was better than nothing. The Association had survived and even gained a considerable influence throughout the country, as well as international recognition. The previous year Ouyang had been awarded the world Greenpeace Prize.

In the recent political upsurge the Association had played a moderating role; apart from announcing its support for 'reversing the verdict', it had done nothing to attract notice, and with little regard for its image had allowed itself to be virtually taken over by bandwagon passengers. But it had won respect for its role as a peacemaker in the increasingly serious rift between the two Fronts. Indeed, Shi Ge had heard not long ago how the news of Ouyang's arrival had been greeted.

'According to a newspaper report I saw later,' Shi Ge said, 'when you got him out of custody Ouyang stated that he did not like to owe a debt of gratitude to a person like me, and that one day he would repay the debt in kind. This would seem like a good opportunity.'

'He'll certainly be glad to do that,' said Chen Pan with a smile,

She had not been gone long before Shi Ge was taken to a room on the third floor. He knew at once that the man seated next to Xing Tuo-yu must be Ouyang Zhong-hua and could see why the man should have so many admirers among women. He had the face of a ballet prince and the unrestrained air of an artist, but looked calm and strong-willed as well. He was perhaps thirty or thirty-five years old and had the figure of a much younger man. He obviously took good care of himself. His well-cut imported suit made those sitting beside him look dowdy.

Of the other men in the room only Xing Tuo-yu, the leader of the People's Front was particularly striking. His face was pock-marked and his hair rumpled and he looked much older than Ouyang. He gave the impression of someone with an iron will, animated by intense fervour. During the 1989 pro-democracy movement he had been in command of workers' pickets and after his arrest, in spite of maltreatment had stood by his principles. When the Democracy Front alleged that the People' Front leaders had sold out in prison, he was the only one they could find no evidence against. Partly for this reason he was promoted from a quite low position to that of leader; he was always in the news and regarded by many as a hero.

His eyes were now fixed on Shi Ge. No one spoke. Shi Ge felt like some kind of rare exhibit, or as if he was in a court of law, since no one told him to sit down. There were traces of blood on his creased and torn clothes, his face and hands. He was very tired and could not stand much longer.

'May I sit down?' he asked.

Xing Tuo-yu did not answer for some time and finally said, 'Yes. I've always wondered what you look like, but I didn't think you'd come here in person.'

'It wasn't a matter of choice. . .' Shi Ge began.

'All right,' interrupted Xing in a tired voice. 'I've seen enough of you, but before letting you go there are two things I want to say. First, that steel wire just now cut off the heads of sixteen of our comrades. I don't believe you personally had anything to do with it. But the Hundred-word Constitution Society wants to cut off the head of the whole pro-democracy movement and you are the man behind that Society. Can you deny it?'

Shi Ge did not answer. Unless he had reliable information Xing Tuo-yu would not have even asked.

The popular political organizations considered the Hundred-word Constitution Society as a common enemy, even by the two Fronts who so violently opposed each other. The Society, which specifically attacked the pro-democracy movement and the democratic system, made no public appearance, but its newspaper, tracts and publications were widely distributed and had considerable influence. Unlike previous official propaganda, the society's arguments against democracy had a good theoretical foundation. They were also lively, attractive and convincing, playing especially on people's fear of instability and chaos. So although it did not show its face, the Society had a large following. It helped to turn people away from the pro-democracy movement.

Naturally, there was much speculation about who and what was behind it. It did not live off contributions; no one apparently supported it financially yet the printing and distribution must have cost great deal. The office—behind an unpretentious door—was cold and cheerless and the few tight-lipped staff members seemed to do nothing in particular, but evidently ran an efficient set-up. Theoretical articles were written and well-printed at a speed which would have been impossible without long-term planning and a large organization.

The Society had announced that 'at a suitable moment' in the future, a Constitution consisting of one hundred words would be made public and that a new social system could be established on the basis of it. This had been given much publicity and the fact that the content of the constitution was still unknown, had aroused much interest and expectation. The 'suitable moment' would come after there had been sustained criticism of democracy, when people had lost their illusions about it.

The People's Front considered this nothing but a façade: the aim was the destruction of the democracy movement, and fuss about a constitution nothing but a cover and a means of attracting attention.

Many people thought that there was a special government agency behind the society, so it was no wonder that Shi Ge had got dirty looks when he was brought into the building

'The second thing is this,' Xing Tuo-yu went on. 'Give this message to your boss. We know all about the tricks you have been up to behind the scenes. Sending women agents to seduce activists who have been forced to take refuge abroad, then handing compromising evidence to the People's Front, giving the statements made in prison by People's Front leaders to a Democracy Front publication. All for the sake of stirring up trouble and turning people against us, while you sit back and rub your hands. This evening's business with the wire was definitely the work of you and your agents. You are trying to get us to fight each other, so that you have an excuse to suppress the movement altogether.'

Shi Ge still said nothing, but he knew that what Xing Tuo-yu said was true. He personally had nothing to do with it, and though he knew nothing definite, realized what was going on.

'You won't succeed. Tell your boss that. There is blood on your hands, and a blood debt must be paid in blood. Soon.' Xing Tuo-yu had been made to suffer and the thought of the heads of his comrades lying in the street now filled his eyes with hatred.

'Now you can get out!'

Ouyang Zhong-hua made an almost imperceptible movement with his forefinger signifying that his debt had been paid.

Shi Ge said, 'Give me back my pass.'

Xing Tuo-yu's eyes froze for a moment. 'You don't forget your shitty pass, do you?'

'If I don't bring it back Central Security will search this building.'

'A threat?'

'No.'

Xing Tuo-yu looked at him with disgust then waved his hand, 'Find the pass.'

Although Xing Tuo-yu was highly intense and excitable, Shi Ge had no fear for his own safety. Even without Ouyang Zhong-hua's intervention, they could not have held him. He was the head of a government organisation: it was easy to imagine what kind of trouble there would be if a government official was taken prisoner.

As he left. he came face to face with members of the People's Front who were seething with rage and in no mood to consider consequences. At the top of the stairs he was merely jostled—everyone on the third floor seemed to know that he was the man behind the Hundred-word Constitution. On the second floor, a woman who smelt strongly of alcohol, half cut and half pulled out several tufts of his hair. The thought flashed through his mind: What will I look like in a few days time, on the General Secretary's official visit to Japan? Between the second floor and the first he almost fell downstairs. Fists and feet came at him from all sides and only by straightening up and protecting his private parts did he avoid falling and being trampled on.

Then the kicking and punching stopped and Chen Pan stood in front of him, breathless, her hair tangled and clothes ruffled. He looked at his reflection in the glass of the door. His lip was split, his nose was bleeding and half of his hair gone. He smoothed the rest of it with his hand, as if he had just got out of a barber's chair. He could see Chen Pan behind, looking at him. Her neck where her collar had been torn open was very white against the darkness outside. Unforgettable.

Tokyo

It was the seventh time Shen Di had been to this underground sex palace in Tokyo. Even if he came another seven times he would never be able to find his way through the interminable corridors, concealed doors, small busy lifts going up and down. There was a slightly eerie silence in the place, that contrasted with the hubbub in the street above—the world of red-light bars.

On this occasion the manager, wearing a kimono, personally led the way. Was it because Shen Di was always free with his money or because 'the major' was finally going to show himself this evening? Although Shen Di had a Singapore passport and his under-arm pistol was German, his instincts were entirely Chinese. He detected on the smiling round face of the manager a certain air of complicity. This evening he seemed to regard Shen Di as 'one of us.'

The manager opened a door at the end of a dark corridor with as low a bow as he could manage and when another almost invisible sliding-door silently opened, invited him to enter. A Japanese girl was kneeling inside to greet him, docile, modest and courteous like a traditional Japanese woman, but the lower half of her body was completely naked, her legs smooth and well-rounded.

The room was very large with a low ceiling and everything had been upholstered with soft material—not only the walls but even the refrigerator, the television and tables—so that one almost felt wrapped in a soft quilt. There was also a large bed on which several people at once could cavort. The walls were covered with Japanese pornographic pictures.

The manager clapped his hands and a tall European girl, wearing nothing but tight black trousers and boots, brought in a tray of drinks. From time to time she tossed her head to throw back her golden hair.

Shen Di was about forty years old, handsome and well dressed, had the appearance of an entrepreneur from Southeast Asia and a veritable money-tree ready for shaking. But he said to the topless girl, 'I need no one.' The manager touched a switch and a screen slowly opened, revealing a glass panel. 'Please choose whatever you wish. He placed the programme on the low table in front of him. 'Please enjoy yourself, Sir.'

Twelve years earlier, when Shen Di had just begun to be sent on missions abroad, he had been fascinated by this kind of establishment. But soon he had seen everything and tried everything. Eight years earlier an army friend of his had developed AIDS. Since then Shen Di had stopped having sex with foreign girls. Even when he was shown each girl's health certificates he remained indifferent. He took care of his body. In his army dossier all his superiors had commented on his strong will.

As if it was no more than a necessary formality' he used the pink microphone to order one of the items in the programme. When lights went on behind the glass screen a Hawaiian man gave a display of raping two Japanese women. Every individual hair could be seen and the groans and cries of the women under the brown body of the Hawaiian came clearly through the loudspeakers.

AIDS had led to great changes in the sex industry throughout the world—changes that had got the industry out of the doldrums and allowed it to develop and expand. Because of fear, erotic pleasure from bodily contact alone had become less popular, but sex in the mind knows no boundaries, and now when people had more money to spend, there was much demand. The glass screen was a one-way mirror so that a client with a reputation to keep up could feel at ease. He could not only watch but also take himself in hand as well if he wanted to. If a client became really excited, there was a communicating door through which he could watch from closer up, even put on rubber gloves and participate. Condoms were available on request.

Shen Di had been here six times—at fifty thousand *yen* a visit. He had no scruples about using public money for such a purpose. But however many times he came, sex by turns, sodomy, naked dancing, homosexual intercourse or sadism—nothing excited him. He came, watched, paid and went—all silently. 'The major's' message had brought him here to wait. 'The major' himself was certainly close by, following him, observing and appraising as usual. But he had not shown himself.

Patience was Shen Di's best assistant. All he knew about 'the Major' was that his rank was self-awarded and that for every ten hits he gave himself a promotion. At least forty human lives would have adorned his epaulettes, if he had worn such things. Shen Di had waited for him on six occasions and had been happy to do so. He was always uneasy if he had to employ someone who was impatient or if he happened to get involved in an affair in which patience was impossible—as in this case.

Behind the glass screen a woman was suspended upside down, another was curled up on a chair and the man was engaged in genital and oral sex at the same time. The animal cries became more drawn out.

Shen Di turned the volume down and flicked on the television set. The press conference at the Chinese Embassy had started and several TV stations were broadcasting it live. The cameras were focussed on the statesman representing the Chinese government. Shen Di saw the familiar face, the exalted expression, speaking, as usual, cheerfully and humorously. The eyes of the world were on the increasing disorder in Beijing, yet here, in Japan, the man went on in a carefree and self-satisfied manner, making jokes, speaking left and right to reporters and showing off his knowledge of foreign languages. Shen Di wondered whether it was deliberate or had he merely been carried away.

Today, the headlines in all the papers were about the Agreement on the Establishment of the Sino-Japanese Economic Cooperation Region, which was heralded as a new departure in relations between Japan and China. The Japanese government was celebrating it in a big way and there was general enthusiasm in China as well. When the two governments had begun full negotiations, Shen Di had received orders from the Intelligence Bureau of the General Staff to conduct an investigation into the role of the Black Dragon Society in this affair. This secret society had been founded in 1901 by Japanese extremists to prepare the way for the seizure by Japan of Northeast China and the Russian Far East. It was rumoured that the society still existed, had become a quite powerful and influential group and was gradually infiltrating the highest levels of the Japanese establishment. By the terms of the 'Sino-Japanese Economic Co-operation Region' the Chinese province of Heilongjiang (the Black Dragon River) would be ceded to Japan for a period of fifty years, in return for a payment, in the form of a foreign debt, of 1470 billion US$, and a 'management tax' amounting to two and a half times what the province paid in taxes at present to the Central Government, subject to an annual increase of 20 per cent. The agreement included detailed clauses to prevent Japanese plundering of the region's resources in the name of development and to ensure the protection of the environment.

The province was in a pitiable state: the land was exhausted, the forests all cut down and there was appalling pollution. In fifty years time, a new Heilongjiang, developed by Japanese capital, technology and management would by handed back to China. Everyone said that it was the best deal ever concluded. Even Japanese research organizations calculated that Japan had nothing to gain. This alone was enough to arouse suspicions. Japan was usually clever enough to avoid getting involved in a bad deal, which was what this shameless sell-out by China was likely to be. The problem of living space was a constant worry in Japan, especially now. A country consisting of a few small islands could not for long compete with the big economic powers. Japan had bought up land and factories in many different countries—by methods which had taken the world by surprise—but that was only a form of economic expansion and an inadequate base on which to build Japan into a first-rate political and military power. The Black Dragon Society believed that only by getting a foothold on the continent could the Japanese nation be guaranteed survival and development. Possibly Heilongjiang and Siberia were going to be the springboard for this historic ambition.

Shen Di was not interested in high-level politics and had little regard for ideological and nationalistic dogma: he merely carried out orders. He knew that those who gave him his orders were at cross-purposes with the man he was now looking at on the TV screen. If Shen Di's investigations turned up anything, it would not be used to warn that man not to be duped; indeed, it might be at that moment that the action would start. His investigations had not gone well. The Black Dragon Society had always been shadowy, and elusive. Each time he thought he had a lead, nothing had come of it. Just when he had begun to get results new orders had arrived.

Shen Di kept one eye on the TV screen and one on the other screen, but he did not fail to notice an almost imperceptible draft as the door opened behind him.

A small man was standing in the doorway, the kind of man who would pass unnoticed in Tokyo, Kyoto, Seoul or Singapore—exactly what Shen Di needed. He looked a little too young at first glance, until Shen Di noticed the wrinkles at the corners of his eyes. People of the East often look far younger than their real age. He was a little surprised at the slender stature and mild manner, and a slightly shy smile. But wherever he went in the world the secret and colourless men he came in contact with, even the top men in the Black Dragon Society, all spoke of 'the Major' with respect and awe. Shen Di appreciated slightly enigmatic people, and welcomed a hit man who did not look the part.

'How are you, Major?' he asked in Chinese. It was the first time he had spoken Chinese on this mission.

'And you?' These two words were enough to dispel Shen Di's last reservation and allowed him to judge how well 'the major' spoke Chinese. He had an accent which seemed to come straight off the streets of Beijing.

'I am now 'lieutenant colonel,'' he said.

Shen Di did not quite know whether to congratulate the Major on this self-promotion or not, so he merely invited him to sit down and at the same time turned off the sound system, so that the woman behind the glass screen became an insubstantial figure in a silent film. Before he sat down however the Major touched a switch on the wall and several lights came on. Shen Di was sure that one or more automatic cameras were hidden in the room and had probably started filming. He did not react in any way. The Major was merely protecting his life and ensuring that he would be paid in full. On the other hand, if everything was conducted according to the agreement, the 'evidence' would certainly not be used—this was the ethical code of the profession. Anyway, with brighter lights Shen Di would also get a better picture from his own hidden camera.

The Major seated himself comfortably opposite Shen Di and said, 'How should I address you?'

'We will use military ranks. I am a colonel,' said Shen Di with a slight grin.

'Should I stand to attention?' asked the other '

'I don't deserve the honour.'

The exchange of compliments over, there was a moment of silence. The Major fiddled with his fingers—his hands were as soft and white as a woman's. He had an unaffected and innocent air, as if he was waiting for a piece of music, or a children's story to begin.

'People say that when you come to meet someone it means that you agree to do business,' said Shen Di in slow and measured tones. 'They also say that if the price is right you accept any target. Is that right?'

'Who do you want killed, Colonel?' It was as if he thought that Shen Di was beating about the bush but Shen Di understood at once that these particular words had been pronounced for the record, for the hidden cameras.

He lit a cigarette and was immediately riveted by the scene being enacted on the TV screen. The press conference had been going on for an hour and a half, when a sweating Japanese newspaperman appeared, grabbed a microphone, and after asking a few questions in a loud voice, announced dramatically that fifteen minutes earlier the Yellow River had burst its banks. The statesman representing China was obviously unaware of the disaster: the agency had made an impressive scoop and he would be humiliated in public. The newspaperman had just finished his announcement and the interpreter had not yet opened his mouth, when a man with a shaven head in the Chinese delegation handed a note to the statesman; it immediately became clear that he was going to reply in exactly the words of the note.

The man with the shaven head had clearly already heard about the flood, but had not wanted to interrupt the press conference. Instead, he had made preparations in case someone raised the question. There was only one sentence in the note: 'We will fill in the breach.' It was enough. As long as the representative did not find himself totally at a loss for words, his honour was saved.

Shen Di was impressed by the man who had written the note; it was the first time he had seen him on this kind of occasion. The presence of such an alert and resourceful subordinate suggested that the statesman was unlikely to be merely a 'transitional' figure. That explained why it was necessary to take the measures that he, Shen Di, had been charged with.

'Do you recognize him?' Shen Di pointed to the statesman, now in close-up.

The Major's voice replied flatly and without emotion of any kind, 'The General Secretary of the Chinese Communist Party.'

The Yellow River

The dull ochre waters of the Yellow River have broken through the dykes fifteen hundred times in the last two thousand years. It has the highest silt content of any river in the world and every year as it crosses the plain four billion tons of fine silt is deposited on the riverbed which rises higher and higher above the surrounding countryside. It is an elevated river. From a distance boats seem to be moving through the air. From Taohua valley in Henan Province down to the estuary, only the great earth dykes on either side prevent the river from breaking out. During all the years of Communist rule the river never once breached its dykes—an exceptional achievement which the Chinese Communist Party claims is proof of its ability to govern the country. This time there may be proof of the opposite.

On the twenty-ninth of July, Typhoon 72 arrived in the region of the Huai and Yellow rivers. On its periphery, a low altitude north-south current came up against a cold and powerful west wind in the middle reaches of the Yellow River. This caused a sudden downfall of torrential rain in Henan province of an intensity rarely recorded in the last hundred years. The personnel of a hydrometric station on the Luo

River that flows into the Yellow River put out a rain gauge and in an instant it was filled almost to the brim and the rainwater contained a dead sparrow. Several tributaries of the Yellow River—itself at maximum level—were also on the point of overflowing. At the Huayuankou hydrological station, the flow was close to the highest post-1949 figure. The Yellow River Conservancy Committee immediately sent urgent warnings to the Central Government as well as to the Henan and Shandong Provincial authorities.

'Politics in command!' was the magic formula of the Chinese Communist Party for governing the country and it was an excellent method of guaranteeing the loyalty of government departments. But when the political situation became complicated the efficiency of government departments declined rapidly. Uncertainty about the verdict on June Fourth had a profound effect on the morale of all government personnel and matters of primary importance tended to take second place. Social disorder also affected organization and the normal circulation of goods, so that when all the preparations had been made an emergency had already become a crisis.

Previously, several million people would be at work on the dykes within a few hours of a breach occurring. Now that the People's Communes had been abolished, the strategy of mobilizing a 'sea of people' was no longer possible. Village cadres now shouted themselves hoarse in the pouring rain, but the peasants were only concerned to deepen the drainage ditches on their own land, to repair their own roofs or cover their supplies of firewood. Those who did answer the call were slow and lazy, interested in the money they could earn, and chose the easy work. It was even more difficult to involve the urban population.

In the afternoon, the thirtieth of July, a breach suddenly occurred in a section of the dyke near a village in Shandong. In one minute, thirty metres of the dyke had been swept away, leaving only a supporting stone wall. An engineer of the River Administration shouted to people to throw rocks into the breach, and a memory flashed through his mind of a similar situation in 1958 when several hundred soldiers had rushed into action and filled in a breach in next to no time. Not now. As soon as he shouted the order all the peasants ran away. As he watched with bitterness in his heart there was a thunderous roar and a yellow torrent rose like the head of a monster and launched itself over the flat land covered with fleeing peasants. He was the first victim, and disappeared under the water calling for the Liberation Army.

The floodwaters covered village after village, with a great loss of life, and cut the Beijing-Shanghai railway, the main artery between north and south China. Six counties and an immeasurable quantity of arable land were inundated. The flooded area extended into the provinces of Jiangsu and Anhui. Factories stopped work and schools closed.

On the thirty-first of July, the heavy rain on the lower reaches of the Yellow River stopped, but up-river from the Sanmenxia reservoir there was exceptionally heavy rainfall. The flood-gates were closed to reduce the pressure and help those fighting the floods downstream. Nevertheless, in the space of one day the reservoir was full.

Rivers in the provinces of Shaanxi and Shanxi were either in flood or had already begun to overflow, and it was feared that if the Sanmenxia reservoir overflowed or the dam was breached, Henan province would be the first to suffer. The three provinces therefore put pressure on the Central Flood Prevention Administration: since Shandong was already flooded, the important thing now was to prevent the flooding of other areas. It was finally agreed to open the flood-gates on the Sanmenxia reservoir.

When this was done 5,000 cubic metres per second of water joined the flood waters of the lower reaches, and once more broke the dyke in Shandong, which had been desperately rebuilt almost entirely. The same night people from several Shandong villages managed to cross the Yellow River into Henan carrying 90 kilogrammes of explosive and blew a breach in the dyke in such a way that the main flow of the river rushed straight at a series of dykes, helped on its way by a strong south wind. The dykes yielded early in the morning of the first day of August and the yellow water poured through the province to the north. Some towns were flooded; others completely surrounded by water. In the neighbouring province of Hebei an emergency was declared. The floods in Shandong on the other hand had subsided to some extent, and in a very short time the breach at Gaocun was filled. The intrepid peasants who had done the work were acclaimed as heroes in the neighbouring villages.

After the decision to implement reform and open China to the outside world, everyone—from the Central Government to local authorities—became obsessed with 'growth' and investment in flood control was continually reduced. The water level of the Yellow River had been relatively low for several years and people had got into the habit of forgetting the river's well-deserved name: 'China's sorrow'. The dykes had become riddled with holes, where badgers and rats increased and multiplied; apart from the actual breaches, all were more or less defective, with cracks, crevices, subsidence and leaks—and constant warnings and alerts were issued.

On August 2nd, extremely violent rainstorms swelled the tributaries that flowed into the upper reaches of the river. In the space of eight hours 452 mm of rain fell. Hundreds of channels were suddenly flooded, destroying the Luhun Reservoir, and a flood wave of 17,000 cubic metres per second joined the Yellow River, immediately raising the flow to 38,500 cubic metres per second—greater than in any recorded flood in the river's history. Much of the great bridge of the Beijing-Guangzhou railway was swept away, and as the flood peak passed Zhengzhou it breached the dykes on both sides simultaneously in twenty-eight places and reached as far as northern Jiangsu and the great city of Tianjin, less that 150 kilometres from Beijing.

When Shi Ge saw the North China plain under water as far as the eye could see, he felt utter despair. Everyone on the Flood Survey aircraft had grim faces, but he was perhaps the only one to understand clearly all the implications of what could be seen. His staff had previously prepared an analysis of a hypothetical Yellow River flood—a scenario which had included neither the increasing political unrest, nor the serious economic crisis and the galloping inflation, which had already reached three figures. The present flood was far more serious than the simulated projection and not only because these things had not entered into the equations.

There was another element. Yesterday the *Liberation Army Daily* had given prominence to an editorial headed 'Patriotism is the foundation stone of the Army' in which it was stated bluntly that 'treachery in whatever disguise will be rooted out by the patriotic People's army.' No names were mentioned, but the previous day the General Secretary had returned in triumph from Japan. The *Workers' Daily* and the *Science and Technology Daily* and the *Beijing Daily* all carried this editorial; but the *People's Daily* and the *Guangming Daily* ignored it.

On the top of a hill stones had been arranged to read 'All thanks to the Liberation Army', and a large number of flood refugees on the hillside waved to the plane as it flew over, taking it for an army aircraft.

When the flood was at its worst the army had finally arrived. Several hundred thousand soldiers had brought in massive supplies of food and medical supplies and had saved lives and property, maintained order and repaired the dykes. The people thanked them with tears in their eyes. But they felt hatred for the government and for the General Secretary who had not hurried home from Tokyo.

Beijing: Western Hills

The red tail-light seemed to flicker as the leading car passed between the soldiers lining the road. Lu Hao-ran normally rode in his own car and being small, never allowed his bodyguard to sit in front and block the view. But in this army limousine with its concealed steel plates, he was accompanied by soldiers, with weapons at the ready. When Wang Feng had telephoned he made a point of saying that the army had a duty to protect its guests in a time of great unease.

Lu Hao-ran normally had little direct contact with the military but his secretary had informed him that Wang Feng, the Deputy Secretary-General of the Central Military Commission wanted to speak to him. This was rather unusual—especially as the telephone message had been scrambled. Wang Feng had merely said that the Chairman wished to see him. He had been very polite, but had fixed 9.50 this evening for the interview without asking whether it was convenient or not. Of course Lu Hao-ran had agreed, and cancelled several meetings with foreign representatives in the Great Hall of the People.

The secretaries had arranged the details, but otherwise the request for a meeting had been kept secret. The car left from a side gate of Zhongnanhai, the seat of the Central Government and drew up in the darkness. Lu Hao-ran was instantly transferred to the limousine.

Before he retired four years ago the 'Chairman' had in fact only been First Vice-Chairman of the Military Commission and he continued to live in his residence in the Western Hills. For the last nine years it was exactly as if he was still in office. Out of respect he was still referred to in the army as 'the Chairman.'

The real Chairman of the Military Commission, who was also General Secretary of the Central Committee and President of the People's Republic, was never called by his proper titles, especially by the top brass. After June Fourth it was obvious that some time in the future it would be necessary to rely on force; so whoever controlled the army would control the country. The importance of the army and its role and status as an obedient tool of the Party was therefore constantly emphasized. The General Secretary, who had managed military affairs for many years, had worked hard to achieve this. Middle ranking officers from the academies had a good opinion of him and he had encountered little opposition. But he was not really in control of the military—an outsider could not be admitted into the inner circle—it merely meant that the army's 'own people' had been kept in the background. To all appearances a tight system had been put in operation according to law, but it was not the real army, the nerve centre of which was in the Western Hills.

Lu Hao-ran had learned from the Minister of National Security that during the past few days high-ranking officers of the area commands had been flown in military aircraft to an army airfield near the capital, then taken in limousines with army number-plates direct to the Western

Hills. They remained there for half a day and were then quickly flown back. The commanders of all the services and departments were received there as well. The military were evidently planning an important move. Indeed the editorial in the *Liberation Army Daily* had made it clear what the general trend was. Lu Hao-ran was confident as he went to meet the Chairman. He needed the military and Wang Feng's telephone call showed that they needed him.

As Premier of the State Council, Lu Hao-ran had more or less equal status with the General Secretary. He had been in charge of the national economy for a long time and had a strong base in the State Council system and an extensive network of contacts. Gradually he became the representative of those who advocated a planned economy. He was respected by several important figures and had been put forward to tackle the 'market anomalies' left over after the economic reform of the 1980s. He was also a kind of counter-balance to the General Secretary, considered abroad as a 'moderate.' The authority of Mao Zedong could still maintain a balance between the various cliques, but antagonisms became increasingly acute after he died, or 'went to join Marx' as he used to say. Everything was changing and there were new groups, alignments and relationships. Lu Hao-ran had been forced to retreat step by step and was aware that he was retreating towards a precipice.

He always thought it strange that he was called a 'hard-liner'—considering himself far too easy-going. Although he advocated tight political control, when this came in conflict with economic development, as a former economic specialist, he invariably yielded to economic necessity and made political concessions. Politics and economics seemed to him to be *always* in conflict. Must he continue to retreat until there was nowhere to go to? There was a logic that no one seemed to understand: the economy could develop only if there was political stability; but there could only be political stability if there was economic development. This had been the watchword for years. On paper, the two things complemented each other and for the sake of the steady development of both he had made many compromises.

Lu Hao-ran believed that as long as economic and political principles were mutually incompatible, political stability would be impossible, whether the economy was developing or not, nor could the economy develop with or without stability. The 'moderate' General Secretary had been playing, to great effect, on the fear of disorder and losing popular support; now he was planning to reap a huge political advantage by reversing the verdict on June Fourth. This was playing with fire.

Lu Hao-ran was well aware that the General Secretary had never been an advocate of democracy. He was taking this risk purely for his own purposes. He wanted to use the political backlash reversing the verdict would cause as a weapon to break the hard-liners.

The problem created by June Fourth was not that people had been killed, property destroyed and international relations damaged. There was nothing very terrible about that. The crux of the matter was that it had led to a crisis of confidence, a kind of psychological loss of equilibrium. The group holding power seemed as strong and solid as ever but in reality it had secretly lost hope. What would the final judgement of history be? The changes in Eastern Europe that had come hard on the heels of June Fourth had increased the feeling of uncertainty in China. At that time experienced men of the older generation were in charge and the crisis of confidence could still be controlled.

Lu Hao-ran did not want to go down in history as a hard-liner. So inflexibility of the will had rapidly given place to infirmity of purpose: which he knew was exactly what the General Secretary was counting on.

It was the 'moderates' who had first called for the 'reversal of the verdict' on June Fourth: for a reassessment of the pro-democracy movement and above all for condemnation of its violent suppression by the army. The 'moderates' hoped to make enormous political capital out of it, especially now when it had widespread support. One hint that the whole June Fourth incident was going to be reconsidered would be enough to make everyone plead total innocence and deny any involvement in the suppression of the pro-democracy movement. Those in power at all levels would lose no time in becoming 'moderates' or even liberals. Such a chain reaction from below could not fail to bring about the destruction of the hard-liners.

Neither Lu Hao-ran nor the General Secretary had been members of the small decision-making group in the top leadership and had no direct responsibility for the suppression of the June Fourth movement, but their respective seats in the Party and government had obliged them to adopt positions. 'Their brains were governed by their backsides' as the mandarins of the Chinese bureaucracy used to say. The hard-liners had used June Fourth to smash the Liberals and as in 1989 in Tiananmen Square, as soon as the first shots were fired the political configuration had undergone a fundamental transformation. Now if the verdict were reversed the hard-liners and their supporters would be finished, stamped out by the moderates.

As soon as he entered the closely guarded courtyard Lu Hao-ran was transferred to a top-class limousine. All over the picturesque Jade Spring Hill, there were sentries and lookout posts. The car followed a winding road for some time then stopped in front of a villa surrounded by ancient trees. Wang Feng was already at the door waiting for him.

'The Chairman had intended to call on you himself, unfortunately he has a cold and asks you to excuse him,' said Wang Feng with a pleasant smile.

'No, no! I am the younger and it is right for me to call on him.' Lu Hao-ran was thirty years younger than the Chairman but twenty years older than Wang Feng, and he realized that he had not been very tactful. 'I have been intending to come and express my gratitude to the army for its help in the flooded areas,' he said, taking Wang Feng's outstretched hand and feeling like an ant trying to shake a tree. Wang Feng was taller than him by a head, handsome and well built and in the prime of life. Although it was summer, his smart serge uniform was tightly buttoned.

'Our units arrived late: for that we deserve criticism,' said Wang Feng.

'Not at all, it was not your fault.'

By comparison with previous floods the army had indeed arrived late, but in greater force. Troops appeared everywhere, on the roads and the railways, and the sky was full of military aircraft. Massive quantities of supplies and equipment were brought in and from morning till night half of China could hear the sound of the army marching song. Even if it had been late in coming the army was praised more than on previous occasions. In the flooded areas most of the local governments were paralysed or had disappeared, and all important tasks had to be performed by the military. In the four provinces and the city of Tianjin, directly hit by the floods, as well as those which had suffered indirectly, the provincial authorities all published articles in the newspapers they controlled praising the selfless and resolute work of the Liberation Army.

It had not escaped Lu Hao-ran's attention that the same newspapers had all, in different ways and without mentioning names, attacked the wealthy provinces of the South, using such phrases as 'enriching themselves at the expense of the whole nation' or 'standing by with folded hands when the country was in danger'. There was much disagreement and hostility between these northern provinces themselves, but on this subject they spoke with one voice. Lu Hao-ran was struck by the fact that the province of Jiangsu, although several times devastated by floods, had not joined the chorus.

He himself was little more than a spectator in all this; to all appearances he took flood relief as an urgent matter though in fact he was not really concerned. The Yellow River flood looked like a natural disaster, but in fact it was man-made—the result of a mistaken policy. People would only wake up to this fact when they were shown the results.

Wang Feng walked with a military stride beside Lu Hao-ran, indicating the way with polite gestures. Five years earlier when he was Chairman of the Engineering Committee of the National Defence Department, he had been the youngest lieutenant general in the army. Now that he had just been appointed concurrently Deputy Secretary-General of the Military Commission of the Central Committee as well, it was rumoured that he would soon be the youngest full general and that he was not pleased at the prospect. In the present system to be a Lieutenant General was to have reached the top, which meant that he would never catch up with his late father, who had been a Marshal in the 1950s. He was said to have remarked that 'a soldier who does not want to be a Marshal is not a good soldier. Now that there's no such rank as Marshal there can be no such thing as a good soldier.'

They went through an entrance hall, two corridors and a large reception room, all quite empty, then in front of a door covered with yellow leather Wang Feng took Lu Hao-ran's hand: 'The Chairman is not very well—the doctor will only allow you five minutes.' Lu Hao-ran nodded, as the other gently pushed open the door.

He found himself in a small reception room. A shrivelled old man sat upright in an armchair, Lu Hao-ran could hardly believe his eyes. It was only four years since the Chairman had appeared in public, but what a change! The tall and imposing figure had shrunk into a mummy, wizened and dried up. His uniform hung on him as on a coat-hanger. His face was wrinkled and his complexion good, unnaturally good. Lu Hao-ran went forward to greet him and his eyes met those of the old man, veiled by a white film. His heart missed a beat. They still had the same severe authority as before and the same power to look deep into one's mind.

The Chairman moved only a finger. 'Sit down.' The once stentorian voice had become weak and hoarse.

In the room, there were only the armchairs, side tables and the carpet—no superfluous furnishing. Hanging on the wall there was a portrait of Mao Zedong, and in front of it, a tall silk screen on which was embroidered, in Mao's lively and vigorous calligraphy, his poem 'The whole river is red.' The poem had once been very well known. Lu Hao-ran knew it by heart, and now he suddenly felt that the words were far, far away and strangely moving.

He sat on the edge of an armchair facing the Chairman, leaning a little forward, his hands between his knees.

'This is the first time we have met,' said the Chairman slowly with long pauses between the words, 'but I know about you.'

Lu Hao-ran nodded. He had seen the Chairman many times, and had even shaken his hand and spoken to him; but he was only a low-ranking Minister at the time and the Chairman could not possibly remember him. By the time Lu Hao-ran became Premier the Chairman had already retired to the Western Hills and no longer showed himself. It was the words 'I know about you' which were important. Of course, the Chairman could know everything about anyone at all, but at this moment the remark signified a kind of acceptance and approval.

'I know that you are the only member of the Political Bureau who is against this shameful unpatriotic agreement, and that you, as Premier, refused to go to Japan to sign it. You did right. You showed backbone. Economic Cooperation Region! All that means is that the Japanese devils are occupying the Northwest all over again.' 'The Chairman' still spoke slowly in the hoarse voice of an old man but Lu Hao-ran could hear the thunder behind it.

'I also know that you have tried to call a meeting of the Political Bureau five times and have called firmly for an end to disorder and condemned the present agitation for reversing the verdict. You have put up a fine struggle and we thank you for it.'

Lu Hao-ran continued to nod his head. He wanted to say that he was glad to have worked for the ideals of the older generation but he refrained. Behind his spectacles, his eyes had become a little watery.

The disorder had been entirely stirred up by the General Secretary who nevertheless pretended to be surprised by it and even totally ignored it. He released those who had been arrested on Lu Hao-ran's orders and a few days ago had announced that he would go personally to Tokyo as President of the Republic to sign the agreement on economic cooperation, asserting that Lu Hao-ran had failed to carry out decisions of the Standing Committee—which was tantamount to dismissing him. Lu Hao-ran had been very gloomy about so many setbacks but the realization that the army still defended and supported him gave him a warm feeling.

'The second-class soldier forgets himself.' The deep lines on the Chairman's face enhanced his expression of natural contempt.

Lu Hao-ran had heard it said that the high-ranking generals in the army always referred to the General Secretary who had never been in the army as 'the second class soldier,' in spite of the fact that he had been Chairman of the Central Military Commission. This was the first time that he had heard it, and from the mouth of the Chairman himself it greatly pleased him.

'We will never agree to it!' The old man said in the tone of voice of someone taking an oath. 'June Fourth was the absolute limit, no one will ever be allowed to go beyond it.'

'I too will never agree to it,' said Lu Hao-ran in a dignified manner.

The Chairman looked at him for a moment, then nodded almost imperceptibly, sighed, and closed his eyes. His arms were now stretched out on the armrests, his legs straight and his whole body absolutely motionless. Lu Hao-ran had a strange feeling that he was looking at a dummy. This man had been a brigade commander during the Long March, full General in the fifties, though not yet someone of great importance. He had been chiefly responsible for the decision to suppress the movement on Tiananmen Square. Now he was the last indomitable standard-bearer of the era of Mao Zedong.

Like a nurse, Wang Feng gently wiped the saliva from the Chairman's mouth.

Wang Feng's father had once been the Chairman's superior officer. Lu Hao-ran observed this bond between the senior member of the old guard and his heir apparent with mixed feelings. He would never have the advantage of such a relationship, so at crucial moments he was left isolated and powerless.

When the Chairman opened his eyes again they had lost their vitality. He was clearly exhausted. The wire of his hearing-aid hung limply down beside his sparse white hair. 'Wang Feng has full powers to represent the army,' he said finally in a hollow voice. Then his eyes closed again.

Lu Hao-ran wondered whether he meant that Wang Feng would now continue the discussion, or that from now on he would take over as the embodiment of the army. The Chairman did not explain and it appeared that the interview was at an end. Lu rose quietly. Once more the old man opened his eyes. 'The army will support your appointment as General Secretary.'

Shandong Peninsula: Naval Base 201

The officer commanding the guard at the entrance to the tunnel took one look Wang Feng's high level pass and immediately brought the guard to attention to present arms. The inspection that followed was by no means cursory. Wang Feng's identity was checked by computer, his fingerprints were matched and his car, like any other, was driven over to an inspection pit and examined for concealed explosive devices. Wang Feng showed some impatience but only in order to test the officer and see whether he would relax his vigilance for someone of high rank. He was more than satisfied.

It had been more than five weeks since he was last here—the longest interval he could remember. The whole time had been taken up with discussions and receiving guests and he had not been able to get away for a moment. Lu Hao-ran had been the last of the visitors and less than five minutes after he had seen the future General Secretary to his car, he had been in the helicopter ready for immediate take-off. He had slept well during the two-hour flight and before landing had phoned his wife to say that he would be home in another two hours or so. He did not tell her that he was in the sky over Shandong or that he would be visiting a submarine.

He drove for five minutes through the brightly-lit tunnel. The officer at the entrance had informed guard posts along the way of his arrival and he was saluted as the barriers opened for him to pass. The tunnel led straight to a dry dock, more than three hundred metres long and two hundred wide which could be filled with water by opening the sluice-gates outside the tunnel. It now contained a large submarine under construction, surrounded by scaffolding.

The dry dock had formerly been used by the navy for secret operations, and had been acquired by Wang Feng with the greatest of difficulty. Soon after he had become Chairman of the Engineering and Development Committee of the Department of National Defence he had ordered the construction of a submarine armed with nuclear missiles. He believed that as far as weapons were concerned the army ought to rely on quality rather than quantity. One submarine with the latest equipment and carrying nuclear missiles was equivalent to an army of more than a million men. With one submarine of this kind aggression by a foreign country, however powerful, could be deterred by the threat of a nuclear riposte. Secrecy was crucial of course. If the enemy knew about the movements of the submarine it would amount to no more than a useless object costing a mountain of gold. Now that the atmosphere was full of spy satellites and infrared rays the construction itself was easier than keeping it a secret.

Wang Feng had obtained this rare facility with the help of the Chairman himself. The tunnel entrance was disguised as the entrance of an underground storage depot, and everything needed for the construction of the submarine was transferred from a genuine underground depot, as if going into storage in another. A whole transport battalion was occupied full-time with this work and none of the drivers were aware of the real nature of the operation. Wang Feng knew that concealment from spy satellites was relatively easy. The real problem was with the large number of people in many different departments who were involved in the project. It was unrealistic to imagine that everyone's mouth could be corked like a bottle, so his policy was to ensure that the various departments only knew what they were directly concerned with. Only he knew the whole picture. To this day even the Military Affairs Commission of the Central Committee, the Chief of Staff and the Commanding Officer of the Navy were not very clear about what was going on or where money had gone.

He stopped the car at the dockside. Crates were stacked everywhere: radar equipment from Germany, American computers, Dutch periscopes, Danish electrical motors and Japanese turbines. More than half the equipment for the submarine was of foreign origin and it had been very difficult to get round the export ban on sophisticated equipment imposed by certain governments. Convinced that without using Western technology it would be impossible to compete in modern warfare he had not hesitated to pay prices several times higher than normal.

A man in naval uniform, without insignia and hatless, appeared and stood at attention in front of him, embarrassed at not being able to salute and not knowing what to do with his hands. Wang Feng told him to stand at ease and greeted him amicably. Ding Da-hai was Supervisor of Construction, but looked like a typical skipper of a Shandong fishing boat, with his broad shoulders and closely cropped hair, except that the lenses of his spectacles were as thick as the base of a wine bottle.

To enter the submarine one had to pass through two guard posts. The first gave access to the outside hull, and could only be found by those familiar with the huge construction. What was visible from the outside was only a mock-up. The real submarine—nearing completion—was concealed inside it and strictly out of bounds to all except those with special passes. This subterfuge, which Wang Feng was rather proud of, was designed to conceal the truth from those working on the project, the majority of whom were not aware of its genuine purpose and even if they saw the two hulls would assume it was merely a new type of construction.

Wang Feng knew that he would possibly have to show the submarine to those who thought they had the right to see it. He was now Deputy Secretary-General of the Military Commission as well as Head of the Engineering Committee of the Department of National Defence. Soon he would be promoted to Secretary-General of the Military Commission and his other office would have to be given up. His successor was bound to ask what was going on. Before that happened it was urgent to finish the project and leave only an empty hull. Then, apart from a few key people whose lips would be sealed and the naval personnel who would take the submarine to sea, no one would know. When he first thought of this it was mainly Western intelligence he had in mind; now it had far greater significance.

He enjoyed making plans and carrying them out. As a child he had dreamed of being a super spy. Later, during the Cultural Revolution whether as a leader of Red Guards, or as party to the plot to assassinate Mao Zedong's wife Jiang Qing, or when sent by his father to canvass the top leaders about some proposal or other, his political ability had grown and blossomed.

By that time his ambition was to become Head of State. Like most of the sons of leading figures in the army he joined up when he was still under age, but unlike many others he did not look upon the army as a sinecure. He firmly believed that 'power grows out of the barrel of a gun,' and for him this meant using the army as a stepping-stone in his career. He did not follow the fashion and learn about the art of war or the usual military subjects but devoted himself entirely to the study of sophisticated weaponry. Future wars would not be fought by soldiers with bayonets. All his plans had succeeded superbly: and he was almost ready to take the last step.

He carefully inspected each section of the submarine, accompanied by the Chief Designer, the Chief Engineer and the construction manager—all rather nervous. Wang Feng had studied guided missiles at the military engineering academy and was familiar with the world's weapons. On specific questions about design, construction and operation, he knew far less than the men who were with him. He had no desire to give them advice, but only wanted to make them nervous and keep them on their toes. For the same reason he wanted all who worked here to not to forget his Lieutenant General's insignia. He needed to say nothing, inspect everything in silent concentration then ask a few penetrating questions. This was enough to make these fellows sweat—like cart-horses under the shadow of the whip.

In fact, as he stood looking at the gleaming brass of the propeller he saw only the floodwaters fanning out over the great plain from the broken Yellow River dyke.

He was very satisfied with the arrangements that had recently been made for flood relief. In the past whenever there was an emergency the army was always the first in the front line and when it was all over everyone forgot about it. Inherent corruption, contradictions and other problems remained the same, indeed became increasingly ingrained and accepted. The selfless devotion of the army had handled a crisis due to mistakes and malpractice, saving the skins of a lot of incompetents so that they could continue to ruin the land and the people.

This time he had secretly prevented the army from reacting promptly, claiming that the slow response was due to various factors, such as the lack of local coordination and the failure of the central government to create the right conditions. As a result all sorts of problems had come out into the open. He despised soft-hearted military commanders who could not bear disasters to strike the country. The loss of a few billion *yuan*—what did that matter, as long as the flood swept away the wrong policies and their advocates? It would not mean the end of the Party and the Nation. This time the army had gone into action later than ever before, yet the people were profoundly grateful, the media were lavish with praise and local support was very solid. It confirmed the truth of the old saying that it is best to wait until the last moment before saving someone's life. More important, the redeployment of the army, of which only the highest ranking officers were aware, had been completed. The fact that the flooded area was so vast, and the situation so chaotic, provided legitimate cover for the large-scale redeployment of troops that he had ordered. The capital had now been discreetly surrounded, the central plain was under control and disposition of troops faced southwards. Under cover of flood relief large reserves of supplies had been built up. There remained only the final step....

The last guard post gave access to the genuine submarine. The basic structure was all there, and the work of fitting had begun. Wang Feng examined the quality of some hermetic sealing and ordered it to be done again. Then he noticed some play in a locking wheel, which could be turned with one finger.

As he did so he saw in his mind's eye the revolving chamber of a pistol ... Yes, the General Secretary would have to die. Wang Feng himself had nothing to do with the June Fourth events but he knew that for the army everything to do with June Fourth was taboo. This had become almost a matter of principle at the centre of military development and thinking. June Fourth was a scar, a hard scab: remove it and highly sensitive nerve endings would be uncovered. Of course, many of the more educated junior officers went on about 'democratic consciousness,' but that was only talk. To condemn the 'suppression of insurrection' on June Fourth would be to mark the army with an indelible stain. Many distinguished generals who valued honour more than their lives would go down in history as criminals. To avoid such a humiliation Wang Feng would be prepared to kill not just one man but ten times, a hundred times as many. The man deserved to die, that is all, and the truth about his death would remain a secret forever. The death of one man is a simple matter, a matter of chance—not like a mutiny or a political struggle. Of course, power would change hands—no one would have anything to say about that—no one would have to make excuses. It would just be accepted in China and abroad. Of course there would be suspicions and speculation but let people imagine anything they liked! He had not yet decided what to do about Shen Di. Wang Feng had already gone to considerable trouble to have him put in charge of the General Secretary's personal security and so insure that the hit-man got away safely from wherever it might be. The hit-man was to be paid six million dollars for the hit. He also wanted a guarantee of safety, an insurance policy against being silenced, so if he were to die in China the video tape of his conversation with Shen Di in Tokyo would be broadcast to the world.

Wang Feng was satisfied that Shen Di could do what was required of him. Once the hit-man got safely away the only remaining danger was Shen Di himself. Wang Feng knew that Shen was not considered unflinchingly loyal—he had helped himself to at least a million dollars of the secret funds entrusted to him for the purchase of missiles. But they had been friends from childhood: for years Wang Feng had looked on him as a younger brother—and was reluctant to dwell on possible dangers.

He watched the testing of an air-seal. The rows of tiny green lights on the indicator screen gave him a feeling of security. But when Ding Da-hai very slightly released the tension other lights flashed red, like fire. . .or blood. . .

At the moment everything was going well, but there was still need for caution. The doctors had tactfully informed him that the Chairman had not long to live; there was evidence of creeping paralysis and several of his organs could no longer function alone. During the recent series of interviews he had been seated in a specially constructed armchair and was secretly connected to various devices that kept them going. His almost transparent skin had been made-up so that guests would not be left the impression that they had been talking to a corpse. No interview lasted more than a few minutes because of 'a slight cold,' and when the time was up Wang Feng continued the interviews. In spite of such precautions every minute took a lot out of the Chairman and emergency teams in neighbouring rooms never took their eyes off the instruments which measured his condition. Indeed, on two occasions immediate resuscitation had been needed. Wang Feng had cleverly covered up the emergencies. No one, not even the Generals the Chairman liked and trusted most, could be allowed to know the truth about his extreme fragility.

Wang Feng's own authority was dependent on the Chairman's survival and in direct proportion to what was left of his vitality. Everything hinged on this fact. Wang Feng had confidence in his own ability but he was aware that his power base in the army was not strong enough. There had been too little time to gather around him and train enough people to control the whole army. Ambitious men over the centuries had used their power over the Emperor to control the 'barons'. But the ancient concepts of loyalty and trust were dead. The power of the Chairman was based on years of dealing with complicated situations. It was strictly personal and could not be handed down to someone else. Eventually the Chairman was bound to die and without him the 'barons' would no longer be under control. They would act according to their own ambitions and interests. Wang Feng would immediately become Secretary-General of the Military Commission and nominally the most powerful man in the army. But apart from a Guards Regiment under one of the regional Military Commissions, he would not be able to deploy a single soldier without going through the Army, Navy and Air Force 'barons' of the various area commands. If they would not obey him there was nothing could he do.

For the time being the army, in its own interests, would probably remain united. After June Fourth its prestige had been increasing but there was more and more dissatisfaction with the army's role as 'the obedient tool of the Party.' Most of the new generation of officers had joined the army during the Cultural Revolution. They had tasted power and learned how to use it; now they longed to repeat the experience. In the present social crisis they felt the time had come for them to play a role and when the Chairman had given them the slightest encouragement they had expressed their pent-up feelings and hopes and shown their willingness to recognize Wang Feng as the representative of the army. But Wang Feng did not trust their smiling faces and evident desire to curry favour with him. He had studied and thought about the 'Lin Biao Incident,' it had taught him never to drop his guard. After all, the top commanders of the Army, Navy and Air Force had all been faithful supporters of Lin Biao. But when he tried to seize power no one would fire a shot for his sake. He controlled a force of five million men yet died alone in the Mongolian desert. Wang Feng did not have Lin Biao's power, nor his network of supporters. To avoid the same fate he would trust no one.

He examined the submarine's command module and felt something like excitement at the array of precision instruments. He loved this wonderful submarine—and it belonged to him. He was determined that he would never hand it over to anyone. In his present position he would be able to find a reasonable explanation when the submarine simply vanished into the ocean without anyone knowing. Meanwhile he would have to work out a way of keeping absolute control of it. For what purpose he did not really know. But one year would be enough for him to be in control of much more than just the submarine and then he would formally hand it over to the navy.

The choice of captain was crucial if he was to be sure that his orders would be obeyed. He must not only have the highest level of technical and operational experience, but also to be free from the control of any department. No one, neither the central government nor the navy, must be able to give him orders. His name should be unknown and not even appear on the muster roll. He must be utterly loyal only to Wang Feng himself.

He did not believe in the 'will of Heaven' and such things, but sometimes he marvelled at a coincidence. There had been little hope of finding a man with the necessary qualifications: a man who could command a nuclear submarine armed with strategic weapons and whose name was not on the register of personnel. Impossible.

Yet Ding Da-hai was such a man. He had graduated with top honours from the Submarine Academy, and had always been given the highest assessment rating. He had become one of the best submarine commanders of the Navy, spent two years in conventional, before moving to nuclear submarines and given command of a missile-carrying nuclear submarine. There were hardly more than a dozen such men in the whole country. But four years earlier, when he was a research student at the Annapolis Naval Academy, he had a fight with an American officer over a woman and fractured the man's skull.

The court in the U.S. had given him a two-year prison sentence. The Chinese armed forces had no place for such a man and when he returned home the Navy had already forgotten his existence. A considerable number of young able submarine commanders had been trained in the meantime. He quietly returned to his village and earned his living as a fisherman. Because of his experience Wang Feng brought him back and employed him as his representative to supervise the construction of the submarine, and he also helped recruit suitable personnel. After Wang Feng conceived the idea of keeping the submarine, he began to think about appointing Ding Da-hai as its commander. He was certainly loyal, but if he was ordered to fire a nuclear missile at his own village, would he do it?

Beijing: A conference room in Zhongnanhai

A young stewardess lifted the lid of Shi Ge's teacup for the third time. When she saw he had drunk nothing, she changed it for a fresh cup and brought a tray of scented face-towels. Shi Ge took one and wiped the pearls of sweat from his brow. Perhaps taking this as a sign of approval she turned up the air-conditioner.

When he came into the conference room before the meeting started, Shi Ge had forgotten to close the door behind him and she had scolded him like a ticket collector on a bus. This short, stocky man had been the first to arrive. He was so ordinary looking, with none of the air of someone in power—unlike those who all arrived later with their staff—that she took him for some kind of assistant who had been afraid to arrive late, or an old official here for the first time. Had he been quick-witted and humorous and easy to get on with, she might have felt some affinity with him. But he seemed taciturn and unimaginative. He evidently had something on his mind and seemed to look at people without seeing them. It was cold in the conference room and although it was her responsibility to regulate the temperature she had no intention of doing so for his sake. She soon realized that she had misjudged him. The important people now arriving were all very friendly towards him, the General Secretary and the Premier who arrived last even shook hands with him. She had heard his name mentioned and knew he was head of something called Unit Sixteen, whatever that was. Apparently everyone paid attention when he spoke in meetings—this much she did know—and she was now rather nervous about her earlier gesture of impatience. At the time he had repeatedly apologized for leaving the door open, but she had been told that big shots never showed their emotions, even when they punished someone.

Shi Ge often came here, but the attendants always had difficulty remembering who he was. He looked so ordinary—this time he had even shaved his head like a peasant. In any case, he was not really an official but a specialist, the kind of man who would normally sit with minor functionaries in the back rows. In fact he was responsible for formulating plans for dealing with emergencies—the term sounded rather better than 'crises'. In the last few years nearly all work involved emergencies, so his sphere of responsibility was constantly expanding. His staff had grown from a small group into what was now the 'State Security Research Institute' with more than three hundred members. Its responsibility now included various kinds of forecasting, the prediction of possible crises and preparation of the necessary measures. To the outside world the Institute was known simply as 'Unit Sixteen' and under this slightly mysterious name Shi Ge had handled many crises. On occasion he was given authority equivalent to that of a Deputy Premier, yet his name was hardly known to the public. After each crisis he quietly returned to the research institute. In the Chinese hierarchy he did not have a particularly high status.

In the last few days the widespread storms in the Yellow River catchment area had died out, and the floodwaters had receded. Relief operations were now in full swing. A hundred thousand troops had set to work and all the main breaches in the great Yellow River dyke had been repaired. Although the flood still covered a vast area, it had stopped spreading and was being gradually reduced by natural evaporation and drainage. The government was now concentrating on reconstruction in the flooded area and providing for the homeless.

At the meeting today three government 'brains trust' organizations were to put forward their proposals for dealing with the situation, which would then be discussed, before the final decision was taken higher up. The Central Government Policy Research Centre and the Committee for Rural Development—both far more important and more highly qualified than Unit Sixteen—were more strongly represented at the meeting but the person who spoke most was Shi Ge.

The three organizations were in broad agreement as to the scale of the disaster: damage to cities, enterprises, oil fields, reservoirs, railways and agricultural land was estimated (at present day inflationary costs) as at least twelve thousand billion *yuan,* or eight percent of gross national product. But there were considerable differences of opinion as to what the consequences might be. The other two organizations stressed the likely effects on the economy. Shi Ge on the other hand, first drew attention to the impact on the country of a mass of homeless flood victims.

'Nineteen million people—a preliminary estimate—have lost their homes, their land and their property. Their only means of survival is to move into other regions; but there is no region that can feed so many refugees. Hunger will probably drive them to violence. This is harvest time, already there has been plundering of crops and of course if the victims have nothing to eat themselves they will join the starving and seize crops elsewhere. Then the situation will deteriorate very quickly.'

'How can you be so sure that the refugees will plunder other people's crops, rather than growing their own? The problem was solved perfectly well in the past when we had disasters of this kind,' said the Deputy Director of the Central Government Policy Research Centre. It was obvious that he did not approve of Shi Ge.

'In the past the state had reserves of grain. Now there are none. That is the difference. Damage to the ecology in the last few years and a general decline in grain production, have resulted in peasants refusing to deliver grain to the state. This year even the reserves for maintaining supplies to the urban population are insufficient, so to feed an additional twenty million flood victims is a sheer impossibility. As to people themselves getting production going again, how can they do that if they have nothing to eat? A hundred and fifty years ago Zeng Guo-fan said, "If the people have no grain they are bound to follow the rebels: if the rebels have no grain they can only become marauding rebels and the country will never see an end to it." Plundering on a massive scale would not only ruin this year's harvest and distribution, it would endanger next year's production, which would be even more serious. Once social order breaks down and there is no longer any guarantee that labour will bring any returns, production will suffer a fatal blow. The following year the situation would be more difficult, with even more destitute people, even more widespread plundering. This kind of vicious circle can lead to a self-perpetuating crisis, even total anarchy.'

'We are not living in the corrupt Qing empire now !' said the head of the Committee for Rural Development indignantly. 'The flood victims are not the Taiping, White Lotus or Nian rebels that Zeng Guo-fan was talking about. We are properly organized and won't allow things to get out of hand.'

The General Secretary had said nothing. From time to time he got up and walked about, or stood with his hands of the back of his chair. Occasionally he wrote a few notes with a thick red pencil. His face was sombre. Every statistic given out by the three specialist organizations seemed like an evil omen, a dark cloud over his head. Lu Hao-ran appeared unmoved, sitting at ease in a spacious armchair looking at the ceiling, with his hands crossed in his lap.

Shi Ge went on. 'The great rebellions of the last century were not only caused by social injustice and government ineptitude and corruption, there was another element—massive over-population. Country people were supposed to stay in the villages, where there was not enough land to go round, or to take up some trade though there was no one to teach them. Fifty or sixty per cent of them had no trade or means of livelihood. There was no way out for them except begging. The number of monks and social organizations such as secret societies increased, as well as vagrancy, banditry and prostitution. This was the seedbed of rebellion. The fundamental cause was the imbalance between population and resources, which resulted in a critical shortage of grain.

'Our situation today is more serious than it was at that time. You say we are 'properly organized' since the People's Communes were abolished and replaced by the land contract system our rural organization no longer exists, except on paper. We have no means of stopping those who have nothing to eat from taking to the roads, and it is highly likely that another 240 million people without work in villages throughout the country will do the same as the twenty million flood victims. In the last few months, on the basis of rumour alone sixteen million people have moved into the Heilongjiang Sino-Japanese Economic Cooperation Region. As soon as the agreement was signed another thirty to forty million peasants are estimated to have begun to move there lock, stock and barrel. When the Yellow River floodwaters recede a large number of refugees will probably join them.'

'Another region which is attracting the same kind of migration is the southeast coast, especially the provinces of Guangdong, Fujian and Zhejiang where there are already 40 million immigrants from other provinces. Very soon, perhaps at once, there will probably be a new wave of migration. There was a time when people like this—the floating population—maintained a certain order and respect for the law; but the resentment of the famine victims is directed *against* law and order. They are as destructive as the flood that drove them from their homes and wherever they go law and order ceases to exist. What will happen next in this chain reaction is difficult to predict, but if we cannot get the situation under control the consequences. . .'

'A great country like ours as frail and weak as you paint it! Beaten by a mere flood!' someone objected, adding—perhaps because the General Secretary was present—that such talk was totally out of place.

'You're right, China is a huge country. But a very big man on a high wire can be pushed off with one finger. In this case, the high wire is the fact that China's population has reached the absolute limit of what our land and resources can bear, and the finger is perhaps the Yellow River. One centimetre on either side of the limit can have totally opposite effects. There is a logical progression of events which cannot be ruled out: floods cause a grain shortage, the plundering of crops leads to the decline in agricultural production and the refusal of the peasants to deliver grain to the state causes famine in the urban areas, resulting in the collapse of the national economy, political upheaval, social conflict. . .'

TheGeneral Secretary raised his hand to interrupt Shi Ge. 'Let us talk about solutions.'

Although his tone of voice revealed nothing, even the young stewardess could see that he was not pleased. Shi Ge left his sentence unfinished, and drank some tea. This time she did not immediately go to fill his cup.

The key to the problem was money and grain—everyone seemed to agree on this—but not with the picture Shi Ge had drawn. The other two organizations both knew that it was necessary to control the twenty million flood victims and prevent them from becoming vagrants or bandits. This meant grain. Specifically it meant distributing to those left in the villages three or four hundred grams of food grain free every day.

Not much, but just enough to prevent starvation and enable people to get their gardens producing again. This was the only way to ensure that production could start again next spring. The state would have to supply approximately 30 billion kilos of free grain every day for at least a year. Making good the flood damage would cost 12,000 billion *yuan*. Work on flood prevention to keep the Yellow River under control would require another 35,000 billion *yuan*. Where was the grain and money to come from?

It could only come from abroad. But now, with the world population explosion and an increasing world shortage of grain, the only major exporters were the USA, Canada and Australia. The relief grain needed would cost at least 30 billion dollars at today's high prices. China was absolutely incapable of spending such a sum in foreign exchange. Similarly, there was nowhere to find the 12,000 billion *yuan*, except by printing money, but that would raise inflation from three figures to four. As to controlling the Yellow River, it was out of the question. The Great Dyke had been breached in innumerable places—if the same thing happened next year, and the year after?

The Committee for Rural Development suggested getting money from Japan, but the idea was immediately rejected. The province of Heilongjiang had been contracted to the Japanese but China had not yet received a penny. The annual management tax did not have to be paid until a year after the agreement had been in operation and all but 370 billion of the US$ 1,470 billion which had been transferred to Japan was a debt repayment. Shi Ge strongly suspected that this financial transaction had been long in the planning and was connected with Japanese ambitions in Heilongjiang.

It was most unlike Japan to make a generous, altruistic offer of help because China was unable to pay its debt—unless of course the plan was to *prevent* China from repaying it, unless Japan finally agreed to write off the debt in exchange for something. Once this was obtained, China would not be allowed to get off lightly again. Recently public opinion and the press in Japan had been hinting that the party cunning enough to get something cheaply would suffer in the end—a clear message to China not to ask for more.

There was an uneasy silence, then a young researcher from the Policy Research Centre spoke. He began by saying that he was going to express only his personal opinion. Everyone understood what this meant. When for some reason or other it was inconvenient for the head of an organization or a senior dignitary to express an opinion, it was commonplace to get someone younger and less important to say the same thing, but as his 'personal opinion'.

He spoke very well, and evidently had a good command of the evidence. He began by explaining the extent of the damage to China which the June Fourth incident had caused and supported his argument with a considerable number of facts and statistics. International investors had lost confidence in the future of China. Foreign investors had only short-term perspectives, and were ready to withdraw at any moment. Since the collapse of the Soviet Union and the dramatic changes in Eastern Europe, China had become an isolated fortress that bore alone the pressure from the West, led by the United States. All sorts of obstructions, difficulties and restrictions were put in the way, causing inestimable damage to China. Overseas Chinese had lost faith in the political leadership of the mother country; their enormous wealth was difficult to move, and often they had little choice but to watch it fall into the hands of others. After the recovery of Hong Kong the flow of capital and qualified personnel abroad had become a flood. In Taiwan the People's Progress Party had replaced the Nationalist Party and was calling for independence, a demand that was rapidly becoming an irresistible force. Every day Taiwan capital was being invested in Southeast Asia. In China, on the other hand, the speaker said, the memory of the June Fourth incident had not 'faded away' as was first hoped and all opposition groups now used it as a pretext to stir up trouble. Shirking and going slow had become a cancer that contaminated every cell in the tissue of society. Opposing authority and creating disturbances are equally common. The supreme ambition of many young people is to abandon their own country and move abroad. Our people serving overseas even keep their money in foreign banks. Quite apart from other adverse effects, the financial loss to China of this practice he estimated, was a minimum of a thousand billion US dollars.

'Without this loss, the political and economic crisis would be far less acute than it is, indeed the scenario might have been completely different.' The young researcher pushed aside his notes and statistics.

'But history does not allow us to speculate about past events, we can only think about matters which we have right in front of us. The leaders of the Central Committee have said that for us, as advisers, there is no forbidden territory. All opinions and ideas are welcome. But now there is no panacea, no magic formula to put forward. We have no choice—I emphasize again that this is a purely personal view—but to ask ourselves: can we not retrieve something from the enormous damage caused by June Fourth and use it to deal with the aftermath of the flood? I am an economist and not much used to looking at questions from a political point of view; but I am sure that if we publicly reverse the verdict on June Fourth, we would not only win back popular support but also change the climate of our international relations. That would immediately result in massive financial and material aid—even more so now when we have been hit by a natural disaster. Western countries have often reacted in this way. In my view, this is the only way out of our present crisis. At least as far as finance is concerned there is no other solution. That is all I have to say.'

The substance of this rather long-winded discourse could be summed up in one sentence: overturn the verdict on the June Fourth incident. For many years no one had formally suggested such a thing. But no one was surprised: it was no bombshell, not even a breakthrough. Long drawn-out discussions had taken place higher up, a decision had been taken and now, using the formula of a 'personal opinion,' the meeting was being used to test reactions to it. Everything had been discreetly planned by the Policy Research Centre on direct instructions from the General Secretary. The matter was now out in the open and if everything went smoothly, this 'personal opinion' would eventually become a decision of the Central Committee and a historical reality. It was strange that Lu Hao-ran remained so impassive. . .

'I too am going to speak from the economic point of view,' said Shi Ge, breaking the silence at this crucial moment. 'It is true that by overturning the judgement on June Fourth we can obtain funds, the question is, how much? A lot can happen between the moment someone appears willing and the moment he actually signs a check. We cannot base our hopes on attitudes. Western countries made a great number of promises to Eastern Europe. but how much did they get? To imagine that the West will make every effort to help us is naive. Even if it were true, China is not Romania or Bulgaria, nor even the Ukraine or Russia. The whole world has not enough resources to help us. What we need is not some imaginary figure thrown up by a game of calculation, but 35 billion US dollars' worth of grain immediately, and the equivalent of 160 billion for reconstruction material, and 47 billion for Yellow River flood prevention—there is no time to lose, we need it at once. Or should we wait for a charity handout, leave our fate in the hands of others? Rather than being a solution to the crisis, the solution itself would be the crisis'.

The young researcher gave Shi Ge a scornful look. 'At this time we obviously cannot rely on our own resources, so the question is: where can we get such a sum except from the international community? Even if they cannot raise the whole amount, it would be better than nothing, and China has nothing.'

'Comrade Shi Ge, talk about your proposals.' This was the first time Lu Hao-ran had opened his mouth during the meeting. The stewardess, noticing that the Premier seemed only interested in Shi Ge, and did not look at anyone else, immediately went to refill his teacup.

'There is somewhere in China where this money can be found,' said Shi Ge. Everyone stared at him. A pause. 'The army.' There was a shocked silence.

'Our annual expenditure on the army,' Shi Ge went on, 'is 85,000 billion *yuan*; this includes thirty million US dollars of foreign exchange, with which we can buy about 30 million kilogrammes of grain. Apart from this, two year's military expenditure will be ample for making good the losses caused by the floods, and bringing the Yellow River under control. But an additional 85,000 billion will be needed for economic development. In this way we will not only be able to survive, but to solve several difficult questions as well.'

'Wait! What do you mean by "additional"? That sounds as if the army will have no money at all!' exclaimed the head of the Central Government Policy Research Centre.

'The army will not need to spend anything. . .' said Shi Ge looking at a reflection on the chandelier. 'It will be disbanded.'

Everyone stared at him in disbelief. Shi Ge began to speak faster, as if afraid to be interrupted.

'The reason for maintaining an army is for the protection of the country, to prevent invasion. But is there any such threat to China? The population is already at saturation point, and there is no room for anyone else to get a foothold; nor are there any surplus resources to plunder. The space occupied by our 1.3 billion people, and their very poverty—this is our best defensive weapon. Anyone who tried to occupy the country would be completely bogged down under the weight of an intolerable burden. I can think of no single country which has the strength to invade and occupy China. Is it really worth maintaining an army at the cost of 85,000 billion a year? Especially when we can guarantee neither the people's livelihood nor the stability of the country? Some may ask, what about the countries struggling for supremacy in the South China Sea where the outcome will depend on military strength? True, maybe Vietnam, the Philippines or Malaysia would like to occupy a few of the Nansha islands, but do a few coral reefs justify the maintenance of a standing army of over a million? Even if there were a lot of oil under the islands, would it be worth spending 58,000 billion every year to get possession of it? It's true there are people clamouring for independence in Tibet and Xinjiang. But to use our army, which costs us 58,000 billion, to intimidate them—which our million strong Armed Police can do anyway—would be less effective in preventing separatism than using the money to finance development. On the other hand, if there is a war to resist invasion, it would be perfectly possible to protect ourselves by raising an army and waging a people's war. The US forces in Vietnam and the Russian troops in Afghanistan both had to pull out badly battered. China is a hundred times bigger than Vietnam and Afghanistan, and could drown all the armies of the world in a sea of a billion people. In fact, the safest and most effective defence is to be without defences. The possession of nuclear weapons alone can provoke a nuclear attack. With a huge standing army there is always the danger of a coup d'état and military dictatorship. If we completely abandon armament, destroy all our nuclear weapons and announce that we will never go to war, we would win the highest praise and respect throughout the world. We would not lose our security but would have an extra 58,000 billion *yuan* every year. With this money the social problems which torment us at the moment could be resolved and we could escape from our present crisis.'

'I've heard people say that he puts the wind up everyone when he talks, but it's the first time I've seen it happen,' said the head of the Secretariat of the Central committee.

Everyone laughed—except the General Secretary. That he did not flare up was already something. Lu Hao-ran did not laugh, but studied Shi Ge closely, to his embarrassment.

The young stewardess did not appear amused but in fact she was happy. She could see that many people present were making fun of the man with cropped hair—as if he was a madman or a fool—although on the surface they appeared friendly towards him. Giving offence to a man like this did not matter and she was relieved.

Yellow River flooded area

What a sunset! Like a dream land—except for the fact that the people around had hardly enough clothes to cover themselves. In the soft light of the setting sun the golden water stretched as far as the eye could see. A grave and melancholy scene—seemingly frozen in time. The tops of trees, the roofs of houses, apparently floating on the floodwater, looked like chessmen arranged in some mysterious formation on a golden chessboard.

Ouyang Zhong-hua knelt and scooped up some water to splash on his face, then began to inspect his 'domain', as he did every day before it was dark. He had a thick black beard that covered his chin and temples and his long hair was stuck together in strands. He was bare-chested, his trousers were shapeless and his embossed leather belt (of French make) was the worse for wear. But he had lost nothing of his distant air of distinction. He stood out like a crane among chickens and people called him 'the city brother'.

It had not rained for six days and the floodwater had begun to recede. Not long ago the island created by the flood, one of the few remaining pieces of ground above water, had been the size of a basketball pitch, now it was more like three football fields and there was even a bay, a peninsula and a valley. Fifty-nine men, thirty-seven women and fourteen children lived there. The dyke had been breached at night. Most of the men had managed to cover themselves with what they could find at hand, the women had only what they had fished out of the water during the last few days.

Now they were gathered at the centre of the island. Some kneeled down, then the others followed. When he had rowed back to dry land at dusk in his rubber dingy, Ouyang had noticed an image, made of stone, mud and branches on the highest point of the island. This idol, the people told him excitedly, was Beauty—what he had told them they should worship. A few days earlier he would have immediately kicked it to pieces; even without limbs or features, it reminded him of the Earth God, the King of Hell and other hateful idols of the past.

He had said nothing. He knew the result of his experiment now. There was nothing to be hoped for and from now on, he need think of nothing.

The ideas of Greenpeace had come to China from abroad, starting with a warning about the threat to the environment, and later condemned the unbridled growth of industry, and 'consumerism', with its endless pursuit of pleasure. Greenpeace urged self-control, respect for the fragile earth and for other species, the creation of a new mode of production and a new way of life. In China, as elsewhere, many people believed that Greenpeace had put its finger on what was wrong with society; but the solutions proposed were extremely feeble and vague. To make people abandon the principal pursuit of human existence from time immemorial—the production and consumption of material wealth—would require more than a few empty words about peace, spiritual values and return to nature, or the equally useless concepts of virtue, morality, control of the emotions, self-restraint and so on.

What could replace these things and become the theme or motive of human existence in the future? Apart from materialism, is there a comparable source of energy, an inexhaustible life force, which can perpetually stimulate humanity? In his key work 'Spiritual Man', Ouyang Zhong-hua had answered that there was such a force—Beauty. He wanted 'spiritual aesthetics' to replace consumerism and channel man's intrinsic desires and potential away from the material world to the world of the spirit. He believed that the 'spirit' was what distinguished man from animals. Therefore the evolution and development of man required the transformation of 'material man' into 'spiritual man'. He called the society of the future 'the cultural form of society', in order to distinguish it from the present 'economic form of society'.

The pursuit of spiritual life was not limited by natural resources, therefore there would be no limits to growth. In the society of the future, material life would be maintained at a level which corresponded to the environment and resources and the main aim of society would be the constant enrichment of man's spiritual life. In the new society, man's greatest satisfaction would be the perpetual pursuit of progress.

This book had been translated into many different languages and made its author internationally famous. His theory became a fundamental part of Green philosophy in China and one of the aims of the principles of the international Green movement and the basis for other theories. There had been conflicting views and much discussion on how the transition from material to spiritual society could be achieved. Ouyang Zhong-hua took no part in this debate: he was too conscious of his prestige and authority to express an opinion that was not unassailable and astonishing.

The flood seemed to be the opportunity he had been waiting for and he had gone off at once to the flooded area in a helicopter belonging to the flood relief service, taking his inflatable rubber dinghy with him. He chose this island, where the refugees were completely isolated, where no political, economic or social agency could reach them. This was exactly the kind of 'sterile culture dish' he needed for his experiment, and had always been searching for.

The 'islanders' were less apathetic now that they had an idol. Their former strange, uneasy feeling in face of the unreal seemed to have disappeared. Men and women, old and young were kneeling round the idol, reverently bowing their heads to the ground, their pitiful backbones moving up and down. Against a background of monotonous droning as they made their vows, the piercing voice of an old woman called upon the Buddhist Goddess of Mercy. Sticks had been pushed into the ground in front of the idol to represent incense and ancestral tablets.

Ouyang was strongly opposed to the idea of waiting passively for billions of 'materialist' people to become 'spiritual' people automatically. It would take a thousand or even ten thousand years. By that time there would be no question of practising Green policies because the Earth would have been destroyed ten times over with not a single green shoot remaining. Nor could he tolerate the thought that the realization of a lifetime's hard work should be entrusted to 'posterity'. Only if he were able to see the results would it be meaningful for him to sacrifice his life for an ideal. However, the most realistic approach, especially in the case of China, was to wait and see and count on future generations. In the space of a single generation who could possibly transform mankind, already riddled with most materialism, into 'spiritual people'?

He mistrusted the idea, yet he deeply longed for a miracle: to reach the goal in one step. He realized that it was useless to discuss philosophy with the common people. The only thing that might perhaps be made to serve the cause was the thirst for religion in the collective subconscious. History proved that religion had a special power to change people's psychological make-up. Under its influence benighted materialists had sometimes been reborn as 'spiritual people'. So he tried to give a religious form to the Green way of life and to its main theme—the appreciation of beauty.

If a 'Green' religion could rapidly develop to the scale of the world's great religions, would it be possible to transform all humanity? The principles of the Greens were mostly based on ancient wisdom and were an integral part of most religions. The traditional Chinese concepts of frugality, sharing, loving nature, having 'a pure heart and few desires', 'being contented with one's lot', the idea of accumulating merit by good works—what could be Greener? Religious feeling itself is a higher form of the pursuit of beauty, and nothing could better provide the basis of unity between the Green movement of the future and the masses.

At first, in this precarious environment, in the shadow of death, Ouyang felt encouraged: a single spark would light the flame of religion! But when he explained again and again to the flood victims that the 'Green religion' had no gods, no paradise, no ceremonial and no monks; that it was not necessary to prostrate oneself or burn incense, they did not take it in at all. In their timid and ingratiating way they remained immovable and finally destroyed his authority as a founder of religion by erecting their idol. They may have made it green with grass and leaves, and called it Beauty, yet in their frenzied worship it was addressed as 'Yellow Emperor', 'God of War' and even 'Chairman Mao'. .

The idol had tipped the balance. He understood now that however complex a psychological phenomenon religion might be, for 'materialist' people there could never be a religion of beauty. They were prisoners of a short-sighted desire for material gain, for blessings in this world, paradise in the next or a good reincarnation. They understood the present flood as a retribution, a punishment for their frantic pursuit of money, which had made them forget the gods. With the gods, things were clear-cut: there was no mistaking rewards and retribution. They could neither understand, nor respect, nor feel awe for 'Beauty'.

The sun sank below the horizon, a white mist rose and hung over the surface of the water. Ouyang thought of Beijing and of Chen Pan and the warm, soft refuge between her thighs. Before he set out she had said that he would certainly be successful. He had only smiled. Unlike her, he had never made a fetish of 'the people'. It was not really a question of being successful: he was in search of a kind of confirmation, so that he could have a clear conscience. If material man could not make the transition to spiritual man then the Earth was condemned to destruction. Although he had worked hard for his ideals he had long thought that destruction was inevitable.

Even this was an inevitable and dispassionate judgement about reality, yet now, surrounded by the yellow water, a new idea had occurred to him: Destruction and the Green movement of the future would go hand in hand—united by death. In death he saw a glimmering of. . .

'City brother, it's time to eat,' said a timid voice. A girl carefully handed him some wheat grain which had sprouted and a piece of pancake, as she did every day. The worshipping was finished and the people were standing in line to get their rations from the oldest man among them. The first portion was given to Ouyang, who received it in his straw hat. The girl did not leave at once. How old was she? He had never asked her. Ten days earlier he had rescued her from the roof of a house which was about to collapse. He had taken her for fourteen or fifteen, but seeing her well-developed breasts under her sleeveless shirt he realized she must be sixteen or seventeen.

'City brother, I did not go with them to worship the idol. I watched the sun go down and really felt what you said—that Beauty is in the heart.' Her eyes flooded with tears and she turned and ran away.

Ouyang drew a breath of damp air. The smallest spark in a person's soul can cause an earthquake in the mind. Yet what did her words prove? That her fellow villagers *could* change? That she ought to survive? He sighed. She was no more than a glow-worm that could not lighten the darkness, but only disappear into it.

He scooped up some water in his tin, and felt nauseated at the thought of all the bodies that floated in the floodwaters. He crumbled his last sterilization tablet into the tin and fine bubbles rose to the surface. A pity he had not brought more of them and more medicines, but even if he had, there would never be enough for all the survivors.

Mechanically he began to eat the wheat grain. He did not feel hunger any more but he knew that he must eat what there was, even if it was like chewing twigs. Every day he rowed his rubber dingy to where there were submerged villages and dived down into the houses, one by one, and searched the storage jars for grain, covered with silt, and tasteless. His knowledge of survival methods, his courage and medicines, his rubber dingy and a lifetime spent swimming in the Yangzi, the Yellow River, in the Pacific and elsewhere, his authority and his deep and mysterious preaching had made him a saviour in the eyes of the flood victims. Some even said he was a god or a supreme leader. He had set up 'tribes', a distribution system, organized work, and introduced order and even law. His thick waterproof diary was almost full, and the scope of his experiment had gone beyond 'Green' religion to methods and organization for survival.

He had been a well-known novelist, but once he joined the Green movement he gave up a promising literary career and wrote only theoretical works. But the fire of literature still burned in him and although what he said and wrote was logical and analytical, his mind was full of colourful and stimulating images. The limitless expanse of yellow water spread out before him in the bright sunlight. Rats scuttled along the rafters of half-submerged houses. There were occasional shots as looters came looking for abandoned property, boat after boat, loaded with clothing from the dead bodies that floated everywhere, white and bloated. Today he had seen a boatload of sightseers, chewing gum and taking photographs. A young man asked him how many watches he had collected, and he had to grit his teeth to prevent himself from throwing the man into the water. The surroundings were making him react very emotionally. Each time he rowed to an island to distribute some of the grain he had collected, the wretched people surrounded and even kneeled down to him.

The idea of launching a replay of the Taiping Rebellion continued to tempt him. He was sure that if he announced far and wide that he was the God of the Green Sect, he would be able to raise an army of a million flood victims. One call to arms would do it! Had he lived a hundred years ago he would not have hesitated. He sighed. This was no time for a straw hero. An army raised by hunger could only be like a violent storm that soon blows itself out. Philosophy—not a knight in shining armour—should be the guiding light of humanity.

He could only think, and write—at least for the time being. He did not intend to compete for fame and popularity with those champions of democracy. The problem of June Fourth, of democracy, constitutions, political parties, who was on top—all that was nothing but stuff being cooked up in a pot. Since the whole cooking pot was going to be smashed there was no point in snatching a few beans. Everything was going to be burned. History demanded a new pot to be placed over a blazing fire so that everything in the world of mankind would be recast, but it must first be created in his brain—that was the mission he felt he had been given. If he did not complete it as destruction approached nothing would survive.

The light had faded and he could no longer see what he was writing. Then, in the light of new moon rising above the water, he could see the undulating back of a man, between the raised legs of a woman. As the weather and people's health had improved, casual sex had become increasingly common. He did not interfere. He had concluded from close observation and analysis that casual sex, temporarily at least, improved the cohesion and stability of a community like this. Couples on the island who did not take part often became selfish and calculating and were rejected as outsiders by the community.

Ouyang intended to have a good sleep. Tomorrow he was going home and would have to row his rubber dinghy all day. His new theories were fermenting in his mind and he was in a hurry to get back to his studio in Beijing and write, to return to Chen Pan's bed, to the world of coffee, perfume, electricity and music. The people here might survive or else they would die. Let it be soon! Total destruction was inevitable and without it there would be no new life.

To hasten the apocalypse was to accelerate progress. Only when materialist man was obliterated could the age of spiritual man begin. Death was the destiny of these people and to save them would be going against history. He yawned.

'City brother, city brother!' the muffled cries of a woman reached him from a dip in the land near the water's edge. The girl who had brought him his food was being held, hands and feet by two men, a third man, naked, was crawling over her.

'Leave her alone!' Ouyang shouted. 'If she is not willing you have no right to force her.' The men jumped up in alarm. Suddenly the legs of the naked man were shaking and his penis went limp and small.

He waved them away. The girl was crying. Her naked body was white in the moonlight, except for the dark patch between her thighs.

Ouyang helped her up, and she clung to him. 'I am a virgin. Only to you would I give. . .' She sobbed still trembling, and hot tears fell on his chest. He stroked her shoulders and his hand followed her spine and rested on her buttocks.

He looked at the moon, then at the men and women copulating on the ground. Many have died and even more would die. . .

Beijing: Zhongshan Park

Chen Pan was very annoyed. Although she was frequently pestered and had a standard procedure—a few words had seen off several crestfallen men—there were too many of them today. Young layabouts, or aging dandies, all looked her up and down lasciviously. It was hardly surprising. She was a well-dressed and attractive woman alone in a public park and Ouyang Zhong-hua had told her to dress to kill. 'That is your weapon.'

'You want me to sell pornography as well?' she said petulantly.

He hugged her and nibbled at her ear. 'Your sex is only for me.'

The sky was very overcast and in the grey light the tall ancient trees in the Zhongshan Park seemed like part of a lifeless stage-set. Ouyang wanted her to meet Shi Ge, not to call on him, just to bump into him 'by chance'. He frequently made such peculiar arrangements and Chen Pan always carried them out. She knew that Ouyang gave a lot of importance to status, and particularly in his relations with the power aristocracy he would never allow it to be thought that he was asking for, or receiving favours. As his secretary—and his lover—she had to respect his wishes but it made simple matters complicated. Ouyang had been away for several days and she had still not encountered Shi Ge; perhaps he did not like to leave anything to chance. Even flies could not enter Unit 16 without a permit and she had waited outside until she felt like an unwanted prostitute. How she would like to set fire to the place with him in it, until the smoke came out of his arse and he jumped out of an upstairs window!

'Hundred-word Constitution! Read the Hundred-word Constitution! One *yuan* a copy!' shouted a child darting among the crowd. From early in the morning this leaflet had appeared everywhere, pasted up, handed out, stuffed into letterboxes, and children were selling it on the streets. Everyone had assumed that a flood of articles would appear before the Hundred-word Constitution appeared, but suddenly without prior publicity it was being distributed throughout the city.

She had seen it twice on her way here, but was too preoccupied with the 'chance meeting' to take much notice. She did not know how long she would have to wait. Probably enough to understand what it was all about, so she bought a copy.

It was a single page with the title Hundred-word Constitution on one side and the text on the other. It described in stark and colourless terms, using only three sentences, a novel system of elections in a succession of small electoral units of between three and nine individuals, or the same number of elected persons representing between three and nine organizations.

1. Persons in positions of leadership in all social organizations shall be chosen by successive multi-level elections, on the basis of *n*.★ Their term of office is unlimited, but such persons may be recalled at any time.
2. Those having positions in several different organizations shall have the right to vote in each.
3. Those who give up positions in order to assist in carrying out public service shall be appointed by the leadership.

★ *n* = more than three, less than nine

As she read, Chen Pan counted the number of Chinese characters—like everyone else probably. Only if everything, punctuation and all, was included, did it add up to a hundred characters. Most people must have felt rather sceptical about the document because of this gimmick, Chen Pan certainly did. The exact meaning was often unclear and it would surely disappoint those whose expectations had been roused by the word 'Constitution', with its evocation of an imposing and solemn statement of principles, which could win people's respect. Yet this had been boosted as the basis of a new law, the key and nucleus of a 'completely new society'. She felt let down and was forced to conclude that whoever cooked up this Constitution lacked wisdom and judgement. The Society had shown that it was no commonplace organization and it seemed odd that the document was so pedestrian and badly presented. Chen Pan was not sure what Shi Ge's role had been but she knew that he was a man who played his cards close to his chest; perhaps this Constitution was the same, concealing more than it revealed.

A man half tripped over her foot and staggered in an exaggerated manner.

'Don't apologize,' he said, deliberately taking the initiative and sitting down beside her, reeking of alcohol. 'Should I call you Miss or Mrs? If you have a husband, it's all the same. . .' Suddenly he swallowed his words: a micro alarm in Chen Pan's hand vibrated audibly, then retracted into its silver grey case. The man vanished.

Chen Pan was very pleased. The alarm was a gift from friend in the police, and it was the first time she had tried it. Many people nearby moved away. They had taken her for a high-class hostess for foreigners, and a prostitute of course in their over-heated imagination. She went around looking at the various fish tanks of all different shapes and sizes. This was the fifth or sixth time that no 'chance meeting' had occurred. Would that bastard come or not? She was tempted to curse out aloud. Some of the volunteer 'spies' of the Green Association had said that he would certainly come to the park today to see the exhibition of fish. They had already gone to a lot of trouble to get on good terms with his housekeeper, who suspected everyone of being a thief. She had told them in her thick Shanxi dialect that Shi Ge had several times promised Yi-wan to take him to see the fish. How long she would have to go on waiting, hungry as she was, in her role as prostitute or plain-clothes woman depended on 'Yi-wan'—whoever he was.

A group of children raced into the park, each with a bundle of booklets, crying 'Hundred-word Constitution! Analysis and explanation at a glance! Multi-level elections. Hot off the press!' The sound of the children's clear voices seemed to lighten the numb apathy of the people in the park. Chen Pan bought a copy of the Explanations. It seemed that all the children of Beijing of about the same age must be running errands for the Hundred-Word Constitution Society, and they had the right words off by heart. They were doing it for money of course. From the beginning, the Society had given its publications free to children and allowed them to fix the price themselves 'according to the market'. It was the summer holiday and a little extra money for their families was very welcome in this time of high inflation. So the children were full of enthusiasm and had their parents' support. To sell the material might limit its effect, but people would probably not read it if it were merely scattered in the streets, whereas if they paid for it they would want their money's worth. Another advantage was that people had a natural sympathy for children. Both the People's Front and the Democracy Front had tried to block the Society's propaganda, but there was nothing they could do to stop its distribution. There was also the fact that the children's families would also read what their children were handing out. A stroke of genius in fact.

Chen Pan went to sit down again. Her legs were aching, and the bench was near to the fish exhibition, where there was still hope for a 'chance meeting'. She abstractedly read through the pamphlet she had bought, to try to get to the bottom of the three clauses in the Hundred-word Constitution and whiled away the time reading the 'Explanations', in which it was stated that the first clause was the crucial one.

The whole purpose of the Hundred Word Constitution was the introduction of the system of successive multi-level elections and its nationwide application. It was perhaps for the sake of precision that the wording was terse, even wooden, but the meaning was not immediately obvious.

The examples were simple however. For instance, a small production team of not less than three or more than nine workers would elect the team leader by a two-thirds majority. The foreman of a workshop comprising a similar number of such small groups, would be elected by the leaders of those teams. The foremen of the same number of workshops would in turn elect the factory manager by a two thirds majority, and the factory managers similarly elect the company director.

The Commentary explained that according to man's physiological capacity for the retention of information, there can be full mutual exchange in a group of five or six persons. The number was not only an ideal electoral framework, but also the size of a unit most easily administered from above. However, in situations of extreme complexity it should not be a rigid and immutable figure. The upper and lower limits of an electoral unit would be established later.

The system was to be applied throughout the country, right up to the top, where the head of state would be elected by the leaders of the seven great regions of China.

The electoral unit being much smaller than in any other electoral system it would not be necessary to fix the interval between elections, nor would there be any need for a special organization to call elections. Even if the heads of the great regions are hundreds of miles apart, with modern means of communication they would be able for instance to hold a meeting at a few minutes' notice and by a two thirds majority vote to recall the former leader and appoint a new one. A person elected would be able to remain in office indefinitely, as long as he is not recalled.

If an electoral system is regarded essentially as a method of appointment and recall, then the Successive Multi-level Election system would be the exact opposite to the system under autocratic government, since appointment and recall will be no longer from above, but from below.

That's a curious reversal, thought Chen Pan, in theory at least. The common people who used to be at the bottom of the heap take the place of the emperor of the olden days. They become the source of the transfer of power, of appointment and recall. But the emperors appointed high officials like governors-general and governors, whereas in this system the people can only appoint village team leaders and cadres. Not the same thing at all.

The second clause, about the right to vote in any organization one belonged to, was perfectly clear. In contemporary society nearly everyone 'belonged simultaneously to several organizations.'

Chen Pan counted her own affiliations: apart from being a Chinese national, she was Assistant Professor and Head of Laboratory in the Biological Engineering Department of Beijing Agricultural University; she was on the Board of the Agricultural Science Society, and Vice

President of its Beijing branch, Head of the Secretariat of the Chinese Association for the Protection of the Environment, Member of the Chinese Art Association and head of her local residents association. Elections would be held in all these and she could vote and be elected. She would be busy! But at least there was an advantage to this system: it would provide plenty of outlets for self-expression, and encourage diversity of activities.

This electoral system would give rise to a form of organization composed of pyramids. The leader at every level would be invested with complete power over each pyramid. The higher the level the larger the pyramid and at a certain point the leader would no longer be able to fulfil his function alone. He would have to delegate functions and power to individuals or planning teams or operational departments, which would be extensions of his own function. So the third clause laid down that in such cases, unlike other social organizations, those responsible would be appointed from above, by the leader, rather than elected from below.

If this electoral system was also applied in the Ministry of Foreign Affairs, Chen Pan thought, the Minister himself would be elected by the heads of the various departments. In this case what guarantee would there be that the foreign policy of the Head of State would be carried out? For the same reason, could the system be applied in the army or the police?

On paper, she thought, this system seemed plausible. But people would say it was nothing but a dream to expect a magic formula of a hundred words to change the world.

Someone was standing by the bench. She did not raise her head but could see a man's clumsy feet, shapeless sandals and baggy trousers. No fop evidently but this kind of man was sometimes more difficult to deal with. He sat down beside her, and cleared his throat then. She took no notice so he tapped with one finger on the pamphlet she was reading.

Chen Pan could not be bothered with small talk and without taking her eyes off the pamphlet, pressed her alarm. No effect. The man was evidently some country bumpkin who did not know what an alarm was.

'It's a serious offence to impersonate police personnel.' Chen Pan looked up.

A shaven-headed man was observing her with amusement. It took her a moment to recognize Shi Ge.

'What happened to your hair?' she said with surprise, and pleasure—which she immediately regretted as too apparent.

'Do you think I'd look better with only half a head of hair?' She thought her laugh must sound a little silly. This really was a 'chance meeting'.

'How come you're here?', said Shi Ge stroking his head, which now had a growth of stubble.

'These things,' she said, pointing to the fish tanks 'are part of my speciality,' and immediately realized that this did not sound very convincing, since she had not been looking at the fish but reading the pamphlet.

A small boy ran over and said something to Shi Ge then, noticing Chen Pan, came up to examine her.

Chen Pan realized that this must be Yi-wan. Although he was dressed like a Chinese child and spoke Chinese, he had blond hair and a turned-up nose. He turned back to Shi Ge, took hold of his ear, and whispered something. 'He asks what he should call you,' Shi Ge said.

'What do you call *him*?' she asked pointed at Shi Ge.

'Elder brother.' the boy said brightly, hoisting up his trousers.

'Why?' Chen Pan could not help asking.

'He's got no younger brother.'

'That's why you call him elder brother?'

'Uncles and aunties all have little brothers, or little sisters,' said the boy.

'Then...of course you should call me auntie.'

'You've got a little brother?'

'Yes.'

'Bigger than me or smaller?'

'How old are you?'

'Four and a half.'

'My little brother is three years and two months.'

'OK.' The boy looked at Shi Ge for an instant, 'You are auntie.'

'I always thought that Ivan should call you "auntie",' said Shi Ge nodding.

'You didn't think I was of an older generation than you?' Chen Pan replied.

'But Ivan's mother and father call me "uncle".'

'That doesn't explain anything.' Chen Pan put the child on her knee. 'Children nowadays are often given American names. Boris and Ivan (Yiwan) were only popular in the nineteen fifties.'

'His mother is a Russian interpreter,' said Shi Ge.

'How come you're looking after him?'

'I borrowed him.'

'Borrowed?'

'I have no little brother myself, so I borrowed him from a neighbour.' said Shi Ge.

'Did you give her a receipt?' Shi Ge laughed, and Ivan took their hands and laughed too.

Chen Pan did not think much of the exhibition of various species of goldfish. They were all well-known and there were no new ones, but Ivan was thrilled to have a specialist to explain things to him. Finally Shi Ge had to offer him an ice cream in exchange for abandoning the fish.

Shi Ge too was interested in what she had been saying, and on the way to the ice-cream parlour they did not stop talking. They chose three portions of what was said to be ice cream made with water from a mineral spring. Water pollution in Beijing was serious and competition obliged the catering trade and manufacturers to label their products in this way. No one really knew whether it was true or not. Even in the park the air was polluted and made people sneeze. The ice cream parlour had private rooms with 'filtered air', for an extra charge of one thousand *yuan* per person per hour. Shi Ge evidently wanted to be generous. He had to feel in all his pockets to find his money.

The private room was quiet, with only a few loving couples. A pianist was playing and singing softly and a large television screen was showing a football match, with the sound off.

'Can your generosity run to extending our lives for another two minutes?' Chen Pan took two deep breaths of what purported to be fresh air.

'Two minutes each comes to six minutes.'

'At 500 *yuan* a minute?'

'That would have been just 3 *yuan* in 1985.'

The ice cream was not bad. Chen Pan was hungry. In next to no time she had eaten more than half of hers. Then she began to turn the conversation round to the purpose of today's 'chance meeting'.

'Perhaps you don't much like serious conversation when you are not at work, but I wanted to ask you: What do you think the result of all your hard work is? Your motive must be to contribute to the well-being of society, of the people, but do you think that people *are* happy?'

Shi Ge smoothed the tablecloth with the back of his spoon. 'Happiness is rather a vague concept and "people" is too wide. All I can say is that some people are happy and some not.'

'Who *is* happy?'

'I think you are very happy...'

'Don't talk about me. I am not having a philosophical discussion with you, I am talking about feelings. Everyone uses the word "happiness" and without arguing for the sake of arguing, everyone understands it. There is no need for a strict definition. Everyone spends his life in the pursuit of happiness, and you, the managers of society, apart from corrupt ones, are all thinking of ways to promote social happiness. But if everyone works hard at it for several thousand years, will people be happy?'

'These efforts have raised the standard of living of our people several times over.'

'The material standard of living, yes. . .'

'You Greens perhaps don't consider that raising the material standard of living increases well-being, but at least it removes the threat of hunger, cold and suffering.'

'When suffering is due to material deficiencies of course the temporary relief can bring happiness. That's the meaning of the saying "suffering is the source of happiness". But when material goods are abundant and people are no longer threatened by hunger and cold, they will get very little happiness from purely material things. Happiness is not a particular form of matter, something with volume and form—like ice cream—which you can dish up on a plate. Or rather that kind of happiness is a personal one, you eat it and it is digested and absorbed and the more you eat the happier you are. Real happiness is spiritual—an interaction between the emotions and intelligence—which is created and functions in the spirit. Material plenty can only spare people biological suffering but cannot give people spiritual well-being. Once man's material needs are provided for, his happiness does not depend on material wealth. However high their standard of material life people will not be happy. They will be increasingly dissatisfied, troubled and desperate.'

'Theoretically I agree,' said Shi Ge.

'I know that you are involved in practical work, but don't use "theory" as a demarcation line. The activity of men like you is limited by a kind of historical inertia. Civilization began with the struggle for scarce resources and you seem to believe that this struggle is bound to be eternal and unchanging and that humanity's well-being depends on continually increasing material goods and consumption. People like you have made the infinite expansion of the economy the supreme aim of social progress, an aim which is shared by capitalism, socialism, left and right, East and West, who differ only on the question of method. Too much has already been said about the crisis caused by your pursuit of unlimited growth in a limited world, so I won't go into that, or the fact that nature has already punished humanity with new scarcities. I will only talk about something which is within the field of vision even of short-sighted practical men.'

'We have recently completed an investigation,' she continued, 'in which we asked several thousand individuals from all walks of life and in different regions, including 1,400 people in other countries, to classify an ordinary day in their life as either happy, satisfying, relaxed, interesting, exciting, one to be proud of, or as boring, unsatisfying, stressful, humiliating, or horrible. We classified the first as happy and the second as unhappy. The statistical result surprised us all: 67 per cent of people questioned were unhappy. Mind you, this was just a superficial evaluation of daily life. If we looked deeper the number of people caught up in all sorts of crises and trouble would be much higher. As regards the overall attitude to life, the number of people whose evaluation was an apathetic "pointless" was more than 80 per cent. Another thing, in towns and cities where living standards are higher the number of unhappy people was several times higher than in the villages where people had a fairly comfortable life, without being rich. In developed Western countries investigations show an even higher proportion of people with grievances. . .'

'I want more,' said Ivan, pushing his empty plate away. He had been well-behaved for a while and though his plate was clean, his nose was covered with ice-cream. Shi Ge gave him what was left of his. Chen Pan wiped his face with a tissue while he shook his head happily this way and that.

'You think that all the work we have done has been a mistake?' Shi Ge asked.

'Not all, but much of it. The fundamental mistake was in failing to identify the source of happiness as being in spiritual rather than material things. Once out-and-out misery was abolished, the pursuit of happiness should have been in the realm of the spirit. All the energy put into material development should have been put into spiritual development. Economic expansion has a limit, but not spiritual expansion, which does not exhaust material resources. In fact, as spiritual life becomes richer people become increasingly indifferent to material wealth. So, as humanity achieves happiness, the earth—now being destroyed by man's greed—will be saved.'

'It sounds very attractive; but the realm of the spirit cannot be seen or touched. What is the measurement of spiritual prosperity, where is the road to it, what can be done to promote it? The concept is a bit woolly for the majority of people.'

'Have you read Ouyang's *Spiritual Man*?'

Shi Ge nodded.

'For the sake of argument I'm going to adopt your overall concept and process of thought, and merely replace material goods in the economic world by what "spiritual man" calls Beauty. Imagine Beauty as a commodity produced in the economic sphere, perhaps the collective product of countless scientists, designers, workers and industrialists, or the product of individual artisans: a commodity having "use value", which can be circulated, exchanged and reproduced. The greater the "volume and quality" of Beauty the greater the spiritual prosperity and progress of society. The "laws of economics" will be replaced by the "laws of aesthetics", the "relations of production" and "force of production" will give way to the production and service of Beauty.'

'I can't just switch concepts like that.' said Shi Ge. 'Material commodities have quality, form, hardness, colour, temperature. . .'

'All those things are also questions of perception.'

'The nature of matter can also be measured.'

'Yes, but measurements have to be perceived by the senses before they are accepted and recognized and are therefore a form of perception.'

'Now we've got into the field of philosophy.'

'So we come to a full stop: in the realm of philosophy everyone sticks to his own perception. But I think that since you can perceive beauty you should not call it empty, illusory or void.'

They were interrupted once more. Ivan could not eat his second portion of ice cream and was smearing it over his face. 'Why didn't you put some on your hair too,' said Chen Pan, cleaning him up.

'The plate's empty,' said Shi Ge, 'otherwise he probably would, just to show you.' He ruffled the boy's blond hair. 'Go on, go and look at television on your own, put on one of those earphones and behave yourself.'

That day at the People's Front headquarters was the first time Ouyang Zhong-hua had met Shi Ge. Afterwards he had enquired about him quite a lot, and had somehow got the idea of asking him to provide a base where his ideas could be tried out. But Chen Pan felt that Shi Ge was concerned only with concrete matters, thinking only about how to act, feasibility and so on. He was not directly opposed to Chen Pan's theories, but for him everything came down to the 'vital link', as if his thought could only extend along a chain of linked elements. As long as there was one link he was not clear about, he would not move forward. He was neither a 'material' nor a 'spiritual' man: Chen Pan thought of him as a 'man of power'. His vitality and life-long efforts could only be applied in the sphere of power, which he was familiar with and where his skills lay. He would never leave it, and it was difficult to conceive of anyone belonging to the structure of power having imagination. Even if a whole delegation presented him with such a request, he would never agree to support such a distant utopia. However, Chen Pan was obliged to comply with Ouyang's wishes and use this 'entirely chance meeting' to suggest something to him, 'purely as a matter of personal interest'.

'You can't expect us to make every link crystal clear by cogitation alone. We also need to draw on practice, to test and perfect our theories. If you were to give us a base in which we can do this, we will give you a complete solution. Will you do that?' Chen Pan asked.

Ouyang had been racking his brains to find somewhere, a base for a social experiment where Beauty would be the central aim and purpose of life. It would involve not only getting hold of an enclave; it had to be somewhere cut off from outside 'power', a state within a state, free from all intervention. In a society where the state controlled everything this was little more than a daydream.

'Let's cooperate,' said Chen Pan after giving a detailed description of the idea of a base, and cleverly linking it with the power structure. 'The base would be a region of social experiment under you, and not only in name since you will certainly get some inspiration from it. Your job is to study and resolve crises so you too should do some experiments. This base could be one of them. Perhaps in the end you will discover that only an experiment like this can show the way to a genuine solution of crises.'

Someone shouting drew their attention to a couple of astonished lovers opposite. There were two ice-cream plates, just ordered on the side of the table. The ice cream which had been on one of them was now smeared all over Ivan's head and the little boy was standing on tiptoe beside the table. Shi Ge and Chen Pan rushed over to him. He was blinking and seemed very pleased with himself.

Shi Ge apologized several times. The young women was very sharp-tempered and gave Chen Pan a disdainful look. 'Huh! A mother who can't take care of her child. . .'

Shi Ge, feeling for money in his pocket hastened to explain. 'I'm his father.'

Chen Pan was both angry and amused. 'You should have said that I'm not his mother.' She too took out some money.

'Tell us what's the relationship between you two and we won't bother with the money.' The young man had evidently being trying to guess for some time.

'All right, all right! I'm too old to be his father' Shi Ge kept nodding, and still tried to find his money.

'That's enough nonsense,' said Chen Pan, throwing down money on the table. She pulled Ivan's sleeve. 'Come on.'

'He's my brother and she's my auntie,' said Ivan pointing with a sticky finger, while the ice cream dripped from his head. People nearby all laughed.

'I'm going to hit you,' said Shi Ge, putting on a fierce expression.

Then he picked up Ivan and followed Chen Pan outside. He found a tap and pretended he was going to douse the boy with cold water as a punishment. Then he tenderly wiped his face.

After that, Shi Ge said nothing for some time, and they strolled in the park for a while. Chen Pan held Ivan's hand to keep him out of further mischief. Somehow the awkward scene had increased her confidence in Shi Ge. He could not really be like the usual 'men of power'—polite, devious and given to flat refusals, otherwise he would not have bothered to reflect on what she had said.

But when it came down to details, he showed all the precision and foresight of a 'man of power'. He seemed to be merely taking a leisurely walk, and only when they were at the gate of the park did he reach a conclusion.

'Your suggestion is perhaps worth a try. I have understood it and will not forget. But my power is not as great as you think and for the moment I cannot agree to anything. Let me give it some careful thought.'

She had obtained nothing, but she was pleased. She had done what had been asked of her, and better than she expected. She had not waited all this time in vain.

Outside the main gate of the park was Tiananmen Square. There were not nearly so many people about as there were in 1989 and now, most people had only come to see what was going on. The loudspeakers of the People's Front and the Democracy Front competed for attention, the statue of the Goddess of Democracy had been erected in the same place as before. People were warned not to give the authorities an excuse to intervene. The Democratic Front had mobilized a lot of students to keep the roads free, and on Changan Street, traffic was continuous, choking everyone with exhaust fumes. On the other side of the street, a truck was parked, in which a large poster had been stretched on which the whole text of the Hundred-word Constitution had been written in characters the size of a football. Xing Tuo-yu was standing in front of this making a speech. He was some distance away and little could be heard against the roar of the traffic, but he was clearly attacking the 'multi-level electoral system' as giving the people no more than the right to elect 'bogus village headmen'. It was the worst case in history of those in power monopolizing all privilege and a brazen attempt to sell dog meat as mutton. Finally Xing took a blazing torch from someone on the ground and prodded each character one by one, so that only gaping holes remained. Finally the whole poster was destroyed.

It had certainly been made by the People's Front, especially for this burning ceremony, as a final reckoning with the Hundred Word Constitution Society The destruction of every character was acclaimed by those present with rhythmic applause. Chen Pan looked sideways at Shi Ge. Ivan was excitedly shouting and imitating each gesture of Xing. In the light of the flames from across the street Shi Ge's face was frozen in a stony expression.

2

Taipei – On the Fujian-Guangdong border – Beijing: Zhongnanhai – Canada: Lake Manitoba – Beijing: Unit Sixteen – The Three Gorges Dam on the Yangzi River

ℛ

Taipei

Nearly everyone was excited about the result of the Taiwan general election. On the face of it there had been a simple change of government. The Democratic Progressive Party, with 52 per cent of the vote, had defeated the Nationalist party (the KMT) and formed a government. In a country with a multi-party system there would have been nothing unusual about this; but the KMT had held power for several decades as the only legal party.

After their defeat by the Communists in the civil war, the Nationalists had retreated to the island of Taiwan in 1949, swearing to 'attack the Communists and recover the country'. It was like a struggle between two brothers, each claiming to be head of the family and responsible for maintaining its unity.

When the Nationalists and their leader Chiang Kai Shek were in power they continually proclaimed their intention to counter-attack, though this was little more than sabre rattling. But Taiwan's economic development surprised everyone, far surpassing that of Mainland China. The island maintained *de facto* independence and became increasingly different from the Mainland in politics, culture and standard of living; the majority considered themselves people of Taiwan rather than of China. So the independence movement developed in what was in effect a independent sovereign state—though not recognized as such by China and most other countries.

The Nationalists wanted to rule the whole of China, not just one island, so at first tried to stamp out the independence movement, but eventually martial law was abolished and other political parties were allowed to exist. The Democratic Progress Party was founded, representing people who were loyal to Taiwan rather than China, and the independence movement flourished. The Party appealed to Taiwan patriotism and won the election.

The majority of the population had been born after 1949, and regarded mainland Chinese as foreigners. After half a century of separation, the only things that interested them about China were its resources and market potential. 'Reunification of China' was nothing but an empty Nationalist slogan. Taiwan was not very big, but life was good; so, what was the point of uniting with a neighbour who might swallow you up at any moment? Most Taiwanese feared that an open call for independence would provoke an armed response from the Mainland. If that happened there would be no question of independence: even survival was uncertain. Profit always comes first in a commercial and industrial society, so the Taiwanese were opposed to a vociferous demand for independence or any other extremist posturing. After all, what's in a name? As long as separation from China was permanent…

The Democratic Progressive Party took this lesson to heart, stopped talking about unification or independence and adopted instead a strategy of maintaining the status quo, expansion and normalization of trade, which was like dividing the family property between grown-up brothers.

This sensible policy enjoyed electoral support. Even the Nationalist party, in deference to the views of the Taiwanese people, toned down its stubborn insistence on unity and now called now for 'two Chinas'—the co-existence of China and Taiwan—but lost the election.

The result had caused a sensation on the island. Only one man seemed indifferent. He ignored newspapers, television, radio and what people were saying in the streets, and took no part in any celebration.

He was in a small wood in Yangming Public Park eating from a bunch of some sort of amber-coloured tropical fruit. The people who normally frequented the park—leisurely tourists, old men practising *taijiquan* exercises, young couples—had all gone to join in the excitement, otherwise they would have found the behaviour of the man rather strange. His eyes were fixed on the bunch of fruit he was eating. He seemed interested only in his reflection in a small oval mirror concealed among the fruit. With great concentration he kept touching his lips and arranging his hair, as if suffering from acute narcissism. In fact, he was adding twenty years to his age

In a few minutes, the casual and pleasure-loving son of a wealthy Filipino family became a stiff and studious Japanese, with a small moustache and old-fashioned gold-rimmed spectacles. His leather backpack, turned inside out, was transformed into a smart brief case; his brightly coloured shirt, also turned inside out, had become sober and old-fashioned. He then walked away with a military step and waved down a taxi with a gesture resembling a salute. When he went to the Ministry of Defence to examine documents in the military intelligence archives, his appearance, speech and identity card did not arouse the slightest suspicion.

There was more documentation on the Chinese Communist Party in Taiwan than anywhere else. Researchers came from all over the world to use the huge mass of material, collected by the military because it was a matter of life and death for the island. When 'the Major' (now with a Japanese name) requested documentation on the relatively narrow topic of 'arrangements for the personal security of Chinese Communist leaders', a whole case of files was wheeled out of the depository: newspaper cuttings, reminiscences, records of interrogations, reports by foreign observers, deserters or defectors—information meticulously collected by intelligence agents on the Mainland over several decades. Although Chinese security practices had always been a closely guarded secret, once every scrap of information had been put together it formed a more or less complete picture.

'The Major' went through it all very quickly. Like every hit man he was a specialist in security and understood everything, however complicated, almost at a glance, especially as he had already spent several days in Hong Kong and knew a lot already. He appeared to have bad eyesight and frequently examined documents through a large magnifying glass, in the handle of which a miniature camera with a silent shutter was concealed. He would study the photographs later, but most of the information was already stored in his memory.

To him there was nothing particularly ingenious about Chinese security measures, nevertheless it was going to be hard to make the hit. He had studied every important assassination in modern Chinese history and knew that apart from a very few that had been carried out in large-scale operations, nearly all had happened in public places, where the target could be seen. Western politicians had to think about votes and frequently appear in public. In the United States the President's precise schedule was even announced in advance, so that however good the security it was impossible to foresee from which window a rifle shot might come.

However, Chinese leaders were isolated and cut-off from society in every way. They lived behind high walls, travelled invisibly in unmarked cars, attended closed meetings and so on. If they needed to 'be with the masses' they could also appear among them, isolated by security men and only appear openly in newspapers and on television. Isolation was the best way to guarantee their safety. The security techniques might be commonplace, but it was very rare for anything to go wrong.

In the luxurious brothel in Tokyo 'The Major' had asked for five million US dollars; or three million if he made the hit in Japan. The Chinese colonel had replied, without turning a hair, 'I'll give you six million, but it must be must be done in China and must be fatal.'

Last night from Hong Kong he had phoned the number the colonel had given him to find out what travel arrangements had been made for the General Secretary's tour of inspection. A long and very detailed programme was read out to him, from which he drew up a complete plan for the activities of the General Secretary in the coming month. 'The Major' went over it again and again. He certainly had no desire to attempt to penetrate Zhongnanhai, the Party and government nerve-centre, where the guards were almost shoulder-to-shoulder. To ambush a convoy of cars in Beijing was equally impossible. No expense was spared for the security of the top leaders and the bullet-proof cars were of top quality. Even if an explosion made one of them turn over several times the occupant would be unhurt. The same with special railway carriages, which were equipped with oxygen and radio and could remain totally submerged for eight hours, if need be. In such situations, even if there were a fifty-fifty chance of success, 'The Major' would not risk it.

There was one thing in his favour: no top Chinese communist leader had ever been assassinated. Vigilance sleeps if every night is quiet. There must be no engagement if victory was not guaranteed.

Nothing could be done in Beijing, he decided. That left the General Secretary's provincial tour of inspection, which was to start at the end of the month. Once he was on the move there would be more chance of him showing his head. He would be mainly in the Yellow River flooded area, in various cities, but was also due to visit the Three Gorges for the inauguration of the first-stage dam.

He would obviously be seeing flood victims on his tour, and for days 'The Major' had been trying, in vain, to think of a way of taking advantage of this. He had been convinced, especially since reading through the material, that this was going to be a difficult assignment. In the first place, it was impossible to find out precisely where the General Secretary was going to be at any given time. Such details were always decided at the last moment and he would have to phone to Beijing to find out. But where would he find a telephone in the flooded area? Everything would hang on that. Secondly, when top Chinese leaders 'meet the people', it was invariably in closed-off, tightly guarded places, which no unauthorized person could enter. If he did not know every detail, how could he be sure that he would be able to use his weapon? Anyway, the first principle of his line of business was to protect oneself, especially in a situation like this where there would be no turning back.

It was for self-protection that he had asked the Communist colonel to tell him who had ordered the assassination. 'Otherwise how can I be sure that you will keep your promise to get me out of China? There's the video of course, which I could make public, but there's no mention of the name of the man in charge, and how many people know you, Colonel?'

It looked then as if the deal was going to fall through. The name had to be genuine. It would be useless to try to fool 'the Major'; he knew too much about the set-up in China.

At first the colonel was adamant, but after a long argument said casually, 'If I give you the name you will get…' (he squeezed his left leg as if giving a hidden signal) 'eight million, not six.'

In Tokyo, when the colonel had proposed six million instead of the five he had asked for, 'the Major' had begun to like him. When the reward was raised to eight million he positively admired the colonel. The man deserved his higher rank!

'I will give you an account number and you will transfer the extra two million to this account. This is what we call in China "presenting flowers to Buddha given you by someone else". The name I am going to give you is worth the whole of China and will make you as safe as Fort Knox.'

The colonel's expression was serene and kindly. The money belonged to the boss, but the account was obviously his. 'The Major' was sure that it already contained a million or two.

'Wouldn't it be better if I just take the whole eight million,' he said with a smile. He was joking of course. He knew that the colonel still held the trump card. Better to have such a man as an accomplice than an enemy.

The name worth two million dollars was 'Wang Feng'.

After going over the General Secretary's itinerary repeatedly, 'the major' finally decided to wait for inspiration. He abandoned the idea of making the hit in the flooded area and saw in his mind's eye—in a flash of inspiration—a whitish-coloured dam at the Three Gorges

He asked the assistant in archives in deliberately bad Chinese, whether there was any material on the Yangzi River dam at the Three Gorges. She searched her computer.

'I'm sorry we don't have much on that kind of engineering project.'

'The Major' laughed. 'Engineering project? The Taiwan army make mistake: if there is war, the Great Dam will be worth ten hydrogen bombs.'

A Taiwan army officer looked up from the catalogue he was examining. 'If you are interested in the Three Gorges Sir, you should go to Canada. They wanted a contract for some engineering work and did a lot of research on the project. They've got more material than anyone.'

'The Major' bowed and thanked him.

'I would like to inform you sir,' the officer added, 'that even without the advice of Japan the Taiwan army understands the military significance of the Great Dam. In fact I have just returned from Canada where I myself was researching that very topic.'

'Sorry,' said 'the major' respectfully. Then he stood to attention and bowed. Forty-three minutes later, once more a lively young Filipino tourist, he flew to Canada.

On the Fujian-Guangdong border

After the passage of the typhoons, the sky was extremely clear in Fujian and there was not a breath of wind. The four typhoons had followed each other with hardly any interval, after which there were rainstorms for twenty days.

The sun, absent for so long, hurt the eyes. Huang Shi-ke was protected from its rays by a large, specially-made parasol held by an attendant. His private secretary was taking notes in shorthand, beads of perspiration on her beautiful young face. Huang Shi-ke felt sorry for her and was tempted to invite her to join him in the shade. He had hardly ever felt the desire to hold or protect anyone; but there were a lot of reporters and officials around, so he held his large grey head upright and pretended he had not noticed her.

Press representatives had been brought from Fuzhou to a town on the provincial border with Guangdong in cars provided by the provincial government. Huang Shi-ke told them that the damage in the province caused by the typhoons was very serious and as Deputy Governor of Fujian and head of the provincial inspection team, expressed sympathy for those who had suffered. He hoped that the press would truly present the facts—the damage was visible for all to see—and inform the world of the heroic struggle of the Fujian people to bring help to the victims of the disaster.

'We in Fujian are determined to rely on our own efforts to rebuild what has been destroyed and make good all losses without adding to the already heavy burden on the state. Nor will we go begging to neighbouring provinces, though we do need help. But we know our country's present difficulties. The provinces and cities which have suffered from the Yellow River floods also need help. The greatest assistance we can give to our country and to the other disaster areas is our determination to be self-sufficient. We ask you to help inform people that at the very moment the Yellow River broke its dykes, Fujian was hit by Typhoon 17. When Typhoon 18 arrived immediately afterwards and inflicted the damage which you have all seen, our situation became desperate. Then there was a third typhoon. It is not a question of our 'refusing' to help the flooded provinces in the north; we have not yet tackled our own problems and simply do not have the means to help them.'

After the great Yellow River floods, several devastated provinces in the north had collectively called for aid and later attacked the south-eastern coastal provinces very savagely, especially Fujian, for callously turning a deaf ear. This put the provincial authorities in an awkward position. It took a reprimand from the central government before a few trainloads of old clothes were sent north; but that was not enough. The only solution was to silence the criticisms by publicizing the extent of the typhoon damage in the province. This was the sole purpose of Huang Shi-ke's tour, of the invitations to the press representatives, of the presents and lavish hospitality they had received and the communication facilities put at their disposal.

Each press representative had been accompanied by someone holding a parasol, and the night life of Fuzhou, the masseuses of Xiamen, the access to smuggled goods, the lavish meals in restaurants, had made them all feel very friendly towards Fujian. They sent off their despatches with emotion, along the lines of what Huang Shi-ke had said.

After speaking to the press, Huang Shi-ke, accompanied by the local county magistrate, then visited the home of a 'typhoon victim'. As he went upstairs he tried hard to conceal his breathlessness. Although Bai Ling remained outside, he was worried that she might hear the stairs creaking under his weight. He resolved to eat less (not for the first time these last few days) and take up jogging—a normal reaction for a middle-aged man with the image of an attractive woman always in his mind. However self-confident in other matters no one can escape the sorrows that come with age, corpulence and wrinkles.

The house had three storeys. The owner, a former fisherman, having become rich through smuggling and taking off emigrants in his boat, had built himself a hideous and ostentatious house. Although it had been in the direct passage of the typhoon, it had suffered little damage. Not a pane of glass was broken, only a few tiles had been displaced. While he had been talking to the press representatives, Huang Shi-ke had noticed this ridiculous house, with tiny mirrors stuck all over it; the sight made him furious. It would only take one reporter to cotton on, especially if he was one of those fellows always on the look out for a scoop, and the whole carefully rehearsed performance would be exposed. Fujian would be lambasted and he would be finished.

Once upstairs, out of earshot of the press, Huang Shi-ke savagely tore into the county magistrate and cursed him savagely in his ugly Fujian dialect.

The damage in the province had been far less serious than this 'tour of inspection' had been intended to suggest. The three consecutive typhoons had only affected maritime shipping and the fishing industry. A few perfunctory relief measures had been taken. But when demands came for help for the flooded areas in the north, the typhoons took on a new significance. The provincial treasure was at stake; properly handled the typhoons would be blessings in disguise.

After meticulous overall planning, the provincial government announced that Typhoon 18 had 'cut communication lines'. By the time meteorological stations in Fujian were able to send their reports to the State Meteorological Administration, the statistics they contained had nothing to do with instrument readings; the figures had been sent from the provincial government by secret and circuitous routes. Even God himself would not be able to detect any discrepancies with reports from other sources.

Most meteorological stations reported 'tornadoes of great destructive force'. Dozens of work teams had gone from the provincial capital to the 'disaster areas' to supervise the collection of data and fabricate reports on the damage. On the route the inspection team and press representatives were to take, arrangements had been made for 'eyewitness accounts' by 'typhoon victims' to be available. Trees and power lines had been pulled down, roofs removed, windows smashed and the ground strewn with all sorts of things the wind might have deposited.

People had always exaggerated the extent of damage in order to get more assistance and compensation. Although obstruction was the norm when things had to be done in the villages, in this case no more than a hint was needed.

Huang Shi-ke was very satisfied with his tour of inspection, although he was still furious about the pretentious—and *undamaged*—house. The magistrate cringed obsequiously, but Huang Shi-ke would listen to no excuses.

An increasing number of people in search of a better life, were going by sea to Japan, Hong Kong, Indonesia, South Korea—almost any foreign country. Those who owned boats had become so rich that they needed trunks to carry their dollars. The proprietor of the house, having made his fortune, had sent a valuable stag antler (famous for its restorative properties), to Huang Shi-ke as a gift. However, 'the waterside pavilion is the first to see the moon' as the saying goes and the magistrate, being on the spot, had certainly received much more than a stag antler, otherwise he would not have been so ready to defend the former fisherman. A man like him, Huang Shi-ke reflected, may suddenly amass a pile of money, yet not lose his peasant mentality. He could not bear to sacrifice his windowpanes, let alone climb up on the roof and remove some tiles, in spite of the fact that the work teams had money with them, and paid compensation on the spot for any 'typhoon damage'. Of course the provincial government had to foot the bill, but it was insignificant compared with what the central government was asking for.

'Get the roof off tonight and smash all the windows facing the sea and all those damn mirrors,' said Huang Shi-ke between his teeth. 'Tomorrow the government consolation team is coming, and if I find the house as it is now I'll have your skin!'

Huang Shi-ke was alone with the magistrate. He had worked in the provincial government for more than twenty years and Deputy Governor for eight, and he always spoke his mind when he talked to county magistrates. Provincial governors come and go, whereas Huang Shi-ke stayed put, spreading his roots and flourishing. Nearly all the county magistrates were his men and in general, his word counted for more than the Governor's. It was he who had stage-managed the 'typhoon disaster' scenario. He was the only man who dared put on such a blatant masquerade.

The town of Xikeng was the last stop on the tour of inspection, then most of the group would return to Fuzhou. Huang Shi-ke was going to the provincial border to meet the Deputy Governor of Guangdong, who was making a similar tour of inspection in his own province. Although it was only a journey of twenty kilometres, Huang Shi-ke had Bai Ling travel with him in his own car to read despatches to him—one of the duties of a confidential secretary. But behind the soundproof glass partition that separated them from the chauffeur, the conversation had little to do with official matters.

Just before Huang Shi-ke left Fuzhou the deputy Secretary-General of the provincial government had introduced the new confidential secretary to him. He had not seen her before and now never stopped thinking about her. What attracted him was not just her youth and sex appeal, her jet black eyes, moist lips and delicate complexion. He had seen plenty of pretty girls. Bai Ling was different.

She dressed simply, behaved with dignity and composure and seemed unaware of her beauty as a capital asset. He found this increasingly appealing. When they were face to face she was suitably deferential, but sometimes, when he stole a sideways glance at her he would suddenly meet her eyes, staring at him, in a way that went to his head. Then there would be the fleeting look of confusion of someone caught in the act and she would seem to retreat into her habitual reserve. Perhaps it was this too which attracted him. He had seen women who only knew how to ingratiate themselves, flirt openly and would jump into bed with you at the drop of a hat. He despised and distrusted them.

He had never imagined that at his age a young woman would steal glances at him like that. They could hardly have been put on. Was there something about him—apart from his power—that appealed to her? Could he experience again the rapture of youth? He was much tempted, dared not believe, and wanted to put it to the test. He felt like a young man in an agony of doubt, caught for the first time in the net of love at first sight. But he was a person of position and standing, not a young man. Whatever he might feel must be kept under control; he must wear a mask of restraint and reserve; he must appear indifferent, detached, and only make extremely cautious soundings, almost invisible like a spider's thread. When 'reading documents' on previous occasions during the tour, they had talked and became more intimate, but he had not received the encouragement he was hoping for.

Although the difference in their status was maintained he, as an older man, showed much solicitude for her. The last time they talked she had told him she was twenty six and without attachments. By modern standards she would soon be considered a 'difficult case'. Huang Shi-ke kindly encouraged her by saying that he could not understand why the 'problem' of marriage had not yet been solved, considering her many qualities. He advised her not to be too choosy.

'Do you want me to introduce you to some fine young man?' He said jokingly, watching carefully to see her reaction. Bai Ling tried to smile, but only succeeded in looking sad. For a long time she watched the fields and houses, then tears dropped slowly from her eyes.

'Bai Ling. Has someone done you an injury?'

'No, no,' she shook her head slightly. 'A wound heals.... I am completely destroyed...'

'No, Bai Ling,' he gently took her hand. 'I can help you.' Her hand trembled and became quite hot, though when she spoke her voice was calm.

'I need your contempt rather than your help. I was seduced by a retired airline pilot when I was fourteen. I understood nothing then. He was kind and considerate, taught me a lot and gave me confidence. I became obsessed with sex. It went on for two years and it became more and more difficult to break it off. No one knew. My parents didn't even suspect anything. Then one day he had a stroke and died, and I became very ill. That was ten years ago. Since then I have not been with a man. Lots of boys have been after me and I tried to get close to some of them, but found that young men got on my nerves. It's more than just a matter of preference now. I like only older men, who are mature and wise and fatherly. I like grey hair, the wrinkles of life and experience, not smooth and immature faces. At first I thought this was because of my first lover and would change with time, but nothing has changed. I control myself though, rather than cause misfortune and retribution. But it is not enough to rely only on self-restraint. To be despised by people—only that can tear out ill-fated love from the heart.' She raised her head finally. 'I want you to despise me.'

The town was already in sight. Huang Shi-ke's head was spinning. She loved old men!...A love which she could not hold in check! Nothing could be clearer. How could he despise her? He felt grateful to the pilot. If they had not been about to arrive at their destination he would have taken her in his arms.

A large green military bus was parked by a small wood on the outskirts of the town. People were waving. Bai Ling quickly wiped her eyes and became the confidential secretary again. Huang Shi-ke was deliriously happy and could not suppress a wide smile. The Deputy Governor of Guangdong took this to mean that the 'Typhoon disaster' plan was going well and seizing Huang's hand, laughed out aloud.

The scenario necessitated the cooperation of Guangdong. Typhoons 18 and 19 had affected both provinces, so it was essential to coordinate their reports. In fact Guangdong had suffered slightly less damage than Fujian, but Beijing had demanded from Guangdong double the amount of money for Yellow River flood relief that Fujian was expected to provide. Guangdong was therefore very enthusiastic about presenting a convincing picture of 'typhoon disaster'. In the town, all the houses had 'lost' their roofs in one street, which looked like a row of irregular teeth. Huang Shi-ke, as producer of this masquerade, felt a little upstaged.

The green military coach looked very ordinary from the outside, but inside was like a five-star hotel suite, complete with a Jacuzzi. Several attractive waitresses served a lavish feast, which appeared as if by magic, produced by a cook who was a master at combining colour, smell and taste.

As the lights dimmed and changed colour there was a discreet sound of music. The deputy governor of Guangdong explained rather apologetically that this vehicle (including the cook and the waitresses) had been hired from the army and paid for in Hong Kong dollars. The

Guangdong provincial government had intended to buy two such coaches, but when there was a government crackdown on importation of such luxuries had not done so, out of a sense of discipline and in fear of denunciation. The army had imported this one as 'military equipment' and no one dared question the price. Nor did Customs present any problem, since the vehicle was brought into the country by a warship. It had been necessary to change its 'capitalist' appearance to one more suited to service in war, or relief work in the countryside, so it had been repainted a dull green.

The conversation quickly turned to the present situation.

After the Cultural Revolution, China had started on the road to economic development, reform and 'opening up' to the Western world. The essence of economic reform was expansion of the economy and decentralization of power, and when central government control was relaxed, the existing differences between various provinces—in climate, geography, technical skills, industrial, commercial development and other things—led to increasingly uneven development.

Economic development of the provinces on the South East coast newly opened to maritime trade, far outstripped that of other provinces. People from inland as well as raw materials and capital flowed into the region and commerce flourished.

After June Fourth the hard-liners tried to reverse this tendency by strengthening the planned economy and central control; but it proved very difficult to remove the effects of reform. Many counties in the South paid more tax on profits than a whole region elsewhere. The clock could not be put back without damaging the national economy. Even if government control were tightened up, the economy of the coastal provinces would not have changed, because people in the upper levels of provincial society had all sorts of ways to protect their interests.

In the inland provinces on the other hand, the economic reforms had not been properly implemented and the big industrial enterprises controlled by the state were still economically strong.

The contrast was so great that some people even spoke of 'two Chinas'. Before June Fourth, the coastal regions were in the lead and the inland provinces followed. When the government became more authoritarian there were frequent political attacks on the coastal provinces, the latest being the demand for massive, punitive contributions to Yellow River flood relief.

June Fourth was naturally regarded as a turning point by the coastal provinces. The only way to return to free development was to 'reverse the verdict' on Tiananmen and end the present state of political inertia. So the coastal provinces had launched an ostentatious public campaign in support of the moderates led by the General Secretary. The crucial question now was what the attitude of the army would be so each province was busily trying to win over the military units stationed in the south.

With the regiments in the Guangdong Area Command there was no problem. They had been stationed for a long time in the province where free economy was most developed, and were far more open than most to new ideas. All the high-ranking officers were involved in commerce and industry. The Area Command itself owned enterprises and now resembled a big financial corporation in uniform, an integral part of the free economy.

This made Huang Shi-ke envious. The army units in Fujian came under the Nanjing command and although Fujian too was a region of free economy, he had not yet found a way to involve them in it. Some entrepreneurs would have openly stuffed money into their hands if only they would open them, but in the Nanjing Area Command, fists were tightly clenched. Each unit was kept under strict control; shut up in their barracks, they had little local contact and took no part in economic activity

So far, a few sons of high-ranking officers had been persuaded to become managers or directors, which they had done more out of defiance than anything else. This was not the same as getting their fathers involved.

At least, the commanders of the Nanjing and the Guangdong Area Commands had not given orders to open fire during the June Fourth days, which would at least give them more freedom of movement when the time came to make a decision. The time was now, but the decision was still uncertain.

Huang Shi-ke asked the deputy governor of Guangdong for help in wooing the military. The daughter-in-law of Commander Bai of the Nanjing Area Command was due to come to Guangdong on business and it was essential that she be secretly helped to clinch a really big deal. Fujian would make up any loss involved. Time pressed and no expense should be spared.

The food was delicious, but Huang Shi-ke did little more than taste each dish and hardly drank at all. He was known as a *bon vivant* and his host expressed surprise at this abstinence. Huang Shi-ke said it was because of high blood pressure. In fact, he was thinking of Bai Ling and her preference for grey hair and wrinkles—she would hardly feel the same about a pot-belly. He had no need to worry about his age apparently, but his figure must be acceptable, so he resolved to lose ten kilogramme's. If only Bai Ling had been sitting opposite him instead of his wretched old Cantonese colleague, this little mobile palace would have been truly delightful.

He refused an invitation to Into, where a Thai girl was waiting in the hotel to give him a 'restorative massage'. He was a little put out. The Cantonese were so indiscreet! 'In a time of trouble like this,' he replied, 'I should be back in Fuzhou.'

It was already dark when he found out that the provincial deputy Secretary-General had gone on ahead, without saying a word, to a small town just across the border with Fujian and had taken Bai Ling with him. He was a little disappointed. When it had been suggested earlier that they spend the night there Huang Shi-ke's heart had missed a beat. It was a quiet, out-of-the-way place where something could easily happen, but he had managed to conceal his excitement.

His only worry was how to find Bai Ling in this dark little town, but when he arrived he was taken by the deputy Secretary-General straight to a dilapidated bathhouse containing a mineral spring.

'This is a cinnabar spring,' said the latter enthusiastically, unaware that Huang Shi-ke had other things on his mind, 'the water is warm in winter and cool in summer, and good for the skin. People say it's a marvellous stimulant...' Huang Shi-ke was about to say something impatiently when the other apologized for wasting his time and left hurriedly. What an idiot!

The water was indeed very pleasant, constantly flowing at blood temperature, gently tickling and stroking the skin, as if cleaning the dust and sweat out of every pore. The bathhouse itself was in a terrible state, like public baths more than ten years ago. The pool itself was cemented and badly made. There were a few wooden benches to put one's clothes on. The plaster had fallen off the walls in several places, and the stars could be seen through gaps in the roof.

A partition made of green plastic panels divided the bathhouse and pool into two. Huang Shi-ke explored with his foot and found that the partition went down to the bottom of the pool and swayed back and forth with the current as the water flowed through gaps between the panels. The light on the side where Huang Shi-ke was did not work, but the strong bulb behind the green plastic was enough to light both sides.

He heard the door of the bathhouse open, the sounds of slippered feet, of a basin being put down on the side of the pool. A woman naturally, since the other side was reserved for women. The light was not on and Huang Shi-ke did not move so she did not realise that there was anyone else in the bathhouse, and was singing light-heartedly. Bai Ling! He could recognize her voice. He heard her undressing, and his heart began to pound.

She got into the pool. The water that had touched her skin now caressed his! He saw her shadow, slightly distorted on the swaying partition; she was naked, moving... showing changing curves and contours from every angle.

The spring water in the pool seemed to turn into alcohol, slightly blue, and burning more and more fiercely. Huang Shi-ke held his breath, controlled his trembling and began to caress the shadow on the partition. Gradually he came closer and closer as if drawn by some mysterious force. Then he stood up and passionately pressed his body against the shadow of hers.

When the partition suddenly collapsed he stood as if dazed, seeing only a yellow radiance, the dark shadow on the partition was gone and now, on its sloping surface her creamy body was reflected. Bai Ling's eyes were wide with alarm. She covered her breasts, with her arm, then her pudenda. But she did not cry out when he strode through the burning water and took her in his arms. She weakly closed her eyes and gave a sigh that electrified him.

Beijing: Zhongnanhai

'*Shou*... Receive energy!' The voice seemed to be carried on an exquisite breeze from beyond the horizon, out of clouds touched red by the evening sun and trailing a long silken net, that gathered up dispersed energy, like a mother's hands gradually coming together... Then the sensation of vital energy flowing into Lu Hao-ran's body gradually faded.

Giving out energy was like bathing in a pool of sweet spring water, receiving vital energy like the caress of satin. The celestial vision, the ripples of gold and silver, gradually dissolved as if in the infinite distance, a whole year had passed, and he returned to the bamboo grove.

'Prime Minister, please come under the covered pathway and rest a while,' said Zhou Chi's disciple deferentially. She was a film actress. Although no longer young she was still beautiful and her voice resembled the pure ethereal '*shou*' of a moment ago, but now had a note of anxiety in it, and there was a hardly perceptible hint of unease in the glance she gave Zhou Chi.

Zhou Chi sat down on a stone bench and looked at the fast-moving clouds. He was completely motionless and dignified, as if bearing an invisible weight. Three other men, also disciples, stood around Lu Hao-ran, forming a triangle, practising *qigong*, their eyes fixed on Zhou Chi.

The Actress held her breath. Then, when she saw a drop of rainfall on the stone bench outside the covered way, exclaimed with astonishment and delight 'Look Prime Minister!' She pointed to the raindrop excitedly, as if she had just been awarded an Oscar. Although the *qigong* exercises had greatly increased Lu Hao-ran's perception of things around him, however hard he looked, it was still only a drop of rain.

'But for the Master it would have been raining by now,' she went on. Lu Hao-ran was completely mystified by her excitement. There was a sudden peal of thunder, and rain began to patter down on the bamboo leaves.

'When cultivating vital energy it's important not to get wet, because you become ill if you stop suddenly halfway through. So the Master stopped the rain,' the actress explained, looking at him in admiration. 'I saw his aura change from green to red and shoot into the sky. It's the first time I've seen him do it. Look, as soon as the Master receives energy the rain starts. Getting it to rain takes a lot of internal energy. How are you feeling Master?'

Zhou Chi smiled but did not answer. He evidently felt it was not worth talking about.

Lu Hao-ran said nothing. He had already accepted a good deal of this esoteric discipline, but his education made him regard such things as 'obtaining rain' as nothing but superstition. He had studied and got his doctorate in Moscow in the 1950s, and had later worked for many years in the fields of science and technology. Nevertheless, there were some things he had seen with his own eyes and could not disbelieve.

On one occasion for instance, a young disciple had chewed into a paste a strip of paper on which Lu Hao-ran had written a few words and added his signature. Then he had turned the paste back into its original form. It was still wet even and what he had written was unchanged.

He thought sometimes that this was nothing but a conjuring trick. Just now, it might have been a coincidence that he had come under the covered way an instant before the rain started. Zhou Chi could easily have controlled the actress by secret signals. But if Zhou Chi was manipulating him what was he trying to achieve?

Zhou Chi looked about thirty, though he was said to be fifty. His eyes were small, bright and very piercing, his face smooth and without a wrinkle. His slightly bent back made him look like a wild leopard cat about to pounce on its prey. He was Chairman of the All-China Qigong Association, which had branches all over the country, twenty six million full members and ten times that number of enthusiasts, who all worshipped him. This gave him power that any politician would envy.

He came twice a week to direct *qigong* sessions with Lu Hao-ran. Three of his male disciples surrounded Lu Hao-ran and transmitted energy to him, the actress contributing *yin* energy.

According to Zhou Chi, this formation produced a sudden intensification in the recipient's unconscious mastery of *qigong* and an increased physical and mental well-being. For someone to enjoy such a privilege had always been 'as rare as phoenix feathers and unicorn horns'. In fact, he said, Lu Hao-ran was probably the only person in recent times to have done so.

Lu Hao-ran had been practising *qigong* for several years, sporadically at first and purely for health reasons, but without any marked effect and without getting better at it. Since he had become isolated and excluded from the political inner circle, his interest in *qigong* had increased. Perhaps he was subconsciously looking for some kind of compensation, or just had more time on his hands. Zhou Chi had been recommended to him by the Minister of Health. *Qigong* made him feel like a new man, full of energy, light and relaxed. It became very important to him and after each session he looked forward to the next.

He had lived most of his life free of uncertainty. Now he kept swinging like a pendulum between belief and disbelief, and it worried him. Yet, he felt a certain awe and veneration... He glanced at Zhou Chi, met the sharp bright eyes, and involuntarily looked away, suddenly depressed. Why was he incapable of recognizing this *qigong* master for what he was—a charlatan and ex-convict from the world of quack doctors and fortune-tellers?

A member of his staff came to tell him that the Minister of State Security had arrived. He shook hands and took his leave of Zhou Chi, but did not thank him. He did not trust him as he once had, yet felt even more anxious to ingratiate himself with the man.

In the car the minister frowned and put his hand out of the window to feel whether the rain was stopping. The action was about to start and heavy rain might ruin everything. They went to a secret room on the 17th floor of a building overlooking Tiananmen Square, where a television screen showed people running for shelter. The pressmen stayed, and put up umbrellas over their cameras.

'As long as the foreign press is here it will be all right,' said the minister. 'Most of the others have just come to watch the fun.'

Lu Hao-ran had come every day lately to see what was going on in the square. This was a special occasion however. The Minister of State Security was here and no one else was allowed in. Automatic cameras, connected to a control room, had been placed in the square and the minister could select what he wanted to see on the screen in front of him.

The pouring rain whipped up a white mist in the square, flags hung limp and motionless and the ink on the posters had begun to run. It was time to begin. The foreign pressmen looked at their watches. There was still no sign of activity. The rain could easily make people change their minds or think it would put out the fire, though with petrol there was not much risk of that.

Lu Hao-ran was wondering whether Zhou Chi could really stop it raining. There was a crash of thunder. Could a man of flesh and bones pit himself against the elements? If *qigong* had such power, all human efforts were puny in comparison. Whether the recent demonstration of 'rain control' was genuine or not, would Zhou Chi agree to use his gifts in his service? When the Minister was out of the room, Lu Hao-ran rang the usual number and said 'Comrade Zhou Chi, in the interests of our country I wish you to stop the rain in Tiananmen Square.' Silence. Not even the click of a receiver being put down. The line must have been cut.

The minister returned. 'The weather people say that the rain will stop in a few minutes,' he said eagerly. Lu found him rather repulsive. He looked at the screen, sure enough the rain was lighter and the sun began to come out. In summer the rain comes and goes quickly and most of the time no one, whether meteorologist or *qigong* master, could get the forecast right.

Lu Hao-ran took up the phone again. It sounded normal. What sort of man was this Zhou Chi? He felt more and more suspicious and sceptical. There was no proof either way of his ability to control the rain.

When Lu Hao-ran had visited 'the Chairman' in the Western hills he had been more or less promised the position of General Secretary, but there had been no hint as to how this was to come about. Wang Feng had said that it was best for him to remain detached and not get involved in anything of major importance. Only one thing was required of him: the General Secretary must, at all costs, be prevented from publicly announcing the reversal of the verdict on June Fourth, which would bring about a drastic change.

Lu Hao-ran was more than willing not to get involved; if the plans of the military went wrong he would not be implicated; he would spare no pains to prevent a reversal of the verdict in any case. The General Secretary's strategy was to use to it bring about the downfall of the hard-liners, win popularity in the country and support abroad. He also intended both to prevent the two factions in the pro-democracy movement from profiting from the occasion, and create bad blood between them.

These two aims could hardly be realized simultaneously and anyway, the second seemed totally unreasonable. But this was all typical of the General Secretary's cunning. He had learned from the experience of

Communist countries in Eastern Europe that it was best not to suppress the supporters of democracy. As soon there was any possibility of obtaining power they would soon forget their principles and sense of shame. Once they saw that the Communist Party was on the defensive and eventually forced to abandon one-party rule, they would step into the breach and show their fighting spirit by attacking each other.

At present the General Secretary was creating the illusion that the Party was in retreat, negotiating with or promoting first some then others, praising some and humiliating others, cleverly stirring up enmity and fanning the flames of jealousy. He was also busy exposing the characteristic weaknesses of the pro-democracy movement: lack of theory and discipline, self-seeking ambitions, internal dissension and ineptitude. People had quickly lost faith in the movement and the support it had enjoyed at the time of June Fourth faded away.

The authorities kept disorder under control so that the movement did no great damage. But the methods of 1989 were not repeated. No time was wasted trying to curry favour with the people and there was no effort to maintain the smooth functioning of social amenities in the capital. On the contrary, they were deliberately allowed to deteriorate, so that superficial chaos got worse and people's living conditions declined. Various departments of the Beijing municipal government neglected their responsibilities: water, electricity and gas were often cut off, foodstuffs and vegetables in short supply. Transport, postal and telephone services almost ground to a halt. Crime increased. Secret police in disguise committed robberies, started fires, and spread fear and insecurity. The media without exception, exaggerated everything and blamed it all on social unrest. People were duly scared and popular support for the pro-democratic movement was transformed into fear and hatred. The authorities were even blamed for not taking sterner measures.

The swing in public opinion had come faster than expected. The time was ripe for an orderly 'reversal of the verdict' that would clear away all the pent-up resentment about June Fourth and get rid of the trouble-makers. Political stability would be guaranteed for a few years. The moderates themselves had expected that it would need another month before the announcement could be made, but the situation had developed so rapidly that they had been forced to bring it forward. It was to be made the next day.

Whatever the army chose to do, the man they called the 'second class soldier' was nevertheless General Secretary and President of the Republic and would speak in the name of both State and Party. To back out now would be no easy matter and might even have disastrous consequences. That was why he was in a hurry to act.

To forestall any attempt to prevent him from making the announcement, the General Secretary had arranged to receive the editor of *The Washington Post* and express 'as a personal opinion' his approval of reversing the verdict. This news would immediately cause a sensation both in China and abroad and if the Central Committee were re-convened the proposal would be passed, because the majority would not dare go against the tide.

The Minister of State Security, the most devious of Lu Hao-ran's subordinates, had put forward a plan of action. The General Secretary wanted to kill two birds with one stone—the pro-democracy movement and the hard-liners. The stone—reversal of the verdict—must have the appearance of a free gift. If there were any suspicion that he had been forced to concede it, popular feeling and the inevitable cries of triumph that would follow would provide 'trouble-makers' with new opportunities and the General Secretary himself would be in bad trouble. The Minister's idea was that the best way of delaying the announcement was to manipulate the pro-democracy movement into *demanding reversal of the verdict immediately*, before he could announce it himself.

But how? Protest, demonstrations and marches no longer appealed to anyone. Hunger strikes had been a public joke since the occasion when TV had shown hunger strikers surreptitiously eating. Everything had been tried except one thing, that had only been talked about—self-immolation. Suicide by setting fire to oneself could not be faked like a hunger strike: once the match touched the petrol the fire did its work and there was no turning back. These days, when only profit seems to count, such an atrocious, totally unprofitable self-sacrifice was almost unthinkable.

The Minister was not given to pessimism. He had succeeded in finding a victim and had notified the foreign press television to come to Tiananmen Square.

A sudden commotion in the crowd was visible on the screen. A man who had just lit a cigarette was being forced to the ground by several plainclothes men, who found a bottle of alcohol on him, sniffed it, then poured the contents on the ground. The news of what was to going to happen had obviously got around.

A large number of police from the Beijing Public Security Bureau, which was loyal to the General Secretary, were now in the square. For their own safety the foreign pressmen had been advised to leave; plainclothes men were everywhere, inspecting bottles and other containers. The police were clearly under orders to prevent the immolation, either by arresting or intimidating the sacrificial victim, so that the General Secretary could announce the reversal of the verdict as planned.

The minister kept changing the field of vision on the screen. Lu Hao-ran felt dizzy and closed his eyes; he did not need to see the whole thing, just to hear about the result. If it failed there was virtually no contingency plan.

'She's coming,' said the Minister in a voice that betrayed both anxiety and satisfaction. The screen now showed in close-up a young woman, her face haggard and pale, with a slight squint, looking dazed and bewildered, her small teeth biting bloodless lips, her trembling lower jaw slightly twisted to one side. She was as thin as paper and her whole body was racked by disease. Though it was not hot, she was in long sleeves and trousers. Her breasts appeared normal. The minister was pleased to see that she was alone and that the police had not noticed her, naturally assuming that someone prepared to die in flames would look determined and strong-willed. This weak sickly woman did not fit the bill at all. In fact, the Minister himself did not have much confidence in her determination.

She was suffering from cancer, both breasts had been removed and her fiancé had left her. The cancer was now general and the doctors had given her only six months to live. She had attempted suicide several times, but on each occasion her family had insisted on saving her life. Security men who had infiltrated the People's Front, had found out about her and she was promised three million *yuan* if she would agree to burn herself alive. She loved no one but her parents and was attracted by the idea of giving a life she no longer wanted in exchange for some real wealth and happiness for them in their declining years. But setting fire to herself was very different from taking an overdose of sleeping pills—too painful, too ugly, too humiliating.

She was not interested in politics and had no desire to go down in history as a martyr. She was unmarried and did not want to burn her clothes, to burn her skin and flesh down to the bones. Pain frightened her more than death. In the end a simple promise made her agree: she would be given some sort of drug beforehand which would allow her to remain conscious and move about. But she would feel no pain, and would 'peacefully enjoy eternal life in the flames'.

At the last moment she hesitated. It was half-an-hour past the agreed time. Several press men were putting away their cameras. She stood motionless as if in a trance. If she made no move no one was going to come forward and set her alight. If the police intervened, in less than ten minutes she would tell everything, and the cat would be out of the bag. Perhaps the investigation would even lead to the secret room on the 17th floor.

'Someone must get her started,' said the minister between his teeth.

He did not have to wait long. Some of his plainclothes police posing as People's Front members seemed to flow over her like a wave picking up a pebble on the shore. All was confusion for a moment. In the secret room it was impossible to see, or hear from the indistinct sounds transmitted by the hidden microphones, exactly what was going on, except that the wave passed round the motionless woman and clashed with police a little further on, distracting the attention of the crowd.

The Minister at the console zoomed in on the young woman. Some sort of liquid appeared to trickle from her trouser legs, but the ground was still wet from the rain and it was impossible to see what it was. 'Rain has its uses.' The Minister was not usually so communicative.

A plastic bag full of petrol strapped to the woman's chest where her breasts had been, was rapidly shrinking. The amount had been carefully calculated to soak through the several layers of clothing she was wearing and insure complete immolation. It was impossible to tell whether she, or one of the plainclothes men had pulled the string to open the bag.

'There's a smell of petrol,' someone shouted. The police immediately began rushing this way and that like a swarm of angry bees. Perhaps this frightened the young woman; a small bony hand came out of her pocket holding a large red lighter. A foreign press photographer with blonde hair, standing nearby gave a shriek and jumped back, adjusting her camera at the same time. Three plainclothes men, noticing the lighter, bounded over like leaping fish, and pounced on her.

The young woman then shouted in trembling voice, 'June Fourth. . .reverse the verdict,' as agreed, so that there should be no doubt why she was burning herself. She had been made to learn several slogans by heart but now she only remembered one. It was enough. The windproof lighter flamed—it had been thoroughly tested—then a man's hand seized hold of it.

Lu Hao-ran almost cried out, it was going to be a fiasco! There was no fire! The flame had not touched the petrol.

In the space of a second, two men caught hold of the young woman—she had no intention of resisting anyway—and she became a ball of fire. The men were thrown back. There was a drawn-out, heart-rending animal scream. Only the two words 'deceived me' were distinguishable.

The young woman ran towards the crowd as if swept along by the wind. People panicked and scattered, shouting, in all directions, falling over and trampling on each other. The foreign press men pushed forward, heedless of danger. Policemen with fire-extinguishers tried to keep up with the young woman who ran, jumped and made sudden turns, at an unimaginable speed. The spray and foam missed her. She seemed to fuse together with the fire. Her clothes lay burning on the ground. Her skin changed colour then suddenly became black.

A police jeep arrived its siren whooping, carrying the type of large fire extinguishers used by the artillery, and started to pursue her, knocking down at least five people, smashing the concrete base of a street lamp, and crushing a pile of cameras and other equipment. When a blast of white powder finally reached the young woman the terrible cries stopped. The cloud of powder dispersed and the fire went out. The young woman fell at the foot of the stone plinth of the Monument commemorating the Heroes of the Revolution. What remained of her body looked like a pile of smoking charcoal; the charred bones of her arms pointed up to the sky. Only the abdominal fat continued to burn with a small flame. The anti-incendiary powder, now burnt black, covered her white bones.

'Idiots!' The minister was furious. 'The extinguishers couldn't save her anyway. They suffocated her instead, before the fire could kill her.' He seemed only interested in the technical deficiencies of his opponents, though in fact he was as pleased as if he had just won money on a football match.

They had succeeded, thought Lu Hao-ran. He felt no excitement. 'Suffocation is less painful...' Then, suddenly remembering, said. 'Was she not to have some sort of pain-killer?'

The minister smiled. 'She was told that just to make her agree to take the plunge. If we had given her something it wouldn't have been such a success. It wouldn't have looked genuine.'

Lu Hao-ran had previously regarded the young woman as no more than an object to be manipulated, a symbol in an equation, like π. Now for some reason he remembered a brief glimpse of her buttocks as she burned—although they were only white for an instant—and realized that she was a human being. The minister said almost boastfully that a few remote-controlled devices had been concealed in her clothing, designed to ignite as soon as she pressed on the red lighter. Whether she had lit the fire herself or not was now of little importance. The minister's men were taking the opportunity of the confusion to retrieve the burnt remains of these devices, in case they fell into the hands of the investigators.

The screen showed people in Tiananmen Square standing in silent tribute, many in tears. But the terrible scene which they had just witnessed seemed to have raised the spirits of the supporters of the pro-democracy movement and this affected more and more people, without them knowing why.

The loudspeakers of the People's Front and the Democratic Front both began broadcasting solemn music, but before long the two factions began to quarrel, each claiming the martyr as one of their members. The minister then arranged for information about her to be given, through undercover agents, to the Peoples' Front, which consequently won the argument, since the Democratic Front did not even know her name. Everyone in the Square gradually started to chant in unison 'June Fourth. Reverse the verdict.' The martyr's last testament.

No one knew the significance of the two words 'deceived me', the last agonizing cry that the promise of a pain-killer had been a trick. Many people took it to be a protest against government duplicity.

The crowd in the square grew bigger. There were clashes with the police, cars were overturned, streetlights smashed and hedges trampled. Then the police withdrew completely, clearly to avoid making things worse. But what had already happened was enough; countless radio messages were already on their way to Western capitals. Security men who had infiltrated the popular groups would continue to stir up disturbances. There would be no announcement tomorrow of reversal of the verdict. It would take at least a month for things to calm down, and by that time the situation would probably have changed.

A perfect operation. But the girl's last pitiful cry still lingered in Lu Hao-ran's ears. He shuddered but not with cold. Perhaps one day he would end up as a pile of ashes. Was the army to be trusted? Could he rely on a promise? He closed his eyes. The hazy scene swayed before him—everything was indistinct and his eyes would not focus. Zhou Chi had agreed to initiate him into the special arts that would give him extra-sensory perception, transmission of thoughts and the ability to see into the future. He had not said why he wanted such gifts. In fact, it was to enable him to see through all the conspiracies that surrounded him. He wanted to ask Zhou Chi whether *qigong* could teach him how to travel through space and time without leaving a trace, how to drive all the enemies of the country—who were of course his enemies too—into a death-trap?

Canada: Lake Manitoba

Close to the shore of Lake Manitoba, in a carefully prepared blind, six metres up a tree, a wild life photographer was woken up by soft footsteps below. As she silently prepared her camera she tried to guess what sort of animal it was. She hoped that it was the cougar the helicopter pilot of the forest protection service claimed to have seen. A good shot of that would be worth something to *Wildlife Photography* magazine. After three days here she had got a few pictures, but nothing which would sell for much.

When the animal emerged from the undergrowth and appeared on an abandoned dam at the lakeside, she almost swore aloud. An animal all right—the highest of the animals in fact, but not one that would interest the magazine. What was worse, with him around no others would show themselves. She could not shout out to him. If she did, there would be nothing for the rest of the day.

She soon became interested. The man put down his backpack and stripped down to his golden yellow skin. He was short and his body perfectly proportioned; he made her think of handsome boys in fairy stories, or of a figure cast in gold. She smiled mischievously to herself as she adjusted her telephoto lens. Since he had disturbed her, she would take a photo of him for a women's magazine. They had probably seen enough of American musclemen and would enjoy looking at an Asiatic Adonis for a change.

She had only time for one shot before the man put on a strange wetsuit and assembled some kind of rifle. After lining up a row of empty cans on the old dam, he got into the water. It was very clear and she could see that the wetsuit had what looked like fins of different shapes and sizes attached to it, that were normally folded but could be opened to act as stabilizers. The depth of his body in the water was evidently regulated by a counter-balanced weight and airbag. Almost two metres down he started to adjust his aim, by means of tubular float chambers on either side of the rifle, linked to a balancing mechanism. The equipment was apparently difficult to regulate; repeated adjustments had to be made before his body was level in the water and totally rigid like a floating log. It looked very strange and furtive.

Yellow autumn leaves on the water then hid the man's movements. The photographer was about to relax her attention for a moment, but there was suddenly the sound of a shot underwater and one of the tin cans on the dam described a curve in the air before clattering down out of sight. The other cans followed. A frightened rabbit racing across the dam towards the brushwood on the other side, was hit when it reached the last can and disintegrated.

The photographer shook with fear and hugged herself. If she made a sound, if the devil emerged from the water and found her and her camera, she would be the next rabbit!

Beijing: Unit Sixteen

Shi Ge was dreaming of the small thin face of his wife. She used to tease him about his increasingly sparse hair and rearrange it with her bony hand, smiling until her eyes almost disappeared. A comfortable feeling flowed through his body like a warm current. He closed his eyes and felt tears forming. He knew this was not really his wife but a light breeze wafting through of the open window. She had been dead for four years from what the specialist called 'environmental pollution syndrome'. When she learned that there were at least ten toxic substances in her body, she smiled slightly and said, 'It's lucky I couldn't. . .' She did not finish her sentence. He had said nothing, but taken her hand. She had often cried because she could not have children and had even suggested he find a younger woman, and had offered to look after the children.

He woke up and raised his head from his desk. Each time he thought of his wife it was like a knife in his heart. Ten o'clock, the time he normally went home. The office was silent. He always expected his wife to be at home, waiting for him. Sometimes she would say, 'The magnolia are in bloom at the Summer Palace,' and if he had replied 'We'll go on Sunday,' her face would have lit up like a child's. But he would have to say simply, 'Yes they are,' like a dull echo.

There were solid iron bars in the window, to deter intruders of course. The building was full of secrets. There were guards on each floor, which were divided by escalators into different sections, where anyone entering had to sign a register and be searched—measures equally effective in preventing people from getting in or out. Secret organizations become like prisons and Unit Sixteen was no exception.

It had been established to handle emergencies round the clock and every day of the year. Everyone was provided with a camp bed and a sleeping bag. When one of the frequent emergencies occurred, the canteen often sent meals up to the offices. Then all communications were temporarily cut, safes and doors were sealed, keys gathered up and the guards changed. All the staff became prisoners.

Shi Ge's supper, in a stainless steel bowl, remained untouched. It looked particularly dried-up and tasteless in the artificial light. He ate a piece of cold meat without the least appetite. The promotion of high yield processed food stuffs, designed to increase production, made meat taste like plastic and unpleasant to chew. Since the death of his wife he was very conscious that the poisons scattered everywhere by man, the chemicals and radioactive material, return to poison mankind itself. When walking in the streets, he often found himself involuntarily holding his breath to avoid filling his lungs with the toxic gases which filled the air. Then, of course, he had to take a deeper breath—as if to make up for the poison he had missed. People are aware that man is poisoning himself, but it does not stop.

He swallowed a slice of beef and suppressed the urge to estimate the amount of poison it contained. Perhaps only in Chen Pan's base would it be possible to escape from this world of poison. Had the telephone not been cut off, he would have liked to hear her voice. She would be disappointed: he no longer had the power to obtain a base for the Greens.

He knew that he had staked everything on a single throw and would not escape the consequences; but had not imagined that the moment would come so soon. An investigation team had been sent, nominally by the Disciplinary Committee, though in fact it was mainly composed of secret police from the Political Control Bureau. This kind of 'investigation in private' was the usual method for examining political prisoners.

The idea of Successive Multi-Level Elections had been in his mind for years. He had been one of the generation of Red Guards sent to the mountains or villages in the 1960s, who tended to be rebellious and worry about the future of mankind. Once this exhilarating, dynamic period had ended, the waves of time had washed away most of their dreams of changing the world, perhaps leaving here and there a more lasting spark. In recent years, this idea had been more and more present in his mind. When he was young, he used to call it the seed of a new era. Now he no longer had such a high an opinion of himself, nor the same energy. He was secretly sick at heart, with anxiety for the future and the feeling of impotence of a tired and overworked man. Now he searched only for a way out of the impasse.

He had worked for many years on his idea until he felt it perfect and without loopholes, but at the same time it tormented him like a brain tumour and was continually trying to escape from the prison of his skull and become a living reality. Yet, when it would finally be presented to the world, it might merely be trampled like a grain of sand under innumerable feet.

Less than half of his staff, who were with him day and night, really believed in his Election System, so the averted looks, sarcasm or ridicule that the Hundred-word Constitution provoked was not unexpected. Perhaps it was not wise to have risked everything by publishing it. As the investigators drove up to the building he saw something like reproach in the eyes of his staff.

Shi Ge was not an impatient man, but there was no more time left. History unfolds at a pace so slow compared with the span of human life that when there is a breakdown of historic proportions, everyone is blinded and confused, as if by a tornado. As long as China remains stable, free speech will be impossible; but if disorder destroys stability, the result will be a desperate life or death struggle. There will be such an hysterical uproar, that no one will be able listen or think properly.

At present, with the movement for 'reversing the verdict' in full swing, and China not yet in a terminal crisis, people were still listening and thinking, so now was the chance. If the proposal for all-level elections did not appear now, it probably never would.

Five million copies of the Hundred-word Constitution had been printed, and more than two million of the Explanatory Notes. The juvenile distributors had done their work well and had gone home with their pockets bulging with money. The so-called Hundred-word Constitution Society contained not a single 'fighter for democracy'. It was a purely commercial set-up. The publishing and printing had been done by dubious periodicals and pornographic magazines, which had made a good profit. Shi Ge did not regret the expense. He had an almost unlimited budget for special propaganda designed to 'influence popular thinking'. Compared with what was spent on combating democracy the cost had been quite small.

Outside Unit Sixteen there were dark areas where the lights had not been switched on. The shortage of electricity was getting worse and partial supply had been maintained by cutting off certain localities entirely. Unit Sixteen was the only building in the neighbourhood that was lit up.

For some unknown reason, interrogations were usually carried out at night. The two section heads from the Political Security Bureau seemed to deal mainly with 'conspiracies'. In this case, Shi Ge, a high-ranking member of the Communist Party and the important department under him, had distributed 'in a conspiratorial manner', several million copies of some sort of 'constitution'. It was unthinkable that there was not some deeper plot behind this. If the intention was not to seize power, why had the word 'constitution' been used? The interrogators put on the table in front of Shi Ge several dozen stills taken from videotapes.

To produce that kind of evidence was costly and time-consuming, thought Shi Ge. His image from several different angles had to be fed into a sophisticated computer, and the data was then used to search through videotapes taken day and night in the square over a period of months.

The prints Shi Ge was shown, were all of him alone, except for one that showed Ivan and Chen Pan looking sideways at him. Even at this moment he had a momentary feeling of tenderness. A happy scene, he thought—and felt a little ridiculous.

'To judge from a little of what we have on videotape you like going to Tiananmen Square,' said one of the interrogators.

'Going to Tiananmen Square is part of my work, just as it is of yours.'

Shi Ge's status was very complicated: he himself was not very clear about it. For many years he had worked very hard helping the Party to govern the country, but after the fever of fanaticism in the Cultural Revolution, he had lost faith in the Communist Party. The gunfire on June Fourth in Tiananmen Square made him realize that this murderous tyranny was done for. But because he had never joined the pro-democracy movement and was considered politically reliable, he was given important responsibilities.

He had anonymously sent money to the families of some of those killed in Tiananmen Square, but had no interest in the present movement to reverse the verdict. He hated oppression of the people, but also those who deliberately stirred up the people and those in power who used the pro-democracy movement in their own struggle for power. He found all sorts of ways to avoid becoming too involved in the 'special assignments' he took on. Consequently, in the pro-democracy movement he was regarded as a spy or enemy agent and was suspected by the political police of being a subversive conspirator.

This was partly because he was capable of a certain wiliness, if not duplicity. He was prepared to cultivate, as is common in official circles, a disarming ease in social relations, as an easy way of achieving one's purpose, and of reconciling even totally disparate and contradictory things by intelligent calculation and planning.

Even more important was Shi Ge's detachment. He belonged to neither of the opposing factions and disapproved of both. The spirit in which he had drawn up the Hundred-word Constitution was to strike with the left-hand at despotism and at the mass movement with the right. He hated tyrannical government as much as tyrannical mass movements, and believed that they complemented and supplemented each other. Oppression caused hatred and violence; the blindness and cruelty of the mass movements inevitably made their suppression more bloody. To attack both these age-old evils together he had to use force to strike at force—and be both spy and conspirator. Wearing different hats was an advantage—he could use one to hide the other.

'The strategy of the Party and government,' said Shi Ge genially, 'is to take advantage of controlled disorder to teach the people a political lesson, to make them realize first, that there is a great gulf between China and Western-style democracy. They are not suited to each other; secondly, that it is dangerous to try and bring them together. I work on the second, which requires ideological guidance, on the principle of suiting the medicine to the complaint. That is why I go to Tiananmen Square.'

'The Hundred Word Constitution is the medicine you are talking about?'

'You should not only talk about the Constitution. The Society has distributed fifty-three different booklets and forty-nine pamphlets explaining the shortcomings of the Western democratic system and correcting mistaken ideas about it. Everyone knows that these publications have been effective.'

'So these other publications were a smoke-screen designed to conceal the bombshell which was to follow?'

'Why not put it the other way round, and say that the smoke-screen came second? The best way of influencing people's way of thinking is through a non-government, non-party organization or society. But if it only attacks the democratic system and has no programme of its own to propose, it will naturally arouse suspicion.'

'So pure and innocent? Why does your programme not support the Party's four basic principles?'

'In work of this kind one has to use roundabout ways—that has been the Party's experience. I think you understand that.'

'Why do you call it a constitution? Mr Prime Minister?' asked the other investigator, who had not said anything until now. Shi Ge laughed wryly.

In order to work out a plan for dealing with a crisis anywhere in the country with the minimum delay, the structure of Unit Sixteen was a mirror image of that of the Central Government. Each ministry or commission under the State Council has its equivalent group in Unit Sixteen, and each had access to all the material, documents, decisions, and so on, of the corresponding ministry and attended its meetings. In short, they made an on-going study of everything in the ministry's sphere of responsibility, in order to work out models of possible developments. This system was an ideal preparation for dealing with crises, but it tended to create a sense of self-importance in Unit Sixteen and give the staff the impression that it was they who really governed the country. They even adopted official titles: for instance, the heads of groups were called 'ministers'. Shi Ge was naturally called 'Prime Minister' and sometimes even addressed as 'Your Excellency.' He had several times tried to put a stop to this game. In order to avoid suspicion the existence of this model government system was kept secret, in vain apparently.

'That's just the young people's joke,' said Shi Ge, rather embarrassed. Someone had talked.

Apart from members of one special group, the staff of several hundred had been unaware of his connection with the Hundred-word Constitution. But they all knew about the Multi-Level Election System and many had taken part in the research. As soon as the Hundred-Word

Constitution was published, they must have suddenly realized what his motive was. Even if they did not disapprove of the system, the realization that a man they had always respected was out to destroy the pro-democracy movement might have made some of them angry and disappointed enough to talk.

He had chosen the personnel himself and the standard he demanded had made it difficult to find them. He often told them that if intellectuals were of any use at a time of great popular discontent, it was in maintaining a level-headed sense of reality. He dared not be more explicit.

Now that the tyrannical government was widely regarded as the enemy, rather than joining the chorus, it was more important for intellectuals to make a rational criticism of 'democracy', that everyone was pursuing like a flock of ducks.

In an age of pluralism, he believed, the pursuit of fashion is encouraging the greatest degree of uniformity in history. The whole world is adopting an identical set of ideas and values, a common style of dressing, the same music and so on. How many people who follow the fashionable demand for democracy really know what it is? One kind of uniformity, imposed at the barrel of a gun, has made people want to resist; the other kind—the product of advertising and propaganda—has made people preen themselves on what they mistake for multiformity.

Democracy is undoubtedly better than autocracy, but that does not mean that they are the only alternatives; nor can the defects of democracy be ignored. The Nazis got into power by democratic election, but the result was a bloodthirsty dictatorship. Now that the mass media control the news, the few who can make themselves heard receive far more attention than the silent majority; and when their tastes and preferences are transformed into fashion by the pervasive influence of the media, they can more easily control the others.

Shi Ge disapproved of those whose hopes for the future depend on stirring up the people into a pro-democracy movement like a raging storm. He believed the masses are irrational, and easily become violent and bloodthirsty. The kind of terror that accompanied the French Revolution, or the Cultural Revolution in China, could easily be repeated. Upheaval of that kind could destroy the old society, but not construct a new one. The main victims of a mass movement are the masses themselves. This is especially so in a huge country like China where there is no tradition of legality and where moral and ethical standards have now been lost.

If a democratic system were established, China would experience more hardship and difficulty than under the present autocracy.

Therefore Shi Ge devoted most of his energy to destroying people's illusions and their blind enthusiasm for democracy; only then could the Successive Multi-level Election System make its appearance. This was his real aim. He could not tell this to his own people, even less to the investigators.

As on previous occasions he courteously declined to divulge who had given him his special assignment. 'I can only tell the head of your Bureau: those are my orders. It is a question of discipline.' These words silenced the investigators, who exchanged glances and left.

Shi Ge began to feel sleepy and lay down on his camp bed. Suddenly, 'the Leftist' entered without knocking, as if they were still together in one of the teams sent to the villages in the 1960s. It was then that he had earned his nickname.

He was now head of the State Political Security Bureau. He was rather shabbily dressed and carried a bottle of 'Five Grain' alcohol and a paper bag full of peanuts. He was acting a part. Shi Ge did not dislike that—at least it showed that he still cherished the memory of those days.

They hardly spoke as they finished half the alcohol, each in turn taking a swig and wiping the mouth of the bottle, like old peasants. The only sound was the cracking of peanut shells. When they were beginning to feel the effects of the alcohol, 'the Leftist' took up a copy of the Explanatory Notes about the Hundred-word Constitution.

'I'm choosing a page at random'. He glanced quickly at the page, marked three passages with a red pencil and passed it to Shi Ge. The three passages were:

> Marxism has concentrated on the destruction of private ownership of the means of production, but neglected another form of private property—the private ownership of political power. By abolishing the former, it has even strengthened the latter. The private ownership of political power is the root cause of the various crises of our society; it is also the reason why socialism leads to a dead end and is no longer what people hope for.
>
> There are two forms of private ownership of political power: one is individual, the other is collective. Depending on whether the means of production are privately or publicly owned they make up the four basic social forms. The most disastrous of these is when the means of production are publicly owned, but political power is in the hands of an individual. The people are powerless. There are no restraints on the ruler. 'Public ownership' amounts to no more than the private ownership by the ruler. This is the reason why this form of autocratic socialism is being universally rejected.

In a system of private ownership of the means of production, even under centralized political power, economic enterprises still have a large measure of autonomy, which provides a form of supplementary self-regulation. But under Communism there is nothing to prevent unrealistic, preposterous or stupid policies of the power-holders from being put into practice. The dangers inherent in the private ownership of power are now greater than at any other time.

It would be better not to 'communize' the means of production if power is not 'communized' as well.

'These are just extracts from a page chosen at random. How many more like that are there?' said 'the Leftist' shaking his head. 'Every attack goes right to the roots. You won't get away with a casual explanation you know,' he added in a heart-to-heart manner, wagging his finger.

Shi Ge had little contact with 'the Leftist' now, though he had known him for a long time. They had been to the same middle school in Beijing and later were both sent to villages in Shanxi province. 'The Leftist' became quite well known there and frequently contributed to newspapers. He had been only two years in the countryside when he was appointed secretary to a People's Commune and member of the county Party committee. That was how he got his nickname.

'Have you seen the General Secretary recently?' Shi Ge asked.

'He's away on an inspection tour.'

'He should have told you.'

'Told me what?' the Leftist asked, surprised.

'About my assignment.'

'I....haven't seen him for a while.'

Evidently the General Secretary had not ordered the investigation. Good. Perhaps it was not going to be difficult to handle after all. Just as he hoped, once the General Secretary was mentioned 'the Leftist' dropped the matter.

She Ge was almost lying on his camp bed. The wine had made him feel totally relaxed—as if he was back in a Shanxi cave dwelling. But now it was necessary to show a little authority and make 'the Leftist' think that he had a well thought-out strategy.

'You may think that the All-level Election System is anti-Marxist,' he said. 'In fact the opposite is true. If the managers of enterprises and farms are selected by this system, society can *only* be Communist. It is the only way to save Communism now that the whole world is returning to capitalism. Criticizing deficiencies of a social system helps it to progress.'

This was slightly disingenuous, though it expressed a genuine conviction. In spite of the worldwide fashion for ridiculing communism, Shi Ge could not believe that the great ideal, that had occupied so many brilliant minds and inspired humanity; an ideal that had swept across the world for a century; had awakened the noblest feelings of mankind and inspired countless heroes to fight and give their lives to end exploitation, injustice, selfishness and greed: that all this had been a monstrous mistake, a shameful self-deception and a futile waste of time.

Shi Ge's values were in essence moral and non-material and he could never be friendly with empty-headed politicians, merchants, pragmatists and docile petty bourgeois, who had lost their ideals and were glad of it. He hated the system of private property they believed in, with its consumerism, greed and competition. If those who had given their lives for their beliefs were not to have died in vain, a way out must be found *beyond* communism, not behind it.

'You think it's right to say that in China power belongs to an individual?' asked 'the Leftist', in a mild—even slightly feeble tone. 'We too have elections...'

'Elections can be genuine or spurious,' Shi Ge replied. 'The crucial difference is whether those who participate in them understand one another or not. Electoral units all over the world are far too big for there to be mutual understanding between the participants. Democratic countries have contested elections, which allow the electors to know something about the candidates. But the bigger the election, the greater is the expenditure on media coverage; so the winner is the candidate with the most financial backing. Political power is therefore the private property of the group which provided the money...'

'In China we have a system for electing the National People's Congress.'

'Which guarantees that power remains private property.' Shi Ge realized that 'the Leftist' was trying to get him to show his hand, but made no attempt to conceal his thoughts. 'The electoral unit in which the so-called "people's representatives" are elected is far too large to allow mutual understanding between electors and candidates.'

'There are no competitive elections in China.' he went on. 'If there were, and everyone voted only for a candidate he knows, the votes would be scattered like sand. That is why a list of candidates is first put forward. But as long as there is no mutual understanding, the electors have no real knowledge of the candidates and there is no valid basis on which to make a choice between one candidate and another. So the official candidate is always elected, whoever he or she is. Even when there is a "multiple-choice" election, the choice is between candidates who have already been "selected". Therefore the "people's representatives" are not in fact chosen by the people, but are appointed by those with the power to select candidates.'

'In our higher level elections, these "people's representatives" are bound to submit to those who appointed them. Even if some of those elected have a will of their own, they don't have the necessary links and understanding with representatives who inevitably belong to larger organizations. So it is essential to put forward candidates who are sure of being elected. In the last analysis it is the high level leaders who control the elections. Once elected an official candidate will always be elected unless his patron dies or there is a coup d'état.'

'And in your system?' asked 'the Leftist'.

'As I said, the basic idea of the Multi-Level Election system is that elections take place in far smaller groups, where there is mutual understanding between the participants: therefore elections are genuine. Many people find it hard to believe that this will make it possible to replace private with public ownership of social power. The all-level election system reverses the existing system of appointment and dismissal of petty officials or functionaries from the top down, and gives the people the power to control the country, right up to the highest ruler. That is genuine democracy.'

Shi Ge stopped suddenly. 'All this is in the "Explanatory Notes", which you have certainly read.' He had, but Shi Ge's long speech had not been wasted. The Leftist' already had his suspicions: this was not a real interrogation. Shi Ge was not a man to play the simpleton, unless he was perfectly well-prepared.

'Does the General Secretary know about the Hundred-word Constitution Society?' he asked cautiously.

'Of course,' Shi Ge replied. 'He personally gave me the assignment.' 'The Leftist' was a little surprised.

In fact, the General Secretary had been interested solely in Shi Ge's idea of using the popular organizations to influence people's minds. The main aim of 'reversal of the verdict' was to lead the people, who had lost faith in the government, away from the lure of democracy. So he had given Shi Ge full powers and the necessary budget, and became his backstage supporter, unaware that Shi Ge was leading him by the nose.

'Has he read the Hundred-word Constitution?' asked 'the Leftist'?

'Of course.'

'The Leftist' breathed in through his teeth, and for some time said nothing. It was true that the General Secretary had read it, and Shi Ge was sure that 'the Leftist' would not dare to dig deeper—certainly not ask the General Secretary himself. The two words 'of course', were enough, even though they were only part of the truth.

Shi Ge, who appeared in good humour, went on eating peanuts, while 'the Leftist' took one or two turns around the room, squeezing his nostrils together by habit. If he did 'investigate' the General Secretary as well, he was bound to get his fingers burned. It was dangerous to touch a thread which led to the top. If there was a shadow of doubt it was best to stop in good time. Shi Ge had been in government long enough to be quite clear about that.

'You have done good work getting peoples' ideas straightened out,' said 'the Leftist'. 'Everyone knows you can dazzle people with words. But you have sailed very close to the wind with your "Hundred-word Constitution" and "Explanatory Notes". You have gone over the limit in fact. You also acted incorrectly, considering that this activity has nothing to do with your organization. I will continue with my efforts, and hope that the investigation can soon be terminated.' He hurried away, and the guard locked the door from the outside.

Shi Ge stood at the window. There were a few distant flashes of lightning in the night sky. The strong spirit still warmed him. He had the same feeling when he had spoken to the General Secretary, but on that occasion there had been no alcohol; the room had been air-conditioned, but he had sweated as much as he was sweating now. All-level elections had seemed far away and indistinct as a dream, but he had talked for all his worth, wanting to make every word penetrate the General Secretary's head. He knew he was being foolhardy, but the hope of success was too much of a temptation. There is no quicker way to achieve something than when the ruler himself suddenly changes his mind.

If the power and efficiency of the autocratic system could be used to promote multi-level elections from above, there would be a peaceful revolution, a smooth transition, at little cost and with a minimum of suffering. If the General Secretary was willing to go down in history as a great man he, Shi Ge, would be glad to be a mere shadow behind him.

If he had not been almost certain that 'the Leftist' would be scared off by the two words 'of course', and stopped his investigation, Shi Ge for all his courage, would not have dared misrepresent the words of the General Secretary: that would have landed him in a real prison. It was true he had read the Hundred-word Constitution, but his only comment had been, 'I think you must be a little mad.'

The General Secretary did not lack spirit and imagination. He had the courage to lease Heilongjiang province to Japan; Shi Ge admired him for it, and had hoped for even greater things. But the all-level election system was different: it would turn the ruler of millions into their servant, and make absolute power a thing of the past. Once this basic principle was threatened, however much imagination or courage a man in power might have, he would be finished. Shi Ge despised the cramped narrow-minded spirit which made a man cling to power rather than win the glory of changing the history of mankind. Countless kings and emperors have come and gone... How few stand out like mountain peaks!

He did not regard the All-level Election System as his own invention. It was part of a whole sequence of concepts that already existed, a realm of ideas of which he had only touched the edge. But he felt intuitively that there was a way out of the blind alley that the world was in, not just an abstract hope, like the 'historical inevitability' the older generation always talked about. He was convinced that the logic of the All-level Election System led towards a new world, the form of which would develop naturally.

He had never found a way of convincing others. People wanted universal systems, complicated arguments and proofs. An election system? That seemed to them like a mere detail. Yet it could be a catalyst. Rather than wear oneself out designing a new world—they were all short-lived anyway—it is better to search for the automatic regulating factor which will allow the new world to appear of itself, make the future unfold, replace the old with the new and decay with lasting prosperity.

For Shi Ge, the system of Successive Multi-level Elections was such a factor. Once its force began to develop it would grow like an embryo into a new world and continually renew itself.

Every system in the natural world, from micro-organisms to the universe itself, arrives at harmony and equilibrium through spontaneous regulation. But man, in his arrogance, thinks he can control the universe and tries to replace spontaneous regulation by human intervention. After a moment of glorious progress, mankind has fallen into a trap of his own making. To attempt to use a complex man-made plan to get out of trouble will do no more than tighten the trap: the only solution is to return to spontaneous regulation. With All-level Elections, the form society takes is no longer determined by the brain of the ruler, but by a great brain made up by, and controlled by, the reaction of millions of cells—which is the basic model of spontaneous regulation.

The important thing was to start, then everything would begin to change, to expand and advance, without the need for pushing, without opposition. But getting started was the most difficult part. Shi Ge had no idea how to do it. So he had decided to stake everything on a single throw, as a hesitant preparation for the beginning, in the hope that people would themselves accept the all-level election system and that the General Secretary would stick to his harmless attitude of puerile mockery.

People had become too clever and it is difficult to become accustomed to simple explanations. The time had come to speak out, to print his proposal in black and white, so that people know it exists. Then, when those who have already travelled the road which leads to nowhere, people who have tried everything and found nothing to save them, might think of trying this. That would be the beginning.

His gamble was worth it.

The Three Gorges Dam on the Yangzi River

The helicopter was waiting for take-off, its rotors turning slowly. Li Ke-ming sat behind the pilot, simmering with rage.

On the other side of the dam, vehicles came and went, people moved about in a scene of rush and muddle. Everyone at the construction administration had been busy day in and day out for more than a month, preparing to receive the General Secretary, who was to cut the ribbon on the new dam at the Three Gorges.

Li Ke-ming, deputy head of Security at the construction site, made the arrangements for the General Secretary's safety during his visit as if for his own father, checking every detail again and again, almost too busy to sleep and eat. He had never before had to arrange protection for someone of such high rank. The whole department was on tenterhooks, fearing the slightest slip-up, and everyone wanted a chance to shine.

'We're only a construction site security set-up,' thought Li Ke-ming resentfully, 'but we're just as efficient as that arrogant Colonel.' Shen Di, who was responsible for the General Secretary's security on this important occasion, had sent Li Ke-ming's men to the outer perimeter of the security zone to serve as messengers. With the General Secretary due to arrive at any minute!

Li Ke-ming swore when he thought of Shen Di. He would like to have slapped that smooth arrogant face with all his strength. The son of a bitch had only arrived an hour ago, and in less than ten minutes had demolished a perfect security procedure, which had taken a month to work out. Apart from the usual curfew, searches, verification of personnel, stationing of guards and so on, Li Ke-ming had arranged for two motorboats with divers to patrol the reservoir, keep watch on every possible target and check on anything floating in the water. He had even arranged for patrols further downstream, below the dam. His own role was to keep an overall eye on everything and command the whole operation from one of the Security Department's helicopters.

But Shen Di, without a word of explanation, had grounded the helicopters, recalled the motorboats and patrols, confiscated their arms and forbade them to enter the central security zone.

Li Ke-ming angrily spat out a dead cigarette butt on to the bulging canvass bag at his feet. He regretted not having walked off and washed his hands of the whole business, instead of insisting on the importance of helicopter surveillance of the dam. The man took no notice, so what was the point? Li Ke-ming had been afraid his colleagues would make fun of him. When they had been expelled from the security zone, they had merely sworn a little; but he was in charge of the operation, and it would have been humiliating to be sent packing without a protest. He had almost pleaded with the bastard, and even tried to persuade him that the helicopter could also be part of the welcoming ceremony.

It was ironic that this ridiculous suggestion appealed to Shen Di. After a moment's thought, he ordered Li Ke-ming to stop the motor and wait orders. Later a canvas bag, bulging with confetti, was loaded into the helicopter. Shen Di radioed to say that when the General Secretary was about to cut the ribbon, he would receive the order to take off, fly to the upper part of the reservoir and release a cloud of confetti.

Li Ke-ming was almost beside himself with fury. The upper part of the reservoir! He almost kicked out the officer who came to inspect the helicopter for arms.

The General Secretary's cortège of dozens of cars had arrived, followed by a noisy crowd, pushing and shouting. The road had been swept and watered again and again, but there was still a cloud of dust. Li Ke-ming had now lost interest, but from habit, watched the scene through his binoculars.

He could not understand the reason for Shen Di's overbearing attitude. The security system was now full of loopholes. A lot of sightseers had gathered at the entrance to the dam, there was no room for the cars to turn and the cortège was forced to slow down. In Li Ke-ming's book, this violated a fundamental rule, especially when the sightseers had not even been checked or organized. They had merely pushed forward as soon as Shen Di had dismissed Li Ke-ming's guards. It was no surprise when a few people in the crowd unrolled a banner reading 'The Three Gorges dam is a disaster for China and a calamity for the people.' There was a scuffle, and Li Ke-ming's heart missed a beat: if someone in the crowd had a gun…

But there were only a few Green activists involved. Li Ke-ming had no time for these people. From the day construction started they had never stopped saying that the Great Dam would upset the environment, increase the foreign debt, lead to inflation, shortage of materials and would cost far too much. It was true that it was going to cost a great deal. Only the first stage was finished and almost all the budget for the whole project had been spent. But look at the size of it! It would be one of the wonders of the world—the biggest hydroelectric station on earth. What was the use of talking only about the environment? There was no lack of grassland. People couldn't live on grass—they were not cows.

Shen Di's voice came over the radio, in a pure Beijing accent and lofty tone that would brook no disobedience. Li Ke-ming thought it strange that so senior an officer should bother himself with confetti and a helicopter.

The helicopter took off. The newly filled reservoir was already a vast expanse of water, yellow in the sunlight. Li Ke-ming immediately noticed a black shape in the water, which moved, then disappeared. A sturgeon perhaps. The water was still yellow with silt and he could not see clearly. The presence of a sturgeon would be a good omen—an answer to the ecologists who had been saying that the dam would cause the extinction of rare species. Li Ke-ming wondered whether to report the sighting, but decided not to. It was too petty a matter for this solemn occasion. If it was a sturgeon, it would certainly not show itself with a helicopter overhead. In any case he did not want to appear to be currying favour.

He asked the pilot to fly near the dam. He was going to make his inspection as planned and to hell with Shen Di. Symbolic perhaps, but he wanted to show he was not just here for decoration.

The cortège stopped in the middle of the dam. A large group of local officials crowded round the General Secretary, who had just cut the red silk ribbon. He was standing, hands on hips, gazing over the water. The cameras were all on him. The television and front pages of the newspapers would show him in this heroic posture. China's dream of creating 'a quiet lake in the deep gorges' had at last come true. After the recent floods, which had left the whole country in a state of shock, this huge enterprise had taken on a special significance, and given people faith and courage. The big shots in the Construction Bureau had even said that the great dam 'is the backbone of China's modernization'.

The radio suddenly spat out Shen Di's angry words, 'Stop dawdling and get to your post at once.' It was difficult not to say, 'Who do you think you are?' The pilot, a close colleague, glanced at him then flew back over the water and hovered.

He cursed as he opened the door of the helicopter and emptied out a bag of confetti, which immediately swirled into a huge bunch of multicoloured flowers. People on the dam chattered excitedly and clapped as the wind from the rotors swept up the coloured paper, some of which was sucked into the cabin of the helicopter, then sucked out again.

It was then that he caught a glimpse of the black form of the sturgeon again, no more than thirty metres from the General Secretary and the officials on the dam. Li Ke-ming seized his binoculars, and then shouted into the loud-hailer, ' General Secretary, look in the water!'

The sound of his voice had hardly died away when, in the bright sunlight, the top of the General Secretary's head exploded like a red flower opening—blood-red petals bursting into full bloom for an instant, then disintegrating. The General Secretary fell. The people on the dam stood petrified, then crowded around him.

For an instant Li Ke-ming thought he must be dreaming. No, he had seen with his own eyes the General Secretary killed, and his body now lay on the ground.

'The sturgeon! The sturgeon!' Li Ke-ming shouted wildly. The water was yellow and still. He immediately became calm. He had been made deputy head of security when he was only thirty, after personally arresting five murderers. Now, if it had not been the General Secretary who had been killed, he would have been glad to solve another murder, nothing pleased him more.

No one knew where the shot had come from: the police and bodyguards on the dam were scuttling about like terrified dogs.

'The killer is in the water,' said Li Ke-ming into the microphone. 'Please send men to close off the two banks of the reservoir. I'll stay in the middle and report if I see anything.'

Strange… Shen Di did not answer.

The helicopter rose to avoid the cloud of confetti, Li Ke-ming leaning out of the cabin door. All the sluices were closed and access to the diversion tunnel barred, so the assassin could not get through the dam and escape underwater. He must still be in the reservoir. A light breathing kit could give him no more than ninety minutes underwater; and using flippers his speed would not be more than five kilometres per hour, or at best twenty five if he had a small electric motor. He was bound to land in less than an hour, and no more than twenty-two kilometres away. He would not come out at the dam, nor on the south bank, which was agricultural land and thick with people. He would probably appear on the north side of the reservoir, where it was hilly and wooded, perhaps five kilometres away where a small plantation came right up to the water's edge.

Li Ke-ming asked the pilot to fly to and fro along the north side, at a height that would keep several kilometres in view. Fortunately there were not too many trees close up to the reservoir, so the view was clear.

While watching the shore Li Ke-ming tried to contact base, but there was no reply: perhaps everyone was in a state of shock and confusion.

'Get me the Security Bureau's frequency,' he asked the pilot.

Suddenly Shen Di's voice came over the radio, without a hint of confusion or panic, but dark and threatening 'I'm warning you, if you tell anyone without my permission what has just happened you will be punished for revealing a top state secret. If you have anything to say you must say it to me.'

Li Ke-ming said straight out what he thought had happened, and asked for another helicopter, for two patrol boats to be sent to the north side of the reservoir and for troops to be sent to cordon off the area and cut all road and rail access. 'The killer will not get away,' he said, his eyes never leaving the shoreline below. 'If you do as I ask I will take full responsibility if he is not caught.'

Silence…interminable. Then Shen Di said 'Return to base! Repeat: Return to base!'

'Message received.'

'How much fuel have you got?' Shen Di's voice sounded almost protective. Li Ke-ming suddenly remembered that before taking off three-quarters of the fuel had been removed from the tank, on the grounds that the confetti display would only take a few minutes. He looked at the gauge.

'Fifteen minutes.'

'Then come back at once. The patrols have already been sent out, and all communications are cut. A helicopter has been sent to replace you, and motorboats.'

'I'll wait until it comes,' said Li Ke-ming. Silence.

They kept up surveillance for ten minutes. The pilot was already uneasy: the needle was almost at red, then there would be fuel for ten more minutes. They were only one minute from base, but there was no sign of the relief helicopter.

Li Ke-ming was not worried about that, but continued to watch the shore through his binoculars.

'Turn back!' he shouted to the pilot and pointed to a small inlet they had just passed over. Something had caught his eye. As the helicopter hovered he adjusted his binoculars.

The inlet was where two sloping hillsides, thickly covered with brushwood, met the water. The reservoir had not long been filled and there was a lot of vegetation still growing in the water. He saw part of a wet black rubber tube near the stem of a mugweed. As the helicopter approached the tube slipped back in the water like a snake, leaving only the tip visible, moving slightly with the ripples.

Perhaps it was an ordinary rubber hose that had been washed up. Or was the killer's mouth at the other end of it? He looked into the distance: two patrol boats had come out but they were patrolling the *south* bank. Shen Di did not believe him and would not leave the south bank alone. But here on the north side, with one boat in support, they could pull up the tube and find out what was there. There was nothing he and the pilot could do alone. There was nowhere to land, and in ten minutes the helicopter would have to head back. Even if there had been enough fuel and there was a man underwater, he would wait until it was dark and slip away.

'Where's the relief helicopter? Why doesn't it come?' he shouted into the mike. No answer.

Should he mention the rubber tube? If it were only a hose pipe Shen Di would have the laugh on him...

Without thinking he reached for his pistol and let out a string of obscenities when he felt the empty holster. He might still have been able to do something if his gun had not been confiscated. He hurled a spanner into the water near the black pipe. Nothing happened.

He tapped the pilot's shoulder. 'Bring her down.'

As the helicopter came slowly down towards the rubber tube, the mugweed bent in the wind from the rotors, which made a swirling depression in the water, deeper as the helicopter came closer. His eyes never leaving the spot, Li Ke-ming put down his earphones and mike, held with both hands on to the sides of the open cabin door and leaned out.

Seven or eight metres away a crouching figure emerged from the mud in the middle of the whirlpool, with arms like the pincers of a crab holding a weapon, which he pointed straight at the helicopter.

'Lift off quick!' shouted Li Ke-ming, as he leaped out of the cabin. He felt something whip past him.

As he landed, he kicked away the man's weapon with his left foot and with the other would have kicked the man hard in the groin had not an ear-splitting explosion thrown him violently into the mud, and he felt a sharp pain from his right foot to his spine. The water surged back, loosening the grip of the assassin's arms and the pressure of his knee in Li Ke-ming's back, which could have broken his spine.

As he stood up, almost up to his waist in water, he saw flames rising from the burning helicopter on a grassy slope about twenty metres away. Immediately his opponent's hand came down towards his neck like a sword. The black respiration tube protruded from his diving-mask, quivering like the tongue of a poisonous snake. A blade of grass was stuck to the window of the mask. As the wave rose Li Ke-ming in one movement avoided the blow, turned round, got up, got free from his assailant. Then he attacked.

He was highly skilled at unarmed combat, but his wounded foot reduced his speed and control and several times he was almost thrown. Fortunately for him, his opponent's movements were hampered by the strange fins on his wet suit, otherwise Li Ke-ming would have been in bad trouble.

The assassin wanted to get away, not to fight, but Li Ke-ming, knowing that he was in no state to pursue him, was determined to arrest him on the spot.

Suddenly burning fuel from the helicopter raced over the grassy slope and continued burning on the surface of the water. The struggle continued. Li Ke-ming's clothes caught fire, but he went on, screaming in agony, raining blows on the assassin. He felt that the man's ribs must be cracking and that only the thick leather-like wet suit stopped him from tearing out his heart!

Suddenly the killer changed his tactics, stopped trying to get away, got his arms around Li Ke-ming and held him in the fire. Fortunately he was wet all over, otherwise the burning petrol would have immediately stuck to him, and flames would have climbed up him as if he were a wick.

Li Ke-ming was now struggling with all his strength to get free. He was almost completely exhausted. The assassin's arms seemed like iron. His face behind the glass of the mask was only a few inches away; his eyes like an alligator's, filled with hatred. Li Ke-ming knew he was in danger of being burned to death. The wet suit gave better protection than a short-sleeved summer shirt, and if they both went into the burning water, he would certainly be the first to fall and the assassin would get away.

The glass in front of the assassin's eyes reflected Li Ke-ming's burnt face in the sunlight and flames, as he dashed his forehead, with all his strength against it. In the instant when the assassin lost his balance and fell, Li Ke-ming quickly scooped up in his hands some burning petrol and threw it into the mask through the broken glass. Then flung himself into the water. Although it was boiling hot, it felt cool and comfortable.

He heard a drawn-out cry. By the time he had stood up and got out of the flames, he saw the assassin running, trying to tear off his diving mask, his hair on fire. Li Ke-ming struggled out of the water and started to follow, but after a few steps the collapsed on the ground. He saw the assassin's back as he ran through the plantation and the smoke from his hair against the green leaves.

Before he lost consciousness, Li Ke-ming remembered that from the helicopter he had seen a search-party approaching. They must have seen the fire and would soon be here. The assassin would not get away...

3

Beijing – Tiananmen Square – Beijing: The Great Hall of the People – Beijing: Central Military Commission – Construction site of the Three Gorges Dam – A village in Shanxi province

Beijing – Tiananmen Square

The sky was overcast and it was raining. High over the Tianyuan Gate the national flag hung damply at half-mast. The guard of honour, wearing black armbands, stood motionless as statues. For the last three days, the official announcement of the General Secretary's death had been broadcast repeatedly by television and radio, between intervals of solemn music. The wording had not changed and no explanation given of the phrase 'a brutal assassination by an enemy of China'.

In Tiananmen Square, at the foot of the Memorial to the Heroes of the Revolution, the few wreaths of paper flowers had wilted in the rain, but the real flowers remained fresh and colorful.

The leaders of the Democracy Front did not know how to react to the sudden death of this powerful, slippery man, the commander-in-chief of the despotic system and their main target. But for him the Democracy Front would not exist, there would have been no meetings, no propaganda and no occupation of Tiananmen Square. He was almost an ally. Now the enemy had gone, their target had vanished, and a slight anxiety was beginning to spread about what the attitude of his successor would be.

Police patrols in the square had been doubled and there were armoured cars and steel-helmeted police with bullhorns and electric batons everywhere. Plainclothes men from the State Security Bureau mixed with the crowd and kept watch on foreign correspondents (who were only worried that nothing might happen), and on uneasy diplomatic personnel, amongst whom were several intelligence agents.

The Square was calm. All amusement centres were closed and many passers-by had stopped to have a look. Even the loudspeakers of the People's Front and the Democracy Front did not really know what to say. Nothing was going on and few people stayed long.

Not many people noticed that several times the usual number of those large luxury coaches used to transport foreign tourists were parked between the History Museum and the Mao Zedong Mausoleum, their curtains drawn. All was quiet there too, and there were no tourists to be seen. The ninety-two coaches looked empty; but inside there were 4,650 well-equipped and travel-weary soldiers, quietly waiting.

Beijing: The Great Hall of the People

Lu Hao-ran had forgotten his pass and was stopped by the guards at the entrance to the Great Hall of the People. There were at least twenty personnel from the office of the Central Committee inside, yet no one came forward to vouch for him. He searched his pockets and brief-case in vain. He must have left the pass in his car, which was already on its way to the underground car park.

He waved to the driver, but decided not to shout. He would have cut a sorry figure and the man would not have heard anyway. The people from the office were laughing. Not long ago they were wagging their tails in his presence, hoping to be noticed. Now, if he asked a service of one of them, he would probably be ignored. He went down the curved ramp to the car park, the light rain falling coldly on his face.

He was usually driven straight to the special lower ground floor entrance to the lifts, like other members of the Standing Committee of the Political Bureau. This time, though he was still a member, the office had only issued him with a pass to the main entrance. There had been no explanation but he knew that his security status had been lowered. He had not made a fuss, knowing that this petty slight was intended to convey to everyone attending this special meeting of the Central Committee that he was not going to be General Secretary, or member of the Standing Committee, or even Premier.

Three days earlier, when the news of the General Secretary's assassination had broken, he had received a call from Wang Feng, asking him to call an extraordinary meeting of the Political Bureau of the Central Committee to be attended by members of the Central Committee at present in Beijing, in order to elect a new General Secretary. Lu Hao-ran had asked whether this had to be done at once.

'Yes,' replied Wang Feng. 'We must act promptly and firmly. Please stress that the meeting is to be attended only by members now in Beijing.'

'A clumsy way of doing things,' thought Lu Hao-ran. Too obvious. Perhaps that summed up Wang Feng: clumsy and unsubtle. Lu Hao-ran had no idea what Wang Feng was planning. He had only told him that he should remain detached, nothing else. Wang was somehow implicated in the assassination. There was no doubt about that, but Lu Hao-ran preferred not to know. He would merely do whatever Wang Feng asked.

The same evening, the Minister of Public Security brought Lu Hao-ran a list of names which, he said, been discovered by one of his agents in the office of 'number two' of the Political Bureau Standing Committee and secretly photocopied. Lu Hao-ran examined it with amazement. It was in his own handwriting and he had never seen it before. It was a list of the members of the Central Committee and the Political Bureau at present in Beijing, who would be at the meeting tomorrow. They were divided according their factions and the way they would vote: thirty three for him and only twenty seven for 'number two'.

Lu Hao-ran thought this plausible. 'Number two' and 'number three' of the five members of the Standing Committee of the Political Bureau were both 'moderates', who had been close associates of the late General Secretary ('number one'). Lu Hao-ran himself had fallen to the position of 'number four'.

The hard-liners were mainly concentrated in Beijing, in the various ministries and commissions of the Central Committee, whereas the majority of moderates, many of whom had enjoyed the benefits of the free market economy, were provincial officials. This was the reason why Wang Feng had asked Lu Hao-ran to see that they did not attend the meeting, but remained at their posts 'in the interests of national security and stability'. With these moderates out of the way the meeting would be attended only by members of the Central Committee now in Beijing, mostly hard-liners. It would only require a little manoeuvring on the part of Lu Hao-ran for the voting to go the way Wang Feng wanted, and as the forged list predicted.

He was surprised to realize that he had never solicited votes or organized cliques; now he had been told by Wang Feng to do nothing. The forged document had obviously been 'planted' on the moderates in order to scare them into bringing the provincial leaders to Beijing and give them sufficient votes to chalk up a victory at the special meeting.

He found his pass in the car and his driver took him back to the main entrance, apologizing profusely. Lu Hao-ran would normally have taken this for granted, but after two days of being given the cold shoulder, he was quite grateful for this courtesy. The Minister of Finance and the head of the State Planning Commission, who entered the Great Hall at the same time, had previously been close friends of his; now they did not even greet him. Their friendly smiles would be used to ingratiate themselves with the opposition.

In the space of three days he had known both exhilaration and despair. As soon as the news of the General Secretary's assassinations had arrived, hard-liners seemed to have received a shot in the arm. The tide was turning and there were opportunities to seize. Lu Hao-ran's spirits rose. Some non-entities among the 'moderates' quickly made it obvious that they were willing to change sides. Lu Hao-ran did nothing except ask for a meeting to be called.

Then he had sunk to the depths of despair. There had been a fleeting opportunity. Missing it was more than a setback: in the present opportunistic world if you did not grab a chance when it was offered you were sure to be dumped. At a moment of drastic change, if you fail to get organized, conciliate, make promises and create a functioning nucleus, no one will be fool enough to support you. People fend for themselves—especially if they have a pass, like those going into the conference hall by the main entrance. But Wang Feng had several times urged him, 'Do nothing. Let things take their course and just watch calmly. This moment is a test for everyone.'

Of course it was impossible to foresee who would pass the test, but Lu Hao-ran had not expected that the treachery of friends would be so virulent, base and infuriating. If Wang Feng had not bugged every room, every telephone, every car, every guesthouse and bedroom, Lu Hao-ran would not have believed it. The tape was in his briefcase, and his heart was cold.

He entered the conference room and went to the seat with his name on it. No one took any notice of him: apparently he was already regarded as a dead tiger. Once they discovered that he was not anyone to be reckoned with, the combat-ready factions—one led by 'number two' of the Standing Committee the other by 'number three' and 'number five'—would start fighting for the position of General Secretary. In little more than a day, the united opposition itself had become a battlefield.

Lu remained silent as the moderates attacked each other, using all the old arguments and theories of their enemies. When they did engage with the hard-liners, they shamelessly used the same arguments—which they had formerly dismissed as self-seeking nonsense. This talk about 'reform' was totally meaningless: no more than a stick for beating the opposition and a ladder for the ambitious.

'Number two' took the chair; 'number three' and 'number five' sat close together. Lu Hao-ran had been allocated a place at some distance from them—unmistakably a 'cold seat'.

The state could not remain without a supreme ruler, even for a day, and although the struggle for power had reached a stalemate, it was essential to decide today from which faction the acting General Secretary should be chosen. Then it would have to be confirmed by a full meeting of the Central Committee.

Battle was imminent and everyone felt the tension. All eyes were on 'number two' and 'number three'. Lu Hao-ran had been written off.

Then everyone noticed a faint buzz of voices outside, sounding at first as if a hive of bees had been disturbed. The impassioned speeches stopped. Everyone listened; never before had a meeting of the Central Committee been disturbed like this. There was an uneasy silence, heavy with apprehension and foreboding.

A sound of coughing and the shuffling of many feet was approaching the conference hall.

They've come, thought Lu Hao-ran.

The door of the conference hall was thrown open, a confused group of personnel was swept in protesting, followed by a large number of silent, well-dressed and dignified people. Some were old and there were some women, but the majority were middle-aged men and each had a briefcase. They stood respectfully just inside the door.

'Who are you?' said 'number two' rather indignantly.

'We are a hundred and forty one members of the Central Committee of the Chinese Communist Party,' said a fat man in a western style suit, standing in the front row. Lu Hao-ran recognized the General Manager of the Baotou Iron and Steel Works.

'What are you doing here?' Number two's tone had become severe.

'We have come to attend the meeting.'

'Who told you to come?'

'The Party Constitution,' said the fat man.

'What do you think you're up to?' said 'number two', pounding the table so that his teacup rattled.

'Comrade,' said the fat man. 'The Party leader has been assassinated. This is a critical moment for our country, and every member of the Central Committee should participate in discussing the future of the Party. Why did only the ninety-five of you—less than a third of the total Central Committee membership—take it on yourselves to decide the fate of the Party. I propose that this emergency meeting be transformed into a Plenary Session. There are 236 members present—far more than two thirds of the total membership, and sufficient for a Plenary Session according to the Party Constitution. Those in agreement please show!'

The hundred and forty one newcomers raised their hands. Among those seated only Lu Hao-ran did so.

The fat man declared, 'One hundred and forty two for the motion—more than 50 per cent. Carried.'

'The meeting is closed.' 'Number two' stood up in a fury and turned to leave the room.

'One moment,' said the fat man. 'This member is contravening the Party constitution and violating inner-party democracy. I propose that he should be removed from his post as member of the Standing Committee of the Central Committee Bureau. Those in agreement please show.'

Again, just inside the doorway, one hundred and forty one hands were raised. This is some fantastic dream, thought Lu Hao-ran, as he raised his hand, which was shaking slightly. He wondered how Wang Feng had managed to obtain such unanimity amongst the newcomers. As in all meetings of the Central Committee, the decision-making nucleus consisted of high-ranking members, such as government ministers and provincial governors. The others were more or less symbolic. If there was a difference of opinion, it was first thrashed out among the decision-makers and unconditionally approved by the others. When Wang Feng told him the previous day that sixty planes had already taken off for all parts of the country to bring these people to Beijing, Lu Hao-ran had doubted whether this would have any effect. Now he knew better.

'One hundred and forty two votes in favour. Carried!'

'Number two' stared at Lu Hao-ran and laughed coldly, then turned and pushed open the small door which gave access to the lift reserved for the use of Central Committee members. As the doors of the lift opened, the lights inside shone on a row of brightly polished steel helmets and a squad of armed soldiers emerged. 'Number two' froze and hastily turned back. In the conference room eyes were on the doorway.

The soldiers did not enter, but through the glass partition wall, their sinister, indistinct forms could be seen, shoulder to shoulder, surrounding the conference room.

The voice of the fat man broke the silence. 'I propose Comrade Lu Hao-ran as General Secretary of the Central Committee. Those in favour raise their hands.'

The hands of all the newcomers were duly raised. Lu Hao-ran raised only his red pencil and, as the fat man was about to announce the result, shook it at him. Silence.

Lu Hao-ran scrutinized one by one, each of those seated, like stuffed hens, in the places reserved for the leaders. The Minister of State Security was the first to raise his hand. He had always been a strong supporter, and could be forgiven for occasional disloyalty. The Minister of Finance quickly raised his hand, as if regretting not having been the first to do so, and managed to put on something resembling a heart-felt smile. He was an opportunist and not above biting his old master's hand in order please the new one. Lu Hao-ran decided to forgive him too. The head of the Planning Commission, the Foreign Minister and the Deputy Premier and many others raised their hands—even members of the opposition began to do so. Then Lu Hao-ran looked at members of the Standing Committee: after hesitating for some time 'number five' raised his.

'Number three' sighed and showed his hand, rather as if he was just rubbing his ear. The last one, 'number two', angrily turned away. Lu Hao-ran made a mark with his red pencil on the paper in front of him.

'Two hundred and thirty five in favour. Carried,' announced the fat man and started clapping. The newcomers followed enthusiastically, the other members joined in grudgingly and with misgivings; but they could hardly refuse to applaud. This was a Plenary Session of the Central Committee, and they had just elected the General Secretary.

Lu Hao-ran stood up. 'Everyone is responsible for the fate of our country. At this critical moment, since you place your confidence in me, I accept my responsibilities without reserve. But before we begin working together, I wish you all to listen to a tape.'

He raised his hand. Wang Feng's assistant had told him earlier that one of the conference hall personnel, wearing a red tie, would be waiting for Lu Hao-ran to give him a signal. Sure enough, a man came up to him with a military gait and handed him a tape. The recorder had been placed ready in advance.

It was a tape made up of many short recordings, and as soon as the voices began to resound in the hall, nearly everyone turned pale. Their secret contacts, bargaining, plans and conspiracies had been recorded and in such a way as to include the names of those speaking, so that there could be no doubt as to their identity. The traps being prepared, the naked bribery and extortion, might not have seemed particularly shocking in private; but when heard over the loudspeakers in front of everyone, they were doubly base and shocking.

Everyone heard himself betrayed by associates, heard things told to him 'as a friend', being repeated to the 'enemy', or heard venomous words of ridicule about himself from someone who had unctuously bowed and scraped to him, not long before.

'These are the voices of Central Committee members,' said Lu Hao-ran in a pained voice, 'of our provincial secretaries, governors, ministers, members of the Political Bureau, and of the Standing Committee! How can they have sunk so low? In spite of the crisis, everyone has only thought of his personal interest, or of his little clique. Can people like this lead our country?'

'Secret recording is against the law!' 'Number two' objected loudly.

'In an emergency, all means of protecting the security of the State are permissible,' Lu Hao-ran replied. 'Even if it is against the law, it is nothing compared with your illegal behaviour.'

'As General Secretary I now give notice,' Lu Hao-ran went on, 'that the 141 members of the Central Committee who have just arrived, are to remain in Beijing to carry on the work of the Central Committee. The others will all be sent to Party schools in the provinces for re-education.'

He then left the conference hall, accompanied by the obsequious personnel from the Central Committee office, who prepared to lead the way and open doors for him before they were pushed aside by tight-lipped soldiers. He alone left the hall. The functions of the Central Committee office had been taken over by that of the Military Commission and an unfamiliar army officer led the way. It was a victory, certainly; but Lu Hao-ran felt lonely and isolated.

The Great Hall of the People was full of troops. The Central Committee guards in their dress uniform had been disarmed. The Armed Police had been dismissed. All communications had been cut, and officers were reporting in by radio to command HQ in provincial accents.

Outside in Tiananmen Square no one knew anything. All was normal; there was a little rain, and a slight autumn chill in the air.

Beijing: Central Military Commission

Wang Feng was not a full member of the Central Committee and had not been at the special meeting that had just taken place. When 'number two' had phoned to sound him out on where he stood, Wang Feng, as representative of the Chairman, had merely expressed the army's absolute obedience to the Party and to the future General Secretary, and offered to provide troops to wait quietly outside the Great Hall of the People in buses in Tiananmen Square, to ensure that the meeting was not interrupted by disorder of any kind.

'Number two' had accepted with alacrity, which gave Wang Feng a perfect pretext to have the Great Hall surrounded. Not being invited to the meeting saved him the trouble of finding an excuse not to attend, so that he was able to have the majority of army members of the Central Committee sent away from Beijing earlier. With the exception of the 'traitors' he had long wanted to get rid of, who had been close to the late General Secretary, the other army dissidents and plotters were already on their way to high level Party Schools 'to study'.

Wang Feng smiled with self-satisfaction. He tapped his elegant fingers on his desk as if on a piano. To have laughed out loud would have been out of place after such a victory; so he merely sipped his coffee and relaxed, savouring his pleasure.

In the middle of his office, a large globe turned at the same speed as the earth, dotted like stars by many tiny lights in different colours marking military targets. Special telephone lines linked him with the seven area military commands, to submarines, to the three fleets, five airforce bases and the seven most important missile launching sites. There was also a wall of fifty-six television screens that enabled him to keep an eye on all departments of the General HQ. When he was resting, Wang Feng liked to watch these screens. He had brought all this equipment with him when he moved from the Works Committee to the Military Commission. A special screen showed the central receiving post of the electronic surveillance department, where twenty officers were busy at work.

Wang Feng had set up the department a month earlier. It employed seventy-three specialists trained in Germany, the USA and Britain and almost two hundred assistants. Most of them were at present concealed in various maintenance rooms of the Great Hall of the People, in Zhongnanhai, the basement of the Central Party School and in various telephone exchanges. The equipment was very modern and could record the slightest sound and transmit it to the centre, where it was selected and processed.

This was one of the reasons for his satisfaction. One small audio-tape had been enough to subdue a group of the most powerful men in China. Of course he could have used the army, but that would have been called a coup d'état and caused a lot of trouble in China and abroad. But by means of one tape they could be legitimately packed off 'to study'. Trial and imprisonment would have been going too far. Party School was perfect: the discipline was often stricter than in prison. Afterwards they could work again.

The 141 other members must not be allowed home yet: their votes might be needed again, now that everyone was shouting about democracy. They could hardly be surrounded by troops, but they had to be guarded for their own safety. So their freedom was not restricted; but when they went out each had to have a pass, a driver and a secretary. They would feel flattered; but their rooms would be bugged and every movement watched. If they were occasionally allowed—as a symbolic gesture—to approve a Central Committee document, they would feel that they were masters of the situation.

Looking at all these screens Wang Feng felt confident he could control not just the army but the whole country, and was grateful to 'the old man' (Mao Zedong) who had made it possible by giving up the position of supreme leader to become Chairman of the Military Commission. 'The old man' hated a quiet life and was not content to control only the army, so he had to made the Military Commission into his instrument for directing and supervising the whole country. From that moment the army had begun to intervene in politics.

'The old man' was no longer living, but his system was. It seemed a waste sometimes, because it cost a lot to keep it going, but when there was a crisis, it showed its immense power. Without it, Wang Feng would not have been able to obtain so rapidly, complete information on the attitudes, background and characters of the 141 collaborators he had selected, or even find out where they were and what each was doing.

They had been assembled in secret, so that their sudden departure would not become known in Beijing through inquiries from agitated local Party organizations. Soldiers in civilian clothes, with bogus papers from the Central Committee office had gone to their homes—sometimes even disturbing them in their conjugal beds—or to their hotels if they were away from home. No news got out. Anyone involved in the operation was kept in isolation until it was all over.

At three o'clock this morning, the 141 Central Committee members from twenty-four different provincial capitals had gathered in Beijing. Before their sudden appearance at the meeting, they had been briefed, had listened to the tape and were aware of the various plots, had been treated to a lavish breakfast and invited to inspect the full-dress guards at the Great Hall of the People. As they did so, a prison van 'happened' to pass carrying a 'traitor' arrested in the act of revealing 'state secrets'. Everything went like clockwork and Wang Feng, obsessive about efficiency, was very pleased.

A buzzer sounded and Lu Hao-ran's arrival was announced. Wang Feng switched on a row of TV screens, which showed the path between his office and the Guardhouse, where a limousine with a military escort had stopped. Strict orders had been given that Lu Hao-ran's safety must be guaranteed at all costs.

As the Lu Hao-ran emerged from an bullet-proof limousine the guard saluted. Wang Feng was a little surprised to see a man and a woman get out as well. He took an immediate dislike to the man, who reminded him of a wild mountain cat, eyes never still, noticing everything, his whole body emanating energy. Lu Hao-ran on the other hand, resembled something a cat might swallow whole. Wang Feng did not like the appearance of the woman much either. She kept behind Lu Hao-ran, it looked as if she would prefer to be walking hand in hand with him.

'Who are those two?' he asked the duty officer over the intercom.

'Lu Hao-ran says the man is Zhou Chi, one of his staff—his *qigong* teacher, who insists on staying close to him.' Wang Feng did not listen any more. He knew about Zhou Chi and the woman.

Why had Lu Hao-ran brought these two charlatans with him? Wang Feng asked himself as he watched them approach. For show? Lu Hao-ran liked to be surrounded by staff and attendants and Wang Feng had provided him with several people to run errands for him. But he evidently did not want to be thought dependent on the Military Commission. Using these two mountebanks was ridiculous, but must be taken seriously.

'Keep those two back and check their identity,' Wang Feng told the office: they would understand, and check up on them in a manner both courteous and intimidating—usually enough to persuade people not to interfere in matters which did not concern them.

Wang Feng had ordered a report from the appropriate department on Lu Hao-ran's enthusiasm for *qigong*. It concluded that he had probably got the idea of making use of the huge number of adepts for his own purposes when he had been politically isolated. There were now almost a hundred million adepts, many of whom had a quasi-religious attitude to *qigong* and their instructors. Zhou Chi was the head of the *Qigong* Association, which resembled a traditional popular sect, with a hierarchy, strict discipline and an ideology that had widespread influence.

Wang Feng had doubts about the analysis: Lu Hao-ran was too weak and lacked character and imagination for such a venture. Perhaps, he suddenly thought, remembering the small bright eyes of Zhou Chi, it was not Lu Hao-ran who was thinking of controlling the *qigong* enthusiasts but the *qigong* master who was trying to control him.

The new General Secretary was already almost at the entrance to the reception room. Wang Feng watched the duty officer conduct him to the door, and as it opened, came in himself through another door.

'How are you...General Secretary?' he said, shaking his hand solemnly.

Lu Hao-ran smiled wryly. 'If I were a real General Secretary you would salute me, rather than offering your hand.'

Wang Feng covered his surprise with a laugh, and mumbled something about 'these democratic times...'

'You could at least have discussed it with me before sending this great pile of appointments to sign,' Lu Hao-ran said mildly, putting them down, unsigned, on the table.

'Permit me to explain, General Secretary,' said Wang Feng, the last two words in a soothing, almost musical tone of voice. 'The provincial appointments are extremely urgent. The former Governors and General Secretaries are in Party Schools now, but we still have to take all possible precautions. Every province has a large organization in Beijing, with contacts and sources of information. We can probably keep the lid on for two days; but if there is a leak *before* the new officials are installed and well-prepared, trouble-makers will be able to stir things up and who knows where it will end. So there was no time to consult you, General Secretary.'

'Who are these people?' asked Lu Hao-ran, pointed to the pile of letters of appointment.

How could he understand? Wang Feng thought. How could he know the time and effort it had taken to train and bring under his control people to take the lead in the country at a moment's notice? Concealing their links with the army had been the most difficult of all.

'Don't worry, General Secretary. There is one thing that is quite clear; all the old provincial governors officials were your enemies. Even if you don't know them, the new ones are not. In fact, I can guarantee they will be loyal and obedient to you.'

Lu Hao-ran hesitated for a moment then said, 'You should tell me now whether you were responsible for that list of people in my handwriting?'

'I can only say I knew about it.'

'And the purpose?'

'Wait until you've signed these papers.'

The list, in his own handwriting, handed to Lu Hao-ran before the meeting, had been drawn up on Wang Feng's orders; it was a plant to outsmart the opposition. It had been entrusted to a double-agent, claiming to be a member of Lu Hao-ran's staff, who had presented it to 'number two' as a pledge of loyalty. The opposition had duly panicked about not having enough votes and had recalled provincial leaders to the capital, where they had all been neatly rounded up by Wang Feng. The tiger had been lured out of the mountains. The opposition was disarmed.

'I don't mind signing the appointments,' said Lu Hao-ran after a long silence, 'but I should have the right to make my own choices.'

'Please do so. Whom do you wish to appoint?' Lu Hao-ran's selection came as no surprise. They were all hard-liners like himself—members of the State Council and Ministers. The importance of controlling the provinces was well known; the new General Secretary was now isolated and powerless because he had not done so.

Wang Feng raised his eyebrows. 'General Secretary. You must be confused. These people are despicable conspirators and deserve to be dealt with. Yet you want to make them provincial governors and allow them to ruin the country!'

Lu Hao-ran went red at this reprimand and could find nothing to say.

Wang Feng feigned surprise, but in fact, he could hardly refrain from laughing at the other's embarrassment. He was very proud of smashing both the moderates and the hard-liners at the same time, and leaving Lu Hao-ran with no supporters. He had good reason for preventing Lu Hao-ran from plotting. It would discourage others from doing so. In this way the hard-liners would be leaderless. Eventually all those involved in intrigues would find bolt-holes and not just wait to get caught. They were bound to get involved in some conspiracy, and even if Lu Hao-ran put up with it, the Party and government would not. The crafty old scoundrels of the State Council would sooner or later be bound to cause trouble. Lu Hao-ran would possibly feel safe with such backing, and even get too big for his boots. Too bad. Now he can go and lean on his *qigong* master!

Wang Feng then relented a little. He had resolved to respect the dignity of the General Secretary,

'There is no time to go over the appointments now. We must decide on the membership of the State Council.' Wang Feng smiled slightly. 'Apart from the Premier, the Ministers of Foreign Affairs, Safety, State Security and Finance, and the head of the Standing Committee of the National Peoples Congress, nominated by the President, you can select the others yourself. As long as you do not choose any of the conspirators we will respect your choice.'

With all those politicians detained in Party schools, it would be difficult to find anyone of consequence. Anyway, the State Council was close at hand, in Beijing: it would be easy to stretch out and grab them.

'Sign, General Secretary.'

Construction site of the Three Gorges Dam

In the hospital of the construction site Li Ke-ming pushed lightly with his toes at the door of his room: it was locked from the outside. The glass of the top part was covered by a curtain, so he could not see into the corridor, only the reflection of his bandaged head, and the clear sky outside the window behind him.

He could not knock with his hands—also bandaged, so kicked the door a few times, not very hard. The curtain was lifted and the astonished face of the head nurse appeared outside.

'I want to urinate.' The vibration of his voice sent a wave of pain down from his chest to his abdomen.

The nurse opened the door. 'How did you get up?' She helped him back into bed. 'I'll go and get you a bottle.'

She was well over forty and had been working in the hospital since the beginning of the dam construction and Li Ke-ming knew her husband. Now her voice and expression were a little odd…

'I can walk, I'll go myself,' said Li Ke-ming pushing past her. The pain almost made him cry out. He had been semi-conscious for several days and it was the first time he had got out of bed. In spite of the extensive burns on the upper part of his body, the speed of his recovery surprised the doctors; after taking a few steps his twisted ankle hardly troubled him.

'No, no! You can't,' said the head nurse very nervously. 'A bottle will do just as well.'

'I wouldn't be able to hold it,' he said showing his arms, like bandaged planks.

'I'll hold it for you.'

'I don't want a woman for that.' He stepped out of the ward.

'I'll do it.' A doctor in a long white gown stopped him in the corridor.

Li Ke-ming looked through the holes in the bandages at him. 'I don't know you.'

'You don't need to. I'm not a woman: that's all you need to know.'

'I don't want you touching my cock,' said Li Ke-ming, deliberately raising his voice.

The man laughed equably and told the head nurse to put a commode in the room

Two other men wearing white gowns were standing in the corridor, looking the other way rather too obviously: one at the top of the stairs, the other at the door to the veranda. Armed guards obviously.

'All right,' said Li Ke-ming in a conciliatory and casual tone. 'I don't mind using one of those things made for foreigners arses, but you must loosen the bandages so that I can move my fingers.'

The head nurse looked at the man. 'A reasonable demand,' he said loftily. The door closed. He was a prisoner again.

What had happened? He kept turning this question over and over in his mind as he lay on his bed. Yesterday the door had not been locked and there was no curtain behind the glass panel of the door. The head nurse had been kind and friendly, there had been no guards and a succession of friends had been allowed to visit him. After his colleague Lao San's visit yesterday evening, everything had changed. Yet Lao San would never have talked.

Earlier, when he had regained consciousness Li Ke-ming had

pretended not to remember anything. All he would talk about to the investigators was his struggle with the assassin. When Shen Di had questioned him and tried to lead him on, he pretended to be even more muddled. He appeared to remember nothing about Shen Di's behaviour that day, and seemed interested only in the possibility of winning a citation.

In fact, he was perfectly clear-headed. When he had regained consciousness in Lao San's arms and heard that the assassin had got away, he refused to believe it. He had seen the search party from the helicopter! Then Lao San told him that after they had searched part of the north shore of the reservoir, they had suddenly been informed that the assassin was on the south shore and were ordered to return. The police cordon had then been removed.

Li Ke-ming understood at once; doubt had become certainty—Shen Di was implicated in the assassination. He had scrapped the original security plan not because it was bad, but because it was too good. Everything he had done was in order to let the assassin make the hit and get away. He had disarmed Li Ke-ming's security men and sent them far away from the dam, because they knew the territory too well. He had forbidden Li himself to contact Security and ask for a patrol boat; had refused to send a helicopter or a patrol to the north shore, and had delayed cutting off access to roads and the railway until it was too late—all for the same purpose. Shen Di had silenced him with the words 'top state secret'.

Shen Di had covered himself well. In an emergency, it is not easy to tell a good strategy from a bad one. At the worst people would say he was incompetent, which was just what he wanted. At the height of the action when he had no room for manoeuvre, he had managed to fool Li Ke-ming. But Shen Di had only to look up Li Ke-ming's record, and sound out his superiors to know that Li Ke-ming was no fool. He had pretended to have lost his memory after all he had been through, and until last night Shen Di seemed almost to believe him. What had gone wrong? Perhaps it was something he had said to Lao San…

A bug! His heart missed a beat. He looked round the room in the bed, the lamp, the table, under the chair cushion. Perhaps it was in one of the pillows at the head of the bed, or behind that black spot on the wall? Bugs could have been put in the room before he was brought there.

He had made a bad mistake. In his work he had never used listening devices. He had not even thought about such things, especially in a hospital. While talking to Lao San, he had turned up the volume on the TV and lowered his voice, as a precaution against inquisitive ears, but useless against computerized bugs.

They had agreed that Lao San would take the Beijing train the same evening. He would get off at Fengtai after midnight and telephone the director of the Police Academy they had both attended, who was now head of a bureau in the Ministry of State Security. Even if he were asleep, he would receive Lao San at once, and learn that the assassination had been ordered by someone high up. Shen Di would be arrested and the whole conspiracy would come to light. A great disturbance in the country would be avoided, and Li Ke-ming would become a hero.

But if things went wrong? Lao San was head of the criminal police of the Security Bureau. He and Li Ke-ming were like brothers; they had grown up together in Heilongjiang province, trained together. Li Ke-ming did not dare think about the consequences of failure; but was tormented by a feeling of apprehension.

The sound of an approaching ambulance filled him with a sudden foreboding. Soon afterwards there was a scurry of activity in the casualty unit on the ground floor then, through the poor-quality flooring he heard heart-rending cries that turned his foreboding into horrifying certainty. He recognized the voice of Lao San's wife, crying and wailing and calling her husband. Why had he gone off without saying anything? Was it to go and see his mother? She wished she was dead like him, crushed by the wheel of a train… 'They said you were drunk but I don't believe it.'

Li Ke-ming lay without moving.

It was too dark to see the hands of his watch. He rose quickly and careful to keep out of sight, looked out of the window. There was a motorcycle outside, as if forgotten by its owner, the keys still in the ignition.

There was a drainpipe from the roof only a yard from the window. It would be easy to get down. His chest was badly burned but his legs were all right. He could now move his fingers a little and there was a flowerbed below the window. Once on the motorcycle he would be far away in no time. With his knowledge of the territory, no one would catch him. He had to get away, and quickly.

That afternoon the investigators had begun to put on the pressure. They had asked why had he called out to the General Secretary telling him to look down into the water, just before he was shot? Why had shouted 'a sturgeon!'? They knew that his family had been killed by the Japanese during the war: did he hate Japan? The General Secretary had signed the agreement leasing his home province to the Japanese, how did he feel about that? When he asked them if they really thought he was the assassin, one of the interrogators took a pistol from his briefcase, with new rust on it.

'You said you kicked the assassin's rifle into the water. We have dragged the whole inlet and have found nothing, except this pistol, an 88. The number is 0503146.' It was his. They asked no more questions but looked at each other with significant expressions and left Li Ke-ming speechless.

Shen Di held all the cards. Li Ke-ming had no idea many people around here were his men, so there was no point in trying to convince the investigators that Shen Di himself was implicated in the assassination. He had no proof. The only other man on the spot was the helicopter pilot, and he was dead.

Shen Di could frame him easily. He would tell how Li Ke-ming had been determined to make a round of inspection by helicopter—many people would testify that he had been abnormally insistent. He could easily have concealed his pistol in the helicopter before taking off. Calling out to the General Secretary to look at the water was to distracted attention away from the helicopter. The word 'sturgeon' might have been a secret signal to the pilot. He had arranged for the helicopter to crash and kill the pilot and stop him from talking. He had burned himself on purpose, and had invented a dramatic story... If this is what Shen Di was going to say, it had a very good chance of convincing people. And they had his pistol...

But if they want to pin the assassination on me, Li Ke-ming said to himself, why not wait for the right moment to show their hand, instead of revealing their evidence in advance? Investigators never did things like that, and these were professionals. But they were anything but stupid: I must work out what the trap is.

The best solution for Shen Di would be to kill me, he concluded. As long as I am alive he has the power to frame me; but this is no ordinary murder, where the case is quickly closed and forgotten; there is bound to be an investigation. I will never plead guilty. At every interrogation and on every possible occasion I will point the finger at him. Even if there is no investigation, people will take an interest in the case and continue to ferret out what really happened. What would I do in his place? Whoever is behind him, however powerful and important, I will track him as long as I live and never give up. Yes, he wants me dead, like Lao San.

Poison in the food or water? An injection? Or simply a bullet? But the murder of someone in his custody would lead to inquiries and might be traced back to Shen Di himself. Perhaps he wants me to kill myself, by showing his hand and leaving me no other way out? He can't think I'm as stupid as that. He can't believe that I would want to die before playing my trump card.

The motorcycle outside was a little strange, the keys were there, as if waiting for me to ride away on it. An ordinary criminal would not be so badly guarded, let alone the man who had killed the Head of State . . . no bars on the window, a motorcycle outside. The guard in a corridor had just been called away to watch TV and was laughing and shouting at the top of his voice. The normal procedure would be to send me immediately to Beijing by special plane, with an escort of at least a company of soldiers, and lock me up in a high-security prison.

There was a slight breeze. Li Ke-ming used the handle of a fly swat to push a tin can off the windowsill and it clattered to the ground. He saw signs of sudden movement in various places outside, then all was still again.

Shen Di is using my own pistol, 'found at the scene of the crime', to force me to attempt a getaway. The bait is the motorcycle and the unwary guards. He is sure this is what I will do, because it is the only way to slip through his fingers, then denounce him and clear myself. Except that I will be riddled with bullets by the men outside 'while trying to escape'. Perfect. The son I have never seen will one day read that his father was an assassin.

He thought of his pregnant wife at his home in Heilongjiang. Luckily, he had sent her back to his mother's house, where the summer would be less hot, and his parents could look after her. If she had not already left, she too would have been killed. She knew nothing, but Shen Di would take no risks.

He had to escape anyway. There was no alternative. Shen Di had worked everything out. But he was not a local man. He would never imagine, and no textbook would tell him, that there was another way out or the trap.

Li Ke-ming put on a waterproof overall that a number of noisy youngsters from the security bureau had used to wrap up some fruit and tins when they came to visit him. It was very thin and light and made of excellent material. He folded his quilt into more or less the shape of a body, then climbed up the heating pipe and crawled through a trap in the ceiling boards. His movements were very slow. He was not afraid of anyone bursting in—not when they were waiting for him to make a break.

The building dated from the 1950s and under the roof, there was an attic, containing a tangle of pipes and wiring and a large number of mice, who never stopped squeaking—perhaps helping to cover up the sound of his movements from the electronic bugs below. All his wounds had reopened, and he felt he was bleeding all over under the dressings. The pain and itching was almost unbearable.

He closed the trap, and carefully crossed to the other side of the attic, glad to find that there was still strength in his legs, and thankful for the little light from below, that came through the cracks and holes in the ceiling.

Through these he could see into a ward, where most of the patients were asleep, a guard in the duty-room was cleaning his gun and there were armed men at each turning in the corridor. The nurses' bedroom, like the last time, was brightly lit. A young nurse, naked, was washing herself.

Two months earlier, Li Ke-ming had been searching the home of an electrical worker caught selling stolen cable, and had come across a pile of photographs of naked or half-naked young women sleeping, washing themselves or just relaxing. They were all all taken from above and from the same angle. The worker first said that he had picked them up somewhere, then that he had bought them; but when he saw Li Ke-ming's electro-shock police truncheon, freshly charged, he had told him about the hospital attic.

Li Ke-ming was relieved—to say the least—that the long thin aluminium ladder was still there. When he came to the hospital with the electrician to verify his story, he had climbed into the attic by means of this ladder, which the electrician had left hidden behind the hospital. After he had inspected the attic, Li Ke-ming had left the ladder there and come down into the corridor in the usual way, telling the hospital staff he had come to inspect the wiring. Since no one knew about the case, Li Ke-ming did not hand over the photos to the court, to avoid embarrassing the nurses. Nor was there any real need to tell anyone about the secret entrance. He thought the electrician had got off lightly and merely gave him two good kicks up the backside. He felt grateful to the young man now.

There was a small square opening in the gable-end of the roof. He took off a half-rotten shutter and felt the cool wind. A few yards away was a cliff and a dark hill above. He poked his head out and listened: nothing. The men waiting for him were watching the other three sides of the hospital. On this side, there was only a steep cliff and the rift where the ladder had been hidden. Who could have guessed that a night prowler would leave such a precious gift behind?

Li Ke-ming eased the ladder out of the opening and propped the end against a small shelf in the rock just below the fissure and adjusted it until the hook on the end of the ladder caught in an iron ring fixed to the stone. He paused to listen again. There was only a sound of distant thunder. He wormed his way out on the ladder and replaced the shutter. Each time he moved his wounds rubbed against the dressings but his body was responding to a desperate emergency and he no longer felt much pain. He had not lost too much blood and could still control his movements and keep his balance. He managed to crawl across on the six-inch wide ladder, and almost fainted when he got there.

He rested for five minutes. Then pulled the ladder back and used it to climb up to the top of the fissure. Then, with the aid of a chain that the electrician had fixed there, he hauled himself up the steep slope to the top, where the menacing form of a high-tension pylon was outlined against the pale night sky. A small path led down to the riverbank. Upstream, the lights on the dam shone like daylight on the fast-flowing river.

He blew up the inflatable compartment of his waterproof overalls, tightened the sleeves, collar and hood. As long as the water did not get in, his wounds would not become infected; a few days' proper rest and they would soon heal.

The current was very strong and once the water was above his knees, it was hard keep his feet. He was not worried, knowing that there were no very dangerous stretches downstream. A few more steps and he was afloat. The dressings on his head were soon soaked; but the fast current would quickly carry him to a place he knew, where small wooden boats tied up. If he could take one and manage to get into it, he would be able to keep water out of the other dressings. Forty kilometres further on, there was the jetty of a small hydrological station. The guard-dogs knew him. He would take the motorboat and before dawn, he would be more than two hundred kilometres away. . . then a car, the train…

His disfigured face was a problem. Even bandaged it would attract attention and might lead to his arrest. The real assassin also had a burnt face, as Li Ke-ming had kept reminding the interrogator. Shen Di would certainly say nothing about that until the hit man was safe—that was an advantage. Apart from his face and bandages, he had no other distinguishing features. The important thing was to get to safety and find someone he could rely on.

A village in Shanxi province

Shi Ge was winnowing. Each time he tossed up a shovel-full of grain into the light wind, it separated evenly: the grain fell to the ground, the chaff and husks blew away. There was already a heap of new grain beside him, golden in the sunlight. The hot sun made him sweat and the air was full of the fragrance of a ripe harvest. He felt almost hypnotized by the rhythm of his movements. It was a long time since he had been so happy.

'Not bad,' he thought as he watched the grain fan out evenly each time from his wooden shovel. Thirty years ago, when he had been a member of a work team of Beijing college graduates living in this village in Shanxi province, he was the only one who could winnow grain. If you threw it up too hard it would land in the straw pile, not hard enough and the grain would come down with the husk still on. He had worked with Gui-zhi's father for a whole afternoon before mastering it.

The pleasant sound of a two-stringed violin came from a pocket radio. Shi Ge sighed with pleasure. Perhaps he should stay and live here, in this bright and peaceful countryside. Even the buzzing of the flies pleased him. He had come back seven times in the last twenty-five years and each time he was tempted to stay; but he always had to hurry back to the noisy, bustling capital. Nowadays a man's worth was judged by how busy he was. Ideals were soon forgotten in all the feverish involuntary activity that was destroying man's humanity and natural virtue, he reflected sadly. People's capacity for communication and interaction was entirely used up in endless looking, listening, talking and reading—there was never any time to spare. The heart has become nothing but a blood pump, and life only a pile of routine matters. In the end, there is nothing but a miserable emptiness, while one's hair grows thinner like trees in autumn.

Shi Ge had experienced both success and failure. All these years he had been as cunning and resourceful as he was able, but on fundamental questions, he had almost been playing devil's advocate. Some people called him 'the black crow'—his croak announced disaster. When they were feeling confident and in high spirits, his ill-omened voice disturbed them, and it was intolerable when he proved to be a jump ahead of them. There were many important people who wanted to bring about his downfall.

The recent investigation was a general offensive against him and had really hit home. Even the little crows under him might have got plucked as well. But Shi Ge's statement that he had the support of the General Secretary had forced them to back down and not enquire any further. Rather than do so and risk finding out that it was true, they chose to act quickly, and wrapped up the case. Unit Sixteen was closed down and Shi Ge dismissed—they could not safely do more. If the General Secretary, on returning from his tour of inspection, asked about the matter, they would simply think up some story and no one would know exactly what had happened.

This was what Shi Ge had been hoping for, and they had not called his bluff. Of course he had not consulted the General Secretary: that would have been disastrous. He had never expected Unit Sixteen to survive and was satisfied as long as not too many of his staff got into trouble. He had shaken hands with everyone, and then taken the first train to Shanxi.

As always, he stayed in Gui-zhi's home. Her father was old and her mother was dead. Gui-zhi had lived with her husband's family until he threw her out. This time Shi Ge had stayed longer than ever before; more than ten days had gone in a flash. Every day, when he was not helping Gui-zhi with the farm work, he would wander round the edges of the fields, looking at the sky, listening to the birds and counting the geese flying south.

In the past, when he resigned or had been dismissed, it had never been long before he was called back; nearly always because things had developed as he had predicted they would. He had often criticized impetuous schemes that caused a brief sensation. When the problems and obstructions he had foreseen became obvious, everyone concerned backed out, Shi Ge was reinstated and eventually solved the problem. This was why people hated him; but he was invaluable to them. He had no desire to be a hero, merely to do what others could not do.

When he started working on crisis management, he had wanted to be the best, the quickest and the most dramatic. Gradually he came to dislike this desire for false glory, and only his strong sense of responsibility made him continue. He had no alternative. He could not sit back and see the monetary system collapse, a wave of panic buying sweep across the country, enterprises collapse and millions of unemployed and their children starve.

Now he felt that this sense of responsibility was meaningless and even criminal. In earlier periods of crisis, China seemed to be getting bogged down. Without a basic change in policy, helping to get the country out of the mud would merely allow the same thing to happen again, each time worse than the last.

Yesterday when they had been drinking together, Gui-zhi's father had said, 'They are bound to call you back—a man of your ability.'

Shi Ge shook his head. 'This time it's different. Even if they call me, I won't go.'

Gui-zhi's eyes had lit up: 'That's what you say now...'

'It's true. What use would it be? One pillar won't save a building from collapsing. In any case, I'm not a pillar—just a maize stalk.' His tongue felt a little stiff; he must have drunk too much.

Shi Ge stuck his wooden shovel into the pile of grain. The wind was almost still now. The radio was broadcasting the news. He sat down, leaning against a pile of straw and rolled a cigarette. He had stopped smoking years ago. The last few days he had smoked all day.

Since the reforms, announcers' voices had become more intimate and natural. Today the tone was once more strident and rousing. The first item of news concerned the assassination of the General Secretary. Everything was now clear. The killer was a certain Li Ke-ming, deputy head of security at the Three Gorges construction site. It was now known that he had shot the General Secretary with a pistol while patrolling the dam in a helicopter

Investigation showed, the announcer said, that Li Ke-ming was a native of Heilongjiang province and that six members of his grandfather's family had been killed by the Japanese invaders during the war. His immediate motive had probably been resentment that his home province had been leased to Japan. His escape showed that he had efficient accomplices. A nationwide search had been launched and there was a reward of more than two million dollars for his capture.

Not being in Beijing, Shi Ge did not know what was going on behind the scenes, but judging from the speed of Lu Hao-ran's promotion to General Secretary it was clear that the assassination was not nearly as simple as the official version made out. The hard-liners had already begun to undo the work of the moderates. The radio was reporting the shattering decision to cancel the Economic Cooperation Agreement with Japan. Other decisions would put an end to the economic reforms, decentralization and the free market policy. State control of the economy would be back with other discredited policies. It had also been decided to impose a heavy special tax to pay for flood relief.

Unit Sixteen had always been neutral in the struggle for power at the top, and Shi Ge did not belong to any faction. For several years, at least since the beginning of reform and opening up to the world, instead of a consistent guiding principle, there had been an incessant swing between two opposite policies: between planned economy and market economy; state ownership and private ownership; between tight and loose control. All the while, the respective advocates of each—hard-liners and moderates—struggled for power.

Continuity and stability were impossible. One step forward, two steps back became the norm and China was caught in a terrible dilemma—a choice between loose control and anarchy, or tight control and death.

There was no middle way; to adopt the advantages of each system would only result in combining their deficiencies. Nor could the Communist Party compromise between tight and loose control, because tight control of the country was the only way its dictatorship could continue. In the end the Communist Party could only take the step it had now taken and install a regime of tight control resembling fascism.

Gui-zhi returned with an empty sack, which Shi Ge filled with winnowed grain. They did not need to speak, each knew exactly what to do. She stood very close to him, her hair continually brushing against his face. Each time she bent down the top of her trousers sagged: from a slightly different angle, he might have been able to see even further. Shi Ge raised his eyes, far away across the low-lying stretch of flat land, to the stretch of hillside. Twenty years ago, it had been covered with lush green grass like a fragrant quilt, and a thick cover of shady trees. Now there were no trees and no grass; just a stretch of scorched yellow earth. Erosion had turned it into a chaotic forest of earthen columns, like innumerable arid phalluses pointing to the sky.

It was there, long ago, that Gui-zhi had first given herself to him, lying on a grassy slope. She was only fifteen, but very passionate. She tightly embraced Shi Ge, making his head spin, then with her small rough hands deftly brought them together.

He was grateful to Gui-zhi for the ecstatic happiness, repeated often in the sun and the trees and the grass. Later, whenever he thought of the village, he felt the ripples of youthful desire, and remembered Gui-zhi's face, washed with tears, when he left to go to university. He had returned to the village seven times, and each time Gui-zhi came back from her husband's home, a mile or two away, to see him. But they had nothing to say to each other, or only exchanged questions and answers like strangers. He did not mention the past, wanting to preserve the memory of her as a fifteen year old girl. But this time…

'Where's that dead dog hiding?' Gui-zhi suddenly shouted in the direction of the straw stack. 'Come on, get yourself out of there!'

Her brother Suo-zhu appeared, grinning. 'I was watching what you two were up to. You don't want him messing with you!'

'I'll cut your tongue out.'

'He's a big shot, sister. He's not interested in a coarse…'

Twenty-odd years ago, Suo-zhu had been a snotty child, now he was tall and strong and had black stubble on his face. A month ago the man who came to collect the grain levy had been beaten up and his leg broken. Suo-zhu had been the ringleader and when the local police had come to make arrests, he had overturned their car. As a result he had been unanimously elected village headman.

Having had his fun, he now adopted a pompous tone befitting his new status. 'Hurry up with the threshing, sister, and get the grain into the store. Yesterday a lot of starving refugees raided Libao village and went off with all the grain they'd just harvested. Imagine that,' he said to Shi Ge.

'Where were they from?'

'Who can tell? They call themselves refugees, but they're the same as bandits. They are from all over the place. People just get together and loot. There are so many of them that no one can do anything. Anyway, hurry up. I have to go to a meeting to discuss how to defend the villages.'

To protect the grain, defence squads of sturdy young men had been formed, which would rush to any village that was threatened. The blacksmiths had all been busy making broadswords and pikes. Ancient blunderbusses had been found and put into working order, and pistols had been obtained on the black-market in exchange for grain. Suo-zhu had one at his belt.

The radio was broadcasting laws against grain raids. There were such a flood of rules and regulations being announced that it would take at least six months before they could be implemented. Only the Military Commission had the means of doing so. A civilian government was now in place but Shi Ge was conscious of the huge shadow of the army behind it, and knew that without its iron hand such radical changes were inconceivable.

For more than two thousand years China could only be ruled by the weight of supreme authority. But now, the greater the strength of authority, the less dynamic is the social organism and the country as a whole. Authority can maintain political stability, but it can only strangle the economy. The heroic dream of making the country rich has encouraged our rulers to introduce reforms intended to stimulate the economy, but they also weaken authority.

The last imperial Chinese dynasty, in its final decade introduced more far-reaching reform than any previous dynasty, and brought about its own collapse in 1911, after nearly three hundred years in power. For about twenty years or more there was no central authority, and the country was torn apart by civil war between rival warlords. Authority was only re-established the by efforts of outstanding men or unscrupulous power hunters such as Mao Zedong and Chiang Kai-shek, after the loss of tens of millions of lives.

If only from a political point of view, it was shortsighted for the Communist Party to concentrate on staying in power, rather than on economic development. Whether the reason for this choice was arrogance or recklessness, the period of reform from the 1980s onwards, weakened its authority more than ever before. In 1911 political authority had collapsed: now the very idea of authority had become extinct in people's minds. Later, with the rise of Mao Zedong, it had been possible to recreate a powerful sense of national unity. But once the natural respect for authority, deeply rooted in people's minds for hundreds of years, is lost, the damage is done. The only resort is force: the army becomes the sole authority

If control had not been relaxed, it might just have been possible to preserve the Chinese social structure for a little longer. But too many powerful and uncontrollable forces were released by the process of reform and opening up to the world, and now China as a whole is sliding irresistibly, like a landslide, towards the abyss. The stronger the resistance to this tendency is, the greater the shock will be. But without resistance the outcome will be as bad, if not worse. There seems to be no possibility of escape from destruction.

These last few years Shi Ge had felt the approach of final disaster. At first only in his dreams, then more and more frequently in his waking hours, but still as a nightmare: a formless, huge, edgeless and implacable convulsion, like a hurricane approaching, shaking the earth and rocking the mountains.

'What's the matter?' asked Gui-zhi, taking his hand.

'Nothing.' The nightmare dissolved. Smoke from the kitchen fires hung over the village.

'Come home now. It's time to eat'.

'I'll work a little longer, call me when it's ready'.

'I can't carry this sack of grain on my own'. Shi Ge looked at her: he had never heard her say anything like that before. When she was young, she had been as strong as any of the young men. Even now she could walk fast with a couple of hundred pounds on her carrying pole. When their eyes met his heart quickened: her eyes were on fire.

He started to lift the sack, but Gui-zhi stopped him. 'I'll carry it, you just steady me.' She was always afraid of tiring him: he took the sack by force.

On the radio a man's voice was talking about peasants all over the country refusing to pay the grain levy to the state. His message was forceful: grain was a necessity for the people of the whole country, like air or sunlight. Peasants occupied the land: their work, their duty was to produce grain. No farmer had the right to refuse grain to the people of the country, only the duty to provide it.

The sack, heated by the sun, felt comfortable on his shoulder. Gui-zhi walked happily beside him. Unlike the last few years, this year's harvest was good, and every family had decided to store as much as possible. The villagers had to keep enough grain for their own use; but they knew that the Yellow River flood had sent the price soaring, and the longer they held on to their surplus the higher it would be.

For most of China's long history, ninety percent of the population had to tighten their belts and consume as little as possible so that others could live in comfort. Their lives of poverty and resignation were short: this was the price they paid for a reasonable balance between population and resources, and for social stability.

Eventually, socialism instilled the idea of equality and later, after reform and opening up to the world, the equality of poverty was replaced by equal opportunity to get rich in a consumer society. Suddenly the demand for raw materials increased several times over. When a hundred million peasants threw themselves wholeheartedly into the mad rush for consumption, it was a mortal blow for China's supply system. Although Shi Ge was no longer obliged to study such important questions, they still weighed heavily on his mind.

Gui-zhi called out to her father to come to eat, as he passed by with a group of men. He said he would come when he was ready, but did not even turn his head. It had been decided to repair the thick wall of tamped earth round the village, built in the old days as a protection against bandits. Since the revolution, there had never been any bandits, so the wall had fallen into disrepair. Now with the village in danger—from starving refugees—each family had contributed money and labour to restore it and Gui-zhi's father was in charge. The village was bigger now, but as soon as the wall was repaired everyone, including Gui-zhi's family, would move back behind it until the emergency ended.

There was little traffic on the main road. Because of the widespread unrest, very few drivers dared go long distances alone and kept together in convoys for safety. Far away, where the road went over a pass, a long line of trucks could just be seen approaching in a cloud of dust and exhaust fumes.

Gui-zhi helped Shi Ge to put the sack in the granary, then turned and stood in the doorway. It was dark inside, only a little sunlight came through the ventilation holes and shone on the yellow maize.

Suddenly she put her arms round him and her head on his shoulder and said, 'I really long for you, brother.'

Her hair, reflecting the sunlight, was still black, and fragrant with the smell of ripe grain. Her rough hands excited him, as they had long ago. He had not wanted this to happen. Gui-zhi was no longer the wild flower of twenty years earlier: she had been married three times. But last night, perhaps because he had drunk too much, her tears had dissolved his hesitation. The first day of threshing, he saw that she was waiting, then her happiness turned to the misery of rejection and she began to cry in secret. Yesterday, when he had taken her hand she had pounded him with her fists and said 'I hate you! I hate you!'

Gui-zhi's breasts were like two round white loaves of steamed bread, each topped with a red date, and warm, as if just out of the steamer. Her belly was flat and smooth, with none of the fatty rolls of urban women. Three husbands had rejected her because she had not produced a child, but she had not aged prematurely like most village women. The dark granary, the golden maize, the warm sacks of grain, the light on Gui-zhi's breasts, aroused Shi Ge more than any soft bed, perfume and tasseled curtains. Is this how I shall live from now on? He asked himself . . .

When they finally collapsed breathless on the maize, they heard a truck stop very close by, and several people jumping down from it.

'Get your clothes on quick,' Shi Ge whispered.

'Hey there!' several voices shouted, and after a pause, 'there's no one in the house.'

'Break into the granary,' another voice ordered.

Gui-zhi, pushing the door open. 'What do you want?'

There were ten or more men outside, in worker's clothes and wearing safety helmets. They were all carrying rifles, and wore old-fashioned ammunition belts made of cloth slung over their shoulders, with the words 'Workers' Militia' stenciled on them.

'We want to buy grain,' said the leader.

'We're not selling,' Gui-zhi replied, blocking the doorway to the granary.

'We know you don't want to sell, but we insist on buying and you won't lose on the deal.' At a sign from the leader, two men stepped forward.

'Sorry, sister,' they said and carried Gui-zhi from the doorway, kicking and cursing, like a chicken held by its wings. The other workers were about to enter the granary when Shi Ge appeared at the door. His look made them stop.

'What unit do you belong to?'

'Datong Coal Mine,' said the leader, guessing that Shi Ge had some kind of authority.

'Let her go.' Shi Ge said, seizing the two workers holding Gui-zhi. They obeyed. Gui-zhi proudly tossed her head and thrust out her chest.

'Who told you to do this?' Shi Ge asked the leader.

'Who told us?' The leader answered by slapping his belly. 'There are thirty thousand of us miners and more than half of us—and our families—have nothing to eat.'

Shi Ge knew before he left Beijing, that the autumn grain levy could not be collected this year. The Yellow River floods, and the panic spread by rumours, had caused widespread hoarding of grain. Grain shops in the towns had been cleaned out, and there was too little in state granaries to be of any consequence. He had not realized that people were already starving.

'The government will deal with the problem.' He said, not believing a word.

To import grain would be like trying to put out a burning cartload of firewood with a cup of water. The only hope was this year's harvest. But how could the peasants be persuaded to pay the grain levy? In the days of the People's Communes, leaders at all levels would make sure that all the grain due would be delivered to the cities. In the 1960s, twenty million peasants starved to death to feed the urban population. That would not happen again. The grain was in the hands of the peasants themselves and no power in heaven or earth or earth could make them surrender it.

'That's enough, old man,' said the leader disrespectfully. 'Fine words don't fill bellies.'

'You are forbidden to steal grain!'

'We don't want to. You look like a townsman, even an official of some sort. I ask you, what are they doing up there in Beijing?. All we ask is that we and our families be allowed to live. We've stripped the factory clean and in the truck there, we've got electric motors, pumps, diesel engines, tyres...and look at this platinum crucible: it's worth more than the whole village. We'll give all the wealth in our town if they'll let us have a little grain.'

'It must be done legally,' said Shi Ge.

'Hoarding grain is illegal!'

'Yes, but the law must be enforced by the state, not by you.'

'We'll all be dead by then, and there'll be no state left,' said the leader with a serious expression. 'We've no time to talk. Load up!'

'Just listen to one more thing,' said Shi Ge, still keeping the workers out of the granary. 'If you take all the peasants' grain, they'll not be able to plant next year. So even if you get through this year, there'll be nothing to eat next year. You'll not only be ruining the country, but condemning yourselves to starvation.'

'If we starve next year, we'll still have lived through this one.' His tone had become very harsh. 'Get out of the way!'

Shi Ge glanced at Gui-zhi. She was absolutely fearless in face of the armed men. Shi Ge was there, and everything would be all right, even if the sky fell on them. He was an important man in the central government even if he had been dismissed—even a dead camel is bigger than a horse—he could deal with these raiders with one finger.

But Shi Ge had no will to resist. Everything the man said was true. The fascist seizure of power in Beijing had been inevitable. When it was a matter of life or death, no one could restore a system of equal distribution and allow everyone enough for survival. There was no choice except life for some and death for others. There was no point telling starving people to obey the law. Their womenfolk were like Gui-zhi, and needed food, perhaps more than she. The miners produced only coal; but in the last few days alone, he had helped Gui-zhi bury six large vats full of grain. Even if the granary was left empty, there was enough to feed her family for a year.

'Sell them some, Gui-zhi,' he said, moving away slightly. Several workers immediately pushed their way into the granary.

Gui-zhi was dumbfounded. Not even the grain raid itself had shocked her so much. After a while she started to cry.

'Aren't you ashamed, brother? Don't you remember what you said to me once...that you'd stand up for us peasants as long as you lived? Now that you're a big shot you let them rob us!'

Two workers carried out the sack of grain that she and Shi Ge had put there not long before.

Gui-zhi threw herself on the sack, crying but defiant. The sack fell to the ground and she wrapped her arms round it, biting and kicking.

It took several workers to get her off, tearing her clothes and buttons and the top of her trousers. In fury, she ripped off her clothes until she was completely naked and the workers dared not touch her. Other workers threw down the sacks they were carrying and fled when she began to chase them.

Shi Ge watched Gui-zhi fighting like a wild animal. Her heaving breasts still bore the red marks of his hands, and between her sturdy thighs the traces of his sperm glistened in the sunlight, and on the sack too, like an unforgettable memento on that bed of happiness. He felt knives in his heart. He could think of nothing he could do and stood gaping. When he was young, he was able to concentrate on one thing. Now his work had accustomed him to consider all aspects of a situation, and the more he did so the less capable he became of finding a solution. This was perhaps the reason why, these last few years he had been increasingly discouraged, despondent and incapable of action.

A shout suddenly came from somewhere above: 'Is Comrade Shi Ge there?'

Unnoticed, a helicopter had arrived and was slowly landing. Shi Ge waved. He was used to his vacations ending this way. Wherever he was they always found him. But why now, when he had no position or responsibility?

The helicopter landed in a cloud of dust not far away.

'Comrade Shi Ge! Please come aboard. The General Secretary wishes to speak with you.' The loudhailer was very clear. The workers all looked at Shi Ge in amazement.

He went up to Gui-zhi, and put her clothes over her. She was covered with earth and sobbing, her face muddy with tears. He said nothing but went straight to the helicopter.

A man in uniform stretched out his hand. 'My name is Zhou Chi.' He ordered the helicopter's communications officer to get Beijing on the radio-telephone; Lu Hao-ran's secretary appeared on the screen and greeted Shi Ge. The screen went black for a moment, then Lu Hao-ran could be seen sitting behind his desk.

'Shi Ge. There is a position I would like you to take. I don't know whether you are interested.' His voice had none of the arrogance of the former General Secretary; it was almost intimate as if he were speaking to an equal,

Shi Ge sighed. He'd had enough. He felt that the wrinkles on his face were very deep; and helpless as if all the bones and tendons in his body were broken and his life finished. How many times had he gone from one post to another? He hated the thought of it.

'What position?' he said, perhaps out of curiosity.

'Deputy Premier,' Lu Hao-ran replied casually.

Shi Ge's heart thumped. Deputy Premier! In his youth maybe, had he dreamed of such heights. Now he was burnt out and had no more extravagant dreams. Yet this one had come to him out of the sky, in this impossible time and this unlikely place.

Zhou Chi regarded him with a slight smile. The sun was going down, the yellow fields and mountain slopes seemed to undulate in the autumn wind.

Had he really had enough? He suddenly felt his blood seething. His weariness and despondency vanished. A completely new future had opened up before him. He was no longer a bureaucrat to be called for or dismissed at the wave of a hand, but a lever to lift the globe. Perhaps he would be able to change the fate of China.

'Well,' said Lu Hao-ran, watching him from the screen.

One word and his life would fly from one extreme to another. Either his lonely ambitions and heroism would be buried in this fractured yellow earth, or else he would stride into history, to be carried towards the future by its wheels, or crushed into a dust by them.

'Yes,' he said without hesitation.

'Then come at once.' The screen went dark. Lu Hao-ran had vanished.

Shi Ge raised his head. His mind could not return to reality.

'Deputy Premier,' said Zhou Chi. 'We'll take off at once.'

'I must say good-bye.'

'No, no. There is going to be fighting here.'

The words were hardly out of his mouth when there was the sound of gunfire. A stray shot glanced off the helicopter. The workers in front of Gui-zhi's door threw themselves on the ground. There were bloodthirsty battle-cries on all sides.

'I must get down,' said Shi Ge, seizing the handle of the cabin door. Zhou Chi held it closed, and Shi Ge could not move it.

'The General Secretary ordered me to be responsible for your safety.'

They were already airborne. A cloud of dust rose. Shi Ge saw Gui-zhi get up from the sack on which she was lying and look at the helicopter. The Village Protection Militia armed with mattocks and forks, commanded by Suozhi, pistol in hand had surrounded the grain raiders.

Gui-zhi became gradually smaller; but her hopeless expression remained clearer than anything in Shi Ge's eyes. She raised her arms, her clothes fell to the ground. The sound of the helicopter drowned her words. A worker tried to pull her down, but she started to run after the helicopter.

Shi Ge moaned aloud. Suddenly she stumbled and fell on the road. Her face was already indistinct and a dark red patch spread across her chest. Although it was invisible at this height, Shi Ge could clearly see a deep round hole between her breasts, her blood was flowing, reddening the wide earth and the sky.

4

Fuzhou – Beijing: The Green Exhibition – In the Wuyi Mountains, Fujian Province – Beijing: Military General Hospital – Fuzhou

ↄ

Fuzhou

The young northerner had been beaten up and his face was bleeding. Yet somehow he broke through the crowd surrounding him, jumped over the barriers along the street and ran off at an astonishing speed, knocking over several people who tried to intercept him. Everyone wanted to catch him, it seemed. Even women and children were shouting excitedly and cursing him in the dialect of southern Fujian.

The young man had been knocked down by a blow from a metal pipe. Huang Shi-ke was sitting in his official car not far away, heard the blow through the tinted glass and saw the man writhing on the ground, then get to his knees and stand up unsteadily. The chauffeur pushed on the central lock switch, just before the young man pressed his bloody face against the window only a foot from Huang Shi-ke. The sight of that face covered with blood and distorted by the pressure of the glass, turned his stomach.

The car then forced its way out of the whirlpool of people, the horn blaring. Huang Shi-ke looked round, but the blood smeared on the window prevented him from seeing much.

The General Secretary had been killed more than a month ago, and throughout South China there was widespread animosity against northerners in general. Feeling had been building up for a long time. Rapid development and the high standard of living in the south had attracted more than forty million immigrants from the much poorer northern provinces, causing a serious economic and social crisis. To make matters worse, after the Yellow River floods several million refugees came south, begging in the streets by day, robbing and looting at night. But the present wave of anti-northern agitation was not the direct result of this. Nor was it strictly political. It had nothing to do with the pro-democracy or 'reverse the verdict' movements, so the government had not yet taken it seriously or suppressed it.

Huang Shi-ke was aware that the real cause was the anger and despair throughout the southern provinces that the policy of the new regime in Beijing had provoked. Each new directive against economic reforms and the free market had raised the temperature of anti-northern feeling.

Beijing had now issued a decree freezing all private bank deposits of over three million *yuan* (about $US362,000), and all foreign exchange deposits. When this news arrived, people surged into the streets as if they had gone mad, northern agencies were burned down, cars wrecked, and anyone speaking with a northern accent was beaten up.

The agitation made Huang Shi-ke feel good. In the past any hint of a disturbance scared him. Now he rejoiced; calm and stability would mean that Beijing had won. If he had not been a little concerned for his own safety, he would have joined in, as if it was a festival. But he did not have much confidence in these mobs. Once they had weapons in their hands they thought they could do as they liked. He knew that the decision to freeze private accounts was the kingpin of Beijing's plan to restore an egalitarian system, eventually return to frugal military communism and put an end to the private economy. Beijing was confident of success. 'Attack the rich and save the poor' had been a popular slogan in China for centuries.

Three million *yuan* was about twenty thousand in 1980 before inflation started! No more than about two per cent of the whole population had that kind of money—let alone foreign exchange. Rich upstarts are always resented, and the attack on a small minority would not affect the stability of the country. However, two per cent was the national average; in the coastal provinces the proportion was far higher. In Fuzhou, the provincial capital, twenty three per cent of the population had more than three million *yuan* in their accounts. Even more had Hong Kong, US and Taiwan dollars. Most people kept their money in the banks because of the interest, so the decree freezing accounts was like a bombshell.

The car moved at a snail's pace. The streets were crowded with rioters, running, shouting and pushing, especially around the banks. Huang Shi-ke imagined the same scene in other coastal provinces and cities. Let those responsible for the coup d'état in Beijing take a look, he thought. Putting the clock back would end in disaster. He was pleased to see that the glass façade of a bank was now cracked all over.

He had not figured out how the coup d'état had been arranged. The procedure seemed to have been legal. The central government unquestionably had the right to replace the provincial authorities and when the new Provincial Governor arrived, Huang Shi-ke had gone with all his staff to express their loyalty to the Central Committee and promised him their faithful service. All provincial officials knew how to do that. The Governor was not a native of Fujian, so there would be no difficulty in turning him into a figurehead. For a whole month, he had been 'getting to know his province', under the guidance of Huang Shi-ke, who took in every word he said. All his orders had been received with respect but none had really been carried out. The Governor was probably quite pleased with himself; he certainly made an effort to win people over and find out about the true situation, but everything he did was sabotaged and nullified, His success was an illusion.

There was one worrying incident however. Two days ago, during a meeting about stamping out corruption, the Governor had produced evidence against Huang Shi-ke's son. Huang knew he was dishonest, but not that he was mixed up with people making pornographic videos. Not only as producer—he had sold several thousand copies on the black market. There was no time to do anything and Huang Shi-ke had no choice but to sign the warrant of arrest. Fortunately, when he visited him in prison, his son had told him that one of his colleagues in the business was 'the Chairman's' grandson, who had made off with most of the profits and enjoyed appearing in the videos himself—not his face, but another part of his body—in close-up.

The new Governor was a former army man, and even though he appeared to be incorruptible, he did not dare give offence to 'the Chairman'. He had no choice but to release Huang Shi-ke's son and announce that the evidence had turned out to be false. Although the score was now even, it had been the first dangerous encounter, and likely to be followed by many others. The Governor's look of hatred told Huang Shi-ke that sooner or later they would cross swords again. How could he have known things that even he himself was unaware of? Who was the traitor?

A long line of traffic was stuck. People were become more and more frenzied. The glass front of the bank building suddenly collapsed completely. Riot police continued to arrive, but they were no more effective than leaves in the wind.

Huang Shi-ke sighed: greed made people insane. Scandals had become commonplace, but he was shaken by the fact that his son was implicated; and had never imagined he could be so shameless. In prison he had a degenerate smile on his face. It would be wasted breath to scold him, but Huang wanted to protect his own political line of defence. His son had been let out of prison and that was bound to make him even more unruly. This society is finished, Huang Shi-ke often thought. Everyone had become so greedy and rapacious, mean, despicable, weak-kneed and vicious. The only aim is to get something for nothing—at the expense of the state and other people, to satisfy their desires without working, or by their wits. Human relations are based on hostility, competition and undermining others… What hope is there for such a country?

The telephone in the car rang. Huang Shi-ke took up the receiver.

'Please use line B.' Bai Ling's formal voice never failed to give him pleasure. Line B was scrambled. Huang Shi-ke closed the glass partition between himself and the driver.

After their encounter at the hot springs Huang Shi-ke no longer had Bai Ling read despatches to him in the car; they were careful not to arouse suspicion and their contact was limited to this stimulating form of secret communication.

Bai Ling's tone of voice was very serious. 'Please look at page three of document number 794.' Huang Shi-ke shook his head. Why was she being so mysterious?

There was a note between the pages, hastily written: 'Do not go to Beijing. You will be arrested.'

'How do you know?' He was shaken; his hand on the phone was damp with sweat. There was no answer.

That morning, the office of the Central Committee had telephoned telling him to come to Beijing at once, the General Secretary wished to see him. A special plane was waiting for him at the military airfield. He had wanted to say goodbye to Bai Ling, but had left in such a hurry that he only had time to take the document case she had prepared for him.

What did she know? He sensed danger and suddenly understood the significance of the strange look in the Governor's eyes. As long as he, Huang Shi-ke, remained in Fujian, the Governor had no hope of taking control and implementing Beijing's policies. He was an obstruction and they were not likely to leave him here. As soon as he reached Beijing, he would be sent to a 'Party school'. He might be arrested as soon as he stepped off the plane. How did Bai Ling know?

He took several deep breaths to slow his heart-beat, and phoned Hangzhou. He knew that two days earlier, the Deputy Provincial Governor of Zhejiang had been called to Beijing to report. He was an old friend, and no less anxious than Huang to obstruct his new superior. His wife answered the phone and told him that since her husband had left for Beijing she had been unable to contact him. Huang Shi-ke forgot to say a few words of consolation and woodenly replaced the receiver.

In the street the police had begun to clash with the rioters, a group of whom had broken down the iron doors of the bank, but found no one there and no money, only a few ledgers and documents. The police used tear-gas and the rioters replied by setting fire to the bank and bombarding the police with tiles from the roof.

They seemed well-organized, obviously wanting to step up the tension and provoke an uprising. Perhaps that would be a godsend, Huang Shi-ke thought. He had never been in a position where he might have to rebel and go into hiding. For decades he had faithfully served the Central Committee and had always been able to adapt to changes and ingratiate himself with whoever was at the top. But he was also suspicious of anyone who wanted to use him as a figurehead for revolt and even if Liu Ya-ji went down on his knees, he would have refused to attend today's meeting. He was furious. He had been forced to join the revolt.

The chauffeur turned to look at him in consternation. Ahead, Molotov cocktails were being thrown and several cars had been wrecked by the crowd. Cars were jammed up one against the other.

Huang Shi-ke opened the car door and without a word disappeared into the maddened crowd. He hurried down a narrow lane until he reached the Blue Lake Guest House, which stood in a large garden hidden by ancient trees. It was a small three-storied building that looked old fashioned and very ordinary; but inside it was sumptuous, with Chinese, European, Japanese and Turkish suites. It had formerly belonged to the provincial government and had been converted by Liu Ya-ji after he had leased it—not to make money by renting it out, but for entertaining important people. He had already recovered his investment several times over... in a variety of ways.

Liu Ya-ji was short and fat, and however closely he shaved, his chin remained a metallic grey colour. When Huang Shi-ke appeared it turned a reddish black with pleasure. 'Deputy Governor. I must bow to you!' He joined his hands in front of his chest and bowed several times.

In the Western Suite about thirty people were sitting in a circle. Most of them were merchants like Liu Ya-ji and they were all among the richest men in the province. There were also a few moderates who had fled Beijing after the coup d'état, some members of the pro-Democracy movement, and activists of the 'reverse the verdict' campaign who had escaped arrest. They all stood up to welcome Huang Shi-ke with the kind of deference reserved for leaders. Huang Shi-ke suddenly realized that he had a new image: not simply as a clever manipulator in the local power network, but a standard-bearer, a leader, a man on whom the fate of a whole way of life depended.

He did not explain his sudden appearance. 'Continue with your discussion,' he said evenly and took a seat. His calm manner enhanced the drama of his unexpected arrival.

The decree from Beijing amounted to a death sentence for Fujian and the other coastal provinces. The reduction of local power and an attack on the private economy would destroy the two motors of development in the south, commerce—especially illegal commerce—and smuggling. Banning the importation of consumer goods alone would close down up to ten thousand shops. The great increase in import duties, the regulations limiting prices, the ban on private wholesale business, capital punishment for smuggling—this was all bad enough. The nationalization of all commercial enterprises with capital over thirty million *yuan* was a veritable earthquake.

'They want to kill us, these northerners, and we'll die with no trousers even,' Liu Ya-ji complained indignantly. He was the biggest commercial entrepreneur in Fujian. His business was importation—or rather smuggling—of consumer goods, and he had networks in Europe, North America, Southeast Asia and Hong Kong. Exactly how much money he had, no one knew. Although a substantial part of it was hard currency in banks abroad, the freezing of accounts had cost him more than half his wealth: nationalization would totally destroy his money kingdom.

Having been in charge of industry and commerce in the province, Huang Shi-ke knew exactly what was at stake. Fujian is mountainous, has little arable land and few natural resources. Thanks to its sea coast the province had achieved a degree of prosperity that was the envy of the whole country. Most of the billions of *yuan* that flowed into Fujian from inland, was to pay for consumer goods, chiefly smuggled goods bought from private commercial enterprises. Only by smuggling could merchants keep down the prices and compete with others.

In the past, even when there had been strong central control, there had been innumerable ways for the province to protect its interests. This time it was different. The new regime had discarded the old indecisive policies, and regardless of development, were brutally re-centralizing power, using fascist-style methods to smash any obstruction or delaying tactics. Beijing was deaf to international opinion and did not care if foreign investors pulled out. But commerce was the lifeblood of Fujian and without foreign investment would become a wasteland.

All the other businessmen present were as furious and vociferous as Liu Ya-ji, gesticulating and banging the tables. Huang Shi-ke gave no sign that he had seen them; merchants were always ridiculous when they suffered a loss. Even when the sword was about to fall on their necks they would still be checking their books. He said nothing —until the end.

'Let us talk about the next step,' the deputy head of the Central

Committee office calmly reminded the meeting. He had been in Beijing when the coup d'état occurred and had sneaked home to Fujian to escape arrest.

Everyone present, including Huang Shi-ke himself, realized that to remain under the new military government would be fatal. No one would escape. For years now people had been calling for a break with 'the Beijing crowd', otherwise the economy would never take flight. It had been no more than grumbling then—they were all Chinese after all. Now it was a question of survival. Independence was the only answer.

The political refugees from Beijing, whose opinion was respected by the businessmen, argued that the market economy and the spirit of freedom were both strong in South China. Even individual small merchants were prepared to fight for their interests. Fujian would not lack allies: Zhejiang and Jiangsu provinces and the city of Shanghai to the north, Guangxi, Guangdong and Hainan Island to the south. The world is highly critical of the Beijing regime, he said, and would welcome independence for the south. It might not be strong from a military point of view, but it had another weapon—its wealth. The combined capital of the businessmen present exceeded that of many countries, and they would prefer poverty rather than go back to the days of 'reform through labour'. Only a leader was lacking.

'Deputy Governor,' exclaimed Liu Ya-ji impulsively. 'You be our leader!'....

'What cheek!' Huang Shi-ke snorted.

Liu Ya-ji said no more. He was confident that Huang Shi-ke would change his mind—for double the sum, or even more. Tomorrow perhaps, the Swiss bank draft would arrive. If he accepted it, Liu Ya-ji would shed tears of gratitude. Businessmen are used to reading a man's face; he was sure that the 'premium' would not be refused.

Huang Shi-ke watched them all encouraging each other and talking about the rosy future with enthusiasm, although everyone knew that autonomy was by no means in the bag, and the future highly uncertain. He asked himself: after a lifetime of effort, should I risk everything on a single throw of the dice?. Whatever its failings, the Communist Party had enough power to smash any rebellion. It had crushed many men far stronger than he. Liu Ya-ji and the other businessmen were going to put up two million US dollars, which would be his if he agreed to lead them. If they failed, with that kind of money he would be able to live abroad, a rich man. Yesterday he had not accepted. Today...twice two is four after all. That would certainly help to compensate for an uncertain future. It showed the importance of choosing one's moment. It was his cue...

'I don't agree with independence,' he said slowly. Everyone looked stunned.

He looked at a carved elephant tusk on a side-table for a moment, for effect. 'Fujian is part of China. No one can change that. We don't want to be a sovereign state—that would be treason. We only want to be able to develop in a direction suited to our way of life. The late Deng Xiaoping's formulation "one country two systems", is perfect for us. It has been applied to Hong Kong, why not Fujian as well? We don't seek to undermine the unity of our country, only to have a different system. That should be our starting point.'

There was a pause, then the former deputy head of the Central Committee office clapped twice with his well-cared-for hands, his face smiling approval. There was general clapping and everyone nodded excitedly.

Suddenly there was a loud exclamation, somewhere outside, resembling the moment in performances of traditional Chinese opera when the villain appears. Everyone in the room became silent. The ivory coloured door with brass inlay was thrown open and a tall figure appeared in the doorway.

Huang Shi-ke went white. He could not believe his eyes. It was the new Governor, with an arrogant and sinister smile on his face. Huang Shi-ke blinked, as if to dismiss an apparition. How did he get here? Outside the window the guards could be seen lolling in the sun. If he had come through the main entrance they would have given a warning.

'Huang Shi-ke!' the Governor thundered. 'Since the day I arrived I've been waiting to hear the words you have just said. I thought you'd be saying them in Beijing, but you've walked right into my net.'

He looked in turn at each of those present and said in a sarcastic tone, 'Ah. Mr Deputy Head, the Central Committee has been looking for you.' He recognized everyone, and teased them as a cat does with mice. He was not so ignorant about Fujian as Huang Shi-ke thought; in fact, he seemed to know everything. He had been preparing a trap: now it was closed.

Half hidden behind the Governor, Huang Shi-ke noticed the shrinking form of the General Secretary of the provincial government. So it was he who had woven the net! The evidence about Huang Shi-ke's son must also have come from this dog. Suddenly he remembered the tunnel…

In the basement of the guest-house there was the entrance to a tunnel which led straight to the office of the Provincial Government. It had been constructed during the Cultural Revolution as an air-raid shelter, and had long been forgotten. The key should be in the administration bureau. It never entered his head that it might one day be useful.

'Phone the garrison to send a company of troops.' The Governor ordered the General Secretary. 'Tell them there will be prisoners, and not to forget the van.' In the 1970s he had been in charge of a scout platoon and had won a citation for the capture of thirty Vietnamese soldiers. Now he was about forty years of age, his face was red. The thirty men present wished they were not his prey.

He told Liu Ya-ji to distribute pen and paper to everyone. 'Get writing! I want your confessions at once. The faster you write, the more details and revelations you provide—who knows?—perhaps your punishment will be lighter.' He patted his side, possibly to draw attention to his pistol. Then he left, probably to check on other rooms. He was obviously delighted.

His temporary absence gave Huang Shi-ke a crucial opportunity. He whispered to Liu Ya-ji in Fujian dialect, 'Get those people of yours wrecking the bank to come here at once, and get them to tell everyone they can that the new Governor is here. He can solve their problems for them.'

'Wrecking the bank! My people?" Liu Ya-ji replied embarrassed, in an unnatural tone.

'Stop pretending. Do it quickly.' Earlier, during the commotion at the bank Huang Shi-ke had noticed that the ringleader was Liu Ya-ji's chauffeur and there were several men with portable telephones around. The businessmen were obviously behind the rioting and whipping it up.

Liu Ya-ji understood immediately what Huang Shi-ke had in mind. At least it would give them time. He took out his portable and went into the toilets.

By the time the troops arrived and took up positions round the guest-house, a crowd had already surrounded the walled garden and were shouting for the Governor. Then stones began to land in the courtyard and rioters climbed over the walls. Very soon the main gate was broken down and an angry mob surged into the garden, trampling the flowers and shrubs before coming face to face with the soldiers. Shouting continued outside in the street, inside there was silence.

'We should leave at once!' said the Provincial General Secretary in a trembling voice.

'Leave?' said the Governor in an arrogant and fearless tone. 'These people want to go to the limit to see if I'm afraid them. Open that door and I'll show them.'

The shouting outside the wall suddenly stopped. Huang Shi-ke could just see the Governor standing defiantly on the balcony.

'I am the Governor.' His loud clear voice, the apparent sincerity of his smile and above all his courage, instantly subdued the enormous crowd. 'You want to see me. I also want to see you.'

Huang Shi-ke beckoned to the people in the room. 'Follow me.'

At the eastern end of the building there was a small staircase leading to the basement. There, behind a rusty boiler and a long disused iron door, was the entrance to a small concrete tunnel, cold and musty, lit by weak yellow lights. There was a runabout with the key in it.

'Don't touch the vehicle,' said Huang Shi-ke. 'Walk on until you reach the provincial government building.'

Everyone crowded into the tunnel, feeling they had escaped death.

'Ya-ji,' come with me for a moment,' said Huang Shi-ke, 'and bring a gun.'

Without hesitation Liu Ya-ji went into the Japanese suite and took a pistol from a secret compartment in a built-in cupboard. It was illegal to own firearms, but pistols were easily obtainable on the black market. Huang Shi-ke did not need to ask whether he had one.

'I don't know how to use it,' Huang Shi-ke said. 'Load it.'

A pane of glass had been broken in one of the windows. He could see the backs of the soldiers, and beyond them the crowd facing the Governor, whose voice came cascading down from the balcony.

'It is useless for you to oppose the state,' he was saying. 'The majority of you, I know, have been manipulated. There are people behind the scenes who have led you astray: I have cast-iron proof of that. If you follow them it will mean ruin for Fujian.'

Huang Shi-ke moved away and beckoned to Liu Ya-ji to take his place.

'Fire a shot in that direction,' he said quietly, pointing to the crowd outside the window.

Liu Ya-ji turned pale. 'Into the air?'

'No, into the crowd.'

'That…'

'Fire immediately,' ordered Huang Shi-ke coldly.

Liu Ya-ji seemed to choke. But with a trembling hand pointed the pistol through the broken windowpane.

'As Governor I will not allow you to destroy your home province, nor will I abandon the responsibility given me by the State. Conspirators behind the scenes will not escape their punishment. Those who continue to make trouble will be crushed.'

A shot rang out. Huang Shi-ke heard it transformed into a high-pitched scream. He saw a young man in the front of the crowd fell, his face distorted by shock, blood gushing from his chest.

Liu Ya-ji ran like a frighten rabbit for the basement. There was complete silence outside, even the hypnotizing voice of the Governor was silent. Huang Shi-ke picked up the pistol from the floor. As he passed through the iron door to the tunnel, there was suddenly a roar from the crowd. The windowpanes seemed to shatter simultaneously. A raging tide of anger burst into the guest-house, shaking the building.

Huang Shi-ke closed the iron door and turned the key in the lock. 'It needs oiling,' he thought.

UNITED PRESS Report October 25th

The people of Fuzhou, infuriated by the government's announcement freezing private deposits, this morning attacked the provincial Governor's residence and clashed with Armed Police. Nine lives have been lost in his disturbance, including that of the General Secretary of the provincial government. The Governor, who has been only a month in office was beaten up by the citizens and is lucky to be alive, but according to a spokesman at the hospital, even if his life can be saved, he has suffered brain damage and will remain paralysed. .

This afternoon an emergency meeting of the Fujian People's Congress standing committee, appointed the Deputy Governor Huang Shi-ke to replace him.

Beijing: The Green Exhibition

The last leaves had fallen. Everything was withered, cold and ashen grey. The poster outside the Beijing Exhibition Centre—nothing but a large green circle on a white background—looked positively luminous. The design was much admired and mainly because of it, everyone spoke of 'The Green Exhibition.'

Chen Pan stood at the entrance, her eyes on the river of people. There was a queue almost a half a mile long at the ticket office and still people were coming. The members of the Green Association were very excited at this success. Chen Pan had hoped that there would be less people on this particular day.

An old man with a stick and a bent back, removed his spectacles and stared at her. She seemed to recognize those eyes. They had an impudent and enigmatic look, which somehow did not fit with his age and infirmities. The limping figure disappeared before she could place him.

Then she saw Shi Ge, still some distance away. He was dressed casually, as usual, and even looked shabby. His corduroy jacket was threadbare in places, his trousers too big for him and his hair, now grown to a formless length, stuck up in several places. He was less well-dressed than the average visitor—no one would have taken him for a Deputy Premier. He gave the impression of free and easy strength that Chen Pan found appealing; she realized that she was beginning to think of him as a man.

Shi Ge handed seven tickets to Chen Pan. 'The price on the market is five times what it should be. I could have made a bit of money,' he joked. Two men, evidently bodyguards, were following him discreetly. Chen Pan had sent him ten tickets, not imagining that the Deputy Premier would be dressed as he was, and have such a small retinue.

'I'd be glad if you could,' said Chen Pan. 'It would be free publicity.'

They had met again almost as old friends.

'Ivan is not with you?'

'I couldn't borrow him this time.'

They had not met since the 'chance meeting' in the park. Chen Pan had been busy organizing the exhibition. Work had started more than a year ago, but it had almost come to nothing. Being an officially recognized organization, the Green Association had escaped suppression by the new regime, but recently it had set up an 'ideological guidance committee'. This was treading on dangerous ground. There had been an investigation into the financial support it had received from the international Greenpeace organization and the Green Party in Germany. The exhibition had been banned on the opening day and more harassment would have followed. Fortunately Shi Ge had managed to get the ban lifted and promised to visit the exhibition incognito and discuss with the leaders of the Green Association their request for experimental bases.

The bustling crowd had no idea that the Deputy Premier had come. It had been touch and go whether this sensational exhibition would be banned and it could be very serious for Shi Ge if his presence became known. Chen Pan had guaranteed that it would not be. That is why she had been waiting for him at the gate. The five secretaries of the Association would meet him elsewhere.

The roof of the first vast exhibition hall was lit to resemble the universe and a strange sound seemed to come from distant galaxies. There were six stands, made up of paintings, models, sculptures, still-life, and with light and sound effects. Each was in a different colour, and they represented various aspects of the human predicament, with more than a hundred actors and actresses representing mankind. The red display depicted, with gruesome symbolism, the horrors of conflict and war. One side of the yellow display depicted deserts, starvation and plague; the other side gold, the worship of money, debauchery, sex mania and Aids. Black was the colour of benighted ignorance, stupidity and other evils. The blue stand was full of machinery of all kinds, operated by men and women in working clothes, and totally expressionless faces, and with metallic sounds coming from their joints.

In the centre was the green display. Here, everything was entirely natural, the trees, grass, villages, streams, even the mud. There was a strong man and an unusually beautiful woman, both stripped to the waist. An angelic child was playing with a frisking lamb. A puppy licked its nose with its pink tongue. There was nothing heavy or complicated about this presentation. But people stood watching it and it made them long for the beauty of natural life.

No one could remain unaffected by this powerful, hard-hitting set of displays. The Green Association had much support from intellectuals, artists and people from the theatrical world, who had contributed their services free of charge, had both designed and realized the displays. Nevertheless the cost of putting on the exhibition was ten times as much as other exhibitions; but ten times as many people came, and it was a sensation in the capital. Since yesterday it had been necessary to restrict the number of tickets sold

It pained Chen Pan to see that what attracted the most attention was anything to do with sex in the various displays. Some newspapers had attacked this aspect of the exhibition as pornographic, and this was one of the reasons why the exhibition had been banned by the Party's ideological watchdog.

Shi Ge stood silent in front of each display for a considerable time and finally, without a word, warmly shook Chen Pan's hand, which moved her more than any praise could have done. In order to get the ban on the exhibition lifted, he had appealed right up to the Deputy Premier himself, who had dug his heels in once his decision was made. Now the military regime had another account to settle with Shi Ge, but he had not been disappointed and felt rewarded for his trouble.

There was a display entitled 'Stretching the Limit', which represented the reply of the Greens to the argument of those who defended unlimited industrialization, claiming that when present resources were exhausted, more would be found, in the sea, the atmosphere or underground. A sphere, that could open like a huge shellfish, represented the earth. On it there were no mountains or, seas or earth. It was totally covered with models of people and products of all kinds—cars, houses, household equipment, television sets, refrigerators and so on. When the sphere opened, one could see that inside it was just the same, filled up with goods and people.

Another display consisted of two homes, one of the present day and one of fifty years ago. Each was constructed in the two pans of a balance, the dial of which faced the spectators. The modern house was full of electrical goods: a refrigerator, TV, air conditioner, washing machine, dishwasher, microwave oven, telephone, video recorder, stereo hi-fi equipment, as well as shower, tables, carpets, and arm chairs of all shapes and sizes. There were also a number of expensive but useless objects: a special stainless steel hammer, serving only to tenderize meat, a wooden statue holding a mechanism for cracking nuts. There were also bicycles, a motor cycle and a car, and the dining table was piled with a mountain of food. The overweight host was continually stuffing himself with food—stopping only to check his blood-pressure, to take slimming tablets, or work for dear life at an exerciser, before returning to the dining room to eat more.

In another room a woman went through innumerable dresses, putting on one, throwing it aside and trying another. Satisfied with none, she phoned a shop to send more. Her child was buried under a pile of toys.

The dial showed the total weight of all this household as fourteen tons, and a panel showed the amount of wood, metal, wool, chemicals, glass, leather, and the amount of energy and raw materials—oil, coal, minerals, timber, animals and plants this family of three required.

Four families lived in the household of fifty years ago. Everyone slept on wooden beds and sat on bamboo chairs. There were only necessities in the house, which consequently seemed more spacious and cleaner than the modern house. Clothes were simple and food light. There was less anxiety and stress than at present, very little waste and consumption was only a quarter of what it is now.

'...China comes top of the world in four things,' Chen Pan said, giving Shi Ge a résumé of the Green point of view. She was glad to talk to him about this, and felt that she was not wasting her time. 'Firstly, our population is the biggest in the world. Secondly, though the land surface of China is huge, most of it consists of mountains or deserts; so the resources per head of population are the lowest in the world. Thirdly, the traditional morality of China is being destroyed by continuous revolution and the cultural attack from abroad. The "new morality" has nothing to give us, so there is a moral vacuum in the country. Fourthly, our leaders now know there is no hope of achieving communism by means of people's conviction and dedication. So they fall back on turning a blind eye, and even encouraging greed, in order to push through their "reform" programme. Of course, greed can temporarily promote economic growth; but if the Chinese people, in their terrible poverty, aim at an American style of life, the unbridgeable gap between the two will give rise to the most voracious greed. If humanity is to be destroyed by its own greed, China will be the first.'

'How can we possibly satisfy the unlimited demands of the biggest population in the world with so little resources?' Chen Pan went on. 'If people can't get what they want by their own efforts, they will take other people's share; such a primitive way of life, combined with the lowest moral standards, will result in a terrible struggle. This kind of pressure is already building up in China. The consequences of the "four firsts" are that demand exceeds supply, and there is inflation, corruption, crime, political discontent and rebellion.

Shi Ge noticed a display of old books about famines in Chinese history. It was explained to him that a certain recurring phrase 'exchange children for eating' meant that people dying of hunger but who could not bring themselves to eat their own children, would exchange them for other people's children. Some old books also mentioned that the market price for meat of 'two-legged sheep', far cheaper than mutton, was in fact a typically Chinese euphemism for human flesh.

Chen Pan suddenly saw the old man with a stick wave discreetly at her. Suddenly she recognized him: it was Xing Tuo-yu. She looked around. No one had noticed. The 'old man' disappeared behind a group of middle-school students. Waving his stick must have meant that he had kept his promise to come to the exhibition. The last time they met he had been a well-known and popular figure. Now he was number two on the new regime's 'wanted list' and his picture had been shown on television and in all the newspapers. She had been anxious about him but assumed that he had hidden somewhere in the mountains, yet here he was playing a dangerous game in public. She would have liked to scold him, but if he wants to put his hand on the tiger's rump, better let him be.

Chen Pan introduced Shi Ge to Lu Shi-jia and another of the Green Association secretaries, a woman. The Association was a loose organization made up of five different groups; it was united on major issues, but not necessarily on every question. The five secretaries were the leaders of these groups, each of which had its own preoccupations and activities.

Lu Shi-jia's group, concerned specifically with the protection of the environment, resembled Greenpeace, and frequently organized high-profile protests that received much publicity abroad. For this reason alone the government had tended to ignore what it called the 'terrorist activities' of the group (such as blocking drainage channels and hijacking rubbish barges) and tolerated the Green movement in general, in order not to alienate foreign investors.

'Perhaps we will be giving you some trouble too,' Lu Shi-jia said.

'You're welcome.' Shi Ge replied in all sincerity.

They left the others and in order to avoid attracting attention, Chen Pan alone continued to accompany Shi Ge.

Chen Pan introduced Shi Ge to 'the Sage', another of the secretaries of the Association, and the only one who was about Shi Ge's age. He was a former professor of system engineering, and interested in research on different social systems with a deep knowledge of philosophy. He was considered in the Association as a very learned theoretician.

His group was concerned with the question of changing the condition of humanity by changing the economic way of life. He considered that the present economic system was responsible for the appalling condition of humanity: unemployment, over-production, inflation and other calamities. The rich become richer and the poor poorer, and life itself becomes a meaningless bustle. He advocated replacing the large-scale economies by small scientific and technological communities.

Finally Ouyang Zhong-hua appeared, meeting Shi Ge by the sales counter, as if by chance. Chen Pan knew that meeting men in authority increased his sense of his own importance and disliked his superior attitude to Shi Ge. He was certainly taller, more handsome, cultivated and distinguished, and most people felt slightly inferior in his presence. But there was no trace of uneasiness in Shi Ge's behaviour, any more than a rock needs to measure itself against a skyscraper.

'I have read your *Nirvana*,' Shi Ge said with a slight smile, shaking hands with Ouyang.

Ouyang's latest book had been written after his return from the Yellow River flood area. It had not yet been published because of the political climate, but it was possible to obtain duplicated copies. Chen Pan was surprised that Shi Ge had read it already.

In *Nirvana* Ouyang Zhong-hua had explained for the first time his ideas on how materialist society could be transformed into the society of 'spiritual man'. He had no faith in the ability of mankind to make the change of its own accord. Too many warnings over the centuries had gone unheard. Humanity was sinking ever deeper into materialism.

The values of people today were centred on 'me' and 'now', and they were not willing to give up anything for the sake of others and the future. In the age of television, when thinkers are looked down on and football stars and sex symbols idolized, what hope is there of persuading people to give up material desires?

Ouyang believed that the destruction of the world is inevitable—and desirable, because it can speed up the birth of the new. He hoped that it would be possible, before the final disaster, to ensure that educated and spiritual people with a high degree of wisdom and self-control could be saved from the general destruction: the only survivors—the seeds of new humanity—who will create the new world on the ruins of the old.

After the collapse of the old world, Ouyang believed, people will have no memory of ease and comfort and their material desires will have abated. It will no longer be possible to motivate people by promising them a wonderful future. Instead the terrible memory of disaster will become part of the collective consciousness of humanity. Fear alone will guarantee—far better than conscious choice—that in everything: reproduction, education, production, consumption and way of life, mankind will acquire the permanent survival instinct of self-control.

This can only be a society of 'spiritual man', a magnificent transition from death to rebirth. The phoenix rising from the fire was the symbol of his powerful, eloquent and poetic book. Not yet published in China, it had nevertheless circulated widely among intellectuals, and had been published abroad, in translation, where it had not been so well-received as his previous book. People thought it original but too sensational.

Perhaps the cold indifference of the public to the 'survival kit' on sale at the exhibition shop, reflected the same sentiment. Ouyang had put together a kit based on his experience of survival in the wild. It contained everything a person might need when cut off from normal supplies: snares to catch small animals, fishing line and hooks, compound salt, a booklet describing how to differentiate between edible and poisonous plants, a magnifying glass for lighting fires, a pocket knife with multiple small tools, compass, alcohol, disinfectant, ointment, phosphorescent paper, needle and thread, windproof lighter, and so on. One of the Association secretaries had been permitted to have these kits produced in the 'Green Industries' which she managed. He had assured her that they would make money; but at the Exhibition people merely laughed. Shi Ge was the first to buy one. Chen Pan wondered why.

'If they were advertised as equipment for adventurous travellers I think they would sell,' Shi Ge said.

Ouyang looked as if he thought it might be a good idea but said 'Mankind is incurable,' then offered to accompany Shi Ge.

Another part of the exhibition was entitled 'The Way Out'. It consisted of a large number of doors. Most of them turned out to be dummies; some of them were three-dimensional projections. Some, that seemed to be real, were half open and one could see a garden or another room; but the unwary bumped their heads if they tried going through the doorway. Some were carefully painted on the walls.

People were laughing and going round and round, trying to find the way out. Ouyang said sarcastically. 'These people think of nothing except enjoying themselves. It's like a doctor who tells a dying man to eat anything he wants. As disaster approaches, these people will have had all the pleasures available and will die contented. But if you teach them self-control and thrift, they die just the same, but think they have missed out on something.'

'Everyone does what he wants and disaster comes sooner?' said Shi Ge.

'Exactly,' said Ouyang laughing, his face radiant. 'And the more thorough it is, the better it will be for future progress.'

Chen Pan was amazed by this laugh, full of uninhibited self-confidence.

'So destruction becomes social progress and acts of vandalism, lawlessness, disorder, all kinds of baseness, lack of moral standards are all noble and praiseworthy.' Shi Ge said.

'That's right.'

'Everyone can do evil with a clear conscience?'

'Yes, and if I were in your position I would give medals to those who did most,' Ouyang replied.

'But not to yourself,' said Shi Ge impassively.

'That's not so sure. If you want to, please don't hesitate,' said Ouyang inviting Shi Ge to precede him—he wanted to see him bump his head.

'I'll follow you.'

Ouyang laughed and went towards a door which was particularly easy to miss. It looked no different from the others, but led, without obstructions, through a dark corridor to a hall in which there were six displays, each of a different colour.

As soon as they entered they could see a crowd of hooligans shouting obscenities at a man and a woman standing opposite each other in the green display. The spectators were scared and quickly moved away. On the display a child started to cry. The actors comforted the child and ignored the shouts.

'Where are the guards?' Chen Pan asked an attendant.

'They seem to have disappeared.'

The hooligans, not content with shouting obscenities, started to throw banana skins at the woman's crotch, and roared at each hit. When the man tried to protect her they threw beer bottles instead. They were certainly not ordinary hooligans and were deliberately trying to start something: each had a kitchen knife or dagger under his clothes.

Chen Pan rushed to intervene, but Ouyang pulled her back. A foreign pressman was slapped in the face for taking a photo and his camera smashed. The staff of the Green Association stood dumbstruck. If anyone had interfered, there would have been a fight.

Only Ouyang Zhong-hua seemed unmoved.

'Deputy Premier...' he said calmly. It was the first time Shi Ge's title had been mentioned. Ouyang did not say any more, but his meaning was quite clear: if a Deputy Premier was here in person what reason could there be to worry?

Shi Ge turned and looked at his two bodyguards. 'If you can handle this on your own it would be better, so as not to make things worse.' It would be impossible to conceal his identity. One of the bodyguards took out a two-way radio.

Chen Pan noticed Xing Tuo-yu, no longer playing the part of an old man, pushing his way through the retreating public. The stick in his hand had became a weapon. 'Don't!' She shouted, as he raised it.

All eyes turned on her, Xing Tuo-yu's as well: only he knew who she was shouting at. As the hooligans began to surround Chen Pan, Shi Ge's two bodyguards moved in. They were not big men but were as agile as cats. Before the hooligans—or anyone else—understood what was happening their obscene shouts had turned into cries of pain.

The leader, who looked rather like a black bear, rushed forward uttering guttural cries and started slashing about with a meat cleaver. The bodyguard facing him stood motionless, then suddenly the cleaver flew into the air and with a sound which set one's teeth on edge, carved a white groove on the marble floor. The black bear's arm hung as if boneless. The other bodyguard kicked at other hooligans coming at him: their faces were now covered with blood and many of them were lying on the floor. It was enough. Some who tried to escape were stopped in their tracks by the order 'Freeze!' Soon all their weapons were on the ground and the staff brought ropes and tied them up.

The public applauded, and especially the performers at the various displays. Chen Pan noticed that Xing Tuo-yu had become an old man again and was leaving discreetly. Reporters who had witnessed this dramatic spectacle, pushed and shoved to question the two bodyguards, who were specialists in unarmed combat, but shrank from this kind of attention.

'Ladies and gentlemen!' Ouyang announced in English with a slight smile: 'Allow me to present the Deputy Premier's two bodyguards,' pointing at Shi Ge not at them. Chen Pan pulled hard at Ouyang's arm, and the cameras caught her expression of fury. She had told him a hundred times that she had given her solemn promise that Shi Ge's identity would be kept secret.

The disturbance itself was a small matter for the press, but the presence of the Deputy Premier at the Green Exhibition was big news. Reporters and photographers converged on him.

His sudden exposure put him in an awkward position. He wanted to hide somewhere. There was a certain sequence in the questions put to him and it was equally difficult to answer them, or to remain silent.

The foreign correspondents wanted to find out why the new military regime had allowed the Green Exhibition to be put on in the first place, hoping to learn something about a possible power struggle at the top.

Chen Pan nudged Shi Ge and signalled with her eyes to follow her, then disappeared into the corridor they had just left. He followed. The corridor was narrow and quickly blocked by the pursuing pack of newsmen. Chen Pan and Shi Ge took the opportunity to run to 'The Way Out' section, which was now empty. Opening a door in the form of a wall mirror, they took refuge in the small space behind it. This took only a few seconds. Then the reporters rushed into the room, and found nothing but doors.

Once safe, Chen Pan silently began to cry, in spite of herself. Through a small crack between the mirror and the wall, they could see pressmen in the room, searching this way and that and bumping into each other. Someone's hands touched the mirror.

There was hardly room to move and she was afraid Shi Ge would sense her agitation. He was very close to her but did not move.

She remembered another night, not long ago, when Ouyang too had been silent and motionless. They were even closer together, in a sleeping bag, but she felt only his inaccessibility, his cold, closed reticence, like ice in her heart. How different was that silence from this! She had cried then, but not so uncontrollably. She was afraid of his silence, but even more of the stream of arguments which she had listened to and later obeyed, by having an abortion. Ouyang could find so many reasons for everything. He made her feel sad, helpless and weighed down. To be pregnant was almost a crime. But the child still lived—in her heart. The doctor told her it had been a boy, and since then, for no particular reason she called him 'little Shasha'. For more than three years he was with her every day and in her dreams, until she was unable to tell whether it was all a dream or reality. She felt so distressed at these memories, by the tension and her failure to protect Shi Ge's anonymity that she cried—in this of all places.

When the pressmen had gone to hunt elsewhere she wiped her eyes, with a handkerchief already soaked. Shi Ge had been at a loss what to do and kept repeating, 'It's all right.'

'It was very clever the way Ouyang did that,' Shi Ge whispered—There were still people visiting the exhibition. He had finally found a way to distract her. There was genuine admiration in his voice. 'I would have done the same in his place.'

From his point of view Ouyang's move had been clever. The news of the Deputy Premier's visit to the exhibition would encourage environmentalists, give the association better international standing and increase its chance of surviving. If it got the Deputy Premier into trouble, so much the better: it would have even greater impact. Chen Pan had promised of course. Too bad. In politics promises are not binding.

'I can't forgive that kind of cleverness,' said Chen Pan.

The light was fading in their hiding place, but she could still see Shi Ge's smiling face—so honest and kind: it made her think of the soil. A sudden emotion made her want to lean on him. It was no more than a flash, but it made her stop crying. She tried to move away from him a little and quickly removed all the tears from her face.

'You must leave quickly,' she urged him. 'We'll have to put off our discussion,' she said in a matter-of-fact tone, putting a distance between them.

'Why?' asked Shi Ge.

'I owe it to you. I've let you down.' The Green Association leaders were expecting a lot from the meeting between them and Shi Ge, which Chen Pan had arranged at their request.

'It was never a question of me being an honoured guest. In fact quite the opposite: I have requests to make of you—not the other way round.'

'Do you mean that?' Shi Ge nodded. She felt his breathing, and her eyes were damp again.

When they emerged from their hiding place, a young visitor asked, 'Is that the way to the exit?'

No one recognized Shi Ge. Chen Pan looked in the mirror, her eyes were still a little red....Then she saw Ouyang's reflection in front of her. He was standing in a doorway watching her. When she looked again he had gone. She led Shi Ge, ignoring the notice saying No Entrance, to a lift up to the third floor, where there was a reception room for honoured guests. She was not sure now whether she had seen Ouyang or not. He and the other Green leaders were waiting for them. Shi Ge's bodyguards were looking all over for him.

The atmosphere in the meeting was a little tense: only Shi Ge and Ouyang seemed at ease. Shi Ge praised the exhibition highly, which pleased the secretaries, but left Ouyang apparently unmoved.

Chen Pan casually glanced at a modern copy of an antique clock. It was ten o'clock: her pulse quickened, almost feverishly. Perhaps today would be different…The thought no sooner entered her head when, as if mocking her, the telephone rang, exactly on time, and made her jump. Everyone looked serious and apprehensive.

Chen Pan switched on the number-finding instrument linked to the telephone, pressed the recording button, switched on the loudspeaker and took up the receiver.

'Yaya Exhibition Centre, Good Morning,' she said pretending to be the switchboard operator

It was the same male voice, high-pitched and cold.

'A bomb in the Green Exhibition will go off in 20 minutes.'

'Hello. What did you say? I did not hear: will you repeat the message please…'Chen Pan hoped to play for time, but the man had already hung up.

As usual, the message had come from a public telephone.

For the last three days it had been the same voice, the same time, the same message. On the two previous occasions the exhibition had immediately been closed, the public and staff dispersed outside and the police called to search the building. There had been no explosion and no bomb had been found, but the public had to be reimbursed and everyone was scared.

'Take no notice,' said Ouyang, as he had the day before. 'We can't let some hooligan lead us by the nose with his practical jokes. Anyone with a coin in his pocket can do this kind of thing; it doesn't mean we have to cancel the exhibition.'

Yesterday the majority had disagreed with Ouyang; today they agreed. Each time the centre was cleared, it took more than half the day to get the Exhibition going again. No money came in, but expenses still had to be paid. Even more serious, if it went on people would stop coming and the staff would all quit. Only Chen Pan disagreed: she did not believe that the voice on the phone was that of a hooligan; but it was not for her to decide. 'If we don't get people out we can at least go somewhere else for our meeting.'

Everyone looked at Shi Ge, who knew that Chen Pan was concerned for his safety.

Ouyang smiled slightly. 'If there's no bomb everyone is safe. If there is any doubt, then the Centre must be evacuated. We can hardly go ourselves and leave the public behind.'

Ouyang's smiling eyes were very cold, thought Chen Pan, as they had been when he saw her emerge from behind the mirror with Shi Ge. His words made her so furious that she wanted to sweep all the teacups on to the floor. She had only to go and get Shi Ge's bodyguards to take him away at once—even if they had to carry him…

'We should continue our discussion,' Shi Ge said.

They came then to the most practical question, the experimental bases, which Chen Pan had already raised with him. But she found it impossible to concentrate on what he was saying: her eyes were on the clock, and its heavy pendulum. When the twenty minutes were up everyone breathed a sigh of relief. Wretched little hooligan! They even felt a little well-disposed towards him. The tension had exhausted Chen Pan, but she forced herself to appear normal. She noticed Ouyang's mocking expression. Whatever he thinks, nothing has happened and that's a good thing.'

For a long time Ouyang had wanted a base in which he could try out his ideas about society. Now, as inevitable disaster approached, what was uppermost in his mind, was to have a kind of refuge where 'spiritual people' could survive to build the 'green' society of the future and bring about the transformation of mankind. 'The Sage' agreed with him and saw in such a base a future for his concept of 'small economies'.

Shi Ge was interested, but he was concerned that the base should be able to ensure the survival of as many people as possible in the event of a major disaster. He seemed to be listening with attention to everyone's point of view but orchestrated the discussion so that a conclusion could be reached as soon as possible.

'I would like to sum up. You all consider that it is necessary to create a different way of life; but you have different concepts of what it should be. Therefore you need to carry out practical trials and experiments. Chen Pan has told me that you need a base in which to do this. I consider that one is not enough. Your ideas are all very valuable. Experiments require comparison, so I have decided to give you six experimental bases—one for each of you.'

They found it difficult to believe: Lu Shi-jia rubbed his ears, the Sage polished his spectacles. The other secretary could hardly contain her joy. Even the smile on Ouyang's face was genuine. Chen Pan was shaken: she was the sixth!

'Since we are not exactly living in a utopia,' Shi Ge went on, 'the real purpose of the bases must be concealed. I can appoint each of you as director of an Environment Protection Region. That is what they must be called and the normal administrative and other work will have to be continued. I don't think that will be much of a burden, since protecting the environment is the duty of your association anyway. For the rest you will have a free hand, except that the bases must not, as far as the outside world is concerned, have any political alignment. Is that all acceptable?'

'Terrific!' The secretaries could not conceal their excitement.

'You said you had requests to make.' Chen Pan's voice was very calm.

'Yes.' Shi Ge looked first at Chen Pan, then at the others. 'I want you all, during your experiments to make the preparations, should it become necessary, to increase the number of bases to sixty, or six hundred and even more.'

'No problem,' said Ouyang Zhong-hua. 'That's what we hope for too.'

Then the bomb went off, with a deafening explosion such as Chen Pan had never heard before, and perforated her eardrum. The building shook, the neat row of armchairs jumped about like frogs. She staggered to her feet. No one appeared to have been injured, but above Shi Ge's head, the heavy brass light fitting was hanging loose from the ceiling. She could not hear her own voice. She had a feeling of emptiness as if there was no floor, there was no sound of footsteps, no time. But she reached Shi Ge, and felt resistance as she pushed him away hard. At the same time a gold-framed glass coffin come hurtling down. She was still conscious and thought only of holding on to her illusion, which was dissolving—as she was...

In the Wuyi Mountains, Fujian Province

There was the sound of an aircraft in the night sky. Then the lawn in front of the villa was lit up by floodlights, and a helicopter, searchlight on, appeared from behind the mountain ridge, like a large night bird hunting for food; flew over the thick forest and hung above the villa, scanning the surroundings, then slowly came down.

Li Ke-ming stood on a terrace nearby. As the searchlight caught him he instinctively moved away and looked for somewhere to hide. Between the rockery with its ancient pines and the pavilion there was nowhere. He did not move, but his grip on the handrail tightened. There was no point in hiding anyway. He was safe here. The place was guarded by a reinforced battalion of the Fujian regional army. Unauthorized entry by anyone, whether by air or luxury limousine, was a capital offence. Supposing he had assassinated the General Secretary, the crimes of the men now coming out of the villa were no less serious.

Apart from Liu Ya-ji, Li Ke-ming had met Huang Shi-ke and the Fujian army commanding officer. The others were leaders of the neighbouring coastal provinces, the commanders of Guangdong and of the Nanhai fleet and several wealthy businessmen.

As the helicopter door opened they all put on their smiles. First, a few fully armed soldiers stepped out, then a young Major-general. Everyone looked at him: there was no one else. The smiles faded away, hands ready to clap were lowered. The Major-general stood facing them, smiling slightly, apparently unaware that he was not the man everyone was expecting.

The Fujian commander broke the silence and began to make the introductions:

'This is Major-General Su, Deputy Chief of Staff of the Nanjing Command.'

'Welcome,' said Huang Shi-ke, putting out his hand, his smile seeming to Li Ke-ming a little forced. 'And Commander Bai?....'

'He had some urgent business and could not get away. I have full powers to act for him and transmit his good wishes.' He saluted—a little arrogantly.

Everyone shook hands with him and mumbled words of welcome. They were all disappointed, even dispirited and worried. As they went inside, the soldiers began patrolling. The helicopter rotors stopped turning and the lights on the lawn and in the porch went out. The moon was high in the sky directly above, not full moon but very bright. There were a few thin clouds. The autumn wind blew across the pine-covered mountains; leaves were beginning to fall.

Li Ke-ming had left Liu Ya-ji's basement after meeting Huang Shi-ke and the Fujian commander and moved to this mountain villa. He was still cautious, but he could move freely about this closely guarded area, enjoying the sun and the sky and the fresh air. He had no fear of arrest and was glad to have escaped from the four walls of the basement room. He felt he had rejoined mankind.

The second day after escaping from the Three Gorges, his wound had become infected. During the night he broke into a small private dispensary and forced the doctor to treat his wounds. At daylight, with a high fever and all the dispensary's stock of antibiotics, he walked unsteadily into the mountains. While the local police and militia were searching for him, he was hiding in the top of a tree giving himself injections.

The worst moments were the two days when he was semi-conscious. As soon as he was able, he had moved into deeper forest, said to be frequented by 'wild men' or yeti. He lived off berries, small animals and grain left in isolated fields. To his surprise his wounds healed and he saw his face for the first time, in the light of the rising sun, reflected in a still spring pool in the mountains. In his career as a police officer he had seen many faces badly smashed up, and he used to think of them as a mental preparation for what might happen to his own. It was not enough. He had never seen anything more hideous. More like rotten tomatoes that had been trampled in the mud than a face. In some places it was bright red, in some places a dirty black. One eye showed a lot of white and the other was almost invisible. All that was left of his nose, mouth and ears were formless slits and holes. His ears had gone, so had his nostrils and his hair. Enough to scare a ghost!

Eventually he laughed—a laugh so full of agony that it frightened the birds and beasts away. Hideous, so what? It would be worth it if he could lay hands on the assassin. Now inside and out he was the same. From now on that's how it would be.

He stole a truck from a forestry centre and drove to a town where he had once worked on a case. The head of the Preliminary Hearing Bureau was a fellow student of the Police Academy. Li Ke-ming did not call on him, but broke into the Bureau at night to use the special telephone line. Under the thick glass on his friend's desk was a warrant for his arrest. The talented young man in the photograph who no longer existed, looked fixedly at him. He first dialled the number of a fellow student in Beijing and said in the local dialect that he was phoning from the Preliminary Hearing Bureau.

'I need to contact the old director urgently, can you tell me how I can reach him?'

'You didn't get the obituary?' Asked the other sleepily.

'What?' His heart suddenly felt cold.

'Gas wasn't turned off properly. He and his wife both of them, in bed…'

He listened no longer and hung up. He had expected that the former director would be under surveillance, not that he would be murdered to prevent any contact between them. Even his high position had not saved them.

He moved about at night, sometimes climbing into a goods train, a cargo boat or heavy truck, going round in circles like a hunted animal. A month had passed and every road, station and public place was still watched. But after a month, he knew every trick and every loophole. If he was occasionally found by a railwayman or a truck driver, he pretended to be a deaf mute idiot who only knew how to beg for food and understood nothing else. His clothes were in tatters, he was black with grime; and that face! He had only to open his eyes wide and could even go into a kitchen and take what he wanted and no one dared interfere.

When he went into Liu Ya-ji's house through the window, Liu Ya-ji was counting gold bars. He almost fainted from fright and could not even call for help, even less take in what Li Ke-ming was saying.

'You've got a gun there. Pick it up and aim it at me; but listen to me and don't call for help.'

The gun made Liu Ya-ji calmer, but it shook in his hand.

'Do you remember your promise? You swore that if ever I needed it you would even give your life to help me.'

'Who are you?'

'Li Ke-ming.'

The gun barrel was lowered.

'That's not his face.' Liu Ya-ji raised the pistol again.

'The arrest notices all over the place say that Li Ke-ming's face is badly burnt, you must have read that?'

'But I don't recognize you. Can you prove you are Li Ke-ming?'

'Li Ke-ming can talk to you about things which happened fourteen years ago. You didn't look so respectable then. You were guilty of embezzling public money and of paedophilia. You were to be released early, because you had reported that certain prisoners were preparing a breakout. But they got to you first and were about to carry out the death sentence they had passed on you. Li Ke-ming, single-handed, dealt with the fifteen thugs and shot their ringleader. Li Ke-ming got an iron bar in his chest one centimetre from his heart. You and he shared a hospital room. Ten days later you left hospital, but Li Ke-ming was there for three months. Now, if you want I will leave immediately; but I'm not going to beg.'

Liu Ya-ji had lowered the gun. 'I was afraid they'd found someone to trap me.'

Li Ke-ming opened his shirt: the fourteen year-old scar was still clearly visible in the huge area where his chest had been burnt.

He had thought of hiding temporarily in the south. All those who knew him were undoubtedly being watched; but they did not know about Liu Ya-ji or the events that happened fourteen years ago. Now the south was seething with unrest and Beijing did not have complete control. It would be much easier to hide here than in the north.

His fate was now bound up with that of the South. If independence succeeded he would survive. The South needed him. Huang Shi-ke had called him a blessing from heaven because now he would defy Beijing. The south would spare no effort to clear Li Ke-ming and help find the real culprit. If Beijing won, he would not escape death, and go down in history as an assassin.

He was not a southerner. His home was in the extreme north, where everything was now covered with snow. The same moon shone on the solemn and quiet scene of his home village and on the frozen Heilong River. Was his wife looking at the moon? he wondered. The son he had never seen must be asleep on the heated brick bed. He loved the rigorous and bleak north, where there was a real difference between the seasons. He longed for the sound of footsteps on the crisp surface of the snow, the steam of his breath. He liked the noise and excitement of the frozen football ground, the sight of hunting dogs chasing a rabbit across the snowy plain, drinking strong alcohol beside the stove—the maternal bosom of all northerners.

Although he had often been received as an honoured guest when he had come to the south on a case, he always felt out of his element. He disliked the separatist plotting and did not want to become anyone's tool. He had saved Liu Ya-ji's life out of a sense of duty. He didn't give a damn for a man like that. Now he had become a guest at the southerners' table and heard them every day curse the northerners.

He became aware of an almost imperceptible sound. His hearing was now very acute and he immediately realized that there was someone close by, moving only when the wind blew. The person, whoever it was, was clearly skilled at concealing his presence. The sound came from behind an ancient pine tree and shrubbery on the top of a rocky escarpment higher up in the garden of the mountain villa.

He approached silently. He had studied the lay of the land the last few days and knew that there was an opening and a small winding stairway leading to the top had been cut inside the rock. Possibly the previous owner of the villa had intended to construct a small pavilion up there. He went silently up the steps, the sound becoming clearer. When he reached the top, he only moved when the other moved. When the clouds hid the moon for a moment he poked his head out and saw a soldier squatting on the ground manipulating some kind of small instrument attached to a low tripod. There was a faint odour of perfume!

Suddenly the soldier turned round in alarm. Just at that moment the clouds unveiled the moon. Li Ke-ming merely raised his head a little more. He could easily imagine the unexpected sight of the King of Hell's face suddenly appearing out of the rock. The soldier's face went deathly white, a scream was suppressed before it was uttered, and the soldier fainted. The military cap fell off and a cascade of hair fell down. It was Bai Ling.

He had already met her. She seemed to have only a small role in Huang Shi-ke's entourage—mostly delivering documents and pouring tea—but each time she appeared, Huang Shi-ke pulled in his belly and sat up a little straighter. That is why Li Ke-ming remembered her. The meeting today was not open to staff members; but here she was dressed as a soldier and she knew how to use the wind to cover her movements.... What was she up to? A thin wire went from her ears to the instrument.

Li Ke-ming squeezed out into the open. The instrument had tiny lights and a tube which was aimed at a window of the villa. A minute tape was turning. He took the ear-piece and could hear the sounds coming from the meeting. He knew of such instruments, which directed a laser at a window and could pick up vibrations caused by sounds inside, but he had never seen one.

There was certainly more to this woman than met the eye. She knew how to evade the guards, how to choose the best listening point and use the instrument. Who was she? She had obviously got Huang Shi-ke round her little finger; but what was she up to?

Li Ke-ming wondered whether to hand her over to the people in the villa or just stop the listening device. Or teach her a lesson only she would understand? He looked at her curled up unconscious body, the line of her thighs and buttocks. So accessible... He felt a surge of desire. After the first sight of his face in the mountain pool, he had dismissed all thoughts of sex. But now, he was so scared to find that his instincts were even stronger than before, that he trembled and refrained from touching her.

He had not decided what to do, but gently put the ear-piece back in her ear. The action was almost enough to sap his resolution, but he did not touch her skin. Then went back down the steps through the rock.

What does it matter who she is, he thought...unless she is a Beijing agent! He owed no duty to the south: let her do what she wanted. She would soon regain consciousness and perhaps think she had hallucinated. The recording was all there; she had not been unconscious long.

Liu Ya-ji emerged from the villa and called Li Ke-ming softly, telling him that he was wanted. As he covered his head with the light yellow hood, he remembered that Bai Ling had never seen him without it until now , and would be unlikely to recognize him.

The Southern Alliance, under Huang Shi-ke's leadership, comprising five coastal provinces, Shanghai and the island of Hainan, was demanding independence from Beijing on the basis of 'one country two systems'. Agreement had been reached after long and intense discussion: they would try to achieve their aim by political means, but it was essential to be prepared for military intervention by Beijing.

The provinces and cities in the Alliance all came under either the Nanjing or the Guangzhou military regions, which controlled all strategic points and could at any time take over local government, airfields and ports, declare martial law and make arrests. Unless the two regional commanders could be won over, autonomy—even for a single day—was out of the question, and armed resistance would be futile. The only solution was for the southern provinces to use their enormous financial resources to 'reach an understanding' with the area commanders. A great deal of money had been spent to suborn the military commander of Fujian Province, but he controlled only a few local armies, and would stand no chance at all against Beijing's field armies. The Guangzhou military region and the Hainan fleet had already promised their support.

The problem now was the Nanjing military region, which controlled four of the rebellious provinces. Commander Bai was known to be incorruptible and kept a tight control over his armies. It was going to be very difficult to win him over, but if it could be done, two fifths of the Chinese Airforce and three fifths of the Navy would follow. With the economic resources of the South, even if Beijing could not be defeated militarily, they would be evenly matched, and it should be possible to reach an agreement of some sort.

The problem was how to convince Commander Bai. Huang Shi-ke had been at his wit's end trying to think of a way when Li Ke-ming arrived as if from heaven. What better way of shifting the inflexible, doctrinaire commander? They would tell him how the Secretary-General had been assassinated by the Beijing usurper and that the new Central Committee was totally illegal. To break away from the Beijing regime was not splitting the country, but defending its integrity.

Commander Bai had agreed to come to the villa himself to hear Li Ke-ming's story and the views of the Southern Alliance. Everything seemed to be in the bag, but at the last moment this beardless, smooth faced young deputy chief of staff with his piercing eyes, ramrod posture and typical Nanjing arrogance, had turned up instead.

Li Ke-ming told his story clearly and simply as he had been trained to do. When he had finished the Deputy Chief of Staff was silent for a while—which puzzled those present.

'What you have told us is coherent and logical,' he said finally. 'But you have left out the most important thing—proof. How can you *prove* that Shen Di deliberately let the killer get away? That your friend in the police was murdered and not killed in a train crash? The murder of the former director of the Police Academy could be a pure a figment of your imagination. Even if Shen Di was in league with the assassin, what proof is there that the top leadership had given the order, or that it had anything to do with recent political changes? Another thing: there is no proof that *you* didn't kill the Secretary-General. You have argued your case well, but the announcement made by Beijing was more convincing. You have said that its version is a total fabrication: can you convince us that yours is not? That it has not been worked out to further the interests of someone or other? Whether you are really Li Ke-ming is doubtful too. A man of your height, made unrecognizable by burns—which also destroyed your fingerprints… No gentlemen, you must present real proof.'

No one spoke. Too much was at stake to risk speaking out of turn. They were all puzzled by the man's hypercritical attitude.

Li Ke-ming understood. He was used to thinking in terms of suspicion and proof. He was not in the least put out by the man's self-satisfied comments: he too had been turning these questions over in his mind.

'I can at least prove that I am Li Ke-ming.' The Major-general turned to him. 'When policemen are killed in the course of duty, it is sometimes difficult to identify them if there are no identifying features and no possibility of using fingerprints, so we all have dental impressions taken. I still have my teeth, so the central fingerprint department can provide the proof that I am Li Ke-ming. As to other proofs you require, it will be very difficult to get them one by one. The ideal solution would be to get Shen Di to tell the facts himself. If that can be done what other doubts could you possibly have?'

'None. Nor will anyone in China or world opinion—that is the important thing.' He seemed to approve of Li Ke-ming's proposition.

'And Commander Bai?' asked Huang Shi-ke.

'His attitude is clear: he stands for justice and legality. If it was really as you have said, and the General Secretary was killed by the Beijing regime, we will root out whoever is responsible and get at the truth. But until you produce proof we are bound to obey the Central Committee and punish anyone who opposes it.'

'Even in an ordinary criminal case proof can't be found in a few days.'

'That's true. A case like this might take years to solve. But the interests of the country make that impossible. So for thirty days, starting from now, the Nanjing command will remain neutral. If you can't produce proof within a month we will wait no longer.'

'If we do give you proof…?'

'Our attitude is perfectly clear.' The Major-general stood up and closed his brief-case.

'A moment please,' said the Guangzhou commander. His rank was higher than that of the Major-general, so he did not need to mince his words. 'You have many doubts, and so do we. You have said you will remain neutral for thirty days: is there any reason that we should believe that? You have examined all our plans: perhaps you will now report to Beijing and get a medal. Perhaps you are even keeping Commander Bai in the dark. These doubt may be ridiculous; but you should give *us* proofs.'

'What proof should we give you, Commander Zhao?' the chief of staff said smiling.

'This is a very scenic spot. You should stay here and rest for thirty days. Commander Bai will surely give you leave,' said Commander Zhao, who was fat and quick-witted.

'I'm sorry,' he saluted 'Another time I would enjoy such a stay.' He turned to leave.

'Are you relying on a helicopter and five soldiers to get you off the mountain?'

'I don't think that will be a problem.' The deputy chief of staff raised his right hand holding a miniaturised transmitter. 'You see the red button under my finger? If I press it, within five minutes a parachute battalion will land here.'

Huang Shi-ke roared with laughter. 'When military men make jokes they're as ingenious as war itself! Commander Zhao, you're no match for the young. But you scared me stiff when you described tying me up on a scaffold yesterday.' Everyone in the room followed Huang Shi-ke's lead and laughed their way out of an awkward situation.

The Fujian commander opened the door for the Major-general. The Nanjing guards had just been released: their uniforms were in a mess and they looked furious. Those who had seized them were nowhere to be seen. A soldier recovered a transmitter from a flowerbed, where it had been hidden as soon as the helicopter landed. It would have started transmitting as soon as the red button was pressed.

'Thirty days.' The deputy chief of staff raised three fingers as the rotors began to turn.

Beijing: Military General Hospital

It was silent as a vacuum in the Beijing Military Hospital. Concrete walls a metre thick kept out the ceaseless hum of the city. In front of a steel door that looked strong enough to resist a guided missile, nurses were entering their code numbers and showing their identification to the video camera. The heavy door opened silently, operated by soldiers dressed from head to foot in white, carrying sub-machine-guns.

After the usual disinfecting procedures Wang Feng entered the central control room. It always reminded him of that of his submarine, still waiting in its secret dock. Both were full of instruments, screens, dials, coloured lights and keyboards.

The doctor in charge was a white-haired, urbane major-general, very different from the submarine commander Ding Da-hai, who looked like a fisherman. Both of them were proud of their respective technical skills: one at taking lives, the other at saving them. Wang Feng needed them both, but what weighed most heavily on him at present, was the necessity to save the dying man, or rather to keep him from dying.

On the other side of a glass panel lay the Chairman, his skin grey. The room was sterile and kept at a constant temperature. As Wang Feng watched, the hydraulic bed rose into a large contraption in which all kinds of electronic and acoustic probes and instruments worked on his body, measuring, injecting, giving oxygen and massage, simulating his breathing, registering his heart beat. It was becoming weaker and the blood-pressure was falling.

'No hope?' Wang Feng asked.

'He won't last the day out,' said the old doctor, who was exhausted.

'The last two times you managed to save him.'

'Now it's different.'

'You are sure?'

The doctor shrugged his shoulders.

Wang Feng looked at the Chairman in the life-support chamber. He needed this man alive, especially now, if only for one day. He had just begun to take control of the country. He was determined to succeed, but was aware of the dangers he faced.

In China there was no longer a procedure for succession that could produce a leader acceptable both to the people and to the various powerful interests. In the old days, succession was hereditary. When an Emperor died even a three-year old son might come to the throne and would be accepted and bowed down to by civil and military alike.

The Communist Party in power had replaced this by the method of 'inner-party struggle'. When the old revolutionaries were still in power, success or failure in the struggle depended on a man's authority, which stemmed from his record and prestige. This was a continuation of Imperial rule in a different guise. Wang Feng remembered how he, like many others at the time, had naively sneered at the adulation of Mao, and the 'cult of the personality'. But Emperors now belonging to the past, there was no other way of creating equally powerful patriarchal authority.

This fact was brought home to him later, when the era of Mao Zedong came to an end. Most of the senior revolutionaries were dead and authority had become weaker. In the wave of liberalization brought about by ill-conceived reform, authority progressively disintegrated, to the satisfaction of those who had nothing better to offer than second-hand western ideas. The loss of authority was a disaster that left China without its cohesive nucleus. Everyone lusted after high office and tried to overthrow others, with total disregard for any kind of order. Chinese history has proved again and again that once this point is reached there is chaos, disintegration and civil war. In the old days a military commander or a prince might usurp the throne or a bandit seize territory and declare himself king. Now reform and decentralization had encouraged local autonomy. Regional government increasingly acted independently and defiantly, threatening a dangerous confrontation with central power.

Mao Zedong's kind of authority no longer existed because there was no one left with enough revolutionary prestige. In any case, the Cultural Revolution destroyed the god-creating tendency of the Chinese people—their desire to worship a leader. Wang Feng was convinced that authority now can only be imposed by force. 'Power grows out of the barrel of a gun.' Control of the army is the key to supreme power. Had he got a firm grip on the key? Wang Feng asked himself. He was confident in his own ability, but that alone was not enough.

Within the army, authority depended on a man's record, his seniority and the support of former commanders and subordinates. Wang Feng did not have such advantages. His rapid rise in the army had given rise to much jealousy. The more senior commanders now accepted him, because they regarded him as the Chairman's spokesman. If it was to succeed everything had to be done in the name of the Chairman—what used to be called 'commanding the nobles by controlling the emperor'. Without the Chairman he would lose the only authority which could bind the army together. The political situation was unstable and there was a threat of rebellion. This was no time to let the Chairman die.

'Shall we inform the family?' asked the deputy head of the treatment team softly. Wang Feng made an unmistakably negative gesture. Apart from the special staff, no one knew the true facts about the Chairman's state of health; even his family thought a short stay in hospital would put him on his feet again. Only Wang Feng could authorize family visits and they had to be well-prepared in advance. The Chairman remained behind glass. The medical records were all falsified.

'Professor,' said Wang Feng to the army doctor, 'can we keep his breathing and circulation going by using an external breathing apparatus and heart?'

The doctor absent-mindedly polished his spectacles. 'He's dead, so what would be the point?'

"That depends on what you mean by dead. Someone who breathes and whose blood circulates cannot be called dead…'

It was not important how he was kept alive, as long as he was not dead and his authority survived. In his last few years Mao Zedong had been more dead than alive—not much different from the body they later put in a crystal coffin. China did not change; but once the doctors proclaimed him dead, his widow was immediately clapped in prison. That shows the power of medicine, and medicine is a creation of man.

The doctor did not think like that. He glanced at Wang Feng ironically. 'Machines are not God.' He was a Major-General—the highest rank in the medical corps—therefore senior to Wang Feng

'The country is in an exceptional situation, we should make judgements accordingly.'

Again the doctor polished his glasses. 'When a body begins to decompose, there's no way of saying that he's still alive. Am I right?'

Wang Feng looked at the electrocardiogram. At each heart beat the green dot just managed to quiver, as if it was on the point of going out altogether. For Wang Feng, life and death applied only to other people, not to the Chairman: as long as people were unaware of his death, he was as good as alive. He did not need long—just one year—then the Chairman could die a natural death and have a glorious funeral.

Everyone who knew the truth would have to be kept in prison for a year, including the medical major-general and the Chairman's family. But…. He looked at the electrocardiogram. He did not like this idea. It was not a question of morality, but there were too many risks involved. Keeping so many people in prison for so long would lead to all sorts of rumours and eventually the truth was bound to come out. Worst of all was the thought of arresting the Chairman's family. Every army commander who came to Beijing invariably called on his wife. She had seven children and fifteen grandchildren, and all of them had large families. Locking up the Chairman's family, Wang Feng knew, would be enough to set the whole army against him.

'Think of something Professor, even if for only a month.' It was the first time the doctor had heard him speak with such a kindly tone. In his long career he had often heard this kind of request and was unmoved by it.

'All scientific methods have already been used. As to non-scientific methods,' he continued with disdain, 'I'm afraid I am not qualified in *qigong* or other esoteric practices.'

Normally Wang Feng would have regarded this remark as

disrespectful. He did not believe in the miraculous powers of *qigong*; but the doctor's disparaging remarks reminded him of the maxim 'When you are ill you should not be choosy about the doctor.' Since there was no hope, every straw should be grasped. If it didn't work, it would only mean there would be another person to lock up. There were so many already, why bother about a stooping charlatan?

Twenty six minutes later Zhou Chi was brought into the control room. Wang Feng was normally proud of his efficiency, but today the delay had been intolerable. The instruments all indicated that the Chairman was in the last stage of heart failure. Wang Feng did not even listen to a report by telephone saying that the leader of the autonomous movement in the South was holding a secret meeting in the Wuyi mountains of northern Fujian.

Zhou Chi carefully inspected the Chairman behind the glass window of the life-support chamber, crouching even more than usual, his eyes only an inch from the glass. As soon as Wang Feng decided to call on a 'magician', he had immediately thought of Zhou Chi. Not that he trusted him—you could never trust these people—but since he was Chairman of the All-China *Qigong* Association, he must be an outstanding practitioner. If it turned out that he was only skilled in cheating people he would get a good view of prison bars—from the inside. It was only because Lu Hao-ran had stubbornly insisted that this fellow be appointed chief *qigong* instructor to the Armed Police, with rank of major-general, that Wang Feng had remembered his name.

'Please have the patient removed from the life-support machine,' said Zhou Chi. He had come in such a hurry that he was still in his exercise clothes, which made him looked even more like a mountebank. The Professor had left, slamming the door, as soon as Zhou Chi entered; he hated magic and took the man's presence as a personal insult.

The technician responsible for the life-support equipment looked at Wang Feng. He nodded, and the bed slowly moved out of the machine until it was in front of the glass window of the life-support chamber. The body of the Chairman looked like a gnawed bone on the white sheet.

'Can the glass panel be removed?' Zhou Chi asked, his eyes fixed on the Chairman.

Wang Feng looked at the doctors gathered around.

'No,' said one of them firmly. 'How can we maintain sterility and constant temperature if it is?'

'It's of no consequence,' Zhou Chi replied mildly.

'To you perhaps, but it is to us,' said the Professor's young assistant, rudely.

Zhou Chi looked at Wang Feng, who gave him an encouraging smile.

'First try with the window in place. Energy can go through air and matter, can't it?'

'It may diminish the effect.'

There was silence in the room as he pressed his hands against the glass. Suddenly a young nurse watching the instrument panels gave an exclamation of astonishment: the blood pressure gauge had slowly begun to rise. The electrocardiogram registered a stronger heart-beat, body temperature increased, breathing became deeper, and there seemed to be a general improvement.

Wang Feng hardly dared believe his eyes. The Chairman's skin began to take on a more healthy colour. It worked. That was the only thing that mattered.

Zhou Chi placed his right hand on the glass and moved it upwards; as he did so, the Chairman's right hand also rose, and fell when Zhou Chi lowered his own, like a string puppet This was repeated several times, with the left hand as well.

This was the first time the patient had moved since he was put in the life-support chamber. Wang Feng fixed his eyes like a man spellbound, on the Chairman's withered hand. Zhou Chi's face was as red as a wrestler's and his body seemed give off an inexhaustible heat. But when he stopped and turned round, his face was white as paper and dripping with sweat—a different man, completely drained.

Wang Feng looked at the instruments, which continued to show an improvement, after Zhou Chi had stopped. The Chairman's complexion was even slightly better than a moment ago, and he appeared to be breathing peacefully.

'You must be tired, Comrade Zhou Chi,' said Wang Feng shaking him by the hand

Zhou Chi nodded. His hand was damp with sweat. Wang Feng took him to a nearby room to rest, and personally poured him a glass of pineapple juice.

'How long will the effect last?'

'Difficult to say.' Zhou Chi replied, sinking into an arm-chair. 'A day or two at most. With direct contact it could have been three to five days.'

'If the treatment is continued how long will the patient live?'

'If it is done daily and without the glass, he will not only live but will be restored to health.'

Wang Feng could not conceal his delight. 'The problem of the glass is easily solved. You have already convinced those pedants. You are better than they are and they'll have to listen to you. From today you must put all other work to one side.'

'Just now,' Zhou Chi said with a smile, 'I used up almost all my vital energy. I can't repeat it without a month's rest.'

Wang Feng became pensive. 'You must have some gifted disciples who can replace you. Say one man every two days—fifteen men on a monthly rota....The state will not forget your trouble...'

'It's no trouble. I don't know who the patient is, but he must be a very important person, and I would willingly give my life to restore the old gentleman to health. But this technique is very demanding. An adept who learns it before reaching the ultimate highest level. can only make a mess of things. That's why I have never taught this technique to anyone. None of my disciples have reached this level, and even then it would need several years of practice.'

Wang Feng was disappointed. He walked round the room with his hands behind his back and stopped for an instant in front of a door. Strange...reflected in the glass he saw Zhou Chi's eyes fixed on his back, with a cunning expression.

If there was no hope, why had the fellow risked using up all his vital energy? He obviously had something in mind. He would first suggest a solution, then talk about difficulties and finally start bargaining. If the price was right he would find a way.

'Think of something,' he told Zhou Chi, who replied, looking elsewhere.

'You could always try a different *qigong* master.'

'I won't consider it. Go on.'

Zhou Chi coughed twice. 'There is something, but it's not really a solution.'

'Comrade Zhou Chi, it is in the interests of the country and you need have no misgivings. Tell me.'

Zhou Chi hesitated a moment, then said, 'This is anathema to the strict school of *qigong*, punishable by death in the old days.'

'Well?'

'I don't know whether you have heard of 'gathering vital energy.' Everyone's body contains energy, but there is very little in those who are not trained in *qigong*. With enough people, a great deal of energy can be gathered and there are no ill effects at all.

'Like giving blood.'

"No, because that does not need many people. The amount of vital energy I transmitted just now would need to be gathered from a thousand people, and they would take six months to recuperate. If I treat your patient once a day for three months, ninety times that is, I would need the energy from ninety thousand young, unmarried men to keep going.

'We have three million young men like that in the army,' said Wang Feng.

'But if they know that their vital energy is being gathered, there can be a conscious resistance, and the transmission fails. If they think they are merely practising *qigong* there is no such problem.'

Wang Feng was silent. There was something about Zhou Chi's small sharp eyes…

'No one can gather energy from a thousand men every two days. The safe maximum is ten men a day. So there must be others to help me.'

Wang Feng made a quick calculation: one hundred and ten assistant 'gatherers' would be needed. 'Will they all be your disciples,' he asked.

'I have never taught that to my disciples, as I said, but there will be no problem finding qualified people. But since all this is contrary to *qigong* principles, it must be kept secret, even though it's being done in the interests of the country. I am not worried about by own disciples, but the others must not be told.'

'Then take your hundred and ten adepts and do the gathering. I will make the necessary arrangements.'

Zhou Chi looked embarrassed. 'It's not going to be easy to start from scratch every two days with a new group of police; it will be difficult for them to get into the right state of mind and unforeseen problems can easily arise. We will have to rush about all day, and if there's a hitch everything will go wrong.'

'What's the answer?' Wang Feng asked pleasantly, watching Zhou Chi seeming to consider the matter, more and more convinced that he already had the answer. Zhou Chi had not been told who the patient was; but by some special power he possessed, he had broken through the defences of Wang Feng's secretive mind. Remembering all that had taken place in the hospital, Wang Feng asked himself whether everything Zhou Chi had said had not been carefully prepared beforehand.

'Perhaps we could start a *qigong* training movement. For the regular army it might perhaps not be suitable, but it would be perfectly appropriate for the Armed Police. They have all been practising the martial arts recently, so it would be logical to include *qigong*. Then a hundred first grade adepts go to a hundred different police detachments and start teaching, while simultaneously gathering vital energy. Every two days ten adepts gather energy from ten men. Then ten second-grade gatherers assemble and transmit to me. For the sake of convenience, the hundred detachments should come from ten different police regiments, one second-grade gatherer to every regiment. The ten regiments should not be too far from Beijing, so I can go by helicopter to each in two days, and be able to get back here. This is the only way we can to be sure of a smooth operation.'

There was one regiment of Armed Police in each province. Wang Feng could see at once that the ten nearest regiments controlled half of China, with Beijing in the middle.

'I'll deal with it at once.' Wang Feng's expression remained unchanged, as if he were organizing a spring excursion; but he was imagining the Armed Police of ten provinces, hypnotized by *qigong* moving on the capital, while Zhou Chi and his adepts recited incantations.

Zhou Chi had not finished.

'I'm afraid that if there's is no official order they won't be allowed to organize themselves and we will have no way of getting the officers to cooperate. I think we should be given an official assignment, because if we fail...'.

Wang Feng looked at him. Zhou Chi's eyes no longer avoided his.

'All right, I'll deal with it.' He had agreed to everything. With *qigong* he could save the Chairman; with the Chairman he could control the army. A hundred-odd charlatans was nothing, even ten regiments of Armed Police would be no problem.

Zhou Chi still had something to say.

'I fear my present position as General Instructor is not entirely suitable now...'

Wang Feng would have liked to turn a flame-thrower on him, but he laughed heartily.

'All right, from today you are Deputy Commander-in-Chief of the Armed Police of the People's Republic.'

Fuzhou

The weather looked promising. Huang Shi-ke stood at the window in his office and looked at the sky. These last few years the atmosphere had been so hazy that even close to the sea, when the sky was relatively clear, the sun was hardly more than a luminous smudge. Today it looked as if the sky had been wiped clean. The good weather made him feel more confident, though his nerves were on edge.

Yesterday he had issued his last order as Acting Governor of Fujian Province, instructing all the banks to unfreeze personal accounts in both Chinese and foreign currency. An hour later, on television he had taken his leave of the people of Fujian.

He had said with emotion that he was still with them in their struggle and had not been able to stand by and allow their hard-earned savings to be taken from them. Beijing had demanded the money from the frozen accounts fifty four times and as a government official it was his duty to obey orders.

From ancient times it had always been said that to be both a loyal subject and honour one's parents was impossible. 'My parents are the sixty million people of Fujian.' He had taken it upon himself to lift the freezing order and was now guilty of the crime of disobedience. He was resigning as acting Governor of the province and going to Beijing to admit his guilt and await punishment, whatever it might be. 'To die for one's country, for the people, is to die an honourable death.'

The banks had been working all night. By six o'clock this morning, it was reported, 93% of customers had already withdrawn their deposits, and the process would be completed in the next two hours. Several billions of *yuan* were now back in private hands.

By freezing bank accounts Beijing had made it possible for the Alliance to get its hands on a huge amount of the population's money, without having to do anything. The decision to reverse Beijing's order had been hotly debated. Some people considered if Fujian won its independence the money would be needed for construction; if not, it would be needed for war. It would be a serious miscalculation not to take advantage of the opportunity of getting their hands on such funds.

But Huang Shi-ke insisted that the goodwill of the people was more important than money. If the people had nothing to gain from autonomy, the cause was bound to fail. With popular support, even more money would eventually be available. He managed to convince the majority. His strategy was right and this was an opportune moment to make himself famous. Government policies were often incomprehensible to the people, but they would look up to and follow a star.

Several highly paid publicity specialists of the commercial and industrial world, employed to create stars, had been at his heels the last few days studying, designing, guiding him, his bearing and appearance—everything from his tone of voice to the script for his TV speech. It had now been broadcast fifteen times. Some of his words were on posters in the streets and there were balloons in the sky carrying his portrait. In the last few days his name had been mentioned more times than in his whole life.

'It's time, Governor,' one of the image-builders told him.

A whole team of specialists entered. Finally someone inspected his clothes, hair, the position of his fountain pen, his briefcase and the way he carried it.

Was he going to be just a shooting star? He wondered. He had never in his life had so many specialists fussing over his image, but he was not in the least complacent. The declaration of autonomy had been put forward a day, but preparations were far from complete. As long as Beijing did not make a move Huang Shi-ke was willing to go on waiting.

The government in Beijing had unexpectedly accepted his appointment as Governor by the Fujian People's Congress. He wondered at the time, whether they were unaware of the existence of the Alliance; but information received two days ago showed that Beijing knew about everything, but had taken no drastic action because of the mutiny of the Guangzhou Military Command and the declaration of neutrality by the Nanjing Command. Beijing had continued to demand the transfer of the frozen funds mainly as a diversion, to distract attention from the discreet build-up of troops and other military preparations.

Beijing's plan of action, according to reports, was to avoid major military engagements. Instead seven highly mobile assault units would make rapid simultaneous raids on the provincial capitals, so that there would be no time to organize resistance. The various leaders of the independence movement would be arrested and brought to Beijing and that would be the end of it. Except that the dissident provinces would be brought under control, discipline would be enforced and purges carried out. The South would be bloodlessly brought to submission.

The last two days the leaders of the Alliance had been scuttling into hiding, or sleeping in different places every night. Huang Shi-ke was in a permanent state of trepidation. But to live in hiding was no answer. The only way out of the difficulty was immediate rebellion, proclamation of autonomy and mobilization. Perhaps that is the only way I can escape death, he had said to himself.

The rising was planned for today. Releasing the frozen assets and Huang Shi-ke's television appearance, had been the prelude.

The specialist left by a side door and Huang was left alone in his office. All day and all night there had been a light in his window, that attracted people to the provincial government building: the devoted Governor was still at his desk!

At dawn he left his office quietly, a plane ticket, bought with his own money, in the pocket of his raincoat. He was going to Beijing to give himself up, in exchange for the savings the people of Fujian had retrieved.

'Governor Huang is leaving!' An anxious voice cried out (as planned) as soon as he appeared. The building was seething with people. The working day had not yet started, but nearly all the staff had arrived and were waiting.

People crowding the corridor silently made way for him; the men with respect and sadness in their eyes, the women with tears. That these government employees (usually too busy finding fault, repeating rumours and slander and taking pleasure in the misfortune of others) should show genuine feeling like this, moved him.

He shook hands with everyone, close to tears himself, and noticed Bai Ling standing behind the others, looking at him in adoration. She knew perfectly well that it was all a masquerade. Yesterday she had showed him his statement of the account in a Swiss bank and documents relating to real estate in Los Angeles also in his name. She coolly put down papers representing assets of five million US dollars, and only said that since he was going to the guillotine she would follow. Now his eyes and hers were full of deep feeling and the sadness of parting. 'Living the part': that was what the producer had called it.

In the vestibule he was surrounded by dozens of foreign pressmen. The anti-North riots and the attack on the Governor, not to mention yesterday's dramatic events, had made Fuzhou a centre of foreign media attention. Huang Shi-ke knew no foreign language and pretended not to understand the peculiar Chinese that some of the correspondents spoke, so he did not answer a single question. But he admired their well-chosen probing questions—their governments had a less accurate view of things.

The Southern Alliance had recently made secret contact with various foreign governments, which had all come to nothing. The West was worried about the line taken by the new regime in Beijing, but was not willing to make any promises to the independentists, who had no visible chance of success. The Alliance had to get going on its own, only if it succeeded would 'friends' turn up.

Huang Shi-ke performed in the manner he had rehearsed with the producer. A good shot of him, he had been told, was one of the best ways of winning public support. So he gave the pressmen plenty of time to take photographs before leaving the provincial government building.

He knew that the huge crowds of ordinary people had been organized, but he had not expected so many. They were everywhere (except the top of the broad flight of steps that was reserved for him): in the streets, on balconies, even on the roofs. Wherever one looked was crowded with people. Surely not *all* of them had been organized, he thought. Some of them had even been standing outside all night. Many people carried portraits of him and posters urging him not to leave. In the streets crowds were shouting their support for him, and he saw for the first time in all his years in government service, the gratitude of the people

The organizers had found, who knows where, a toothless man who looked over a hundred years old who told the Governor how his lifetime's savings from farming and raising pigs had been taken from him.

'It is you who have returned the money and I am putting it back in the bank.' He shakily held up the banknotes to pass them to Huang Shi-ke, who stretched out his hand to prevent him.

'Governor, you must not go to Beijing! There is a traitor there and he will kill you.'

'I personally do not matter,' Huang Shi-ke replied nobly, 'as long as the people do not suffer, I am ready to face anything!' He raised his head and looked at the seas of silent people: 'Fellow countrymen, take care of yourselves!'

The old man had spoken his lines rather woodenly, but his acting had been very effective. Though there were no loudspeakers, the scene had been arranged to take place in front of the provincial government building and everyone could see.

Finally the old man knelt down, and one after the other, several hundred people in the crowd knelt down too.

Huang Shi-ke had felt that kneeling down was too old fashioned. But the producer wanted scenes which would look good on film, and had arranged for a dozen or so people to kneel in front of Huang Shi-ke. No one had expected it to catch on! Huang Shi-ke was very moved. The foreign pressmen had never seen anything like it. In the script Huang Shi-ke was supposed to support the old man for the benefit of the photographers, but feared he would be unable to control his emotions and ruin the scene. So he only said in a slightly choking voice, 'I would sooner the state betray me than I betray the state,' and went over to where his wife was waiting in the car.

He told the driver to go to the airport. But after a few yards, the street was blocked by kneeling people. Huang Shi-ke could no longer tell who was acting or who was not.

The driver got out of the car and knelt down too, saying 'I too am Fujianese. I cannot drive you on the road to death.' The crowd surged forward, opened the folding hood and at a signal lifted up the car to shoulder height. The producer had insisted on a convertible. Huang Shi-ke would not be able to wave properly out of an ordinary car, especially if it was being carried.

Huang Shi-ke looked uncomfortable, but stood up and raised his two arms to the crowd. This carefully rehearsed gesture was a great success. He had never thought of himself as glamorous. Anxiety about his girth was dissipated all at once. Of course Bai Ling did not want him to lose weight!

Everyone saw his wife's white hair and kindly face. They looked like a virtuous and happily married couple. A great man in politics could not do without a virtuous companion at his side.

The convertible, carried high above peoples heads, led the procession. The mighty crowd advanced through the main street, clearly more than the two hundred thousand expected. There were flags and posters on balconies along the street. Leaflets fluttered down like snow from high buildings, as car-horns blared and there was shouting and declamations on all sides. The slogans shouted sounded increasingly like a political programme.

'Fujian belongs to the people of Fujian!'

'Fujian people refuse to be slaves!'

'Retreat means obliteration!'

'Fellow countrymen, take your fate in your own hands!'

'Independent, our life will be better.'

'Northerners, keep your poverty for yourselves!'

Huang Shi-ke's anxiety and doubt had been swept away. He felt strong. He was being carried along by the footsteps of history! A breath of sea wind blew in his face. He had finally felt what it was like to be a colossus, standing above the people, leading them towards a new world!

Police in cars and on motorcycles, made a passage through the crowd for a large broadcasting van, which stopped in front of the marchers. An impassioned and excited voice announced:

'Fellow countrymen! A meeting of the Fujian People's Congress has just met, and I solemnly announce its decision. From today Fujian is autonomous! The former Acting Governor Huang Shi-ke is elected Prime Minister of the Fujian Autonomous Government!'

There was an earth-shaking explosion of acclamation. Huang Shi-ke stood straight and motionless, looking at the sea and the blue sky.

The same day the Fujian People's Congress addressed a message to the people of the whole country and to the People's Congress of each province, which ended:

We advocate the immediate calling of the National People's Congress, the revision of the constitution, and the transformation of the present system of centralized control into a unified, peaceful and mutually supportive Chinese Federation, on the basis of local self-determination. As a member of the Federation, Fujian will unreservedly respect and uphold its sovereignty, obey its constitution and within the world family, make a great contribution to the prosperity of the Chinese people.

5

Beijing: Zhongnanhai – Shandong Peninsula: Naval base 201 – Fuzhou – Zhejiang Province: The Xianxia Pass – Nanjing Command HQ – Zhengzhou City, Henan Province

☙

Beijing: Zhongnanhai

The days were growing shorter, it was already dark. The lights in General Secretary's official residence were on, but only the Actress was there. Lu Hao-ran felt slightly anxious.

'Has Zhou Chi not arrived?' he asked as he threw down his briefcase on the sofa. He had not really intended to ask.

'He can't be found.' The Actress said, standing up respectfully. 'I've left messages for him all over the place telling him to come at once.'

Lu Hao-ran sat down and immediately felt more tired. He spent most of his whole life sitting and did not even want to stand up. He took off his spectacles, pinched the bridge of his nose and sighed deeply.

The Actress put a covered cup of green tea at his elbow and looked at him with solicitude. 'Would you like to do some *qigong* exercises?'

'I'll look at the video tape first.' He wanted her to massage his shoulders, but hesitated to ask.

He had told her to bring the tape at noon, so that he could watch it before the meeting; but the time had been changed. She had been waiting four hours.

It was a copy of an interview with Li Ke-ming, the most wanted man in China, put out by Fujian Television and broadcast over and over again in the seven provinces of the Southern Alliance. In the north it appeared to have been secretly banned. There had been no official announcement, so no one knew who had banned it, for what reason or even whether it really had been banned. It could not be seen in any public place, nor had it been mentioned at the top-level meeting Lu Hao-ran had just come from. It was as if the tape and the sensational news it contained, had never existed. Lu Hao-ran would have not have heard of it had the Actress not obtained a copy through her contacts with television people.

During the interview Li Ke-ming categorically denied assassinating anyone and accused Shen Di, who had been responsible for the security of the General Secretary of being an accessory. He claimed that the assassination had been planned and carried out the orders from the very top.

The interview had been designed to have the maximum impact. Li Ke-ming described the assassination very clearly and in vivid detail, his suspicions at the time, the behaviour of Shen Di, the murder of his friend and of the Director of the Police Academy. He answered questions, various documents and pictures were shown, and specialists were seen examining an imprint of Li Ke-ming's teeth, which proved his identity. His face was not shown, but in spite of the gauze mask he wore, his suffering, anger and sincerity were apparent.

But the fact remained, that apart from Li Ke-ming's testimony, there was no evidence, even against Shen Di, that would stand up in court. It was the best the Southern Alliance could do at the moment, but could hardly justify their formal declaration of autonomy that had just been announced on radio and television news. If the video had been widely diffused—even if the evidence was inadequate, the combination of the two would have a powerful psychological impact. What people want to believe is more important than proof. People nearly always take the side of the small man who has been hurt—or someone who chooses to play that role.

Li Ke-ming made a good impression. The mask inevitably led people to imagine what the damage was like (which may have been worse than the reality), but spared them the horror of seeing it. Sympathy was increased by the knowledge that his wife, far away in the northeast, had just given birth to a boy who had not yet seen his father. The producer in Fujian announced that the studio had sent people to Heilongjiang to film his wife and baby and a moving scene of both of them crying was shown. The footage was taken in a hurry, it was explained, because Li Ke-ming's home was under close surveillance. His family was obviously poor and it was snowing outside.

It was clear that Li Ke-ming had not known in advance about this footage. He had become very tense; his injured hands, in gloves, gripped the arms of his chair as if he wanted to crush them. He said nothing but the pain was visible in his silence.

The experienced producer did not interrupt, but allowed the spectators to share his grief. The cameras closed in on him. The red rims of his eyes could just be seen through the gauze mask.

Lu Hao-ran was not interested in this deliberately tear-jerking scene, but he believed what Li Ke-ming had said. For this minor security officer from the Three Gorges construction site to challenge Shen Di to a public confrontation was pointing the finger of accusation at his very nose! Not that Shen Di would be able to see this film. Not in China anyway, since he had vanished soon after the assassination. After the declaration of autonomy by the southern provinces his home, as well as those of his parents and some of his friends, had been simultaneously broken into. Nothing was taken and no one was hurt. The raiders had not been identified.

The southern provinces would certainly not be content with winning sympathy by means of the TV broadcast. They would want caste-iron proof against someone at the top, to justify their action.

Lu Hao-ran had known nothing. He had deliberately looked the other way of course. He should have realized, after being summoned by the Chairman, that something was in the wind. Wang Feng had asked him to arrange for Shen Di to be put in charge of the General Secretary's security, which he had taken to be a simple transfer and thought no more about it. He had never met Shen Di and had absolutely nothing to do with the assassination, but would anyone believe it?

When the film came to an end, the Actress asked 'Do you want to see it again?' Lu Hao-ran shook his head and looked gloomy. From now on, for his own sake, he must keep his eyes open. Not because he knew now who had ordered the hit—that had long been obvious to him—but because he might be the next. If Wang Feng thought he was an obstruction, he would not hesitate to get rid of him.

So he asked no questions. He was a puppet. When he was elected to the position, he had intended to stir himself and be a real General Secretary. Now he thought this ridiculous and pathetic: someone placed at the top by others could not become their master. Sometimes Wang Feng humoured him, as if throwing a bone to a chained dog. But he had lost the will even to hold on to the bone, let alone trying to control anything himself. The ashes of his ambition had been fanned into a few last flames of hope; they had now been utterly extinguished. Everything was easy to handle now that he had no will. He would call a meeting if Wang Feng wanted one, and would go to find out from him what it was for and how to conduct it.

The Fujian declaration had been made thirty-eight hours ago, followed by Guangdong, Hainan Island, Zhejiang, Jiangsu, Shanghai and finally Guangxi. Six hours ago the People's Congress of Jiangsu province had announced its support for transforming the republic into a federation. No other provinces had expressed an opinion, but popular support for a federation was obviously growing.

There was great unrest in the minority regions of Xinjiang and Tibet but also in Heilongjiang. Nearly a hundred million people from other provinces had moved there. Everyone was expecting great things of the Sino-Japanese Economic Cooperation Region. The unilateral decision of the new Beijing government to cancel the agreement had aroused fury and despair. After the Fujian declaration, many people began to think of demanding self-determination, separation from Beijing and cooperation with Japan. There had been demonstrations and illegal organizations had paraded with the banner of an autonomous government.

The provincial officials selected by Wang Feng were now in control, except in Fujian, where they had been arrested. The crisis in the country was extremely serious, and required determined action. But only at the meeting today had a decision been reached on what that action should be.

Lu Hao-ran drank his tea and absent-mindedly chewed the tea leaves that floated on the surface. The decision did not affect him in the least: he felt neither alarm nor responsibility for what might be a momentous decision. He was a mere spectator.

There had been much discussion in the meeting on the action the new government should take: political or military.

Those who supported a political solution argued that the crisis itself was political and economic. It could only be solved by relying on the unity of the people and on social stability. If force were used, the result would be civil war, involving great loss of life and destruction. It would be far better to use political pressure, negotiation, judicious compromise, to postpone the reckoning and avoid making things worse.

The main supporters of this line were the members of the standing committee of the Military Commission, including the deputy chairman, and the chairman of its political bureau.

Wang Feng played the part of a modest junior officer. He had thoroughly briefed Lu Hao-ran, who in addition to being General Secretary was also Chairman of the Military Commission. He said that the crisis was caused by the Party and government constantly backing down and relaxing control, out of fear of disunity and instability in the country. Consequently, it was losing all authority. The inevitable result would be the break-up of the country and the end of both the party and the state.

Lu Hao-ran proposed immediate military action against the Southern Alliance and the suppression of rebellion by military force. Martial law should be proclaimed throughout the country and the roots of trouble eliminated. 'If necessary we should not shrink from severe and rapid large-scale physical elimination.' Lu Hao-ran said this in an impassive tone of voice, but spread a cold cloud of apprehension over the meeting. All the members of the Political Bureau supported him, but only one member of the Military Commission.

Wang Feng said nothing—his views had just been expressed. His roots were in the army, but he had a far better control of the Political Bureau than of the Military Commission. He had organized the coup d'état in the Political Bureau single handed and had appointed every member of its Standing Committee; the big-shots in the Military Commission were the same as before. Wang Feng was a junior officer with the shortest service record of any of them. It was all upside down: the civilians were out for blood, the military were cautious and pacific. If Shi Ge had been a member of the Political Bureau, it would not have slipped so easily into the role of Wang Feng's mouthpiece, Lu Hao-ran reflected. It was not that he disapproved of tough measures: he had always thought that was the only way to save the country.

But he did not feel the same about a decision taken by him and the same decision taken and carried out by others. He was an indifferent bystander, but he wished there had been one member of the Political Bureau who could stand up to Wang Feng. Shi Ge would have done so, but whatever Lu Hao-ran could say, Wang Feng had flatly refused to allow Shi Ge on the Standing Committee of the Political Bureau.

Lu Hao-ran, whose former supporters had now gone over to Wang Feng, did not want only colourless yes-men under him. He remembered how Shi Ge had openly advocated disbanding the army. Of course that was no more than an intellectual's fantasy, but at least it showed his attitude towards the military. He had been dismissed as head of Unit Sixteen because he had personally organized opposition to reversal of the verdict and to the so-called pro-democracy movement. This increased Lu Hao-ran's respect for him. As for the 'Hundred-word Constitution', Lu Hao-ran had not understood a word of it and dismissed it as a utopian dream; but he recognized that Shi Ge had considerable standing in intellectual circles and to promote him would prove his own discernment. What was more, the promotion would earn Shi Ge's gratitude. If he applied his well-known gift for dealing with crises to the higher levels of government, who knows? He might become a valuable right-hand man.

Lu Hao-ran had tried to appoint one military man for each civilian, but it had not worked out as he had expected. Shi Ge had nothing but a title: his appearance at the Green Exhibition had lost him even that. He only escaped more severe punishment because Wang Feng wanted the government to give the impression of stability and calm.

Zhou Chi had also been promoted and instead of coming here every day as he used to, he now went to Wang Feng instead. Lu Hao-ran knew that he was 'collecting vital energy' for the Chairman. He appeared to keep nothing from Lu Hao-ran, but he trusted Zhou Chi less than before. There was always something hidden and mysterious behind that unruffled expression.

Lu Hao-ran felt as heavy as a stone statue and kept yawning. He had a tingling in his nose as if there were a sour cherry in each nostril. Everything looked fuzzy: perhaps there was something wrong with his eyes, or his spectacles. It was almost a week since Zhou Chi or any of his disciples had appeared, and he felt worse every day. He was sure it was the result of having no group *qigong* exercises.

Since starting group exercises with Zhou Chi, *qigong* had become even more important to him. The sense of attaining a wonderful new plane had become an essential part of his existence. At first, when Zhou Chi and disciples had taken the trouble—and considered it an honour—to come to his official residence to practise *qigong* with him, he had not yet felt this. Only in the last week, after they had disappeared, had he realized that he had become addicted to *qigong*. He was suffering withdrawal symptoms, making him want to scream and roll on the floor. Exercising by himself was no better than a glass of water for an alcoholic. He hated Zhou Chi now and wished he would come back at once.

'Will you let *me* help you, General Secretary?' the Actress asked diffidently.

Lu Hao-ran sighed, but already he felt more relaxed. The Actress was far less skilled than Zhou Chi and his disciples, but better than nothing. He sat in the correct position on the sofa and began to regulate his breathing. Though his eyes were half shut, he could see the Actress sitting opposite him on the floor like a beautiful statue of the Goddess of Mercy, her face red with excitement and pleasure because he had accepted her offer.

But no cool wind came and enveloped his body. Instead, random thoughts, worries and memories, like the contents of an overturned rubbish cart, invaded his mind. No sooner had he managed to concentrate on *qigong* than his thoughts slipped away to the Chairman—the strength of his authority, his relations with Wang Feng, his signature...

In the meeting that morning there had been a deadlock: some members wanted military action against the southern provinces, others a political solution. Wang Feng had said nothing. Each member of the standing committee of the Military Commission held strategic positions in the army. It would only take one of them to dig in his heels and the whole army might be paralysed. More than half them now opposed a military solution. At this critical moment a high-ranking officer entered and handed a sheet of paper to Wang Feng, who read it impassively, then passed it to the chairman, who read it several times before returning it to Wang Feng. 'All right, that's what we will do.' There was a hint of resignation in his voice, but no sign of disapproval.

Wang Feng put the sheet of paper into an overhead projector and the message was projected on to the wall, much enlarged. It had been typed on a voice-activated keyboard, which could recognize 'the Chairman's' voice, but no other, according to an explanatory note at the top of the page.

I have a few suggestions:

1. The Military Commission should obey the Political Bureau and faithfully serve the Party.
2. The unity of the country must come first and everything else take second place. If we have to fight we should not hold back.
3. To avoid a chain-reaction and a worsening of the situation, there should be nationwide mobilization.
4. I suggest that, in accordance with the regulations for emergencies, a wartime leadership command be set up, headed by Lu Hao-ran. Wang Feng should be appointed as his military assistant.

At the bottom there was 'the Chairman's' signature and the time—thirty minutes earlier. All eyes were fixed on the signature, enlarged ten times. The hand was shaky but it was unquestionably genuine, as familiar to all the higher ranks in the army as the palms of their own hands, for it had been on nearly all their promotion warrants, that had brought them step by step to the top. Though it had not been seen for a long time, it had lost none of its authority. It had the effect of a huge hand smoothing over differences and was accepted without hesitation or resentment. The military commanders who had been opposing the Political Bureau were now glad to become faithful servants of the Party once again.

The signature seemed to grower bigger and bigger and when Lu Hao-ran slightly opened his eyes the Actress seemed to be dancing inside it. He tried to stand up but his body refused to move. A smouldering fire in his mind suddenly lit up, as if fanned by a bellows; the scorching heat flashed through all the veins in his body. The signature, now enormous, seemed at any moment about to fall and crush him into the fire. Suddenly a breath of cool wind flowed over him; refreshing spring water flowed into his mind. The burning signature melted away. His crimson body relaxed and became as transparent as glass. The fire was transformed into dense vegetation, that instantly produced a mass of dewy flowers. Then his eyes opened, the chains on his wrists and feet soundlessly disappeared. In only a few seconds his body was filled with vitality, and he knew that Zhou Chi must have returned. He was quietly standing in the doorway, his hand gradually drawing something back towards himself.

Lu Hao-ran could not move his lips and made no sound. Only one step further! He felt an inexpressible terror. A little longer and he would have fallen into a terrible abyss; if Zhou Chi had not arrived at the critical moment and helped him, he could have been burned by the fire and transformed into a frenzied wild beast or a frozen corpse. He said no word of thanks. There was no point. His shirt was damp with cold sweat and he could not move a muscle on his face.

'You must not exercise with the General Secretary when I am not here,' said Zhou calmly to the Actress.

She had no idea what had happened. 'You scared me stiff, General Secretary!' No one answered.

The *yin* and the *yang* had to be in harmony, but the exercise just now had produced the opposite effect: they had mutually repelled each other and were heading towards extremes.

'I have not seen you for a long time,' said Lu Hao-ran looking indifferently at Zhou Chi.

'I haven't had a moment. More than ten provinces in two days…' It was difficult to see whether he was tired or flattered.

'Has it really been so hard?' Lu Hao-ran said, a little sourly. Zhou Chi had told him that the 'collection of energy' had become a big operation because it was an opportunity to gain control over the Armed Police. Lu Hao-ran had guessed that it was not essential for the survival of the Chairman, considering Zhou Chi's ability; but a kind of bargaining counter and a clever way of getting a hold over Wang Feng.

'Collecting energy does not need very much effort, but getting the Armed Police into *our* hands' (he stressed the word almost imperceptibly) 'needs much more,' Zhou Chi replied.

'By the time the Chairman has recovered we won't have got our hands on anything!'

'He won't get better,' said Zhou Chi. 'He's a dead man, except that they keep his heart and breathing going.'

'Can a dead man sign his name?' Lu Hao-ran did not conceal his suspicion. He had himself ordered Zhou Chi to prevent the Chairman from dying—but not to bring him back to health. If that should happen

Wang Feng would become even more powerful and there would be no chance of getting out of his clutches. The best solution was to keep the Chairman between life and death and wait for an opportunity to swing things in the direction he wanted. But Zhou Chi's absence had aroused his suspicions, and the sight of the Chairman's signature increased them.

Zhou Chi smiled and took from the desk a special kind of brush used only by important officials for signing documents.

'You sign,' he said, handing the brush and a piece of paper to the Actress, who signed her name in bewilderment and with a flourish.

'Lie down on the sofa.'

Zhou Chi placed his hand on several specific points on her body and the Actress fell into a deep sleep-like state. 'She is now in the same state as the Chairman,' he said. 'Only her heart and breathing are functioning.' To prove it he shook her and called her name a few times. There was no reaction. He propped her up. 'Now her position is the same.'

'Watch.' He opened his right hand and held it in the air above the Actress's arm and moved it back and forwards from her shoulder to her hand, stopped then raised it above her right hand holding the brush. As he did so the Actress's hand was lifted up as if by invisible threads and guided to the paper. Then his left hand covering her temple gradually became a reddish colour and her hand slowly moved involuntarily, making her signature with the same flourish as before.

'Can you tell the difference?' he asked handing the paper to Lu Hao-ran. They were identical. He realized that this performance was designed to show that it was not easy to forge a signature. The most skilful forgery would not pass the security bureau's computers: each signature had to match the original in more than a hundred details. The Chairman had been unconscious but the nervous functions connecting with signing were the same as before. The rest was simple. The text was pieced together from previous recordings of the Chairman's voice.

This trick enabled Wang Feng to control the destiny of China, in the name of the Chairman, while he himself appeared to be even handed and reasonable, keeping in the background, and reaping the greatest possible advantage.

Backing the Political Bureau meant backing himself; by using military connections he strengthened the position of the army in order to promote his own interests. He had mollified the various power factions within the army, making them so drunk with the prospect of increased power that they no longer needed to squabble. At the same time he had increased the power of the man who controlled the Military Commission—himself.

However, the most important result of 'the Chairman's suggestions' was that it provided the basis for a wartime leadership, that had supreme power over the Party, the government and the army; that could declare war or end it; that could change the law, dismiss the government and declare martial law. The fate of the Chinese people had been put in the hands of a few men, an inefficient bureaucratic system replaced by a dictatorship.

Such emergency measures had never been used before, and very few people understood their full implication. In theory Wang Feng's role was 'to assist' Lu Hao-ran; he was 'number two,' but Lu Hao-ran being only a puppet, he was in fact 'number one.'

Formerly, it was only possible to combine Party and government functions in a roundabout way. Now as wartime leader, he could legally control everything.

'It was Wang Feng who got you to do it?' Lu Hao-ran asked, with a sidelong glance at Zhou Chi.

What he really meant was 'Why are you working for Wang Feng?' If Zhou had not suggested that he could get the moribund Chairman's signature by means of *qigong*. Wang Feng, with all his power, would never have thought of such an extraordinary thing. Lu Hao-ran felt a little jealous.

'If Wang Feng wants war,' Zhou Chi said, 'it's best to let him have it. As long as things are calm we continue to be his slaves: our chance will come only if things start to go to pieces. You see, it's your interests I have in mind.'

There was something hypnotic about Zhou Chi's eyes and Lu Hao-ran's anger dissipated like smoke in the night. This man's demonic fascination was irresistible. In his presence, fixed by those eyes, Lu Hao-ran was like someone with no thoughts, only a white emptiness, eager for Zhou Chi's orders to fill the void.

'I must have gone to sleep,' The Actress woke up, and looked at Zhou Chi in embarrassment.

'We'll help the General Secretary to exercise now,' he told her, sweeping Lu Hao-ran with his luminous eyes.

He placed his hands on the Actress's back. 'Now put out your tongue.'

'Cover her tongue with yours, General Secretary.' His eyes had become more intense.

A weak signal of understanding reached Lu Hao-ran's consciousness: this is how he gets me under his domination, and keeps me prisoner by means of *qigong*. Gradually he strips me of my dignity, the only weapon I have against him. When I obey him and put my tongue into that woman's mouth in his presence, he is trampling on my self-respect. I submit and allow myself to be humiliated. I become a disciple and he will control me, not only in *qigong*....

The power flowed into his body from Zhou Chi's hand on his back with an inexpressible warmth and strength; the weak voice of reason disappeared completely.... In the vast expanse of an undulating sea, the Actress's tongue became a pulsating cowry shell, full of cool, sweet juice. .

Zhou Chi's hands pressed their bodies together....

Shandong Peninsula: Naval base 201

The commander's cabin was minute, very narrow and less than two yards long. But Ding Da-hai knew the submarine and everything in it so well that he could almost see it gliding through an ocean trench, following an alien ship or rocking slightly in an undersea current. At the moment it was resting motionless on fine sand at the bottom of the sea.

He remembered the interminable ten days and nights twelve years ago, submerged in the South China Sea, near a Vietnamese naval base. Now he was waiting near his own naval base and his mission was much more secret; the submarine must be kept not only from foreign eyes but from Chinese eyes as well.

He switched to the computer screen which showed satellites that were above at present. Every hour an average of thirty-three military satellites passed overhead, many of them about this time. A British satellite was about to pass over, followed two minutes twenty-six seconds later by a Russian satellite. Three minutes later an American one would come over from a different direction, then Japanese, Australian and French.

Spy satellites could detect the presence of a nuclear submarine underwater from the heat given off by the reactor. But Chinese naval scientists had developed a highly efficient cooling fluid which could absorb an enormous amount of heat. A complex computerized control system ensured that the cooling liquid emitted by the reactor was always at the ambient sea temperature. Ding Da-hai had been assured that even at full speed a satellite directly above it would not be able to detect the submarine. But a defect in the cooling system had been discovered. It was the first time out of dock and at the height of satellite activity overhead. Ding Da-hai was taking no risks, so the submarine lay on the seabed close to the main drainage duct of the naval base, where any emission of heat would not be noticed.

After the lock-gates of the dry-dock had opened, the submarine emerged from its huge shell like a moth from its chrysalis, and came to life. All tests had been completed and it was eight days since it had last returned to the secret dock for adjustments.

Ding Da-hai loved the submarine like a partner for life, clever and responsive. In addition to the two regular low-noise propeller screws aft, the submarine was equipped with a computer controlled system of water propulsion which enabled it to move slowly but silently underwater with no risk of detection by the most sophisticated sonar equipment.

Suddenly a metallic sound from the galley startled Ding Da-hai. In dock he would not have noticed it, but at sea it was different. All surfaces were covered with rubber, the crew wore rubber-soled shoes, tools were made of plastic if possible and everyone whispered. Silence was the most important rule—a matter of success or failure. For Ding Da-hai it was already instinctive. He enjoyed the silence of submarine life. Any sound had a physical effect on him. This time it was more important than ever to avoid discovery by anyone: that was Wang Feng's solemn and imperative order. Everything would depend on it. He went to investigate.

The sound in the galley was caused by a tin falling on to the stove. A junior lieutenant from the engine room who had just come off duty snapped to attention, but did not dare meet Ding Da-hai's eye. The cook had been emptying the contents of a tin into a pan fixed to the stove and his hand had slipped. There were no movable cooking utensils and no need to cook. Everything came out of tins and only had to be warmed up. The lieutenant had just spent five hours in a diving suit outside the submarine making an adjustment of some kind, so the cook had broken the rules and added two eggs.

Ding Da-hai turned off the stove and said almost inaudibly: 'You are both forbidden to speak for forty eight hours.' The offenders came to attention to acknowledge the sentence. Being forbidden to speak for two days was a severe punishment when there was little else to do to pass the time.

Near the naval base this kind of noise was far too frequent, and unlikely to attract attention. Those fancy naval men ashore would probably not realize where the sound came from, Ding Da-hai said to himself. But if it had happened outside Chinese waters, there might have been serious consequences.

He told the cook to prepare a 'sick list' meal for the lieutenant, which was somewhat more palatable than the usual food.

Shortly afterwards he felt a vibration from the special watch that Wang Feng had given him. It was strong enough to wake him up at night and he wore it permanently on his wrist, even in the shower. The signal meant that there was a message for him on the receiver.

He returned to his cabin and saw a red light pulsating in the coded lock of a steel drawer on his desk, showing that a message had been received. Unless the red light showed, even if he knew the code the drawer would not open. Once the code was confirmed, the fireproof, explosion-proof steel drawer opened automatically.

It contained a radio receiver that accepted only signals from Wang Feng's transmitter, and printed out a message. On a thin strip of paper: *Go immediately to the 51 kilometres post on the Qingdao-Qingshan road and wait for me.*

When he surfaced in his power-assisted scuba suit and removed his mask, the cold wind struck his face. The sky was full of stars. He took deep breaths of the moist sea wind. He was accustomed now to the coffin-like peace of the submarine and its stale air; but since childhood he had spent most of his time on a fishing boat and often dreamt of the wide sea and the sky, the shooting stars and the storms.

The road passed close to the sea at the point chosen by Wang Feng. Ding Da-hai hid his diving equipment among the rocks and climbed up the cliff. He could see the 51 kilometre signpost, white and eerie in the starlight. Beyond a low hill, the sky was lit up by the lights of the naval base. The sight warmed his heart: he could see the village where his family lived—the first house on the eastern side. In dreams too he often saw these lights: like seeing a lighthouse through the periscope.

A car without lights approached silently along the indistinct road. Ding Da-hai did not notice it until it was almost alongside. He knew that Wang Feng was obsessive about precision: if he said he would be at the 51 kilometres post, he would stop exactly there. It was one of his qualities that Ding Da-hai admired and was fascinated by—it was part of his demonic power—and Ding Da-hai unconsciously copied him. When he saluted, he was exactly behind the post.

The car door opened automatically. 'Get in please,' in Wang Feng's masterful but courteous voice. Only a constellation of coloured instrument lights was visible. There was a low sound of electric motors and metal blinds came down inside the widows. A faint light came on in the car. They shook hands.

It was not the first time that he had been in this car—an expensive mobile office, very much in Wang Feng's style. It was an elongated limousine, with the unnecessary seats removed. It had a desk, folding bed, refrigerator, as well as an impressive array of incomprehensible electronic equipment. It made Ding Da-hai feel that he was on a visit to the future. He had worked under Wang Feng for four years and knew that he was mad about science and technology. Since he had the power to get anything done merely by lifting a finger, he chose to use complex and expensive equipment to do it for him; but no one could accuse him of preferring leisure to working. Much of his success had been thanks to this craze of his.

The electronic clock in the car showed the time in all different parts of the world. Wang Feng looked at Beijing time and said: 'I'll give you three minutes to tell me what you think about the technical trials.'

Before Ding Da-hai could start a buzzer signalled an incoming telephone message. Wang Feng switched off all communications. Ding Da-hai had only three words to say, 'All went well.'

The terse answer pleased Wang Feng. He already knew everything about the tests and only wanted to assure himself about the commander's state of mind.

'The operation starts tomorrow,' he said as if mentioning a small matter in passing.

Ding Da-hai had taken part in all sorts of operations in the Navy. This one was different: it had no code name, no written schedule, no documents and no coordination with anyone else. When Wang Feng said 'the operation', Ding Da-hai knew that it meant making this nameless submarine disappear into the ocean and remain hidden at all costs. It was to have no contact with the outside world, nor accept any orders except those that would arrive in the steel drawer in the commander's cabin. Without orders to the contrary, the submarine was to remain at the bottom of the sea.

This had been decided before the construction of the submarine. A year's provisions had been stored aboard as well as desalination and oxygen generation equipment. Ding Da-hai did not know what the purpose of the operation was. Wang Feng only told him that the submarine must be capable of remaining a year at the bottom of the sea. Not a word more. Ding Da-hai said 'Yes sir!'

A coloured map of the world appeared on a computer screen. Wang Feng made a series of dots on the Chinese mainland, from each of which he drew circles with a radius of 6800 km. In the Pacific he also drew an irregular wandering line.

'The submarine must not operate outside these lines,' said Wang Feng, making the map zoom in on the coastal cities within the semicircles. Islands, ocean currents, and marine trenches were all clearly marked. The exact position for every change of direction in the Pacific was accurately given. Wang Feng handed a print-out of all these to Ding Da-hai.

Six thousand eight hundred kilometres was the range of the nuclear missiles which the submarine carried. As long as the submarine remained inside the area covered by the semi-circles, any of these targets was in range. It was perfectly clear that this was a threat not to foreign countries but to China. But as usual Ding Da-hai only said 'Yes sir,' as if he had not thought of this.

Wang Feng looked closely at Ding Da-hai for a moment. 'You know about the present situation in our country?' He had never spoken like this before, unlike his blunt and incisive orders: he seemed to want to talk. The commander could not say that his knowledge was up to date; the submarine had a sensitive receiver on board which could receive signals from nearly the whole world. He had heard reports of the fighting in China, and had listened carefully, but only as a military man, in order to have in his head a precise map of the operations. He did not want to bother his head with political squabbles: no one could make out what the truth was anyway. If every soldier made his own political judgement the army would not know whose orders to follow and would become useless.

'A soldier does not need to understand, only to obey,' Ding Da-hai replied. Wang Feng looked pleased.

'The break-away southern provinces will get nowhere and will soon be eliminated. But the situation is difficult and complicated and at a time like this can change very rapidly. The Party and government will use all possible means—including nuclear attack—to preserve the unity of our country and protect the interests of our people. Your duty is to attack without hesitation wherever you are ordered to attack.'

'Yes sir.'

Wang Feng produced a small metal box on a fine chain. He turned the miniature combination lock a few times and the box sprang open: inside was an integrated circuit the size of a thumb-nail. 'This is the coded circuit that starts the arming sequence of the missiles; it is the only way of bypassing the safety device on the warheads. It is the key for launching the missiles.' Wang Feng closed the box and handed it to Ding Da-hai.

'The code to operate this device is your date of birth. You must always wear this round your neck. You can only receive orders from my transmitter. I only hope we will never have to use it. But if I send you the order it will be the decision of the Standing Committee of the Central Military Commission. There must be no mistake. Understood?'

'Understood.'

'Good.' Then Wang Feng became almost kindly. 'Before we part I have a small gift for you.' He handed an envelope to Ding Da-hai. It was an ordinary brown-paper envelope with the name 'Central Military

Commission' printed on it in red. Ding Da-hai did not quite know what to do.

'Open it.' Wang Feng encouraged him, looking at him through half-closed eyes.

It was a pair of Senior Captain's epaulettes. The commander was dumbstruck, and his face became bright red. His immediate reaction was to stand up and salute but he only banged his head against the roof of the car.

Wang Feng smiled. 'Let me put them on you.'

Ding Da-hai owed everything to Wang Feng and worshipped him. He had come out of prison in the United States with a heart of ice, was arrested by the Chinese Military Attaché and sent back to China, where he was reprimanded, interrogated, humiliated, laughed at and discharged. Instead of being a favoured, talented officer in the navy he had become dog shit. Wang Feng had taken him in hand, and had given him work, salary, somewhere to live and most important of all an officer's self-respect. When he was appointed commander of the submarine and restored to his former rank of lieutenant-colonel, he had wept. The navy was his spiritual home, even if he only had a mine-sweeper to command. Wang Feng had given him the diamond in the navy's crown! The dream of a lifetime. A submarine with forty nuclear warheads which could paralyse any nuclear power in the world. He had the key round his neck, and would soon have two bars and four stars shining on his epaulettes. For Wang Feng he would go through fire and water and die a thousand deaths! But no words came. The light reflected on his spectacles hid the tears in his eyes. When Wang Feng removed his Lieutenant's epaulettes and attached the new ones, he could hardly control his impulse to kneel at his feet.

As Wang Feng's car left silently and disappeared into the distance, Ding Da-hai stood at attention, long after there was nothing to be seen. Several minutes passed. The car would be carried in a special helicopter to Beijing. The situation there was very tense and he felt proud and honoured that Wang Feng had come specially to see him.

Before leaving Wang Feng had reconnected his communications network and there were all sorts of sounds of bustle and urgency. Driving back, and even in the air, Wang Feng would be dealing with all sorts of military affairs and other business. In an inner pocket of his Lieutenant-General's uniform, there was a transmitter the size of a packet of cigarettes. It was the only one in the world that could contact the submarine. It could use the radio network anywhere in China to transmit by satellite to the submarine wherever it might be: an invisible thread linking Wang Feng to Ding Da-hai and his submarine.

Under the dark expanse of the sea lay Ding Da-hai's alter ego, silent and unseen. Behind him, where the sky was lit up, was his own harbour—his warm and welcoming home. Tomorrow he would set out on a long and lonely voyage. Sailors as they cast off always look back to their home port. He had intended to look for a last time, from where he was, at the lights shining from the windows in his home. Instead he strode straight to it, through the reeds that swayed and rustled in the wind.

Partly for reasons of security the crew of the submarine all lived in houses specially built for them. Ding Da-hai had chosen mostly former fishermen like himself, thinking that young gentlemen from the cities would be unable to put up with the hardships of life at the bottom of the sea.

Through a gap in the pink curtains (made for his wedding) he watched the evening ritual of foot washing: his son's feet. like two white fish playing in the black pottery foot-bath, next to his wife's.

He heard the sound of childish laughter, and heard his son ask where 'Ba-ba' was. His wife looked anxious and careworn.

'Ba-ba came to see me again last night.'

'You were dreaming.'

'He said he would take me fishing.'

During the holidays the boy had asked him several times, but the submarine was nearly finished and he had no time. Ding Da-hai felt guilty. His son had not forgotten... He longed to let him jump up into his arms, to show him his new epaulettes. As he moved a little to take a last look at his wife and his son, the peak of his cap brushed against the cold glass of the window.

'Who's there ?' His wife called out nervously.

He moved back from the window, and saw the curtains drawn open. He saw his son climb up on the window-sill, his mother's arm around him. The light above made her eyes look like dark hollows. He felt a sudden sadness and a leaden foreboding. As he backed away something got caught on his sleeve, but he dared not stop to disentangle it.

'Baba!' he heard his son call—but perhaps it was his imagination. The sound came from far away, but very clearly.

On the hillock he turned for the last time. There was no light in the window, but his wife and son must still be looking out. Perhaps their eyes met in the darkness...

In the light from the naval base he found that there was a hook caught in the sleeve of his uniform, and a nylon line, tied to his son's fishing rod—just a piece of bamboo.

Fuzhou

The brown arrows on the map, representing units of the Beijing army, all pointed south. The largest was in the neighbouring province, pointing straight at Fuzhou. Facing it, in the Wuyi mountains there was only a thin red line: Fujian troops defending the pass—like a grasshopper trying to keep a cat at bay.

Though it was the beginning of winter Huang Shi-ke's whiskey glass was full of ice-cubes. His brain felt as if is was on fire, but drinking ice-cold whiskey was like pouring oil on it.

On the western side of the map, yellow arrows and threads marked the northern defensive positions of the Guangdong army. It was a fairly strong army but its purpose was to defend Guangdong, not Fujian. Blue dots in Anhui and Jiangxi, the two provinces north of Fujian, marked the position of the forces of Nanjing Area Command—which was still neutral.

The strategy of the Beijing army was simple: to make straight for Fuzhou, the centre of the Alliance and the least capable of military resistance, while avoiding other military action. Once Fuzhou fell the effect on morale would be enough to make the other provinces capitulate, cause a split in the Guangdong command and bring the Nanjing command to its senses.

So far the scale of military operations was limited. Beijing was relying mainly on political pressure, scheming and manipulation; while consolidating its forces and only going into action if there was armed opposition.

Parts of other provinces had joined the autonomous movement for reasons of their own. The local political heavyweight might have ambitions to make himself a 'little emperor' with his own domain, or perhaps wanted to be associated with the wealthy south. The money provided by the Southern Foundation, started by industrial and commercial interests in the Alliance, also played a role. It had only to put a few cases of banknotes in front of such personages and they would join at once. Not that they would count for much when the Beijing troops arrived. They would either surrender at once or make themselves scarce. Nevertheless, they would possibly hold up the advance of the Beijing armies, anxious to consolidate their rear before attacking Fuzhou.

There was silence in the room and a strong smell of whiskey and cigarette smoke. The seven Chiefs of Staff continually corrected the operations map. The enemy was advancing irresistibly, but without haste. Sooner or later Fuzhou would be like a turtle in a jar. Whether it was because of the whiskey or the lighting, Huang Shi-ke felt that the faces of all those in the room looked black and sinister. He held out his glass to Bai Ling—he was drinking more and more the last few days—she filled it, mostly with water. She was the calmest person in the room.

There was no question now of playing for time. At midnight tonight, the thirty days time limit set by the Nanjing command, would be up. The Southern Alliance had not succeeded in finding evidence of Beijing's complicity in the assassination. Nanjing would abandon neutrality and recognize that the Southern Alliance was in rebellion. There were almost three hours left, but Huang Shi-ke felt he was already a condemned man, three hours from death.

The only valid proof would be Shen Di himself; but he had vanished without trace. Fifty three teams had been sent to track him and had come back empty-handed. They had found out that Shen Di had no friends and no contact with relatives and must have gone abroad. That is all. He had been trained from an early age for high level intelligence work, had travelled abroad and could speak five languages fluently. In twenty years he had woven a world-wide network of contacts, at all levels of society. He was a citizen of the world, where he was like a fish in water and could hide more easily than in China.

The difficulty in carrying out a proper search in China (except for the South) and abroad, made Huang Shi-ke realize the weakness of provincial governments in comparison with the Central government. The absence of specialized personnel, built up and trained over decades, of intelligence services, foreign affairs organizations, contacts in foreign countries, of an adequate communication system. Huang Shi-ke had to rely on the provincial security departments and old hands in the army, who seemed able but had a limited vision, like frogs in a well. They were quite helpless in anything which had an international dimension. Even to find Burundi or Jamaica on the map would take them ages, let alone lay their hands on Shen Di. But then, Huang Shi-ke thought sadly, I'm only a frog in a well as far as politics is concerned.

Blue is normally a peaceful, tranquilizing colour, but the blue lights representing the garrisons of the Nanjing Command, spread all over the Southeastern region made Huang Shi-ke think of the eyes of a pack of wolves. The ambitions of the Alliance seemed ridiculous. Two provinces and the city of Shanghai had not dared to make a move because the Nanjing Command had not yet decided whether to support it or not. Fujian had had no choice. But what was the point of the defences in the Wuyi mountains if the whole province was dotted with Nanjing Command garrisons? Huang Shi-ke knew exactly how many tanks, rockets, artillery and aircraft each blue dot on the map represented. As soon as Commander Bai gave the order claws and teeth would replace the wolves' eyes, and Fujian would be torn to pieces.

The communications centre in the next room had been trying to contact the Nanjing HQ for the last thirty days; but it seemed to be a silent and impregnable fortress—nothing came out and nothing went in. Emissaries had been sent there, but were turned away by the sentries. Telephone calls were not put through, telegrams disappeared like stones in the sea. But ten days after Liu Ya-ji sent ten million *yuan* to the commander of a Nanjing garrison near Fuzhou, an extremely severe reprimand had been received by telephone from HQ in Nanjing forbidding any underhand tricks, otherwise neutrality would be ended. The only hope now was to beg for an extension.

Huang Shi-ke's glass was empty and he wanted a refill. Instead Bai Ling deftly removed it and to counteract the effects of alcohol gave him a herbal remedy, without which he would never have got through the last two days with a clear head. She, rather than his wife, was always by his side now, almost every minute of the day.

Thanks to her he seemed sober—on the surface at least—and was neatly dressed, in contrast to the untidy, drunk and stupid members of his staff.

When he heard a shout from communications room 'Nanjing Command is on the line,' he hurried out, almost choking on his herbal tablet and knocking a glass of water out of Bai Ling's hand.

Direct communication was about to start. Huang Shi-ke waved everyone out of the room except Bai Ling, who wiped his mouth and straightened his collar, then quickly moved out of sight. The handsome, arrogant Deputy Chief of Staff of the Nanjing Command appeared on the screen.

'How are you Governor?' The use of his old title showed that Nanjing did not recognize his election as Prime Minister of the autonomous government. But it was no time to complain about that . . .

'We are now sure that Shen Di is hiding abroad.' Huang Shi-ke replied.

'That must be the case, even if there is no proof. And now?'

'We are pulling out all stops. The international agency we have employed is searching all over the world. We have organized special units in all the services, which are on permanent stand-by, and have agreements with certain governments...'

'But you don't know where he is, do you?

'However...'

'Do you?'

'That's right.' Huang Shi-ke was trembling with fear, but it was essential to speak naturally. 'Frankly, Major-general, could you find an ordinary looking man of average height, somewhere in the world, in only thirty days?'

'I'm sorry Governor, this is not the time for such questions. I am not concerned with your problems.'

'Give us another ten days, Major-general.' Huang Shi-ke was perfectly aware that even with a hundred extra days they would find no trace of Shen Di, but a slight delay was better than putting one's head on the block straightaway.

'Impossible,' the Deputy Chief of Staff said bluntly. 'We gave you thirty days and were accused of criminal disobedience by Beijing. There are still two hours and a half to go. If you do not produce your proof, at midnight you must surrender unconditionally. Otherwise our troops will go into action and any resistance will be dealt with.'

'Why not allow us to surrender now?' Huang Shi-ke asked.

'We are soldiers and mean exactly what we say. Before midnight we do not consider you as rebels, so why ask you to surrender? Until midnight then. Goodbye.' He did not smile. His tone was arrogant and brutal. Huang Shi-ke sat dazed and silent until Bai Ling took his hand.

He followed her mechanically outside into the fresh air. A confusion of dark clouds swept in from the sea, was lit up here and there by the beams of anti-aircraft searchlights. Huang Shi-ke's HQ in Fuzhou was on a small island in the Min River which had been a tourist attraction. On it there was an ancient wall and inside fortifications and defence installations. It was very close to Fuzhou, but cut off on all sides by the river and easy to defend against surprise attacks.

Bai Ling took his arm and they went onto the town wall. She said nothing, apparently wanting him to relax in the night air. Apart from those directly concerned very few people understood—or perhaps wanted to understand—that the crisis that was imminent.

Fuzhou was lit up as usual and the sounds and music coming from the bars and discos on the riverside made it easy to imagine that the sweeping beams of the anti-aircraft searchlights were fireworks or stage spotlights.

But at midnight paratroops and airborne vehicles might be dropping through the clouds. The order would be given to the rocket launchers, the anti-aircraft guns, machine guns all to open fire. Or would the paratroops float down unmolested to subjugate us?

Gunboats patrolling the approaches to the island swept past. One of them came rapidly through the only passage through the underwater defences to refuel. The island was well-defended, but since Fuzhou itself was not…

What next? The question was never out of Huang Shi-ke's mind.

From a military point of view there was no hope of effective resistance. That left only the people of Fujian. They supported autonomy and had begun to organize. If at midnight every road, railway and airfield were blocked, the garrisons surrounded by masses of people, perhaps the Nanjing attack could be stopped. For two or three days possibly, Huang Shi-ke thought. But to expect people to hold out longer with no supplies or back-up... If the Nanjing troops executed one or two of them on the spot, the rest would become as docile as lambs or mice.

He looked at Bai Ling. She was calmly gazing at the riverside. How young and beautiful she looked. How much better to be here with her than the hasty intimacies of his office. If one day he was cut down from his high office, could he hold on to her? He decided that whatever happened he would not flee to Guangzhou: he would be no more than a guest at table or a homeless dog. In any case how long could Guangdong hold out?

A seaplane covered with camouflage netting was waiting at the jetty, its fuel tank full and the pilot in the cockpit, ready to take off. To go abroad was the last choice and perhaps the most realistic. But where? The speed and range of the seaplane being limited, it would be best to cross the straits to Taiwan. Six months earlier, when the Kuomintang was still in power there, this would have been easy. But the policy of the present government of Taiwan towards the Mainland was one of mutual non-interference: and avoiding anything which would alienate the Beijing government. Relations were far less hostile now than they had ever been. Since Fujian's declaration of independence, Taiwan had renounced any public or secret contact with Fuzhou and had warned the Taiwan people not to give assistance in any form to the independent alliance. So Huang Shi-ke had no hope of even being allowed to pass through. He might even be handed over to Beijing.

He would have to fly to the Philippines, buy Philippine nationality (it would cost US$100,000), and go to the West. Not that he liked the idea: not a single Western country had offered him asylum in spite of his four million dollars in the bank and his apartment in Los Angeles. But to die wearing a Filipino hat would be disrespectful to his ancestors.

'Prime Minister.' Huang Shi-ke was startled by the voice behind Bai Ling. His arm around her suddenly stiffened. He turned and saw Li Ke-ming's mask, grey in the darkness. 'Have you got something on you that emits a radio signal?' Li asked.

Huang Shi-ke was completely bewildered.

'The observation post upstream has detected a radio signal coming from the island, in that direction.' Li Ke-ming pointed to a place where he and Bai Ling had been standing not long ago.

Huang Shi-ke shook his head. 'That's impossible. How could I have a thing like that?'

'The young lady then?' Li Ke-ming's face could not be seen, but his intensity was palpable.

Bai Ling smiled. 'Do you want to search me?'

Li Ke-ming was like a statue. Bai Ling continued to smile, but her arm around Huang Shi-ke transmitted her fear.

Li Ke-ming said nothing and left. Could the signal have come from Bai Ling? Huang Shi-ke wondered. She still snuggled up to him and once more he felt that there was something mysterious about her. She had warned him not to go to Beijing and said it was intuition. He did not ask about a radio signal. In another hour and a half it would all be over and nothing would matter any more.

He asked Bai Ling to get in touch with Liu Ya-ji and tell him to come back to the island before midnight. If Huang Shi-ke was to fly to the Philippines he would have to rely on Liu Ya-ji's contacts there. The plane could not leave until he arrived. Passing by Li Ke-ming's command centre he stopped for a moment. He felt he had nothing more to do, but was surprised at the amount of activity going on.

Li Ke-ming, responsible for the defence of the island, was simultaneously talking by radio telephone to the radar station, the patrol boats and the anti-aircraft unit, while watching the screens of each observation post. A cigarette was stuck in a small hole in his mask, which made his head look rather like a bomb with the fuse already lit. Huang felt that this man ought to be entrusted with more important work. He was the only man there whose work was faultless. He was not necessarily more able than anyone else, but he had no thought for himself. He considered himself as already dead, had no feelings and no thought for the future. But whatever he put his hand to, he did not let go, it became his purpose in life. He ought to put his hand to more important things, but it was already too late.

A loud incoming message drowned Li Ke-ming's voice. 'Observation Post 'number three' reporting....something floating down river...narrow, four or five metres long and low in the water....about 150 metres away....current is 0.9 metres per second. Can't see it clearly now...'

Li Ke-ming gave his orders. 'Searchlights one to eighteen: direct your beams upstream, don't leave any areas of darkness. Patrol boats three and five proceed at once to intercept the floating object. The rest, keep to your stations and keep your wits about you.'

One after the other, the searchlights lit up the surface of the river.

Two patrol boats raced upstream, bows high out of the water, a white turbulence behind.

'I can see it now. It's a fisherman's boat, a sampan.' This from No. 3 observation post.

'What's in the boat?' Li Ke-ming.

'Nothing, it looks...No. There is something, a bale of some kind...'

'Launches 3 and 5. Check there's no explosives on board. Follow the usual procedure.'

In spite of the searchlights visibility was poor. Li Ke-ming' eyes remained glued to the screen, as if the whole island was about to be blown out of the water. He stuck another cigarette in his mouth.

Later a report came in saying that the patrol boats had secured the sampan, 650 metres from the island. There had been no explosion. There was a confusion of voices: 'There's only a sack...poke it with an oar...there's something soft inside...not so hard... Steady. I'll go aboard first....There's a fuse sticking out of the sack!.....it's nothing....If you're not worried about being blow sky high I am!'

An exclamation of surprise, then 'There's someone in the sack!

'Dead or alive?'

'Alive. He's breathing, but unconscious.'

'Search him and the sampan,' said Li Ke-ming and ordered out another patrol boat to join the two others at once.

After a pause, 'Nothing else in the boat. Nothing on the man except a small tube with a label on it.'

'What's on the label?'

'Just one word: "sniff".'

'Repeat that.'

Another screen lit up. The communications launch had joined the others. All eyes were fixed on the screen, which became gradually clearer. All the boats brought their lights to bear on the scene. Several members of the crews were kneeling in the sampan, which was tossing slightly in the current. The video camera zoomed in as a limp, well-dressed man was pulled out of the thick felt sack.

'Focus on his face,' said Li Ke-ming.

Someone supported the unconscious man's shoulders, another lifted his head by the hair.

For a long time Li Ke-ming was silent: he seemed to have turned into stone, and Huang Shi-ke did not understand. He had never seen him so shaken. Even when talking about the imminent attack by Nanjing he had pointed at the ammunition cases and said calmly, 'When that's finished so are we.'

He turned. There was something extraordinary about the mask and the mutilated face behind it. A thin wisp of smoke rose from the shapeless stub of a cigarette stuck in his mask, from behind which came the soft, almost inaudible, portentous name: 'Shen Di'.

Huang Shi-ke was dumbstruck, his mouth fell open.

Li Ke-ming spat out the stub of his cigarette, like a bullet. 'Bring him back straight away, with the greatest care. If anything goes wrong you'll all be in big trouble.'

Five launches, each carrying two floodlights, went upstream to escort the others in. The river was lit up like daylight and surrounded the patrol boat. On the video screen in the command centre Li Ke-ming could see that Shen Di had been transferred to a steam launch and was surrounded by several armed members of the crew, two giving him artificial respiration and the others standing guard.

Shen Di was brought in. There was no sign of any wound, but he appeared to be in a coma. His breathing and pulse were normal, but the doctor could not bring him round, try as he could. Li carefully examined the tube which had been found on him. It looked like a fountain pen, but once the top was removed he could see there was a pressure button on one end and a nozzle on the other. He looked at the word on the label, 'sniff.' Evidently Shen Di had been made unconscious in some special way and the nasal spray was for reviving him.

Li Ke-ming told someone to bring a police dog, put the nozzle into its nose and pressed. The dog sneezed and shook its head and there was a strange, unpleasant smell, but the dog was otherwise unaffected.

He then did the same with Shen Di, who opened his eyes and regained consciousness at once. He sat up straight, holding the arm of the chair and looked around him.

'This is Fuzhou, I take it?' he asked, as if he had already thought out what he would do. He expressed no surprise and smiled at Huang Shi-ke. 'Congratulations, Prime Minister!'

No one said anything—neither questions nor answers. It was hard to realise that the man hunted for so long was in front of their eyes. Even Li Ke-ming was silent, as if the dream would burst like a bubble if he opened his mouth. Shen Di seemed very natural and there was no surprise or fear on his face.

'Anaesthesia tends to make people very thirsty,' he said pedantically. Someone poured him a glass of water. Huang Shi-ke looked at his watch: forty-seven minutes to midnight: there was not much time. However Shen Di got here he must be made to give evidence before Nanjing made its move.

Shen Di looked at his watch too. ' We should hurry.'

'You think so too?' asked Huang Shi-ke cautiously, hardly believing that he was willing to cooperate.

'Of course,' Shen Di almost giggled. 'It's you who are wasting time. Now that I am here you can simply ask me to talk. Although I was hiding, I was really hoping you'd find me, to tell the truth.'

'What do you want?' Huang Shi-ke asked, still rather gingerly.

'Let me first tell you what I've got to offer. First, I can tell you the inside story of the conspiracy; second, I can give evidence to the Nanjing Command; third, I can hold a press conference and announce to the world what actually happened.'

Huang Shi-ke could not believe his ears.

'And what do you want from us?'

'First of all, get rid of those cameras. Inside China there must be no recording equipment or anything written down. The press conference can be held once I am out of China. Your photographers can be present then.'

Huang Shi-ke instantly dismissed the photographers. Shen Di was obviously not going to give anything away until the price was agreed and his future guaranteed. It was a reasonable request.

'What I want from you is a just price. It's like in publishing, the holder of the copyright....'

'How much?'

Shen Di languidly waved his hand. 'For telling the inside story from beginning to end, in a place where I am satisfied there is no hidden recording equipment of any kind—in the open air for instance—two million dollars. Another two million for giving evidence to the Nanjing Command. For the press conference it will be certainly more, but we can discuss that later.'

Later the bastard would probably want ten million, Huang Shi-ke thought, at last believing him. Even revolutionaries did not choose to die rather than submit nowadays. It was a thing of the past. People like Shen Di would not sacrifice themselves for an ideal, or belief, leader or their own country. The only thing that interested them was doing business and they would sell to anyone prepared to pay a good price. If they got caught, they would find a way of saving themselves and making a good profit by following market principles.

There were only thirty-four minutes left.

'I wish you first to phone to Nanjing,' said Huang Shi-ke.

'All right. Add on another hundred thousand,' said Shen Di, very pleased.

'We can pay you, but we have to know what your evidence is, whether it is true or false.'

'I have already said: first pay two million, then I'll choose a place and tell you there. I am your prisoner and not so stupid as to get myself deeper into trouble by peddling counterfeit goods.'

'There's no time. Why not phone Nanjing and we will give you a hundred thousand at once.'

'Prime Minister. We should not mix up the proper order of things in a deal like this. I can't phone Nanjing without telling the whole story and giving evidence. That comes to four million one hundred thousand.'

'There is only thirty minutes before midnight…'

'I know what midnight means to you, and I was worried about you even when I was abroad.' Shen Di then wrote down a series of figures on a sheet of paper. 'This is the number of my Swiss account. Phone the bank and credit my account with 4.1 million $US. It can be done in ten minutes. Once I get an assurance that the money is in my account I will phone Nanjing.'

'For a provincial government to draw such a sum there's a whole procedure to be gone through. Can the President of the United States take four million out of the Treasury in a few minutes?' Huang Shi-ke asked.

Shen Di shrugged his shoulders: that was not his affair. He drummed his fingers on the arm of his chair and looked around him. Huang Shi-ke really wanted to plead with this scoundrel, who seemed most unlikely to be moved. He looked at his watch, and finally steeled himself. 'All right. I'll give you four million now and the rest later.'

Shen Di magnanimously waved a hand.

'The hundred thousand is not the problem. Someone who can pay four million is not likely to quibble about that; and in any case, we'll have more business to do.'

Huang Shi-ke felt like putting his fist in the smiling face. The four million was exactly what he had in his own Swiss account. He was deliberately being stripped clean. An hour ago, his only hope for the future was the deposit note he had in an inside pocket. Now it had all been thrown away.

The transaction was completed in ten minutes, as Shen Di had said. He put on an air of someone whose word is his bond, and as soon as the transaction was confirmed, casually sat down in front of the telephone. As the call was being put through he looked at Huang Shi-ke and then at Li Ke-ming, and said,

'Mister Police Officer, I have a question I would like to ask you. Ever since you held me at pistol point in that bar in Bangkok, I have been wondering….and still don't understand. I know you are a very able man, perhaps even a genius, but how did you manage to operate abroad wearing that mask? And how could you find me? All the secret agents of the seven provinces put together could not have done that.'

Li Ke-ming did not answer. Huang Shi-ke thought he must be with his own horrible memories. When had he held Shen Di at gunpoint in Bangkok? Everyone knew he had never left the island, just as they knew that Shen Di was sitting there. They were all completely confused. Then the screen lit up. Nanjing was on the line.

Zhejiang Province: The Xianxia Pass

A van, apparently broken down, had been at the top of a pass in the desolate mountains of eastern Zhejiang for several days. No one would have noticed that it was very close to a hidden manhole, or that a thin wire led from the van to an underground communications cable.

It was night and there was no one about. Inside the van, at nineteen minutes to midnight, a lieutenant in civilian clothes was recording a telephone conversation and translating every word almost simultaneously into a secret code and transmitting it.

There were three voices on the line. The lieutenant knew (he had been listening in for nearly three hours) that one of the voices was that of 'Deputy Governor Huang Shi-ke'. Another was 'Deputy Chief of Staff Xu'. The name of the third had never been mentioned, but his voice had been recognized by computer as corresponding with the voice of '001'. The lieutenant did not know who '001' was; but in the instructions he had received from Beijing, there were three crosses after the code name, meaning he was the most important target.

The line was silent for a long time, then the voice of the Deputy Chief of Staff could be heard, asking, 'Can you give proof of your identity?'

001 laughed. 'I'll give you a name from the distant past—Xiao Mei. I'm sure you remember that evening in the basement of your home. We were fighting for first turn and I punched you. You turned round and saw that a drop of blood had fallen on Xiao Mei...Do you want me to go on?'

'Does that policeman from the Three Gorges project say you're genuine?'

'If we had found him earlier we should have recruited him. Everything he said was guesswork, but it was all more or less accurate. I admire someone like that.'

'I don't suppose it was you who wanted the dirty work done?'

'Of course not. I'm not high enough to take his place.'

'Who was it then?'

'You must have realized. Someone who wanted to be boss even as a child. Who was playing with a globe all the time, and could think up plans which made young men's eyes pop?'

'Him?'

'Who else could give an order like that?'

'No one above him?'

'That I can't say. In our job communications are all one way.'

Then Huang Shi-ke's voice, saying 'It's going to be midnight soon.'

The Deputy Chief of Staff seemed to wake up. 'I'll order all troop movements to stop for two hours. But you must come straight away to Nanjing, old friend.'

Huang Shi-ke had the last word: 'The plane will take off in less than fifteen minutes.'

Only a second later, the Lieutenant transmitted the last coded word, and stretched. Everything had been sent to Beijing, but he had to wait until six the next morning, when the captain woke up and took over. To pass the time he liked listening in on radio communications. Outside the van, there was only the sound of the wind, but the earphones were full of all sorts of sounds. He half closed his eyes. Sometimes, on short wave, he could hear pop music or a criminal talking to someone from a train on his portable.

Then suddenly the voice of 001 broke in: 'Three fighters!....Not Nanjing planes come to meet us?...Then hurry up and intercept them!...Return to base full-speed!...Fucking hell! There's three more behind.... Hello, hello! Where are you from? Repeat: Who are you? Don't fire! We surrender!'

Disaster was imminent and made him incoherent. The lieutenant heard an explosion, and then shouting or perhaps the roaring of flames, he could not tell. It was not difficult to imagine a plane, hit by a rocket, hurtling down towards the earth. The last recognizable word was 'parachute'.

The lieutenant held his breath for at least ten seconds. Then a voice said: 'Attention all aircraft. Attack the parachute by turns. It must be destroyed before it lands. Repeat, destroyed. Aim at the man's head.'

Nanjing Command HQ

In the Nanjing HQ, the video recording had been replayed five times. Commander Bai made a sign that it was enough. He was short and stout but had all the authority of a great general. The Deputy Chief of Staff, who looked down on almost everyone, was extremely deferential in his presence.

'You are sure it was Shen Di?' asked the commander, his small eyes still on the screen.

'Yes, I have known him for a long time…unmistakable.'

'What is this Xiao Mei business?'

'When we were young we both, well…had relations with my father's nurse.'

Commander Bai was not interested in this kind of thing.

'Wang Feng was your superior?'

'No, just the eldest.'

After a moment Commander Bai said, 'This video tape is useless: Wang Feng's name is not even mentioned. Does Fujian have a recording of Shen Di's evidence?'

'No. Shen Di didn't want to allow others to have the evidence so soon. He knew we would be recording him, so he said nothing.'

'Wang Feng has got rid of this witness, so how on earth can we clear this matter up?'

'Perhaps it's better like this,' the Deputy Chief of Staff said cautiously. 'If Shen Di doesn't re-appear, we have no reason to go on defying Beijing, whereas if he had given evidence we would have been forced to move against Wang Feng. But this is not the time either for deferring to Beijing or attacking. We should wait and see how the situation develops and allow Beijing to consume its resources. At the moment we have insufficient cause either to submit or attack. As things develop we may have more or less reason… according to our needs.'

Commander Bai stood up, walked a few times back and forth on the carpet, straight as a ramrod, as if on the parade ground. Then he turned to the Deputy Chief of Staff. 'Call off the standby. Inform Fuzhou that until the situation is completely clear we will observe indefinite neutrality.' He paused. 'Arrange for a secret team to start work under the Chief of Staff, drawing up a plan of attack on Beijing.'

Zhengzhou City, Henan Province

Shi Ge told his driver to leave the dirt track at the site where the new Yellow River dyke was being constructed and get on to the main road to Zhengzhou. But the road had been damaged in at least twenty different places, and several trucks were stuck there, their drivers cursing and swearing.

Shi Ge left the car and walked up the huge newly constructed earth embankment. It looked well-built. The top was smooth and level, and the slope at the correct angle. But a few blows with a spade revealed cavities—called 'honeycombs', under the surface, where hard lumps of earth had been merely piled up and covered, without tamping it all down. Some were big enough for a child to hide in. All day he had come across these 'honeycombs'. It was a new way of cheating that was spreading rapidly since the first frost. Frozen blocks of earth, concealed by a layer of normal earth took up more space and earned the labourers an extra ration of grain. But there was no more frozen earth at hand because it was early in the winter and the frost had not yet gone very deep. So the labourers had removed the surface of the earthen track, instead, which was well compressed by the passage of trucks before being frozen.

Of course once it thawed, the places filled with frozen earth would become mud holes. There was saying 'a dyke hundred miles long can be destroyed by ant's nests'. Let alone 'honeycombs!'

Shi Ge was tired of getting angry about it. He knew that there would be no reaction on the faces which surrounded him. The labourers wore all sorts of old clothes, given by people in the towns as their contribution to flood relief. Many of them, already well worn, had quickly become rags and tatters, some still showed traces of foreign letters and designs. Some hardly covered the labourers' chests and bellies; some were worn over dirty village-style black clothes. There were men wearing women's hats with feathers, summer hats or crash helmets, making them look strange and rather pathetic.

One of the most important operations, after the military took over the country, was to assemble an enormous number of homeless refugees from all over the country to work on Yellow River conservancy projects.

The decision had been taken to cut a new bed for the river, 500 metres wide, thirty metres deep, from Zhengzhou to the sea—a distance of over 600 kilometres. The new bed would mean that the Yellow River would flow below the surface of the surrounding land and the earth excavated would be used to raise a huge dyke on either side. The maximum flow would be twenty times more than that of the old bed and enough to accommodate safely the worst flood in the last two thousand years. It was a project of such magnitude that it had never been considered before.

At least thirty million people had been put to work on construction sites along the Yellow River diversion. There was no need for the state to provide mechanical equipment. Everything—digging, carrying and tamping—was done by human labour. This deliberate return to methods more ancient than those used to build the Great Wall or the Grand Canal, was designed to kill two eagles with one arrow: to reduce costs by an astronomical figure and at the same time settle homeless people—at least temporarily.

Shi Ge knew, better than most, that this had involved draconian measures and a large number of troops. The destitute wanderers were now like destitute criminals condemned to forced labour, living in rudimentary tents and provided with neither fuel nor bedding. A strong labourer working hard could earn no more than 150 grams of grain daily, and without the little extra the 'honeycombs' brought in, would have less than half what he needed.

It was difficult to provide even the ration they got now. The grain was obtained by reducing the amount available for the urban population and by forcing peasants in areas not affected by the floods to pay their grain levy. This caused other, extremely difficult, problems.

The only way of maintaining stability now was by terror. Throughout the country, several thousand military courts were authorized to carry out summary execution. Announcements of death sentences were pasted up on walls and notice-boards everywhere.

An overseer recognized Shi Ge and hurried up.

'There's nothing we can do, Deputy Premier,' he said helplessly, referring to the 'honeycombs', and shaking his electro-shock baton in the direction of stony faces around him. 'I'm one man in charge of five thousand and I can't be in two places at once. These people are lazy and cunning. I've only got to turn my back and they are up to some trick or other.'

Naturally he pretended not to see what was going on. He had a police baton powerful enough to intimidate twenty people, and a loaded pistol at his belt. He was scared. More than thirty overseers had been killed on the project because they were too brutal. The millions of ignorant and expressionless faces, voices which could only say 'Don't know', seemed like an impregnable wall. But behind it, there was not just stupidity and ignorance. Without planning, resolution and courage they would not have abandoned their homes and become destitute wanderers and learned all sorts of tricks which allowed them to survive. They were no longer honest, docile peasants who could be ordered about. Among them were sellers of men, smugglers, bandits, prostitutes, gamblers and conmen.

The military authorities had told Shi Ge that there were all kinds of secret organizations on the site, formless, and invisible, hidden by a screen of 'stupidity'. They were like the river itself, liable to flood, and the only thing that kept them under control was the army—thirty divisions in all. If *that* dyke did not hold a human flood would soon cover the whole country. The Yellow River had long been 'China's sorrow'. This was more terrifying: a sword hanging over the country, which sent cold shivers down the spine.

'Do the work again,' Shi Ge ordered.

The overseer turned, raised his baton and repeated the order.

Shi Ge knew that even if he remained there watching, it would not be done. The dykes were hundreds of miles long. Once spring came the frozen earth would sink, and new earth would be added. In any case, settling the floating population for as long as possible was even more important. To do the work again ten times did not matter. The labourers had got a little more food by cheating. It was a drop in the ocean compared with nationwide corruption.

Long-term planning on flood control had been based largely on the research done by Unit Sixteen. But when Shi Ge had first suggested using Yellow River conservancy projects to solve the problems of the homeless, his idea had been to use the money saved by disbanding the army to employ and provide for them. Now the army was forcing them to work without pay. That was the difference. Shi Ge had been totally excluded from the decision-making process, but put in charge of its implementation.

It was not unusual to put a Deputy Premier in nominal charge of a project of this magnitude. This time it was different. When Wang Feng announced his appointment, Shi Ge was ordered to direct the work *on the spot.* This was in effect, a punishment for his visit to the Green Exhibition.

The exhibition and the various incidents had been widely reported abroad. Shi Ge was said to be the man behind the Exhibition, who headed a new, enlightened group of Central Committee members and had two masters of martial arts as his bodyguards. Several foreign newspapers asserted that the hooligan trouble and the bomb explosion were both the work of the 'Ideological Guidance Committee' controlled by the military government.

In China the whole affair was greeted with total silence, and no direct action was taken against Shi Ge—an intelligent move, since nothing more was said about it and the foreign press soon lost interest. He was discreetly removed from Beijing and sent off, with thirty million homeless refugees, to direct the Yellow River diversion project.

He was pleased to do so. A few days after being nominated Deputy Premier, he realized that he had been appointed purely as a make-weight in political deals. If that was all the General Secretary wanted, Shi Ge would make use of his name to do a few useful things, such as making the Green Exhibition possible or supervising the Yellow River diversion. At least that would be serving China.

On orders from the overseer, Shi Ge's car was carried over the part of the track which had been dug up, by the labourers repairing it, while the drivers of the stranded vehicles watched with astonishment and wondered who it was that was so privileged. The very ordinary Chinese-made jeep was dusty and battered. Shi Ge himself was wearing baggy work clothes and his shoes were covered with mud. One of the drivers shouted indignantly, "Why don't you carry mine?' The overseer replied 'I piss in your face!'

On reaching the main road Shi Ge changed places with the driver. Before he came to the construction site, he had never the time or the opportunity to learn to drive. He enjoyed it and also had a little scheme in mind.

The last of the three checkpoints was at a gate in the wire fence surrounding the whole work site, like a huge sack containing twenty million people, who could get in but not out. It was manned by armed soldiers and there were sentries, watch towers, and patrol cars as far as the eye could reach. A continuous stream of homeless people from all over the country was being herded by soldiers through the gates.

However much Shi Ge disliked such draconian methods, he could not deny their efficacy. The floating population had been reduced in number and order was restored in the country. Apart from the few provinces which had declared their autonomy, the rest acknowledged the authority of Beijing. The economic crisis was still very serious, but Beijing, using force and threats, had obtained more funds from the regions and the people than at the time when the economy was flourishing. The army was at war, and was expanding at the same time. There was also the great Yellow River project: Shi Ge was astonished that four thousand tons of grain every day could be provided to feed the labour force. If half the army had not been tied down enforcing martial law, the rebellion in the south would have been suppressed by now.

Shi Ge was in two minds about this war. He disapproved of all kinds of war, civil war especially. But he knew that if the south was allowed to become autonomous the whole country would disintegrate. Once the unity of the nation breaks down into a number of separate regimes, each prefers to be the head of a chicken rather than the tail of an ox. The result would not be partial autonomy but the collapse of the whole.

Apart from war, what else could prevent this break-up? Fascist dictatorship seems the only solution for China. But long ago, after much study, Unit Sixteen had reached a different conclusion: if a fascist dictatorship was again established in China, it would be the beginning of the disintegration of the country, or else, before the collapse of China, a fascist dictatorship would certainly take over. Fascism was both the last defence against disintegration and also the accelerator of disintegration.

At the gates a guard recognized the Deputy Premier's car from its number plates, but did not know who to salute. The driver, sitting next to Shi Ge, and the bodyguards behind were all too young and Shi Ge, who had bumped into the gatepost, did not appear to be the regular driver.

Driving on to the concrete road leading to Zhengzhou, Shi Ge resumed his train of thought. If terror was maintained, perhaps disintegration could be avoided. Terror preserved order, order saved the economy, the economy created social stability. This had happened in the past. China has had several thousand years of experience in the use of terror. But because of the huge population, the machinery of terror has often grown so monstrous and costly that it has brought about the collapse of the government that created it and the disintegration of the country.

Today the army is no longer like a solid iron block. It was the defection of the Guangdong Command that encouraged the seven provinces to proclaim their autonomy, but the Guangdong army itself has no hope at the moment of holding out against Beijing, and Guangzhou itself will soon be attacked. But the Nanjing Command had made Beijing very uneasy by opting for indefinite neutrality. The prospect for the survival of the state was bad. If a vase is already falling to pieces, it is too late to tie wires round it.

The broken-down jeep was ideal for the earth tracks in the construction site, but on the main road, even with his foot down Shi Ge could not get it to do more than a hundred kilometres an hour. He had happily agreed on the phone to pick up Chen Pan at the railway station; but the train must have arrived at least two and a half hours ago, and he had only reached the outskirts of the city.

He drew up at a bus station in the suburbs and said to his men, 'Bring that thing over here,' pointing to a concrete bench about thirty yards away.

'What for?'

'Bring it. Quick!' The three men, totally bewildered got out and went towards the bench.

His two bodyguards, experts in the martial arts, who had been enrolled in the Armed Police by Zhou Chi, had demonstrated their prowess at the Green Exhibition. The concrete bench that normally took a crane to lift, had in fact moved a little when they tried to raise it.

Shi Ge was not skilled enough to shout out of the window while driving, so he drove a little further and stopped.

'Don't waste your energy. Wait for me in the guesthouse.' Normally his bodyguards never left him, but he did not want them around when he met Chen Pan.

When they understood that they had been tricked the men started to run after the jeep. Shi Ge managed to get it moving again just before they could grab it. He saw them in the rear mirror, stamping their feet in anger and could not help laughing. He was thoroughly pleased with himself, in spite of having bumped into a post. He had chosen a battered jeep on purpose.

That day at the Green Exhibition, when Chen Pan had pushed him out of the way before the light fitting fell on him, she had suffered a broken arm and three ribs. She was only just out of hospital. In Beijing he had often been to see her, but they had not met since Shi Ge was given his present assignment. She had phoned the day before to say that she was about to take over her duties as director of the Fanjingshan Nature Reserve. She had arranged to meet him in Zhengzhou, where her laboratory was.

Last night Shi Ge had not slept well in the tent which had been his home for the last month. He thought he had better look out some presentable clothes before setting out, but they all seemed more or less the same, so he wore his ordinary working clothes—more suitable for inspecting the work site than for a secret meeting.

While waiting for Chen Pan, he regretted his choice: she might take it as showing off or inviting pity. Indeed, when she saw his clothes she did have an expression of commiseration.

To distract her attention he asked her to show him her laboratory, which was on the roof of the biology department of the Institute of Nutrition. It was, in effect, a large plastic greenhouse and in spite of the cold north wind, was heated by the bright sun. There was a pleasant smell of different kinds of growing plants that produced edible oil or fruit. Chen Pan was a visiting professor at the Institute and one of those in charge of the laboratory.

There was no soil and the plants were between rows of plastic tubes which provided them with a nutrient fluid. Cultivation without soil was nothing new: what was interesting was the purpose of this laboratory, which Chen Pan explained:

'There is a shortage of arable land in China, and the situation is getting worse because the expansion of towns and cities takes up more and more of it. But there is space lying idle: on the roofs of buildings. This amounts, roughly speaking, to a million and a quarter hectares, which is 1.1 percent of our arable land. What we are working on here, is not how to provide five star hotels with fresh vegetables in the middle of winter, but how to make use of this roof space.'

'In theory,' Shi Ge remarked, 'with sufficient investment, tomatoes can be grown in the Himalayas.' It was the midday break and they were alone in the laboratory now.

'We are trying to work out a way of reducing capital investment to the minimum, to below the value of land at least. We use this plastic hothouse because we have to keep the experiments going during the winter; but future users will not need to use them because cultivation will follow the seasons. In the north there is one planting season, in the south two or three. The tubes lie directly on the surface of the roof, not in frames, which reduces costs. Large-scale production will make the plastic tubing very inexpensive. The tubes will have to be changed about every five years and the cost would be about the same as the value of land.'

'The key question,' Chen Pan continued, 'Is the composition of the nutritional fluid. Chemical fertilizer is costly and relatively difficult to produce and may also have undesirable side-effects. Are you interested in having a look?'

'Of course I am,' said Shi Ge.

Chen Pan led him over to a rather strange looking apparatus, consisting mainly of stainless steel containers of various sizes (whose bright surfaces reflected their distorted images), linked to a fermentation vat with a solar-powered heater.

'The fluid is made of processed natural material.' She pointed to the steel teeth in the mouth of a crushing mill. 'This will grind up any natural substance: vegetable waste, weeds, excreta, ash, natural fibres and so on. There are many things usually regarded as waste, or even harmful, that we crush and put in the fermentation vat, using this potent, fast-acting ferment.' She took a pill about the size of a broad-bean from a glass jar on the table. 'We use only one pill per vat, which is then warmed by solar-heated water. Fermentation takes two hours, and the liquid then goes through the separator. What comes out is a superior nutritional fluid made of natural substances.'

Beside this machine was a pile of trailing cucumber stems. Chen Pan took up some with a garden fork and put them into the crushing mill, and told Shi Ge that it could be powered by electricity, or an engine, by wind or water or, if necessary, by hand.'

'Let me try by hand,' said Shi Ge. The cucumber trailers were easy to grind; but the speed of the separator was higher and it was quite difficult for one man to turn.

'We can also add a treadle for one person or several,' Chen Pan said rather proudly. 'If material is free and natural or human energy is used, you can imagine the low cost of the fluid.'

'What size of "plantation" could one machine handle?'

'With more fermentation vats and round the clock operation, three or four hectares.'

'What's the cost of the equipment?'

'It's the most expensive item, of course. At present prices one unit would be more than 4 million *yuan*.'

Shi Ge was silent for some time, his mind busy with mental calculations. He arrived at the conclusion that with 357,000 units, enough grain could be produced to save 20 million people from starvation and settle the floating population. A month earlier, when he was responsible for agriculture and the environment, he might have thought it worth a try.

'In such a huge country as ours,' he finally said, 'one can always find encouraging statistics.' He curbed his enthusiasm and spoke as a man of experience. 'There would be a lot of factors involved in developing this technology. For instance, it would cost a fortune to adapt and consolidate the roofs; urban water consumption would increase enormously, which would cause difficulties; new methods of sorting rubbish would have to be worked out, and some way of dealing with the residue....' Then he realized he was deliberately thinking of difficulties. Perhaps what he said was reasonable, but this was not the time: he had seen the despondent expression on Chen Pan's face and stopped in full flight. He wanted to stroke her hair and tell her he really wanted to help her. He sighed.

'To tell the truth, the idea is a good one, but at present I don't have the power, and even if I had, this is not the moment to put it into operation. It would need time, and China has no time left. It would need order and stability, which don't exist any more. Even if the whole 1.25 million hectares were used, it could only provide 1.1% of total crop production. We have a *fifteen* percent deficit of grain and this will double in no time. So it would be hard to justify spending an enormous amount of energy for the sake of a 1.1% increase. What China needs is a miracle. Otherwise we should use the time and spirit left to us to prepare for the final moment.'

Chen Pan raised her eyes. 'Collapse?'

Shi Ge nodded. There was a shudder in the look they exchanged.

Chen Pan opened a cock on the fermentation vat, and started the separator. Her injured arm still hurt sometimes. 'I'm taking this unit to my base at Fanjingshan.'

'Good idea.' Shi Ge helped her to reload the crushing mill with the trailing stems of cucumber plants. 'Then there's our bargain...'

'I thought you had forgotten that.'

'Do I look like someone who makes bad deals?'

'Well you don't exactly look like a grasping merchant,' Chen Pan replied. 'Do you know what they said when they told me you'd arrived? "There's an old peasant 'uncle' downstairs who wants to see you."'

'I don't know about "peasant", but "uncle" is right.' He remembered the look the woman had given him when he presented himself at the desk and asked for Chen Pan in Shanxi dialect.

'I'll cook you some of my new hybrid vegetable. You've got time to take a bath. There's been a lot of sun today, so the water is very hot. I'll wash your clothes in the meantime and put them through the dryer, so they'll be ready when you've had your bath.'

He did not really want to take a bath. She had sensed as much, and had made it difficult for him to refuse. 'Then there's our deal to discuss, so we mustn't waste time.'

For several weeks he had not touched hot water. On the diversion site the thirty million labourers did not even have fuel to heat water, so he had forbidden his staff to do so for him. Now the pleasure of lying in a bath of hot water gave him a frisson of pleasure.

The 'bathroom', was no more than a small part of the laboratory, surrounded by screens. The sun shone on the plastic above his head. The washing machine was humming away, and there was a pleasant clatter and smell of cooking. He felt a rare sense of well-being. This was a home, like the dreams which often came to him in his loneliness. He closed his eyes to fix the dream in his memory. At the end of one's life. few such scenes are left in the mind—the rest have dissolved like smoke.

'Tell me more about your Multi-level Election System,' she suggested.

Chen Pan was just the other side of the plastic screen; he could see her vague outline and the colour of her clothes, so close that he could stretch out and touch her. He suddenly felt shy of his nakedness.

'I only mentioned it at the Green Exhibition. But I had the feeling, especially at the Exhibition that although the ideals and the philosophy of the Green movement are outstanding, the political ideas are very feeble. You seem incapable of explaining how your ideals are to be made into reality. You seem to think it will sufficient to awaken the understanding and self-awareness of the masses—both of which are incredibly weak—and your problems will be solved. So you concentrate almost entirely on research, appeals, mobilization, education and so on, which are all soft, indecisive measures. The trouble is that you have not found the kind of social structure which can transform Green ideals into reality. You can't adopt the "hard" structures of Western democracy or of Eastern autocracies because both can only pursue unlimited economic growth, either because they are forced to curry favour with the electors, or else out of motives of self-glorification. This is totally contrary to Green principles. You have not found the social structure that can integrate the philosophy of the Green Movement and ensure its survival and development and eventually its realization. All your attempts to do so have failed.'

'The Successive Multi-Level Election System I have worked out, was not designed with the Green ideals of philosophy in mind. But I now believe that it is the only social system that can ensure that the future will be Green. So, though I said I wanted to strike a bargain with you, a quid pro quo, in fact it is a contribution to the Green movement.'

'Unscrupulous merchants always pretend to be something else.' Chen Pan said. 'How do expect me to believe that rosy picture?'

'Let me take an example.' Shi Ge went on. 'You Greens are always blaming the people for not making a conscious effort to abandon their endless pursuit of consumption; for not realizing what the long-term consequence will be; and for being unwilling to make any sacrifice in order to avoid it. This barrier is the greatest difficulty you face. In the Multi-Level Election System, only at the lowest level can those elected be said to be in direct contact with the electors at the grass roots. At higher electoral levels, the knowledge, education, experience and access to information of electors and elected increases and there is far less chance that mass prejudice and short-sighted and selfish views can influence decisions, and a far *greater* chance that decisions will be taken with the interest of the whole of society, even of mankind, in mind. Otherwise the blind folly of consumerism will surely end in the destruction of the environment and of humanity.'

'I agree with you on that point,' Chen Pan interjected. 'But when I was in hospital and reading the pamphlets that were distributed in the park that day, I could not help feeling very doubtful whether a simple procedure for organizing elections can possible change humanity. It seems to be expecting too much.'

'Yet, in the world today the fundamental difference between democracies and autocracies as you know, is one that concerns procedure: Western democracies have a system of competitive elections and in autocracies elections are controlled or rigged. System and procedure are of vital importance. Democracy is nothing but a concept, but for it to be put into practice it is necessary to create a very precise and coherent system. Popular mass movements in China since 1919 have always shouted loudly about the *concept* of democracy, but no one ever came up with a detailed system and procedure that might make it into a reality. The result has been that even within such movements themselves, a kind of democracy has been practised which is either a democracy in name alone, or else is a kind of dictatorship of the majority. Both these invariably develop into the dictatorship of a few. The system of autocracy is deeply ingrained and everyone has become accustomed to it.'

'The Successive All-level Election System is based on the concept that all elections to-date have been conducted in units that are much too large, and consequently not genuine elections. If it were put into practice it would produce startling changes and very far-reaching effects. You should transcend psychological barriers and trust to reason. This system can bring about an entirely new kind of society.'

'The ultimate,' said Chen Pan.

'That's another psychological barrier. The Multi-Level Election System is not the future, not the aim in itself, but a means of reaching the future. Man has always used poetic imagery to evoke an ideal future and encourage himself to go forward. But once ideals are realized, they fade sooner or later or become reactionary. But if there is no ultimate in human development this does not means that mankind is condemned to endless despair, backwardness, mistakes and bloody conflict. The Multi-Level Election System is a way out of mankind's difficulties. It is like a superior automatic train that carries man safely from one station to another. The travellers—society—will no longer be in danger from a violent, tired or drunken driver. The train will never disintegrate at the bottom of an abyss, killing half the passengers. The precise nature of the future is not the concern of the train, but its progress makes the future perfectly clear. No "saviour" is needed. There will be no more obstructions, there will be no getting lost on the way and humanity will be for ever on the right road.'

'You've become positively poetic,' Chen Pan remarked.

'I originally thought only of how to make this train and get people to get aboard, and was not concerned with its destination. But since I have known you I have, consciously or not, come to realize that the destination is the Green world.'

Chen Pan laughed. 'A magician as well. But after a compliment like that I can only accept your "bargain".'

'That's what I wanted to hear.'

He had spoken the truth. In this chaotic and despairing world, the Green movement, its philosophy and activity as well as the refreshing qualities of its supporters had come like a ray of light in his troubled and perplexed mind. For him, Chen Pan was a product and a symbol of the Green movement. His faith in his Election System had been revived.

It was a long time since he had felt so relaxed. His soul was hovering in the steam and in the sunlight above. The feeling of home became stronger, the image of his wife appeared in the steam clouds, then merged into Chen Pan. From the smells he tried to guess what she was cooking. Then he smelled dry clothes and had to get unwillingly out of the bath.

On the working surface where there was also a weighing machine and various other things, Chen Pan had spread two sheets of clean newspaper and put five dishes of various kinds of vegetables, that looked so fresh they might have been growing there in the dishes.

'There's also some marrow soup. It will be ready in a minute.'

At the other end of the table Chen Pan, still wearing an apron, was gluing something. Shi Ge, more comfortable in his clean clothes, asked her what she was doing.

'I'm mending my baby's trousers.'

In front of her on the table was a shrivelled inflatable baby doll. Chen Pan was sticking a patch over a puncture on its knee.

Shi Ge stopped her. 'Don't do it like that. The glue will go through the hole and stick everything together inside and your baby will be crippled.

'What a fool I am.' She covered her eyes with her hands.

'It will be all right if you blow it up first.'

'You'd better help me. My hand's shaking.'

It was made of thin plastic—such cheap dolls could no longer be found now—a boy of about a year old, with pouting lips, a slight squint and a lively, mischievous expression. His arms and feet were in a boxing position, one foot was in front of the other and he wore flared red trousers. The patch was a piece of yellow plastic that Chen Pan had cut out in the shape of a dog. Shi Ge clumsily applied the glue.

'Don't stick it on the wrong way up.' Chen Pan warned him.

'People say those with good eyesight often squint,' he said defensively. Chen Pan looked at him, with narrowed eyes.

'It has a certain charm.'

He said nothing. He felt a little embarrassed under her prolonged regard, the trace of a smile in her eyes.

Once the patch in the shape of a little dog was stuck on, there was no trace of a puncture, and the trousers looked better than they had before.

'Shall we patch the other knee.' Shi Ge suggested.

'What for?'

'For symmetry.

'That's an out-dated aesthetic principle.' She tickled doll under the arms and around his waist and he wriggled, full of life and vigour, even cried out as if he could hardly catch his breath for laughing. His movements were entirely those of a real son rather than a toy.

'So this is the "little brother" you told Ivan about: Shi Ge said.

'What do you mean? That he's inferior to Ivan's little brother?' Chen Pan took her baby in her arms and examined him, his pouting mouth and his slightly squinting eyes. He seemed to be sharing her indignation.

Shi Ge raised his head and laughed. In the park that day Chen Pan had told Ivan that she had a 'little brother', and he had never forgotten this. He did not really know why he had indirectly made enquiries. There was no trace in any official record. But who knows, perhaps the child was with Ouyang Zhong-hua. Now, finding the true identity of the 'little brother' he felt a strange joy.

'I mean nothing of the sort. Ivan will certainly like his "little brother".

Chen Pan stopped frowning, and told the child, 'Don't glare at him like that. Give him a kiss.'

Shi Ge duly kissed the smooth plastic face, rather shyly.

'He's called Shi Ge,' Chen Pan told her child. 'He has no "little brother" so you and Ivan call him "elder brother". You introduce yourself and say, "I'm called Shasha".' Chen Pan squeezed the doll in such a way as to make it sound almost recognizable as his name. Then she put him in Shi Ge's arms and went to see whether the soup was ready.

Behind the table Shi Ge had noticed a row of what looked like some kind of gourd, close to the bottom of the plastic wall of the greenhouse. It had trailing stems, but no leaves, and the fruit itself was very smooth, large and round; it looked extremely unattractive. Like a rare kind of tumour. It was growing directly from the nutrient tubes on the ground. There was only one row but they were evidently planted at different times. First they were mere buttons, then fist-sized and so on. The colour changed from white, to green and then red. The last looked at least 15 or 16 kilos and had already begun to dry.

'Come and eat,' said Chen Pan, putting the soup on the table.

'What is that?' he asked pointing to the row of strange plants.

Chen Pan smiled wryly. 'Those things have become a real drag. Because stem tubers can't be grown direct from the plastic tubes, we tried with potatoes and did a lot of experiments. We finally developed a cross between potato and two different kinds of gourd. This is the result. We call it *shugua* (potato gourd). At present most of the nutritional fluid is absorbed by the, inedible parts, the trailers and leaves, especially in soilless cultivation: this is a problem we really wanted to solve. *Shugua* is very suitable for this kind of improvement: the trailers and leaves have been reduced to a minimum, so they take less time to ripen, we've discovered. This is the result so far. The smallest *shugua* you see there was planted before dawn this morning, the biggest twenty days ago. At peak it can put on one and a half kilos per day. So our plans were successful, the only trouble is that it is not pleasant to eat. The other part of the laboratory is piled high with it and no one wants it. So we use it for making the nutrient fluid. But we keep a row going because we don't want all our work to have been for nothing. If you are interested I'll give you some. Now you must try my cooking,' she added serving the rice.

'What is the nutritional content?' Shi Ge asked.

'Not bad at all. Starch and protein about the same as potatoes, vitamins and amino-acid slightly higher.'

'No harmful effects?'

'Of course not. It's just that the taste is peculiar, even pigs won't eat it. Are you thinking of taking up farming, or what? Come one. The food will get cold'.

'I'd like to taste your *shugua*,' Shi Ge said. He was very hungry and the smell of the dishes on the table mouth-watering. But he wanted to judge the *shugua* when he was still hungry.

'How do want to eat it?'

'First raw, then cooked a little, then roasted. Then with condiments added, then what about fried?'

'It looks as though I've cooked you a meal for nothing. Why not sauté and steamed as well?'

The taste was indescribable—it seemed to have inherited all the less appetizing flavours of its progenitors—and even when salt or sugar or any other condiment was added, the strange taste remained. Roasted, it seemed a little better. But with the best will in the world it was difficult to imagine it as a food. Shi Ge tasted it conscientiously, the tough and the tender. Even the seeds which were ten times worse he chewed and swallowed while Chen looked on. 'I can't say it makes my mouth water to watch you.'

'I did better than the pigs,' Shi Ge replied, managing to smile as he fought his nausea. 'Could someone dying of hunger survive on this alone?'

'Yes, and even be healthy.'

'People would rather eat it than die?'

'Of course. If there was nothing else.'

'If grain and vegetables were available, even in small quantities people wouldn't eat it; but if there came a day when more than a billion people were faced with empty granaries and land on which grain wouldn't grow?' Shi Ge asked.

Chen Pan stared at him but said nothing.

'Another question. What is the yield?'

'Fifteen tonnes per hectare.'

'About six times that of cereal crops, or about twice by weight. But the growing time is only about twenty days whereas for cereals the maximum is five times that. That's ten times the yield for cereals. Do you realize the significance of your invention? Shi Ge asked with an intense look in his eyes. 'I'm not saying it's epoch-making, because I hope and pray that the day will never come; but if or when it does, this will allow us to stretch out a hand to help our people. It is really a godsend! I have never hoped for miracles, but perhaps this is a miracle you have created.'

'I have never considered it like that,' murmured Chen Pan confused.

Shi Ge got up and walked several times from one end of the laboratory to the other, silent for a long time and deep in thought, his eyes apparently fixed on nothing. Leaves moved as he walked past. Chen Pan followed him with her eyes. Finally he came and sat down and once more tasted a piece of *shugua.*

'Don't go to the Fanjingshan base, it's too far away. I need you and the whole staff of your laboratory. Stop all other research and put everything into the large-scale production of *shugua* seeds and the enzyme for the fluid. But above all, put everything into improving and building complete units. At the moment I cannot give you much money—not more than a billion *yuan*—to pay for a few thousand units. Perhaps the most important thing is that while you are doing all this you should organize an industrial enterprise that can immediately go into large-scale production when needed, and in the shortest possible time produce large numbers of units and all necessary material. Perhaps that day is not far off.... I won't ask you whether you are willing or not. Only you can do it. I can't give you any official appointment, so work under the name of your laboratory. The source of the funds must be kept absolutely secret.'

The state allocation for the Yellow River diversion was a thousand billion *yuan.* After deducting the cost of food for the labourers and cost of baskets, carrying poles, tents and so on, only 200 billion remained. For Shi Ge, on his own initiative, to allocate half of that sum was an extremely serious crime, even though he was Deputy Premier. But there was no alternative. In any case, if the worst happened, and the population was wiped out, it would not matter if floods reached the sky.

It was a gamble. If the day did not come, or came later, he knew he would pay with his life.

When Chen Pan asked him what to do with the products, he merely told her to put them into stock. If China was granted a breathing space it would be no more than a billion-worth of rubbish. If he was not sentenced to death, he would end his days in prison. He was already a thorn in the flesh of Wang Feng and the army. It was the only chance. As Deputy Premier he had not done a single thing that no one else could do. He had no desire for a higher position—even this one was not for long. If he did not commit this crime, he would have been Deputy Premier for nothing. Since he was not bothered by the prospect of prison and did not fear death, it was worth making some final preparations for China. When the day came it would be his last contribution. He knew in his heart that a world-shaking disaster was now unavoidable and imminent.

6

In the Wuyi Mountains – Taibaishan Nature Reserve – Fuzhou – Taipei: The Presidential Palace – Montevideo – At sea, South of Taiwan – On the Fujian coast

ꕥ

In the Wuyi Mountains

It was raining. Li Ke-ming stood motionless in the grove of young bamboo and watched the road far below through his binoculars.

He had ordered the road blocked over a length of almost a mile, by dynamiting the steep slopes and cliffs on either side and had calculated that it would take the Northern Army engineers the best part of a month to clear it. He had not foreseen that the enemy could bring up equipment that would make the road serviceable far sooner. Now a strange, powerful-looking machine, of a kind Li Ke-ming had never seen or heard of before, was at work down below. It was short, almost square, on huge wheels, equipped with a powerful engine and very manoeuvrable. It had a pair of long, highly mobile arms that lifted heavy sheets of steel from the top of the machine and laid them, one after the other, over the rocks and rubble blocking the road. A squad of army engineers on each side joined the sheets together, attaching supports when necessary and formed a steel road over which vehicles could pass. The machine advanced until it ran out of steel sheets, then went back to have more loaded by a crane from heavy trucks.

Li Ke-ming watched this monster lay about seventy yards of steel road and thought: if we don't stop it, the armoured cars and troops will soon be flowing like a flood through the valley.

The nature of the terrain was the only really effective defence that Fujian had against the powerful Northern Army. Eighty per cent of the province is mountainous, and the few roads that exist are narrow and notoriously dangerous. The Wuyi range is perfectly placed from a strategic point of view; joined to other mountains north and south, it guards the whole of the northwest part of the provincial boundary for a distance of over two hundred miles. This is why Fujian, throughout history, has always been considered 'easy to defend: hard to attack'.

The strategy of Li Ke-ming, in command of the Fujian troops, was to block enemy access to the mountains by any road that could be used by tanks, motorized vehicles or artillery. Incursions by infantry presented no problem, but the autonomous government of Fujian dreaded a large-scale motorized attack. He had given orders for a whole series of literally earth-shaking operations. Special detachments were sent into the neighbouring province and under the noses of the Northern Army, had blown up 37 railway bridges, 152 road bridges, 18 railway tunnels, 42 road tunnels; all mountain roads and defiles that could be used by tanks or trucks had been blown up or blocked. The advance of the Northern Army had been brought to a halt. All airfields in the province had been made unusable—including those which were regarded as possible escape routes for Huang Shi-ke and other leaders of the Southern Alliance. The northerners had control in the air, but could not land airborne troops. Parachute troops were less dangerous, since there was more time for the Fujian troops to ensure that they did not reach the ground alive.

The Southern Alliance began to feel that after all Fujian could be defended: Li Ke-ming had no illusions. The enemy advance had only been slowed down; sooner or later Fuzhou was bound to fall.

It is cold in the mountains, especially during the winter rains, when the damp air seems to absorb the heat of one's body. It had been drizzling all day and large drops of rain dropped down Li Ke-ming's neck from the bamboo leaves.

The soldier behind him was hunched up and shivering. Sapper Zhang was a demolition expert—one of the best in the world in Li Ke-ming's opinion, though not very popular with the troops. He was a native of Fujian, therefore defending his own province, otherwise Li's strategy could not have been put into operation so quickly and with such devastating results.

Li Ke-ming lowered his binoculars and stretched out two fingers behind him. Someone put a cigarette between them and he stuck it in the hole in his mask.

'That big rock over there,' he said to the sapper, pointing to an enormous rock, weighing several hundred tons, shaped vaguely like a cone, point downwards. 'Can you bring that down on them?'

'It looks perfect for what you want to do; but that's not an ordinary rock. It's called the Swaying Rock, because in a force six wind you can see it move. It's mentioned in ancient writings as much as a thousand years ago.'

'I'd like you to go and have a look.'

'You want me to blow it up?'

'Yes.'

'But it's a scenic curiosity…'

Face to face with the goose-yellow mask of rain soaked gauze, the sapper swallowed his words.

'Go.' said Li Ke-ming. Then, to his Staff Officer, 'Send out a squad to cover the sapper and the explosives. Inform Outpost Nine and co-ordinate your movements with them.'

Everyone was a little afraid of Li Ke-ming—mainly because of his mask—and was very polite to him. There was a cable-way to the outpost, about 50 yards lower down in a plantation. It would take only ten minutes to haul the sapper and his explosives up to the rock.

Li Ke-ming's strategy was a form of guerrilla warfare. Every group of soldiers, either hidden in caves, woods or camouflaged on high ground or in valleys, was linked by telephone or hidden paths. They never showed themselves until it was necessary. Any direct confrontation with the far more powerful enemy would be the height of folly. If the Northern Army had decided on a lightning attack, Fuzhou would already have been lost. Fortunately the mutiny of the Guangdong Area command and Commander Bai's declaration of neutrality had obliged Beijing to bring back troops from far-away in west and northwest China. Perhaps Beijing was also hoping that Commander Bai would come to his senses: instead, Shen Di's sudden reappearance and his testimony only strengthened his neutrality. Fuzhou had been given a temporary respite.

Li Ke-ming returned to the shed in the bamboo grove. Placing the charges would take some time. In order to avoid discovery, no fires were allowed in the various positions and everyone was freezing. The altitude, the cold and damp contributed to the sick-list far more than wounds, and its effect on morale was worrying. But Li Ke-ming preferred it like this; the enemy troops were even less adapted to this climate.

His permanently rain-soaked mask continually sent cold air into the depths of his brain. His home in the far north was colder than here, but there was a crackling red-hot stove and a heated brick bed to sleep on. Here it was endlessly overcast and the cold was like needles of ice. It was difficult even to imagine his wife on the snow covered plain, far away in the north.

There were ten radio transceivers in the bamboo shed, handling incoming reports and sending instructions to each unit along the whole length of the Wuyi front. A telecommunications expert from the Fujian army HQ, familiar with the problems of interference in the mountains had established an efficient radio network. The Northern Army had no such advantage and their communications were often crippled by interference and Li Ke-ming's sophisticated jamming equipment. He could also get information from aircraft and satellite reconnaissance by radio from Fuzhou. Every day he sat down with a map in front of him and gave instructions by radio to all units under his command.

Up until now they had not fired a shot at the enemy. But yesterday the dams of seven reservoirs had been blown up and half a division of the Northern Army wiped out. There were many such reservoirs in the Wuyi mountains. Charges of dynamite had already been placed in all the dams and could be detonated by his units concealed nearby. Proper use of this weapon would be equivalent to ten divisions.

At first Li Ke-ming had little confidence in the southern armies. The small, skinny southerners seemed to have been sapped of their energy by greed and money, and were always busy with their own petty calculations. Danger or difficulty used to make them take to their heels; but when the northern troops advanced and threatened their homes, their will to resist gradually developed. Their houses, property, way of life and values were all tied up in the province. If it fell into the hands of the northerners they would lose everything, they would be robbed bare and sent to live as criminals in the 'reform by labour' camps. A large number of young men had joined the army of the autonomous government, and every town had set up a self-defence contingent. Many factories had gone over to producing arms and military equipment. The whole province was protected by an anti-aircraft network. The people of the Wuyi mountains had undertaken to supply food to the soldiers and provide intelligence on enemy movements. With their help the advancing enemy had been slowed down by guerrilla tactics and the obstruction of roads.

Outpost Nine reported that the charges were in place and asked permission to detonate.

'Tell them that the sapper is in charge of the operation; he will give the order not me.' The request annoyed him. It held things up and increased the danger that the message would be intercepted by the enemy. Whoever was detailed to do the work must have full responsibility. Bureaucratic habits seemed to have followed him even here.

It was still raining. He left the shed, completely hidden in the grove of bamboo. Just outside, he saw the Shaking Rock sway and slowly detach itself from the mountain top in a cloud of dust, followed by the crash of the explosions, echoing round the mountains. The huge rock thundered down, rolling and bouncing over all obstacles and ripping up a wide passage through the trees and bamboo. The sapper's calculations had been good: the rock hit the steel road.

Li Ke-ming's eyes never left the road below and the long-armed monster. The driver must have heard the explosion, but could not see the reason for it, because of the hanging precipice over the road. The mechanical arms continued to do their work... If only the Swaying Rock would smash it to pieces it would be like breaking a leg of the Northern army. Li Ke-ming raised his clenched fists to encourage it

It missed. But by so little. The driver, warned by rocks falling down the cliff, had suddenly reversed at maximum power. An instant later the huge rock hurtled down, missing the monster by twenty yards or more. Li Ke-ming turned away despondently.

The triumphant cries of the others made him look again. The monster seemed to jump up in the air, throwing the steel sheets off its back, then hurled itself at the Swaying Rock, its two arms gesticulating comically, as if to embrace it. There was an impressive burst of sparks as it struck; in the violence of the impact the monster was smashed to pieces. Li Ke-ming dared not believe his eyes. The steel road looked like a hideous wounded dragon with a broken back, in a cloud of dust.

Li Ke-ming stretched out two fingers behind him, but no one gave him a cigarette. The Shaking Rock had fallen on one end of the section of steel road, and in a seesaw effect the monster on the other end had been thrown into the air. What a stroke of luck!

The enemy reacted with fury and opened up with all their weapons, firing at random, imagining perhaps that the southerners were laughing their heads off behind every tree and rock.

Before long there was a familiar sound of helicopters in the clouds. Li Ke-ming had never heard so many at the same time. Forty modern helicopters appeared like vultures from the rain-clouds, as if tipped out of a bucket. They split into pairs that each concentrated on one of the twenty mountain peaks around. First came the incendiary rockets, which laid bare the hills, stripping trees, bamboo and all vegetation, leaving only scorched earth and no place to hide. Then, while one of each pair circled and covered it, the other hovered over a hilltop and fully armed troops were lowered one by one. Some immediately set about digging-in, others went gradually down the mountain slopes with flame-throwers, burning everything in sight. The troop-carrying helicopters were relayed by others and in next to no time 1,600 special troops had occupied all the surrounding mountain tops.

Li Ke-ming ordered his troops to concentrate their fire on the hill-top emplacements, and the anti-aircraft guns to fire at the helicopters. Up until now the enemy had relied mainly on infantry offensives, easy to deal with. This new plan of action was far more dangerous. Once the enemy controlled the high points, the Fujian troops below would lose the initiative and the enemy would be able to control a large area and clear the road blocks. Had the helicopters arrived half an hour earlier, the Swaying Rock would still be a scenic curiosity, where it had been since the beginning of time.

Li Ke-ming watched his anti-aircraft guns fire uselessly at the helicopters. Their small calibre shells had no effect; but whenever the firing increased, the helicopters used their rockets and turned the southern positions into a sea of fire. Once the enemy's positions were consolidated the helicopters flew off, but would soon be back with more troops and occupy more positions. He was not afraid: there were thousands of mountain peaks. You occupy them by day and we'll retake them at night. In the forest there are only our own people. Who gives a dog's fart for their crack troops?

He was wrong. A squadron of fighters roared out of the clouds and dived, low over the bamboo grove. Li Ke-ming saw a small parachute released from one of them, from which something bright, in the shape of a hemisphere, was suspended. Before he could see what it was, his adjutant pushed him down to the ground. There was a small explosion, and when he looked again he saw that the whole side of the mountain and half of that next to it was on fire. A similar hemisphere, carried by another fighter had exploded and released into the air a cloud of oily vapour which spread out to a diameter of about half a mile, before it ignited.

This was the most devastating part of the Northern Army's new strategy. They held only the high points but were systematically burning the whole area, leaving no trees, no grass, no living thing. What sort of enemy was this? How could they be attacked?

The bamboo grove was already on fire and the heat on his cold face made him shiver.

'Bring the radio-transceivers.' He jumped up suddenly. The Staff Officer would never get up again.

He ran through the flames—almost enjoying the heat—and thought of his home in the Northeast and the crackling stove, his wife's warm quilt and strong alcohol warming his gut.

'We're pulling out. Bring the transceivers.'

Taibaishan Nature Reserve

It was Ouyang Zhong-hua's idea to start the Soul Memorial Library. Chen Pan had done much of the work, but it was only since all the roads out of Taibaishan had been blocked by snow, that she had found time to enter into 'the world of souls'.

No more than a part of the original collection had been brought and lodged in the highest cave, where it was dry, in sealed folders and boxes. Ouyang regarded the writing of memoirs as one of the greatest of man's inventions, enabling people's souls to be permanently preserved after their material bodies had disappeared, thus realizing man's ancient dream of immortality. Memoirs had always been conserved of course, when fame or commercial value ensured their survival, making the writing of memoirs a special privilege of the great and famous. Ouyang wanted all memoirs to be conserved.

Chen Pan was rather more concerned with the reform of traditional funeral customs. People spent a great deal of money burying dead relatives, and tombs, mounds and memorials took up space, rapidly becoming scarcer, that could be better used for the benefit of the living. Rather than spending money on people's physical remains or ashes, why not commemorate them in a way closer to human feelings. Memoirs have a greater aesthetic value and are more economic of space and resources. Reading about the lives of one's ancestors, their thoughts and feelings, is a better way of remembering the dead than polishing some gloomy-looking funerary urn. This was the starting point of green ideas on the subject. Chen Pan realized that people's souls were immortal after reading some manuscripts. However long ago the author of a memoir died, his or her life was lived again as Chen Pan read it. Most memoirs were simple and rude in comparison with the memoirs of great men. The writers had no duty to make judgements about history or create an image. She laughed, cried, loved or meditated with the authors. Very few living people revealed themselves so unreservedly. She felt she was with close friends when she read about the simple everyday lives of these living souls. The last few days Chen Pan had only to enter this cave and all her troubles were forgotten.

Suddenly a loud voice was heard, echoing through the caves. 'Chen Pan. Long-distance call from Zhengzhou!'

The centre of the nature reserve was a series of inter-linked natural caves in the side of the mountain, of all sizes and on several different levels. As well as living quarters and guest-rooms, there was an assembly hall, a recreation centre and a gymnasium. Nearly all the caves were linked with the administrative office by a speaking-tube made of bamboo, through which messages could be transmitted over a considerable distance. For the sake of tranquillity the cave that housed the memoirs was not connected to this system, so when a loud voice was heard calling Chen Pan to take a long-distance call from Zhengzhou, she hurried to the nearest speaking-tube and shouted, 'I'm coming. Don't get cut off.'

She had been waiting for this call, but since it had started snowing three days earlier, it had been impossible to get down the valley to the office and she had almost given up hope. It was no longer snowing, so to save time, instead of taking the winding wooden stairway, she slid down the snow-covered slope to the bottom and went to the administrative office, in a brick building. The Nature Reserve, was now one of the six bases of the Green Association, and the director, known to everyone in the association as 'the Sage', was shouting into the telephone, as if expecting to be cut off if he stopped.

In Chen Pan's absence the head of the laboratory in Zhengzhou was in charge of the *shugua* project. He told her that all was well and asked her to wait patiently at Taibaishan until the roads were cleared. The project was very secret and he could not say more, but Chen Pan was relieved. She had made all necessary arrangements before leaving and had drawn two days of food supplies in advance. The snow had forced her to change her plans. She told him that it was no longer snowing and that she had hired two local people who knew the way and would soon start the journey back to Zhengzhou. Neither of them had mentioned the 'provider of funds'. Only she knew that this was Shi Ge. Communications between them were one way: she never contacted him and had been worried that he might have been trying to contact her the last two days and that her absence would cause delays. The fact that the 'provider of funds' had not been mentioned reassured her.

Before coming to Taibaishan she had told Shi Ge that she was confident of being able to persuade the base to accept the Successive Multi-level Election system. The Sage was a theorist and was hopeless as manager, and organization in the base was chaotic. Now was the opportunity to put it to him. She had been in close contact with Shi Ge in connection with the *shugua* project and had become enthusiastic about the Multi-level Election system, which he loved to talk about. He jokingly called her his first disciple. However, the *shugua* project now took up all her time, so she tried to persuade Shi Ge that the Multi-level Election System could just as well be tried out in one of the other bases. He refused.

The state of affairs in the base made her very unhappy, but not enough to diminish her enthusiasm for the vitality of the Green way of life. Now that it had stopped snowing, the rock painting and the ice sculpture, that she found imposing and moving, were again visible. They had been inspired by Ouyang's ideas about the pursuit of beauty and its place in the spiritual world of the future, replacing the present materialism and consumerism. More than a hundred people had been involved in their creation, often working in cradles let down on ropes from above.

The painting covered the whole of the southern face of the mountain and incorporated natural features of the rock into the design. It was a mystical painting that seemed to portray the history of humanity itself, man's sorrows and hopes and his inevitable extinction. It was a testament left for eternity.

Not so the ice sculpture: it would melt in spring when the sun returned. There was a waterfall not far from the caves, about sixty feet high. In winter it froze solid and had been carved into a sculpture of a man and woman making love. Chen Pan had been taken inside it by one of the principal artists, and through the male figure's seminal duct into the woman's uterus, which contained an enormous foetus. Her guide told her that, in proportion, she was about the size of an egg. He had pointed out that they were standing approximately where—according to the laws of nature—an egg and a sperm (about his size)—would meet. Chen Pan refused this rather original invitation, but she was not offended. The artist's heady enthusiasm moved her.

When she was called to the telephone, Chen Pan had been reading a memoir that revealed an astonishing and moving secret. If the Memorial Library had not existed, the secret would have been lost without trace, like countless others. The author had requested that no one should read his memoir until five years after his death and Chen Pan was the first to do so. There were other memoirs that were to remain sealed for a century. The library scrupulously respected the wishes of each writer and Ouyang had been trying to get the People's Congress of the province to pass a resolution obliging police, security and other government organizations to do the same. But the new military regime in Beijing, after arresting innumerable living people, began investigating the memoirs; so in order to protect the tranquillity of the 'souls' and avoid implicating the living, it had been decided to transfer all the memoirs marked secret to Taibaishan.

Unlike the other bases, the Taibaishan Nature Reserve not only had the relative comfort of numerous habitable caves, but was even able to heat them, thanks to the existence of a hot spring, from which the water was piped under the stone flagging in many of the caves

There was even a heated swimming pool—a large cave with a naturally concave floor. As Chen Pan passed by this, she noticed that there was a young and attractive Belgian girl in the water. Ouyang, in swimming trunks, was sitting on a rock watching her. The Beijing regime restricted the entry of foreigners into China, otherwise there would have been many more at the base. Chen Pan did not much like the Belgian girl, not because she was flirting with Ouyang—she was used to such things—but because she had come here purely for emotional stimulation, not to observe and learn.

Ouyang pretended he had not noticed Chen Pan, but purely for her benefit dived into the torch-lit pool to join the girl. He was like a spoilt child. Whenever he could not get what he wanted he took his frustration out on others. He must have heard when Chen Pan was called to the 'phone and was now sulking because he assumed it was Shi Ge on the line? She had been furious in the past whenever she found out that Ouyang was having an affair with another woman, though she knew that he was only amusing himself. It was natural, she felt, that such an exceptional man could not let himself be monopolized by one woman. She felt no flush of jealousy now.

Meeting Ouyang this time at Taibaishan, after two months apart, had been a turning point in their relationship and for the last few days they had not slept in the same room.

She had hurried to Taibaishan to attempt to put the Multi-level Election system into operation while he was away; otherwise there would be little chance of success. He was not interested in ideas that were not the fruit of his own genius. Moreover, the Sage's request for help was an opportunity for him to get control of the base. He hoped to get all six of them under his control—particularly Taibaishan, because it had the advantage of being not far from the railway.

Taibaishan had become the biggest of the six bases in terms of members but also the most heterogeneous, because the Sage lacked judgement and never refused anyone who wanted to join the community. His narrow shoulders were accustomed to supporting the head of a philosopher rather than an administrator; the confusion and increasing tension had become too much for him. He had several times asked to be replaced and said so to Chen Pan as soon as she arrived.

'The trouble is,' he complained, 'Shi Ge doesn't concern himself with our problems and the authorities won't do anything as long as he is Deputy Premier; but If I formally resign they'll appoint someone of their own choosing and we'll lose control of the base. A way round this problem would be to make my position purely nominal: I would just sign things and call meetings. The actual running of the base should be put in the hands of someone competent, such as…'

Chen Pan interrupted him. She knew what he was going to say. Ouyang's gift for organization was well-known and the success of his base at Shennongjia was the envy of the other five. She did not deny it, but she had come here so that Shi Ge's ideas could be tried out and did not want the base to fall into the hands of her former lover.

She still respected Ouyang, but no longer took everything he said as holy writ. She was not conscious of any direct connection between her changed attitude and her friendship with Shi Ge. Indeed, when she compared the two men, she thought Ouyang had more points in his favour. For some reason or other, her contact with Shi Ge had made her more independent and less submissive, and she was slightly surprised that she could not only see the faults in Ouyang's character but even stand up to him.

While Ouyang was absent, Chen Pan had been tirelessly talking about the Multi-level Election System and explaining its advantages. The general level of intelligence in the community was very high and people were quick to grasp new ideas. So there was great interest in Chen Pan's proposal, but no unanimity because everyone had his or her own opinion. At the meeting of the General Assembly, Chen Pan's motion that the system be adopted got a majority of only one vote—she had hardly hoped for more, but it was not enough.

After more discussion and a second vote, she might have got an adequate majority had not Ouyang made a dramatic entrance at the critical moment. He appeared at the meeting after returning from a long and difficult journey of four hundred miles, bringing back a large consignment of supplies from Huangdiling, in spite of martial law and road-blocks everywhere. He was greeted with clapping and shouts of welcome. People crowded round him and forgot about Multi-level Elections. Ouyang enjoyed this kind of performance and revelled in the applause.

The general assembly had just been beginning to understand the full significance of what Chen Pan was proposing, and the majority of those who had not voted for it were nevertheless opposed to keeping the old administration and merely changing the director.

The Sage chose this moment when everyone was excited by Ouyang's arrival to suggest that here was the man to take over as director and called for an immediate vote. A lot of people raised their hands. The result was three votes short of a majority. The Multi-level Election system seemed to have been forgotten. When Chen Pan stood up to protest, she saw the mocking expression on Ouyang's face, which made her—unjustly—put all the blame on him. Though he seemed indifferent, she was sure that he had returned only because the Sage had asked him to take over as Director immediately.

Members of the Green movement were mostly the kind of people who dislike both leading and being led: to get three votes short of a majority was quite an achievement. For all his recent equanimity, when Ouyang was alone with Chen Pan, perhaps because of exhaustion and disappointment, he blamed both her and the Multi-level Election system, and said spiteful things about Shi Ge for his neglect of the bases. For the first time, Chen Pan did not passively allow him to let off steam.

He was surprised and he stalked stiffly away. In the past, it was always Chen Pan who softened first, and he waited for this satisfying outcome, but Chen Pan had not come to him to make peace.

Electric light in the caves was provided by a wind-powered generator built by Xing Tuo-yu, who was an electrician by trade. The former commander of the People's Front and many others who had been involved in the pro-democracy movement, had been forced to go into hiding after the military coup d'état and had taken refuge in the Green bases to avoid arrest. They still had to use false names and dared not leave the bases, but at least they could see the sun and the sky and lead a more or less normal life. Xing Tuo-yu however, considered the safe and isolated base an ivory tower. Having to live there made him edgy and cantankerous, and he sometimes refused to do work that was alien to his world and not sufficiently down-to-earth; he had for instance refused to install electric light in the Memorial Library for this reason, though he claimed that there was not sufficient current. Anything to do with children was another matter and he was now busy with the lighting in the infant school.

There was a 'painting class' going on, though in fact there was no teacher. The children were free to paint what they liked, or to watch and comment on the paintings of others. The adults present were mostly successful, even famous, artists.

Not many parents brought their children to the base so the dozen or so children were 'little treasures' as well as 'guinea-pigs' on whom the Green methods for creating 'the new man' were tried out. In its early years, the Green Association had demanded that education should receive at least half of the investment and effort that was devoted to economic development. But gradually, the Greens had come to realize that the only kind of education capable of changing humanity was not that of knowledge or ideology, but of feeling and emotion, which is the source of peace, harmony, tolerance and fraternity, and is incompatible with materialism.

The children in the nursery school were introduced to poetry, art, music, knowledge of the world and its people, and the understanding of nature. The group studying educational planning considered that these subjects were those best suited to the cultivation of feeling and emotion. Many members of the community took part in educational planning—for the last few days Chen Pan had been talking to the children about animal husbandry and how plants grow. In art classes, she merely helped the real artists.

She enjoyed painting, especially landscapes that were dream-like, strange and full of feeling, rather than realistic. Today, perhaps because she had been moved by her intimacy with the unknown author of the memoir she had been reading, she was working on a very small painting that was both mysterious and unrestrained, expressing both passionate yearning and torment. The landscape seemed to extend into the far distance with terror and dark forms in confusion. But at the end of the earth, where the sun shone, the sky was painfully beautiful.

When he had finished his work, Xing Tuo-yu stood and watched until Chen Pan had finished the painting. He was the sort of man who despises art and artists yet he seemed profoundly moved by it. Chen Pan, feeling quite honoured, wrote a dedication and gave it to him.

'The paintings have to be left here for a few days for the children to see,' she told him. 'When the paint is dry, just take it if I have gone by then. It doesn't matter if I'm not here, since it's got your name on it.'

'I'll miss you, if you leave,' Xing Tuo-yu said with feeling that softened his scarred face.

They walked together to a large cave next to the school that was called 'the big theatre,' where plays and other performances by the members of the community were presented. It was also used as a meeting hall. At present it was empty and there were musical instruments and props still lying on the natural stone platform that served as a stage.

'Tell me more about that election system of yours,' said Xing Tuo-yu, making histrionic movements with a wooden stage sword. Chen Pan was surprised. In the community he was one of those most hostile to the Multi-level Election system. Her memory flashed back to the scene in Tiananmen Square when he furiously burned the Hundred-word Constitution poster.

Xing Tuo-yu had little formal education, and had not understood much of the rather theoretical explanation she had given at the assembly, consequently had showed little interest and voted against it.

After summarizing what she had said, in simpler terms, Chen Pan ended by saying: 'A function of the Multi-level Election system is that it promotes unity and mutual understanding between people. This will initiate an irreversible evolution in which cliques, political parties, and interest groups that all cause enmity, conflict and killing, will eventually disappear. Then the ancient Chinese ideal of Great Harmony can become reality.'

'I think you're laying it on a bit thick,' said Xing Tuo-yu.

'I thought so too at first, but I have come to realize that the possibilities of the Multi-level Election system are almost limitless.'

'Wishful thinking makes every prospect seem rosy,' said Xing Tuo-yu pensively. 'Who would have thought that the pro-democracy movement on Tiananmen Square would ever sink so low as to encourage competition, rivalry, factions and jealousy. Backward people of that kind should have been thrown out of the movement. Such people were always trying to get ahead of others. Cutthroat competition got worse and worse until in the end people lost all sense of reason and self-control. Sometimes I have to agree with those who say that the quality of democracy depends on the quality of the people. We have nine hundred million peasants. Almost half of them are illiterate and couldn't even sign their names on a voting card.'

The assassination of the Secretary-General had been used by the Beijing regime as a pretext for large-scale suppressive measures. This time no tanks were used, but the pro-democracy demonstrators on Tiananmen Square scattered as soon as they saw the troops arrive. This pitiful performance left Xing Tuo-yu with a bitter sense of shame and had almost destroyed his faith in the pro-democracy movement.

'When do you think democracy in China will be feasible then?' Chen Pan asked. 'In two hundred years from now when the whole population have university degrees? Having a university education is no proof that someone understands democracy. Student movements in China, including June Fourth, have always been the same. Even if all the professors got together, they still would have no idea what kind of democratic system we should have or how to introduce it. Some people think that democracy is a proof of civilization: therefore not possible in China. What we need is an electoral system based on the principle that every sentient person, whether peasant of illiterate, can give expression to his or her will in a way that encourages social harmony. That's exactly what the Multi-level Election System is. Of course it is difficult for an illiterate person to grasp the intricacies of rival political programmes, or pass judgement on great affairs of state. But no-one, however well-educated can understand a small village better than those who live there, or be better able to evaluate and exercise a measure of control, if necessary, over the elected authority in his or her village. In small villages people could vote by show of hands if the need arose.'

'In practice,' said Xing Tuo-yu, slashing about him with the stage sword, 'Your system would have to be applied right down to the most basic levels of society and that would be very difficult and wouldn't necessarily involve everyone.'

Some theorists in the pro-democracy movement had suggested that China and its population being so big, and in view of the expense involved, there need only be token polling stations in remote rural areas and villages far from cities—where up to sixty per cent of the country's population lives. They claimed that most of the peasants would not bother to vote anyway and that limiting rural voting would raise the general level of the electorate.

'It will certainly be difficult to put the Multi-level Election system into practice,' Chen Pan went on, 'But definitely easier than general elections on the Western model, which require a huge organization imposed from above. The Multi-level Elections operate from the bottom up and elections can be held anywhere, whenever necessary and among any number of electoral units or levels.'

Xing Tuo-yu was silent for some time. 'I'm only afraid that it won't be so good as it sounds.'

She did not try any more to convince him. The vote had gone against her and she felt she was wasting her time. Shi Ge had said once that people are often impervious to reason. Reason is an attribute of the conscious mind, whereas man's roots are firmly in the unconscious. If he disbelieves something on that level no explanation will have any effect.

A little girl emerged from the latrines, very delicately holding her nose and came up to talk to them. Xing Tuo-yu listened to her in astonishment; Chen Pan realized that she was speaking in Spanish. There were many people in the base who knew one or more foreign languages and some of them were invited to serve as teachers. Foreign languages were taught every day except Saturdays and Sundays and from after breakfast to supper-time, the children were supposed to use only the language of the day. Today it was Spanish. Though neither of them understood the child's words, it was obvious that she was talking about the latrines.

Although the ventilation in the caves was excellent and care had been taken in the construction of the latrines, the stench was overpowering. The normal rota of teams responsible for the latrines seemed to have temporarily broken down and the buckets were all full to overflowing—everyone pretended not to notice. It was difficult to maintain a high standard of hygiene in this much frequented place. Each time she entered, Chen Pan sighed for the three-star toilets of the 'materialist world', with their fragrance, stereo music, pristine porcelain and mirrors.

Although Xing Tuo-yu tried to stop her, she went into the latrines with a determined look on her face and came out carrying a bucket full of excrement. Xing Tuo-yu followed her, and being stronger, took up one in each hand. She carried the bucket a few steps then put it down, not because of the weight but to get a breath of fresh air. To her surprise the bucket was nearly knocked over by a head which emerged from a cavity in the rock as she was passing.

The head belonged to one of several people in the community who liked exploring inside the mountain: he had a coiled rope over his shoulder and carried a torch and an ice-pick. According to them, only a small part of the existing natural caves were in use. There was a whole world of caves, some of them very spectacular, often taking a whole day to reach. They were now surveying these caves and intended to make a map and open a potholing centre. Perhaps they would find more habitable caves.

The potholer happily rubbed his head—he had no helmet—and took up the bucket.

'There's something that Ouyang Zhong-hua has left out,' he said as they walked along. 'The future world of "spiritual man" ought to include some "materialist enjoyment centres". Enjoyment is a form of culture that should be preserved and developed. Of course, if spiritual man does nothing but enjoy himself he will soon get fed up, but with no enjoyment he will become dull and boring. Not too much, not more than a month every year—like a holiday. Going to the enjoyment centre will be like going to a five-star hotel, using high quality cars, eating, drinking, gambling, whoring, indulging oneself to the utmost—and really learning by experience about the depravity of consumer society. Then they will return to the world of spiritual man and to beauty—or carrying buckets of shit. In this way both spirit and flesh will be enriched.'

The desire to have the best of both worlds was often expressed in the community, usually said in a joking manner, but there was genuine concern. The Greens advocated 'moderate comfort', but in the present context it was difficult to define what 'moderate' meant. Aesthetic satisfaction could not, it seemed, entirely make up for material deficiencies and sometimes the latter would ruin the former: carrying a shit bucket gave no one aesthetic satisfaction.

Xing Tuo-yu came back to help Chen Pan and as soon as he saw the bucket in the potholer's hand he stopped. He had little respect for intellectuals who spent their time finding holes in mountains or studied snow or ice. He thought they should do something more useful.

The cess-pit was a cave on ground level and all the excrement from the latrines of more than ten levels ended up there. There had been talk of turning it into a methane generating plant and use the solid residue as fuel. But it was found that the cave leaked, so it was decided to leave things as they were.

Chen Pan offered to solve the problem by providing the community with a nutritional fluid processing plant. Once excrement is fermented and separated, all that remains is a clean residue and a fluid which could be used to grow vegetables for the community. The shortage of food prevented it from expanding. The chickens and rabbits that were raised could only provide enough for the children. Chen Pan constantly thought about how to remove the unpleasant taste of *shugua*, but she had neither the time nor the necessary equipment to do anything about it. Biological experiments frequently involved ten or even a hundred man-years before they bore fruit. She often wondered whether really advanced research would be possible in the Green society of the future.

Although the glass in the window of Chen Pan's cave-room was of very poor quality, full of impurities and uneven, it kept the cold out and let in some light. Equally poor quality glass had been used to make a mirror, the position and angle of which could be adjusted to reflect light into the cave. The glass had been made in the riverside workshop, that worked round the clock producing not only glass, but various tools, water pipes, paint, theatrical props, iron and stone vessels, and so on. Cloth was woven and dyed there and there was a pottery kiln. It was open to anyone, and many inventions were produced there.

The workshops were the result of the Sage's vision of an ideal society. He considered that excessive specialization was responsible for contemporary man's alienation and dehumanization. The division of labour in society had played a vital role in the development of production and technology; but nowadays when people have an easy life, they easily become idle and decadent and their frantic consumerism leads to waste, destruction of the environment and unemployment. Now is the time to bring the division of labour to an end. The thirst for knowledge should replace the desire for comfort as the main motivation of labour. An important principle in the community was that the distinction between physical and mental labour should be progressively abolished and that members should engage both in collective work for the common good and in the pursuit of spiritual beauty. Mental and physical work should become perfectly complementary: mental effort is rest from physical effort and vice versa.

The Sage had a list of all the unsolved economic and technical problems there were in the base posted up, and individuals or groups were asked to produce a solution to as many of them as possible. The non-stop operation of the workshop was the result of this stimulus. His ambition was to make the base self-supporting. There were many scientists in the community, but most of the solutions to the Sage's list of problems were for craftsmen to solve. The library had a collection of books and papers on handicraft techniques used up to a hundred years ago; these attracted more readers than the fat volumes on modern science. Artists, usually considered to have the least to do with material production, showed their natural gifts when something of a specific form was needed. They were all keen to take part and what they designed were also works of art. The absence of glass had been one of the difficult problems that concerned everyone in the base. After much planning, the production of glass started, by which time, almost half the members of the community had become involved. Although the quality of the glass was poor, every piece—with its impurities and uneven surface—was a work of art.

Certain things had to be done even if they interested no one. Culinary artists enjoyed cooking, but not preparing vegetables or washing rice; botanists enjoyed plant breeding but not hoeing, fertilizing or watering the vegetables. Cleaning the latrines was the most unpopular task of all. Such things were therefore done by rota. It was not only the rough physical work that people liked to avoid; the work most sought after by materialist man—that of administrator—was another.

The pursuit of beauty may require no organization at all, but economics—however simple—does. The nature reserve had been a Green experimental base for three months and up until now, the community had depended on the 250 kilos of grain and 200,000 *yuan* that was required as a contribution from each member upon joining. If production could not be properly organized before spring, they could only eat what they had and wait for disaster.

Organizing large-scale production was not just a matter of making a list. Ploughing, sowing, reaching agreement with near-by villages, relations with the state, the distribution of materials, protection of the environment and innumerable other questions had not yet been dealt with.

The Sage knew that all these things had to be done before the spring sowing; at least he was not vain and had no illusions about his ability. He had decided to resign as soon as possible in order to give maximum time for his successor. He wanted Ouyang to replace him, not only because his organizational ability was greater than that of anyone else in the community, but also because Ouyang agreed with him that the base must become self-sufficient, though not for exactly the same reasons. Ouyang's view was that 'spiritual man' could only escape the inevitable social collapse if the survival bases were already self-supporting. All efforts should be directed to this end. The Sage continued to lobby in Ouyang's favour and completely stopped carrying out his functions in order to put pressure on the members of the community to resolve the problem quickly. In the absence of any kind of administration, the canteen had yesterday only provided one meal because of the shortage of supplies.

Chen Pan knew the Sage well. He was excitable and choleric, but this behaviour was not in character. Yet there was a need for some kind of pressure. The general assembly had not voted for Ouyang Zhong-hua as director; nor had there been enough votes in favour of the Multi-level Election System. There the matter rested. If nothing was done, the present muddle would naturally continue. If the community began to suffer the consequences of the present chaos, it would not be difficult to obtain a majority in Ouyang's favour—another three votes would be enough. Chen Pan was certain that this was not the Sage's strategy, but Ouyang's.

Earlier that year, at a village fair in the Northeast with Ouyang, Chen Pan had seen an inflatable baby doll hanging up like a lantern. Still hoping that he might be capable of a little natural kindness, she asked him to buy 'little Shasha' for her, then teased and pestered him into holding it in his arms in full view of the public as they walked through the fair. Her unplanned pregnancy made her float on a sweet sea of happiness; but to tell him about it, needed all her courage. Only in the darkness, relaxed after making love, in the warmth of the tent and with 'little Shasha' beside them, did she find the courage to tell him she was pregnant. She had always considered him a genius and admired him because he could always get the better of anyone in an argument or debate. But now, when she obstinately refused to listen to the reasons why she should not have the baby, he finally told her to choose: if she insisted on having the child, he would leave her. She cried bitterly. Everything he said was right. At any moment he might be arrested and even killed—he did not want the child to suffer. But she hated the pressure he put on her, his peremptory and authoritarian manner, disguised as calm reasoning. He was not offering a choice, but showing the whip. She gave in of course, but from then on whenever he behaved in this way, even if he was in the right, she wanted to close her eyes and block her ears.

Supper was only rice gruel and pickles. Everyone had been busy all day, in the workshops or out in the cold painting or sculpting. They were hungry, and complained. Chen Pan helped in the kitchen and somehow a meal was produced for the children. It was Theatre Day in the base and people from the various camps outside also came, expecting the usual theatrical activities: performing or rehearsing plays, or discussing scripts with everyone who wanted to participate. Theatre Day was a day of celebration and an opportunity for the whole community to get together. People continued to arrive from midday onwards. But today, no group activities had started and it was already dark. If it had been merely a matter of discomfort it might not have mattered, but people were hungry: beauty was not strong enough to compensate for that.

When everyone had assembled in the 'big theatre', the Sage again said he wanted to resign. Because of the civil war, half of the grain that members had contributed on joining had not yet been delivered. One of the last two consignments had been seized by the military, the other by famine victims. Like it or not, the base dedicated to Beauty was being transformed into a base for survival, as Ouyang had said. Priorities were different and strong leadership more important than ever. Ouyang Zhong-hua's ability and achievements, the Sage said, were well known, and he now proposed that the General Assembly elect him as director by acclamation rather than voting. Many people began clapping, but perhaps because people were hungry, there was no enthusiasm.

In the light of the flaming torches, Ouyang had the solemn air of someone about to take office in a time of crisis. This tended to inspire confidence that to follow his leadership would not be a mistake.

The Sage was about to bang down his hammer to announce the decision when a enigmatic voice was heard from the back.

'When there were not enough votes, we had only gruel to eat: if he takes over, will those who disagree have only the northwest wind to drink?'

Silence. This cynical remark from the semi-darkness seemed to express the feeling of many people and perhaps explained the half-hearted applause earlier. The Sage appeared very uneasy, his thin body twisted and turned and his eyes looked this way and that.

'Our present stocks of food, apart from grain, only allow us to provide for the children.' He said. Now winter's here, and with civil war going on, even the big cities have no vegetables. One of our two greenhouses collapsed under the snow, and the vegetables we planted in the other were killed by frost...'

A tall man rose in the front row. Chen Pan recognized a member of the Lanzhou Glacier Research Institute, who had been both to the North and the South Poles and was well respected in the community. His camp was on the highest peak in the Taibai mountains. 'The details can perhaps be worked out later. We need a decision this evening. Everyone is hoping to clear up some problems.'

'What problems?' The sage said cautiously, on the alert. There had been much discontent the last few days in the scattered communities.

The man from the Lanzhou Institute turned to the assembled members. 'We should ask Chen Pan's advice.'

'I'm here,' said Chen Pan, raising her hand in the last row. Someone brought a flaming torch nearer and all eyes turned to her.

'We would like to hear more about the Multi-level Election system,' he said.

Chen Pan was surprised and delighted.

Everyone listened to her in silence, then after she had finished speaking and had answered a few questions, there was some clapping—a little scattered—but for Chen Pan, an unexpected reward. She did not dare look at Ouyang, but felt his eyes on her.

'Thank you,' said the glaciologist with a courteous bow. Then he turned and said to the Sage, 'I propose that we now take a vote—even if only symbolic—and then adopt the Multi-level Election system by acclamation. Chen Pan is a guest and a woman who deserves this recognition as an expression, at least of our serious interest.'

The Sage seemed to take this as a kind of consolation, politely expressed appreciation of Chen Pan's suggestion and gratitude for her help to the Taibaishan base. Then he called for a vote.

Chen Pan had not expected to see so many hands raised. But when the votes were counted it was found that they were several short of a majority.

'There's another vote here,' said Xing Tuo-yu standing up in the back row, his hand raised. Seven of his comrades of the People's Front who had also taken refuge here in the base, immediately raised theirs too. They always stood together.

Fuzhou

In the bunker the shrill sad sound of the sirens was inaudible, but not the bombs although the Beijing army had announced that no harm would come to the people. Probably because Beijing was exasperated by Fujian's determination not to surrender and decided to terrorize the population, so ever since Guangzhou had fallen to the Beijing army a few days ago Fuzhou had been heavily bombed every few hours.

It was cold in the bunker and there was no heating. Yet Huang Shi-ke was sweating from every pore, and sticky. He knew this must annoy Bai Ling but he could not help himself, and insistently snuggled up close to her. He found no comfort except in the contact with her body. He knew there was not much time left. What should a condemned man cling to if not to the person he could not bear to lose? He had never been so desperate. Even when Nanjing's time limit was running out he could still escape. But now the seaplane had been shot down and in any case no aircraft could even take off because Beijing controlled the air and had also laid mines in the river. During the night parachute troops had landed on the sea-shore to avoid the Fuzhou air defences, and were consolidating their position. Fuzhou was cut off by land, sea and air.

After the defensive line in the Wuyi Mountains had been broken the Beijing army advanced down the valley of the Min river towards Fuzhou. Other strategic points had then become irrelevant. Everything now depended on the slow retreat, with heavy losses, of the exhausted Fujian troops under Li Ke-ming. After a battle the previous day the Min river flowing through Fuzhou ran red. In a few days the survivors would be in Fuzhou. Most of the province of Guangdong was in the hands of the Beijing army, which was now only about 100 km away

Huang Shi-ke closed his eyes and had visions of the slow and agonizing death reserved for traitorous ministers of the Emperor of former times. Though the gleaming knives soon vanished, the cold in the bunker seemed to slice his flesh and he clung tighter to Bai Ling. His sweat had soaked the quilt and fear made him moan and groan. She was silent, lying naked in his arms, giving him no tender consolation and showing no trace of fear. When he began to weep she looked at him.

'You despise me, don't you?' Huang Shi-ke said.

She did not answer. At headquarters these last few days only she had appeared indifferent to the danger. Li Ke-ming at the front was determined to go on fighting whatever the outcome and Bai Ling had become the main link between him and headquarters. She seemed to have a thorough understanding of military matters and warfare. When she sat at the radio and listened in exhilaration to the sounds of battle and Li Ke-ming's hoarse voice giving orders, Huang Shi-ke felt very small.

'You despise me, don't you?' he repeated tearfully. He had forgotten what tears were, yet in the space of a few days he had become a weakling. 'I'm not afraid of death,' he said, 'only of losing you. The thought of never seeing you again....' Bai Ling sighed slightly

'I have a last request, Bai Ling,' he went on. 'I refuse to become a trophy for the northerners and be humiliated in their courts,' He took her hand and led it to a small bag hanging on a cord round his neck. 'This is poison. All I ask is that you let me look at you when I swallow it, so that we can be together always...' He could not go on.

'You ask whether I despise you,' said Bai Ling in the darkness. 'Yes I do, very much so.' The coldness in her voice stopped his crying immediately. 'What I loved in you was your maturity and strength—not behaving like a woman intent on suicide. You were not like this before. You didn't lose hope when Nanjing's neutrality was almost brought to an end. You held your head up to the last and a miracle happened. Why have you given up hope now?'

'Yes, it was a miracle. But only God creates miracles.'

'You Communists believe in God?' Huang Shi-ke was puzzled. Bai Ling herself had been in the Party for several years, why did she say 'you communists'?

'It's because I don't believe in God that I no longer hope for a miracle.'

'Then you don't believe that Shen Di was dropped from Heaven?'

'That's still a mystery to me.'

'When you were about to fly to Beijing who told you that you'd be arrested?'

'You 'phoned me…'

'How did I know?'

She had always said it was intuition. Now she was clearly telling him that it was a lie.

'To have found out that you were going to be arrested in Beijing is nothing to speak of. But to track down and capture Shen Di and deliver him to your doorstep was something far beyond the ability of your Southern Alliance to achieve. If you have been protected in the past why should you not be helped in the future by the same power.'

'Power?' Huang Shi-ke's throat tightened, he could hardly get a word out. 'Who…?'

'Who could it be? You should have guessed.' Bai Ling's voice became very gentle, and she let out a word which fluttered round in the darkness like a pigeon.

'Taiwan.'

Under the damp quilt Huang Shi-ke's body became rigid.

'Then you…'

'I am with Taiwan Military Intelligence, on special assignment. Five years ago I took the identity of a girl from Fuzhou who had escaped to Taiwan. Your provincial Secretary General is head of Taiwan Military Intelligence in Fuzhou and he got me into the provincial government.'

Bai Ling's voice was soft and tender and pleasant to listen to, but her words had as much effect on him as the bombs landing on Fuzhou.

'And your pilot friend…?' he asked apprehensively.

Bai Ling laughed. 'That was a touching story, wasn't it?'

Everything seemed to fall to pieces about him. The enemy aircraft shrieked overhead and bombs kept falling.

'And the hot springs?' Huang Shi-ke could not help asking.

'There was no special plan, but of course it was not just chance. If you had not pulled down that plastic curtain I would have found a way to do it.'

He clenched his teeth and did not ask about the glances she used to give him: of course they were false. Everything became clear. She liked old men? Naturally that went to his head and stifled any suspicion.

In silence Bai Ling lay on him writhed like a snake, rubbing against his body.

'You used me,' he said hoarsely.

'You should say I helped you.' Bai Ling kissed his neck. 'What have I ever done for you that was not in your interests?'

He thought of the radio signals penetrating the dense darkness from close to his body. Li Ke-ming had caught her in the act, but shielded by him she had had nothing to fear.

'I don't like being used.' He felt suffocated. For the first time he felt the weight of Bai Ling on his body.

'But you like being helped. When Shen Di appeared you wept with joy.'

'I don't see the point of these mysterious games you've been playing.'

'Of course it was not just to give you an unexpected and pleasant surprise. If there had been enough time we would have delivered Shen Di earlier, when Beijing might already have been at war with Nanjing. But he wasn't easy to catch and we only succeeded at the last moment, and getting him out of Thailand and secretly back to China was very complicated. When I was in radio contact that night there was no guarantee that they could deliver him on time. But they did well, our people, don't you think?'

'Why did the person who caught him pretend to be Li Ke-ming?'

'Because he's easy to impersonate, of course. He only needed a mask. At the time we couldn't let anyone know that we were involved. Our position is a bit delicate. That's why we had to pretend a little to you.'

Pretend a little! Huang Shi-ke groaned. Bai Ling's lips wandered over his chest and belly like a pigeon pecking...He was no longer twenty years old and could not imagine making love with a special agent. But in fact Bai Ling had done no harm and had given him so much joy; why worry whether her feelings were true or false? He had no choice now but to let himself be used. That was the way of the world now: use and be used'

'Now what?' he asked.

He was surprised now that he had not seen through her earlier. In the darkness he could sense that she had a smile of triumph.

'Appeal to Taiwan. Our army will help you regain the initiative.'

Huang Shi-ke switched on the light and poured himself a drink. The sound of bombs exploding seemed to come from the west now. Water was seeping down the concrete walls of the bunker, like snail tracks.

He had not thought of this possibility before. Taiwan had an army of eight hundred thousand—only a quarter of that of the Mainland—but better trained and equipped. Taiwan had a strong economy and incomparably more foreign currency reserves. Even if Taiwan only supplied arms the Alliance would not be in so disastrous a situation. Moreover, if Taiwan intervened there would certainly be a dramatic tilt of the political balance towards democracy. For several years the economic achievement of Taiwan had been obvious to all; but for economic and political reasons Beijing had been making concessions to Taiwan. Family contacts and trade relations increased and with the increased circulation of Taiwanese products the image of Taiwan on the Mainland had greatly changed and made the 'communist model' of development seem inferior. This development might have increasingly important political consequences. The problem was that the Nationalist Party (KMT) had lost the elections and the Democratic Progressive Party was now in power, and intended to have nothing to do with the Mainland and would not interfere with Mainland matters at any price. The Southern Alliance had several times failed to establish relations with the new government.

Huang Shi-ke finished his drink. 'You don't mean to say that the Taiwan government has also been pretending?'

'The Democratic Progressive Party is just the little finger: the army is the fist. It is we who have helped you and will continue to help you. Don't forget: it is we, not the DPP who represent Taiwan.'

Then there was a deafening bomb explosion; the light went out, a corner of the concrete wall collapsed, the whole bunker rocked and began to fill with water. The command centre above was flattened. Huang Shi-ke had the impression that the whole Min river was flowing into the bunker. He jumped off the bed and went barefoot towards the door, water already up to his ankles. In the darkness he bumped into the door, which had been blown open and a shattered mirror fell in pieces into the water.

'Don't move,' shouted Bai Ling. She found a torch and put on her clothes.

Huang Shi-ke stood, ashamed beyond words, blood on his forehead was dripping into his eyes. In the light of the torch his protruding belly looked green. He felt incomparably ugly and shook from cold and terror.

'There's not much time,' said Bai Ling, helping to dress him.

'What should I do?'

'Go to the radio station and read out this statement.'

Bai Ling looked at him encouragingly. There was a sheet of paper in her hand. He took it mechanically. Pieces of the broken mirror flashed in the rising water.

'Just for reading this Beijing will have my head.'

'They won't let you keep it anyway.'

The air raid came to an end. Everything was silent. The water continued to rise.

Taipei: The Presidential Palace.

The President stood looking out of the window at the flowers and shrubs lit by yellow globes. The dark outline of the trees swayed eerily, resembling enemies stealthily moving into position. The radio was still tuned to Fuzhou, which had evidently suffered serious damage: there was constant interference and sometimes it could not be heard at all. Nevertheless all Taiwan had heard the broadcast.

The President was suddenly afraid: the moment had finally arrived.

Fujian Radio had stopped all programmes and repeatedly broadcast Huang Shi-ke's appeal for help. The President had never taken Huang Shi-ke very seriously, but this appeal made him change his mind. Even an experienced Taiwanese politician could not have spoken so well. It was pitched just right for the occasion and in terms which were genuinely Taiwanese. It was stirring, but made no short-sighted and hackneyed call for unity, unlike the usual Mainland broadcasts to Taiwan. Just because of all this, it was going to be more difficult to handle.

The President focused his eyes on the glass of the window and saw reflected there a row of epaulettes and shining hat badges. The Chief-of-Staff and the commanding officers of the Army, Navy and Air Force were sitting stiff-backed on the sofa. They were all approximately of the same stature and reflected in the glass, looked like a row of toy soldiers. The head of Military Intelligence sat at the end: his rank was lower than the other officers but not his importance. The only man in civilian clothes sat casually in an armchair, more at ease in these surroundings than the President, whose position he had occupied for six years: the present incumbent for only six months. Though no longer President, as Chairman of the KMT, Nationalist Party, he had only to clear his throat and the whole island felt the tremor.

The eyes of the six most powerful men in Taiwan were on the President's back. He felt the room oppressively hot. He had been woken up in the middle of a dream twenty minutes ago when Fuzhou had began broadcasting Huang Shi-ke's speech; yet these men had arrived together at the Presidential Palace. No child could believe that this was by chance. Not long ago he had assumed that as President he would be able to control everything, but he had been unable to find any trace of plans make by the previous, Kuomintang, government for an attack on the Mainland.

For decades the nationalists' call to 'counter-attack the Mainland' had been nothing but an empty slogan. June Fourth marked a turning point: from then on it became a practical policy. But after the elections all the relevant documents had been removed from the Presidency and nothing could be done by the new President to nip it in the bud.

He finally turned round to face his visitors.

'My attitude has always been clear. Taiwan must be completely separate and independent when the Mainland falls apart if we are to avoid being blown to pieces at the same time. This is the only intelligent policy and the only guarantee that we will survive and continue to develop. As for Fujian's appeal, we can only express our desire to help and the impossibility of doing so.'

'This is not just a question of helping Fujian,' said the KMT Chairman, not hiding his impatience. 'It is a question of saving our country from disaster! We have waited for half a century to counter-attack the Mainland. We have the opportunity now and if we do not take it, by the time Beijing has put down the rebellion of the Southern Alliance and recovers its stability it will be too late. Your party has always accused us of shouting about counter-attacking and doing nothing. Now let us suit our action to our words.'

Both men knew that this was indeed the last chance to recover the Mainland. With passage of time the descendants of those who had come from the Mainland after their defeat by the Communists, had become 'Taiwanized'. Taiwan not China had become the focus of their patriotism. The last of the old generation was facing retirement, their successors would have no interest in attacking the Mainland and Taiwan would finally become independent. But for the moment a struggle was still going on between the nationalists and the independentists. Although the President had long since decided to adopt a policy of independence, no announcement to that effect had been made. It would have been perfect if the civil war on the Mainland had been delayed for three or five years. Unfortunately an opportunity had appeared now and those people who had been shouting for a whole generation for a counter-attack were not likely to let it escape them.

Huang Shi-ke, in his broadcast, had referred to Taiwan's investments in Fujian—another question that troubled the President. As the sentimental attachment of people in Taiwan to the Mainland became weaker, the desire of Taiwanese to invest their money there increased.

It had fallen off for a while after June Fourth, and the government had energetically imposed controls and guidance in order to reduce the rush to invest. However, there was too much money lying idle in Taiwan. The Mainland was offering preferential terms as an enticement and by now several hundred million dollars had been invested there, 60 per cent of it in Fujian. Taiwan investors saw the Mainland as the last really big market in the world. But would Taiwan be able to monopolize this market, the dream of capitalists all over the world? Even within the KMT the will to reconquer was being sapped by the lure of profit. Commercial and industrial interests were very powerful in Taiwan and from the beginning of the civil war between the North and the South, had criticized the hands-off policy of the government and demanded aid for Fujian.

In his broadcast appeal Huang Shi-ke reminded Taiwan that if the autocratic Beijing regime succeeded in suppressing the independence movement, all their investments would disappear. It was ironic that there were many among those urging the government to intervene in the civil war on the Mainland who were 'genuine' Taiwanese—not descendants of refugees. People are willing to fight to the death for the sake of money.

'Whether from the point of view of politics, economy and culture, Taiwan has moved further away from mainland China,' the President said, 'so what is the point of sticking together or for us to attack them. Whether we can succeed is questionable anyway but what good would it do us to control the whole Mainland? Productivity here is 12,000 dollars and on the Mainland eight hundred. How can we possible co-exist? Taiwan would not be able to bear the economic burden and there is no certitude that the Mainland would ever make up the enormous discrepancy. We are two different worlds. The realistic thing to do now is for the Mainland to split up. Why cling to attitudes of half a century ago?'

'Mr President,' said the Chairman of the KMT, leaning back in his armchair, yet seeming to talk down to the President from a great height. 'Fifty years is nothing but a snap of the fingers in the long march of history. After five thousand years of history are we, the Chinese people, to be separated by a difference in productivity? You have only been in this residence for six months, but for fifty years we, the KMT held office here. It was we who raised the productivity of Taiwan; why should we not do the same for the Mainland?'

The Chief-of-Staff spoke before the President had time to reply. 'I am a soldier and speak purely from a military point of view. Do you think, Mr President that if Beijing recovers full control over the whole country, the independence of Taiwan will be tolerated? We would be in desperate straits if they attack or blockade us; however developed our economy may be, it would be difficult to fight a protracted war of resistance with our small population and resources. If you do not intervene on the Mainland that does not mean that Beijing will return the favour. To imagine that relations with the Mainland can ever be on an equal footing is wishful thinking. From a military point of view defence never produces victory, merely a different degree of defeat, while attack is the best means of defence. Leaving aside the question of attacking the Mainland, if we can help Fujian to get free from Beijing, this would create a buffer zone between us and Beijing which would at least increase our security. If the Mainland shifts from a centralized system to a federal system, that would be even better for our security. In a pluralist political system based on territorial entities, there would be no strong demand for an unified, indivisible China and no means of preventing regional independence. Of course, if we liberate the Mainland, democracy will be introduced and there will be a way of settling these questions once and for all.'

As the Chief-of-Staff was speaking the three top commanders kept nodding their heads. They were all members of the KMT. The President had been involved in politics for many years but only now that he had reached the highest position in the state, did he realize the strength of the KMT. He had been a Communist when the Nationalists held power in China before fleeing to Taiwan, and had only seen their corruption, inefficiency and incompetence: the KMT was rotten all through and fated to disappear from the stage of history. Now the position was reversed. The KMT was no longer in power in Taiwan but the President had not failed to see that it was indestructible, omnipresent, its power penetrating into every corner. Most of the army officers were members and their ideas were all animated by the spirit of 'counter-attacking the Mainland.' Who could stop them now that there was an opportunity to wipe out the humiliation of defeat and flight more than fifty years ago?

The Chief-of-Staff had obviously foreseen the present situation and had thought long and carefully about it. The President wondered why he had not seen so far ahead. He had been hoping that on the Mainland all efforts would go into economic development and become so dependent on the international economy that Taiwan would slowly achieve independence in a roundabout way by playing its cards right. The assassination of the Secretary-General and the political changes in Beijing had put paid to such illusions.

Seeing the President lost in thought the KMT Chairman said mildly,

'Your Progressive Party, only came into existence in 1975, when the late President Jiang Jing-guo lifted the ban on political parties; now it is you who are President. It should not be forgotten that the former President's intention was solely to leave behind him a final plan for recovering the Mainland: by lighting a beacon of hope for our fellow countrymen on the Mainland, so that our political freedom and economic prosperity would inspire them to overthrow the cruel dictatorship of the Communist Party. Our fellow countrymen have now risen up. If we ignore them how can the soul of President Jiang Jing-guo rest at peace?'

The President signalled to a secretary to turn off the radio, and sat silent for a while.

'I cannot lead the people into war for the sake of a political motive,' he said finally. 'I intend to call a referendum on Taiwan's independence. After the people have made their choice we will discuss the next step.'

This was his last throw of the dice. The KMT influence was strongest in the upper levels of society and in the power cliques. The PPP had calculated that if there was a referendum, 60% of the population would vote in favour of independence. Decision by majority vote is the cornerstone of democracy and however powerful the KMT might be it would not dare oppose such a decision. Beijing was too preoccupied with its own affairs and incapable of starting a war with Taiwan. So once Beijing had recovered its strength 'the timber would have become a boat', and nothing could be done about it.

'A referendum.' The Chairman of the KMT smiled coldly. 'Are you thinking of using a referendum to escape from reality? Even if all the votes are in favour you still have to keep your feet on the ground. There are links which cannot be broken by votes. Taiwan and the Mainland are joined by a common heritage. Do you think that a vote by 25 million can count as a majority vote? How many generations have shed their blood for Taiwan: should they not have a vote? Will over a thousand million of our countrymen on the Mainland be allowed to vote? Are you going to decide the fate of the Chinese people by an empty piece of "democratic" theatre? If things are so simple the First Emperor need not have unified China! Mr President, this line of thinking is a little infantile.'

The President did not meet the KMT Chairman's eyes and did not answer. His silence showed that he had not changed his mind and did not need to discuss these high-sounding principles and rhetoric. He was President of the Taiwan people of today. Moreover, if he went against the principles of the PPP he would have no legitimacy.

'Your Excellency.' The Chief-of-Staff was more respectful than the

Chairman of the KMT. 'The decision of the army has already been taken and you will not prevent us from acting by refusing to ratify it.'

'That is unconstitutional!' said the President, raising his head in astonishment.

'If you cannot lead the country properly,' said the Chief-of-staff in the same courteous tone, 'We will impeach you, according to the Constitution, in the interests of the country.'

The President tried to laugh coldly, without much success.

'Impeachment has to follow a procedure. Do you imagine that the people of Taiwan will agree to it?'

'In wartime there is a wartime procedure; the people of Taiwan will not even know that you have left office.'

'What do you mean?'

The Chief of Staff lowered his head modestly. 'Whether you agree or not we are going to fight this war under your leadership. If you agree you will go down in history as the great president who restored the glory of the Chinese race. If you don't agree, from now on you will see only us. We will report to you, consult you and get all our instructions from you. All you need to do is sign. After the victory we will apologize to the people and ask for punishment.'

The President's blood was seething, but he silently paced the carpet and without showing his feelings, considered whether to call the Presidential Guard and put these traitors under arrest. He immediately dismissed the idea: if they could draw up battle-plans involving several hundred thousand troops, they were not going to be caught napping by the Presidential Guard.

He turned and sat down in the spacious armchair behind his desk. 'Why do you choose to intervene on the Mainland just when the Alliance is about to go under?'

The Chairman of the KMT turned away to admire a fine vase full of flowers, as if to say that everything was now up to the military.

'In that way,' the Chief of Staff explained, 'we can inflict the maximum possible damage on the Beijing armies. Modern warfare is a competition involving a high level of expenditure, superior, costly and high-tech material. The latest intelligence indicates the reserves of the Beijing armies are already very low. Lack of parts and maintenance have grounded half of their aircraft and forty per cent of their tanks and armoured carriers are immobilized. Shortage of fuel has led to a serious crisis in transport and supplies fall far short of requirements. Their mobility has visibly decreased. Now is the best moment to attack. For political reasons we also need to reduce the power of the Southern Alliance. Although they have broken with Beijing that does not mean that they have become sworn enemies. Allowing the south to retain too much power will make them more difficult to control. Of course, once we have recovered the Mainland there can be no question of allowing them to flirt with independence again.'

'The greatest threat from the Mainland,' said the President, tapping on his desk with a pencil, 'is not the Beijing armies, but their nuclear weapons.'

'That's correct,' the Chief of Staff replied with a faint smile. 'However, the ABM Convention has relieved us of that threat.'

The importance for Taiwan of the ABM Convention was that it removed the darkest shadow hanging over Taiwan's dream of independence. China, as a member of the Security Council had tried to obstruct the adoption of the treaty, but dared not come out openly in favour of 'first use' of nuclear weapons and had finally abstained. The fact remained that Beijing was bound by the Treaty.

'We will not be taking action in the name of the government of Taiwan,' said the Chief of Staff, 'or the army. Our soldiers will be called 'people's volunteers'. This will give us more latitude as far as international law is concerned.'

'Maybe,' said the President, realizing that argument was useless but determined to make his point. 'No matter how weak the Mainland may be, a thin camel is still bigger than a horse: whether or not we win in the end, our troops are going to suffer heavy casualties. How are we going to explain that to our people?'

'Of course we are not going to rely on military means alone. The desire for change on the Mainland increases day by day; we only have to tap this source of pent-up energy and will win without fighting. Our specialist has already made a great deal of preparation for this.'

The 'specialist' was the head of Military Intelligence, the little old man responsible for the subversive operations on the Mainland for more than half a century

He explained leisurely that as a result of several years of reform and decentralization there had been a great increase in local power on the Mainland. In several provinces and cities a completely independent system of local government had developed that could become the basis of greater independence. It was this trend that had led to the formation of the Southern Alliance.

'Other provinces are frightened of Beijing and give the appearance of toeing the line; but as soon as proof of the illegality of the Beijing regime is known there will be a surge of opposition. The landing of our troops in Fujian will encourage revolt in other places—even if the Alliance is defeated. We have 37,000 agents undercover on the Mainland who will simultaneous take action and start a major rebellion.'

'The Nanjing Command has so far not lost one man out of its half a million troops and is enough of a threat to us, not to mention the East China Fleet,' said the President.

'You know the nickname of Commander Bai of the Nanjing military region, Your Excellency? The Fox. He pretends to be upright, direct and just; but he is an experienced man, astute and ambitious, who has been waiting for an opportunity to grab the southeastern provinces and make himself into a little emperor. Our intervention will suit him, and unless we provoke him he certainly won't fight us. On the other hand we can give him plenty of reasons—even encouragement—for advancing on Beijing.'

'How?' asked the President.

'By providing proof that the Beijing government is illegitimate. If we produce positive proof that the late Secretary-General was assassinated by those now in power, the Mainland will split overnight.'

'Can you find proof?'

'It's in the bag.'

'Well?' The Chairman of the KMT walked back to his chair leaning on a stick. The President threw down his pencil on the desk: 'I'll wait until you produce it.'

Montevideo

The Major was tired but happy. His games the previous night with three girls had been a little too wild. One of them, new to the trade, was delicate and shy and very stimulating, another was extremely attractive and the third very passionate. He indulged himself in this way once a week and paid five times the normal price. All the girls had to be different each time and go to hospital for a check-up first. He was not concerned about the money. Now, after a Turkish bath and a massage, he felt clean and relaxed and he liked that. It was the same each time. He was himself, tainted by no one.

He was drinking the most expensive French wine to be found in Uruguay. It was the reason he frequented this bar. For several days he had been drinking nothing else. He was looking at the statue of Jose Artigas in Independence Square and the pigeons fluttering about the bronze rump of his horse in the warm sunshine.

Since he had finished his job in China his life had been one of leisure. The six million dollars would last him for ten years. He always kept in his wallet a one dollar bill—the extra dollar that he had been paid, a sign that the client was satisfied. He kept it as a memento. He was not a man of much feeling but he felt proud of his success in China. Cosmetic surgery had removed all trace of the burns, but the memory of that sea of fire remained with him.

A car had drawn up in the parking area and a Chinese was leaning against it reading a newspaper. The Major felt a twitch in his spine. There was nothing unusual about the man's posture, but he felt death in the air. He had often leaned against a car reading the paper when he was hunting. Not far off, another Chinese was taking photographs of the Salza Palace. ...The same feeling...

He looked away. His expression did not change, nor his colour. He believed he was going to pay dearly for the wine: normally he did not go to the same bar or restaurant several days running.

In complete silence the two Chinese sat down at a table nearby and three others joined them. Suddenly the Major flew sideways out of his chair, his hand already on the butt of the automatic in his under-arm holster. He only had to roll over a few times on the ground and the automatic would clear a bloody path for him. The five men were staring at him in stupefaction, motionless as if completely nonplussed. The Major understood. As he leapt up he had felt a slight prick in his side.... There was no spectacular rolling fire. He fell heavily to the ground, his body stiffened and began to shudder.

The five Chinese stood woodenly to one side waiting for someone to come. One of them slipped the Major's automatic back in its holster.

'Epileptic fit.' He heard the Chinese kneeling over him say in English. He began to froth at the mouth and his eyes turned up, leaving only the whites visible.

'I'll go and call an ambulance,' said the waiter in consternation.

'We'll take him straight to hospital,' the Chinese volunteered. He's Chinese after all.' The Major felt his body leave the ground.

'Thank you, thank you.' The waiter's voice was the last thing he heard.

At sea, South of Taiwan

On a luxury cruiser, without lights, a press conference had just come to an end. The cameras were no longer pointed at Li Ke-ming, the recorders had been put away. He raised his hand and tried to wipe the sweat from his forehead, forgetting that he was wearing his fine steel mask.

Bai Ling had told him one day that only bank robbers and terrorists wear masks like his. 'It will make a bad impression. You need something more original. The new mask of thin steel sheet, very light, and oxidized (it appeared slightly blue), had been made for him in Taiwan. It had a hinged jaw-piece and light-sensitive lenses to spare his eyes. It was comfortable, even when he wore it for long periods. Li Ke-ming often forgot its existence. Not others. The Reuter correspondent coming out of the light-proof door looked at him like something from another world

'You should have confidence in modern cosmetic surgery,' he said and Bai Ling translated.

'Are you suggesting I should leave the war to take care of itself and spend a month in an American hospital? Then go and die on the battlefield with a brand new face? No need. The bullets and flame throwers will do the face-lifting for me.' Li Ke-ming was antagonized by the pity—though not the shock and horror—in the man's eyes. The new mask seemed to make people slightly more frightened of him. Bai Ling on the contrary was fascinated and continually looked at him with a slight smile.

Forty correspondents from the world's most important news agencies had now been conducted out of the saloon on the lower deck. A helicopter was waiting on deck to take them to Manila. As soon as they reached there, news and pictures of the press conference would appear all over the world.

The press conference had been called in the name of the Fujian Autonomous Government, but Li Ke-ming was aware that everything, the luxury cruiser, the squadron of fighters overhead, the arrangements with the Philippine government, the submarines at sea—all had been provided by Taiwan.

He had been taught almost from infancy that the white sun on a blue background was the flag of the enemy, the Kuomintang, and it felt strange when he saw it on microphones thrust at him at the press conference, and had to explain how he had been wronged and under its protection claim justice. The power of the KMT was impressive.

The last to come up from below was the Major, still with a rather nonchalant expression and escorted by Taiwan secret service men. His appearance caused a sensation among the correspondents. He had been the star of the press conference. Dozens of governments and agencies had been trying to find the assassin, who had vanished without trace. He told without emotion how he had shot the General Secretary. He also produced video tape, which showed his meeting with Shen Di in Tokyo, the leg of an apparently naked woman could be faintly seen in the background. At first both the Major and Shen Di had flatly refused to talk, not wanting to implicate the manager and proprietor of the sex palace in Tokyo. But after Shen Di had carefully put a check for two million dollars in his wallet, he said very distinctly 'Wang Feng'. The video showed the date on the newspaper the Major was reading at one point during their encounter, as additional proof of authenticity. Each correspondent was given a copy of the video and a transcription of the conversation in English.

As he came out of the saloon the Major stopped in front of Li Ke-ming.

'I will always remember the way you jumped out of that helicopter.'

Li Ke-ming regarded him for a moment: there was no trace of irony or provocation on the Major's face. Even if it was not respect in those clear eyes, he spoke as if to a friend.

'And I remember how you lay floating in the water, aiming your rifle.'

'Then let us say goodbye,' said the Major offering his hand.

Li Ke-ming thought he ought to say something. But what? He lightly shook the other's hand. The Major would now be out of work for ever. Every day a bullet of revenge might hit him or he might be caught up in the snares of the law. But no fear showed on his face. Li Ke-ming could hardly imagine, looking at those childlike eyes, that many people had died at his hand. If he were to meet him again he would be unrecognizable: perhaps his eyes would be blue. Cosmetic surgeons might replace his Asiatic features with European. Taiwan would give him a new nationality and identity. He would live like an earthworm for the rest of his life. Taiwan had paid him six million dollars to persuade him to give evidence. This was generous. He had in effect been paid twice for the assasination: the first six million was what Wang Feng paid for getting control of China, the second payment was for giving Taiwan a pretext for realizing its dream of re-conquest. Li Ke-ming realized that he and the Major had something in common. Except that the Major, though at the mercy of the Taiwanese, had taken six million dollars from them whereas he had got nothing—except a steel face.

It was pitch dark on deck yet not a single star could be seen. The cruiser was nothing but a dark outline against the moonless sky. Taiwan was taking every precaution to keep Shen Di alive. The island screened the cruiser from detection by the Mainland, but everyone was on maximum alert. Another helicopter arrived and was guided down by infrared rays, then took off almost immediately with the Major and the security men, and skimmed away like a dragonfly over the surface of the sea.

'We are alone now,' Bai Ling said, relaxed. 'Come to my cabin in a little while.'

Li Ke-ming looked about him: Bai Ling had gone, leaving behind her a whiff of perfume in the sea air. If the silent crew and the bodyguards could be counted as machines he and she were indeed alone on the cruiser. The thought excited him. Seaspray from the bows felt salty in his mouth. He stood for ten minutes in the darkness without moving.

There was a curtain over the door to Bai Ling's cabin; he could see light inside.

He heard Bai Ling's voice saying, 'Please lock the door.' His heart began to thump. The room was warm and scented and he felt slightly dazed.

'Come in.'

This was the most luxurious suite on the cruiser, consisting of a saloon, with a white carpet almost as thick and soft as a mattress, where Bai Ling stood. She had changed into a clinging pink silk dress, her shoulders and arms were bare. Her smile welcomed him. 'Come and sit here,' she said, pointing to the comfortable sofa.

Li Ke-ming sat upright, as if hypnotized, and could not get a word out. He had known her always as the serious and formal Deputy Secretary General of the Fujian Provincial Government. She had represented Fujian at the press conference—though the correspondents did not know that her appointment was for the occasion only—and had organized everything. Even the Taiwanese took orders from her. Li Ke-ming had of course never been in her room before let alone seen her in a dress that showed her nipples.

'My mission is completed now,' she said, her caressing the carpet restlessly with her stockinged feet. 'I feel relaxed, so relaxed. I have done my duty well. It wouldn't have been easy without your help.'

Li Ke-ming swallowed and forced his eyes away from her legs.

'I didn't help you.'

'Oh, yes,' she said, looking at him ardently. 'At that villa in the mountains you found me listening in on the meeting, but you didn't tell anyone. Then the day Shen Di arrived you picked up my radio signal, but you didn't do anything about it. It would have been easy for you to give me away and the whole plan would have been messed up.'

'That wasn't helping you. It's just that it wasn't necessary to give you away. The first time, I didn't want to interfere with something that was not my business. The second time, I suspected that Shen Di's arrival had something to do with you and that you were helping Fujian…'

'Of course, those are good reasons,' Bai Ling interrupted, putting her hands on his arm, and looking at him with burning eyes.

Li Ke-ming was speechless. Ever since that night in the mountains the memory of her form in the moonlight had continued to fan his desire. In innumerable sleepless nights he imagined stripping and possessing her. Whenever he saw her so intimate with Huang Shi-ke it was like a hot iron in his skull. He looked forward to catching a glimpse of her, secretly watched her, kissed the things that had touched her. He had never felt like this before. His wife had been the only woman in his life. His sexual demands had not been very great because he always feared the fire inside him would change something in his body and turn him into an uncontrollable sex maniac. But this fear never suppressed the demon that was now rising inside him, tearing away the barriers of his calm and good sense.

'Your face is so cold,' said Bai Ling, stroking his steel mask; 'but I can feel the flames in your heart.' She went over to the drinks cabinet, took out two crystal glasses and poured a thin stream of wine into each. As Li Ke-ming looked dizzily at her back the straps slipped from her shoulders and the silk dress fell from her like a waterfall, and he saw her full soft buttocks and thighs like a sudden burst of almost blinding light. She turned and came towards him. Li Ke-ming was paralysed. The luminous vision turned to face him glowing ten times brighter and came close. Li Ke-ming was as if stunned. Her smooth and lustrous abdomen was on a level with his eyes, above the palpitating rounded young breasts, and below between jade-smooth thighs a burning chrysanthemum bloomed.

The glasses in her hand chimed a music of celebration. The fragrant wine flowed intoxicatingly into his mouth... He found himself in the bedroom, some of his cloths scattered on the floor behind him. He instinctively pulled down his shirt—he was still sufficiently in control of himself to do that. From the waist up his body did not look like that of a human being. But Bai Ling wanted him naked and even took off his black leather gloves, leaving only the steel mask. Then she backed off a little and looked at him with wide-open eyes, then with fear and ecstasy joined with him.

'The lower part of your body is so smooth so strong and handsome and your emblem of manhood so imposing. Oh!...wonderful, wonderful,' she murmured dreamily. 'But why is the rest of you like this? What are you? A god or a devil? Something from hell?? Have you come to punish me, to rape me? Come on then, come on!'

For the first time in his life Li Ke-ming saw, in a large full-length mirror on the wall, the reflection of his whole body. It was a freakish combination: the lower half young and handsome, the legs powerful and between them a tall erect form. The upper half of his body was hideous and demonic—an expanse of pitch, a pile of frozen rubbish, mangled flesh and skin mixed up with foul and revolting things. The expressionless steel face made the sight even more horrible. Such a monster should never as much as touch a woman again, but he was incapable of curbing his passion, which surged up within him. Bai Ling was cowering in a corner.

'Whore!' He spat word at her between his teeth and threw himself like a wild animal.

At the moment when the earth shook; Bai Ling cried out like a lost soul. Her beautiful eyes, dazed and terrified, swept over his whole body. Again as they struggled he turned his head to one side to watch their bodies as they moved. Terror and pleasure for her were one.

In this storm of cloud and rain the turbulence of a memory came between them. A case he had dealt with once of a woman, with a man's help, who had sex with a donkey and it gave her exceptional pleasure! He was now a donkey!

'Whore!' He struck hard at Bai Ling lying under him, and saw her eyes become even more excited. She liked it. His twisted hands like burnt branches kneaded her soft white breasts. She writhed as if in a life and death struggle. He thought how easy it would be to bite her breasts and drink the spurting blood, sweet and hot and intoxicating—incomparable.

On the Fujian coast

It happened just after dawn on the day of the Spring Festival. A sleepy sentry outside a Beijing army fortification on the Fujian coast was huddled up against the cold, thinking of the kitchen stove at home where the stuffed dumplings would soon be cooking. His comrades inside were still sleeping, warmed by the tot of strong spirits that had been issued to everyone the night before. He stamped his feet for a while, wishing for more.

Today the coastal defences were to be extended against a possible invasion from Taiwan. The Fujian rebels had appealed for help three days ago. Nothing had happened since then and the troops thought that Taiwan was planning to declare independence and would not want to get involved in the shambles on the Mainland. They hoped to God it was true: if there was no invasion the war would be over in a few days and they could all go home. The officers seemed relaxed, otherwise no alcohol would have been issued, even if it was the Spring Festival.

The sentry heard a low rumbling almost indistinguishable from the sound of the waves breaking on the shore. He raised his head and was surprised to see that it was already daylight. A dark swarm seemed to be flying across the sea: surely there were no locusts on Taiwan? His thought flashed back to the fields at home, the crops that could be stripped bare in no time at all. He fired a whole clip of cold bullets into the air: the only effect was to alert his comrades.

Before they were entirely awake, the fortified position became a sea of flames. The bombs exploding, intensified in the mountainous terrain, had filled the air with pieces of rock and brought down part of the sea cliff. The sentry was buried under the blockhouse, now reduced to ruins. Just before he died he saw a line of landing craft stretched out in front and uninterrupted flashes of gunfire.

At ten thirty that morning the mines in the Min River, placed by the Beijing army had all been exploded by the high-speed Taiwan minesweepers, using lasers, opening up access to the port. Large troop carriers then followed each other up the river towards Fuzhou. About a hundred vehicles of all shapes and sizes parked on the runway of Fuzhou airport, dispersing from time to time to allow large transport planes to land.

In the air F21A fighters, assembled in Taiwan, had shown their superiority in the air battle which had just terminated, by shooting down twelve out of twenty-seven of the Beijing fighters.

At Xiantou, down the coast, the Beijing army had sunk more than half of the Taiwan landing craft, but elsewhere there was hardly any resistance.

As the Taiwan troops entered the city in troop-carriers, the citizens of Fuzhou felt they were watching a film. At the head there was a banner saying 'Taiwan People's Volunteer Army'. None of them were wearing any insignia on their helmets—otherwise it looked like an ordinary army. The soldiers all seemed very young, proud and disciplined. More and more spectators crowded the pavements; a few started clapping and others followed. The 'volunteers' saluted.

7

Beijing: The Central Military Commission – Beijing: the Temple of Heaven – Headquarters of the Nanjing Area Command – Beijing: Zhongnanhai – Chinese Missile Base 0142

☙

Beijing: The Central Military Commission

Half-frozen snow, blown off the roofs by the helicopter rotors, clattered against the window panes. Curfew was in force and the wide street outside the Central Military Commission had been cleared and cordoned off for the green helicopter troop-carriers to land. Wang Feng watched the battle-weary Special Troops jump down from each: they looked tough and reliable.

His first decision after the Taiwan troops attacked, was not to send reinforcements to the front, but to bring these Special Troops to Beijing. Helicopter troops were no match for the enemy fighter planes but they could give him total control of the capital. Two of the helicopters had been shot down by Taiwan fighters, but otherwise the force was intact.

Beijing Military Intelligence had been keeping a close watch on Taiwan since the beginning of the civil war, continually assessing the likelihood of an attack on the Mainland. The Taiwan army kept putting up smoke-screens to conceal their real objectives, but the general consensus in Intelligence was that they would avoid getting mixed up in mainland affairs: their military preparations appeared to be purely defensive.

When the news broke that Taiwan had attacked in force along a wide front Wang Feng saw red. He was incensed by the incompetence of the intelligence services with their astronomical budgets: their agents must be living it up abroad—if they hadn't been turned by the enemy—and sent in nothing but false reports. No one could be trusted these days: devoted service was a thing of the past and, if it comes to pickings for the greedy, the East is no match for the West, nor the Mainland for Taiwan.

The attack from Taiwan had been sudden and rapid. Beijing had superiority in the air but had not thought of establishing a network of aerial defences, so it was now too late to protect airfields or deal with the enemy's parachute and airborne troops. Many towns had been taken in the space of thirty-two hours. Even the difficult passage through the Wuyi Mountains seemed to have been no more difficult than going through an open gate. The lightning attack threw the Beijing troops into confusion and they had no time to establish a defensive line or develop a strategy of obstruction as Li Ke-ming had done. Beijing's campaign against the Alliance, so near to victory, had turned into a rout.

This was not Wang Feng's most serious worry: Taiwan was small and relatively weak. The press conference at sea the night before the enemy offensive, was another matter. He did not care about world reactions to the sensational disclosures made by Shen Di and the Japanese hired killer, but their effect inside China could be disastrous. He had always kept tight control over the media, but there was no hope of smothering that kind of news nowadays. It was being spread all over the world from geostationary satellites in the Pacific; the Voice of America had doubled its Chinese language broadcasts and was reporting the progress of the Taiwan troops as they advanced. Radio violation of China's air space was no less serious than the military invasion.

Wang Feng lowered the blind and walked back on the soft red carpet to his own office. His enemies had at last succeeded in forcing him into the open ground: the spotlight was on him and they all had him in their sights. Yet he felt that the fire-power they held in reserve was infinitely more murderous.

He was linked by hotline to top commanders all over the country. Not long ago they were proud to have the privilege of speaking to him every day. Now the phones squatted there in silence. Those who had been competing for his favour yesterday were today coldly calculating when to strike. If he let them be, it would only take one of them to turn on him and the others would join in and tear him to pieces. He had to find a good long whip. . . . If one dog wagged its tail and licked his hand, the others would fight to be next in line.

He stood in front of the phone to Nanjing Military region. It was no different from the others, except in the feeling it aroused in him. He always treated all the senior commanders with deference and respect, but Commander Bai, 'the Fox', was the only one he really feared. Wang Feng had once considered bringing him to Beijing to be Deputy Chairman of the Military Commission and Minister of Defence, because without direct command of troops he would be powerless. He had long felt in his bones that it would be this man who would ruin everything and his premonition was being proved right. Even in the days when the other phones were ringing incessantly, the hotline to

Commander Bai had been silent. Wang Feng could almost hear the sound of marching feet. . . .

His hand hovered over the phone for a few seconds before lifting it. He was connected immediately, as if someone was waiting for the call. The screen was black: officers were not allowed to see their superiors on the videophone.

'Commander Bai?' Wang Feng said smoothly. Silence. 'Are you still neutral?'

'It's a little difficult. . . .'

'Why?'

'Because I promised Huang Shi-ke and the others that I would march on Beijing if they gave me proof that you were behind the assassination of the Secretary-General. I have that proof now. I would be happy if there were any doubt about it, but there is none.'

'So you are withdrawing your troops from Fujian and Jiangxi provinces and handing them over to Taiwan.'

'I am acting on a request from Fujian and have no contact with Taiwan.'

'But their troops are invading your territory.'

'That's your responsibility, not mine,' Commander Bai retorted. 'Why kill the Secretary General? You're still young and could have waited for your day to come.'

'Commander Bai, do you remember the opinion you expressed when you came to the Western Hills last year to see the Chairman? If you don't, there's a full recording of the interview in the archives of the Military Commission. The changes in the Political Bureau were the result of an unanimous decision of the army, you included. Do you want me to call a press conference and tell everyone about this?'

'But. . .we didn't give you authority to assassinate anyone.'

'Assassinate?' said Wang Feng evenly. The other's agitation made him smile slightly. 'Come, assassination is a fact of life in high places, that's why the carpets are always red. Moral indignation is out of place. The duty of soldiers is to obey orders. Do you think I should have disregarded that fundamental principle?'

'Whose order was it?'

'I thought that was obvious.' Wang Feng sighed and deliberately hesitated for a few seconds. 'The Chairman's.'

Commander Bai was silent for a moment then he laughed. 'Young man, all of us have been talking about how you use the Chairman's authority to get what you want, even now when he is very ill and can't even speak.'

.As a rule no third person had been present when he talked with the

Chairman, so he could later put words in the old man's mouth and present them as genuine. That did not stop others from regarding them as lies. Sometimes even he was confused.

'It's true that the Chairman is not well; but he can still speak. I am with him now and he would like a word with you.'

Wang Feng was conscious of the effect of this bombshell. He touched a button that linked the telephone to a computer. When the Chairman became moribund and had to be kept alive by means of *qigong,* Wang Feng had set up a secret technical team to work out a computer programme that could imitate the Chairman's voice instantaneously as the words were typed. When it was perfected even Wang Feng could not tell the difference. The programme even included different tones of voice depending on the circumstances and various sounds, coughing, wheezing, stopping to take a drink of tea. This was the first time Wang Feng had used it.

'Now listen to me, young man,' said the Chairman's voice. 'Don't make a fuss about petty details especially when we are face to face with the enemy. Why are you so muddle-headed? What did I tell you when I sent you to take charge in Nanjing? I said you were to cope with Taiwan—not to take sides with Taiwan against Beijing. We've been fighting Taiwan for more than fifty years: that's what matters. Everything else is irrelevant.'

Each time there was a pause in the Chairman's reprimand, Commander Bai said 'Yessir! Yessir!' like a soldier on parade. Wang Feng imagined him sweating and probably standing to attention.

'If I had heard the Chairman's instructions earlier. . .'

Wang Feng cut off the rest of the sentence, realizing that the Commander had only dared interrupt to test whether it was a recorded message he was listening to. No doubt he was wondering why the Chairman had said nothing when he first heard about Nanjing's neutrality.

The Chairman's voice resumed, as if ignoring the interruption. 'I was hoping that you would come to your senses. You are the most senior commander in the army now and I saw no need for anyone else to know about your imprudence. In any case, I am retired and didn't want to interfere too much. I know you don't think much of Wang Feng: but we must get the war over and done with, then he can return with me to our old home. He has no personal ambitions. I told you long ago. He represents me, that's all. Everything he says and does is according to my wishes. Why are you so intolerant?' He coughed.

'Chairman. . .'

'Don't say any more. I want to see your report tomorrow.'

'Turn on your screen.' Wang Feng said, and saw with special pleasure that the Fox's face was white—it was usually dark red—and pearls of sweat were dropping from his nose. He was not the cause of the man's humiliation, but he had created it. He typed the last two words 'Do it!' and closed the communication.

It was unwise to say too much. A disloyal subordinate had been brought to heel, that was all. But if Commander Bai now decided to toe the line and attack the Taiwan forces, both he and his army would have to come north and who knows what might happen. However, with this machine Wang Feng could show him the whip again, and often. He sat still for some time, mentally preparing a list of others 'the Chairman' would be talking to.

A buzzer interrupted his thoughts and a secretary announced the arrival of the Chairman's wife and daughter. Wang Feng was astounded and shaken. He turned on the video screen and saw the Chairman's black car in front of the building. Two cars belonging to the Armed Police had stopped at the entrance gate. The Chairman's daughter Ying-ying, was helping her mother out of the car; both looked as if they had been crying.

He had a premonition of extreme danger, without knowing what it was. He wasted no time thinking about it: if there was danger the first thing to do was to put everything else to one side and find out what was wrong. He quickly removed all the papers from his desk.

'Bring them straight in and forget the formalities. Detain those two police cars and hand the men over to the special troops.'

As Ying-ying and the old lady entered the building the first police car was seized, the second got away with a screeching of tyres, followed by a fast army jeep carrying a number of the special troops. These men were trained in the open countryside and neither understood nor had any respect for civil authorities; they were also more reliable and more likely to keep their mouths shut than the troops of the Military Commission. Wang Feng quickly went down to the reception room to welcome his guests.

He greeted the old lady, led her to a sofa and sat down beside her.

'Why did you deceive us?' she said tearfully.

He turned to Ying-ying standing beside him. 'What's this all about?' She was about forty years of age and a major in army communications.

'Why didn't you tell us that father was dead?' Ying-ying said indignantly.

'And what's all this *qigong* trickery you've been subjecting him to?' Her mother added.

'You have been listening to rumours,' said Wang Feng. 'Who told you the Chairman had died?'

'Zhou Chi. . .and he gave us a demonstration of what you have been doing to him!'

'Zhou Chi?' said Wang Feng, disconcerted but suppressing his anger. '*Qigong* is a form of treatment. China needs the Chairman alive, just as you do. That is why everything has to be tried, even if Zhou Chi is a charlatan.'

'But that's not his story.' Ying-ying's eyes seemed to show that she longed to believe him. 'He told us you have been using father for your own purposes and that you forced him to keep father's body from decomposing by means of *qigong* and cheated everyone, including us, by making him appear to move.'

The widow was sobbing now. She was a simple woman from the countryside and the idea that anyone could use her husband's body for a dishonest purpose, was a serious humiliation for her; like the violation of a grave, which would prevent the soul of a dead man from resting in peace.

'Do you believe me or Zhou Chi?' Wang Feng had known the widow and Ying-ying from childhood. When his parents were put in prison during the Cultural Revolution, the Chairman's wife had more or less adopted him.

'We wouldn't have come if we didn't believe you,' Ying-ying replied. 'Zhou Chi told us that if we found out that father was dead you would have locked us up, so he wanted to send us to Commander Bai in Nanjing for safety. Perhaps he doesn't know how close to you we have always been. How could we just take his word for it? So on the way from the airport I told father's chauffeur to drive straight here. I thought it was strange when I saw the Armed Police following us. . .'

Wang Feng took her hand. 'Of course your father is alive: his heart is beating and his breathing. . . . . .' Then he remembered that both depended on Zhou Chi and he might have stopped them.

'His heart and breathing have both stopped?' He asked gently.

'Zhou Chi says that for months. . . .'

Wang Feng ran into his office and switched on one of the video screens. He could not tell whether the Chairman was breathing or not, but the sheet had been thrown aside and although the equipment was still in place there were no doctor or nurses to be seen. They would never have dared abandon him if he was still alive.

Zhou Chi had seen to it that Wang Feng did not know about Chairman's death until half an hour later, giving himself just enough time to get the old lady and her daughter on to a plane for Nanjing. After the invasion by Taiwan and the revelations about the assassination, Zhou Chi must have decided it was time to do some fishing in muddy waters. Commander Bai thought he had just received a dressing-down from the Chairman in person. If anyone but the Chairman's wife told him that her husband was dead by that time, he would not have believed it.

Wang Feng had no illusions: as soon as they learned that the Chairman was dead and the sword of his authority no longer hung over them there would be nothing to stop the senior army officers hostile to Beijing from having his hide.

The army would be divided and Zhou Chi, at the head of the Armed Police, would be able to take control of the undefended capital. Wang Feng would be 'brought to justice', and the Secretary-General Lu Hao-ran would be used to control the 'barons' of the Communist Party. The charlatan would then get his dirty hands on the whole of China.

Wang Feng gave orders for the intensive care unit to be sealed off immediately and everyone privy to its secrets put under guard. On a video screen he watched Ying-ying comforting her mother in the next room and gave orders that they be taken care of, but not allowed to leave or see anyone.

'Have the Special Troops guard them and when they leave, take them out through the tunnel. Don't let anyone on the staff see them. They must be treated with respect and provided with anything they need,' he told his secretary. He had the utmost confidence in the man, who had been with him for many years, and needed no more than brief and explicit orders. Today they were unusually detailed.

'Say there is a military emergency and I will not be able to see them off myself. Convey my excuses.'

He switched off the video camera in the reception room, then walked backwards and forwards in his office, very troubled. Suddenly he heard a woman's voice on the other side of the leather-covered door. He felt like blocking his ears, but turned on the camera again.

The old lady, surrounded by Special Troops, was screaming like a mad woman. 'Wang Feng! You have no feelings. You are a traitor, a bandit and a cheat. God and my ancestors will not forgive you!' Ying-ying seemed stunned.

Wang Feng found himself close to tears. He remembered how she looked when he left his adopted home. Everyone feels something special for his first girl-friend, but he had resolved that his feelings must never again be allowed to lead him into trouble. He had already suffered the consequences of not having Shen Di killed. His enemies were closing in on him: once the death of the Chairman became known he would have to face them alone.

He strode about for a long time then sat at his desk and took his precious transmitter in his hand and touched it lightly. It was no bigger than a packet of cigarettes. He thought of the sea and its dark depths, of Ding Da-hai's rock-like head and the marine life around the submarine. . .

He still held the trump card—one that no one else knew about. He did not want to play it yet, just to contemplate it and calm himself. The moment had not yet come. 'Victory comes to him who brings up his reserves last'—the oldest principle of the art of war.

Beijing: The Temple of Heaven

It was pitch dark. The sombre outline of trees stood out against the sky. In the park of the Temple of Heaven, as in other special parks, visitors are asked to leave at dusk. Yet the headlights of Lu Hao-ran's limousine swept over crowds of people sitting under the trees and in open places, almost filling the park. No one moved and there was no sound.

Lu Hao-ran was full of admiration for the order and self-discipline that *qigong* gave those who practised it. Wherever crowds of ordinary people gather there is always quarrelling, rowdiness and petty crime. But the same people, once they take up *qigong,* are quickly transformed and reborn and become models of self-control. Beijing is very cold at night in February, but the crowds of people were sitting so quietly they would even have put soldiers to shame.

Lu Hao-ran was more and more convinced that *qigong* was the best possible thing for China. If the whole population were like this there would be no disorder or suffering, and all worries and stress would disappear. He had suggested to Shi Ge that *qigong* be used to solve China's crisis in agriculture and resources. Once people reach a certain level in *qigong* they would no longer need to eat rice and other staples and would obtain energy from light and the air. Even if only half the population reached the level of 'abstaining from cereals', China would no longer have a problem of grain production. Shi Ge had merely given him a strange look. Lu Hao-ran sighed: Shi Ge was intelligent, but after all he was an ordinary mortal and could not appreciate the mysterious perfection, the profundity and breadth of *qigong*.

Subsequently Lu Hao-ran had put his idea to the Qigong Association and in the space of a few months the newspapers reported that fifty thousand *qigong* followers had already reached the level of 'abstaining from cereals'. Lu Hao-ran felt that the key for resolving the crisis of humanity was in his hands. He was convinced that *qigong* would lead mankind to a new era, and that his name would go down in history.

Consequently he was not worried about the present crisis China was facing, or anything else for that matter.

His limousine stopped at the head office of the Qigong Association and in spite of the bustle there and outside, he was in a state of transcendental serenity.

The plan was flawless. It only remained to wait for the Armed Police from ten provinces to occupy Beijing and arrest Wang Feng. Lu Hao-ran had not been implicated in the assassination of the Secretary-General and had been continually persecuted by Wang Feng, so felt he had every justification for taking the lead. Once Beijing agreed to the Alliance's demand for independence, the Taiwanese would have no reason to continue their aggression. Commander Bai would be won over if Wang Feng was handed over to the Nanjing command. Zhou Chi, in return for the position of Premier, would call upon the twenty million *qigong* followers to support Lu Hao-ran. He was perfectly aware of Zhou Chi's intentions: he wants to use me and my authority as Secretary-General, because a *qigong* master at the head of the Chinese state would not be acceptable either here or abroad. He needs someone more respectable as a front.

Considering his former position Zhou Chi ought to have been savouring the prospect of becoming Premier; but the unexpected disappearance of the Chairman's widow and daughter had upset his plans. The eyes that had always looked down on everyone with the overbearing arrogance of the founder of a powerful sect, now showed strain and apprehension.

'You can't go back to Zhongnanhai today, Secretary-General,' Zhou Chi said. 'We'll have to act earlier than we intended. The Armed Police are assembling and can move on Beijing tomorrow. I have arranged for three thousand young people from the Association to wait here in the park and be ready to help them. We'll have to use armed guards as well. We *must* get the Chairman's widow and daughter out of Wang Feng's hands, otherwise there will be no way to neutralize the military. I've sent five teams to work on it. There's no point in using a lot of men, the important thing is to work skilfully.'

Lu Hao-ran's personal bodyguard consisted of twelve men—all highly trained and carefully selected members of the Armed Police and experts in *qigong*. Zhou Chi had spared no effort to ensure Lu Hao-ran's protection, but without waiting for the Secretary General to reply, he made a sign to the men and Lu Hao-ran watched them being driven away.

'Do you remember,' he asked Zhou Chi, 'a question I put to you last year: can *qigong* be used to bring about the death of China's enemies?'

In spite of the darkness it was clear that Zhou Chi was taken aback. Lu Hao-ran went on, 'You answered me with a question: "How did Lin Biao die?" That's all. It stuck in my memory. Now perhaps is the time to give me a real answer.'

Zhou Chi smiled. His anxiety and tension seemed to have gone. 'If Wang Feng flies over Mongolia he may suffer the same fate as Lin Biao. But that is not necessary at present. I want to measure my strength against his. I want to make him submit to me before he dies.' Lu Hao-ran looked into the dark night. If thirty thousand followers gave out energy all together? How much would that add up to? He saw the blue-green hemisphere of the *qigong* platform, like a tower against the sky. Recently, thanks to *qigong* he had reached a higher plane: not long ago he had only been able to see one person's aura, now he could see the aura of a whole group of people practising *qigong* and it filled him with an uncontrollable joy.

'Let us start,' Lu Hao-ran said.

'Start?' Zhou Chi raised his eyebrows. 'All we have to do now is wait.'

'I'm not talking about seizing the city. Today is the fifth day of the Lunar New Year. . .'

Zhou Chi understood at once. He had fixed the day himself, on each day of the month containing a 5 there would be group *qigong* exercises at the Temple of Heaven. In the previous month there had been two, on the 15th and the 25th and on each occasion Lu Hao-ran had been in seventh heaven. Now he could not understand why Zhou Chi frowned: he had stressed the importance of the first day of the first month himself.

'At this critical time Secretary-General. . . .' Zhou Chi did not know what to say.

Lu Hao-ran had never bothered with the lunar calendar in the past: now he could hardly remember the normal one. For him all other days of the month were a preparation for the three special days.

'There's plenty of time,' said Lu Hao-ran impatiently. 'Everything is ready and we are certain of success anyway.'

'Another day,' said Zhou Chi with the expression of someone with a sore tooth.

'No!' Lu Hao-ran almost shouted. He suddenly felt cold and an unbearable darkness invaded his mind. In fact it was not so much the group *qigong* itself as the anticipation of it that invigorated and made him feel good. As soon as he knew that there was to be no prospect of *qigong*, his spirits collapsed like a deflated balloon. 'No, no,' he almost whined. 'I can't wait. I feel terrible. . .'

'Secretary-General!' said Zhou Chi in a kindly and persuasive voice. 'Before long we must start to move. It will be a decisive moment, we need all our strength and can't afford any distraction. Every moment counts, if we are to be sure of victory.'

Lu Hao-ran was not listening. All these words—victory, action, political situations—were so remote. The State—and political power were insignificant. A single desire burned fiercely in his mind and made him implacable. He glared in fury at Zhou Chi from behind his spectacles.

'You want to be Premier, all I want is *qigong*. I'll give you what you want—you give me *qigong*.'

'Very well, Secretary-General.' Zhou Chi bowed his head deferentially.

Lu Hao-ran saw a large golden star in the sky to the south. He was not quite sure that there should have been a star there; but he could see it distinctly, like a jewel in the dark night sky.

He stood on the circular terrace of the Temple of Heaven where every year the emperors of old performed the ceremonial sacrifice to Heaven. The white stone paving and carved balustrade looked like something out of a dream. Carpets had been laid down in the form of the 'eight diagrams'.

Young men and women, lying naked on the carpets, represented the *yin* and *yang* respectively. Lu Hao-ran had already taken off his clothes; the cold winter wind was pleasant on his skin, like a light and fragrant spring breeze. He had never felt so strong and healthy. Normally, if he did not wear a hat—even in the car—he would catch cold. He felt he was an incomparable spiritual being.

He saw Zhou Chi raise his hands from the ground towards the sky, gathering energy from earth and heaven. A gush of warm energy, as if from a hot spring, caressed Lu Hao-ran's face and flowed into him from the bodies around him. He felt it surge into his lower abdomen—the source of primary vitality—and infuse his blood vessels and his soul.

At his feet the three young virgin men lay on their backs, their ensigns of manhood majestically erect. As Zhou Chi drew in his hands towards his chest, Lu Hao-ran, raised by some buoyant force, lightly stepped over the three young men on to a carpet that led to the centre of the Temple of Heaven. In front of him the Actress, also naked, stepped over the three naked virgin girls before her, and approached Lu Hao-ran with the same floating movement, very slowly. Both were drawn forward and in the middle of a circular carpet the *yin* and the *yang* came smoothly together.

Lu Hao-ran, who had long since thought himself incapable of sexual intercourse, felt fifty years younger and was surprised and delighted by his vigour. The vital energy of the cosmos gave him unprecedented, superhuman power. In that moist place, soft as a bed of down, which responded contentedly to every movement, primal energy gushed into his body like a celestial river at each pulsation and his winged soul soared in the cosmos. The golden star in the western sky grew brighter and bigger.

Was it the thunder of the cosmos? An awful roar came rolling down from above, followed by a whirlwind as if the vault of heaven was leaking. The gold star, now a dazzling light, came very close. An ominous feeling invaded Lu Hao-ran's abdomen. He felt as if his body had been frozen violently by the sudden growth of an icy mountain. The actress fell to the ground from his arms like a stone.

'Nobody move!' A voice from above. . . . The tone was quite mild, but it had the effect of a thunderbolt.

There was no golden star. The searchlights of five helicopters lit up the naked men and women on the Temple of Heaven, frozen in positions of terror and astonishment.

One of the young men jumped up and made for the darkness, perhaps to find his clothes. There was a sharp burst of fire from one of the helicopters. A line of red marks appeared on the man's bare back and he fell at Zhou Chi's feet.

The order not to move was repeated from a loudspeaker, in the same tone of voice—not stern but infinitely menacing.

Lu Hao-ran, in a daze, saw other helicopters with searchlights appear from all directions, flying low and all repeating the order not to move as they hovered in a circle round the park. One of them fired a rocket at the Qigong Association building, which went up in flames. Lu Hao-ran saw no one putting up any resistance. Perhaps the rocket was intended to intimidate the thirty thousand *qigong* followers who were now being rounded up.

Zhou Chi was as if nailed to the ground. He was the only person in the *qigong* group who was dressed. His long gown covered with hexagrams was stained with blood at the hem.

Another helicopter arrived, camouflage green and with a more powerful searchlight. A cameraman leaned half out of the cabin door on a safety belt. Lu Hao-ran quickly turned his face away. In his mind's eye he suddenly saw the huge reflection of his own shrivelled body. He was freezing and wanted to throw up. He was old and ugly. A nauseating exhibit.

His terror increased. The first man to emerge from the helicopter covered him with a military overcoat and helped him aboard. Only then did the photographer begin taking close-ups. No one would recognize him from the first shots of the scene. Lu Hao-ran felt increasing sick. Suddenly he saw Wang Feng's face.

'I have come to fetch you, Secretary-General,' Wang Feng said with contempt. Lu Hao-ran began to vomit. . .

Wang Feng did not look at him again but got into the helicopter, followed by impassive and intimidating Special Troops.

'Remove his gown,' Wang Feng ordered from the helicopter, pointing at Zhou Chi on the platform of the Temple of Heaven, which was like a well-lit stage.

Zhou Chi bared his teeth like a wild animal, bellowed something and brushed aside the soldiers holding him. At a sign from Wang Feng a squad of Special Troops raised their rifles.

'I have always wanted to put your *qigong* to the test,' said Wang Feng sarcastically. 'If you have not stripped in three seconds I will demonstrate that you are not invulnerable to bullets.' He did not count, but stood tall and straight, with his hands behind his back.

It took less than three seconds for Zhou Chi to tear off his gown. A photographer's assistant in military uniform pushed the terrified Actress into his arms and the photographer took pictures from all angles.

A large number of troop-carriers entered the park. In the green helicopter, a voice suddenly announced over the radio 'The Chairman's widow has been kidnapped!'

Headquarters of the Nanjing Area Command

The Chairman's widow was crying bitterly in the short, club-like arms of Commander Bai. His face was darkly purple and the old scars on his forehead were pulsating with anger. Major General Su, his Deputy Chief of Staff, had heard him let off a torrent of curses before, but never with such ferocity. Yet somehow the obscenities he uttered sounded righteous and moving, rather than base.

'Elder sister,' he said eventually. 'The Chairman has departed. Consider me as one of your family. I will look after you. Wang Feng—that dog's spawn—will not get away with it. You'll see him get what he deserves if I have to skin him alive myself!'

These were exactly the kind of words the much-wronged widow needed to hear. But Major General Su knew perfectly well that if anyone was hoping for the Chairman's death it was the vehement, outspoken and passionate Commander.

The Chairman was the only man he feared. This was why the Commander had not joined the Southern Alliance, but had adopted a position of uneasy neutrality. He knew that China had been transformed into a racecourse and that victory would go to the fastest horse. The Chairman had been the only man in the country who could give direct orders to Commander Bai's troops and make them disobey their commander. The old man died just at the right moment; it was a signal for the race to start and a gift from heaven. This evening, the Deputy Chief of Staff said to himself, his Commander would celebrate by drinking a whole bottle of twenty year-old liquor.

Major General Su helped the exhausted widow into a limousine, which was to take her to hospital for a check-up. Before she got into the car her daughter wiped her swollen eyes and said to him in a low voice, 'Don't be too hard on Wang Feng.'

The Major General sighed inwardly. Women! He lightly shook her hand (which in earlier days he would never have dared touch, even in his dreams), and told her not to worry.

Who was going to be hard on whom? He thought, watching the car leave. Now that the truth about the assassination had come out and the Chairman was dead, Wang Feng was in a difficult position; but it would be underestimating him to imagine that he was finished. In his youth Wang Feng had been the leader of a band of young officers of his age, and was much admired by the others because he had an extraordinary gift for finding a way out of difficulties.

They were full of praise for the way he had dealt with Zhou Chi, making sure that the event was presented simply as the rounding-up of a hooligan assembly. The following morning when TV new showed the arrest of Zhou Chi, viewers could not take their eyes off the television screens: they had never seen such a large number of naked men and women before. In next to no time everyone knew about it. Millions of people had a superstitious belief in Zhou Chi, but the faith of most of them was instantly destroyed by the disgraceful spectacle.

The Armed Police who had been preparing to seize Beijing were thrown into confusion by the revelations. Who would want to risk his life for such a scoundrel? When it came out that Zhou Chi had used his *qigong* followers to collect energy from the armed police for himself, in order to increase his sexual prowess, tens of thousands of armed police were mad with fury and in many units, followers of Zhou Chi were arrested and executed. In this way Wang Feng had no difficulty in winning over the armed police, who had been intent on rebellion. The Deputy Chief of Staff did not know most of the details, but for him it was further proof of Wang Feng's genius.

When he returned to the office he found Commander Bai listening—as he had already done several times before—to a recording of the astonishing telephone call of the previous day. The widow had told him that yesterday morning at 10.30 she had seen the lifeless body her husband. Yet the phone call came at 10.41 and the voice was undoubtedly that of the Chairman. It was incomprehensible. If the widow had not suddenly appeared, the troops of the Nanjng command would have opened fire on the Taiwan army at one minute to midnight, even if 'only for the form'—if such a thing is possible.

Commander Bai, stopped striding about the room and ordered Major General Su to have the Chairman's widow and daughter sent to Commander Liu in Chengdu immediately.'

'To Chengdu?'

Without further explanation Commander Bai continued to pace the carpet. It did not take more than an instant for the Deputy Chief of Staff to understand: Lieutenant-General Liu was the senior commander who had been most intimate with the Chairman. The widow's tears would arouse him to fury. He had only tolerated Wang Feng because the Chairman had insisted; now, even if he did not immediately launch an attack on Beijing, he would not interfere if the Nanjing Command did so. Without the Chengdu Command on his side Wang Feng was in serious trouble.

The Situation in China.
Extract from THE TIMES Editorial

Since the recent declaration by the Nanjing and Chengdu Area Commanders of their rupture with the Beijing regime, other regions have come out in rebellion. Lhasa was the first to revolt, and a delegation of twenty leading monks has set out for India to bring back the Dalai Lama to head an independent Tibet. The Tibetan population in neighbouring provinces have expressed their support. Xinjiang immediately announced the creation of the Eastern Turkestan Republic to which the huge southern part of the province has pledged allegiance. The Kazakhs in northern Xinjiang are actively discussing independence.

Dissidents in both Tibet and Xinjiang have experienced bloody suppression in the past, and their hatred of Communist rule has now taken the form of blind 'ethnic cleansing'. No precise figures are available, but according to individuals who have managed to escape, Han Chinese who did not leave before the events have almost all been killed, including women and children.

Several hundred thousand Moslem inhabitants of Northwest China have also revolted, seizing seven county towns and setting off a series of massacres. Armed groups of ethnic minorities have come out in rebellion in other provinces. In some cases such action has been prepared long in advance. In others, groups or even individuals have taken the opportunity presented by the general breakdown of authority in China to set up little kingdoms in the mountains. They all make lavish use of words like 'republic' and 'democracy', but with a few exceptions it is hard to find any evidence of enlightenment.

Informed opinion has long considered that the last chance for China to avoid a serious system breakdown was before the events in Tiananmen Square in June 1989. If the Chinese communists had been wise enough to abandon one-party rule—or had been forced to do so—inevitably at serious risk to themselves, and had allowed an opposition to develop, the continued stability of China might have been assured.

When people become disillusioned and hostile to an existing regime and there is no peaceful alternative in sight, the result is often social disintegration and violence, and the emergence of predatory and primitive power groups—a process that has often been repeated in Chinese history; and will be repeated as long as China and particularly the Chinese Communist Party persist in their outdated hostility to any new form of unification.

Some people fear that it may be ten or even more years before a new political power emerges and there is an end to the chaos. . It has happened before. But this time, after their defeat by the Communists in 1949, the Nationalists fled to the rich island of Taiwan and created a prosperous modern state that one day may become the nucleus of a new Chinese unity.

The Taiwan army has asserted that its troops on the Mainland are volunteers. Officially they are fighting under the banner of the Southern Alliance and never speak of 're-conquering the Mainland'. They claim to have intervened because the autocratic Beijing government is illegitimate, has lost all support and is driving the people into rebellion; and that if the Southern Alliance, which they support, succeeds in creating a federal democracy Taiwan will become part of the new China.

The truth is however, that Taiwan wants to rule China. Its forces have advanced rapidly at lightning speed, and are now less that 800 km from Beijing. The only obstacle is the Yellow River where the thirty divisions supervising the diversion of the River, are making a last stand. The 30 million labourers have all fled and are doing as much damage in the rear of the Beijing forces as a whole army run riot. The fate of Beijing will be decided in a matter of days.

Western governments are beginning to look about them to see who has the power to replace the Beijing regime and rule the whole of China. Most of them favour Taiwan. The US state Department has sent people to Taipei and to Fuzhou to discuss diplomatic relations. Yesterday the Assistant Secretary of State publicly expressed the hope that the crisis in China will be solved by a referendum. The attitude of the European community is close to that of the US; that of Russia is less clear.

After the collapse of the USSR it was assumed in the West that Russia would become a second-rate power and no longer represent a significant threat. Russia's weak position in international affairs may give rise to a sore feeling of humiliation and rekindle her imperial pretensions.

In Moscow's strategic thinking the common frontier with China, several thousand kilometres long, makes China of more immediate concern than the West. The break up of China would be less of a threat to her security than its transformation into an united, pro-western country.

Russia is calling for an end to civil war in China and urging the belligerents to negotiate the division of the country according to the territory they presently control. In this way Moscow hopes to realize Stalin's dream of a partition of China north and south of the Yangzi River. This geo-political solution would condemn North China, constantly threatened by the richer South, to become a faithful 'friendly neighbour' of Russia. Therefore Moscow will not allow the situation in China to become worse and will not hesitate to express its 'wishes', which will certainly not coincide with those of the West.

The international situation makes the future direction of China even more uncertain. Every power group in China is seeking allies and supporters. Secret negotiations are taking place. China is changing and at present no one dares predict what the future may bring. What we see now is reminiscent of the beginning of the twentieth century, when China was without a government. However, history never repeats itself exactly. We shall have to wait and see.

★ ★ ★

Beijing: Zhongnanhai

Everyone had been expecting a thaw, but it was snowing hard. The sky was very dark and the snow very white, except on the streets, where it had been churned up by the traffic and looked horrible.

Shi Ge drove into Zhongnanhai. Soldiers at intervals holding small flags indicated the way to the conference hall. The officer on duty looked surprised and perhaps a little suspicious: the Deputy Premier had not been seen for some time and had neither driver nor bodyguards.

His two *qigong* bodyguards had vanished without trace, after the arrest of Zhou Chi. Shi Ge had returned to Beijing when the Yellow River Diversion Zone became a battlefield; no one needed him and no one asked for him. He remained alone in his room for three days looking at a map and never took a step outside until, unexpectedly, he was summoned to the meeting.

Since the emergency, policy decisions had been made by Wang Feng and a few others almost without any discussion or consultation, let alone voting. Today however, it looked as if all top government, army and Party leaders had been ordered to attend.

The conference hall was very hot, in spite of the acute fuel shortage, and better lit than most places, making one forget how dark the sky was. The atmosphere was grim and oppressive: no one spoke or moved about, but sat dazed and isolated from each other. Occasionally there was a clink of teacup lids, which almost seemed to make people nervous.

On the desk in front of each seat was a copy of the latest report on the military situation. Shi Ge chose the seat at the end of the last row. Contrary to normal practice the report gave an analysis of the military situation and admitted that there was now no possibility of organizing an effective counter-attack. It was estimated that within eight hours the enemy would be in the vicinity of Beijing. If the Government troops were sent to hold up the Taiwanese advance, Beijing would be left poorly defended and Commander Bai's Nanjing troops, who were close by, could then take Beijing.

Shi Ge noticed that hardly anyone else was reading the report. They probably felt that it would make no difference anyway. He too felt totally at a loss. He had long been considered a specialist on emergencies. Whenever there was trouble of some kind, even if it was not something that concerned him directly, a flood of ideas would come into his mind. Not now. The old hands at politics were more cautious than he. They had no power to save the situation, so they would do nothing. The country was like a big building: in the past, if there was a leak somewhere or some masonry coming loose, a competent repair man could find a way to deal with it. But now it was as if every brick had turned into powder and there was nothing anyone could do.

Lu Hao-ran and Wang Feng entered last, the Secretary General in a wheelchair pushed by two attendants. Shi Ge had heard that he was ill, but had not imagined that it was so serious. He looked like a lump of clay, and neither moved nor looked about him, yet there were no obvious signs of illness. What struck Shi Ge most was his profoundly dejected and mournful expression, as if there was no soul in the empty husk of his body.

By comparison Wang Feng's appearance and manner were astonishing. He was under attack from all sides, denounced the world over, his defeat inevitable and he was destined to eternal damnation in the lowest level of hell. Yet he showed no sign of anxiety or despair; he even appeared more spirited and fearless than usual, impressive in his spotless general's uniform and utterly self-confident.

'I declare. . .the meeting open,' said Lu Hao-ran in a feeble and indistinct voice, stopping in the middle as if uncertain what to say. 'I call on Comrade Wang Feng.'

The latter, with none of his former modesty, took the seat of honour as a matter of course, as befitted a man who dared to take responsibility and show his heroic stature, however serious the crisis.

'I am not going to speak about the situation,' he said, tapping on the report front of him, 'but of the factors which have led up to it. For the last two days disruptive elements have been stirring up trouble everywhere. Students' demonstrations and public petitions are demanding my resignation, as if the present condition of China, including the present war, were entirely my fault. They seem to think that peace will be restored as soon as I resign and am put on trial. It is not surprising that a small handful of enemies of the State should take advantage of people's ignorance, but there are even some senior people in the Party, the army and the government who seem to believe these things. So I must make the matter clear.'

'If Taiwan, Fuzhou, Nanjing and other rebellious regions guarantee to cease fire immediately if I resign, withdraw their troops and abandon the demand for independence, I will accept every injustice, whatever the consequences. But I know they will not do so. I am not their target. They want to wipe out the Party and the government and divide up China, so that they can all have their own little kingdoms. They want to kill everyone here, to tear down the five-starred red flag of our People's Republic and fly the white star of the Kuomintang and Taiwan in its place.'

'How has China reached such a state of disunity? We who have been so strong and proud, who defeated the eight million-strong army of the Kuomintang. Our Party is the biggest in the world and our people used to be united as one. That glory is a thing of the past. Because of Wang Feng? If I have made a mistake, it is in acting too late. I did not achieve power soon enough to correct bad policies and stop traitors from bringing the country to its knees. China cannot be ruled simply by managing the economy. More than a thousand years of history has proved it. The core of China is its spirit, and once that spirit dies, China will disintegrate. But so-called reformers have destroyed China's spirit and put money in its place, drawing the whole people into a race for profit. Again and again we have said that we would uphold the authority of the Centre, because otherwise we cannot guarantee the integrity of China. Authority is above all a question of spirit. If everyone pursues profit there can be no authority and ambitious men will work incessantly to establish their own power bases. It was such people who opened the gates to the Taiwan army. Are we to go on retreating with the enemy's noose already round our neck or shall we change the situation at one stroke and smash the enemy?'

The old politicians did not even open their eyes. They were no longer moved by impassioned speeches and had no illusions about 'smashing the enemy at one stroke'.

'Perhaps you think that these are just empty words,' said Wang Feng calmly. 'With all your experience you can't think of a way. But I can!'

He turned to a large map on the wall behind him and with a pointer stabbed the circle representing the city of Taipei.

'We will make a nuclear attack here,' Wang Feng announced with a radiant smile.

Shi Ge went cold all over. He looked at the others present: no one seemed to share his emotion. They had opened their eyes for a moment, then closed them again. All army officers knew about the Anti-ballistic Missile Convention. The result of a nuclear attack on the Taiwan capital would be that Beijing would be destroyed; unless China flattened Russia, the United States, Britain and France simultaneously before they could act. Pure science fiction. If Wang Feng was going to do something desperate in order to save himself without considering the consequences, the old guard were not going to keep him company.

Shi Ge knew that Wang Feng was not a man to lose all touch with reality; his self-satisfied smile showed that he knew what he was doing and had something up his sleeve.

'Don't despair, Comrades,' Wang Feng said with a genial smile, 'I have not forgotten the ABM Convention. If you read the text carefully—in any language—you will find that the Convention forbids the use of nuclear weapons *against another country*. Not in one's own country. Taiwan is part of China, as the United Nations and almost the whole world recognizes. As do the 147 countries we have diplomatic relations with. Therefore an attack on Taipei will not contravene the Convention and the UN will have no reason to take action against us. I can guarantee that foreign countries will do nothing but protest. They are constantly talking about human rights, but when it's a question of millions of innocent people being killed they do nothing, as long as their own countries are not affected. In any case we are acting within the law. In the unlikely event of the UN deciding to punish us, the fact that Taiwan is universally recognized as a Chinese province, with Taipei as its provincial capital, means that the UN would only be justified in attacking one of our provincial capitals but not Beijing. They may attack Nanjing, or Fuzhu, Guangzhou or Chengdu. . . let them choose. But I issue this warning: China may not be a major nuclear power, but we have 1700 nuclear missiles, enough to wipe out half the cities in the world if Beijing is attacked. No one will dare, Comrades, believe me. You have seen enough evidence of the weakness and incapacity of the international community. International condemnation for June Fourth never harmed a hair of our heads because we are the first or second biggest country in the world, and no one dares pick a quarrel with us. We only have to take courage and victory will be ours!'

The gloomy faces seemed to show some signs of colour. The shrunken skin seemed more elastic, as if a refreshing spring wind had come from Wang Feng's mouth and breathed life into the withered bodies.

'Taipei is like the head of a snake,' Wang Feng went on, turning to the map again, 'and with snakes you aim for the head. The army will be thrown into confusion and bolt back to Taiwan to restore order there. If they make another move, which is unlikely, we will strike again and solve a fifty-year-old problem by forcing them to surrender. The attack on Taipei will also be a strong warning to the other rebellious people in our country.'

'Comrades, the choice before you is between the end of the Party, the break-up of our country, disaster for our people and eternal disgrace for all of you present today, or the sacrifice of Taipei in exchange for peace and the unity of our nation. Remember, the US atomic bombs on Hiroshima and Nagasaki only made Japan surrender a few days earlier than intended and saved the lives of a few thousand American soldiers. Yet history has not condemned that action. Our reasons for attacking Taipei are a thousand times more valid. Comrades, it is now time to decide.'

Shi Ge stood up, like a schoolboy, though it was not customary to stand before speaking in such a meeting. Perhaps he wanted to intervene before anyone could express support for the proposal. Wang Feng had summoned all these people to the meeting only to avoid having to bear alone the responsibility for a nuclear massacre. Now the fateful decision could be presented as a decision of the Party, Army and Government together. The ABM Convention excluded the ultimate weapon as a realistic possibility from people's minds. But Wang Feng had shown the way round it—a dangerous one—but a way all the same.

Shi Ge had been reminding himself to be careful, but he knocked over his porcelain tea-mug. The tea soaked the documents in front of him and dripped on to the floor. Wang Feng looked coldly at him with narrowed eyes. Shi Ge controlled his voice with difficulty: there was nothing to be gained by getting excited.

'What you said earlier is right: China no longer believes in anything and there is no authority people can respect. Therefore to wipe Taipei off the map with nuclear missiles can only give us a temporary respite. We cannot create authority, or faith or morality with missiles, and they won't free us from crises, disorder, disunity and separatism. You can't fire missiles at all the towns in China, and at all the mountains where rebels are hiding. What if there is a rebellion in Beijing? Nuclear weapons can kill others: they can also destroy us.'

'So what brilliant suggestion do you have?' said Wang Feng standing with his hands behind his back. 'If you have an alternative we will all stand up and bow to you.'

Shi Ge picked some sodden tea-leaves from the table and absent-mindedly chewed them. There were certain things he would never have dreamt of saying in such a gathering, but this was no time for caution.

'Every system has its life span,' he said. 'Shouting "Long live!" one thing or another is just wishful thinking. Our political system has reached the end of the road. Why make a useless effort to save it by slaughtering the people of our own country with terrible weapons of mass destruction? Why inflict a wound that will never heal? We ought to be more rational, to understand the way the world is developing and consciously go with the current of history, not against it. That is the only choice we have. If we can no longer create anything, at least we should not sow destruction. Is it so terrible if China is no longer one huge country? Why insist on unity if people do not live any better for it? We are not nationalists and we should not sacrifice millions of lives for the sake of a meaningless concept. The crisis, rebellions, the attack by Taiwan are signs that we—all of us here—should go, leave the stage, dissolve the Party and become ordinary people again. Perhaps we will lose our lives, but there are less than a hundred of us. How can we send three million people in Taipei to their death?. . . .'

'That's enough,' Wang Feng interrupted. 'we know all about your ideas.' To the others present he said, 'This man, a member of the Political Bureau of our Party, and Vice-Premier of the State Council has proposed the dissolution of the Party and approves of Taiwan's attack. We will deal with him later. Those in favour of a nuclear attack on Taipei please raise your hands.'

Shi Ge leaned forward. The last drops of water in the tea-leaves seeped through his fingers. He wanted to make these comatose zombies wake up, to pound on the desk and shout 'Don't raise your hands! Don't commit a crime against humanity.' But no eyes met his. His passionate words were no more than a wind that rises suddenly in the desert and just as suddenly vanishes. There was no reaction from the blank and wooden leaders of China. One after the other they drearily raised their hands, as if to the slow beat of a funeral march—withered yellow hands, without life—in silence.

'Approved unanimously.' Wang Feng's raised hand came down in a chopping movement, as if cutting off Taipei from the world.

'I don't approve.' Shi Ge heard his own voice, coming from far away, hoarse and unintelligible, like a cry from some dry and distant planet.

'You? ' Wang Feng gave a snort. 'Do you think you have any right to disagree? You don't have any right at all, even to approve!'

Shi Ge seemed totally at a loss what to do. He took up the teacup to drink. It was empty. He reached for a thermos flask, knocked over his chair, looked this way and that, as if he had forgotten where he was. Then he opened the thermos, poured boiling water over his hand instead of into the cup, then dropped both. The vacuum flask exploded with a muffled sound, the tea-mug bounced without breaking. Shi Ge held his head in his hands and fell to his knees.

' I must put my head under the cold tap,' he mumbled, moaning with pain.

Wang Feng looked down at him, as if he were a slug.

'Go on. Clear your head, then we'll make it even clearer for you.'

The snow on Changan Street was thicker and more slippery than before. Cars and trucks crept along cautiously. In the rear mirror Shi Ge saw the gate of Zhongnanhai disappear in the falling snow. His scalded hand was very painful. But if he had not put on that performance of someone cracking up, Wang Feng would not have relaxed his vigilance and he would not have been able to escape through the toilets. The officer on duty at the gate had again looked at him, but with even more bewilderment than before. The car was covered with snow and Shi Ge had scraped enough of the windscreen with his hand to make it possible to drive. Now the snow was melting and the wiper was working.

He did not know what to do, or whether anything could be done. One thing was clear: he must make it known that a nuclear strike on Taipei was imminent; perhaps the scale of the disaster could be reduced. There was no use shouting about it in the street: he would be taken for a madman. The media. . .? Taipei would already be reduced to rubble by the time the information was verified and a decision taken. Now that Beijing was at war with Taiwan all communications had been cut. Send a telegram to the UN? Who would believe it? Even if they took it seriously, getting the news through all the layers of bureaucracy would be worse than taking a slow train.

A foreign embassy, he suddenly thought. An Ambassador would have a hot line to his Head of State. If Taiwan got the news from an embassy in Beijing through the UN, it would not be taken for a hoax. He reached for the car-phone. . . No. Embassies get too many hoax calls. He was a member of the government. He must go himself and make them believe him. Preferably to an embassy where he was known. Not so easy. . . He was not in a senior position and not much in the public eye. Few foreigners would recognize him. If he appeared at the door, it would take too much time getting let in, and they might not listen to him anyway. He regretted never having a taste for diplomatic affairs or wasting time at receptions. But he must know someone. . . .

Then he remembered a Secretary at the Australian Embassy. Two years earlier, at a reception he could not avoid, he had found himself next to her. As it happened, she wanted him to choose a Chinese name for her; this made him remember that she was called Josie. She had told him her phone number and he had made a pun of what it was in Chinese, so he remembered that too. She would probably take some time to remember him: he was a man of little importance to her. But when he announced his name over the car-phone, she said, 'Mr Vice-Premier, so you remember me?'

'I need to see your Ambassador. Please meet me at the Embassy door. I'm coming at once.'

He was already in Tiananmen Square. The traffic lights were red and there was a long line of stationary vehicles. He turned into the part of the street reserved for bicycles and went on, ignoring the lights and spraying the traffic policeman with slush. The car, with its Political Bureau number-plate made the policeman stare.

It was fourteen minutes since he had left the meeting. Wang Feng must already have discovered that he had escaped. The officer of the guard would have reported that Shi Ge had driven away in a hurry, bumping into another car but had not stopped. Wang Feng would have already taken action.

A traffic policeman put out his arm to stop the car, then ran towards the telephone, only to be hit by a skidding vehicle and thrown up on to the bonnet. Shi Ge accelerated away against the lights and edged his way into the line of cross traffic. A jeep bumped into him from behind and he bumped into the bus in front, half tearing away his offside mudguard. He was not a skilled driver, but he managed to get away and avoid worse damage. Then, as he drove east along the broad street he noticed that passers-by were all looking upwards. In the side mirror, maladjusted after the slight collision, he could see an armed helicopter flying low in his direction.

If he had kept in the heavy traffic it would have been more difficult to find him, but by crossing when the lights were red he had allowed those in the helicopter to identify his car. They were not likely to lose him again, now that his car was visibly damaged. At the railway station he accelerated past police forming a road-block of vehicles. An instant later it would have been completed. He crashed through the opening just in time, shattering the side windows. The helicopter came closer, its rotors whipping up the snow and blowing it into the car like bullets from a machine gun.

He turned abruptly into a small side street beside the International Hotel, narrow enough to force the helicopter to gain height. He did not approve of high-rise buildings, but felt grateful to the space-saving architects. . . . the higher the better! The collision had made his car-horn sound continuously, as if it were a fire-engine, and pedestrians—not even very close—got out of the way.

In the small street the snow was not compacted by the traffic and he was able to drive much faster without skidding, but in the rear mirror he could still see the dull green helicopter, watching him as a cat watches a cornered mouse.

To reach the Australian Embassy he had to cross a two-way ring road. As he left the group of high buildings he saw the helicopter hovering close by. The door was wide open, and there was a heavy calibre machine-gun pointed in his direction and Special Troops with rifles and flame-throwers. Just as they seemed about to open fire a heavy truck loaded with bags of cement, emerged from a building site. Shi Ge desperately swung round and drove the car up against the truck, putting it between himself and the helicopter. There was a sound of metal crunching and scraping. The truck driver seemed not to realize that anything unusual was happening until firing from the helicopter made him lose control of the truck which went zigzagging all over the road. The bullets hit the piled-up sacks of cement, raising a huge grey cloud, like a smoke-screen.

Shi Ge's car lost both doors on one side, but broke free from the truck. His face was covered with cement, but he was pleased to find that the car still worked. He trod on the accelerator and, taking advantage of the smoke-screen, raced for an underpass where he stopped and got out of the car. The truck had crashed into a thick wall along the pavement behind and was half way into a courtyard. Some people nearby rushed up to watch, thinking a film was being shot.

Shi Ge saw that the helicopter was on the bridge waiting for him to come out on the other side. Even if he ran all the way it would take him at least half an hour to reach the Embassy. When a wire ladder began to descend from the road above, his blood ran cold.

He jumped back into his car and prepared to turn it round in the opposite direction. At this moment he saw a limousine approaching. . . . flying the Russian flag. The Ambassador's car! He was saved. He quickly drove up close behind it. A soldier half-way down the wire ladder fired a short burst without aiming. The bullets hit the bonnet and one of them grazed Shi Ge's neck. He first thought, 'This is it' as blood ran through his collar into his shirt, then, more calmly: if there are only Special Troops in the helicopter they won't recognize the Russian Embassy car nor realize the gravity of wounding the Ambassador, even by mistake. Wang Feng dared not offend Russia.

There was no more gunfire and the helicopter swung away. No, Wang Feng would not have let the Special Troops handle this alone: they did not know his car and were not familiar with the streets of Beijing. There was someone in the helicopter who did; the Russian Ambassador's car was Shi Ge's protection.

There was a line of bullet holes in the rear of the embassy limousine and the occupants were very alarmed by the helicopter low overhead and a battered wreck close behind. The driver put his foot down. Shi Ge kept up with him and each time the limousine slowed down, he deliberately bumped into the back of it.

The helicopter gained height to avoid some wires over the road, then returned to the attack, trying to come down on the roof of Shi Ge's car to separate it from the other car. The occupants of the embassy car were scared out of their wits. The driver—a trained security man—was convinced an attempt was being made to assassinate the ambassador and just as Shi Ge had hoped, swerved violently on to the pavement then followed a small road into a group of tall buildings. Shi Ge then parted from the other car, leaving the embassy driver baffled and kept to small access roads.

There were no tall buildings in the embassy quarter, but the helicopter was prevented by international law from pursuing its prey there. The soldiers drew back into the cabin and the firing stopped.

Shi Ge was able to think calmly again. He did not want to scare the people at the Australian Embassy. His car was a wreck and the sound of the horn was very peculiar now that the battery was running down. When Josie saw him get out of the car at the Embassy she was speechless. He was covered from head to foot in powdery cement and was grinning like a clown, as if his appearance, the blood on his neck and the sorry state of his car, were all part of the comedy.

Shi Ge loudly greeted her in English and before she had time to reply, took her arm and confidently led her into the Embassy, worried by the presence of the Chinese sentries at the gate of the Embassy. Fortunately they had no knowledge of what was going on. By the time they heard the loudhailer on the helicopter order them to arrest Shi Ge, he was already on Australian soil.

Josie, who thought by this time that she had found an explanation for the strange appearance of Shi Ge, his car and the hovering helicopter, froze into diplomatic formality, concealing her excitement and anxiety.

'Mr Vice-Premier, if you have any special request we will have first to consult our government, because the implications. . .'

'I have no such request,' Shi Ge replied with a slight smile, guessing that Josie thought he had come to ask for political asylum. 'I only want to request His Excellency the Ambassador to transmit a message, then I will leave at once.' He took her nervous hand, and went up the steps.

Although Shi Ge spoke excellent English, the ambassador, a tall white-haired gentleman, did not appear to understand, but his intelligent eyes widened.

'An imminent nuclear attack. Not a second to waste.' Shi Ge made an effort to speak more clearly. 'I request Your Excellency to ask your government to inform the United Nations and Taipei immediately, as well as the US and Russian governments. They must put pressure on the Chinese authorities and get Taipei to disperse the population. . . . I beg you to phone at once.'

The Ambassador was still staring. This was a strange and theatrical way of communicating news. But was it credible? To make such an announcement was a weighty matter. No diplomat could be expected to know what to do, or even pick up the phone without some sort of guarantee. . .

'Your Excellency, I am Vice-Premier. I could not possibly come here to play a trick on you.' Shi Ge abruptly walked to a window and pulled aside the curtain. 'Does this make it look like a practical joke?' The Embassy was surrounded. Military vehicles were arriving; troops with steel helmets were jumping down and surrounding the Embassy. Outside the gate a few officers were standing, legs apart, their hands behind their backs. A command truck with high radio antenna was parked behind them. At each corner of the embassy compound, a helicopter was hovering. Josie gasped and put her hands to her head.

An embassy official burst into to the Ambassador's room and started to say something. The Ambassador stopped him and took up a telephone on the desk. 'The Ambassador to China wishes to speak to the Prime Minister.'

'Someone from the Chinese Foreign Ministry is here, Sir.'

'I'll not see him,' said the Ambassador firmly.

It was very quiet in the room. Outside the windows the helicopters roared.

When the Australian Prime Minister came on the line the Ambassador said. 'According to the Chinese Vice-Premier . . . hello . . . hello.' He shook the phone and tapped it, and shouted, in vain.

The line had been cut. Shi Ge's heart fell.

'Try the radio,' he suggested, as the Ambassador replaced the phone. They went to the radio room; almost all of the embassy staff followed.

After repeated efforts the radio operator gave up. 'The van outside is blocking our signal.' There was a deathly silence.

Shi Ge saw the grief on the Ambassador's face and Josie's expression of despair. Outside the office the embassy staff stood shocked and apprehensive. Shi Ge said 'Thank you' almost inaudibly, and they made way for him. His mind was empty. He saw no nuclear explosion, no Taipei—only Gui-zhi's naked body and the blood flowing out between her breasts and dyeing the sky red.

It was still snowing. Everywhere was white. The snowflakes swirled in changing configurations round the helicopters. A few officials from the Ministry of Foreign Affairs were in animated discussion with the senior staff of the embassy; they fell silent as Shi Ge passed. Outside the gate were silent soldiers and officers and a searchlight on top of a vehicle continually sweeping this way and that.

A distant memory of infancy came into Shi Ge's head. It was a grey day . . . white snow damp air . . . a cold wind that penetrated one's clothes. He watched the snowflakes floating down. His mother's face kept interposing itself as she stooped to kiss him, leaving a tickly sweet fragrance. He tried to push her to one side so that he could see more snowflakes. . . Now he wanted to see his mother again, but there was only snow.

As he went down the stone steps Josie held him. 'You don't have to go, you can ask for asylum. You are protected here by international law.'

He did not hear her. He thought of Gui Zhi's burning hot body in the fragrance of harvest time, now becoming one with the cold yellow earth.

'Stay here, we will protect you,' Josie said, with tears in her eyes.

He strode out of the Embassy gate, the staff all watching him in silence. He went up to the Armed Police and held out both hands. A tall officer handcuffed him—gently, as if he did not want to hurt him.

Before getting into the police car Shi Ge looked back once. The helicopters had gone. The snow lay quiet. The sky was pitch dark. On the clean snow the whole staff and the white-haired ambassador stood. Josie's shoulders were shaking.

Chinese Missile Base 0142.

If there had been someone passing by, he would not have believed his eyes. A stack of rice straw does not split in the middle as if cut with a knife, then move apart, revealing a large round plate made of concrete and steel. But since the straw stack had been put there, no outsider had been within miles of it; no one had seen the 96-ton cover opened by an explosive mechanism inside and watched the smoke disperse.

There were a few rustic dwellings, but no trace of the missile silos, no busy control centre or modern installations, no machinery, no electricity wires and no human beings. However, deep underground there were sounds of rapid and well-rehearsed preparations.

Some mice emerged in panic from their nest in the straw, their noses twitching, sizing up the changes in their place of habitation.

A sudden loud explosion blasted all the mice head over heels and a silvery missile twenty metres long and two metres in diameter was pushed out of the shaft. A terrifying scream turned into a deafening roar and white flames spewed out of the end of the missile. Then it disappeared into the sky.

All the mice were roasted and the straw–stack became a bright ball of fire. The missile was already far away, trailing a white plume.

8

Taipei – The Government of the People's Republic of China issued the following statement – Beijing: The Central Military Commission – Guangxi Province: Nuclear Missile base 1358 – Beijing: The Military High Court

ଔ

Taipei

At 12.41 a nuclear bomb exploded 3,000 metres above the Hilton Hotel in Taipei, the capital of Taiwan. A heat-ball close to the temperature of the sun emitted a blinding light that was seen by awestruck fishermen off the coast of Fujian. The clothing of hundreds of people at the railway station and all the curtains at Taipei Hospital caught fire simultaneously. The paint on every vehicle in the streets was burnt or blistered and all that remained of the trees were charred trunks. Glass melted, newspapers, canvas and rubbish was immediately incinerated, plastic became instant chemical fumes. Two petrol stations exploded and before the sound reached the next street, the shock-wave had become a huge ball of fire many hundred metres in diameter, which at the speed of thousands of metres per second swept everything away in its path. The blazing petrol stations were engulfed in a powerful blast of air that blew out the flames; tons of petrol from one of them poured into the street and caught fire again.

In seconds the centre of the city became a pile of rubble. The Hilton Hotel was blown away like a castle of playing cards. One wall was thrown more than a hundred metres before disintegrating. The people did not suffer much: their lives came to an end before they knew it. Most of them were buried under mountains of rubble. No building could withstand the force of the explosion, no one, nothing was left alive. Vehicles were thrown about as if they were made of paper. People outside were swept into the air, among flying girders and concrete. Within a radius of three kilometres of the Grand Hotel nothing escaped destruction, apart from a very few people who jumped or fell into water.

There was a deep anti-nuclear shelter under the presidential palace; but the attack was so sudden that not a single person had time to take refuge there. The President was reading an official document as he ate his lunch. The shock made him stab himself in the mouth with his fork. Then he was thrown against the thick stone wall. The roof of the palace, with its magnificent hanging lanterns, flew away and the sun, which had abruptly come so close, melted him like a candle.

Further away from the centre, where the shock wave was weaker, only the frame of the Sun Yat Sen Memorial Hall remained, like the vestige of an ancient edifice. The damage to high-rise buildings was far worse: all that was left of the Yuanshan Hotel was the steel structure, which collapsed to one side in a heap like wickerwork. At Songshan Airport a plane on the runway had been blown away, its wings ripped off; the remains crashed into the hills north of Keelong.

The number of dead was slightly less than in the centre, but still very high. The survivors mostly suffered from burns or injuries caused by flying masonry. Some were buried alive under collapsed buildings and had no choice but to wait for death, Wild animals escaped from the zoo and ran in terror this way and that. A wounded lion roared loud enough to shake the heavens.

It only took one minute to kill 600,000 people. Then a huge mushroom cloud rose to a height of 15 kilometres over the ruins of Taipei. All was silent, there were fires everywhere. Everything destructible was destroyed. Buildings and streets no longer existed, only rubble. Thousands of factories and shops and a third of Taiwan's universities were destroyed. The headquarters of the two main political parties, the President and elder statesmen, all ministries and other government buildings, the police headquarters, the Municipal government—all ceased to exist.

Taiwan took a long time to react. The destruction of Taipei left the island without a government, without information. People had to rely on a few local authorities to take whatever action they could. Local radio stations broadcast news to the whole island, but at first only caused panic. In mortal fear that Beijing would continue to destroy towns and cities, people fled from the urban areas, blocking transport; many were trampled to death. Local officials thought only of their own districts. Keelong alone sent a relief team of 400 doctors and police, which was like trying to douse a fire with a glass of water. Nor could they handle the enraged and desperate people whose loved ones had been killed.

Only the army was capable of providing authority and organization to deal with relief. But the army was on the North China Plain and it stopped advancing as if stunned.

The Government of the People's Republic of China issued the following statement:

> The separatist regime that occupies the Chinese province of Taiwan has launched a general military attack, in a vain attempt to overthrow the legal and internationally recognized government of China. Its armies have killed thousands, destroyed towns and caused damage to the economy. The government of the People's Republic, after repeatedly exercising restraint, and in order to put an end to the fighting, preserve national unity and relieve the suffering of the people, therefore carried out a limited nuclear attack on Taipei at 12.41 (Beijing time).
>
> The Government of the People's Republic of China solemnly declares:
>
> 1. That the purpose of this attack is solely to put an end to the fighting and restore peace by inflicting the minimum of damage. This is the will of the Chinese people and a decision which has been forced upon them.
> 2. Taiwan is internationally recognized as an integral part of China. This attack is therefore purely an internal matter and does not violate the Anti-Ballistic Missile Convention. It is not a threat to any country in the world. China has always and will continue, to deal with this question as an internal political matter . . .
>
> The Government of the People's Republic of China reiterates its unchanging stand: China will never be the first to make a nuclear attack on any other country, and approves and advocates the complete banning and destruction of nuclear weapons. The Chinese people sincerely hope for friendly coexistence with the people of the world, and will never stop working for this end. At the same time we warn all aggressive elements: China will retaliate against any nuclear attack on our country, in accordance with the Anti-Ballistic Missile Convention.

Beijing: The Central Military Commission

The guesthouse of the Military Commission was a large mansion that had belonged to a prince of the last imperial dynasty. It had been entirely restored and, though only separated from the other buildings by a wall, it was a different world. Surrounded by an extensive park with artificial hills, fishponds, half-hidden paths, bamboo groves, pine trees, conservatories containing rare plants and birds, and a small stream—now frozen—with a beautiful white marble bridge over it. The rooms had been restored to their former splendour, but with modern furniture, so that the guesthouse looked like a cross between an imperial palace and a luxurious western mansion. Very few outsiders knew about the guesthouse and very few Area Commanders had ever stayed there: it was something one could boast about.

From the start of the civil war Wang Feng had occupied No. 1 suite (decorated in the Suzhou style). The guesthouse had five suites, each with its own courtyard. Today he moved into No. 3, which was in no way inferior; but by moving to what might appear a less prestigious suite—a detail which would not be overlooked—he was expressing his apology and repentance to the Chairman's widow and daughter.

As he listened to a secretary reading the day's reports, his orderly helped him change his uniform for a well-cut western style suit. He was pleased with his appearance. He liked his uniform too, with its shining epaulettes, but since the end of the civil war he usually appeared in public in civilian clothes; in these democratic times the leader of a great country ought to look like a man of culture. It was the first time in two weeks that he had found the time to have a haircut, which made him look more dynamic. He was slightly thinner, but the signs of stress had gone and he was calm and contented.

The orderly emptied the pockets of his uniform and arranged various objects on the table. The precious transmitter was in an inner pocket, where it had been since the submarine had put to sea. The official procedure for the deployment of nuclear weapons required a complicated joint authorization; but the transmitter enabled him, with the touch of one finger, to order the submarine to fire its twenty twin-head nuclear missiles at a target decided by him alone.

He had been confident that this time he would not have to use the transmitter. He knew that the meeting of yes-men would unanimously approve the attack on Taipei, whatever the cost, and authorize the use China's nuclear weapons. They might be at loggerheads most of the time, but when the fate of the Party and the State was in the balance they would stick together, come what may. His only mistake, he reflected, was letting Shi Ge get away. It had not interfered with his plans, but in the eyes of the world the image of a leadership united as one in face of the enemy, had been tarnished. The treacherous buffoon would not get off lightly!

Today's reports were mainly about world reaction to the attack on Taipei. Wang Feng listened carefully. International hysteria was to be expected. However Hungary was the only country to break off diplomatic relations, because their unfortunate Minister of Commerce had been killed in the attack. Too bad, Wang Feng thought, that's what comes of flirting with Taiwan. He had feared that all the important countries would withdraw their ambassadors, but the US had left a temporary chargé d'affaires, and the Russian ambassador had hurried back from Moscow.

Sanctions had been imposed: bans on trade, loans, the sale of weapons—the old story. No-one of any importance had raised the question of the ABM Treaty. The policy-makers avoided the subject and shifted responsibility on to each other.

The Secretary-General of the UN had admitted that this was an exceptional case; that the ABM Treaty was not entirely applicable and that a meeting of the Security Council would be necessary. It was a victory. China has the right of veto in the Security Council, and no decision against her interests could pass that hurdle. Even if a two-thirds majority of the General Assembly voted for a change in the UN Charter, by the time action had been decided on it would be too late. Moreover, a new Charter would not be applicable retrospectively. It was a real masterstroke. Wang Feng congratulated himself. The UN was stymied and China in the clear.

As to the sanctions, they were not worth the paper they were written on. Those imposed after June Fourth had not affected China in the least, except to teach the way to get round them and import whatever she wanted. Businessmen are only interested in money and there were always plenty of loopholes to be found. Public opinion might cause a temporary rumpus but it wouldn't last. People are good at forgetting. With a little patience everything would return to normal. The fading memory is a great ally, as June Fourth has shown. Grit your teeth and hold out for a year or two; everything will return to normal and you will get away unscathed.

He took the transmitter from his pocket and examined it for a while before putting down on his desk. He did not want to have a hard object in the pocket of his suit this evening. For a while he would have no need of it to give himself peace of mind. It was less than two hours since the attack on Taipei, and already the Taiwan army was beginning to retreat all along the front. The lower ranking officers had not been told of the nuclear attack on Taipei, but before long the Beijing army broadcast the news and panic spread like an epidemic. What had been an orderly retreat, turned into a race to get home, more like a landslide.

At least ten divisions were wiped out by units still loyal to Beijing. If the Nanjing and Chengdu regional armies had not mutinied, but attacked the Taiwan army from two sides, it might have been totally annihilated. Wang Feng ordered the Beijing forces not to pursue the retreating enemy too closely, for fear that the two regional armies would seize the opportunity to take Beijing in their rear. The total destruction of the Taiwan army would be the next step; the priority now was to restore order throughout the country.

The evening meal was announced. The orderly quickly put away Wang Feng's uniform and said, 'I'll go and inform the old lady.'

'No, I'll go myself.'

After the nuclear attack on Taipei, Wang Feng had sent a final order to the Nanjing and Chengdu area commands giving them 48 hours to surrender; otherwise the two cities would suffer the same fate as Taipei. This was a gamble. Wang Feng did not want to use nuclear weapons against part of mainland China so, on the grounds that 'a dead pig does not fear scalding water', Fuzhou was not included in the threat. Otherwise he might have been presented with a difficult choice between using nuclear weapons against the city, or seeing his new strategy of nuclear terror shown up as an empty threat. He would then have little chance of dealing rapidly with Nanjing and Chengdu and their powerful armies. The attack on Taipei had convinced everyone that Beijing would stop at nothing. No one with any sense was going to declare independence if there was any danger of a nuclear punishment.

The Commander of the Chengdu Military Area, Lieutenant General Liu, had phoned this morning informing Wang Feng that he had decided to come to Beijing and give himself up. He was a good and honest man and incapable of action which would harm his country and its people.

'You should never have neglected your duty to defend the country on account of a personal misunderstanding,' Wang Feng said to him over the phone. 'Do you think I would ever forget my debt of gratitude to the Chairman? When you come here you will understand. Send the old lady and Ying-ying and come yourself. The death of the Chairman and his funeral make their presence necessary and you will wish to take part as well.'

As soon as the military aircraft from Chengdu arrived in Beijing the Commander was taken to a military prison, to await judgement and sentencing. The Chairman's widow and her daughter were lodged in the first and second suites respectively.

At first when the old lady saw Wang Feng she turned away, began to curse him, then burst into tears. Just as he had expected. He knew her very well. Ying-ying tried to console her mother, did not look at Wang Feng either and cried too.

Wang Feng stood in front of them, a General more than six feet tall, his head bowed, like a guilty child. He knew the old lady's mind: if she could be made to remember the child he had been all those years ago, her anger would soon vanish. That was exactly what happened. She stopped cursing and her words and heart softened: Wang Feng knew it was the time to speak.

'Dear Aunt. It was a terrible blow when I saw the Chairman was dead that day and I lost my head. He was assassinated by enemies in order to plunge the whole country into chaos and I could think of nothing except how to deal with the emergency. They wanted to use you and Ying-ying to further their own ends. The political struggle occupied my whole mind, and I feared for your safety but did not think how much I had hurt you. I have become nothing but a political machine, thinking only of upholding the Chairman's noble cause but wronging his family—which is also my family. After you had been taken away I did not sleep for several nights and swore to ask for your forgiveness as soon as I saw you. I do so now, dear Aunt.'

Wang Feng took a step back, went down on his knees and bowed his head in calculated humility. This had more effect than words. The old lady genuinely relented. Ying-ying looked at him in astonishment: she knew from childhood that he would never admit being wrong. Now the man who bore the responsibility for the whole of China was on his knees and only an arm's length away.

'Ying-ying, help him up.'

'I will not presume to stand if you do not forgive me...'

'Don't make my old eyes blind with tears. You have explained to us as members of one family that you were thinking of us, so what is there to forgive?'

Ying-ying helped him up.

'Dear Aunt, the Chairman is no more. I will be your son.'

He and Ying-ying escorted the old lady into the dining room of his suite, where a meal of the highest quality, prepared by a famous cook, had been laid out.

After eating a little the old lady, who was tired, was taken in a wheel-chair by a doctor and a nurse to the Suzhou Suite.

'Don't bother about me,' she said to Wang Feng before leaving, 'Look after Ying-ying. She's been really heart-broken because of you.'

Ying-ying blushed. Wang Feng did not know whether the old lady was aware of their past relationship but she could hardly have mistaken the evidence of her daughter's present feelings.

Wang Feng dismissed the servants and as they sat alone, opposite one another, a secret phone call he had been waiting for arrived. The Nanjing Deputy Chief of Staff reported that in the meeting which had just taken place, the majority of army commanders, under pressure from the people and from officers and soldiers native to the province, had agreed to surrender to Beijing. Commander Bai however, had refused and had been planning to get his way by force if the decision went against him. To that end he had instructed the Deputy Chief of Staff to see that there were armed soldiers standing by. They had entered the place of meeting, but instead of coercing the others to support Commander Bai—as he had wished—they had shot him dead.

The Chief of Staff in the name of the whole of the Nanjing command now formally surrendered to Beijing and expressed the hope that there would be no investigation of any of his subordinates who might have supported Commander Bai in his treacherous acts.

'Tell them,' Wang Feng said in a formal and impassive voice, though the news had put him into the best of spirits, 'that we demanded unconditional surrender and cannot at present agree to anything else. However, the Central Committee seeks national reconciliation and has no desire to make things worse by an inquisition.' He then said some complimentary words to Major General Su.

As soon as the Taiwan troops had withdrawn the Deputy Chief of Staff had secretly indicated that he was entirely at Wang Feng's disposition. The meeting in Nanjing had then been arranged between them. Commander Bai's hold over his subordinates was very strong, so they had decided that he must be killed. Wang Feng had promised the Major General that he would be rewarded, but while saying this, resolved that as soon as things settled down a little he would be got rid of too. He had been close to Commander Bai and must have been involved in all his plans, yet he had killed his former commander without the slightest qualm in order to ingratiate himself with a new master. Wang Feng's voice became affable and pleasant as he appointed the Major General as his deputy to receive the surrender of the Nanjing Command troops.

Ying-ying sat watching him during this exchange and other telephone conversations. Her look stirred tender thoughts in him, making him put aside the phone and meet her eyes. She dropped hers, then raised them again, just as she had another evening, under the light of a hanging oil lamp, when they were young.

'Do you think I'm cruel?' he asked. She nodded, almost imperceptibly. He sighed. He ought to have been full of energy and enthusiasm. Instead he felt gloomy.

'Do you remember, the night before I left to join the army, I told you I wanted to be the Napoleon of China?' Ying-ying nodded. 'With an ambition like that a man has to put aside many things. . .feelings. . . emotions.' He felt near to tears. 'I no longer want to be a Napoleon. But China needs one.'

His eyes were damp, with happiness or sorrow he hardly knew, nor whether on account of the past or of the future. He took Ying-ying's hand and she silently fell into his arms.

Guangxi Province: Nuclear Missile base 1358

Wild flowers scattered all over the hillside, and lit by the sun behind, shone like many-coloured precious stones. It was the beginning of Spring—the best season in Guangxi—when the air is full of an intoxicating fragrance. As he lay prone on the ground a bee kept alighting on Li Ke-ming's watch, bringing memories of his childhood on the banks of the Heilong River—where the wild flowers would not bloom for another two months.

The sun had almost set and the ground-level buildings of the base were already in the lengthening shadow of a mountain. Two soldiers were squatting at the side of a basketball court eating. Perhaps they spent all day underground. From time to time the put down their bowls and made motions of shooting a basket, or stretched their arms or legs.

The base looked vulnerable to attack, even the sentries seemed slovenly and careless. But Li Ke-ming was in no doubt that there were all kind of hidden surveillance equipment. If anything abnormal were detected, in no time there would be no one in sight. Everything was underground, where no outsider could ever hope to enter. There would be traps everywhere, from minefields to tactical nuclear weapons—enough to wipe out several divisions without the least damage to the underground installations, and the missiles could easily be fired automatically. Most of the nuclear bases were on the territory of one or other of the independent or semi-independent regimes yet, up to now, no attempt had been made to capture one. They remained firmly under Beijing's control. But vigilance had been relaxed otherwise the two soldiers on the basketball court would not have been there so long without any officer intervening.

Li Ke-ming once again looked around him. All his men were still lying in the undergrowth completely motionless. He was pleased. The slightest alarm in the base, and a nervous finger on the button would bring down the steel gates underground and all his efforts would be wasted.

After the Taiwan army's retreat from the Mainland, Fujian was again in imminent danger of attack by Beijing. Everyone thought that Fuzhou would be the next target for a nuclear attack. The population of Fuzhou was fleeing with their belongings in blind panic to villages in the mountains. Even the autonomous government fled to a mountain in the suburbs.

Li Ke-ming's system of defensive blockade had been extended and virtually turned Fujian into an island. There was no defence against nuclear attack, and nothing could prevent Fujian troops from deserting in large numbers. After the nuclear attack on Taipei thousands of

Taiwanese had fled to Japan, the US or Europe. Few people in Fujian were wealthy enough to do so, and in any case could not obtain visas. So, like the Vietnamese boat people they had no choice but to take their chance at sea in small boats. It looked as if terror alone would bring the province to its knees.

Li Ke-ming had been almost the only Fujian army commander who was holding out at the front when he was called back urgently to HQ, where Huang Shi-ke and a general from Taiwan gave him orders to capture a Beijing missile base in the nearby province of Guangxi.

'As long as Beijing's missiles are aimed at us all defensive methods are futile,' Huang Shi-ke said. 'The only hope is to threaten Beijing in the same way and force the government to renounce the use of nuclear weapons. We need a breathing space and something in our hands to negotiate. A coup like that will also give confidence and courage to our people. The future of Fujian is in your hands.'

When Li Ke-ming left Fuzhou for Guangxi with his small assault force, Bai Ling had appeared at the roadside and squeezed in beside him. All the time he had been at the front he had thought of her day and night. He had been bewitched since the night on the ship and had little thought for anything except wild sex. After being called back to Fuzhou by Huang Shi-ke, he had once managed to embrace her, and was nearly caught in the act. Now she had left that fat and feeble old man to come with him—a man who had to hide his face behind a steel mask. He could refuse her nothing. So he took her as well as the nine students from Taiwan who were with her.

He ought to have refused, he told himself, even though it was true that he had not enough men. Nevertheless, if Bai Ling had not insisted, even pestered him, he would not have agreed to take strangers—especially not Taiwanese—on this operation. Two of them were Bai Ling's cousins, who had come from Taiwan with the idea of taking revenge on the Beijing regime for the destruction of Taipei. Li Ke-ming had seen many groups of such hot-headed young men. They were very brave but lacked experience. He decided to keep them close to him, Bai Ling as well, just in case.

The sun had set and the wind off the mountains was cold. It was time. Bai Ling who was lying beside him in the undergrowth, suddenly put her hand on his thigh and as usual it sent an electric current through him, but his mind had become clear. The three squads behind him seemed ready, and he gave the signal to move off.

This particular base had been chosen, on the basis of information provided by Taiwan intelligence, because there was only one control centre to be captured. In large bases with more that one, they would have had to be captured simultaneously, to avoid automatic locking of the missiles.

Li Ke-ming had asked for a supply of an odourless narcotic gas that could be introduced into the air-conditioning system of the control centre. He specified that it must be easy to carry, effective in a large space, do no lasting damage to the victims and that he must be provided with an instantly effective antidote. He had no knowledge of chemistry himself, but the way Shen Di had been put to sleep had impressed him; he was confident that Taiwan could satisfy his request. The Taiwan general at Huang Shi-ke's HQ made a note and the following day a special plane delivered sixteen cylinders resembling scuba-divers' air bottles.

The General from Taiwan applauded Li Ke-ming's plan. The base was hidden underground but was linked to the outside world by ventilation ducts: any attack must start from there. For various reasons they were facing different directions; and there was no means of knowing in advance which of them would be in use at any particular time. Therefore the commandos had to attack from all four points of the compass simultaneously so as to be sure that the gas was effective.

Soon after dusk Li Ke-ming crawled into what looked like a cave until he came to a barrier of heavy steel bars; by the light of his torch he could see a succession of others like it. At the end of the tunnel he could see the dark mouth of a vertical shaft. Good. This ventilation shaft was the one in use.

After a few pairs of gas cylinders had been brought up into the cave, Li Ke-ming ordered everyone else out. Each pair consisted of a yellow and a black cylinder joined by a three-way valve that mixed the two gasses in the right proportion.

After putting on a gas-mask, he carefully opened the valves. The gas was immediately sucked into the ventilation shaft. Before leaving the cave he looked at his watch: twenty minutes to wait.

Dealing with the sentries was no trouble and was done in silence by the four groups acting with perfect coordination. An officer of the guard lost his life, but managed to set off the alarm in the base. He saw to his horror before he died. that the gate barring access to the lift was open; he heard the urgent howl of the alarm. . . . nothing else.

If the huge reinforced steel door to the control centre had been closed, no explosive charge could have opened it. There was just enough space for someone to pass through. Two sentries were senseless on the ground; the hand of one of them only a few inches away from the mechanism controlling the door.

Li Ke-ming was the first to enter huge, brightly lit underground cavern, extending in all directions—like a maze. The gas had now all been expelled by the ventilation system, and he and his men removed their masks. The personnel were lying everywhere in different attitudes, as if put to sleep by an evil magician in a story.

The only sound was of a rock-and-roll band, coming from all the loudspeakers. In the central control section army personnel were slumped over computers, screens and dials—an eerie and sinister sight.

Li Ke-ming ordered his men to search and occupy all parts of the base and lock up all the unconscious personnel. Once this was done he ordered the missile specialists of the Fujian Army to take over. His job was done. It only remained for him to take Bai Ling and the nine Taiwan students to guard the control room.

Within seconds he realized that he had made a fatal mistake. The elder of Bai Ling's cousins was giving orders in the manner of an experienced military officer. Two of the students closed the door of the control room and took up the best defensive positions nearby like well-trained soldiers. The other cousin stationed the remaining students at various points. Li Ke-ming then realized the truth of the saying 'even a hero can be hoodwinked by a beautiful woman'.

The 'students' had none of their former clumsiness and ignorance: they appeared perfectly familiar with everything in the control room and each was a skilled operator who went to his particular task without waiting for instructions. The controls were rapidly made operative, computers began working, diagrams appeared on screens and all sorts of lights went on.

' Hey!' Li Ke-ming shouted. 'Keep your fucking hands off!' He was not clear what their intention was and pretended to be a little dumb.

Bai Ling gave him an amorous glance. 'Don't worry they're just as expert as these ones are,' she said, handing the papers of the unconscious technicians to the 'cousins'.

Li Ke-ming had already noticed that they both had their rifles trained on him from behind. He knew he must do nothing until he found out what they were intending to do.

After the elder 'cousin' had the papers, a colonel and three other officers were picked out among the technicians, and Bai Ling restored them to consciousness with the same kind of spray that Li Ke-ming himself had used on Shen Di.

The cousin then nodded to a big 'student' usually addressed as 'fatty' by the others. This man had always appeared simple and straightforward and often had tricks played on him. Now his face was abruptly transformed into something savage and ferocious. He lifted the colonel off the ground by the collar as if he were a chicken.

'Tell us the code!' The colonel looked at him coldly and said nothing.

Li Ke-ming assumed that 'the secret code' was the key to start the firing process or perhaps to arm the warhead.

The fat man seized hold of one of the Colonel's fingers, waved a small razor-sharp knife in front of his eyes and pared away the flesh from his finger as if sharpening a pencil, leaving only the bone. It was done so fast that before the colonel could cry out a second finger had been pared.

'I don't know it. I don't know it,' the colonel screamed, struggling violently. 'Fatty', immovable as a mountain, seized the man's hand held it up in front of his eyes, showing him his five flayed fingers, stuffed the parings that had fallen on the table into the Colonel's mouth, then slapped his face with his own mutilated hand.

'One last time: what's the code?' 'fatty' threatened, preparing to start on the other hand.

The colonel managed to give the figures he knew and immediately the three majors completed the code. The face of one of them had been mutilated. The other two spoke of their own accord, less for fear of pain than because of the ghastly horror of what they had seen. Only the most experienced interrogators reached this standard.

Once the code was entered, the activity in the control room became frenzied. There was a sudden, palpable surge of energy that made one gasp, and made the pieces of human flesh dance on the table. The rock-and-roll sounded louder and more intense. Everything seemed drawn into a confusing and mysterious field of high velocity. The base personnel had recovered consciousness and now became extremely nervous.

Li Ke-ming moved very slightly. The barrels of two automatic rifles pressed into his back.

'What the hell does this mean?' he objected loudly. 'We're on the same side!' It was a reasonable protest, but the guns still pressed into his back.

'You're right. We are, but I want you to put your rifle aside for the time being.' The elder 'cousin's' voice was very amiable and without its usual fawning tone.

Li Ke-ming pretended to be very angry and let loose a stream of angry obscenities—in order to concentrate the other's attention on his steel mask—and propped his rifle against the wall beside him in such a way that the trigger-guard was touching a lever at the side of the instrument panel cover. Then he angrily raised his hands in the air in order to relax the vigilance of the 'students'. 'Does that satisfy you? What the fuck are you doing anyway?'

Bai Ling came gently forward. 'Ke-ming, don't ask, it's nothing to do with you and. . .'

'I'm not speaking to you, you whore,' he interrupted her angrily.

'You should tell him,' the elder 'cousin' said. 'He's been good to us and we should thank him for bringing us here.' He turned to Li Ke-ming 'We're going to make Beijing look like Taipei—wipe it off the map.'

'What do you mean?' Li Ke-ming pretended not to understand.

'By doing what they did to Taipei.'

'But our mission was to occupy the base, to force them to negotiate—not to fire a missile and start a nuclear war.'

'That was *your* mission, and you have accomplished it. The next step is our business.'

'Who gave the order?'

Bai Ling put out her hand as if to stop the 'cousin' from explaining. But he continued, 'It doesn't matter. We have cooperated and he has a right to know.' His rank was evidently higher than Bai Ling's and to him Li Ke-ming was a person of no great importance. 'It is a decision of the army, which is the only authority now that can govern Taiwan. We have to win back people's faith in us, to put an end to the demoralization caused by the destruction of Taipei and the resentment against us. We have to retaliate. You are a soldier and I need not tell you that our honour has been trampled on, our families have been killed. We personally would like to destroy Beijing a hundred times over!'

'You're not afraid of another attack on Taiwan? How many missiles are there here? Even if you fired the whole lot how much of the country could you destroy? Beijing has enough missiles to turn your island into scorched earth and leave not a single person alive.'

'That's why we suggested that the Fujian government should arrange for this attack and occupy this base, not us. Beijing will find out that you led the attack, and even if they don't we will have vanished. They will blame you and if they want revenge they can attack Fuzhou.'

As the 'cousin' was speaking the other 'students' were working fast. They were clearly well-trained specialists in missile technology and had a complete grasp of the systems in use on the Mainland. Preparations were almost finished. The missile was now aimed at Beijing rather than New Delhi. The prospect of imminent success made the elder 'cousin' show off a little.

Bai Ling looked at Li Ke-ming with pity in her eyes.

'I don't believe that Beijing will be able to retaliate. Look, the four officers who each knew parts of the firing code, are all wearing different uniforms, because they belong to four different services. The order to fire can only be given on the authority of all four. If we destroy even one of the HQ—they are all in Beijing—the missile bases will all be paralysed. Once Beijing is wiped out the whole of the Mainland will break up in independent regions. This is not just blind revenge—it is the only choice we have. If we do not destroy Beijing Wang Feng will use nuclear missiles to force us to give up Taiwan. If we obliterate Beijing, even though we have lost Taipei, the whole of the Mainland will be ours.'

The preparation for firing was complete. The 'cousin' looked around him with an arrogant and cruel expression, and, as if greeting the moment of historical destiny, proudly touched a switch on the control console. A panel slid silently opened, revealing a large, bright red button. The countdown began, adding a cold and alien beat to the rock-and-roll still blaring from the loudspeakers. . .twenty seven, twenty six, twenty five. . .

Li Ke-ming again raised his arms. 'I'm not going to watch you do this terrible thing. . . I'm turning my back.' The armed men behind him kept their eyes on his raised hands and did not notice that he had managed to hook his foot into the strap of his automatic rifle, so that the trigger was touching the lever beside it. He gently exerted pressure.

Suddenly bullets were flying in every direction as the recoil made the lever jerk backwards and forwards. No one could make out where the surprise attack was coming from and instinctively dodged and ducked. In an instant Li Ke-ming had his weapon in his hands, and with his back to the wall, covered everyone in the control room.

The elder 'cousin' went white. The fat man was ready to throw his knife when a burst of fire hit him in the throat. The knife flew out of his hand, described an arc in the air and its sharp point stabbed the floorboards. The other 'students' threw down their arms.

'Why?' The elder cousin asked with a forced smile. 'We're friends, allies.'

'I don't want to kill you, just prevent you from destroying Beijing.'

'What has Beijing done for you, except try to kill you and make you as you are now?'

'You're right,' said Li Ke-ming sombrely. 'But since I was a child, I have heard and spoken the name "Beijing" every day and can't do without it.'

'You idiot!' Li Ke-ming did not hear him.

13. . . . .12. . . . .11. . . .

Bai Ling had begun to move lasciviously in time to the music. Her clothes seemed to fall off her as if in an animated cartoon. Her breasts swung and bounced, her red, moist nipples like berries in a spring wind.

Her honey-coloured panties fell into a pool of blood still flowing from the body of the fat man. Her full, rounded buttocks became a ball of blazing flame and the flower between her legs as she kicked them in the air gave out an electric charge that made Li Ke-ming tremble. All he wanted at that moment was to be transformed into a cloudburst and throw himself at the fertile mother earth.

.....4......3.....2.....

Bai Ling approached dancing nearer and nearer to the control console, then all of a sudden flew towards the bright red button like a shooting-star.

'Stop!' Li Ke-ming's shout cut through the thickening silence. One shivering burst of flame came from his rifle. He stood as if dazed, his expressionless steel face like granite. On Bai Ling's jade-white back, small red dots slowly became bigger, like flowers opening in the snow. Bai Ling fell to her knees, and turned to look at him for the last time, then abruptly raised her hand to the red firing button.

His trigger-finger seemed not to belong to him but to some force from another world. A burst of fire severed Bai Ling's hand like a knife, the hand that had led him to a paradise of delight. Her hand, its fingers almost touching the button, now lay lifeless on the control console. She waved her handless arm and fell to the ground.

Li Ke-ming gave a cry like a dying leopard and turned his automatic rifle on the 'students' just as they were picking up their weapons, then kept on firing and howling at the same time, and when one magazine was empty took up another rifle, and turned everything in the control room into an unrecognizable mass of rubbish, flashing short-circuits and smoke. In the middle, Bai Ling her beautiful naked body and the pure white breasts, looked like a sleeping goddess.

Beijing: The Military High Court

It was the most public trial by the Court since martial law had been declared. Although the press was not allowed in, the authorities chose representatives from various walks of life, who were allowed to watch on closed-circuit television in an adjoining room.

Shi Ge's name was now known world-wide, his fame surpassing that of many presidents, film stars and billionaires. He was considered a great martyr, the 'conscience of the world' and his name was put forward for the Nobel Peace Prize. There were petitions and demonstrations demanding his release. Various governments urged Beijing to make a public statement assuring the world of his well-being. The open trial itself was the response to international public opinion.

As soon as she was led into court, Chen Pan realized that any hope of pressure from abroad being effective was illusory. The procedure was very correct and formal, but it was clear that Wang Feng and his yes-men were determined to make Shi Ge pay the full price for his action.

Since being arrested herself Chen Pan had thought only of Shi Ge. Whatever trumped up charges might be levelled against him, from a legal point of view, he was undoubtedly guilty. For a Vice-Premier of the State Council to reveal—in wartime—a top state secret to the enemy through the government of a third country, was impossible to justify in the eyes of the law. International opinion, based on moral considerations, was irrelevant. That is why the authorities were so self-confident. TV cameras were standing by, ready to broadcast the truth to the world.

Chen Pan was seated in the witness-box between two policewomen. She was accused of being Shi Ge's accomplice. This was the first time she had seen him since she heard on Australian radio about his astonishing act. She had hurried from Zhengzhou to find out what had become of him. On the third day she had asked permission, although she knew it was pointless, to visit him in prison. It was then that she too had been arrested.

Shi Ge was in the dock. He was thinner, which made his forehead seem larger, his scanty hair was unkempt—he looked rather like a famous photo of Einstein. He had not asked for an advocate to defend him and did not challenge the charge of treason. He was interrogated many times and simply answered 'yes' absent-mindedly, as if all this was nothing to do with him. Only when he heard Chen Pan called did he raise his eyes.

His expression showed nothing, not even that he recognized her. But their eyes met, and for her everything else around her momentarily disappeared from sight.

She had never paid much attention to his appearance. Now she felt that a mature, wise and strong man is far more good-looking than a handsome, immature young man. A man can become more, not less attractive with age; because his looks reflect his spirit. Here, in this ominous setting, she again made a comparison and saw that Shi Ge was more handsome than Ouyang, handsome enough to break her heart.

'The witness must answer the question,' said the Judge impatiently, hammering the table with his gavel. Chen Pan was not aware that she had been asked one. So far, the questions had been long-winded and tedious and she had responded mechanically: was she a member of the Green Association? She had admitted it. The Association had been banned and one of the charges against Shi Ge was that he had 'protected a reactionary organization'.

'Please explain these contracts you signed a few months ago,' the prosecutor repeated holding up some photocopies.

'It was. . . .well, the laboratory needed. . . .'

The prosecutor fanned out the photocopies like a pack of cards. 'The laboratory needed what? These contracts are for the purchase of 4720 SJ-8 machines for the production of nutritional fluid, 18 tons of catalytic agent, 30 million metres of plastic tubing, and contracts with a group of enterprises. The amount of money that passed through your hands alone, adds up to more than 20 billion *yuan*, which is enough to buy your whole institute 100 times over. Its requirements seem a little excessive, don't you think?'

'The court requires you to tell the truth,' said the judge in a loud and imposing voice. 'You are warned that you will take full responsibility before the law for false testimony and the concealment of crimes.'

Chen Pan was silent for a moment. It was useless to conceal the truth: the court clearly knew everything. But there was something in the look Shi Ge gave her which seemed like a question. He did not know the results of the assignment he had given her; they had not met since then. She was going to make this like a progress report on the task he had given her. Perhaps she would not see him again.

'If it was possible,' she said looking at Shi Ge, 'I would order even more. In another two weeks I would increase my order to three billion *yuan*, excluding the down payment. It's a question of saving millions of people from starvation and we should not hesitate to use unconventional measures. Our orders have exceeded the budget by one billion *yuan* and I'm not sure that we will be able to pay the difference, but at worst I will be charged with corruption. The product is there in storage and can fulfil its function if the need arises. Expenditure has exceeded the amount agreed on—it wasn't enough anyway. It was essential to spend the extra amount in order to win confidence and build up a group of companies. Everything was going well and it's a pity we have no means of carrying on.'

Shi Ge had given her ten billion *yuan* from government money allocated to the Yellow River diversion project. Chen Pan used it with the utmost economy and did not draw any if she could help it. She was aware that his unauthorized use of this money was bound to come out, and thought that if the figure was smaller his crime would be less serious. She would rather have borne the blame herself.

There was a smile in Shi Ge's eyes which only she was conscious of, and she was happy to have given him pleasure. She felt her eyes fill with tears.

'Who provided you with funds for this swindle?'

'I object to the use of such words.'

'The witness must answer,' said the judge.

'Only if the prosecutor withdraws his misleading and insulting words.'

'The record will show that you just now admitted to being a swindler.'

'The witness must answer the question.'

'I refuse.'

'The witness must understand. . .' began the judge.

'I provided that money,' Shi Ge announced. 'I also asked her to keep it secret.'

The judge narrowed his eyes. 'The court did not give you permission to speak.'

The court had not devoted much time to the main charge in the indictment—that of treason. It was clear-cut: the accused had admitted the charge and the verdict was not in any doubt. The court was more interested in the question of the misappropriation of funds. The authorities realized that condemnation of Shi Ge on the main charge would not damage his reputation and was fishing in other waters.

'I ask the witness,' the prosecutor continued, 'what is the nature of your relationship with the accused?'

'I don't understand your meaning,' Chen Pan replied her heart drumming violently the figure of Shi Ge, as clear as ever. She stared at him, as if waiting for something.

'I will make myself clear. Are you the accused's lover?'

Sooner or later this was bound to come up. A Vice-Premier in collusion with his lover embezzles an enormous sum of public money to obtain goods on false pretences—that was the picture they wanted to present to the world. A hero praised world-wide, shown up as a common criminal who tried to cover his crimes by betraying his country. Chen Pan realized that the best thing to do was to deny categorically she was his lover—the more firmly the better—and object strongly to such a slur on her character; but she hesitated. . . .

'Please answer the question.'

The voice of reason warned her: deny it at once, forcefully! You'll ruin him! Let people understand that you are innocent, that you've never been his lover, or ever hoped to be. . . Never hoped that one day. . . .? At this moment, perhaps of final parting, to reply with an icy 'no', to pretend to be offended at the very suggestion, and imply that nothing was further from her thoughts? To let him take that answer with him to an eternity where nothing can be retracted?

She would speak out. Tears obscured her sight. Everything was indistinct. Except they were alone in the world, face to face, close to and far away as the brim of the earth.

'The witness must answer.'

'Yes, I think so,' she said softly to Shi Ge. 'I hoped so much. . .I. . .'

Shi Ge stood motionless. She saw him blush like a youth. All sounds in the court were far away in the distance. The calm light of their eyes was a bridge between them.

'I should give your clothes a good wash.' She said.

'I dreamt of you last night.'

'There's something I always wanted to tell you,' she said.

'Tell me. I'm listening.'

'My little Shasha would like you. . .to be his father.'

'I have always wanted a son.'

'You agree then?'

'I agree.'

'I want to cry.'

'You are very beautiful.'

'I'm so happy.'

'In the next life I must be born a little later and be young like you,' Shi Ge said.

'No. No. Your age doesn't matter.'

He disappeared from her view, as if following a winding track to a door at the back of the court. She found herself being seized forcibly by the two policewomen. There was an uproar in court and the judge was pounding the table and shouting. The great outside doorway open like man-eating jaws swallowed her. She struggled and managed to turn her head. The milling crowd already blocked her view.

'I love you!' she shouted desperately.

Two hours later she heard that Shi Ge had been sentenced to death. He had fourteen days to live.

9

Another missile base in South China – Beijing: Central Military Commission – Shennongjia Nature Reserve – From the diary of the UN Secretary-General – The Pentagon – The South China Sea: depth 460 metres

ca

Another missile base in South China

All missile bases had been on maximum alert since the capture of Base No. 1358 by a mysterious commando unit. In spite of this, another base had been seized without the least resistance—or so it appeared—no one knew how.

Communications had apparently not been interrupted, yet no warning had been received by central control. Everything seemed normal, except that a missile had suddenly shot out of a silo; otherwise no one would have known that the base had been captured.

Anyone with an acute sense of direction who saw it would have noticed that the missile was headed in the general direction of Beijing. But a ballistic expert, even with the naked eye, would have felt there was something wrong. Perhaps those who had seized control of the missile base had been in too much of a hurry and were not sufficiently familiar with the firing procedure; or simply because the Beijing soldiers manning the base (who were also Communist Party members) had managed to put a spanner in the works, the firing angle had been a hair's breadth off course from the start. But by the time the missile entered the atmosphere at 25,000 km per hour, and reached a height of 1,200 km when the warhead began its return to earth, the deviation was no longer microscopic, but very great. It was going to miss Beijing by a long way.

Both the capture of the base and the reason for the error will remain secrets for ever: because a second missile, hard on the heels of the first, did not wait to leap out of the silo before exploding. It left total destruction behind it, turned into an exploding star that flew into the ground at a speed of 200 metres per second, severely shaking the surrounding hills.

Fifteen minutes later the first missile exploded in Siberia, in a sparsely populated forest region, not far from Nerchinsk, where in the seventeenth century the first treaty between Imperial China and Russia was signed. Fifty kilometres of the Trans-Siberian Railway was destroyed, leaving a tangle of rails and burnt sleepers.

Beijing: Central Military Commission

At 22.37 hours, the Chinese fire-fighting contingent sent to Russia reported that the fires near Nerchinsk had been put out. The joint Sino-Russian statement issued later, made no mention of the fact that all but 20,000 of the 200,000 Chinese labourers sent to help the Russians fight the fires had vanished into the mountain forests nearby as soon as the last fires had been extinguished. Short of rounding them up one by one, they would not be coming back.

Wang Feng was relieved. This was the first good news for days. Fortunately the snow in that part of Siberia had not yet melted and the strong spring-time winds had not started, otherwise two million labourers would not have been able to put out the fires in just a few days. Hundreds of thousands of hectares of forest had been destroyed, the Trans-Siberian Railway would be cut for a few days, but less than three thousand people had been killed and the nuclear fall-out was negligible, given the size of Russia. This made it easier to minimize the incident: all that Wang Feng had been hoping for. Beijing wanted harmonious relations with Russia—the only country that did not want to 'teach Beijing a lesson'. In any case, the two countries shared a long frontier and it was always dangerous to offend such a neighbour.

As soon as he heard that a missile had landed in Russia, and before Moscow had time to protest, Wang Feng offered an indemnity of two billion dollars. The actual damage came to less than a fifth of that, but Wang Feng was not tight with money.

He also instructed the Foreign Ministry to accept all Russian reproaches and demands without question. A sovereign state is naturally responsible for anything that happens on its territory. Wang Feng was infuriated by accusations abroad that Beijing was not in control of the situation. No country could guarantee total immunity from such terrorist acts. The generous indemnity had its effect and Russia became more understanding. But Wang Feng was quite sure that once detailed discussions on compensation began, the Russian bear would show its teeth. He intended, once Taiwan had been taken over, to pay Russia out of Taiwan's enormous foreign currency reserve. If the Russians were in a hurry to get their money, they should help Beijing recover Taiwan.

He had no interest in the 180,000 Chinese labourers who had disappeared into the forests of Siberia: that was Russia's problem. At first he had proposed to send troops to put out the fires. They would have been far more efficient and would not have run away. Russia categorically refused: first a nuclear missile then the Chinese army! But people were needed to fight the fires, so two hundred thousand Chinese labourers were 'mobilized', meaning that destitute Chinese peasants were rounded up. Russia was huge, full of forests, wild animals, edible mushrooms and plants, whereas in China people are squashed together like ants, on worn-out land. It was not surprising that they wanted to stay there. In fact, people wondered why even twenty thousand of them had returned. If the Russians could not force the others to leave they could be considered as a human indemnity for the 3000 killed by the missile—sixty Chinese for every Russian. If they asked for more, so much the better; a few hundred million for instance. Heilongjiang had already become a powder-barrel of overpopulation: 180,000 less in that province would not even be noticed.

Even as a child Wang Feng feared nothing. Yet now that he had made himself the most powerful man in China and had armies and weapons at his command for the first time, he felt as though his chest was full of knotted weeds.

No sooner had he ordered the nuclear attack on Taipei than the certainty of victory gave way to the torment of waiting, and fear that a missile would land on his own head. Paying the generous indemnity to Russia was nothing—even more would have been worth it. The thought that the rocket was intended for Beijing made his blood run cold; but for that blessed deviation the capital would no longer exist.

Nuclear terror had by no means put an end to all the rebellions. It had no effect at all on the shepherds in the snows of Tibet or the Uighur horsemen in the Northwest. They cared nothing for cities. In any case, apart from a few cities bigger than provincial capitals, four thousand others and twenty thousand small towns feared nuclear missiles no more than fleas fear big clubs. You can't frighten fleas with a big stick. Most of the rebels were constantly on the move. However, the nuclear game has started and is not going to stop because I want it to, Wang Feng thought to himself. Military Intelligence reported that Taiwan was already on its feet again in spite of the nuclear attack and had started to counter-attack by capturing nuclear bases on the Mainland. On the first occasion disaster had been mysteriously avoided, but a few days later another base was taken and a missile fired.

Wang Feng had then ordered the disarming of another base that was vulnerable to attack, by destroying the firing programme. It was just in time: a few hours later it too fell into the hands of Taiwan commandos.

Panic spread, not only in Taiwan and Fujian but also in Beijing and throughout the country. After the rocket was fired from inside China—the one that landed in Siberia—the people of the capital began to flee the city in large numbers; many had moved out already because of the shortage of food. Now that everyone was saying that Beijing would come under attack the exodus became a flood. Even old fogies who had held important posts in the government and Party for years, handed in their resignations, or just left. Transport was totally inadequate and roads out of the city were clogged with people: on foot, on bicycles, in Pedi cabs, carrying children, old people and property. There were traffic jams twenty or more miles long.

Wang Feng made no attempt to stop this exodus. It would have been impossible and pointless. The more people left, the less was the burden on the authorities, the more stable the city. He approved all resignations. Anyone who wanted to leave could do so, even the vice-chairman of the Military Commission, the Premier of the State council, and members of the Political Bureau. After the attack on Taipei, he had become supreme leader—though his official status had not changed—so no one opposed him and there was no procedure to be gone through. Former leaders had become ciphers. It was not that they recognized his authority; they only wanted someone to relieve them of all responsibility. Perhaps they feared the judgement of the International Court—or of History. They were highly skilled in trimming their sails to the wind. Let them go and save their rotten lives.

His miniature transmitter lay on the desk in front of him. He took it in his hand and gazed at it for a long time. The last two days it had been switched to 'stand-by' and was connected with a nuclear missile base in Inner Mongolia. With one movement he could launch a missile at the base in South China captured by commandos from Taiwan. His whole life he had longed for such power; but to his surprise he felt the need for someone to share this decision.

The base had been disabled by the premature firing of the second missile, but the missiles were intact and the personnel from Taiwan had enough technical skill to repair other damage. The captured Chinese technicians would certainly cooperate under the threat of torture. According to Beijing specialists there was only a hundred to one chance that they would succeed. That was what Wang Feng had been told by other specialists about the likelihood of any Chinese nuclear base falling into the hands of the enemy: three already had. That shortened the odds. A missile on Beijing would be disastrous.

The captured bases were under attack by Beijing troops but there was no certainty that they would be recovered rapidly. Wang Feng had put the transmitter on 'stand-by' so that if the Taiwan technicians managed to repair the firing system, the base could be destroyed by a missile before they could fire on Beijing.

Only he could press the button. The decision was his alone; but it was a difficult one. The base was in enemy hands and there was no source of information. Even if there were, would it be reliable? No intelligence could ever be one hundred per cent. In this case it had to be.

He had not slept for three days and nights and was very tired. His brain felt dried up and painful. Everything was hazy, even the transmitter looked unreal. If the missile had to be used, the sooner the better. The nuclear game had started and must be played out. Nuclear weapons were now the basis of power. There was nothing to be gained by holding back,

But that base was not on Taiwan, nor abroad, but on the Chinese Mainland itself. To use a nuclear missile on his own country: who could imagine what that might lead to? China was not like Siberia, half uninhabited forest. The base that blew up and killed several tens of thousands of people and burned villages around; that was the fault of Taiwan. The attack on Taipei was taken by collective decision at the highest level. Now he was alone.

He saw in his mind a sea of fire and Beijing slowly disintegrating. Missile after missile flying across the sky in a dotted line. He should have woken up but he was so sleepy that he took no notice. He returned to his childhood and spring walks on the grassland, the fragrance of the night and flowers. A girl lying with him on the grass called him softly 'Your hand. . .what are you doing?' He had touched the downy grass between her legs. He had felt ashamed and explained confusedly that he had been asleep and that his hand had moved on its own. The girl stopped scolding and put his hand back between her legs, where it had been before.

Suddenly he saw a masked bat shoot like a rocket out of the atmosphere aimed straight at him. For an instant the shrugging wings blotted out the burning sky and he saw a ferocious face and two bright, intense eyes. A split second before it reached him he stretched out his hand. . . . .and woke up. His finger was on the firing button. He was not afraid and did not draw back. The button lit up and silently pulsated. He pressed it for a full ten seconds, then stood up, moved his shoulders as if doing exercises and sent for his secretary.

'Send out the following proclamation,' he said calmly, then took a few steps, while he considered the wording. 'For each of our missile bases seized by Taiwan troops we will destroy one Taiwanese city.'

The secretary left. It was very quiet and difficult to imagine that in South China, where Spring had nearly come, the shock waves and thunder of a nuclear explosion were about to shake the earth and the hills. He lit a cigarette; he had never been much of a smoker: now he felt the need more and more. He could not think clearly. Why had Zhou Chi's face appeared behind that torn mask?

Zhou Chi had been condemned to death. He had requested to be allowed to purge his crime by using *qigong* to control the Taiwanese who had seized the bases and make them withdraw. Wang Feng had agreed. But Zhou Chi had escaped with the aid of a crowd of his disciples as they were practising *qigong*. His escape was very strange, because the guards watched as if they were dreaming and did nothing.

Wang Feng wondered why he had ever trusted the man. He recognized that he believed him more than before. . . Only people who have no confidence in themselves place their hopes in strange powers where truth and falsehood are mixed.

Shennongjia Nature Reserve

In the wide blue sky there were only two clouds resembling fluffy snow-white sheep's wool. The larger one lay behind the highest peak of the Shennongjia range, which looks like a half-open umbrella: the smaller of the two seemed to be leisurely following the sun. The warmth made people feel lazy and after the cold winter every muscle longed to loosen up. But when Ouyang saw a thin man standing in front of him, every nerve became taught as a bowstring.

The man had two long yellow protruding teeth and when he smiled he looked like an old horse with a bellyful of malevolent intentions. Behind him was a group of dirty and mean-looking armed men, with donkeys carrying empty sacks.

Ouyang Zhong-hua lay on the grass and did not move, sighed inwardly, toying with the stone wine cup in his hand and glanced at them loftily. They must be a bit simple-minded: how could so many armed men expect to be allowed into the base? They were probably going to ask too much. If he put a foot wrong he would not be able to handle this without a hitch. The defence force of young peasants had still a long way to go before they would be effective.

'Heard you wanted to exchange grain for guns,' said the thin man with an oily smile.

Since the beginning of the civil war there were a large number of firearms in the rural areas, some picked up on the battlefield, some sold by deserters. Ouyang had recently put out the word that the base wanted to exchange grain for guns. These men were the first to respond and they had a lot of guns, but Ouyang felt a tingling in his armpits.

He filled up the cups of the two guests lying on the grass with him, directors of other Green bases, whom he had invited to a picnic, which he called a 'Roman-style three couch banquet'. It had just started.

The two guests watched the scene being enacted with interest. With the air of an old merchant used to bargaining, Ouyang entered into negotiations with the thin man, and they finally agreed on 60 kilos of rice per rifle and 40 kilos for a hundred rounds of ammunition. The local price of a Swiss watch was about one kilo of rice, ten kilos for a colour TV.

Last year's harvest of grain had been requisitioned by soldiers and factory workers or looted by destitute people and bandits. It was nearly time for planting and there was barely enough grain for seed. Nor was there much grain left in the base. Fortunately Chen Pan's laboratory had provided equipment and technology for the production of *shugua* and although it was almost torture to have to eat it, a great deal of grain was saved.

'Take them through the passage to load the grain,' Ouyang ordered Big Ox, with apparent satisfaction. It was not something he had ever said before and hoped that Big Ox would cotton on.

He didn't. 'Through the passage? What for?'

Ouyang lifted his wine-cup and glared at Big Ox as he drank.

'Don't waste time. We can't bring all the rice out here to pay for these guns. Our friends have been generous and there's no reason not to trust them. Take them by the road to the tunnel and straight to the granary to load up.'

Big Ox still did not understand, but Ouyang's expression had its effect and prevented him from asking simple-minded questions. Hearing the word 'granary' the man with the yellow teeth followed Big Ox with alacrity.

'I'll be there before you,' said Ouyang coldly as they disappeared from sight. He had prolonged the bargaining in order to work out a plan of action. The man with the yellow teeth, a former regular army officer and deserter was far more intelligent than Big Ox, and Ouyang would have to watch his words and say as little as possible. His two guests were interested to see the exchange and insisted on coming along.

The centre of the Shennongjia base was a huge fortified village, such as there were in former times, where bandits or rebels used to hold out for years. The wall, several miles long, was formed by natural features like cliffs and precipices, joined up by man-made walls, and surrounded land that had been cultivated for generations by mountain people. Local peasants employed by the base were working round the clock to complete the defences.

Another team was enlarging a natural tunnel at the end of which was a kind of natural amphitheatre surrounded by cliffs. Apart from this the only other access to the amphitheatre was by way of a narrow passage way through a natural fissure in the rock, much longer than going through the tunnel, so that by the time Big Ox had led the thin man and the others into the amphitheatre, Ouyang and his guests were already seated at a bamboo table, chatting and drinking tea. The rice had been brought to the mouth of a tunnel half-way up the cliff and was being lowered sack by sack by pulley. Imagining that the granary was up there, the thin man's eyes lit up, and immediately became positively obsequious to Ouyang.

Big Ox, who was almost six foot six, could carry a sack under each arm, while others could manage only one. He had worked at odd jobs in the mountains, and had become highly expert in martial arts. His teacher admired Ouyang's understanding of Taoism and knowledge of the world and believed that China would have need of Ouyang, so gave Big Ox to him with the injunction that he should serve Ouyang for the whole of his life as if he were his teacher.

The thin man opened a sack and let a handful of white rice slip between his fingers. His yellow teeth seems to have grown longer. He signalled to the men behind him to load the donkeys.

'It's stupid to exchange guns for rice,' he said pointing his rifle at Ouyang, who did not move but continued to watch the rice being loaded onto the donkeys. 'These day if you haven't got a gun all the rice is going to be eaten by others; but if you've got a gun you've got rice. We'll just take this for today and tomorrow we'll be back for more. It's not as if we don't know the way. . .'

'You'd steal our rice!' Big Ox's stentorian voice reverberated in the amphitheatre and even brought down some loose stones.

The bandits all raised their guns, rather as if they were hoes, but nevertheless managed to aim them.

Ouyang signed to Big Ox to calm down.

'That's right, looting,' said the thin man waving his rifle. 'You think this is just for trading? With guns who the fuck needs money? Bullets don't have eyes, remember. Till tomorrow.' He swaggered off at the head of the donkey train and entered the passage.

Ouyang remained sitting under a wild peach tree with his two guests, who clearly found his behaviour bewildering. The tree was in bloom and a large brass gong was hanging from one of its branches, still swinging a little. It had been put there just before the bandits entered the amphitheatre.

The last of them backed towards the passage, rifle at the ready.

Thinking the these unarmed city gluttons hardly warranted such precautions, he made an obscene gesture before turning to catch up with the others.

The passage was so narrow in some places that there was only room for one man at a time to pass. The donkeys loaded with sacks of rice often got stuck and the bandits had to push and pull. Ouyang smiled coldly, delicately picked up a stick (the bark was still on it), and made a signal without turning round and beat once on the gong. *Daoong!*

Small rocks began to rain down into the crevice from above. A few seconds later—*Daoong!* Just as abruptly, they stopped.

In the passage some of the bandits were lying still on the ground, others were on their knees. Most were bleeding. They were all stunned and scared by the unexpected and incomprehensible attack. There was screaming and shouting, the donkeys kicked and reared and all the sacks of rice had fallen to the ground.

'Put down your weapons!' Ouyang ordered.

The order seemed to have the opposite effect. It seemed to have awakened them from their stupor.

Daoong! Daoong!

Again the offensive lasted only a few seconds, but there was much more blood this time.

'Put down your guns!' They did not have to be told twice.

Big Ox roared, making even more stones fall into the passage, then jumped down behind the bandits and picked up a rifle.

The thin man already had him covered. 'Don't fucking move!' he shrieked like a fox caught in a trap, his yellow teeth bared to the maximum. He was hiding behind a protruding rock and was barely hurt. He wasn't a bandit leader for nothing: after being caught in an ambush he had immediately seized the initiative. Ouyang was taken by surprise. Now that Big Ox was in the passageway he could not use the gong again. The thin man kept Big Ox covered and shouted to his men, who had been standing like wooden hens, to pick up their weapons. Big Ox was determined to fight his way out and ignoring the guns aimed at him, sent three of the bandits flying with one kick as they stooped to pick up their rifles. The thin man hesitated: it was only the presence of Big Ox that stopped the rocks from falling again. While he hesitated Big Ox rushed him. The thin man stepped back and fired a shot. It seemed to have as little effect as firing at a sandbag.

Big Ox now had a rifle, but using it as if it were a stave, thrust the barrel at the thin man's throat. Perhaps because of the bullet that had hit him, Big Ox's muscles suddenly contracted and his finger involuntarily pressed the trigger. There was a burst of fire, scattering half the man's brain over his face. Big Ox was dumbstruck and did not seem to know how to stop the automatic rifle. It continued to fire until the magazine was empty.

The thin man lay motionless. His face was unrecognizable, except for one long yellow tooth. The bandits were paralysed with fear; those who had picked up their rifles quickly threw them down again. There was a stench of death and urine.

All the guns were collected without difficulty.

There were cries of triumph and joy among the young peasants, all strong, loyal and obedient like Big Ox and had been selected by him personally. They were as excited as children at the success of the ambush—except for Big Ox himself, who was leaning on a rock vomiting. The wound in his side seemed to impress the young men far less than the remains of the thin man's face and the solitary yellow tooth. Ouyang put his hand on Big Ox's broad muscular shoulder, which now looked bowed and pathetic.

'Is he dead?' To Ouyang, the eyes of Big Ox looked more like those of a frightened sheep. Although he was mad about martial arts, Big Ox had never hit anything with a stave except stuffed dummies and his first bloody killing had shaken him. Ouyang was not pleased that the iron pagoda of a body contained such a soft centre. He needed a killer, someone with strong nerves and no feelings, someone who would deal with an enemy without emotion.

'Of course, he's dead.' Ouyang replied. 'It was either him or you... and me and my guests here and our young men. We thank you and so would the countless people who have suffered at that bastard's hands. You should be proud of yourself.'

Big Ox relaxed, stopped vomiting and looked with gratitude at Ouyang Zhong-hua. His wound was quite serious and he was carried to the clinic in the base.

The young peasants fell in. They were still awkward in their movements, but were now in fighting spirit. Ouyang called them the Green Guard. Big Ox was his second-in-command and a former army major had been given the post of instructor. Ouyang could hardly explain to him that in order to keep the Green Guard under his own control, he preferred the dull-witted but loyal Big Ox to a former army officer. The Green Guard now had twenty-six new rifles. It was a good start and Ouyang was elated.

Without showing his satisfaction, he apologized to his guests for the violent and bloody scene they had just witnessed. Some of the Green Guards moved everything needed for the 'Roman-style three couch banquet' to an elevated place with a view, where the smell of blood was soon dissipated by the fragrance of flowers.

One of the guests, a Secretary of the Green Association and director of one of the bases, was a spinster, whose remarks and tone were invariably negative when speaking to any man she was interested in. Now however, she was glancing sideways at Ouyang in visible admiration, excitedly waving her stocky hand and instructing him in Green principles.

Ouyang responded to her onslaught with a slight smile and an accommodating manner. He admitted that to recruit forces and buy arms was very ignoble, contrary to the principles of non-violence, even degenerate. 'But I think that a principle should not be turned into dogma. In a world soon to be plunged into terrible violence, if we don't prepare to resist violence, not only our Green ideals but our civilization itself will cease to exist.'

'I agree,' said Lu Shi-jia, Director of another of the Green Bases, looking at her. 'Don't forget you have just been protected from violence by violence.'

'That's not true. If there had not been a question of bartering rice for arms, the bandits would not have come here. If they had not been stoned they would have left of their own accord and there would have been no loss of life.'

'First of all,' Lu Shi-jia argued, not so politely as Ouyang, 'bandits don't only attack those who want guns. Secondly, if they had not been stoned, they would have come back. If the bandit chief had not been killed, we would all starve.'

Ouyang interrupted their argument.

'Of course I don't approve of or advocate violence. In an orderly society, even an autocracy, non-violence is desirable. But what we are faced with now is a cataclysm: order will exist no longer, civilization will be replaced by barbarity. Survival will depend solely on struggle and even killing. A world without violence would leave people defenceless against aggression and annihilation. To sit waiting for death to strike in the name of non-violence is absurd.'

'Several times in the history of our country, the state has collapsed and the result was not always so terrible as you describe it,' the woman said.

'The fundamental difference now,' Ouyang replied, 'is the simple fact that our population is now 1.3 billion. No collapse of a state has ever involved even a third of that number of people. Collapse means that all systems of production, distribution and transport are wiped out. Each person will have to fend for himself and find enough to eat. Everything will come down to the basic question of food.'

'China's present size and environmental conditions enable us to feed our population; but only on condition that we have a highly organized and efficient system, working at utmost pressure and extracting natural resources to the absolute limit. This has to be supplemented by organized international trade. Natural disaster, social disorder, civil war, separatism, the cutting off of international trade—any one of these things can lead to famine. If these disasters all threaten us at once, famine is bound to sweep away all social organization, and that will drastically reduce the amount we can extract from natural resources. How will we feed the population? Nature can provide wild fruits, birds and animals, roots and bark, which in the past have enabled perhaps several hundred million to survive by wandering all over the country in search of food. In the past the collapse of the state has not led to the obliteration of the Chinese people. Now the situation is very different. The gifts of nature have now been very severely depleted, while the population has increased enormously. This terrifying discrepancy is several times more serious than at any time in the past, and will bring about a disaster several times worse.'

'Don't forget that our reserves are much greater than they ever have been. The global grain reserve is enough to provide for world consumption for ten months.'

'Yes, but that reserve is constantly decreasing,' Ouyang replied. 'In the first place, the series of natural disasters last year reduced it to six months, and that is an optimistic estimate. Secondly, China's total reserves are far below the world average, and state reserves are even lower: enough for the whole population for only *two months.* Thirdly, since last year's Yellow River floods and now the civil war, this miserable reserve has been reduced to almost nothing. Fourthly, in a disastrous situation where order and the rule of law has broken down, consumption is faster, there is less planning and the reserves dwindle faster. This is especially true of private, non-government reserves, which are reduced to nothing by banditry, looting and the proverbial orgy of eating and drinking before the curtain falls. After a major disaster, even if agricultural and other food production is re-organized, it will take a hundred days before anything can be produced. In the meantime how are 1.3 billion people to survive? Is there anyone who can survive three months without eating?'

'So you think the big disaster will mean the obliteration of our people?' the woman asked dejectedly.

'In history civilizations have been destroyed more than once. The Chinese have survived for a very long time and we have no reason to believe that they will not continue to do so. I estimate that about 800 million will die—at least.'

They were all silent and thoughtful. The spring sunlight and the breeze had vanished, leaving the two directors with a feeling of terrible foreboding.

'How have you arrived at that figure?' Lu Shi-jia asked with a grim smile.

'Not by attempting to estimate the number of dead. The products of nature I mentioned just now could possibly provide the minimum food required to support a maximum of 500 million people. That is the most merciful estimate. It means that 800 million will have to die if the others are to live.'

'The basic reason for the coming disaster is the imbalance between population and resources. So we can foresee that whatever the exact form the catastrophe may take, the result will be the obliteration of a large part of the population by war, starvation and epidemics until population and available resources correspond. Then perhaps there will be a possibility of bringing the situation under control.'

'The five hundred million will only survive if some kind of social system is created very quickly. The longer it takes, the fewer survivors there will be.'

There was gloomy silence.

'If the survival ratio is 5:8 maybe we will be among the eight hundred million,' said Lu Shi-jia intending to lighten the atmosphere. The effect was the opposite.

'Not just possible, but certain,' said Ouyang. 'A feral strength and ability to survive—since the source of life is the stomach—will be far more important than philosophy or literature. Peasants, mountain dwellers, vagabonds, thieves, bandits and robbers will survive. Those of us who are only good at thinking, frail and ineffectual intellectuals, most specialized workers, urban people, the old, women and children: all those who are not familiar with wild plants and animals, who have no rough and primitive strength, who are incapable of brutality, who cannot bear hardship and suffering, these people will die among the eight hundred million, together with their culture, civilization, knowledge and spirit, leaving only five hundred million animal-like people—the only survivors in an animal world.'

'I don't believe it,' said the woman putting up her hands as if to cover her ears.

'It is said that God's prophecies always ended with the rider: "no one will believe me".' Ouyang replied. 'I am even less likely to be believed'.

'This is why you want to organize an armed force?' Lu Shi-jia said meditatively.

'Some may think that people hiding in the forests and obtaining their own food and producing *shugua,* are bound to survive and have no need of an armed force. But they would not be living in a "Peace-Blossom Garden",' some kind of isolated paradise cut off from the ruined world. Feral people keep their eyes open. You have just seen for yourselves how famine evenly distributes starving people over whole regions. There will be hardly anywhere to hide. There will be no rule of law and no production, so plunder and pillage will become the main way to survive, if not the only one. *We* may not be able to go out and plunder, but we can at least ensure that we are not victims of those who can. If we cannot even do this, all our ideals, our experiments and even ourselves, will be wiped out. In a violent world we can only protect ourselves by violence. Whether or not Green ideals can survive depends on this, not on non-violence.'

Ouyang took a few steps, holding a heavy stone wine-cup of great beauty, made by an artist in the base.

Under the blue sky and slowly moving white clouds, a sparkling waterfall and everything as far as the eye could see, was washed with the gold sunlight, like a dream of peace. Elsewhere in the world there was war, famine, fire, disorder, and flames. What a contrast!

'...What's more, the reconstruction afterwards may require even more violence,' Ouyang added.

He did not continue. It was not the time to say more, though he felt this was the true starting point of all thinking and preparatory work for the future. Survival was not his aim. The prospect of calamity did not trouble or frighten him. On the contrary, he welcomed it. Having come to the conclusion that there was no hope of overthrowing the existing social system from the outside, his only hope was for collapse from within. He had waited for many years: a hard, lonely and seemingly endless wait, until the bitter gall seeped out of him on to the white pages of his notebooks. He had begun to despair. How long could this society, sick to the heart, go on living? Perhaps it would not take a whole lifetime before the old society, that which for a thousand years no power could overthrow, came crashing down before his eyes to die a natural death. Then on the desolate plain covered with the ruins of the old world, the moment will come when a mysterious green morning star will rise and be transformed into a sun.

His ambition was unlimited. The freedom from restraint, the simplicity and tranquillity he called for in his teaching had never inhabited his own mind—a volcano that erupted with infinite longings and uncontrollable passions. He did not consider this at odds with his philosophy, because he believed that the aesthetic world of 'spiritual man' would be divided into different levels, in most of which there would be a place for both simplicity and freedom from restrain. Only at the highest level of the world of Beauty would there be highly esteemed, brave and selfless heroes. His ambition was not of the common variety that could be satisfied by power or glory. It was a natural demand of his burning blood, which called on him to take the destiny of mankind in his hands. He had to fuse with immensity—as great as the universe—in order to function. For the sake of this he had given up any thought of power, fame or wealth. All these things had been within his reach. But he would take no road that did not lead to the summit. He had chosen the Green movement because he knew that this was the banner of future mankind. He needed nothing. . . .home, wealth, position, comfort: the things that ordinary people wanted. His only desire was to change the course of man's history, to re-order the world.

What he needed now was an armed force and a political party. The Green Association was a loose alliance of various tendencies, in which everyone had his own opinion and went his own way. It was not suited to the situation and would not serve his purpose. A strong unified organization with iron discipline was needed to bear the responsibility for China's fate. He had invited his two guests in order to discuss how the Green Association could be transformed from an ineffective debating society into a strong fighting force. There were difficulties. Their philosophy made most Green supporters hostile to political parties, power, discipline and so on. But when people's very survival was threatened, such principles had to be abandoned. Strengthening their awareness of the threat to survival was already a breakthrough.

The bloody scene his guests had just witnessed was more convincing than any argument. Lu Shi-jia was entirely won over. The spinster, although her words were caustic, was at heart willing to cooperate. Ouyang more or less controlled four of the six Green bases. The remaining two he wanted to take over as soon as possible. Taibaishan and Chen Pan's base at Fanjingshan, both of which had adopted the All-level Election system, which seemed to be working well. But Ouyang believed strongly that democracy is a luxury of stable societies, something that people took to, like alcohol, because it made them feel good, but which at the critical moment would not enable them to bear the burden of turning the tide. With the approach of utter lawlessness and barbarity which will follow the collapse, people would realize that only he, Ouyang Zhong-hua, could save them.

He needed an extensive base area, where there was plenty of space and raw materials, and from which it would be possible to launch attacks or to retreat into the mountains and valleys. There must be peasants to grow grain and factories to produce arms and fortified towns that could resist attack. In such base areas, tens of thousands of the finest people could be provided for and people of ability trained for future reconstruction. The nucleus of a new China would be created there.

Three of the Green Bases that Ouyang already controlled—Shennongjia and two others—formed a triangle of 300,000 square kilometres on the map. This is where he planned to establish his base area. The blueprint was detailed and growing like a living thing.

All this was within his reach. But there was always something missing, deep in his heart, an emptiness that no great cause could fill. He made plans and was always busy; he needed a party, an army, a base, and other things but he had never admitted to himself the furtive, hidden message of his pain and longing: that he needed Chen Pan.

He knew that Chen Pan had been given a prison sentence of five years for misappropriating public funds and he knew everything she had said in court, but no one knew for certain in which prison she was being held. Every night when all was quiet he dreamed of her, together with the kindly, tired face of Shi Ge, old before his time, in a prison cell of stone. When the vision dissolved grey water-lines, like tears, seeped into his eyes.

From the diary of the UN Secretary-General

The last few days, China has been constantly on my mind. In that crazy country everyone seems to be preparing their nuclear weapons. Yesterday the rebels in the south fired a nuclear missile from a captured base that destroyed half of the city of Zhengzhou. Beijing immediately destroyed the base it was fired from. The CIA reports that eleven bases have been surrounded by rebel forces. No one is clear how many independent regimes have been established. Major cities in the rebel territory such as Fuzhou, Guangzhou and Lhasa have been abandoned, and no longer exist as targets for Beijing's nuclear blackmail. Taiwan is reported to have paid South Africa more than 15 times its value for a submarine carrying 18 nuclear missiles with a range of 4,800 km, which is now speeding towards the China Sea. It is estimated that within days Beijing will be within its range. Indiscriminate nuclear bombing seems about to start in China if it has not already done so. The whole world is convulsed by these developments.

Without involving the UN, the United States and Russia have secretly drawn up plans and demand that any action they take must be in the name of the UN, which displeases me greatly. My first reaction was to refuse. However, given the present state of the world, there is probably no other way of preventing nuclear holocaust.

It is not difficult to accept the aim of 'total abolition of Chinese nuclear weapons'. Of course, neither Beijing nor Taiwan is going to meekly hand over their nuclear weapons and the means to make them. So in this case 'abolition' must mean the destruction of Chinese nuclear installations and weapons anywhere in the world—including Taiwan's recently acquired submarine. The essence of the US-Russian plan is to make China a non-nuclear power.

This is acceptable. But the attack must be simultaneous. If the destruction of only one of the 137 nuclear missile bases on the Mainland of China, or of any nuclear device in the air or at sea is delayed for even a few minutes, there can be a terrible nuclear counter-attack. The only way to prevent a nuclear war is to launch a nuclear war!

Russia's fear of a nuclear civil war in China is understandable, considering that the two countries are neighbours and have a very long common frontier. Not to mention the fact that already a missile from China has landed in Russia. Many of the Chinese missile sites were built with a war with Russia in mind. Many of the missiles are aimed at her large cities. If one of the many rebel forces were to capture a base and fire a missile, it would probably explode over a Russian industrial centre, military installation or large city, unless the target coordinates have been changed, which seems unlikely. Given the present state of public opinion in Russia, it in unthinkable that the arrival of another foreign missile on her territory will be tolerated.

The US also has her own interests to think about. After June Fourth, there was constant friction between China and the US and the former friendly relations were not restored. Last year, when the regime and political line in Beijing changed, the White House finally lost patience and has now apparently placed its hope for a reliable political force on the alliance of independent southern provinces.

US relations with Taiwan have become closer, although the Taiwan government has been criticized for its weak reaction to the bombing of Taipei. In the present civil war in China, in spite of any strange exploits the Southern Alliance and Taiwan may pull off, they can never stand up against Beijing's nuclear superiority. The action the US and Russia envisage will deprive Beijing of its only card, protect the southern provinces and Taiwan, and respond to the criticism by the US public. In addition, the US in its arrogant and overbearing role as world leader, is untiring in its urge to interfere and correct other countries.

Britain and France have reservations about the US-Russia plan, but in the absence of any better solution, have voted for it; but refuse to participate directly in a nuclear attack.

The UN should play a role in this. Beijing has adroitly insisted that the destruction of Taipei was entirely a matter of Chinese internal politics. Here at the UN many people were secretly pleased, because it has provided a reason for not having to punish China for a breach of the ABM Treaty. Quite apart from the loss of life it would involve, everyone is afraid of China's reaction to such punishment. I recall the surprise that greeted Mao Zedong's remark that China had no fear of nuclear war because even if several hundred million people were killed, China would still be the most populous country in the world. The Chinese regard life as an organic whole, not in terms of individual lives, as we do. Therefore to inflict punishment on the principle of an eye for an eye would be futile.

However, failure to react rapidly would do inestimable damage to the reputation of the UN and make a mockery of the ABM treaty.

The US and Russia have estimated that about 200 nuclear missiles is the minimum required to destroy China's nuclear installations. On nuclear sites they will primarily use ground penetrating missiles which explode at a depth of 50-80 metres, with great destructive effect on underground installations. They cause little damage above ground and the nuclear fall-out is minimal. Most Chinese missile sites being in isolated locations, though a few naval missile bases are near cities, the attack, I am informed, will not cause much destruction to industrial production. China is thickly populated, but loss of life will be small by Chinese standards.

I am anxious about the effects on the environment, and especially the danger of nuclear winter. Although many scientists dismiss the theory of nuclear winter, the TTAPS research report has partially confirmed its validity. The US and Russia have given an absolute guarantee that, in any case, it would take the equivalent of a thousand megatons of TNT to produce such an effect. They will use less that 2% of that. But the extensive destruction and over-exploitation of China's forest cover has left many mountains bare. This is bound to increase the likelihood of nuclear winter.

I reminded the Russian Foreign Minister that the Chinese people are easily roused to xenophobia and that an attack on Russia by an army of several million regular troops would be extremely difficult to deal with. He replied with a smile that Beijing will have reason to be grateful to Russia. The missile bases in South China that are Russians targets, are all in the territory held by rebellious regimes. Their destruction will make it easier for Beijing to suppress these regimes afterwards, as constituting a threat to the country's security. Targets in North China will be the responsibility of the US which is protected from a Chinese attack by the Pacific Ocean.

While acting in the cause of world peace, the two countries are guided by their respective policies towards China: Russia as an immediate neighbour, while the US is more oriented towards South China, Taiwan and Hong Kong.

The 'exchange of battlefields' allows both protagonists to combine conflict and cooperation, to give the appearance of being allies while in fact undermining the other and avoiding hostility or collision, at least in those areas most concerned with their vital interests. This is acceptable: there are no disinterested gifts in politics. But I sense danger in it—the spectre of decades of two-power confrontation. China will probably continue to split apart, and those on either side of the rift will clash.

The crucial task now is to prevent a major nuclear war. If China's ability to produce nuclear weapons is left intact, in a short time we will be faced with a new threat, and vengeance is even more dangerous. Therefore it is essential to destroy not only nuclear weapons but all of China's nuclear research institutes, factories where missiles are built, all equipment, blueprints, technical records and documentation. Once this is done, it will be necessary to establish a system of international control and ensure that China should never possess nuclear weapons again. Only the UN can do this. Indeed, it would be an excellent opportunity to transform the UN into a genuine world government rather than a mere a talking shop.

The Pentagon

Lieutenant Commander McGowan had been studying a satellite photograph half the size of the table for at least half an hour. It showed part of the Chinese naval base on the Shandong Peninsula. In spite of all Chinese security precautions, US intelligence had long known that under a certain cliff on the coast there was a tunnel large enough to admit a submarine. Last year it was known for a fact that inside it a new submarine was being fitted out.

The photograph had been taken about five weeks earlier on a routine reconnaissance. It had not attracted any attention at the time, but since the establishment of the US-Russian command for the attack on China, the photographs had been sent with other material to McGowan's group which was responsible for selecting the Chinese naval targets to be attacked.

In principle all relevant intelligence material had already been sorted out, and useful information detected by computer. No one wanted to waste energy going through old documentation. But the occasion was too important and no stone was to be left unturned, especially anything concerning easily concealed targets under the sea. The slightest negligence might mean disaster. So all material had to be searched three times. The satellite photograph had already been examined twice. This was the third time. McGowan had found nothing which conflicted with earlier analyses, and was ready to send the photograph back to the archives, but he felt that there was something unusual about it. Two days ago, in the middle of the night, when he was half asleep, the image of the satellite photograph had appeared in his mind.

What puzzled him was the very faint trace of a line. That seemed to come from the tunnel and make its way like a winding thread to the main drain of the naval base, which the satellite photo showed to be a source of heat. The line was barely visible, almost like a minute flaw in the paper or in the developing process. But it can hardly have been by chance that it came from the tunnel.

He had an enlargement made of that part of the photo and after subjecting it to further analysis, concluded that the line also represented a slight increase of heat. He was one of the best submarine detection specialists in the US navy and could identify a submarine from satellite photos of water disturbance caused by its propeller. But this line was far fainter than any worthy of notice and it was not surprising that the computers had failed to detect it. It was now essential to know more.

He had already requested the US-Russia joint command HQ to undertake a world-wide satellite reconnaissance of the sea, for the umpteenth time. China's sixteen submarines had shown up as clearly as fish in a tank; not one of them had escaped detection even for a minute. It looked as if China had invented a magic submarine, which left only a minute trace and could remain underwater for 133 days, which was clearly impossible.

Unless it could be proved that the submarine was still under construction in the secret dock, the whole plan for a nuclear attack on China would have to be put on hold until the mystery was solved.

You never know what the Chinese are up to, McGowan thought to himself. They were a stupid and pig-headed lot, but there were some who had real genius. He remembered that when he had been an instructor at the Annapolis Naval Academy, there had been a Chinese called Ding or something, who looked like a blockhead but had stumped him in front of everyone. Ever since then he had been wary of the Chinese.

The phone rang and the head of the Far East section of the CIA told him that the submarine was still in the underground dock.

'It was actually seen?'

'Do you think I'd report hearsay?' The CIA man said indignantly.

McGowan had gone straight to the President through the joint command to get him to compel the CIA to provide the information before eight o'clock this evening.

'We risked blowing the cover of one of our best operators. Although he's high up in the Chinese army, we gave him only two days to get into the dock. Sooner or later someone's bound to get suspicious. He even managed to get a shot of it with a miniature camera.'

'Fine.'

'It's not fine for me.'

'I'm sorry.' If the CIA man knew the importance of the information that his mole had obtained, he would not have been so touchy. But probably only the head of the CIA knew about this matter and then only in general terms.

When the CIA man told him that his operator had found out that 133 days ago the lock gates of the underground dock had been opened to let sea water in—part of the tests that the sub was going through—McGowan felt greatly relieved. Everything was clear now. It was winter when the gates were opened and warm air could have come out of the dock and because of the difference of temperature, the water would have been attracted to where the temperature was higher, that is to say to the mouth of the drain, and showed up as a slight trace on the infra-red satellite photograph.

It had taken a lot of work, but he was now at ease. He calculated the amount of nuclear energy needed to destroy the dock and added a little. Penetrating missiles would not go through the rock so the submarine would only be destroyed if the blast at the entrance was strong enough. One kilometre away, there were three other Chinese submarines at anchor. One dual-head missile would be enough. There were military targets all round and though the shock wave would be enormous, not many civilians would be killed.

The South China Sea: depth 460 metres.

Ding Da-hai suddenly opened his eyes and was fully awake, as if he had not been asleep at all. His heart was beating very fast. He always slept for exactly five hours, no more and no less. He found he had only slept for three hours.

He did not want to sleep any longer: it was impossible anyway. He had been on edge for several days, knowing instinctively that some great danger was close, without knowing what it was. Unknown dangers are the worst. Half dreaming, he had tried to guess why the China Sea was covered with sonar buoys. Why there were so many unmarked helicopters active in the sky? Why were things like sonar nets been pulled this way and that in the sea above? Why had there been a sudden increase in the number of spy satellites over East Asia, like red eyes staring at the Chinese Mainland and the sea? Why had the atmosphere been full of coded signals? And had both the US and Russia used the same code, and if so why?

Eight hours earlier the flood of coded messages had suddenly stopped and both US and Russian radio stations simultaneously went off the air. These ominous signs filled him with foreboding. Normally in war these things meant that preparations were completed and action was about to start.

When something finally roused him, he doused his face with cold water and went to the control room, where he spent nearly all his waking hours. He immediately discovered that the silent coded signals had just started again, and the duty lieutenant had been about to call him. He put on the headphones and found that even more stations than before were continually sending and receiving messages, they were clearer, and the tone was also different. Although he could understand nothing, he had the impression that the general tenor was one of self-congratulation.

The nuclear submarine lay calmly in a trench. Volcanoes were emitting heat, which allowed the submarine to maintain a reasonable temperature and use less reactor coolant. Something had happened in the world above; the best thing to do was remain on the sea bottom.

There was a coloured curtain in the control room. The image on the screen behind was very strange, having no depth and emitting no light. A coloured outline moved, flashing with a whole series of numbers; this was the sonar profile digitalized by the computer. Had there had been a whale outside, its form would have appeared on the screen as a blue silhouette, the figures at the side representing the whale's sonar co-ordinates. If the whale came nearer, the size of the image would became larger and vice versa.

Twelve hours earlier, Ding Da-hai had seen the *Qingdao* pass by. The sonar screen immediately recognized it, as one would an old friend. It was also a missile-carrying nuclear submarine under the command of a class-mate of Ding Da-hai at the Submarine Academy. Ding watched the *Qingdao* go in a northwesterly direction with a critical eye. Only later did he notice, deeper in the sea, a Taiwanese submarine following the other submarine like a sea-snake. Ding silently swore at his colleague: he was evidently still the self-satisfied know-all he had been before and had relaxed his guard. He could not warn the *Qingdao*; the enemy submarine was too close. Yet one torpedo would send it to the bottom. He was sure that the enemy submarine intended to capture the *Qingdao* and use it to terrorize or attack the Mainland, just as they had done with the missile base they had captured on the Mainland. He would not move, but continue to lie on the bottom and do nothing, even if the Taiwanese submarine went into action close by.

At that moment, the reef itself began to shake. The bulkheads shuddered and a blinding streak of light flashed on the sonar screen, something that only happened when the submarine was near the surface in a very bad storm.

But on the bottom of the sea at 460 metres, nothing had changed except the flow of the current. How could there possibly be a storm? The computer clearly seemed in doubt as well; the rumbling reverberation inside the submarine was clearly audible, but nothing unusual showed on the screen, except that fish were darting about in an agitated manner. Yet the sonar video had not broken down. A submarine earthquake or volcanic irruption or a seismic sea wave? No, the volcanoes appeared perfectly normal. The sound waves came from far away and were very powerful. There . . . . .on the top right corner of the sonar screen, a white point of light had finally appeared, extremely bright and surrounded at first by a red ring. A nuclear explosion! That was exactly the sonar image of a nuclear explosion deep under the sea. Ding Da-hai had seen one only once before, during training. He had never thought to see a real one. The whole sea had shaken. The co-ordinates showed that it was 140 nautical miles away.

Had the *Qingdao* been destroyed by a missile from the Taiwan submarine, or was this the result of all those coded messages? Nuclear attack was the most effective way of destroying a submarine. One nuclear warhead could ensure that any submarine in a radius of eight nautical miles would be destroyed: any within fifteen miles would be seriously damaged or put out of action. But unless there was a full-scale nuclear war and it was intended to wipe out an enemy's total nuclear armament with one strike, no one would use such a powerful weapon and pollute the ocean on such scale just to knock out one submarine. Was there a nuclear war between China and a foreign country?

The *Qingdao* cannot have been the target: the explosion was too far away. The underwater shock wave had mostly been absorbed by the resistance of the water. The submarine, jolted at first, now merely swayed gently in the new current. Ding Da-hai took no action of any kind, and did not sound the alarm to wake the crew. More than half an hour after the explosion the sonar screen showed its effect in an area of more than 140 km in diameter. The coded radio signals resumed after the explosion and in the hour that followed, he had heard people excitedly reporting how much damage had been done. If his submarine was detected, it and the *Qingdao* would be destroyed. The best thing to do was to remain calmly on the sea bottom and not move.

He put on the radio headphones and tuned in to Qingdao radio. The members of the crew liked to listen to news about their home port. There was no signal; all he could hear was a rustling sound. Qingdao had disappeared. He searched rapidly in one wavelength after the other, and heard broadcasts from different countries in different languages. No other radio station seemed to be off the air. . .

An announcer, speaking English, in the excited tone of a football commentary, reported that the United Nations, in order to prevent the outbreak of generalized nuclear war, had decided to eradicate China's nuclear capacity. The United States and Russia had jointly launched an attack, the former north of the 30th parallel, the latter south. The attack was now finished and had been a complete success. All targets had been hit simultaneously, including the nuclear submarine recently acquired by Taiwan, which had been sunk in the Indian Ocean. Two long-distance Chinese cruise missiles with nuclear warheads were destroyed by US missiles over Northeast China. This was an exemplary victory in military history, the target area being so large, the accuracy so great and the coordination so perfect. Its greatest significance, the announcer said, was that it was the first war in human history to use weapons to destroy weapons, in the interests of peace and for the benefit of the people, not only of China, but of the whole world; the first war in which there was no enemy, no defeat and no conquest. A great victory for the whole of mankind!

Ding Da-hai felt as if a steel claw was tearing at his heart. Empty, desolate and numb, so numb that his whole body felt cold as ice, his bones and muscles as if made of steel and plastic.

The officers on duty in the control room were all at their posts. They were only permitted to listen to the radio during their recreation periods. He switched off the radio with a finger that already felt stiff with *rigor mortis*. The image on the sonar screen had already expanded into what looked like a target with coloured rings. It took up the whole screen and gave off a blood-red light.

His mind was clearer than it ever had been before. Against a background of infinite chaos in the form of nets heaving in the distance, were a whole series of things to be done, each very distinct. He located a circuit panel in the bulkhead between the missile silos and the gyro-stabilizer room. In this corner, where no one ever came, he had to rely entirely on a small flashlight held between his teeth. His hands were perfectly steady. He loosened two small screws, switched the wires, changed their tags and removed the end of a wire. He did not need to consult the wiring diagram. In four years, he had come to know the innumerable circuits like the palm of his hand. No one would notice. But from now on every radio on the submarine would be irreparably short-circuited as soon as it was switched on—except the one in his own cabin.

He inspected the crew's quarters, officers' mess, and the bunkroom from top to bottom. Most of the crew were asleep. The stale air was constantly replaced by artificial air that always smelled the same. In the crew's recreation room, lit by a few weak fluorescent lights, a few men were playing poker, in silence; there was something dreamlike about the scene. No one had been listening to the radio.

The back of each seaman's bunk was covered with photos of his family: each man's lighthouse at the dark bottom of the sea.

He felt a sudden tightness in his throat. He had chosen only experienced seamen. All were married and had children, and lived in the newly constructed housing in the base near Qingdao. . . . . He had not yet thought about the base. Perhaps it was a sea of fire or white smoke, or under dirty sea water. . . Looking at the pictures of these women and children, he began to tremble. Near him a sleeping sailor was murmuring. It sounded as if he was dreaming of making love with his wife, and his tender, passionate words were profoundly moving. His wife looked down on him from the wall, smiling.

He suppressed this sudden trembling, lifted his head and drew himself up straight. Behind the thick lenses of his glasses, there was a determined look in his ice-cold eyes. He returned to his cabin, locked the door and sat in front of the radio without moving for two hours. The UN announcement regarding the nuclear devices used in the attack was very insubstantial, saying hardly more than they had been limited to the minimum, that for most targets penetrating missiles had been used, tactical and even standard missiles. Nothing had been said about the targets that had been attacked. . . Perhaps there was a gleam of hope in the darkness. If all the other nuclear submarines had put to sea and US Intelligence had not found out about the submarine built underground, there would have been no necessity to attack the Qingdao Naval Base. Or perhaps it was known that this submarine was now at sea and that the one in the underground dock was an empty shell. No, that was impossible: if they knew it was at sea, they would definitely not attack other targets until they had hunted it down and destroyed it. He knew Americans and the way they thought.

He hated the US to the depths of his soul. Before going there he was very excited. For a young Chinese naval officer who had grown up in a fishing village, America was as mysterious as another planet. But from the day he arrived there, he felt out of his element. He was the only Chinese in the Academy. The skyscrapers, the sea of lights, the traffic, the rock-and-roll, the blazing, swirling colours, were like a frenetic dream that gave him no rest day or night. He did not know how to use a knife and fork, how to get anything out of a vending machine or how to find his way about town. He knew nothing about boxing champions or pop stars. He knew neither when to speak nor what to say, or to wear, and had no idea of protocol or etiquette. The more nervous he was, the more ridiculous he became. As soon as he discovered or began to feel that all the Americans around looked at him with derision and contempt, exchanged glances, waiting for him to make a fool of himself, he stopped having anything to do with them. He put all his energies into study, and was hardly ever seen without a book in his hands. He stopped greeting those he met by chance and strode off, as if on parade, as if he had not seen them. He quickly became known in the Academy as an oddball and was referred to as 'the Chinese tin soldier'.

One day a girl called Betsy, who worked in the library, burst into his room and said that they saw each other every day and it was a pity he never took any notice of her. Very soon she undressed. He was speechless, but did not resist much. Finally, like a wild bull he threw Betsy down on the bed. That night, for the first time, he felt relaxed. He wanted to be friends with Americans and to learn everything they knew and no longer be a tin soldier.

But Betsy did not come again. In the library she pretended not to see him. He felt like a lost soul. But that did not prevent him from defeating five of his American class-mates, one after another, in the class submarine war-game. One of them was a big man two metres tall—a racist, with a freckled face and blond hair like frost. Within three minutes, Ding Da-hai got him with three torpedoes. Afterwards during recreation, the big man strode over to the window where Ding was staring out blankly and said 'How come your dick is not as hot-stuff as your torpedoes?' Then, seeing his look of perplexity, said viciously, 'Betsy took a bet with some of us, to test whether the Chinese tin soldier has a dick. She said that in bed you were just a bottle of fizzy water. . .take off the top and bang! There's no more fizzy water left!'

Apart from a surge of mad fury rising in his blood, Ding Da-hai had no memory of what happened afterwards. The other student was boxing champion in the Academy, but he never had a chance. His face was like a soft pumpkin by the time Ding Da-hai could be restrained by several of the other students.

In court later, witnesses testified that Ding had been roaring like a wild animal, and had a diabolical expression on his face. They said that he hit his opponent as if he wanted to kill him. Ding Da-hai accepted the judgement impassively. The court was too small in comparison with his hatred.

His son's fishing rod was leaning against the bulkhead in his cabin. That night when he stood outside his home in the darkness, the fishhook had got caught in his uniform, now he felt as if it were piercing his heart and the fishing line stretched all the way to where his home had been. It must have been the US that had the task of attacking the naval base where his home was. He did not take the fishing rod and stroke it for a long time as he usually did. He took off his wrist watch, and carefully wiped the vibrator inside the back. Although it was made of an alloy which could never rust, he was worried at not having received a signal for so long, and wondered if it had become less sensitive. He watched it as if waiting for it to call him.

10

The state of China – Beijing: The Central Military Commission – The South China Sea: depth 460 metres – From 'Libération Daily' (Paris) – Beijing – The Chinese-Russian frontier in Heilongjiang – State Security Ministry Report to Huang Shi-ke (Top Secret) – Beijing – A report received by the US Central Intelligence Agency – A Buddhist nunnery near Beijing

ꝏ

The state of China

A total of 205 nuclear missiles were used in the attack on China—76 of them by Russia and 219 by the United States. The most powerful missiles were only used to ensure the destruction of six Chinese missile silos very deep underground. Considering that this was the biggest nuclear attack ever launched, the damage inflicted could hardly have been less. No more than two million people were killed or wounded. The main industrial centres and plants, apart from a few towns in the vicinity of naval bases, were entirely undamaged. It was called a 'perfect surgical operation.'

Had it been possible with a clear head and expertise—like the military specialists who had planned the attack—to calculate its results on powerful computers, or even count gains and losses on their fingers, China would have realized that it had lost only the weapons capable of destroying her. Productive capacity was hardly affected. Two million poor and backward mountain people were killed of course, but more than ten million people in the cities survived. Neither the United Nations, under whose name the attack had been carried out, nor the international community, would stand by and see China perish. Millions of dollars and rivers of food and materials would be sent; far in excess of the damage that had been caused. The Chinese people should therefore rejoice and be grateful and the attack would be an epoch-making triumph.

However, at this moment, the Chinese people were no more capable of making such a calm and dispassionate assessment than a wild animal, just pricked with a needle, will rub the spot and say thank you for the immunization. Their nerves were at breaking point: famine, death, and international sanctions had come down on them one after the other like rocks from a mountain during an earthquake.

There were dead bodies everywhere, even in the subways under Tiananmen Square. Every day, the bodies of homeless, starving and diseased people were removed and carried away. With the coming of spring, epidemics quietly began to spread, carrying off whole families.

Hospitals were short of medicines; the haggard and exhausted staff could only carry out the simplest of treatments.

Ninety percent of motor vehicles were off the road because there was no fuel and the roads to the crematoria were blocked with handcarts carrying dead bodies. The crematoria too suffered from shortage of fuel and there were far from enough furnaces. The stench of putrefaction spread for miles around.

Water and electricity were available only at fixed times and for very short periods. Most factories were closed for lack of raw materials. There was no market and the workers had no means of getting to the factories. A few vital enterprises were kept going by force: the workers, under strict military control, were virtually prisoners.

Household gas was provided only twice a day; explosions and gas poisoning were common because people often forgot to turn off the taps. Those who lived in big buildings and high-rise accommodation, burned books and furniture in makeshift stoves and there were frequent fires that spread rapidly in the howling spring wind. In the streets the only vehicles were wailing fire engines.

The majority of people stared woodenly at nothing, with blank and unfocused eyes, as if totally detached from what was going on around them. They had no work, no income, and no hope. There was nothing in their lives except to wait for the daily distribution of 100 grams of grain. If they waited patiently, it was because for countless generations their forebears had squatted at their doorways, waiting, watching the world go by. But behind their expressionless faces, every nerve was taut as a bowstring. Two hundred and five missiles had been enough.

People first learned about the attack through rumours. The state television stations had at first continued to broadcast the usual programmes as if nothing had happened. Then there was only music, finally just coloured lines on the screens. Later a few people had heard from foreign broadcasts that there had been a nuclear attack. The news then spread like lightning and became exaggerated in the process. Some people said that half of China had been destroyed! Crowds gathered in the streets and even illiterate old women told how missiles had been falling like rain and bombs turned cities into large holes in the ground.

Chinese in general tend to weep only when they see the coffin:

disasters elsewhere hardly affect them as long as they and their families are all right. Even when they rouse themselves from their apathy, they rarely show any sign of agitation. Those who repeated rumours added products of their own imagination, such as colour and detail, like professional storytellers, causing more laughter on the streets than usual. However detached from the troubles of others, they were increasingly anxious about their own survival. The repercussions of the massive nuclear attack, even when indirect and fortuitous as a ricochet, could also grow into something massive, equally violent, irrational and uncontrollable.

The first disturbance in Beijing started with a petty incident that occurred in a narrow street called *Wangfutang Hutong* or Palace Granary Street, where there was a middle school, now used as a food distribution centre. After the nuclear attack, people collecting their food allocation no longer observed the established days for the different districts and a crowd of about ten thousand people had gathered at the gate of the school. Their reasoning was very simple: if the government collapsed tomorrow there would be no distribution.

A platoon of soldiers was on duty, but they were in no position to lay down the law to so many desperate people and it was decided to continue distribution all night and give out rations for the following week.

At first everything proceeded in an orderly manner, but too slowly. People were hungry, tired and cold. Owing to the power failure there were only a few candles at the distribution counters, but everywhere else was in total darkness. A young man at the counter got into an argument with one of the staff (who were also hungry and tired) about whether he was entitled to a ration for his son, who had died only a day or two ago. The exchange became more and more heated and finally the young man made off with a small plastic bag containing 700 grams of low-grade flour. It was this that led to the rioting.

People started taking whatever they could. The candles blew out. Those at the back of the crowd, fearing that there would not be enough for everyone, pushed violently forward. The soldiers fired blindly in the darkness, hitting people in the crowd as well as those manning the distribution centre. Many more were trampled to death. In next to no time, more than fifty tons of food were looted, and the school was set on fire. There were dead bodies on the ground, which was white with flour. The crowd grew bigger. At first their object was to obtain food for themselves and their families. Order had already broken down and there would be nothing for those who did not join in the looting. Food shops, grain distribution centres, canteens and restaurants were all stripped like trees in the autumn wind. As people's fury and hatred grew, private houses were looted as well. Someone only had to shout that there was grain in a certain house for it to be attacked and looted, set on fire and the occupants killed. In the darkness fires could be seen all over the city.

Half an hour after the first outbreak, several thousand rioters surrounded the Bank of China building not far from Granary Lane. According to rumour the bank was full of 'foreign money', just what people needed to escape abroad. Truck jacks were used to make an opening in the railings, windows were smashed. Police and soldiers arrived, but without light they were unable to take effective action and before long flames were pouring from every window. In another part of the street, the building of the People's Political Consultative Conference was also on fire.

The looting rapidly spread to the whole of Beijing—partly because the telephone system was still functioning. Troops and armed police attempted to suppress the rioting by force and killed thousands; but they were soon over-stretched and less effective, while some of them even joined the rioters. They knew from experience that it would not be possible to put an end to the chaos and that the government would soon collapse: only fools would hesitate to grab what they could.

Thousands of Beijing citizens took refuge in foreign embassies. Many people wanted to take advantage of the opportunity while the authorities were fully occupied with the rioting to take their valuables and go to live in 'the free world'. They had been waiting for a long time for the necessary papers. The embassies of prosperous countries were packed; there was nowhere to sit down and sanitary facilities were totally inadequate. Latecomers went to the embassies of third world countries, even Burma and Vietnam. At first most embassies were panic-stricken by this invasion, but they soon realized that the crowds of people who had visas were naturally well behaved and formed a solid wall that protected the embassies from being plundered.

There were political demonstrations. University students with red flags took to the streets with loud-hailers, cursed the government for leading China into disaster and called on people to join them, to occupy Zhongnanhai and take over the government. The banners of the Democracy Front and the People's Front were seen again and there were appeals for international recognition and support.

However, food was the sole concern of nearly everyone: to obtain as much as possible by any means, in order to be able to live a little longer. Forty railway wagons loaded with rice arrived at the railway station and the rice disappeared without trace within half an hour. Those who arrived too late caught up with some of the more fortunate ones in the streets, attacked them and took their rice. Looting spread like a prairie fire. No shop, or department store escaped. Once they reached the city limits, the looters turned their attention to villages in the suburbs, and to the peasants' grain, pigs, sheep and chickens not long out of the egg. Once the peasants came to their senses, they started raiding other villages with increased violence, killed people from the city, destroyed roads and railways and looted all goods they could lay their hands on.

On the evening of the nuclear attack, the same scene was repeated in twenty-four other big cities. Whether coordinated or not no one knows. The Voice of America, the BBC and Hong Kong Radio all gave frequent reports of these events in Beijing and their live coverage undoubtedly contributed to 'unrest' elsewhere. The following day looting was nationwide. In towns and villages, north and south, people took to frenzied looting. It was the only effective activity. People looted alone, or in gangs, or between gangs. If they did not get what they wanted, they fought; if they did not win they fled. The strong killed the weak and were themselves killed by those even stronger. Vagabonds, refugees and starving people streaming everywhere brought violence to a peak. The whole country was in a paroxysm of terror and consisted only of individuals fighting and devouring each other. All its arteries and nerves had ceased to function: goods had stopped moving. The railways were piled up with obstructions, the roads full of holes and wreckage. China was paralysed. Government collapsed at all levels. Local leaders could no more restore order than a locust can stop a cart. Law and order no longer existed, only looting.

Innumerable people who had lost their families and property joined the huge mobile army of homeless and hopeless people—the 'floating population'—which became like an uncontrollable flood. Wherever they passed abundance became poverty and poverty, death. In isolated villages, not a blade of grass was left.

Such floods surged and raged totally out of control and with increasing violence all over the country up to the last barriers—the frontiers of China—like an earthquake under a reservoir.

Beijing: The Central Military Commission

Wang Feng had sat all night in his office, lit only by the fires burning all over the city and reverberating with the sound of gunfire from armed helicopters. In the faint rays of the rising sun, blood red like a winter sunset, the fires seemed to be gradually wiped away. He sat motionless, with a fixed gaze and an expressionless face. It was the shortest night in his life. Eventually the dawn came, like blood, but the dawn nevertheless. Living people no longer looked like the dead. The Earth still turned and time was running out. He finally stood up. A pall of dark smoke hung sadly over Beijing and, in the slanting rays of the sun, made the city look like a dream world. No one had ever seen such a sinister red sun. A helicopter flew across the sky, so low that one could see the faces of the special troops who had stopped the rioting last night. The streets were strewn with red flags and dead bodies, like sheaves of wheat in a field at harvest time, but lying in pools of blood. The rioting seemed to have ceased at daybreak. There were columns of smoke everywhere but nothing left to loot. It was very quiet: the silence of an ancient battlefield, like one of his childhood dreams. The lights, colours and atmosphere were the same, except that there were mountains instead of tall buildings all around. In his dream he was standing on the highest peak in the Alps, clothed in the rays of the rising sun, a sharp curved cavalry sword in his hand. Now he had no sword, nothing.

He pressed a button to summon all his secretaries. The building was very quiet. They silently filed into his office, unshaven and with bloodshot eyes, pulling on crumpled military uniforms as if overnight they had suddenly become slovenly. They looked at Wang Feng as they might at a sick man dying.

He gave orders to summon the Russian and United States ambassadors and gave very precise directions about how they were to be notified, escorted and received, what carpet should be put outside the entrance and what music should be played. He seemed to have spent the whole night thinking about these things. For this relatively simple matter, all the secretaries were required and the ambassadors were to be received as if they were Heads of State. From their expressions, the secretaries wanted to ask what this was all about. They had never done anything but obey orders: today it was different. This was the end and they felt they had a right to ask questions.

'Carry on,' Wang Feng said dryly.

Only one secretary said anything. 'The Americans have withdrawn their Ambassador. There's only the Chargé d'Affaires.'

'It makes no difference.'

The Central Military Commission, re-named Headquarters of the Commander in Chief of China, was now the sole source of authority in the country. Wang Feng had made himself Commander in Chief but was really indifferent to such formal titles. All the top leaders had resigned after the nuclear attack. Wang Feng did not care: they were all totally useless anyway, but he was glad that his own staff were still at their posts and would now enable him to accomplish his final task. He had no illusions about the loyalty they expressed: it had everything to do with the fact that the basement store-room of the Military Commission buildings was perhaps the only place in the whole of China with a large stock of food, where the personnel and their families could take refuge and have enough to eat. It only takes a small amount of food to buy loyalty now. . .Wang Feng sighed.

He felt totally listless. Even when he heard on the radio that Major General Su, on behalf of the Nanjing Regional Command had publicly approved of the destruction of China's nuclear weapons by the United Nations, he did no more than laugh scornfully. Such men were experienced at pledging allegiance—to those with most power. How many times had it happened in the last few years? Now the pledge was to the United Nations but the tone and language was typically Chinese—and comic.

Wang Feng knew he was finished as soon as he heard of the nuclear attack. Without nuclear weapons, he could neither hold China together nor resist external aggression. It was too late now to appeal to nationalist sentiment or use anti-foreign feeling to unify the people. Patriotic feeling no longer existed. Years of worshipping the West and denigrating China had made the Chinese ashamed of their own country. Nationalism had become nothing but the empty slogan of the die-hards. No one had any enthusiasm for the nation or was willing to shed blood for it. The death of a people starts with the heart. Radio stations all over the country were reporting declarations of allegiance to the United Nations by people who were merely taking advantage of the country's situation for their own benefit. What benefit? They themselves were doomed to obliteration, the cretins. Everything would soon be finished, including their shameless lives.

The head of the Foreign Affairs Bureau came to report that the United Nations had set up a special committee for aid to China, and that a large number of aircraft carrying relief supplies had already taken off.

In a fury Wang Feng issued a statement that if any hypocritical attempt was made to deliver supplies, aircraft violating China's airspace would be shot down. The Chinese people 'would rather starve than eat filthy dog-food'.

But several provinces and cities had already announced that aircraft bringing aid would be welcome. The United Nations accused Beijing of indifference to the fate of the Chinese people and declared that there would have been no food riots if relief had been accepted. The Beijing authorities alone were to blame. The Chinese people were called upon to make their own decision. If Beijing closed the door, the aircraft would land at other airfields.

Wang Feng only replied, a little absent-mindedly: 'I know. You may go.'

A white telephone on his desk rang. He stood over it for some time; it was a telephone reserved for special calls. Somehow he knew that it was the same person who had rung several times after the attack. He took up the receiver.

It was Ying-ying. There was both pleasure and anxiety in her tone. Wang Feng was silent, wanting to hear more of her voice, whatever she might say. 'Hello, hello.' He hesitated, then pressed a button that told the switchboard operator to dismiss the call, and heard him say firmly that the Commander in Chief was not in his office.

'Be sure to get him to call me,' Ying-ying said, close to tears.

The sun was brighter and the smoke slightly thinner. Wang Feng shook off his melancholy and telephoned home. As usual his wife said little. She had lived with him for ten years and knew that this suited him. He too said little, except to tell her to take the child and go to her old home. 'Your relatives all loved your father and will look after you.' He was conscious that this might make her anxious: it sounded as if she was to be on her own from now on. He rang off quickly.

He told a secretary to arrange for his wife and child's removal from Beijing and to send six month's food supplies to the Chairman's widow and daughter. That seemed to be all.

He told an orderly to prepare his full-dress uniform, reserved for special occasions, which he had never worn. He had been made a General only a few months ago, though it seemed ages ago. He had lost weight, but it fitted him well and looked perfect. The orderly opened the box containing his decorations and he chose the least impressive, his first medal, awarded when he was a low-ranking and overworked young officer at a missile base in the Gobi Desert.

The aide-de-camp responsible for etiquette and ceremonies came for him. The ambassadors were about to arrive.

In the corridor he saw the naval officer he had sent to report back on the situation in the submarine base after the nuclear attack. There was a blood-stained bandage round his head and his clothes were stained and torn—part of Shandong province was evidently in rebellion. The officer's report was no surprise to Wang Feng: there could have been no other outcome. But instead of bare names and figures, the report told him of the blood that had flowed, the fires and the wasteland of ruins in the light of day. He put the report into a pocket of his uniform and shook the officer's hand with feeling.

The cars of the two diplomats arrived simultaneously, as Wang Feng had ordered, and drew up at the ends of two red carpets, flanked by the motorcycle escorts. The carpets had been laid to form a V and the guard of honour stood to attention on either side of each.

As the ambassadors got out of their cars two military bands played their respective national anthems. An aide-de-camp led each along one of the legs of the V to the apex at the imposing entrance to the Headquarters of the Commander-in-Chief. Both men were familiar with diplomatic ceremonies, but they had never seen anything like this. The national anthems were being played, *simultaneously*. Guards of honour were only for Heads of State: but these were not even saluting. Why were there so many officers of all ranks, from general to second lieutenant, drawn up at the entrance? It was all wrong. It did not look at all like a surrender ceremony. In any case no one had declared war on China, so there was no need. Perhaps the Chinese had finally come to their senses and realized that they could not oppose the whole world, and wanted to show their respect for Russia and the United States hoping for their forbearance.

The two men met at the point of the V just as the two national anthems ended. An officer shouted 'Salute!' The great doors opened and Wang Feng emerged. All the Chinese troops saluted and the band played the Chinese national anthem.

Wang Feng looked very distinguished, tall and straight, the sun on him, as he came down the steps with great dignity. The two ambassadors stood side by side with smiles that did not even crease their faces, and stretched out their hands. Wang Feng looked closely at the two faces, slowly stretched out his hand and said,

'I don't see your Presidents, only their representatives. . .' Then he suddenly slapped their faces, so hard that they fell down on the red carpet, bleeding from nose and mouth.

The band continued to play the Chinese national anthem and the flag of China with its five stars fluttered in the wind. All the soldiers continued to stand to attention and salute. The two men made an effort to stand up and regain their dignity, but they were dizzy and could not keep their feet.

Wang Feng looked at them until the last strains of the national anthem died away. An orderly handed him a white towel; he wiped his hands, as if after a banquet, and threw it down at the feet of the two ambassadors. Then he saluted all the officers and under their astonished and admiring eyes, went back into the Headquarters.

The secretary on duty in the emergency office stood up as Wang Feng entered.

'Tell everyone,' Wang Feng said in an unusually amiable tone of voice, 'that the Headquarters of the Commander in Chief is now abolished. Then instruct the service department to divide up all the food supplies between everyone, after which they must go and fend for themselves.'

The secretary could hardly believe his ears, but dared not say anything. 'Go,' Wang Feng said, patting him on the shoulder.

His office felt like a tomb, silent as if even the air was dead. He carefully locked the door, went to his desk and took the miniature transmitter from an inner pocket and placed it in front of him.

When he had heard about the nuclear attack, shock and panic had swept everything else away, root and branch, leaving in his mind only the solid image of the submarine. His network of communications with all the missile bases, nuclear submarines and nuclear weapons units no longer existed, which proved that they had all been destroyed. Not his submarine; it had no connection with the others. He knew, as soon as the United Nations had announced the '100% destruction of Chinese nuclear weapons', that it was safe. A hundred per cent minus one nuclear submarine.

He was the only person in the world, apart from the crew, who knew of its existence and that it carried forty nuclear warheads. Others who had known were now buried in the underground dock destroyed by the Americans.

He opened the lid of the metal box and looked at the row of miniature keys. He checked carefully that everything was working normally and the battery was fully charged, then he started feeding in his coded message. It was not an order and did not mention the missiles. It was simply a list of names.

The officer he had sent to report on the damage to the naval base in Shandong had informed him that the families of all officers and men on the submarine had been killed in the United States nuclear attack on the Shandong naval base. Wang Feng had asked him for the names of all those killed, without exception, and the exact circumstances where possible. This would be more effective than anything less detailed.

He took care to make no errors. He was in no hurry: there was nothing else for him to do. He entered the list of dead, nothing else, as if it were a normal procedure before a mass funeral. It was enough, far more than enough. There was no accompanying order, only the list; Ding Da-hai would understand that this meant death. It would mean releasing a diabolical force of hatred and destruction, that needed no order, nor was he responsible for its actions. Wang Feng had sent the list of dead out of the kindness of his heart: that would be the verdict of history. From now on everything would be done by this force, and far more thoroughly than he.

Once all the data had been entered Wang Feng made a careful check. As he did so images suddenly appeared on the blank TV screen in front of him. An announcer said that the television station had now pledged loyalty to the United Nations and was back on the air again. Soon afterwards the screen showed some heavy Russian-made transport helicopters land on a runway at Beijing airport that was covered with vehicles of all kinds to prevent ordinary aircraft from landing. What appeared to be relief supplies were unloaded from each. Then light armoured cars and jeeps carrying soldiers wearing the blue helmets of the United Nations peace-keeping force sped on to the runway, knocking over several piles of what appeared to be relief supplies. The jeeps took up positions at strategic points while the powerful armoured cars cleared the runway of obstructions in next to no time. Then with a thunderous roar, huge transport planes with an escort of fighters began to land.

Turning back to the transmitter, Wang Feng lightly pressed a round orange-coloured button surrounded by a white ring, that programmed the transmitter to switch to cyclical mode until the battery was completely discharged. A pin-light glowed red. The radio signals were already passing through the atmosphere, bouncing off a satellite to reach the submarine deep under the sea.

The High Command Headquarters was deserted. Wang Feng's car was the only one left in the car park. He stuck the transmitter out of sight under the dash-board with some strong glue he found in the secretariat. He had nothing particular in mind. The future owner of the car, whoever he might be, would be sitting on a radio wave. People would never get to the bottom of it. Let them puzzle it out.

The sun was still red. . .very unusual at noon.

When the armed jeeps flying the United Nations flag arrived at the Headquarters of the Commander-in-Chief, they saw only a young general in a spotless uniform, tall even by western standards holding himself straight, as if on parade, at the point where the red carpets met. On his face was an expression that puzzled those who had come to arrest him: the slight smile only seen on the faces of men who have once held the destiny of the world in their hands.

The South China Sea: depth 460 metres

The tape came slowly out of the receiver, at no more than five words a second and piled up in front of Ding Da-hai. The names that appeared after each number, conjured up familiar faces, one after the other, old and young: as if at a get-together of the crew's families, when the old entrusted their sons to his care and their children kissed him. Now, on this rice-coloured paper, they were no more than dust and ashes.

The printing was too slow. The tape was too long and he wanted to pull it out by force. Can no one be still alive? The word 'deceased' appeared endlessly, again and again. He would give anything for his own name not to appear.

'Number 126.' No. . . .

'Number 127'. . .then the name of Ding Da-hai's father. 'Body not found; mother. . . .wife: burned to death. . . son Ding Xiao-long: blinded in both eyes fishing on the shore, also burned. Fell off a cliff trying to find his way home.'

His brain exploded into a fog of blood, and a violent black wind blew against his face. He felt himself become as rigid as a stone. His eyes felt dry, his eyelids were of gritty sandpaper; but tears were flowing backwards down into his heart, stifling his breathing and strangling his arteries. He felt he was frantically waving his arms to dispel demonic figures.

The naked body of his wife shrank to the size of a child, like the black stone of an olive. Her eyes opened painfully, looked at him and looked at her son, whose skin had fallen off like cracked plaster and was scattered over the ruins that had buried his parents. Only his skeleton remained, his two sightless eyes hanging on his chest. From all around came the child's cry: 'Ba-ba! Ba-ba!'

The little boy's fishing rod still hung on the wall of Ding Da-hai's cabin. He took hold of the sharp barbed hook (it had a slight blue tinge) and jabbed it into the muscles of his forearm. Then slowly pulled it out with a piece of his flesh on it, like bait. The sharp pain was a kind of release, bringing him to his senses, and the nightmare visions gradually dissolved. Again and again, he stabbed his arm with the hook puncturing an artery. He looked closely at the fine fountain of fresh blood and saw nothing else, no images. He saw only the blood carrying away the heat of the violent frenzy in his body. The blood vessels under his skin levelled out, his jaws relaxed. He pressed on the artery until the bleeding stopped, then bandaged his arm.

Tape still flowed from the receiver. It already covered his knees and part of the floor, and some of it was sticky with his blood. He saw that it was repeating the same message over and over again like an endlessly repeated nightmare. He pushed the receiver into the safe. The printer stopped, but the red light on the code lock had immediately lit up and the alarm watch on his wrist vibrated. If a message came when the receiver was not open he was warned by the vibration of his alarm watch. It was not a powerful vibration but very clear, and if it went on for long, whether in his wrist or his mind, it was enough to shatter his nerves.

His mind became clear: there ought to be an order with the message; just to know about the deaths was not enough. He needed instructions, as black as death, clear and merciless. His arm was no longer bleeding; his hand was white as a dead limb. He punched in the code and the receiver slid out from the safe. The red light went off and the alarm watch stopped vibrating. The tape began sliding out like a snake.

It was the same list again. There were no orders on the tape, only the list of dead. . .dead. . .dead. He wanted instructions. All he got was death.

He switched on the radio receiver. All over the world the broadcasts spoke only of China. The latest news was that Wang Feng had been arrested by the United Nations forces. Ding Da-hai felt more lonely than he ever had. Wang Feng had never once contacted him since their last meeting yet, however deep and dark the sea was, he always felt that the submarine was held in some superhuman hand, that eyes were watching him wherever he might be. Now he seemed to be sinking like a leaden weight. Without that steady hand, the submarine had lost all contact with the world of man and had become a coffin containing 127 men, bound for the darkness.

He could not understand why Wang Feng had only sent the list and no orders. Because he had no time? Or was there some hidden meaning? One thing was clear: from now on he had to make his own decisions.

He pushed the receiver back into the safe, the tape stopped, and his watch was vibrating again. He took it off and put it on the desk, where it continued to palpitate like an epileptic mouse. Disturbing. He tried putting a glass over it, but could still hear the chattering. Not until he had wrapped the watch in a piece of bloodstained bandage torn from his arm, put it back under the glass and put two heavy books on top did he escape from this nightmare.

He screwed up the tape into a ball, took off his blood-stained clothes and stuffed them along with the tape into the kitchen waste grinder. He waited until the tape must have been ground into paste that would dissolve in sea-water.

Then he gave his orders over the loud-speaker to the crew. There was a bustle of activity in the submarine: everyone seemed pleased. He felt that the burden of his loneliness would drive him mad.

From 'Libération Daily' (Paris)

Few men can have experienced more dramatic changes of fortune in so short a time than the former Deputy Prime Minister Monsieur Shi Ge. He was recently awarded the Nobel Peace Prize for his single-handed attempt to give warning through the Australian Embassy in Beijing of the imminent nuclear attack on Taipei, for which he was sentenced to death for treason. He was saved from execution at the eleventh hour by United Nations troops, and the same evening his appointment as Prime Minister of the new Government of China was announced.

In the last two days he has received messages of congratulation from more than 162 countries, a sign of the goodwill and hope he inspired in the international community. However deserving and suited he may be to this high position, the fact remains that he was not chosen by the Chinese people but by Russia and the United States who, having defeated China with nuclear weapons, now occupy the country in the name of the United Nations and act like colonial powers.

The new Premier owes his appointment not only to his courageous act which made him world famous, but also to the fact that he was never implicated in the crimes of the former government and won the respect of Taiwan for refusing to condemn its demand for independence. He will have an important role as a mediator between the United States and Russia as they plan the future of China.

It has already been decided that North and South China, including Taiwan will be reunited in a single sovereign state. This is sensible, because a divided country will cause antagonism and conflict and the recent action, for which a high price has been and will continue to be paid, will have been in vain. However, years of hostility and division can never be wiped away by formal unity.

The prominent position of Russia in the recent action is a signal of danger. Russia's vital interests are more closely involved than any other country in the future of China. Russia's re-emergence as a great power, if only in the region of China, gives grounds for great uneasiness.

Russia has deployed 130,000 troops in China—seventy per cent of the occupying force. But Moscow has only agreed to contribute 4.5% of relief supplies. The economic situation in Russia is poor, and the government and people blame this on the West, particularly the United States, which is accused of having ulterior motives. The truth is that the United States is extremely wary of Russia regaining its former power.

However, it was politically impossible for the United States to attack China alone. It was essential to involve Russia but also in total contradiction with United States' strategy.

The question now is whether the United States can prevent the increase of Russian influence in China. This can hardly be doubted. But the two nuclear powers have their own intentions and whether they can genuinely maintain the unity of China remains to be seen.

The most urgent matter at present is the restoration of order in China. The nuclear attack has paralysed the transport network. If it cannot be put into operation rapidly, the future of the country hardly bears thinking about. This is undoubtedly something the United Nations and the two powers had not foreseen or taken into consideration.

The whole world is worried about the situation in China, not just for humanitarian reasons but also for fear that the shock waves of the Chinese disaster will spread to the rest of the world. The scale of the famine is unprecedented. This is not going to be like famine relief for Zambia or an earthquake in Afghanistan. The efforts of a few pop stars are not going to raise the funds needed. The majority of developing countries have problems feeding their own population, so the burden will have to be borne by the developed countries, whether out of a sense of morality, or virtue, perhaps also for political reasons. Already supplies have been mobilized on an unprecedented scale.

Shi Ge was well-known for his ability to deal with crises. China now is on the knife-edge between survival and extinction and he is no more than a pawn in the hands of the United Nations. Will he succeed in this, the greatest crisis of our times, or will he go down in history as a theatrical figure who likes to be at the centre of the stage?

Beijing

As Shi Ge came quickly into the reception room, more than thirty white-haired nuclear specialists stood up—they had been waiting a long time. The oldest unrolled a white cloth on which he had written, in blood, big red letters 'Chinese born: foreigners' slave. Never!'

To complete the destruction of China's nuclear capability, the United Nations had decided that all the most important nuclear scientists and technicians must be exiled to other countries. The terms were to their advantage: they could choose the country they would go to; parents, spouse and children would be immediately granted work permits; the country of their choice would pay all the costs of setting-up home and would find them jobs. For the countries which would receive them this was a windfall. For these 9,000 highly-qualified Chinese specialists who had formerly been subject to strict security rules and were not allowed to go abroad, it was like a gift from heaven; so there was no question of forcing them and there was a general atmosphere of rejoicing. Only these thirty elderly scientists had refused.

'My apologies,' said Shi Ge, taking his seat, and immediately came to the point. 'I have no time to go into details although I would have liked to do so. The government will put this banner in a memorial hall, but you must go. You are the best of our nuclear specialists, at the top of your profession, and respected world-wide; but the doubts and anxiety of the world community will not be eased unless you leave the country: the anti-nuclear agreement be regarded as incompletely implemented. This can have many repercussions for China which will affect everyone. I hope that your own patriotism will allow you to defer to the interests of the whole country. . . .'

'I don't agree,' someone said indignantly. 'Those interests were betrayed by your first act on taking office—signing the anti-nuclear agreement. It's true we can now get international aid, but in the future how will China defend itself? I didn't come back to China after fifty years abroad to see it colonized by the United States and Russia.'

'Any colonization, in the future, my friend,' Shi Ge paused, then added with a cheerful if enigmatic expression, 'will be colonization turned upside down.'

No one understood what he meant by this and he did not explain. He looked at his watch. 'There is no time for discussion. I would ask you to remember one thing: every second that passes a hundred or more of our people die. While we have been talking that makes a few tens of thousands. There is no time to lose: go abroad at once. Anyone who refuses will simply be put on to a plane.'

He quickly took his leave of them. The old man who had spoken refused to shake his hand and said fiercely 'I have always hated traitors.'

'Go, my friend,' Shi Ge said gently.

There had been a dust storm the last two days. The air was full of dust and in daytime the sky was a strange dark yellow colour, as at dusk sometimes; the wind howled like a banshee—worse at night. After nightfall, any outside light looked like an orange ball, bright but solemn.

Shi Ge rinsed his head with cold water, then stood for a moment looking out of the window. Since he had been taken from the place of execution several days ago and brought to Zhongnanhai, he had not slept and he had difficulty in staying awake. The secretary behind him coughed to remind him that the Ministers were waiting for him.

He had not felt any different at his transformation from condemned traitor to Head of State. The night before he was to have been executed he had a vision of the earth and the sky devouring each other. That was in a blood coloured dream. Now everything was yellow; but his mood had not changed, as if he were still under sentence of death. Except that now, it was not a question of his death alone, but of the whole Chinese people in his charge. To die, to close one's eyes and instantly dismiss all troubles, was one thing: responsibility for the lives of over a billion people was a different matter. When the United Nations Special Committee for Aid to China had invited him to become Prime Minister of the Provisional Government, he immediately agreed. He did not behave as politicians nowadays usually do. He needed no time to consider the offer. His ideal had always been to help create a prosperous and glorious China: now it seemed that he had been born for this inevitable disaster.

He made only one condition before accepting: he must have total control of the transport and despatch of international aid, including the quantity and nature of goods, the date and place of importation and their destination; no aid supplies should be directly handed over to any local authority, group or ethnic minority. Since he was the Premier Minister of a sovereign country, this demand did not seem to him excessive. Nominally, the United Nations Special Committee for Aid to China was an international organization headed by the Deputy Secretary-General of the United Nations. In fact it was dominated by the United States and Russia, both of whom tried to manipulate him in their own interests. He appeared to yield to both, giving administrative and military control of North China to Russian nominees, and control over the internal affairs and economy of South China to Huang Shi-ke and the Taiwan elected authorities—both supported by the United States. He also appointed Huang Shi-ke First Deputy Premier.

As for himself, apart from control over aid supplies, all he wanted was control over organizations connected with aid, foreign affairs, transport and foreign exchange, and would not interfere in anything else. A modest sphere of authority for a Prime Minister.

Russia and the United States were surprised and delighted by Shi Ge's attitude. Authority in China was divided between these three, and Shi Ge was the weakest. Political analysts concluded that he lacked ambition and had no long-term view on the fundamental question of what system, economic model or political form China should adopt. They predicted that he would not last very long.

His own colleagues were puzzled. Twelve hours after his nomination as Premier, his former staff from Unit Sixteen reported for duty. Like him, they had yearned for a better future and hoped that one day they would take over the running of China. They could not understand why the man they used to call 'Premier' or 'Your Excellency', now a genuine Prime Minister, had become so dull and uninspiring. This feeling was uppermost in their minds at the ministerial meeting he had called.

The Minister for Rail Transport began by asking Shi Ge to explain why relief supplies from Europe and Russia were to come by rail to western Xinjiang rather than to Inner Mongolia or Manzhouli—an obviously easier, safer and less costly route. It was obvious to everyone that the Minister was having difficulty controlling his anger. The other Ministers round the table seemed to agree with him.

A little over half of international aid had to be transported on the Europe-Asian Railway thousands of kilometres across Russia, and the closest point of entry to China was in western Xinjiang. This region is very far away from the industrial areas of eastern China and other areas of dense population. It would be extremely difficult to find enough transport to take the supplies to a more central destination, especially in view of the fact that a 'Republic of West Turkestan' had been set up by rebels in Xinjiang and the railway linking Xinjiang to the rest of China had been cut. Shi Ge's insistence that 53 per cent of aid should be channelled through Xinjiang obviously did not make sense and would put an intolerable burden on such Chinese transport facilities as had survived the nuclear attack.

Transport was one the very few things under Shi Ge's direct control and he had set up almost twenty different departments for this alone—for railways, roads, maritime and air transport, security, and so on. In fact his administration seemed to be almost entirely concerned with transport, and the four Ministers he had chosen were the most capable of his former subordinates in Unit Sixteen, as well as experts in international affairs. This too was something that his colleagues found hard to understand.

'Petroleum products will enter through Inner Mongolia. It will only be food supplies that will be delivered in Xinjiang,' Shi Ge explained. 'This will save the United Nations Aid Committee more than ten thousand tons of fuel and we will be credited with the equivalent sum of money. The United Nations will make another considerable saving in transport costs because most of the food supplies will remain at various places in western Xinjiang. Distribution networks will be set up to feed the millions of homeless and starving people from the rest of China who will be encouraged to make their way there.'

'I want the Xinjiang railway to be reopened immediately,' he went on, 'and locomotives and rolling stock brought in from all over the country. Part of the fuel imported through Inner Mongolia will, first of all, be used for this purpose. Sufficient means must be made ready as quickly as possible to take millions of people to Xinjiang.'

This was an order as well as an explanation, but one that made the Ministers frown. From the moment he took office, Shi Ge had pursued this strategy of moving the floating population to the border regions of China, including the southeast coast, using food as the inducement. The food distribution centres were being gradually moved further away from areas where homeless and destitute people were most numerous; since their primordial aim was to find food, they naturally followed. This strategy originated with Shi Ge's conviction that the floating population was the biggest hindrance to the re-establishment of order and the reconstruction of the country.

Three of the border regions were already full to the point of explosion. The rich coastal areas had long been complaining about excessive immigration. The Sino-Japanese Economic Region had attracted so many people to the Northeast that there had been no room for more. The civil war had made nearly 200 million people homeless. The ministers were all agreed that the restoration of production—particularly of grain—was the first priority. Foreign aid could not feed a billion starving people. For this reason alone, it was essential to get the floating population away, above all from the main agricultural regions.

One of the four border regions had a relatively small population in comparison with its size. The other three were close enough to be reached on foot. But Xinjiang was too far from the centre, access was only possible through the Qinghai plateau, where survival was difficult, or by crossing the Xinjiang Desert or the Gobi Desert which was impossible. It was this region that Shi Ge wanted to fill up not only by rail: he also directed that all available heavy trucks be assembled and turned into double-decker buses with trailers, that could carry 250-300 people. Ten thousand must be ready in ten days. The department of road transport was made responsible for opening the route from Dunhuang and Hetian, along the Old Silk Road, south of the Tarim Basin. 'There is another way of moving these people,' Shi Ge resumed. 'If the relief stations are carefully located, it will be possible for people to travel long distances by foot and on bicycles. There are three hundred million bicycles in China, a large proportion of them now abandoned in the big cities. They must be collected and distributed to the refugees free of charge. In this way the speed of travel will be enormously increased. There must be a supply of spare parts available and roadside repair shops. In short, all means must be used to despatch to Xinjiang those who cannot be absorbed by other border regions. This is our most important task at this moment.'

'What about the future?' asked the Minister responsible for air transport. 'Do you remember in Unit Sixteen, you asked me to research the problem of resettling people? After two months' work, my group came to the same conclusions as you have: that only Xinjiang has sufficient space to absorb large numbers of refugees. But I told you then that the absolute limit was 15 million people and that they would have no land to cultivate, no waste land to open up and no work. International food aid will not be enough for even 200 million. I'm sure you are aware of this.'

Shi Ge wearily twiddled his pencil. 'What I am thinking about is the present, then we'll think about the future.'

'That's not what you always taught us...'

Shi Ge raised his pencil but said without raising his voice, 'In the past I have never said to you "the matter is decided, this is what you must do". What I am saying now is: Please do as I ask.'

There was an awkward silence in the meeting. Shi Ge looked at his watch, and several others present did the same.

'How can we be sure that the line will not be blocked?' asked the Minister for Rail Transport.

In order to move the floating population it would first be necessary to get the railway through the rebel areas of Xinjiang and protect supplies passing through. The victims of famine were not the only people interested in getting to where the food was. To beat off rebels familiar with the territory and supported by local people, would not be easy and, considering the length of the line in West Xinjiang, unthinkable without considerable military forces.

The head of the Transport Security Bureau had been the head of the 'national defence' section in Unit Sixteen: he was the only person present who did not question Shi Ge's Xinjiang strategy. He was a military specialist, and the protection of transport in Xinjiang was a large-scale military operation, for which his Ministry was responsible.

He explained that since the nuclear attack, China's armed forces had been reduced from 77 to less than 50 army groups. Thirteen existed in name only, the others had not been completely reconstructed and consisted mainly of semi-independent garrisons that the newly-formed central military command could not effectively control. The overriding preoccupation of every unit was how to avoid starvation. A large part of China was now bleak and desolate waste land: looting—the traditional expedient of soldiers—was no longer enough and many units had disintegrated. Soldiers fled home, many became armed bandits. The armies had no source of food or fuel of their own and would take orders from anyone who could provide them. Shi Ge had given up his nominal military power, but control over supplies made it possible to organize them more effectively. Under orders from the Transport Security Department, nineteen armies had begun to regroup. Troops of the Lanzhou command stationed in Xinjiang had already started advancing towards the rebels. Troops were being stationed along the road and railway to ensure the safe transport of goods and refugees. Other troops, together with the United Nations Peace-keeping Force, also under the direction of the Transport Security Department, protected distribution centres in other border regions and in the coastal areas.

In the small hours the arrangements for the transfer of population to Xinjiang were completed. There were only four hours left for sleep. Several people lay down on sofas or in the conference room and fell asleep instantly.

Shi Ge was told by his secretary that a bed had been put in his office. He was struggling to keep his eyes open and after putting his head under the cold tap, said 'I will be back in four hours.'

The sandstorm seemed to be burying Beijing. Thousands of tons of fine yellow earth were falling out of the sky on to the city and miles around. As soon as the wind dropped a little, all flat surfaces were immediately covered with a thick layer that was swept up into the air again as the wind freshened. In the beams of the car's headlights, it looked as if solid matter was swirling about and hiding the road.

Driving was only possible by using an infrared night vision instrument. It was the first time Shi Ge had driven Wang Feng's car and he was taking great care. The United Nations Peace Keeping Force had given him the car only the day before and it had taken him twenty minutes before he could even start it. The other special equipment in the car he had not even touched.

He drove west along Chang'an Street. There were United Nations troops at every crossroad, wearing strange looking goggles and capes. Apart from them, there were no other cars or people. The streets were deserted, no lights were visible and there was no sound, except that of the wind. On the night vision screen, unreal looking buildings loomed up and disappeared, and occasionally at a crossroads, a solitary statue might appear. Shi Ge felt as if his skull were full of pieces of lead and he was looking through glass a kilometre thick. Everything was indistinct.

He should be able to see Chen Pan after eight o'clock. At his request United Nations authorities had found her in prison somewhere in Shanxi province and had sent her home to Beijing. Since then he had seen her at a meeting—not quite as long as this one—to discuss the question of *shugua,* but there had been a table between them and many other people were there. He had not been able to find time to see her again. He could not even telephone.

If he had any desire during those days waiting for death, it was to see Chen Pan. She was continually in his thoughts. He had never experienced this kind of longing before and had always laughed at love-scenes in novels—and almost despised the author. He thought that love between men and women counted for very little in real life. When he finally discovered that he had been wrong, and that love is something beyond description, it was already too late. Unless tonight. . .

He had brought a present for Shasha. It looked a bit shabby now. In prison he had torn some cloth and thread from his jacket and found a piece of thin wire to use as a needle. He had never done any sewing before, but he had made a little satchel for Shasha's school-books and was rather proud of it. There had been bloodstains on his clothing from the wound he had received when the helicopter fired at his car. Though he had washed the cloth again and again, he could not get it completely clean and there were marks on the satchel.

He had asked a warder to get the satchel to Chen Pan somehow. The warder had laughed sarcastically and told him to do it himself. . . Now he was going to.

He drove more slowly when he came near to the residential area where Chen Pan lived. He felt a little confused. He was longing to see her, in prison his longing had been love; but there was something else, he urgently wanted to talk to her about his plan.

It was too vast. He felt almost as if he was going to commit a crime. One man, unknown to everyone in the world was deciding the fate of over a billion people. It was an arrogant fantasy of divine omnipotence. He had not merely conceived, it, but was working against time to make it a reality. Each step was irrevocable. How could any man keep this secret, this plan and all the responsibility for it to himself?

It was the only reason he had agreed without a moment of reflection to become Prime Minister. The plan had been conceived in three days while at his residence in Beijing, after the civil war had put a stop to work on the Yellow River diversion. He had covered the walls with maps and for three days had not opened the door or gone out. Later, in prison, he had ample time to turn the rough outline into a detailed plan. For years he had been responsible for planning for emergencies. In prison his mind incessantly produced all sorts of imaginary situations. He understood very well that only someone in the highest position in the country would ever be able to realize this plan but never imagined that he would be that man.

He dared not reveal anything, even to his ministers. If there were any leak, all progress would be obstructed. A billion lives depended on absolute secrecy until the very last moment. Even with his most trusted colleagues, he involuntarily imagined the sort of things which happen in thrillers: one of them might talk in his sleep, or be tortured or even, like him, might want to share with someone else the burden of a secret too heavy to bear alone. Alone with this immense secret he needed a warm being to merge with, an answering voice to give him corroboration. He wanted a warm bosom in which to bury his head, express what was hidden in his mind, gain strength and self-confidence. There was only Chen Pan

He drove slower and slower until the engine was almost silent as if the car was propelled only by the wind. Chen Pan's apartment was more difficult to find than he had expected. He remembered the number and had a map of the residential area, but the night vision apparatus could not distinguish the numbers on doors and buildings, which all looked the same. He looked at the map again and went round in circles. There were no streetlights and no one in sight. Even the apartment blocks looked like ghostly buildings in which there was no one left alive.

Then he saw a figure pass between two buildings. He drove closer. The man had a pack on his back and looked as it he had come a long way. In the dust-filled air one could only see a few yards, but the man found his way without hesitating, like someone returning home. A piece of luck.

Shi Ge was about to sound his horn to attract the man's attention when he realized he knew him. This was the way to Chen Pan's apartment, the right directions and signs, just as on the map. The man heard nothing against the howling wind. He entered the foyer of Chen Pan's apartment block. From his self-confident air and the way he walked, Shi Ge recognized Ouyang Zhong-hua.

A candle was lit in Chen Pan's room. As Shi Ge looked, suddenly in a dream-like state, he felt a dark bottomless pit open under him. Unintentionally he touched a switch: a coloured map appeared on the videophone screen in front of him—a map of China. From the centre of the country, radial lines were drawn, each marked '6800 km', and a meandering line went out into the Pacific.

Almost immediately Shi Ge fell asleep, his head on the steering wheel.

The Chinese-Russian frontier in Heilongjiang.

Spring had hardly reached the 50th parallel this year. Normally at this time, the ice on the Amur River—which is called in China the Heilong River—would have begun to break up noisily. It was still solid. Only at noon, when the sun was at its strongest did the surface of the ice begin to melt—as if sweating. An hour or two later it froze again. Russian light tanks patrolling the frontier still drove fast over the river, trailing white clouds of powdered ice.

The ice was becoming thinner. Although the temperature of the air was below zero, it was no longer as cold as in winter, when the ground is frozen several metres down. The water flowing below was beginning to melt the ice. Tens of thousands of people continually arriving on foot from downstream brought news that the ice was breaking further and further at a rate of about 30 miles a day.

The area a little south of Aihui was full to the limit with refugees. The ground was hardly visible under the teeming mass of humanity. There were tents and makeshift shacks everywhere. Smoke from innumerable small fires hung over everything. The last surviving forests of North China had been here: now no tree was left standing. Those not already burnt had been cut down and were closely guarded. Without a fire no one could avoid freezing to death; people were continually being killed, fighting for a few sticks.

The refugees had been drawn to this area by the forest and the river. Armies of starving people had looted everything in the cities then the towns and finally the villages. Anything edible was eaten, anything man-made destroyed. Now there was nothing else to do but make for the 'empty North where life is good', to the land 'where you can kill a deer with a club and ladle fish out of the river'; 'where pheasants fly straight into the pot'; where venison, salmon and bear's paws would be on the table. This was the vision the starving people had before their eyes. Perhaps it was not far wrong half a century ago.

When locusts descended like a black cloud, the crops would simply vanish for miles and miles around. Now it was many times worse. There was a plague of humanity, of starving people, bigger and more destructive than locusts.

Every day more and more dead bodies could be seen. For those still alive, they were no more worthy of attention than autumn leaves, even if there was a relative lying among them. They had no strength left to weep and only one thing in mind: to go on, to find new forests, and fertile land, where there were wild animals and birds, where fat salmon leapt out of holes in the ice.

They stopped on the banks of the Amur River.

From the air it must have been a strange sight. The frozen river looked like a meandering crack that had opened up in the plain; China on one side, Russia on the other. A huge area of the south bank, where the Chinese refugees had halted, was an ugly black colour. The snow had been trampled into mud, and a black cloud of smoke hid the sky. The ruined towns and villages were like piles of rubbish. By contrast the Russian side opposite was clothed in a dazzling, silvery white. There was hardly anyone in sight, only trees and scattered, tranquil dwellings.

On the map, the frontier between the two countries is represented by a line in the centre the river: in reality it was a line of dots, each of which was a Russian half-track armoured car of the frontier defence force and the line next to it had been made by their tracks on the ice. Here the contrast was even more striking. The Russian side of the frozen river was a clean expanse of ice, smooth as glass. On the Chinese side innumerable holes had been made in the ice, showing the black water of the river below. There were millions of Chinese refugees everywhere, their black hair forming an enormous fur spread over half the river.

The holes were for fishing by the typical method of the far north. The fish are attracted by the light and oxygen from the holes, scattered like stars above them, and as they fight each other to get near, they are caught on wooden hooks or in nets. Sometimes fish leapt out on to the ice. Half the ice-covered river was holed like a sieve and the fish were continually in danger. Not only that: there was a hubbub of voices and a mass of people above who smelled bad. Though their brains are small, the fish eventually had the sense to swim under the ice to the Russian side—having no conception of such things as frontiers and sovereign rights. The river they had lived in for generations had suddenly become narrower by half.

The fishing stopped and the holes froze over. The refugees crowded together to keep warm, all eyes fixed on the expanse of forest and fertile land. They saw a fine stag standing on a hillock, its huge antlers high in the air. For many decades wild animals had been crossing the frontier into Russia escaping from China where there were no trees, no grass and no peace—only people who hunted them for their antlers, their furs or their meat. The stag seemed to look disdainfully across the river, as if remembering the place he had left behind.

Suddenly from downstream came the unmistakable sound of the ice breaking up. Shortly afterwards loudspeakers began to broadcast the voice of a history teacher from a town nearby. 'What you see over there used to be Chinese territory until the Russian Czar seized it by the unequal treaty of Aigun that China was forced to sign in 1858.' After this rather pedantic start, the speaker rephrased it. 'Over there is the treasured land of our ancestors. The hairy devils took it from us by force.' This was the kind of language everyone in China had heard every day for thirty years when China and Russia were deadly enemies.

'Now the land that was once ours, is in front of you: a vast space, with endless forests, fertile land, wild beasts and birds. In summer tons of fruit fall from the trees and lie rotting on the ground.'

As the voice of the speaker became louder and louder, like the roar of the tide, the Russian troops came out into the open and hastily set up their weapons. The immense crowd instantly became silent. Russian half-tracks roared into position. In silence the refugees at the back began to push forwards; those in front, on the river bank were pushed on to the ice. Some fell into the fishing holes. But the silence was not broken. The Russians driving the armoured cars seemed to become flustered and drove fast towards the refugees, hoping to scare them into moving back. Some were crushed under the caterpillar tracks, splashing blood on those near. It was impossible for the refugees to turn back.

Behind them the impenetrable and silent wall of humanity grew thicker and more solid. Russian loudspeakers shouted threats and warnings in Chinese, and ordered their troops to make ready to fire. But to open fire on a 'charging enemy' on this scale is only possible when there is some incident, a trigger. There was none in this typically Chinese, creeping, inch-by-inch advance.

It was impossible to see where the mass of humanity ended: it certainly far outnumbered the available bullets. Soon the trigger incident occurred. The ice on the river was already thin, weakened by the fishing holes and the combined weight of the thousands refugees. Suddenly there was a loud crash and the ice split down the centre of the river for a distance of almost a mile. Many refugees were tipped into the water and a few Russia armoured vehicles sank rapidly to the bottom of the river. There was a deafening scream and thousands rushed in terror to the Russian side, where the ice was stronger.

The Russian troops were paralysed. They hesitated to fire on people who were only trying to save their lives. Their own instinct was to run, but before they could do so, they were buried by the flood of refugees rushing forward to break through the frontier defences. Russian soldiers were overwhelmed and trampled underfoot in the pure white snow, that soon became black mud.

Once a breach had been made in the Russian defences refugees ran madly to the bank of the river and jumped; perhaps in a second or two the ice would give way completely, to stay meant death. Better to be shot than die slowly of starvation.

In no time, the breach was eleven miles long. The ice continued to break up. Thousands fell into the water and were drowned: even more were pushed in by the crowds massing behind. Hardly any of these reached the other side alive: no one could survive more than a few minutes in the icy water. More and more refugees started to run upstream where the ice had not yet broken up and crossed there.

Russian troops opened fire, hesitantly at first, and cut down the refugees in swathes. Dead bodies piled up on the ice. But the refugees hardly noticed: there were dead bodies everywhere in China. People walked across them as if they were no more than rags. When the Russian soldiers saw these people, with frenzied eyes, clamber over dead and living, most of them understood that their weapons were useless.

Among the mass of dirty, distorted and savage faces, there was one that was perfectly calm and even pleasing to the eye; but showing no emotion, and for that reason, all the more frightening.

A Russian second lieutenant with a machine rifle froze at the sight of this apparition from hell not knowing whether to fire or not. As he hesitated, the apparition's hands, in thin black leather gloves, broke his neck like a chicken.

Li Ke-ming had come home to the north to find his wife and child. He was now free. Being on the wanted list was a thing of the past and even his steel mask no longer surprised anyone. He was an ordinary man among the crazed and dazed people, thinking only of his family. He had shaken off his former feeling of desperation. The village was nothing but a pile of charred ruins. Only one corner of his home remained, where an old man was raping a young woman dying of starvation. No one knew where his family or his parents had gone to. Relatives and friends he had grown up with, schoolmates, teachers, neighbours were all gone. There were only unfamiliar and distant faces, haggard from starvation and madness.

Li Ke-ming was now accompanied by seven or eight men, armed with rifles taken from Russian soldiers. They were silent and kept close to him, perhaps out of fear or because he had a presence that commanded obedience and they recognized him as their leader. Li Ke-ming and his men drove upstream along the river bank, in a snow truck, loaded with weapons and ammunition and wiping out any Russian troops firing at refugees trying to cross the river.

That night about 30 million refugees forced their way into Russia, having breached the frontier defences over a distance of more than 180 miles. The Russian city of Blagoveshchensk, about sixty miles north of the frontier, was ablaze and everything, especially food and clothing, had been looted clean. However, very few of the refugees took to banditry or violence. Once safely across the river the majority hurried north, towards the mountains and forests.

Just before dawn the Russians regained control of the frontier. Small groups of refugees continued to arrive and awaited their opportunity to cross the river in the veiled light of dawn. For miles the great slabs of frozen ice mangled the floating bodies and the river ran dark with blood. Upstream, the ice had not yet broken up and was piled layer on layer with dead bodies.

The thirty million refugees fanned out when they entered Russia, like a flood across a desert. Russian helicopters following saw them break into ever smaller groups, until they disappeared into the endless sea of Siberian forests

State Security Ministry Report to Huang Shi-ke (Top Secret)

We have a report that a Russian local defence corps at Belogorsk has captured a Japanese secret agent among the Chinese refugees who have penetrated Russia. Under threat of execution this man admitted to being a low-ranking member of the Japanese *Black Dragon Society*. He had joined the refugees, disguised as a Chinese, before they broke through the frontier, his mission being to incite them to enter Russia by force, then help them set up a base in Russia. He claimed to have received no other instructions, but admitted that there are numerous other agents of the *Black Dragon Society* with the same mission. They have all received long-term training. The agent is in the hands of the Russian authorities. The incident was reported in the Amur newspaper, but no further information has reached us.

According to state intelligence services, the *Black Dragon Society* was founded over a hundred years ago. It has always worked in the shadows and maintained strict secrecy. Even today its regulations, membership, precise activities and plans are entirely unknown to outsiders. It is rumoured that many people in Japanese political circles are members and that their number is increasing.

The backbone of the society is a group of young activists who see themselves as saviours of Japan. Their aim is to fight for the expansion of Japanese territory. There has long been anxiety in certain circles in Japan about the small size of their country and the danger this presents for the future. In recent years a stream of sensational articles in the press reflects the persistence of such views.

It is clear that the *Black Dragon Society* intends to increase its influence by controlling and organizing young patriots and finally seize power. Its long-standing aim has always been the annexation of Northeast China and the Russian Far East. Russia is powerful enough to prevent this from happening. But Japan's active promotion of Heilongjiang Province as a 'Sino-Japanese Economic Cooperation Region', and the considerable increase in Japanese investment in the Russian Far East, are part of a new strategy of economic penetration, inspired and directed by the *Black Dragon Society*. The captured agent admitted that his long-term future and cover would be as a Japanese merchant in the Far East. It must be assumed that Japanese activities among the Chinese refugees are part of this strategy.

In view of the importance of this question, we suggest that our research on the *Black Dragon Society*, interrupted by recent political changes in our country, should immediately be resumed and should be given high priority in funding and personnel.

Beijing

Chen Pan, on a plane returning to Beijing, was reading a speech Shi Ge had given at the Green University, in which he had said:

> Which is better: public or private ownership of the means of production? To all appearances this question has now been answered: private ownership is far more effective for increasing material wealth. So public ownership is being repudiated all over the world. However, central to the Green way of thinking is the conviction that the unbridled, headlong pursuit of material wealth is leading the world to destruction. The only way of avoiding the obliteration of mankind is to call a halt to perpetual and unrestrained development and adopt a way of life based on self-control and moderation, a reasonable level of comfort and facilities, and 'purity of mind and few desires'.
>
> I firmly believe that private ownership, with its intrinsic greed, will never voluntarily abandon the race for expansion and ever more development.
>
> I have been troubled that Communism has been so misrepresented and abused that it is now hated. I have never believed that the communist ideal is nonsense: indeed the philosophy of the Green movement is evidence of its validity. Only public ownership is consistent with the Green ideals of virtue, frugality, rational planning and public spirit that will allow humanity to escape from the unbridled greed that accompanies private ownership. Only through public ownership can we achieve the self-restraint that can save mankind. Then the innumerable people who have fought for this ideal will be vindicated: they shed their blood and gave their lives, not to create a monstrous caricature of Communism, but to open up a difficult and essential road for future generations of humanity.

Chen Pan boxed these passages with a thick red pencil. Several Western newspapers had concluded from these remarks that Shi Ge was still basically a communist and made sarcastic comments about his continued attachment to public ownership.

Chen Pan was moved by these words, Shi Ge's profound love and concern for humanity and his desire to pay tribute to the preceding generation of revolutionaries.

As the plane approached Beijing, only Chen Pan noticed signs of alarm on the faces of the cabin crew. The ship merchants, who made up more than half the passengers, were making a lot of noise and there was a strong smell of alcohol. Several scientists on their way to study the climatic effects of the nuclear attack, kept their heads obstinately buried in their scientific papers.

Chen Pan had never been afraid of flying. But during her travels, that had taken her all over the world, she had experienced an abortive hijack attempt and a bomb scare, resulting in an emergency landing, four last minute flight changes and repeated searches and had now become tense each time she got on a plane and had sworn never to fly again.

While flying across Mongolia, she heard a low muffled sound, that seemed to be coming from the hold. The plane bumped a few times. The smile on the face of the Dutch air-stewardess's face became fixed and false. Chen Pan asked no questions but concentrated on leafing through her newspapers and magazines, then re-read the passage from Shi Ge's speech again.

The honeymoon was over between Shi Ge and the international press. The United States and Russian authorities found him far less obliging and cooperative than he appeared. They had assumed that they held the reins: now they found that he did. Shi Ge relentlessly played on the feelings of guilt in the United States, Russia and their allies, for having brought about the destruction of China, but remained cordial and friendly when pressing them for more aid. He did not hesitate to create suspicion about the ulterior motives of one country in order to increase the contributions of another. The result was that there was almost a competition among nations to increase their aid and the amount first promised was soon doubled.

In one western newspaper he was called 'the world's top blackmailer', though in fact he very rarely showed any partiality. Russia strongly demanded that he find some way of preventing Chinese refugees from flooding into Russia; Shi Ge replied that Russia only had herself to blame by causing so much suffering in China by the nuclear attack. Nevertheless he broadcast a personal appeal calling on the refugees to return home and appeared to be actively trying to solve the problem. His appeal naturally had no effect. No one knew better than he that China had not nearly enough food to guarantee their survival so did nothing to stop the continued flow of Chinese to the frontier.

In order to explain and justify the attack on China, the United States Vice President paid a visit to Beijing and urged the immediate trial of Wang Feng. The New York Times reported that he was entertained to lunch in Zhongnanhai staff canteen, 'Shi Ge put the last of the white cabbage soup in the Vice President's plate and said "Wang Feng used three nuclear missiles, the United States one hundred and fifteen and the Russians seventy six. Do you think the trials should be in alphabetical order, or according to the number of missiles each country deployed?'"

In general what most affected world opinion of Shi Ge was the massacre of rebels in Xinjiang. He had the reputation of a great humanitarian and the scale of the killing involved in the opening up of road and rail communications in Xinjiang aroused much anger. The majority of the population of Xinjiang are Moslems and regarded Shi Ge's Transport Security Bureau as satanic criminals with blood on their hands: they had punished any attack on the road or railway by inflicting ten times as much destruction on attackers. Chen Pan was much troubled by this. She thought Shi Ge's government should have been more patient, and tried to solve the problem by negotiation. She could not understand why the government would not tolerate the slightest delay and met all obstruction with extreme violence. The Moslems also accused the government of trying to smother their independence by filling up the province with Chinese refugees. International human rights organizations too condemned the massive shift of population as a disguised form of genocide.

Chen Pan could not believe this was true. Shi Ge had taken what for him was the unusual course of resorting to military force to put an end to a local rebellion. Under Wang Feng's brutal totalitarian regime Shi Ge had publicly expressed approval of Taiwan's demand for independence, so why would he have taken such violent and excessive measures against Xinjiang, half of which was desert?

Most people in China did not understand Shi Ge. He appeared to them to be going the same way as most modern leaders, who are acclaimed with enthusiasm and hope when they come to power, but soon disappoint people. In Shi Ge's case this seemed to have happened with exceptional rapidity—in two months.

Chen Pan had met a maritime transport expert in Amsterdam, who said that Shi Ge's actions confirmed the fact that power corrupts. This moody young man knew about Chen Pan's position and, perhaps because he had had a few drinks, started to tell her about his own highly secret mission. Shi Ge had sent him abroad to buy up as many sea-worthy ships as he could find, however old. A large number of other people had been charged with the same mission. As scrap-metal, the ships were cheap, the young man said, but China was in ruins and there was scrap-metal everywhere, so why waste money buying it from abroad? Some people thought the ships were for transporting foreign aid, but the countries providing aid delivered it themselves. In any case the old wrecks would be useless once foreign aid came to an end. But orders came for bigger and bigger ships, capable of considerable speeds—it was crazy. Prices sometimes plummeted if one waited, but the order was to hurry, the young man complained. This mad rush to buy ships also played havoc with market prices, and the price for old ships increased one and a half times in two weeks. Ship merchants were like snakes coming out of hibernation and occupied half the places on this plane

If Shi Ge had been corrupted by power, Chen Pan reflected, no one would misunderstand him. If power had gone to his head and he wanted to 're-unite the empire', why had he tolerated Tibetan independence and other little separatist 'kingdoms' in the country? All Shi Ge's plans and actions had this in common: everyone found them incomprehensible: they were not stupid blunders—which are easy to understand. She knew that her work during the last two months would not be understood by the majority of people. But she also knew that Shi Ge's plans were far more intelligent and far seeing than people thought. Whether he was right or wrong history would judge.

Just before landing at Beijing, the calm voice of the pilot announced, 'We are having a little technical problem.'

Chen Pan closed her eyes. The stewardess, a professional smile concealing her agitation, began to check that all safety belts were fastened. The passengers realized there was a serious problem.

The merchants all fell silent and stopped drinking, the stewardess crossed herself and asked the passengers to clasp their hands behind their heads and sit doubled-up. The aircraft violently hit the runway and bounced, Chen Pan's accumulated anxieties disappeared: at least she had seen no flames or damage, just the runway, down which the plane was sliding, no longer level but at an angle. There was an ear-splitting scraping and screeching sound coming from below, as well as heat. She remained curled up in her seat, pressed hard against the arm-rest and heard the meteorologist next to her moan something about god. The other passengers seemed to have lost the power of speech.

Then there was a loud crash: the safety belt tightened and she felt lifted into the air, her head hit the back of the seat in front and she felt the pressure of the whole row of passengers behind. The aircraft seemed to be turning over completely. But with the tail up in the air, the movement and the scraping noise stopped. What peace! She felt as if in a vacuum. The stewardess shouted several times before the passengers, still crouched over holding their heads, took any notice. She saw the emergency doors open, the solid earth and the sky above and a hazy cloud of smoke. There was a smell of over-heated engine oil.

'Get out quick!' someone shouted.

People began to react. Chen Pan tried to undo her safety belt, but she seemed to have forgotten how to make the simplest movements. The meteorologist ran over, undid the belt, lifted her up and threw her bodily through the emergency exit. She slid through the strong smelling rubber escape chute, her skirt above her thighs. She fell on top of a bearded ship merchant, who seized her arm and ran with elephantine steps over the grass. Chen Pan noticed a dead sparrow, and some mice scuttling away. Fire engines and ambulances raced up, sirens wailing, The aircraft had neither exploded nor caught fire but was merely stuck nose first in the grass beside the runway, its tail in the air. The starboard engine was smoking and one of the wings was broken, showing the struts and mechanisms like intestines.

Once they knew they were safe, they embraced each other joyfully. A ship merchant kissed Chen Pan and lifted her high in the air and she was passed on from one man to another; the bearded man breathed alcohol fumes in her face. She was finally rescued by the meteorologist, continuing to play the role of the chivalrous knight.

The airport building was far away and looked like a wooden toy. Nearly all regular flights had been cancelled and the airfield was empty. Most governments had warned their citizens not to go to China: Chen Pan had been to four different countries before she found a plane for Beijing.

No vehicles had come to meet them. Essential services such as flight control, ambulances and security had been taken over by the military, everything else was paralysed. The passengers had to walk to the customs office in the main building. Chen Pan remembered that her passport was in her handbag still on the plane: she would have to wait until the baggage was discharged. Never mind, she was alive and had arrived and the sky was blue.

It was not yet hot, but the airfield was like a skillet. There seemed to be no sign of nuclear winter. In the late 1980s, some influential scientists put forward the theory that when nuclear explosions reached a certain level, the extreme heat would cause enormous quantities of dust from stone, earth, and smoke from burning cities to be thrown up into the atmosphere, forming a global screen that would prevent sunlight from reaching the ground. The temperature in the upper atmosphere would rise and that of the earth fall by 10-25° or more, creating an artificial winter that might last several weeks or months. World agriculture would be destroyed and with it humanity. There would be no victor. In the attack on China, it was said, the number of nuclear devices used were not sufficient cause nuclear winter, but had provided a valuable field of research.

The climatologist who had come to the rescue of Chen Pan had been in China five times in the last two months. He was not in the least encouraged by the good weather, and remarked philosophically that any unusual change, even for the better, can be a warning of danger. His slightly distracted expression reminded her of Shi Ge and made her feel well disposed towards him.

Shi Ge himself was far away. Since he became Premier, she had seen him only once, at a meeting in his office, together with various officials and her colleagues. Shi Ge was on time to the minute. He shook hands with her exactly as he did with the others and his eyes scanned her face, revealing nothing. He spoke only about *shugua*: nutrient, ferments, equipment—nothing else, and made decisions one after the other. He gave orders for the organization of an educational network to teach the method of producing *shugua* throughout the country in the shortest possible time, and called for maximum nationwide production of nutrient fluid and all other necessary equipment. He also asked for more research to reduce the ripening period of the *shugua*. Even Chen Pan could not understand why he asked for the small *shugua* production equipment to be collapsible and easy to transport over considerable distances. Shi Ge did not explain, and there was no time for discussion. Everyone was acutely conscious of his authority and the distance he seemed to have put between them and him. He commanded obedience. He was not the amiable and simple man they were used to. Chen Pan was a key person in the development of *shugua*, not only as the principal inventor of the process, but because of the production enterprises she had already set up. However she was now neither excited nor moved: when she spoke it was to the Premier—not to Shi Ge. He was far away.

After the meeting he asked her to remain behind. Her heart bounded suddenly... But he also detained someone else, the Chief Assistant, with his pen and notebook. In a manner that showed that he was still Premier and nothing more, Shi Ge instructed her to go abroad immediately, taking copies of all information concerning *shugua*, samples of equipment required to produce it and of the *shugua* itself. She was to give it without reservation, to any country, enterprise or research organization in the world that expressed interest. After which Shi Ge, in the name of the Chinese government, would request countries giving aid to China to start production according to the technology and blueprints provided by Chen Pan, and supply China with *shugua*. It was impossible for China's failing production to provide even one percent of the *shugua*. What was needed was quantity—of steel, plastics, money and energy. The world was already incapable of providing China with adequate supplies of food and *shugua* was the only hope. If the countries that were interested and now had all the necessary information, would go over to something on the scale of an emergency or wartime arms production, hundreds of millions of Chinese, otherwise condemned to starvation, would have a chance of survival.

Since then Chen Pan had not seen Shi Ge. Everything was arranged by the Chief Assistant, who was competent and amiable; but she secretly hated him and was often unreasonable with him.

For the last two months, she had shuttled from one country to another. After the first press conference she had given in Japan, *shugua* had caused a sensation throughout the world, and she received invitations from a large number of countries. Industrial firms and financial groups offered her astronomical salaries. The press followed her everywhere. Organizations connected with agriculture, animal husbandry and the environment were all very excited. Solicited in this way, Chen Pan's attitude was very simple: she treated everyone alike and gave them each a complete set of documentation, drawings, a bag of seeds and a video tape showing specific procedures, for which she asked only cost price and expenses.

The speed at which *shugua* production started in developed countries astonished Chen Pan. Government and private' investment was phenomenal, as was the scale of labour recruitment. Not only the food industries but several others, and the military as well, wanted to use the technology.

Chen Pan went from one country to another giving guidance. Her expertise was widely respected, but she gradually realized that, as their research advanced, she became regarded as an outsider.

This embarrassed her and made her feel ridiculous. She still continued to help anyone who needed her at no advantage to herself, in fact her income got smaller and smaller. All because Shi Ge had not recalled her. . . Perhaps he had simply forgotten her. The chief assistant phoned every day to greet her and ask how she was. She asked him nothing, but she would have liked to take him by the throat, just to make him say the name 'Shi Ge'.

The passengers, delighted to be alive, went half way round the outside of the airport building until a sullen official led them through a small insignificant-looking door that no one had noticed, down a winding corridor to Customs. The whole building was deserted and gloomy—like a tomb in a dark forest—in contrast with the bright sunlight outside. There was waste paper and rubbish everywhere and a powerful stink from the toilets. Outside the locked glass door of customs, traces of the rioting were still visible. There was nothing for sale: all the shelves in the shops were bare. The waiting hall was deserted—apart from the sparrows.

Someone outside knocking on a window attracted Chen Pan's attention. It was Ouyang Zhong-hua. The sun was behind him, but she could see his face distinctly, his smile and white teeth. On the phone she had told him that the plane was not on schedule and he should not come to meet her. He pressed his hands flat on the dirty glass of the window. The glass was very dirty. She put her hands over his. His sensuous mouth formed a kiss. She smiled, a little confused and went to catch up with the other passengers in front of the closed door of customs.

No one knew when the baggage would come from the plane. Ouyang had disappeared, which made Chen Pan feel less uneasy. She had resolved several times not to allow herself to sink again into an intimate and difficult relationship. When she was abroad, she had thought it would not be difficult. He might not want to accept it at first but after all, he was a reasonable man who respected others. She felt less sure now. What if Ouyang, without saying anything, had taken her in his arms and silenced her objections with a kiss? Would it have been like that night all over again? How many times had she told herself that it was different, that this was their final parting? Yet he had made a long and difficult journey on bicycle and on foot from who knows how far away. How could she have the heart to reject him? It would wipe out the memories of past joy and leave a wound that would never heal. If they were to separate, there must be a transition, not a sudden break. She felt resentful about Shi Ge as well. From the moment she had come out of prison, she had waited for him. She had waited half the night, then it was not he who had knocked on her door but the other. She could not resist: her need was too great and she made no distinction between the two. Ouyang was a man, and she needed him.

She did not know whether Shi Ge had heard those last three words she had shouted as she left the court. Even if he had not, she had surely made it sufficiently clear in what she had said from the witness box? From that moment, she had completely given her heart to him. But she had since lain in Ouyang's arms. She did not regret it and did not blame herself. But when she saw Shi Ge again, a twinge of remorse stopped her from saying anything more, as if perhaps what she had said in court was the result of a passing emotion. It would be in bad taste for a self-respecting woman to take the initiative, especially to a man in his position. She could not talk of love to Shi Ge when she had just come from the arms of another man: she must wait until the smell, sweat, and fire were forgotten. So she had said nothing and had gone abroad the same day.

When she reached Japan on her way home, she heard that Shi Ge had nominated Ouyang to the post of Director of the National Bureau for the Protection of the Environment. Now a suspicion came into her mind that she felt a little ashamed of: perhaps Ouyang had come to Beijing, not in order to see her as he claimed, but in connection with this work.

Ouyang had founded a 'Green Party' and in doing so had split the Chinese Association for the Protection of the Environment. There were now two large and mutually hostile groups. The Green Party was well organized, with a clear-cut programme and strict discipline and was far more effective than the Association. It was now a political party second only to the Communist Party. The chief assistant explained to Chen Pan that the aim of the Green Party was to start survival bases all over the country—an extension of the former six Green bases. The Association was an organization for the future, while the Party was much stronger and more suited to the present crisis. This was probably in Shi Ge's mind when making the appointment.

A 'phone call from his chief assistant confirmed that Shi Ge had indeed decided that the role of the Green Association was to plan for the future. Its immediate responsibility was setting up and running a Green University for which most of the leading members of the association had been recruited as teachers. It bore little resemblance to a normal university but was more like a factory in continuous production. At every session of 25 days, the numbers of students, recruited from all over the country, doubled. All of them attended classes, leaving only the minimum of time for sleep. The All-level Election System was at the centre of the study programme. Shi Ge's intention was to disseminate the idea throughout China, and as soon as they entered the university, the students were organized into groups and held elections according to its principles. The experiences of the Taibaishan and Fanjingshan Nature Reserves in adopting the system were invaluable in refining Shi Ge's original conception. The students also studied Green philosophy and social theories, and learned how to grow *shugua* and use natural sources of energy

At present there were branches of the Green University at Shanghai, Guangzhou, Wuhan, Lanzhou and Shenyang. On graduating, all students went back to their various regions and started courses to teach others what they had learned.

In his last phone call to Chen Pan, the Chief Assistant had told her that many of the teachers were exhausted by their heavy work load and that the Premier had decided that Chen Pan should return to China. Apart from teaching at the Green University, he had other important work for her to do, the details of which he would explain when she arrived.

Chen Pan's first reaction was: so that's all he wants me for.

These thoughts were interrupted when two men approached her. One of them produced an identity card in a leather folder bearing the pulse-quickening scarlet seal of the Ministry of State Security.

'Please come with us,' the man said in a cultured voice and made a polite gesture to precede him.

'What for?' Chen Pan asked with a slight tightening in her throat. No answer. His politeness did not conceal the confidence in his own power.

'My baggage is still on the plane.'

'Don't worry. We will deal with it.'

She knew it was useless to say anything more, and did not believe that this interpolation was a matter of any importance. She said goodbye to the meteorologist and the ship merchants, who seemed a little anxious about her. She left with the two men and passed straight through Customs without stopping. Outside, Ouyang Zhong-hua was waiting for her.

'What's going on?' he asked. the two men were slightly taken aback by Ouyang's sudden appearance and his haughty demeanour.

'These two men from Security want me to go with them,' Chen Pan said. .

'For what purpose?'. They evidently did not intend to explain. He took out his identity papers. 'I am Director of the National Environmental Protection Bureau. . . .'

'. . .Ouyang Zhong-hua.' One of the two men interrupted. 'There are no environmental problems here.'

'Broadly speaking, the law is also part of the environment.'

'I apologize, Director, if I have misunderstood, but your Bureau seems to want to interfere in everything,' said one of the men with an insinuating smile.

Ouyang turned to Chen Pan: 'Don't worry. You don't need to say anything to them to them. It will soon be sorted out.'

Chen Pan was reassured and on the road into the city she was pleased to see Ouyang in a car close behind. She had resolved to bring their relationship to an end when she next saw him; now she had begun to weaken.

Tiananmen Square was quite clean and patrolled by United Nations soldiers in steel helmets. The car did not drive into the Ministry of Security, but passed behind the Great Hall of the People and into the underground car park. She saw Ouyang being stopped by the guard. The car went down the winding ramp to some lower level. She had no idea that the Great Hall, proclaimed as a symbol of the power of the people, contained so much that never saw the light of day. Because of the shortage of electricity, there were very few lights and it was as dark as a forest.

This was the First Deputy Premier Huang Shi-ke's headquarters. He evidently had an organization of considerable size, that was independent of Shi Ge. The United States intended that as soon as stability was restored, there would be a general election in China and the creation of a legislative assembly that would draw up a constitution. A government and a Head of State would then be appointed. The United States had Huang Shi-ke in mind: he was far more favourable to capitalism than Shi Ge.

The Russian point of view was different. Moscow insisted that no one had declared war on China. The United Nations had merely removed the nuclear weapons of both participants in the civil war. Therefore China was not a defeated country and neither the United Nations nor any country had the right to meddle in her affairs, or oblige her to change her political system or social structure. Her sovereignty must be respected as the Charter of the United Nations demanded.

On one point however, the United States and Russia agreed: they both regretted the choice of Shi Ge as Premier. No one had given so much as a hint as to whom the Russians would support as his successor. All things considered, it was not going to be easy to find anyone who was a match for Huang Shi-ke, and if Huang could dispose of Shi Ge, so much the better.

It did not take long for Chen Pan to realize that Huang Shi-ke's security department had brought her here in order to help frame Shi Ge. When she mentioned that it was he who had ordered her to transmit the *shugua* technology freely to any country interested, she noticed a glint in the eyes of the small man—from Fujian—who was questioning her.

'We know about that, of course, we only wanted confirmation. I hope you will continue to be frank and sincere with us.'

'I don't understand what there is that warrants the intervention of Security.'

'Before I reply, permit me to ask you two questions.' The man leaned forward in his high-backed chair, his arms crossed. 'First, do you think that foreigners will give you all the details about the improvements they make?'

This was difficult to answer. She was on her guard. In fact she only needed to go into their laboratories and see the improvements herself. 'I don't think they could conceal anything really important.'

'OK' he nodded. 'Am I right in saying that the factor that most affects the spread of *shugua* as a foodstuff is its taste?'

'That's true.'

'At present foreign countries are energetically trying hard to remove the unpleasant taste. Did you know that in Japan they have succeeded?'

This was a shock. On her last journey Chen Pan had been five times to Japan and had heard and seen nothing about such an important break-through

'Impossible,' she said, 'I have been to all the Japanese laboratories.'

He sighed and shook his head. 'You are too naïve.' He turned to his switchboard: 'Bring me sample number 079.'

Someone wheeled in a small trolley on which there was a ice-box containing a slice of *shugua* in a transparent box.

'It cost us three lives to get this sample,' the small man said. '*Shugua* is your invention, so you have a right to taste it.' He carefully cut off a piece hardly bigger than a grain of rice and handed it with a pair of tweezers to Chen Pan. She examined it. It was slightly green and less translucent than usual.

She chewed carefully between her front teeth and transferred it to the tip of her tongue. As she did so she became tense: innumerable experiences of this sort had turned the process of tasting into something intensely nerve-racking. She was particularly sensitive to the strange taste of *shugua*—even thinking about it made her slightly nauseous. Strange, there was none of that pungent smell that irritated the nostrils. There was still a little astringency but there was even a trace of sweetness. Although it was not pleasant to eat, it was far from inedible. It would certainly be all right for fodder and it would not cause vomiting in humans. There was a great change in texture as well; it was like eating a vegetable rather than plastic. It was difficult to get the real taste from the minute sample she had been given but the slice had been carefully replaced in the ice-box and taken away.

Chen Pan was pleased. She admired the achievement of the Japanese scientists, but was annoyed by their duplicity.

'They didn't tell me,' she said, reluctantly swallowing the *shugua* sample.

'My second question is this,' said the security man with an expression of sympathy. 'Were you aware that during your two months abroad at least ten attempts were made to kill you?'

'Kill me?' said Chen Pan incredulously. 'Why?'

'Two different interest groups were involved. One of them wanted to stop you promoting *shugua* technology in order to keep it for themselves, or prevent you from publicizing details of their progress. When they needed your help they could not prevent you from knowing about certain aspects of their progress. But once they had finished using you, it was safer to get rid of you. The other group wanted to prevent the technology from getting out at all, because *shugua* production damaged their interests.'

'Fortunately those who *did* need you, went to a great deal of trouble to protect you and several times saved your life. Eventually they too may want you out of the way. Interpol has been protecting you because attempts on your life have often been arranged as aircraft accidents, which of course put a lot more people in danger. The plane you came on had been tampered with, of course. There is no real reason now for killing you, but the assassins were probably trying to make up for so many failures. You have been lucky.'

Chen Pan felt weak, at the recollection of each moment of danger in the last two months. The man put a folder of Interpol reports in front of her. 'All this shows,' he said, fetching two cans of Coca-Cola, 'that the people you have been dealing with are not as you imagine them. They are not trying to help China; but are determined to monopolize *shugua* themselves. Do you think that Premier Shi Ge does not understand this simple fact?'

Chen Pan finished her Coca-Cola.

'I don't understand what you are getting at.'

You should understand.' He pushed another can in her direction. 'Our country is in dire straits and—almost miraculously—has this precious plant at its disposal. We should have made maximum use of it. As you know, Japan immediately gave us to understand that if we gave them sole right to use this technology, they would pay us a sum equal to twice our annual state revenue. With that amount of money, China could have recovered in no time. Instead, the right to use the technology was given away left and right. That was a serious error of judgement to put it mildly. To be more accurate, it was treason!'

This was not unexpected: it was the first attack on Shi Ge. A good way of stirring up popular indignation. Giving away something for nothing! And to foreigners who have just humiliated us. In the world of politics, you can call a sesame seed a pumpkin and get away with it, so why not make the Himalayas out of this one?

'You should realize,' said Chen Pan angrily to make her seem self-confident. 'Shortage of raw materials is the main problem in the world today, and that is what makes monopolies profitable. We don't have the means at present to produce *shugua* on a large enough scale. The world shortage of food will not be solved by allowing one country to have a monopoly on *shugua* production; but it will make a lot of profit for those who have the monopoly. Such people are capable of creating shortages in their own interests. The only way to solve the problem of shortages is to make the technology available to the whole world. The policy is intelligent and far-seeing. The governments and financial groups that go to any extremes to set up monopolies are following their acquisitive instincts. They will not succeed; but will destroy themselves. The cultivation of *shugua* will spread to the whole world and the shortage of food will cease. Then China will really benefit. Already there are several countries that genuinely want to help us, what prevents them from doing so is that they themselves have no great quantities of food.'

'Your kind of idealism is very far from reality,' said the man with severity. 'By the time the whole world becomes prosperous, there will be no more Chinese left.'

'Even if we do sell the technology,' Chen Pan replied, 'by the time all the interminable discussions and red tape in modern commercial transactions are finished, more than half the Chinese people would be dead. We may receive mountains of gold and silver but we can't eat it. But when everyone cooperates, look how fast things can be done...'

'What has that got to do with us?' The man from Security interrupted her angrily. 'It's true the Russians have set up thousands of production plants using the information you gave them. For what purpose? Certainly not for our benefit. They have cut their aid to China by half because of the refugees who poured into Siberia. But the aid did not go to those refugees. All the refugees get from the Russians is bullets. Russia is producing *shugua* in order to solve its own food supply problems. With the millions of dollars they save, they can import food. United States farmers are violently opposed to the manufacture of *shugua* equipment because of the threat *shugua* represents to their grain exports. They are only concerned about their own future, and in the end China will get nothing! Don't imagine that *shugua* belongs to you to do whatever you want with it. You used funds and research facilities provided by the state. *Shugua* is the property of China. The Prime Minister has no right to bankrupt the country.' Chen Pan looked for a moment at the man's face, that suddenly became calm.

'What makes you think that I will help you attack Shi Ge?'

'We are acting in the interests of the country and don't want to attack anyone. We are not asking you for help, only that you speak the truth, not invent explanations. Even so, your testimony has been recorded, and is legal evidence.' He stopped for a moment and a different look came into his eyes.

'Another thing, purely personal—but perhaps of more interest to you for that reason—which you will be pleased to know about.'

He took a photograph from his folder and put it in front of her. It was taken with an infra-red camera and showed a man on foot and a car nearby. Though the figure was small and indistinct, she recognized Ouyang. In the background she could see windows. Ouyang was walking past a tree towards a building—she recognized her own apartment block. The photo was dated and the location recorded. It was taken that night. . . What was that car doing there? Obviously Ouyang had not seen it. The engine was running, judging from the photo. Had it just arrived or was it following Ouyang? There was a sandstorm that night and the sound of the wind was so loud that even a tank would not have attracted attention.

He put another photograph in front of her. This is like a slide-show, she thought. It was taken from the same spot but pointing upwards. Ouyang was not on it. She saw a light in her window. She only had candles at that time. In the foreground was the car.

Another photograph. The light in her window was out. The car had not moved. The photo had been taken two hours later.

Chen Pan smiled coldly.

'The spy in that car had a hard night,' he said. 'It looks obvious to me. . . makes one wonder why he bothered to wait so long.' He looked as if he could hardly help laughing. He was just about to say something when the buzzer on his desk switchboard sounded and a red light went on. He hastily left the room, but had time to say, 'The spy was Shi Ge.'

So he did come. Was it some obscure quirk of fate that he was twenty metres behind and that when she opened the door for him, it was someone else; and he saw this happen?

How many times in some aircraft, or in a foreign airport, sleepless in a hotel, or gazing through a double-glazed window at a sea of snow, or at a ceiling in the semi-darkness, or with a solitary glass of wine, how many different explanations had she considered? But not this one.

She had decided never to tell Shi Ge about that evening: it was not important for the future. Over-scrupulous honesty is often the enemy of sincerity. Anyway, she asked herself, what right have you to talk about honesty? He was keeping watch outside the whole time. She felt a flush of resentment. So that's the sort of man he is, jealous and self-important. But at least he had reacted. His way of breaking off their relationship was to turn and go, without a word; since then he had been nothing more than the self-important Prime Minister. He should have given her a chance to explain. Perhaps he had no time. . . And what explanation? Such things could never be explained and the frustration of this was like a dark and bottomless pit, from which a black wind blew white ashes, like snowflakes, into the sky. In spite of herself all her feelings, ability, thoughts seemed to dissolve into ashes floating upwards, and she was falling, falling. . . .

She saw the small man come back and heard him speak without listening. She followed him, in a daze, floating. The light in the lift was very bright. There were dark-tinted mirrors and multiple reflections of herself. Then she saw the sunlight through a window, abnormally bright.

An old man with a grand manner greeted her with a fulsome smile and put out a large fleshy hand. Ouyang was standing next to him.

Light was reflected from the yellow glazed tiles of the Imperial Palace nearby. She realized that she was on the top floor of the Great Hall of the People; the old man must be the Deputy Premier, Huang Shi-ke. It was the first time she had seen him. He was different from his picture on television or in newspapers. He seemed amiable and gave her a favourable impression. The Security man left after a docile apology to Chen Pan. He had apparently being reprimanded for something or other. A secretary brought champagne. Chen Pan, shading her eyes from the light, looked at a calligraphy scroll hanging on the wall, something about 'completely recovering the ancient mountains and rivers'.

Chen Pan quickly composed herself: everything became clear. Perhaps Huang Shi-ke wanted to do Ouyang Zhong-hua a favour hoping that it might help to undermine Shi Ge. It would be worth while to be on good terms with the Green Party now that its influence was growing. Chen Pan felt that she was about to be released, which meant that the case against Shi Ge must be complete.

Huang Shi-ke brought her a glass of champagne. 'I envy you young people,' he said, with a gesture that included Ouyang. 'Especially young lovers. Your beauty and your future makes old people like me quite sad .... But of course it is useless to be envious. We should drink to happiness and life. Come!'

Ouyang raised his glass with a smile. His face was suffused with pleasure, his eyes were on Chen Pan.

One full glass of champagne remained untouched.

A report received by the US Central Intelligence Agency.

Secret instructions have recently been sent by Moscow to Russian intelligence organizations and personnel in China requiring them to find the Secretary-General of the Chinese Communist Party, Lu Hao-ran, with the utmost urgency. He disappeared without trace before the arrival of the United Nations Peace-keeping Force and has not been seen since.

The entry of large numbers of Chinese refugees into Russia has become an extremely serious problem. Moscow has lost all confidence in Shi Ge, who has not only taken no measures to control the refugees but has been secretly encouraging them to cross the frontier. Moscow is urgently looking for someone to replace him, someone capable of counteracting the influence of Huang Shi-ke in order to insure that the Beijing government is friendly to Russia.

Russia is no longer a communist country but, in its own interests, will not hesitate to support a communist government in China; for the simple reason that a puppet government cannot be other than autocratic and undemocratic. There is a certain logic in this. The United Nations does not consider that China is a defeated or an occupied country, therefore former leading figures have not lost their legal status.

Consequently, Lu Hao-ran continues to hold the position of Secretary-General of the Chinese Communist Party, President of the People's Republic and Chairman of the Central Military Commission. In name at least, he is the Head of State and supreme leader of the country. If the Russians are allowed to find Lu Hao-ran, it will be difficult for us to oppose his return to power. Lu himself is a nonentity but he is at the centre of a complicated power structure and his resumption of power will be the source of problems and dangers difficult to foresee, and will obstruct the implementation of our China policy.

In the long term, the containment of Russia's imperial ambitions is extremely important for the future of the United States. The invasion of Russia by Chinese refugees is an unexpected windfall that will turn Russia's imperial dream into a non-starter without our having to confront Russia directly or expend lives and raw material.

In the short term, it is in our interests to consolidate the status quo, make sure that Russia does not escape the troubles caused by the China tangle, and prevent her from controlling China as she desires. For these reasons we must find Lu Hao-ran and ensure the Russians never find him.

A Buddhist nunnery near Beijing.

In Lu Hao-ran's mind, time had become something empty and without dimensions. He did not know how long he had been here. Since the night of rioting in Beijing when Zhou Chi suddenly appeared and lifted him with infinite lightness from his sickbed, all he remembered was coming here through a confused alternation of darkness and the light of fires. Since then he had been in this dark secret chamber and not seen the light of day.

He was wearing a light blue nun's robe and hat. His head was shaven and shiny. He had lost his spectacles long ago, which made the darkness even more opaque. But his mind was extremely clear. He no longer needed anything worldly. Even eating, which had troubled mankind for ages, had become unnecessary to him. It would have been better if Zhou Chi had not insisted he drink a bowl of milk every day. In the two weeks since he had started to abstain from cereals, he felt every day as if he was flying to a peak of boundless radiance. The foreigner who had come here with Zhou Chi said that he looked very like an old nun. In fact in the *real* world, the difference between male and female was merely skin-deep. Zhou Chi was intolerably worldly, Lu Hao-ran reflected.

He knew that it was not Zhou Chi who had changed: it was he himself who was flying upwards. He used to need him as if he were a god. The day Wang Feng had thrown him into prison, he had clearly felt the rim of death pressing against his spine. He did not know what had changed him. Since he had lived in the dark chamber, he had miraculously thrown off the past. What group *qigong* exercises had failed to give him he had mastered himself and had suddenly and effortlessly expanded and dissolved in the dark universe. He needed no group to collect or transmit energy at will. He could shrink into the size of a needle's point and swell to equal the whole of heaven and earth. He felt there was a river of sweet dew flowing, filling the darkness and from his skin penetrating the depths of his body, filling it with happiness like water in an ancient well. The last bond was cut. He had perfected himself. What a word, so simple and yet unclear. But he was sure of it. Looking back, everything was so insignificant. There was no suffering, no happiness in the world: the searching and fear were futile. To be perfected or not was nothing but a doorstep: cross it or stay outside. He had never been one to prostrate himself at the feet of a great master, but now he knew there was no great or little in the world, no master and no disciples. He himself had gone far beyond any great master and was wandering leisurely on the rainbow at the horizon while men like Zhou Chi were bustling about in the minuscule world of man.

A prolonged intestinal rumble interrupted his measured breathing: he should not have drunk that bowl of milk. Two weeks without wanting to defecate had led to an increasingly formidable build up in his intestines. He had thought to dissipate the turbid gases by means of *qigong*, but that was easier said than done.

Zhou Chi and the foreigner arrived in a most surreptitious manner, their faces hidden by the nun's gowns they were both wearing. The foreigner had a photograph in his hand and looked at Lu Hao-ran from all angles for some time before showing that he was satisfied.

From a single word the foreigner said in his own language, Lu Hao-ran judged him to be Russian. He spoke excellent Chinese and expressed his dissatisfaction about the state of Lu Hao-ran's health. That was probably the reason why Zhou Chi had been insisting on a bowl of milk every day. The two men were clearly bargaining, as if for a draft animal worth a great deal of money. Lu Hao-ran closed his eyes and said nothing, as if he had heard nothing.

Zhou Chi repeatedly assured the Russian that this place was completely secure. To prove it he gave an order to a young nun who always slept in the room next to that of Lu Hao-ran. The young nun stretched out her hands, palms forward, and an oil lamp hanging on the corner of a building opposite was extinguished. Lu Hao-ran had seen her strike a man dead by the same movement, a violent character who was trying to rape her. She had then thrown the corpse into the secret room, as if it was no more than a ball of cotton. On another occasion she chased away a band of vagabonds who were looting the impoverished nunnery. Lu Hao-ran had to share his room with the corpse for several hours.

To put the Russian at his ease, Zhou Chi ordered two extra strapping nuns to join the guard outside the secret room. Before leaving with the Russian, he told Lu Hao-ran that he would be taking him to Beijing tomorrow.

In the middle of the night confused noises came from the ante-room, as they had every night since the young nun had been sleeping there: but tonight the noise was three times louder. Lu Hao-ran did not know anything about the young nun's way of life but he had read that there was often homosexual promiscuity among nuns. The racket went on half the night then suddenly stopped completely. Lu Hao-ran's belly ached terribly, and he had more and more difficulty in bearing it. Normally if he only wanted to urinate, he used a small pipe in the secret room, otherwise—as now—he had to go outside, where there was a temporary privy, used during building work. He had often bumped into the young nun there in the middle of the night. She would merely roll her eyes in the dim lamplight and seemed not in the least bashful.

He took up the oil lamp from the altar niche. The heavy copper lamp-stand was icy cold in his right hand. There was a black cast-iron handle in the stone wall. You had to push it to the left than pull it back to the right, and a stone door swung open without a sound. Who knows from what century it dated or what its original purpose had been, but it was perfectly made: though the door weighed several tons, it was as easy to open as a book.

Strange, Lu Hao-ran thought, there was a large cupboard for

scriptures and in the worm-eaten back panel of this where there had always been a small door, there was now only a large, naked black hole. As he stepped through an unfamiliar hot smell entered his nostrils and there was some thick, sticky liquid under foot. He shaded his eyes from the light of the lamp with his free hand, enabling him to see into the room. There were naked bodies all over the bed and on the floor, so tangled up together that it was difficult to make out any one human form. But a closely shaven head was very clearly visible.

The oil lamp fell from his hand; it did not go out but burned even brighter. He saw the eyes of the young nun staring, lifelessly, like those of a dead frog. He saw her pubic hair, surrounding what proved without doubt that the young nun was a man. A real nun he had brought here to pass the night with him, was still under him, and between her withered breasts was a large bright red wound.

This was the last thing Lu Hao-ran ever saw. He did not see whether it was a club, a dagger or a pistol with silencer that put an end to his life. But as his sight vanished, he heard a voice say something in a tone of admiration. Yes, it was in American English. . . This was Lu Hao-ran's last judgement.

11

Xian and Taibaishan – Near the Great Wall, North of Beijing – An ocean basin in the Pacific – Westward from Xinjiang – The Chinese-Russian Frontier, near Manzhouli – The Southeast – North China: Zhangjiakou

Xian and Taibaishan

The helicopter was to have refuelled at Xian before going on to Taibaishan; but Ouyang Zhong-hua had seen before landing that the oil depot was nothing but a large black hole. When he pushed open the door of the helicopter a nauseating smell of old cinders hit him. The carcasses of several hundred trucks were piled up all round the crater, and white smoke like gauze still hung above smouldering tyres.

The manager, a strong fellow who seemed unshaken by the catastrophe, greeted them with a black toothed smile.

'You're too late', he said with the butt of a cigarette between his lips.

There was an oil depot in each of the provincial capitals to supply anyone arriving by car or helicopter who could prove they were on official business. The United Nations Peace-keeping Force had yesterday delivered by air thirty tons of petrol and eight of diesel oil. Ouyang had arranged for the depot to be notified that he was authorized to refuel the helicopter on arrival.

The cigarette butt moving in all directions like the barrel of a gun, the manager described how, after the departure of the United Nations aircraft, trouble had started, as might be expected, when vehicles people had stolen, found or seized by force, descended on the depot in a disorderly mass. Since there were no pumps, they had all come with any receptacle they could lay their hands on and began using buckets, wash-basins, even cooking pots, to fill their tanks. There were soon several hundred vehicles, all jammed together, so that those who had filled up could not leave. People jostled each other, petrol was spilt and the air, already heated by all the engines, became thick with petrol and exhaust fumes. Perhaps someone lit a cigarette, or perhaps there was a spark. Who knows? For whatever reason, thirty tons of fuel exploded like a bomb.

The pilot refused to fly on to Taibaishan. The helicopter was already low on fuel, and if there was not enough for the return journey to Xian there was no means of getting some sent.

The depot manager found a hand-pump on wheels and they took some fuel from one of the aircraft to fill up the tank of one of the many vehicles abandoned in the streets that an aircraft mechanic had put into working order.

Ouyang Zhong-hua, his secretary and bodyguards drove to the city. The great Dayan Pagoda, almost 1,300 years old, had been blackened by the smoke from the burning depot. There were no birds to be seen and no sound to be heard.

The streets were swarming with rats, like a swirling tide of filth. At an intersection there was a large, bulging pile of them, composed only of the tails of hundreds of rats. When Ouyang's bodyguard fired a shot, hundreds of heads and little red eyes appeared. When he fired again most of the rats scuttled away, revealing two human skeletons, arms around each other. A knife was buried in the chest of each. Only scraps of flesh remained between the bones. Soon more rats came and buried their heads to get at it.

Ouyang was astonished that he felt a sense of beauty, like a great swelling current. He had been several times to Xian and disliked it each time, as he did all Chinese cities. He had come to understand why he was moved by the silent expanse of the Gobi desert to the northwest and the high plateau further west. It was because they were deserted, dead lands that made him solemn, pensive and conscious of eternity. They enveloped him in solitude and made him detest everything dying: a sick and filthy body on a bed, the stench of putrefaction, the groaning and vomiting. Each time he saw withered plants covered with the grey dust raised by the wheels of passing vehicles, or a dried-up river bed like a scab, or a stream reduced to the size of a worm, watermelon skins, empty condom packets, metal utensils piled up at the corners of streets, old people and young desperately searching for water, he thought of a description he had read somewhere of a small town that was dying. North China was dying of drought, the South of damp and mould, the coast of drugs and stimulants. China was really dead now, therefore the most detestable city had become a thing of beauty.

'Take me to the Museum of Terracotta Warriors,' Ouyang said. His secretary, who was driving, looked surprised but turned the car and said nothing. It was in the opposite direction to Taibaishan, a round trip of fifty miles. The buried army of life-size figures had suddenly come to mind and Ouyang wanted to see it again. Perhaps for the last time.

He had not imagined that the sight could be so saddening. The thousands of terracotta soldiers that once had stood erect were now lying down, as if the whole army had been wiped out. Previously, visitors could see them only from the galleries that crossed the excavation where the figures had been found and were exhibited. The museum had been burnt to the ground and everything was open to the sky and the scudding clouds. Ouyang went down into the excavation. The soldiers, now fallen and broken, presented a sight more imposing than when they were drawn up on parade. Fine sand carried by the wind had begun to cover them layer upon layer. Soon the plain yellow earth would bury them a second time. Would they ever be found again? He saw the body of a fair-haired foreigner who had been crushed by the broken figure of a general. China had no defences now, neither in the air nor on the frontiers; international robbers of antiquities had come to China as if it were their own back yard, to dig up whatever they wanted—smashing what they could not carry in order to increase the value of what they took. The foreigner was probably a victim of gang warfare among these 'collectors'. Bullet holes were visible in the figures near the body. Sand blown by the wind already covered their faces and his feet. O China! Is this your history, a great pit full of broken figures?

The road to Taibaishan was in a pitiful state, like any other road in China now. Road maintenance no longer existed. There was no other vehicle in sight. Potholes and the ruts carved by tanks crossing the road made the journey excruciatingly uncomfortable. What remained of the Wei River, heavily charged with mud and sand, flowed sluggishly as if at any moment it might come to a stop, gasping with exhaustion. A succession of tomb-mounds of ancient emperors could be seen on the plain, increasing the feeling of approaching death. Not long ago the countryside was a boundless expanse of green, but the winter wheat planted last year had been trampled into the mud. A few cadaverous men squatted there searching for seeds that had not yet become soggy, which they ate, mud and all. Dead bodies lay face down on the ground.

People had turned their backs on mines and factories, schools and cities and running, crawling and weeping had thrown themselves on the fields. They had turned this splendid, flourishing land into a lifeless world for the sake of the commonest, cheapest, simplest little cereal grains, the most basic and essential sustenance of the whole country. Even the dead were still peering with sightless eyes into the earth.

The Ministry of Agriculture had reported that this year grain had been sown on only a third of the arable land. Ouyang Zhong-hua suspected that this was no more than a rough estimate. Moreover, the figure included winter wheat planted last year, most of which had long been plucked off the stalks and eaten. There would be no harvest this year. After spring sowing there would probably be no harvest either, because starving people were scratching up the seed before it could even sprout. Sowing was only a part of the process: there had to be enough grain to feed people for months. What was the use of an autumn harvest if people had already died of starvation? Or if the growing crop was looted before it ripened? The experts may say that there will be only 30 per cent of normal planting; but the truth is that next year there will be no harvest, because there will be no seed to plant. Therefore there will be no harvest the following year—or ever again.

A band of staggering people had cornered a wild dog that lived on dead bodies. It was big and well-fed and easily escaped them and loped off. The kind-hearted driver fired a shot at it out of the window of the car and the dog fell. In no time it was eaten raw by the starving people, who fought each other savagely—to the point of drawing blood—over a piece of dog-meat.

After the disappearance of grain, a new food-chain had evolved. Wild animals such as dogs, rats and carrion crows, propagated rapidly and also became food for the starving. People learned how to collect maggots from dead bodies, wash them and half dry them in the sun, to reduce the taste of human flesh. Some people lay down and pretended to be dead, bore the pain of an attack by carrion crows and sometimes managed to catch one and eat it, feathers and all. This would keep a person alive for a few days.

Ouyang looked silently out on this scene. The day of disaster was approaching. The great calamity he had been hoping for had begun. The new world of the future could be born only out of this disaster. But the foretaste of what was to come was so horrific and tragic that it froze even his blood, though he had the reputation of a man of iron and stone. Once begun it could not be reversed. As always new life was distant and hazy—more than hazy. The only thing to strive for now was to avoid death, before the future could even be contemplated.

The Environment Protection Bureau he now headed, Ouyang reflected, ought to be called the Life Protection Bureau or, even better, the Bureau for the Preservation of a Minority of Lives. However much the Bureau expanded, however hard he and his colleagues worked, the survival bases would be insignificant; however much they grew, they would never be able to resist the flood tide. Most of the new bases had been set up in desert oases or on high plateaux or off-shore islands. The purpose was not so much to save people as to hide them or, to put it another way, to save the minority it was necessary to isolate them geographically, so that they would not be engulfed by the majority. The original six bases of the Green Association were not located with this in mind. All of them could easily be reached on foot and the protected plants and animals of the nature reserves had attracted starving people like a magnet. The Taibaishan base had already been attacked and was in the hands of destitute marauders.

There were more and more dead bodies on the road and the car had to swerve continually, making Ouyang's head spin. He was wondering whether it would have been better to abandon the Taibaishan base, rather than sending Big Ox to recapture it. It was the bigger of the two surviving bases, its loss would weaken the Green Association but strengthen the Green Party. Nevertheless, he felt a little nostalgic about the rather theatrical aesthetics of the Taibaishan community. Moreover, the twenty-five tons of compressed rations and tinned food secretly stored there was a good reason for not abandoning it. But the main reason was Ouyang's pride. He still resented his rejection in favour of the Multi-level Election system. To have the base under his control would give him some satisfaction. His own base at Shennongjia was strong as a rock, while Taibaishan, under that hare-brained democratic system, had been overrun. That was more convincing than any theoretical explanation.

Recovering the base would not be difficult, but he had not foreseen that it would turn the Association against both him and the Green Party. He had been obliged to come in person to deal with the problem: the behaviour of Big Ox. The commander of the Green Guard may have been stupid, but he had realized that Ouyang wanted to take control of Taibaishan and that the best moment was now, when the leading members of the community had gone to teach at the Green University. This was no more than his typically peasant cunning, but this stupid fellow had taken it as his bounden duty to carry out the take-over himself and not leave it to someone else to do. So as soon as he arrived at Taibaishan, he considered himself King of Taibaishan, and the Green Association, even Ouyang himself, would have to knuckle under. During an argument with the Sage, he twisted his arm behind his back so hard that he broke it—and laughed.

The Green Guard had been waiting for a long time when Ouyang's car arrived at the county town. They were passing round a bottle and wolfing food from tins. They were all armed to the teeth with various weapons, from the latest automatic rifles to big swords with red tassels and had cartridge belts slung over their muscular bare chests. In the space of a few months these once proud, and honest young peasants had become utter devils. When they recaptured the Taibaishan base, their indiscriminate killing was the reason for the hatred the Green Association members felt for them. The Taibaishan radio described the way they took pleasure in killing, sparing neither the women and children nor the old. People were used as targets for shooting competitions and so on. Ouyang did not entirely believe this: intellectuals tended to exaggerate, but he believed that the young peasants of the Green Guard had indeed sold their souls for fresh blood.

When the Shennongjia base was being extended as well as during the Spring ploughing, protection had been necessary from the hordes of starving people, bandits and gangs of deserters from the army. Fighting was frequent and savage. The Green Guards had become brave fighters, and had captured enough arms to fill two cave dwellings. But even the best of them, developed an abnormal self-confidence in their own power. They became cruel and heartless when they saw terrified people go down on their knees and beg for their lives, or the blood that flowed when they fired. Peasants, after all, are not notoriously soft-hearted.

Ouyang made Big Ox get into the back of the car, where he sat with his automatic rifle between his knees. When Ouyang reprimanded him for the way he had behaved he merely grinned as he refilled the magazine and seemed to be hardly listening. He still obeyed Ouyang, but no longer worshipped him as before. Ouyang suddenly felt he could no longer be sure of him. The Green Association had reacted very strongly against the Green Party on account of Big Ox's behaviour. Ouyang had sent a message through the Taibai radio station ordering Big Ox and the Green Guard to leave Taibaishan immediately and wait for him at the county town. He was informed that Big Ox had refused on the grounds that he had not understood the message and did not believe that it was Ouyang's voice. He had also said that if anyone tried to pull a fast one on him he would smash his head in. Ouyang then obtained a short-wave transmitter and repeated his order to Big Ox in person. The fact that Big Ox was sitting in the back seat of the car proved only that he had obeyed Ouyang's order; it was enough.

Without turning round and with deliberate severity Ouyang said, 'There's an ancient play about an officer who, after offending a civil official, has himself bound and tied with thorn twigs goes to the official's house, as a sign of repentance. That's what's going to happen when we get to the base.'

'What? Put on a play?' Big Ox said with a laugh. The thought appealed to him for an instant. . .

'If you laugh again I really will give you a birching.'

Ouyang disliked this kind of bantering reprimand but it was necessary. The incident with Big Ox had done Ouyang no good politically. He had become known as someone who did not shrink from employing people who were extremely violent. What made him furious was that there should be such violence in the Green movement. Big Ox deserved to be severely punished, but this was not the moment: Ouyang needed him too much.

On entering the Taibaishan Mountains, the car left the main road and took a track. Ouyang relieved his secretary at the wheel. Before he had driven twelve miles, he saw that the pass ahead into the mountains was blocked by several hundred starving people with wild, dishevelled hair and dirty faces distorted by suffering, some with teeth bared like animals, making threatening gestures as they piled up rocks to block the road. Others ran towards the car, brandishing clubs and crude spears, their clothes so torn and tattered that they looked like feathers.

'Run them down,' Big Ox shouted . 'If you stop we're finished.' He took up his automatic rifle and tried to lean out of the window of the car, but his broad shoulders stuck in the frame and his automatic shot holes in the roof of the car.

'Don't fire!' Ouyang ordered furiously. A glancing bullet had hit the secretary's leg and he was screaming with pain. The faces of the destitute people could not be clearly seen. Ouyang was determined not to turn back—it was too late in any case. If he drove on over those emaciated bodies, it would be like crushing dry twigs. Big Ox was right: if they stopped they would be dead men.

The roadblock was complete. The ditch on the left was a dried bed of stones and mud, and it was about ten yards lower than the road. The car could easily turn over. In the instant when the clubs were about to strike the bonnet of the car, Ouyang accelerated and turned the steering wheel violently to the left. The brakes were totally ineffective. The bottom of the car scraped over stones with the noise of squealing like a pig being killed. The car seemed to take off in a cloud of dust. The dry bed of the stream was smoother than the road.

Ouyang felt relieved but not relaxed. He wondered whether the encounter with the starving people had been a matter of chance; or had the Taibaishan base been attacked again? Without the Green Guard it was defenceless. After finding his way on to the track again, Ouyang drove as fast as possible, the cold mountain wind blowing in through the broken windows. Big Ox was reloading his rifle. The administrative office of the base was in sight. Alerted by his secretary, Ouyang saw, on the slope to the right of the road, a man running unsteadily, covered with blood and followed by a marauder with a spear, getting closer and closer. Suddenly the running man tripped and fell flat on his face. The other man slowly raised his arm with all the pleasure of someone about to impale a toad. Ouyang put his hand on the arm of his bodyguard, who was preparing to fire. He had recognized the Sage, whose arm had been broken by Big Ox. He could hardly believe that he could run so fast. He nodded to Big Ox, who fired a burst—he never bothered to aim. The spear swayed and slowly fell backwards. If Big Ox had fired another burst, the assailant would have been cut in two.

Ouyang carried the Sage to the car. 'It was Big Ox who saved your life,' Ouyang told him in a matter-of-fact tone. A life for a broken arm: no one would deny they were quits. But the Sage's hatred of Big Ox was very deep: he was not forgiven.

He did not look at Big Ox, but said to Ouyang, 'The base has been captured again.' That was obvious. Ouyang said nothing. 'You must go and save our people,' the Sage went on, grasping his arm. He was almost incoherent. He had apparently heard several hours earlier that fifteen or twenty members of the community had not escaped and were now prisoners of the marauders.

'Save them? How?'

The Sage searched for words. Behind his crooked spectacles, which had lost an ear-piece, his eyes looked strange. His only quarrel with Ouyang and the Green Party stemmed from his hatred of violence; he had said that it would be better to lose a hundred bases rather than allow Big Ox and his brutes to kill indiscriminately.

'Think of a way,' he begged.

'I approve of non-violence,' said Ouyang coldly, 'and look forward to a world without it. It seems to me that you would prefer to reason with the marauders and get them to leave. Well then, when it comes to reasoning with people, you are the obvious choice.'

Big Ox began clapping maliciously.

'You are being difficult,' the Sage said angrily. 'How can they be reasoned with? They are beating our people to make them say where the secret stores are. . .'

'What did you say?'

There was a pause. The Sage closed his eyes. 'This is no time to discuss principles. They'll soon have all the stores and our people will be dead.' He was embarrassed and on the brink of panic.

'Then you must tell me what must be done,' said Ouyang. 'This is a Green Association base and we will naturally follow your plan and not go against your principles like the last time.'

The Sage clung to Ouyang. 'Xiao Bi is there and her whole family. I saw some of the marauders push her down on the ground and. . .I beg you to save her. . .'

Ouyang felt disgusted. He knew Xiao Bi. She had formerly been the Sage's housekeeper. She was young enough to be his daughter. For that reason, the Sage had sent his wife and children abroad and had refused to teach at the Green University. Instead he had brought Xiao Bi and her family here.

Once more the unsolved question flashed through his mind: Who are the survival bases for? Who was to be saved and why? The mandate of the

Environment Protection Bureau was explicit: the bases were there to allow the survival of the 'finest' people of China so that they could provide the spark for the reconstruction of the country. But did such people exist? What could be seen everywhere was the decline of morals, the loss of integrity, the death of the spirit. What better proof that a whole people is doomed! What the Chinese people lack is not knowledge or technical skills, but moral integrity and souls The first two can be taught and preserved, but integrity and the soul are the product of centuries of evolution. What hope is there of creating a new world of 'spiritual man'? As always, this question no sooner came to his mind than he dismissed it, pushed it down to the lowest level of his consciousness. It was out of bounds, a threat, a knot impossible to untie. Better die than thinking about it.

'I'm not interested in your Xiao Bi.' Ouyang felt like slapping the Sage. 'Just tell me what is to be done.'

'You've got weapons. . .' the Sage replied in a faint voice, seeming to shrink into something soft and round.

'Make yourself clear. Weapons for what purpose?'

'They're not afraid of anything else. . .'

'So we just show them our rifles? Ouyang said fiercely. 'Or do we use them?'

The Sage blinked pathetically, on the edge of tears.

'Do we fire?' Ouyang repeated, more patiently.

The Sage nodded weakly.

'In the air?'

The Sage burst into tears. 'Don't force me. . .'

Big Ox laughed and jumped up and down. 'Make *him* fire. He's a holy man who won't even step on an ant.'

'Hold your tongue,' Ouyang told Big Ox. 'I'm not forcing you,' he said to the Sage. 'This is a matter of principle between us and it must be made clear. When we save people we don't want to be accused of crimes of violence.'

'I'm not accusing you. They are bandits and deserve death. Wipe them out. Quickly. . . Save Xiao Bi.'

Ouyang turned away in disgust from the pitiful wrinkled face. Bandits? What are bandits? Everyone is just trying to stay alive. Everyone who does not want to die is a bandit now.

'All right. I believe you are a man of honour.' Ouyang could not keep a hint of sarcasm out of his voice. When the time comes don't forget what you have just said.'

'You go,' Ouyang ordered Big Ox. There was no need to send his bodyguard as well. One automatic rifle with enough ammunition would be enough to disperse the marauders. Better not to create more killers. . .

'I'm not going. Let him go and kill them himself!' Big Ox said, but he was already keyed up like a wild beast that had scented his prey.

'Big Ox . I beg you. . .' The Sage slid out of the car and almost knelt at his feet.

Ouyang pushed him back, not wanting to watch this degrading scene. To Big Ox he said, 'Limit the killing. . .if you don't want to go to Hell.'

Big Ox laughed. 'I'm going there anyway.' The automatic rifle in his hand looked like a toy.

'Don't harm our people,' Ouyang shouted after him. 'and kill as few people as possible.'

How many is a few? Ouyang wondered. The way Big Ox ran off impatiently made him realize how far Big Ox had retrogressed in the last few months and had become a wild beast, bloodthirsty and totally without self-restraint. In this world, to be strong was to be a wild animal like him. Enlightenment and reason had given way to barbarity and muscle. An oppressive sense of dread such as he had never known before invaded his mind like a thick fog.

There was a sound of rapid fire. He drove to the top of the hill and saw Big Ox, legs apart, mowing down row after row of the starving raiders. It looked as if cardboard figures were being knocked over on a hurriedly erected stage set, rather than a massacre. Except for the sound of piercing screams. Yet even that might have been taken for some loud, high-pitched noise. Big Ox did not stop firing except to change magazines. He was standing legs apart, mouth wide open, blabbering as if in utmost pleasure. He had cornered all the marauders and no one was going to escape.

Ouyang took his bodyguard's rifle and fired into the air, hoping to stop Big Ox. But this had the opposite effect, since Big Ox thought that others were coming to join him.

Ouyang's shoulders drooped. When he closed his eyes he could see the whole great land of China, its rivers and mountains, covered with a blanket of white bones. Who could prevent the annihilation of this people? It was doomed to disappear and the process had begun. Did a degenerate, backward people whose spirit was dead have any reason to continue its physical existence?

The motive force of social transformation has always been to satisfy people's desires. But the Green society of the future intends to restrain peoples' desires: only fear will make them accept, a memory of terror that will make them tremble even in their dreams, that will forge the collective consciousness of man: only that will make it possible to realize the transformation. What greater terror can there be than the annihilation of a people? Big Ox was only a minute instrument carrying out his first great massacre. No one could save these pitiful people, no one could save the disaster stricken nation. China was finished, it was fruitless trying to prevent it. Only welcome this inevitable, world-shaking and unparalleled annihilation.

Ouyang had a vision: boundless glaciers were creeping forward, dazzling the eye. . . .herds of dinosaurs looking up to heaven and bellowing a long and mournful cry.

Near the Great Wall, North of Beijing

This part of the Great Wall, which starts north of Beijing and ends at Jiayuguan, nearly two thousand miles to the west, was built under the direction of a famous general of the Ming dynasty. From the tallest tower on the wall Beijing is visible, a hundred and twenty miles away. Much of it crosses mountains at dangerous-looking angles. The beacon and defensive towers are closely spaced, sometimes only ten yards apart and each different. The wall was designed, not only to stop the advance of an enemy, but also to allow fighting to continue on the wall itself.

Chen Pan had not realized that it was possible to be so tired. She leaned against the battlement, aching all over. All day and every day since the establishment of the special training course, she had been on the march, over the mountains, or roads selected for their difficulty. The training included survival techniques, hunting, identifying edible plants, how to survive hunger and thirst, how to make bivouacs and live outside in the worst possible weather, how to deal with snakes, light a fire in the rain, avoid illness, handle psychological problems: everything that might be encountered in the most difficult situations.

There were 531 men on the training, 164 instructors; and they had a complete set of *shugua* production equipment of an improved design, made up of small units easy to transport. The plastic tubing could be taken apart into lengths that one person could carry, together with the *shugua* growing from it and the nutrient fluid, so that growth was never interrupted. Whenever necessary the complete unit was assembled and the nutritional fluid topped up. All the factories were now producing such units as fast as possible. Technical problems had been basically solved. But Chen Pan, like the others did not know what the purpose of all this training was, or why the *shugua* equipment had to be portable.

She need not have come out on exercises and was the only woman to do so, but the mobile production of *shugua* was new, and since she had to teach a course on it, she wanted to see how it worked in practice. She also wanted to know exactly what the training consisted of. She had personally selected all the trainees and felt a strong bond with them.

When she had been called back from abroad the Chief Secretary had been very reticent on the telephone, but his tone implied that this mysterious 'important work' was something out of the ordinary. Even when she knew what it was, she still did not understand why it was being kept so secret.

A special committee had selected a little over fifteen hundred of the best students of the Green University based on results in each part of the course, as well as on their imagination, will-power, organizing ability, independence, sense of responsibility, logical thinking, state of health and so on. Finally, Chen Pan was to assess each individually and decide whether he could be confidently entrusted with the fate of several million people.

She thought this absurd. But the Chief Assistant was very serious. 'This is what the Premier wants and he chose you himself.'

So she came to the Green University as a kind of 'Inspector General'. The selection committee passed on to her a detailed dossier on each person and the members had been told that the final decision was hers. She thought it was a ridiculous idea because she did not believe that she was qualified to make judgements on so many fine people. Apart from that it was not a bad method. All those involved were men and in the circumstances, it was probably better to rely on a woman's intuition rather than on 'experts'. Of course it must be a woman with a highly developed intuitive sense, trusted, unprejudiced and honest. In the eyes of Shi Ge she was just such a woman.

It was in the middle of this heart-warming thought that Chen Pan lost her self-confidence. It would take her two years to read through all the reports and she only had five days. She had been chosen because she was the sort of person who could ignore the reports: they had already been examined several times by different people. In the end she abandoned any thought of basing her judgement on reason. She did not even ask a person's name, merely said a few words, asked some question or other, and met only once and in public. She made her mind blank and allowed each man to project himself, so to speak, so that she could obtain her first reaction: yes or no. She did not alter her judgement whatever her subsequent doubts might be. A member of the administrative personnel was beside her, nodding or shaking his head as she did. Then the names were taken down in two separate registers.

She had been given no quota, merely told to select those she judged qualified, and felt for the first time what it was like to have power. Those she selected were immediately formed into the 'special training unit'. The programme of training had been drawn up by Shi Ge in his capacity as Director of the Green University. Neither the Executive Director nor the commander of the battalion knew what the purpose of the training was. Nor did she, though few people believed her. The other two, she reflected bitterly, had at least talked to Shi Ge, but the only contact she had been granted was through the tiresome Chief Assistant.

The sun was already in the west. The clouds, the mountains—everything—glowed as if covered with gold leaf, concealing other colours, the mountains, clouds—even the mighty wind. Only if one looked closely could one see the green tinge of moss on the ancient bricks of the Great Wall, and the miniature flowers growing between them. The whole Special Training Unit was assembled on a part of the Wall that was sloped like a lecture-theatre, facing a platform on which four hundred years ago, the great general Xu Jiguang announced the disposition of his troops. Now it was to be used as a stage for a speaker who had not yet appeared. The place for a helicopter to land was marked out on the platform.

Xing Tuo-yu, as deputy commander of the unit, once again took the roll-call. He was one of the first persons Chen Pan had selected. Instructors had been positioned as guards. The place had been carefully examined several times for intruders, although it was difficult to image that anyone would come here. Nevertheless, curfew was in force and the guards were placed at a distance where no one, including the instructors themselves would be able to hear anything said in the open-air 'lecture theatre'. Chen Pan was present not because she was privileged, but because everyone assumed she knew everything, so no one told her to stay away.

She leaned limply against the battlement of the Wall and had no intention of leaving. She could hardly walk and wanted to hear what the lecture would be about.

The trainees in the row next to her were collecting ants. They tasted good with a little salt and it was part of their training to compare the taste and nutritional value of various insects. Since starting this part of their training they had not been provided with any grain at all. Apart from the growing *shugua* they carried, they had to find all other food for themselves, in the wild. Surviving according to the principles they learned was part of their training. The instructors received a daily ration of 200 grams of biscuit and 100 grams of tinned food. Chen Pan was exhausted. She could hardly imagine the exhaustion of the trainees who had survived on the insects they had managed to find. Those who had not been chosen were lucky. Someone began to sing, in a hoarse voice:

I walk the ancient road,
A road that is desolate and cold.
The trees are wizened with age.

I walk in the northern desert.
The desert is desolate and vast
Once there was water, now the rivers are dry.

The sky became increasingly bleak. Fiery clouds began to pile up and wind began to howl through the battlements, as in tales of ancient warfare, when arrows fly from crossbows.

A helicopter appeared like a bird out of the sky, its rotors forming a transparent semi-circle of golden light. Its body and glass reflecting the rays of the evening sun, as if it were on fire too. It flew straight to the meeting place on the Great Wall and came down towards the landing space until the skids were a few inches from the ground. Someone opened the cabin door and stepped out. The helicopter rose quickly, as if suddenly pushed out of the way, and flew off, leaving Shi Ge alone on the platform.

Chen Pan felt as if the wind, her hunger, even her heartbeat had all stopped. In the dream-like light, only he seemed to exist. He looked older. It was only a few months since she had last seen him, but his hair, gently blowing in the wind, was already grey-white and there were deeply-engraved wrinkles on his face. He still looked kindly. But whereas in the past this kindly look concealed his strength, now, although his slight smile was extremely kindly, the impression of strength was dominant. She was sad to see him so much aged.

'Please come closer,' was the first thing he said. 'I am not going to use a loudspeaker or shout. I have come to meet you here in order to avoid the listening devices which are everywhere in the city now. I have been given a guarantee that no unauthorized person is nearby. But the secret that I am going to tell you is so important that I am obliged to speak almost in a whisper.'

His voice was very calm, but it did not entirely conceal his unusual agitation. Everyone pressed forwards. Chen Pan did not move: she had been in the middle, now she was at the back. Perhaps because the wind was in the right direction, or because of the special nature of the occasion, each word Shi Ge said seemed to have been whispered in her ear. Every intake of breath, every nuance of his voice was clear.

'I can tell from your eyes,' Shi Ge said. 'That you all wish to hear what it is that I am asking you to do. You had the right to know from the moment the training course was set up. Thank you for your silence and determination. Thank you for suffering hardships without knowing the reason. Silence and determination are both difficult, especially together. Even if I knew them, it would be impossible for me to tell you the full extent of the difficulties you will undoubtedly encounter in the future. Perhaps in the history of mankind, no harder task has ever been attempted.'

The sun's rays began to be tinged with red. There was silence on the Great Wall, apart from the low soughing of the wind in the desolate weeds.

'I need not tell you about the situation in our country. The reports you have been given every day to read, are all that I have seen myself. Neither you nor I can say what the future will be. That is something the survivors will have to think about. What we are faced with is death on an unprecedented scale. In a month's time China's reserves of all forms of food will be exhausted. The day is rapidly approaching when even natural sources of food, such as edible species of animals and plants, even the bark of trees will be exhausted. International aid can no longer provide what we need. Yesterday's imports were only 17% of what they had been: two weeks ago, we were able to feed 170 million people, saving them from death by starvation. Now we can only feed 30 million. Mortality now stands at 3.5 percent and in the near future that figure will double. We estimate that three weeks from now mortality will rise to twenty or thirty percent, even more perhaps. Three to four hundred million will die of starvation. What about the longer term? The remainder of the population will be left in this desolate country to wait for the day when time and nature re-establish a balance between population and resources. This will involve perhaps a billion deaths from starvation. A billion is merely a statistic; but imagine them all as someone's brothers and sisters, wives and children.'

'My friends! History has put the fate of the Chinese people in our hands. We must lead our people to escape from death, to resist the inevitable, no matter what immutable laws or regulations, or even God himself, stands in the way. You are those who will have to fight all impregnable fortresses that will obstruct the migration of the Chinese people. China must leave this land of no hope, only that will allow these billion people to live.'

'In the world of today, the concept of sovereignty is as sacred as Holy Writ. The whole world has been divided up by state frontiers, armies, weapons, and barbed wire. Some countries are huge and rich, with fertile land and forests; some are poor and crowded, or full of deserts and barren mountains; in some countries the land is overcrowded, in others there is fertile land where no one lives. Some land is crowded with people, while elsewhere there is land which has never been put to the plough. Inside our frontiers there are dead everywhere, but if we look beyond the frontiers, we can see unused spaces and resources. History has imposed on us an unquestioning respect for sovereignty, but when the lives of several hundred million people are at risk, sovereignty must take second place. There is nothing more important than the right to life. This principle should be universally accepted. China has no other choice but to save a billion of its people by a mass migration that will break through the barriers of sovereignty.'

'It is you who are going to lead the people out. This is the reason why you have been through all kinds of difficulties and hardship in your training. This migration will be a tremendous shock to the world, and if any news of it leaks out the reaction will be so violent that the whole plan will come to nothing. I am sure you understand the necessity for vigilance and secrecy. There was no choice but to keep the truth from you, just as there is no choice for the Chinese people but to migrate.'

'From very early on, the pressure of population forced Chinese to emigrate. Today they number 60 million. In earlier times they were not well thought of in China because they had left their ancestral homes. But the new wave of emigration towards the end of the 1970s changed this attitude and many people thought that going to live abroad was a road to wealth, comfort and a successful life. Those who did so were wise and enterprising and not just going abroad as cheap "coolie" labour. Their departure was noticed and others were encouraged to follow. So there has been some psychological preparation for mass emigration.'

'In the 1990s the number of people who left by boat increased enormously, and not long ago seventy million people broke through the frontier into Siberia and Outer Mongolia. This was the spontaneous beginning of the great migration. What we must do now in the shortest possible time is to increase this migration to the greatest possible extent, so that we save the lives of the maximum number of our people from extinction.'

Shi Ge made very few gestures as he spoke. In the failing light of the sunset his darkening figure stood out more and more clearly against the sky.

'Now let us look at the routes the migration will take. You have all memorized a map of the world in your minds. From now on you must get used to the fact that only there will you find this information. The most important route will certainly be to the north. Siberia is three times bigger than China and its population is less than 50 million. Outer Mongolia is nearly 1.6 million square kilometres, and its population less than three million. The natural resources of these two regions together can feed four to five hundred million people. If we deduct the indigenous population and our 70 million migrants already there, Siberia and Mongolia can still absorb 300 million of our people. Our common frontier with these two regions combined is several thousand kilometres long.

Apart from the northeast, where the frontier follows the course of the Heilong and Ussuri Rivers, access to the rest of the frontier can be on foot and the migration should present no great difficulties.'

'The second route,' Shi Ge went on, 'will be along the Old Silk Road through Afghanistan, Iran and Turkey to Europe. Although there is not much space in Europe, its wealth should enable it to feed 200 million—at least we hope so. We have little chance in Asian countries: most of them are as poor and crowded as China. Japan and South Korea are rich but minute. So for the remaining 300 million, we have to consider sending them across the ocean. The USA, Canada, Australia are all rich and spacious countries. The problem is how to get them there.'

Chen Pan naturally thought at once of the young government official she had met in Amsterdam who had been sent by Shi Ge to buy up old ships. If he had spent more money, she reflected, and bought up all the old ships in the world, it would still not be enough for 300 million refugees. But, as Shi Ge was explaining, a large number of ships and boats had been assembled in ports along the coast, that could take people abroad. A billion destitute people had been cleverly enticed to the border areas and the sea coast to await the moment when they would simultaneously sweep over all barriers or embark on ships. People would suddenly realize why the route through Xinjiang had been kept open, even at the cost of bloodshed and why such an immense movement of starving people had been put in motion. Xinjiang was of vital importance: it was the gateway to Siberia northward, and westward to Europe by the Old Silk Road. Several hundred million could cross the frontiers there. To get them to Xinjiang was an achievement comparable with the building of the Great Wall.

O Shi Ge! Chen Pan's eyes flooded with tears. She looked at him standing there alone, speaking without brilliance or ostentation with the utmost simplicity. Yet with his silent, hidden strength he was preparing to do something God himself could not conceive of. She suddenly realised the significance of his order to hand over full information on *shugua* technology to all countries unconditionally. It was so that the Chinese refugees should have enough to eat when they had left their homeland. Perhaps it would not be enough, but it was at least giving all there was, and not relying on others.

The sun turned red. In the east a silver moon rose as the sun set. An eagle circled high in the sky. Shi Ge's voice seemed to merge with the wind on the Great Wall.

'My friends. This migration is going to be extremely difficult. A spontaneous break through a frontier is not likely to be repeated. Russia has sent large forces to protect the frontiers in Central Asia. In summer the

Heilong and Ussuri Rivers will no longer be frozen over and will once again become serious barriers. The frontier in Outer Mongolia is defended by Russian troops. Between Xinjiang and Europe there are four countries and more than 3,700 miles. To get to Australia and the USA there is the Pacific Ocean to be crossed. On every route, without an extremely strong and able leadership among the refugees, it will be absolutely impossible to operate on a large scale. Spontaneous and scattered attempts to get out of the country will not help our plan.'

'We need men whom people will naturally turn to because of their character, knowledge, wisdom and authority, who will become the nucleus of groups numbering hundreds or tens of thousands and more. They must be superlative organizers who can provide structure and order amongst people who have lost all other hope. They must be outstanding strategists who can keep the initiative in the most adverse situations. They must be gifted natural diplomats able to win the sympathy and tolerance of governments and peoples in situations where there is great hostility. There need not be many such people: five hundred and thirty one will be enough. You are these future heroes!'

'It is not my role to discuss the details. Aircraft will come for you very soon. Specialists will tell you about the plans, your tasks, technical matters, briefing and so on. Tomorrow you will go to your posts and the migration will start immediately. I now ask you to make a choice. It was not possible to do so earlier and I apologize. But this is the last, the only opportunity. As far as character, power of reflection, physical strength and skills are concerned, every one of you is capable of surviving in China in the most difficult conditions. If anyone survives, it will be you: you have no *need* to leave the country. What awaits you if you do is endless wandering, hatred and scorn; you will be chased away and suffer hardship, oppression and insult. You will have to face all kinds of armies, weapons, whips, concentration camps, even death. Your lives will be a continuous succession of difficulties, and the burden of responsibility for tens of millions of lives will weigh on you until you are tired to death. You will have to carry silently in your hearts the suffering of the whole people, wind and rain, the heat of the sun, all kinds of hazards and an interminable journey. You must each make yourself an indispensable linchpin, without any official appointment, and no support from any power structure. You will have to depend entirely on yourselves from beginning to end.'

'You will be nameless heroes. There will be no record of your acts, no laurels, no acclamations. The government will not help you, whatever the circumstance, or admit that it sent you, that in any way it organized or put the migration into operation. If you are beaten or tortured, or even taken out and shot, your country can do nothing for you. The government may even have to condemn your activities and apologize to the world.'

'I ask you now to make your choice. Anyone who does not want to undertake this mission has the perfect right to withdraw immediately. If this is what anyone feels called upon to do, I beg him not to hesitate. The battalion commander will make all the necessary arrangements.'

Shi Ge was silent for at least three minutes, turning his head to look at the sunset beyond the waves of mountains. The wind blew this way and that. Among the trainees no one moved. Chen Pan was in tears. Shi Ge then looked steadily at these young men, so calm in the face of death.

'Dear brothers. Look again at our country, while the sun still shines; at the mountains that have seen five thousand years of history. Look at this Great Wall built by our distant ancestors, look at every plant and tree, watered by their blood. How beautiful our country is, our rivers and mountains! How many great minds, how many heroes have paid homage to its beauty! But now. . .now. .' Shi Ge's voice broke and his eyes filled with tears. 'Whether the flame of China continues to burn, depends on you.' Suddenly he bowed low to his audience.

Chen Pan held her hand tightly over her mouth, and sobbed.

In the failing light of the sunset, helicopters appeared out of the splendid clouds edged with fire. The eagle circled higher and higher until it became a barely visible dot.

An ocean basin in the Pacific

It was pitch dark except for light emitted by some species of marine life. The sun never penetrated to this depth. Even a large object could pass by unseen.

The submarine moved very slowly, followed by a blue electric eel that had made its home somewhere in the superstructure. At the stern, under the hull, multiple jets propelled it forward at the speed of 3.5 knots. The submarine hugged the edge of the basin westward, keeping in a deep sea current. Another thousand sea miles and it would reach the American continental shelf.

On the surface a typhoon was blowing, whipping up huge waves and causing havoc in the submarine sonar detection base in Hawaii. But in any case the submarine made no sound and could not have been detected even if there were no typhoon.

It was like a wild animal and understood when to crawl forward to reach its prey. Patience was the key. Opportunity was always there. The important thing was to avoid detection before pouncing.

Westward from Xinjiang

News suddenly started to spread among the Chinese migrants massing in southern Xinjiang. France, Britain, Germany, Italy, Switzerland—almost all the important wealthy European countries had decided to open their frontiers to Chinese refugees and allow them to settle there. They were all to be given work, lodging and would receive relief money. For people getting only half an American 'famine biscuit' a day, this news was like a drowning mariner sighting land. These countries, where in the minds of the refugees bread grows on trees and rivers run with milk, had been inaccessible because they had no passports, no visas and no foreign currency. Now these things were no longer needed. The people of these countries were so rich that they did not know what to spend their money on and like all foreigners are happy to help people so that they would go to Heaven, just like Buddhists in China.

More details were added as the news spread more. But this rumour was not like others. It did not spread gradually, but was heard by a hundred million people simultaneously like an explosion. If anyone had followed the thread, like that of a spider's web, it would have been obvious that the rumour had been spread deliberately.

Among the migrants there were a number of people who were both ordinary and special. In outward appearance they were much the same as everyone else but their temperament and character were distinctly different. They had the easy manner of intellectuals but their knowledge and ability to survive and their competence and willingness to turn their hands to any kind of work, was exceptional. They had all arrived among the migrants quite recently, but already groups had formed around each. They all had miniature solar-powered radios, and regularly listened to broadcasts from Beijing through ear plugs. The broadcasts were in a secret language, such as were used in Secret Societies, and they all listened on the same day and at the same time. They also received news from various western government broadcasts, and the crowd around could hear English, French, German or other languages, which none of the migrants could understand. Fortunately there was someone to interpret. But whatever was said in the broadcasts, the translation was always the same. If the few people who understood a foreign language had not been deliberately kept out of earshot, they would perhaps have heard something about a new German car or a review of an opera in Paris. In this way the rumour was picked up from several different sources simultaneously, and naturally had the effect of a bombshell among the migrants.

One rumour became increasingly clear and precise: the Kunjirab pass into Pakistan was open and the government had agreed to let Chinese refugees cross the country on their way to Europe. They would even be provided with transport. There was another rumour to the effect that because of the dense population in Europe only a very limited number of people would be admitted. Entry would be stopped once the limit was reached.

About 200 million refugees were led westward by this news. After Russian aid stopped and aid from other countries was much reduced, relief stations in West China progressively closed, so even without the rumours the refugees would have started to move. The rumours immediately 'suggested' the best direction.

Twenty million migrants near Taxkorgen, in the extreme west of Xinjiang, only about 110 km from the Kunjirab Pass and the frontier with Pakistan, were the first to move, assembling in the region of Kashi, Shule, Wuqia. Others at Yecheng and Shache (Yarkant) realized they were falling behind, and went on fast with great determination—sometimes marching day and night. Another large contingent that had assembled further north, heard not a whisper of the news about Europe, but did hear a rumour of a flourishing land to the north, and therefore set out for Kazakhstan and Siberia.

Along the two main roads through Western and Southern Xinjiang, as well as on local roads and tracks, there was a constant stream of refugees. So many that people were forced to walk in the desert alongside the road.

Everywhere there were people carrying *shugua* equipment; in most cases the early, heavier version. The 100 metre long plastic tubes in which the *shugua* were growing, were carried on a whole series of bicycles joined together, which greatly limited the speed of the march. The majority of the refugees now lived on *shugua* alone. It mattered little how heavy the equipment was or how unpleasant it was to eat; it was better than dying by the roadside.

When Beijing first sent the equipment most people were not interested. But as international food supplies dried up, *shugua* teams formed around each production unit and made themselves responsible for production and distribution. Almost all of them practised the Multi-level Election System, because the lives of the migrants depended on *shugua* and whoever mastered the production technology, was naturally in a position of power and became the nucleus of each group.

All those who joined the refugees with the *shugua* equipment were from Green University and its regional branches. Their function was to spread the Multi-level Election System among the refugees. They did not believe in the rumours about Europe, but did nothing to obstruct the movements of the their *shugua* teams, because they knew that nothing could be worse than staying where they were. Some probably smiled secretly, having perhaps expected this move.

The production of *shugua* was far from enough. Very little material was available for making the nutritional fluid; water was also in short supply. Because of these reasons, the *shugua* teams often ignored the people kneeling along the roadside begging for *shugua*. Fighting often erupted and many production units were wrecked. To put a stop to the violence, a rumour was spread that at Taxkorgan, there was plenty of *shugua* equipment and mountains of nutritional material for making nutritional fluid. Make for Taxkorgan at once, before it's too late!

Even before they arrived there, people could see helicopters landing. A whole fleet of heavy cargo helicopters dropped supplies of material and the newest models of the equipment that could easily be dismantled; the tubes now had valves at each end so that the fluid could be retained during transport. The equipment could be operated by one person, which increased the speed of production. A work team from somewhere or other, was methodically organizing migrants who were completely destitute into groups, as well as urging members of the older *shugua* teams to infiltrate the new groups, so that they were not deprived of technical know-how and organizing experience. Since the new equipment was technically superior, it was not difficult to persuade them. They also recruited other refugees to make up for those who had left.

An increasing number of migrants were organized in this way and the self-governing capacity of the migrants was greatly increased. Several team leaders joined together and elected the higher-level leadership and more and more organizational levels were established, proving that the Multi-Level Election system has distinct advantages in such unstable situations.

Beside the Yarkant River, there were piles of dried material. No one knew exactly what it was. It looked like dried dung, but contained what looked like fragments of bone. The refugees who had come north in the railway wagons wondered what this material they were sitting on was. They soon learned that it was raw material for making the nutrient fluid for the *shugua*. Even without the use of a crushing mill, this material could be mixed with water and put in the fermentation vats. This was exactly what was wanted, because it would probably be impossible to obtain what was needed to make the fluid when passing through foreign countries. Many of the refugees used their trousers as sacks, stuffing them full of this material and, carrying it on their shoulders. Without it there would be no *shugua*. The heavier it was to carry, the fewer people would starve.

The refugees climbed up the Karakorum highway to the Kunjirab Pass and entered Pakistan. The work team leaders, who had all been very sceptical about the rumours, could hardly believe their eyes: the frontier was open and the refugees were calmly crossing into Pakistan in an endless stream.

All the signs were that Pakistan was prepared for what was happening. From the Kunjirab Pass to the frontier with Afghanistan there were troops, police, reserve forces, tanks, armoured cars, and machine guns drawn up to form a corridor. Artillery was in place on strategic hills and there were helicopters overhead. Close by powerful loudspeakers warned people—in Chinese—that their safety would not be guaranteed if they left the corridor. At night the refugees had no choice but to pass the night sitting on mats, the women huddled together for warmth.

What astonished everyone was that the Pakistan government sent a large number of trucks of all shapes and sizes, most of them pulling trailers to take the refugees further. Many of these vehicles had come from China and there had been no time to paint over the markings. Fuel for the trucks came through a special pipeline from China. A Chinese was directing the *shugua* teams on to the trucks, while Pakistan army and police, under his direction, kept order. Before embarking in the trucks, those with bicycles had to hand them over to some of those travelling by foot, to make the journey easier for them. In fact, when they saw trucks falling from the precipitous roads into deep canyons and bursting into flames, they had few regrets at not being able to travel in such relative comfort. Especially as the trucks were packed and overloaded. Many of the weak did not survive the journey, but those who rode in the trucks could travel in half a day the distance that took several days on foot. Apart from stopping at regular intervals to allow Pakistani vehicles to pass, they travelled day and night.

The convoys stopped in Afghanistan but bypassed Kabul and made for the frontier with Iran. Afghanistan had also made a corridor for the refugees to pass, but far less strict than that of Pakistan; hardly more than a few soldiers sitting in machine-gun posts, watching the strange sight of an endless river of people. People also came from the villages to watch. From the Kunjirab Pass to the Iranian frontier, a distance of about 1,240 miles, took fifty hours by truck, but forty days on foot. The bicycle teams transporting the *shugua* tubes took twenty days.

When the Turkish ambassador to Pakistan was invited to the embassy by the Chinese Ambassador, he assumed that it would have something to do with the world-shaking problem of the Chinese refugees. Turkey would certainly be one of their next stopping places and, although there was still Iran to cross, Ankara had been sending urgent messages every day instructing him to report on the situation.

In the basement of the embassy was a round tent-like screen made of some kind of special metallic matting, connected to the electricity mains:

it was the most up-to-date baffler against electronic eavesdropping available. The Chinese Ambassador courteously led the Turkish Ambassador into the 'tent'. The latter was very surprised to find a Chinese Deputy Minister of Foreign Affairs already there, having received no hint of his presence in Pakistan.

The Deputy Minister was new, and unknown in the world of foreign affairs. When he spoke, he had none of the agile language of diplomacy but was serious and sure of himself. He first explained the efforts China had made to prevent refugees flooding into neighbouring countries and admitted with great regret that these efforts had failed. The flood was too great and had broken through the frontier of both Pakistan and Afghanistan, and it was now impossible to stop them, let alone bring them back. China had no choice but to go with the tide and ask the Turkish government for help.

'What sort of help?' the Turkish ambassador asked uneasily. For security reasons there was no interpreter present, but both of them spoke English.

'By allowing our refugees to go through your country on their way to Europe.' The Deputy Foreign Minister looked at the Turkish Ambassador's beard.

'Absolutely impossible,' the latter exclaimed. His surprise was caused less by the prospect of a flood of refugees passing through Turkey, than by the fact that the Ambassador could even make such a request. He had been a diplomat all his working life and thought that his Chinese counterpart must have gone mad: it was like asking a neighbour to help by pulling his house down.

'Our people will do no more than pass through. They are just like you and me: they know that only Europe has the ability to save them. No one will remain in Turkey; their passage will take no more than forty days: even less if Your Excellency's government can provide them with transport, as Pakistan has done...'

'Impossible. This is absolutely unprecedented!' the other replied firmly.

'Precedents are man-made...'

'But such a precedent would destroy the very concept of sovereignty. It would be a threat to world order.'

The Chinese Deputy Foreign Minister shook his head, perhaps in regret. 'This is not a question of making a precedent. But sticking to the letter of the law is no solution: on the contrary, it will bring about disaster. Forget about principles of foreign relations and look at the actual situation: two hundred million Chinese refugees are assembled on the frontier of your country. How can you stop them from entering it? By killing them? Turkey is not going to kill two hundred million people for the sake of sovereignty. Modern standards of civilization would not permit it. Nor does the Koran. Nor do you have enough troops to slaughter two hundred million people. Perhaps they could prevent two hundred migrants from passing in an orderly way through a corridor, but not a huge flood that would cover the whole of your country and drown your sixty million inhabitants in a sea of refugees. Your politics, economy, culture, society—all would be swept away. I am confident that Your Excellency, with your wisdom and experience can envisage this prospect very clearly, and will persuade your government to make the only wise and reasonable choice.'

The Turkish Ambassador was silent for some time. He was trying to envisage two hundred million people. Finally he said, 'It is not yet the moment to discuss this with my government. Wait until they have crossed into Iran.'

Everyone knew that Iran had a way of looking at things that was different from other countries and made her neighbours a little nervous. Now it had become a shield to hide behind.

'Iran has already agreed,' the Deputy Foreign Minister said. 'Iran understands that the disaster that has overtaken the Chinese people is due to the oppression by the superpowers, and that it is only right that they and their allies—the wealthy countries of Northern Europe—should bear the burden. Throughout history Asian and Third World countries have suffered from colonial depredation. Now whole continents that are not yet developed, but have abundant resources, are being colonialized by the superpowers. The world is over-crowded and resources are almost exhausted: the time has come for "counter-colonialism". How many millions of your people have already moved to Europe because of poverty? In the past the colonizers were the great powers, now they are the people of poor countries. The weak have an account to settle with the powerful. Teheran is well aware that the Third World cannot possibly defeat rich countries by military means. Their only weapon is poverty. The government of Iran has already agreed to provide transport by rail for our refugees. With the cooperation of your country, the railway wagons can go from Mashad direct to the frontiers of Greece and Bulgaria. The crossing of Turkey can be very rapid. This helps the refugees and greatly reduces the length of their stay in your country, which is very much to your advantage. I request your Excellency to consider this very seriously. If you refuse it is certain that the refugees will break through your frontiers anyway. In that case your people will not tolerate your government detaining two hundred million refugees in the country and you may well have a war on your hands. . .'

'This is blackmail!' the Turkish ambassador protested angrily.

'Not at all. The Chinese government wishes to make a deal with you. We have no money to offer you, but we have priceless treasures and antiquities enough to recompense your country. We also intend to grant you a permanent enclave within China, as an expression of gratitude for opening your frontier to let the refugees pass. Do you not urgently need a port on the Pacific? We offer you a choice of Qingdao, Dalian, Ningbo or Wenzhou... '

The Turkish ambassador showed interest when he heard the mention of an enclave. 'What else do you want apart from free passage and rail transport?' He had abandoned none of his caution.

'Some basic necessities for survival, such as water...'

'No one could provide enough food for so many,' the Ambassador interrupted.

'Our specialists made available to you what is necessary for the production of *shugua*, to supplement what the refugees produce for their own needs. We hope that you will be able to provide some *shugua* and grain as soon as possible. In addition we hope you will provide a little extra material for the production of nutrient fluid. On our side, we will send you the medical equipment and medicines we have received from world aid. A major outbreak of plague would be terrible for your country.'

'Will the refugees be allowed to cross Greece and Bulgaria?'

'Please do not worry about that. Both countries have agreed to create a corridor, so the migrants will not enter the interior of either country. The corridors will pass through Macedonia and Yugoslavia, and, from then on, Turkey will not be affected.'

The Ambassador hesitated, then said 'I must get confirmation from those countries.'

The Deputy Foreign Minister smiled. 'I beg you not to do so. No government is going to confirm such an agreement. Nor can your government ever admit to having allowed the refugees to cross Turkey. You can only say that they forced their way through the country.'

'Is that what Pakistan and Afghanistan have done?'

'As I said, our refugees entered by force.'

The Chinese Ambassador, who had sat silent through this, knew better than anyone how many sleepless nights and hungry days it had taken for the whole staff of the Embassy to arrange this 'forcible violation of frontiers'.

While the Deputy Foreign Minister and the Turkish Ambassador were meeting in Islamabad, another Chinese Deputy Foreign Minister was in a secret meeting with the Iranian Ambassador in Damascus and told him,

'Turkey has already agreed.' Within minutes the Turkish Ambassador heard that Iran had agreed. Officials from the Chinese Foreign Ministry were also busy in Sophia, Athens and Belgrade. During this time the Chinese Foreign Ministry was worked off its feet. To the west of China only two Deputy Foreign Ministers were involved and almost a thousand personnel. In other places they were being withdrawn.

The Chinese–Russian Frontier, near Manzhouli.

The weak light in the cabin of the helicopter came from a single shaded bulb that added to the impression of stealthiness. A Japanese technician behind Li Ke-ming kept fussily adjusting the angle. Li Ke-ming disliked the way he kept his feet firmly on the frame and wondered what was the reason for his apparent anxiety and restlessness.

When the operation was being planned Li Ke-ming had insisted that to be effective he must appear to be floating through the air. Only that would produce a strong enough impression on the panic-stricken refugees and make them turn back from certain death. With an ordinary cable and harness people would be able to see at once that he was hanging from the helicopter.

On the frame provided by the Japanese, he would appear to stand steadily in the air, as it were, and would be able to make certain movements. The plan had been put forward by 'the man from Beijing' and the most difficult problem had been finding a suitable frame. A Japanese special agent who was present immediately undertook to procure one and in thirty hours the design, construction, testing and revision had all been completed. The frame had arrived in an almost silent helicopter, also required for the operation.

Two Japanese technicians who had come to take charge, bowed in the usual Japanese way and said a few words in Japanese, which Li Liang translated: 'They are asking you to go up and carry out a test in the helicopter.'

Li Liang, a distant cousin of Li Ke-ming, had been a section head in the Heilongjiang Foreign Trade Department and spoke both Japanese and Russian. He was now interpreter with the refugee guerrilla force. Since the fighting started on the frontier with Russia, he had not left Li Ke-ming's side.

The helicopter rose. This new Japanese helicopter was several times quieter than an ordinary one. In the thick, cloudy darkness and with the sound of the wind and people on the ground shouting as cover, it was not necessary to fly at more than 100m, and no one on the ground would see that Li Ke-ming was suspended underneath it and indeed seemed to be flying. Li Ke-ming felt uneasy that both the pilot and the technician were Japanese. But for the fact that only they could provide what was needed so quickly, he would never have allowed them to meddle, or put himself at the mercy of foreigners whose motives were far from clear. He had asked Li Liang to accompany him, not only to interpret, but also to have someone reliable with him.

Li Ke-ming was lifted out of the helicopter and let down on a thin black hollow cable that did not reflect light and was therefore almost invisible in the dark. He could be lit up from head to foot by means of a optical fibre cable, with a switch in the cabin. Extremely fine steel cables linked various parts of his body to different points on the frame. In this way his movements and gestures could be controlled from the helicopter.

The wind was strong and buffeted his steel mask. Without the sophisticated control that could be exercised from the helicopter, the frame would have been blown about in all directions. While adjustments were being made to suit Li Ke-ming's weight, he took the opportunity to examine the lie of the land in the direction of the frontier, ten kilometres away through his binoculars.

On the Russian side of the frontier, a kaleidoscope of searchlights was visible. There were occasional bursts of machine-gun fire here and there. On the Chinese side, all was dark and silent. But below, along the 70 km stretch of frontier west of Manzhouli, ninety million refugees were assembling and increasing in numbers by the minute, under cover of the night. When would the 'spontaneous' crossing of the frontier begin? The man from Beijing had insisted that they must wait for it to happen.

'We already have forty tanks,' Li Ke-ming had told him, 'and thirty-eight guerrilla units in Russia. That will be enough to open a breach in the frontier so that the refugees can get through.' In two months Li Ke-ming's guerrilla force had grown from his original following of a few men to nearly a hundred units and had become the largest Chinese guerrilla group operating inside Russia. They were intensely loyal and disciplined, but this 'man from Beijing' (no one knew anything else about him) had no sooner appeared than he seemed to be on an equal footing with Li Ke-ming, if not higher.

'No. No,' he insisted. 'If we initiate an operation with tanks inside Russia that would be an invasion. We must at all costs avoid hostilities between China and Russia. It is not only here that our refugees are going to cross, but along the whole frontier. If four or five hundred million of our people are going to survive there, it's essential for the Chinese government to maintain a neutral position and have some room for manoeuvre. Military action can only be undertaken by the refugees' own guerrilla force.'

'Sooner or later the tanks will have to be used and cross the frontier,' Li Ke-ming said.

'That's different. If it is not a deliberate attack on the frontier, but a response to a Russian subterfuge—a trap for instance—they could not hold the Chinese government responsible. We would argue that the tanks were abandoned by Chinese troops and appropriated by the refugee guerrillas when they secretly returned to Chinese territory.'

Abandoned? Who would believe that? It was the 'man from Beijing' who had led the guerrillas to the tanks. Their engines were not yet cold, the fuel tanks were full and they had plenty of ammunition. When this man first appeared in the thick Russian forest, his arm was in a sling made from parachute nylon. Li Ke-ming was sure he had been sent by the Chinese government. He knew all about the assembly of 190 million refugees in the region of Manzhouli. In fact he had details of the whole operation in his head, as if he had organized it himself. In the northeast this was the only sector where the frontier did not follow the course of a river that would prevent the refugees from crossing. It was protected by strong and resolute Russian forces. The 'man from Beijing' had come to ask the guerrilla detachment to come back from the Russian side of the frontier and help the refugees cross. Since being framed for a crime he had not committed, Li Ke-ming had a hatred for anyone in the government, but this man had won his confidence.

Li Ke-ming's only reason for living was to fight for the right of his countrymen to survive. The guerrilla detachment had many times defeated Russian attempts to wipe it out and had fought constantly to enable the refugees to establish a base in the vast Russian Far East. His guerrillas had once cut the Trans-Siberian Railway and prevented the Russians from bringing up reinforcements. They had even occupied a town and painted in large letters on a wall the words: 'Lenin gave back the Russian Far East to China.' Nearly all the refugees regarded Li Ke-ming almost as a god who was trying to save them. They called him 'the iron-faced general.'

He agreed without hesitation to the request of the 'man from Beijing' and immediately sent an order to the thirty-eight guerrillas units to go with him to Manzhouli.

As they approached the city they found that just north of the frontier the whole Russian population had been evacuated from a triangle formed by the Ergun River and two railway lines, forming a large pocket, the entrance of which faced the 190 million refugees massed on the other side of the frontier, in China.

The railway lines, forming two sides of the triangle, looked from a distance like hurriedly constructed walls, being entirely covered with passenger wagons, in which Russian troops had set up machine guns, in two rows, one above the other, so close as to be almost touching.

A captured Russian soldier admitted that their orders were to prevent the refugees from charging across the railways and denied knowing anything more. But he had a gas mask in his pack, and said everyone had been issued with one. Li Ke-ming and 'the man from Beijing' were very alarmed by this, but could no longer doubt what they suspected after hearing a report from a Japanese intelligence agent.

This man had frequently offered to help the guerrilla unit. Li Ke-ming had always chased him away from the secret camp and reprimanded Li Liang for bringing him. Now it was vital to know what the Russians were planning. The Japanese agent, who spoke Chinese very well, put his finger on the map. 'This is the China-Russia frontier where we are now. Elsewhere it is protected by the river which is now in flood and impossible for the refugees to charge across. This is why the Beijing government has sent all refugees from the northeast to Manzhouli, where there is no river.'

'That has nothing to do with the Chinese government,' said the 'man from Beijing' dryly.

'But it has something to do with the secret Green University training course,' said the Japanese agent with a radiant smile.

'Can you prove there *was* such course?'

'No. I do not intend to try.'

'Then don't repeat rumours.'

Li Ke-ming had heard of the Green University because there were graduates among the refugees who were trying to introduce some sort of election system; but this was the first time he had heard of a training course. The reaction of 'the man from Beijing' convinced him that it really existed and he had some connection with it.

The Japanese agent, who only wanted to show off his knowledge, went on with his explanation.

'The entry of Chinese refugees into Siberia is a catastrophe for Russia. There is much unrest in Central Asia already because of ethnic conflict. The huge territory of Siberia is still stable. But if they cannot prevent several hundred million Chinese flooding in, Siberia will become Chinese, and without it, Russia might well disintegrate. So they will stop at nothing to prevent this.'

'The Russians know about China's policy of concentrating refugees in various places,' he went on. 'They can hold the Manzhouli section of the frontier, but attacking the refugees once they assemble, will only make them disperse and that will be even more difficult for them to handle. The water in the Urgun River will go down in a few days and, over a distance of a hundred or more kilometres, they will be able to wade across the river and cross the Mongolian grassland to the west. If the Russians attempt to defend the whole line, they will lose the advantage of concentrated fire. They have realized that passive resistance is useless. The only way of stopping the 190 million refugees from entering Russia is to wipe them out.'

'That is what they are planning to do. They have deliberately opened a breach of 70 kilometres in the defence line, and when the refugees attempt to break through, they will be met with immense Russian firepower from the other side. The refugees will be thrown into confusion and will rush in the direction where there seems to be no danger. That is to say into the pocket. Once all 190 million are there, the entrance will be closed. Then up to a hundred tons of grenades and rockets containing VX sarin poison will rain down on them. Death will take no more than seconds. The depopulated triangle will suddenly be populated again—with 190 million corpses. Although the cost of burning them and cleaning up will be immense—millions of roubles—it will be far less than the loss of Siberia and the disintegration of Russia.'

'. . .Ten times worse than Hitler. . .' Li Ke-ming was so shocked he could not get the words out. 'How could they face the world?'

'They won't need to make any excuses,' said the Japanese impassively. 'They'll cover it up, that's why they are going to get the refugees to cross into Russia first. Then they'll announce that they have disappeared into the Siberian forests and indignantly deny all accusations.'

There was a deathly silence. 'Why are you telling us this?' Li Ke-ming asked in a husky voice.

The answer was ready. 'If I speak of humanity you will not believe me, so I will be frank with you. Japan's present prosperity is extremely precarious. If we do not obtain more space and resources for our future generations, they will live permanently in fear. For us, as for China, Siberia is like a Promised Land. But we cannot get possession of it on our own: we are not strong enough. That is why we are helping the Chinese refugees. Numbers have become a weapon. However strong Russia is militarily, she can do nothing to prevent several hundred million Chinese from settling and multiplying in Siberia. Sooner or later it will inevitably belong to the yellow races. We and you come from the same stock. Japan's wealth and technology plus China's population can transform Siberia into a new homeland of the yellow races. For the common interests of our two people, we naturally cannot stand by and watch the Russians destroy the greatest weapon we have for the conquest of Siberia.'

The helicopter slowly came down. The winch started to bring Li Ke-ming back into the cabin. The frame was now properly adjusted and it only remained to wait for a spontaneous breakthrough to begin, tonight.

'Wait!' He had seen the lights suddenly go out along a part of the Russian frontier, and in the vast triangular space where the trap had been prepared, no lights could be seen.

This could not be the work of the guerrillas, he was certain, because the previous day he had sent a unit to cut the power-lines to the searchlights. He had waited all night but the searchlights remained on and his guerrillas did not return: they must have been killed. The refugees were terrified at the brutality of the Russian troops and would certainly not dare to attack them. If the guerrillas had succeeded in extinguishing the searchlights, the refugees would probably have taken the opportunity of sudden darkness to start breaking through the frontier. Li Ke-ming was convinced that it was the Russians themselves who had turned off the searchlights, with exactly the same purpose in mind. Both they and the refugees were impatient for the breakthrough to start.

A sound like the roar of the tide came from the direction of the frontier, like an endless succession of waves breaking on a shore. Li Ke-ming felt as though he was suspended over a dark ocean, suddenly whipped into violent waves by a submarine earthquake. The breakthrough had started.

The Manzhouli railway on the west side of the trap was still brightly lit. Searchlights swept back and forth. On the higher ground, against the light, tiny figures of people could be seen falling under the machine-gun fire. Crowds of refugees were running, like an immense flock of sheep fleeing from the long whip of a shepherd, towards the other railway line, to the protection of darkness, where there was no firing; only darkness like a wide-open welcoming gate.

The helicopter did not need to land. Li Ke-ming used the radio to contact the 'man from Beijing', who was directing the operation on the ground. The forty tanks hidden in a mine began to move, the deafening roar of their engines made inaudible by the sound of the huge mass of refugees. The tanks were all manned by disbanded soldiers from the former tank regiments, who had joined the guerrillas. The 'man from Beijing' had miraculously 'come across' several tank instructors who, as chance would have it, were familiar with this variety of tank and trained the crews in a few days. However, if the Russians had not deliberately left the trap open, even ten times as many tanks would not have been able to cross the frontier. There were no mines, no anti-tank rockets, no Russian troops even. It had never occurred to the Russians that anything but helpless refugees might enter the trap—and destroy it. The helicopter flew across the frontier into Russia. There was no moon, only the swirling black clouds, and a few drops of rain. Li Ke-ming would not allow himself to be winched back on board the helicopter: he could see better from where he was.

The Russian railway line to the west was lit up by searchlights, and a row of powerful beams was directed eastwards. From the long fortified wall of passenger wagons, innumerable machine guns were firing at the sea of people surging this way and that like a herd of terrified wild horses. At the frontier with China, the Russian troops turned their weapons in the opposite direction and, by their fire power, forced the fleeing crowds in a northeasterly direction, to where the Russians had prepared to use their poison gas. The gunfire had the same effect on the migrants as a precipice does on water. They threw themselves like a torrent in the direction where there was no gunfire. On the dark earth, there was a dotted red line. A large number of the guerrilla force had been positioned among the refugees. Each guerrilla had a flashlight covered with a red cloth, pointed upwards. They had orders to remain always in the front line of the crowd to show Li Ke-ming which direction they were moving in. They were moving very fast. A flood of people 70 km wide was being drawn forward by the instinct of self-preservation and fear of massacre, towards a darkness where there was no hope of life.

Li Ke-ming and his colleagues had been racking their brains for hours, trying to think of a way to make the ocean of refugees change direction and save themselves. They could be informed of the Russian plan by word of mouth; but that would only make them afraid to cross the frontier, which was their only hope. .

What if they crossed the frontier and, then under the leadership of the guerrillas, fought their way through the fortified railway to the east? However, no one believed, that in their desperate state, the refugees would remain sufficiently calm and rational to obey the guerrillas.

Time pressed. Mortality among the refugees was increasing by the hour. Finally the 'man from Beijing' went off alone and lay in a wood for two hours, working out a plan. When he told the others, they were sceptical. Everyone said it was unthinkable and would not believe it was the only way to get the refugees over the frontier. But there were no other suggestions. . .

The helicopter flew a certain distance over the immense crowd, then returned. Li Ke-ming checked on the direction then gave the order to start. The fine optical fibre draped around his whole body made him clearly visible from the ground, but from a distance it was impossible to identify the source of the light. It would be best if the 'deity' suddenly appeared when it was almost dark, flying fairly close over the refugees.

'Fellow countrymen!' Li Ke-ming shouted into a small microphone hung round his neck; powerful loudspeakers amplified his voice so that it sounded like thunder. He heard people below shouting, 'It's the Iron Masked General!'

He was already a legendary figure among the refugees and for several days 'the man from Beijing' had been spreading the word that as soon as they were in Russia, they would see him showing the way. Now he was flying in the air above them! His steel mask shone gold, he carried a rifle and a sword, and the long feathers of his martial head-dress, still used in Chinese operas, wafted in the wind as he floated in the air like a mythical warrior. This was what the thousands of upturned eyes most longed for—a god come to save them. The crowd finally overcame its forward impetus, stopping in the darkness of Russia.

'Fellow countrymen, you are fleeing for your lives, but you are going in the direction of death. In front of you there is a Russian trap and you are about to walk into it. They are waiting for you with poison gas and want to wipe out every one of you. Once the poison touches you, you will begin to itch, then to vomit. Your heads will go round and you will fall. Your vision will be distorted. You will be covered with blisters. Your skin will rot away. Finally you will bleed to death. If your nerves are damaged by the poison, you will go mad, kill your own loved ones, bite your own children. No one will remain alive.'

'Fellow countrymen! You must turn back. The only hope of life for you is westwards. The Russian population has not been moved away, so they dare not use poison. Don't be afraid of them firing at you from the railway. Our guerrillas have brought up forty tanks and are at this moment opening the way through. There are thirty-eight guerrilla detachments to lead you. Once you are on the other side of the railway, go northwest, towards the Elena River Basin and Lake Baikal. Huge forests and rich land awaits you. Fellow countrymen! Unless you turn back at once you will all be killed.'

The dotted red line of lights did not move. Li Ke-ming switched off the microphone, and told the pilot to fly a short distance at right angles. He was very agitated. He had said what he had to say—and only once. To say too much, to make it sound like a motherly entreaty, and the message would lose its power to frighten people into action. The helicopter must fly a small distance each time before he spoke again: fewer people would hear but those who had already heard it, would hear it for a second time. Eventually everyone would be warned. But would the people in front turn back? Could they resist the pressure of others behind pushing forwards? The Japanese technicians had guaranteed that the loud speakers could carry a distance of four kilometres. Beyond that people could only follow those in front and push their way back too. If a large enough mass of people did not turn, they would all be wiped out.

When Li Ke-ming had repeated his message for the third time, he finally saw the red line marking the position of the first group of refugees begin to recede. Very slowly at first, then faster, and by the time he had spoken for the fourth time, they were already running. He breathed a sigh of relief: the tide had turned. Now that the first wave had changed direction the rest would follow.

Wherever the helicopter passed, the red lines were moving back. A mass of refugees 43 miles wide could not turn in its own space. The line of red lights in the front had now become the last line, and the crowd hesitated. The shouting of the guerrillas with the torches was probably the turning point. The refugees still flooding across the frontier were pushed westward and the Russian trap was broken open.

The guerrillas' forty heavy tanks made a breach 30 miles wide in the fortified Russian railway line. The Russians had never imagined that the refugees had tanks at their disposal; their weapons were ready for bones, flesh and blood, not for tanks. Russian reinforcements were cut off by an ambush of guerrillas. Bombs dropped on the refugees had no effect. By the time the tanks had all been destroyed by air-to-ground missiles, their mission was accomplished. The presence of Russian inhabitants west of the railway made it impossible for the army to use heavy artillery. By the time a new day dawned, more than half of the 190 million refugees were in Russian territory.

The helicopter from which Li Ke-ming was suspended took advantage of the darkness to slip past Russian helicopters not far away. Light from the optical fibre was out, and the speed of the helicopter made the cable attached to the frame stretch out almost straight behind it and Li Ke-ming was battered and blown about by the air current. Below were the mountains of Russia, dark and silent. Li Ke-ming was overflowing with joy, like a waterfall. He wanted to sing out loud in his toneless voice so that the mountains echoed.

'Winch me in.' He signalled to Li Liang over the radio. The speed of the helicopter increased. Li Yuan must have forgotten him in his excitement. But soon the helicopter was flying so fast that he could hardly breathe, and the wind was whistling through his mask. He could only just make out the shape of the helicopter, like a great owl, flying sideways at full speed. Why didn't Li Liang reply? Perhaps he hadn't heard. No, the cable was moving. . . . But not pulling him in. . .he was getting further away.

'Li Liang! Are you mad?' He suddenly felt cold sweat, over his whole body. There was no sound in his earphones. The strap of his theatrical headgear felt as if it had dislocated his neck. A surge of bloody anger filled his chest. The darkness in front of his eyes seemed darker still and full of tiny coloured stars. He held the head-dress with one hand and fumbled for his dagger with the other. His only clear thought was: Don't cut an artery! He struggled to get the knife under the strap and just as he was about to lose consciousness, managed to cut loose the head-dress, which was immediately carried away. Then he felt himself strike something in the dark emptiness. His leg felt like jelly. Acute pain made him fully conscious. The dark shape of a mountain grew more distant. The dagger had saved his life, otherwise he would have been dashed bodily against the mountain, not just his leg.

'Li Liang you bastard, I'm blind!' The shock had switched on the microphone round his neck: his voice was amplified by the powerful loudspeakers under the helicopter and sounded like a thunderclap. He could hear the panicked voices in Japanese: they must be afraid the Russians had heard.

'Li Liang. . .speak Chinese, you dog-spawned traitor! You've sold out to the Japanese!'

Another peak approached in the darkness. He slashed at the winch cable with his sword, but it only screeched off the hard steel core. The hill came closer. If he had not been strapped to the frame he could have pulled himself up the cable and stretched out his legs to brake the impact of landing. But his body was like a clumsy lump of metal. Only his hands were free. The sword in his right hand hit a rock and sparked. His left hand was smashed, every finger broken. Bone splinters and small stones clattered against his steel mask. His earphones were shrieking. He was being dragged by the helicopter over the top of the hill.

'Li Liang! I'll butcher you, or I'm no man!'

'Forgive me, spare me' his cousin cried. 'It's the fault of the Japanese. They were afraid of the refugees having their own leader and turning against them. They want to make slaves of them. I've seen their cruelty. But I could not go on living like an animal; they promised to take my whole family to Japan. Forgive me. . .I. . .'

He heard a shot in the earphones, then silence.

'A curse on all you Japanese,' Li Ke-ming screamed like a wild beast. Another hilltop. The helicopter tried to come down and smash him against it to prevent him from getting away. There seemed to be no hope. . .except to try cutting the cable again. After hitting the rock his sword was now more like a saw and each cut he felt the core of the cable was giving. In his earphones he heard the pilot of the helicopter scream and saw the outline of a Russian fighter burst through the clouds. Another hill loomed up in front and just as he was about to hit it the cable broke and he suddenly became weightless, then fell into the soft darkness.

He thought at first that it was eternal night and did not expect to see light, but the dew on his mask dripped into his eyes and diluted the blood that sealed them closed. He saw a pale red glow in the clear sky, like Bai Ling's lips. When by the light of the moon, he had washed Bai Ling's body in a clear spring, her lips were still tinged with red like the glow on the horizon. He kissed her lips, and copulated with her dead body. But her eyes were closed forever, no matter how he called on her and pleaded. The red glow expanded, the clear morning air vibrated with the song of birds. His wife appeared from among the trees carrying her child and weeping, but dared not approach. He felt a little ashamed, but stretched out his hand to her. She was his wife, after all, the woman he had always been with. His son was tightly wrapped in white cloth: it was difficult to believe that the bundle contained a living being. Was it time to go home? Yes. What he had to do was done. To go home was perfect.

His mind became clear for a moment. He remembered the helicopter, the winch cable, Li Liang and the Japanese, and in the depth of his mind he laughed. Do you think China is finished now you have killed me? He would have liked to shake hands with 'the man from Beijing', if possible, even hug him. . .but probably not; men were shy about that.

Somehow the whole sky had become red. Some Russian soldiers bent over and looked at him and were excitedly saying something. With his short sword and his last remaining strength he cut a red flower on one of the faces bending over him. He felt the weight of the bullets enter his body and smelled the odour of the Russian earth—the same as the earth at home.

The Southeast

Innumerable ships were moored off the long coast of China, and the famine refugees had been watching them for several days. Construction vessels kept coming and going and small craft carrying passengers shuttled back and forth. On each ship there was welding going on; cranes were at work and there was the sound of foremen's whistles. The old ships from abroad were being towed into harbours and repaired. It looked as if perfectly good ships were being almost completely dismantled. Even guns and radar equipment were thrown into the sea like rubbish. Ships were called back from abroad, others brought to the coast from inland waterways. All naval vessels were turned into transports. Ten of thousands of fishing boats—whose owners had been given material inducements—dropped anchor at various moorings where they were converted and loaded with supplies of fuel oil and drinking water. A large number of them loaded supplies straight from ships carrying international aid.

No one gave any explanation for all this activity until the day it was announced that international aid had come to an end and there was no more food left in the country. Immediately strangers appeared among the starving people, assumed the role of leaders and set up a Refugee Action Group. A day or two later, along the whole coast, they simultaneously gave the order to 'seize the ships!' It was obvious that this is what the ships had been waiting for.

The newcomers insisted that the 'seizure' of the ships should be entirely peaceful; indeed, there was no resistance. The Chinese troops guarding the ports did not interfere; as for the UN troops, they had not noticed any 'incident.' Small boats were also commandeered in the harbours to take a member of the Refugee Action Group to each of the ships moored in the roads. When each appeared on the bridge of the ships, it was a signal that the 'hijacking' of the ships had been completed. The captains and the crew from then on were 'acting under duress' and had no choice but to take the ship wherever the 'pirates' wished.

The Action Group then began to embark the refugees, still in their *shugua* production teams. There was some confusion, but in general everything was done in an orderly manner. The *shugua* equipment was put on the decks, where the plastic tubes were laid out and benefited from the reflection of light and warmth.

As soon as they boarded the ships, the refugees saw that in the tanks of oil tankers or the hangars of aircraft carriers, in all the ships, wherever there was room, shelves had been erected, wide and long enough for a person, and with head-space enough to sit. Whatever they were intended for, the refugees quickly appropriated them to sleep on. Though they were packed tight as sardines, nearly everyone was delighted. The long voyage would be far easier. Those in charge also realized that the bunks increased enormously the numbers that could be carried.

There was silence when the ships sailed, even infants stopped crying. In the bustle of boarding, people had forgotten that they were seeing their homeland for the last time.

Ships of over 300 tonnes set out immediately for the other side of the Pacific. The innumerable small boats, fishing boats, sampans as well as small cargo or passenger ships and motorized fishing boats, were divided between two routes: those setting out from the east coast of China made for Japan, those from the south coast for Australia, with landfalls in the Philippines and Indonesia. These small boats, were everywhere, like a swarm of locusts, as far as the eye could reach.

There was panic in the Philippines and Indonesia. Both had been pestered these last two months by 'boat people' from China and were extremely apprehensive of an even greater plague of 'boat people' now that China was beginning to break up. But no one had imagined for a moment that the exodus would be on such a scale. Secret reports from diplomatic sources put them at their ease somewhat. Beijing informed both governments that neither of the countries were the destination of these boats; but because they were coastal rather than sea-going vessels, they were forced to keep close to land for safety as well as for supplies. Beijing reminded the two governments that one only needs to take a few steps to dive from a springboard and that if they were not prepared to tolerate the proximity of the springboard, the locusts that covered the sea might well gnaw it to pieces. The Philippine and Indonesian governments understood that this cryptic message meant that they should provide food, drinking water and refuge in case of storm. They had no choice but to grit their teeth and agree.

Japan closed the Korean straits and harbours on the west coast of Kyushu, directing the boat people to Kagoshima, where the Japanese government had assembled, commandeered, rented or bought huge sea-going vessels. The Chinese refugees embarked on them enthusiastically and discovered that there was enough water on board for an ocean crossing and Japanese-made *shugua* equipment. The freshly-harvested *shugua* tasted much better than their own.

No one could explain why Japan was being so kind and benevolent. But the government announced to the world that Japan was not able to accept so many Chinese refugees, nor could she condemn them to death by turning them away. Japan would therefore provide sea-going ships and food and let them choose their own destination. Even so, the Japanese captains who had agreed to command the ships knew that the destination had been decided long in advance: the United States.

The Japanese Ministry of Transport had set up a transit directorate at Kagoshima on the understanding that once the refugees were transferred to the sea-going ships, the boats that had brought them would be abandoned. For this purpose tugs had been assembled to clear the bay. When the time came to do so, it was found that the boats, still manned, had put to sea, the larger boats towing the smaller ones. The sight of them going back to China to pick up more refugees was a shock to the Japanese who wondered how many more there were to come.

Many people fled from Taiwan and Hong Kong out of fear of invasion by refugees from the mainland, for whom they were both desirable destinations not far away. They had not collapsed economically. Natives of Hong Kong and Taiwan who had money or special skills obtained visas and fled. The majority of ordinary people did not have the means to do so. The officials in the two places, who remained at their posts out of a sense of duty, had to find a way of protecting those who stayed. Beijing proposed a bargain. If the authorities in Hong Kong and Taiwan agreed to turn a blind eye when millions of tons of shipping in their ports were hijacked—repeatedly even—Beijing would guarantee not to encourage refugees to settle in Hong Kong and Taiwan. In this way, no government would be blamed. The captain and crew of each ship, 'under duress', would be obliged take refugees to North and South America and Australia, then return to the China coast and be hijacked again, until there was no one left to take.

The mass migration of Chinese famine refugees started down the Mekong and Salween Rivers. Starving people on the high plateau of Yunnan province made rafts out of bamboo, or tyres, oil drums or anything else that would float, and passed through Laos, Burma, Thailand and Cambodia. Immense numbers drowned in the rapids of the upper reaches and in some places the rivers were almost blocked by piled-up wreckage and dead bodies. In spite of this, floating down river was a short cut and a way of avoiding slogging through the sub-tropical jungles. Bit it was not a success.

It was difficult for the refugees to remain organized during the arduous journey and impossible for them to take their *shugua* equipment with them. They became captives of the river, vulnerable to dangers, starvation and suffering. The worst aspects of human behaviour gradually showed themselves: the looting of riverside villages became increasingly common, often involving the destruction of whole villages and the massacre of the inhabitants. The organizers had overlooked the fact that within China there was a shortage of material from which rafts could be made. Once there was none left, the refugees inevitably raided across the borders of neighbouring countries, cut down woods and destroyed buildings, leaving desolation behind them.

The tolerance and understanding that the Beijing government had carefully cultivated in countries along the route of migration was lost. Measures were taken to block, chase away and suppress the intruders. Local people organized resistance and took bloody revenge on the refugees, with great loss of life on both sides—but ten times more among the refugees.

They could not all be killed: there were too many, nor prevented from moving on. In the end, up to ten million refugees reached the coast, covered with mud and wounds and leaving a trail of blood. They immediately set out southwards on foot towards the Malay Peninsula. Whatever the shortcomings in planning and choice of routes, the survivors never forgot the repeated encouragement of the organizers, who told them there would be thousands of ships at the southern end of the Malay peninsula to take them to Australia, a sunny and hopeful new continent, as beautiful as paradise.

North China: Zhangjiakou

Under intolerable pressure from millions of Chinese refugees, Russia finally realized that it was impossible to prevent their entry by merely defending the thin line of a frontier. Shi Ge as the head of the Beijing government kept apologizing and promised to control them, but continued in secret to do the opposite. The only solution, Moscow decided, was to establish a broad 'buffer zone'—in China.

It was exceptionally wide, comprising the area of China north of the Great Wall, the whole of the Northeast and Xinjiang—an area of three million square kilometres—almost the size of India. The whole area was occupied in the space of a few days by the Russian army. It was called a 'separation zone'.

'North of the Great Wall' is a vast area and a vague formulation. In fact what the Russians chose to occupy depended on communications, the presence of towns, geo-strategic and other considerations concerning their future administration. The city of Zhangjiakou is *south* of the Great Wall, but that did not stop the Russians from making it their military headquarters.

It was at exactly 19h27 when a Russian colonel responsible for a satellite ground communications station in Zhangjiakou detected a peculiar phenomenon: the ground station suddenly switched on automatically and sent a signal to a communications satellite above the Pacific Ocean. The initial signal that had been picked up was coming from a very weak moving source, clearly a vehicle, that was found to be approaching Zhangjiakou from the south along the road from Beijing at a speed of 80-100 km/h.

A signal in top-secret code, able to transmit an order to a ground station was a matter to be taken very seriously and there was much speculation about who was in the vehicle and why was it approaching Zhangjiakou?

It was not until he was fairly close to the city that Shi Ge thought about Wang Feng and why he had wanted a car that was not registered with the licensing authority. He had been groping among the nameless levers and switches under the dashboard and must have inadvertently touched something, because the car was now riding much higher on the suspension. Shi Ge regretted not having known how to make this adjustment earlier: he would not have been slowed down so much by the pieces of smashed rifles that littered the road in some places. He no longer bothered to slow down and from time to time there was a sound like the clash of swords under the car. Fortunately the tyres were special. It was gratifying to him that the rifles were now nothing but scrap-metal.

The army commanders had accepted his order to disband the armed forces as if they were being asked to die for their country. He had assigned to the army the task of reopening road communications, for the purposes of internal migration, and to ensure the safe transport of international aid. The mission was already completed. Now international aid was coming to an end and the army with it. The millions of weapons belonging to organizations that no longer existed, or no longer under control, would bring disaster rather than order. Innumerable people could be killed. The best final contribution that the army could make to the future of China was to disband itself immediately. A force of 'military police' was set up to handle the assembly and destruction of all weapons, particularly small arms. These were laid out on the roads and flattened by tanks. Explosives were used to destroy aircraft and artillery. When this was finished, tens days' rations were issued to every soldier, and all units dispersed unarmed. It was the first time since the mid-nineteenth century that the Chinese army had been totally disbanded. The warships that generations of distinguished Chinese statesmen had seen as symbolizing a strong and prosperous new China had already been stripped down and used to transport the refugees abroad.

Huang Shi-ke had sworn to punish Shi Ge as a traitor who had ruined the army and the country. Two days after the Russians had invaded North China, Huang Shi-ke had fled to Nanjing and formed a 'Government of National Resistance' mainly as a protest against Shi Ge's order to offer no resistance to the invasion. After the destruction of the Chinese army, the Russians entered what was to all intents and purposes an empty land—as far as military resistance was concerned—and the speed of the occupation corresponded with the speed of the troop transports. Shi Ge's only reaction was to call upon the people to exercise restraint, to submit to the Russian authorities and cooperate with them. This was superfluous since the Chinese people had lost all will to resist. Just as the Russians said, the Chinese refugees had occupied 10 million square kilometres of Russia, so China was hardly in a position to talk about resisting invasion.

Huang Shi-ke's real motive was different. The former Deputy Premier had long wanted to rule China himself and this was a suitable opportunity. On reaching Nanjing he proclaimed himself President and urged all countries to withdraw recognition of Beijing and the whole people and all organizations and groups to obey the new government.

There had been almost no reaction in the world to the Russian occupation of north China. All countries that felt threatened by the arrival of Chinese refugees sympathized with Russia. The USA alone immediately recognized Huang Shi-ke's 'Government of National Resistance', moved its embassy to Nanjing and, 'in accordance with the request of the new government' began to despatch large forces to China. Although on the surface relations between the US and Russia were more hostile, both of them wanted to avoid a clash. Huang Shi-ke's 'resistance' remained purely verbal, as the US demanded. The US defensive line was along the Yangzi River, about 1000 km south of the Russian army. The US and Russian troops under UN command were permitted to withdraw from territory occupied by the other and it looked as if they were playing a balancing game: I take a piece, you take a piece. No country in the world wanted a premature confrontation and apart from the embassies of a few Latin American countries, which followed the US embassy to Nanjing, the majority stayed in Beijing. So in fact Shi Ge's government controlled more than half of the country, though it had no legal status.

Feathery clouds bunched together to form a fiery phoenix floating in the rays of the sun, already on the horizon. The blue outline of mountains gradually merged with the evening sky. Towns and villages became more frequent, showing that Zhangjiakou was not far away, but in most of them there were only empty houses and shop signs, no sign of life. China could no longer be saved by reconstruction. The United Nations, Russia, the USA and Huang Shi-ke were all wrong. China as an organized entity was finished. It only remained to dissolve it, disperse all its people and save them from being buried in the ruins. Consequently Shi Ge considered that there was no need to get excited—or even pretend to—if Russia invaded or if Huang Shi-ke set up a government or the US sent troops. Whether his own government survived or not was of no importance, since the migration was almost completed. There remained only one thing to be done.

He arrived at Zhangjiakou. In front of him, where the road meets the railway, there was a row of tanks and a large number of soldiers dug in behind a forest of arms. Shi Ge, aware that at this time any careless movement might be fatal, stopped a good distance away. The Russian troops were not normally so tense. China was incapable of recovering her lost territory and the US forces were far away. It was a special security measure, that showed that Japanese Intelligence was right: the man Shi Ge wanted to see would be spending the night here.

The computer in Wang Feng's car had a translation programme, and Shi Ge entered a sentence in Chinese saying: 'I am alone and have no weapons and only request to see the officer in charge.' It immediately came up in Russian, and he read it out letter by letter. The car had an adequate loudspeaker but he was not sure he had made himself understood. The result was better than expected. Two armoured cars approached and pulled up one in front and once behind his car. A handsome young captain emerged from one of them and saluted. Perhaps he saw that the car, though very dirty, could not belong to an ordinary person. When Shi Ge used the computer to ask in Russian to see the commanding officer, the captain hesitated but did not seem surprised.

The commanding officer was a very tall Lieutenant General. Before his arrival, Shi Ge had answered questions from several of the guards, without saying anything of substance, nor had he revealed his identity.

'What have you come for?' The Commanding Officer's appointment clearly had something to do with his ability to speak Chinese and his natural rigidity was softened by his imperfect pronunciation.

'To see your President.' The Lieutenant General looked surprised.

'Who are you?'

'The Prime Minister of China.' This reply surprised him even more. He stared at Shi Ge and politely rose to his feet.

'I must admit,' he said, 'that when you came through the door your face seemed familiar, but your appearance on television is more. . .conventional. This manner of meeting made it difficult to connect you with your high office.'

Shi Ge smiled. 'Let us call this a visit incognito.' He was immediately invited to sit down and offered coffee. The Lieutenant General spent some time stuffing a large pipe, lit it and silently smoked for a moment.

'The person you wish to see is not here. I will transmit a message.'

Shi Ge looked at the design on the wallpaper and pretended not to have heard. If he had not been certain, he would not have risked coming. The information had been confirmed by other sources. Although diplomatic relations with Russia had been broken off after the invasion, a small group of the embassy staff had remained in Moscow to handle communications and knew of the Russian President's visit to Xinjiang and Helongjiang and the journey across Russian occupied territory. Information as to where he would spend the night came from the Japanese.

'Please do not waste time trying to guess.' Shi Ge cut short the other's prevarication and handed him a map. 'If China wanted to harm your President, it would not have been necessary for the Prime Minister to come in person. In any case, if we wanted to see him dead this would have been far more effective. . .'

The Lieutenant General took the map as if it was a bomb.

This was not far from the truth; but a bomb so huge could not be held in the hand. It was enough to blow up the whole city of Zhangjiakou. When Shi Ge had first seen this map, which had also been provided by the Japanese, he felt a kind of nausea at the thought that science and ruthless evil could be so well combined. Ten years ago Japan made an enormous profit and cheated China of a large sum of money by constructing a large chemical enterprise at Zhangjiakou, with many subsidiaries in the city and the suburbs. For safety reasons combustible or toxic chemicals were stocked in tanks at Yantong in the suburbs and fed through pipes to the central pumping station as needed, then distributed to the various production units through a complicated maze of pipes. The Russians had occupied Zhangjiakou but Yantongshan was outside their territory and it had not occurred to them that old stocks of chemicals could be very dangerous. The Japanese motivation, in sending the map, seemed to have been to further Chinese interests, and their suggestion was this: if the Russian president were killed in an explosion, the government would become destabilised and chaotic and the Russians would stop rounding up and slaughtering Chinese refugees. This was an extraordinary opportunity. But for such a chance combination of factors, it would take a miracle to assassinate a Russian President.

Shi Ge did not mention the role of Japan but simply explained to the Lieutenant-General some of the details of the map. If several powerful generator-trucks were used to replace the city's electrical supply, which was not working, the pumping station at Yantongshan could be put into operation. The Japanese had provided a formula, whereby a deadly liquid could be prepared from various chemicals and pumped silently under pressure into the underground pipes in the city. The green valves marked on the map are those which men would be sent to open at the appropriate moment. The blue valves are permanently closed. Yellow ducts are those that would be temporarily connected. This could be done by a few dozen men familiar with the pipe system sent here for the purpose, and would only take a few hours to get the toxic fluid flowing through the city. The places marked in red are where mines have been placed in pipes and are controlled by radio from anywhere within a 50 kilometres circumference from the city. This would cause an enormous fire, and after three such explosions all life in the city would be destroyed and the President would die.

Beads of sweat appeared on the Lieutenant General's face, which had turned from ruddy to white. The Russian's hairy hand reached for the phone, but Shi Ge had not finished.

'Three things: first, there are no mobile generators at Yantong. Second, I have already sent people to cut the pipeline between there and the city. Third, please take me to the President. Don't worry, I'm not going to let myself be blown up.'

From then on there were no difficulties. When Shi Ge finally took his place in the military limousine, he could hear Russian tanks roaring out of the city on their way to occupy Yantong. If time had permitted, Shi Ge reflected, the Japanese would have made their 'suggestion' to the Nanjing government or, if not too many mobile generators were needed, would have done the job themselves; but they would have to have enough technically competent people—disguised as refugees—to do the work on the pipelines. The President would certainly have been killed.

Shi Ge did not believe for a moment that the Japanese had the interests of the Chinese refugees in mind—that was not likely, these days. In return for their help in transporting refugees to North America, Shi Ge had given Japan three oilfields in China. In next to no time they had been working again and shipping the oil like mad to Japan. If the Russian President were killed, the Russians would undoubtedly take it out on the Chinese. Japan was hoping to use China as cannon-fodder and pick up the benefits. If their President was killed, the Russians would undoubtedly inflict a terrible vengeance on China and Japan would be there to pick up the pieces.

After passing several checkpoints the limousine turned into a garden and stopped. There was none of the tension so palpable elsewhere and no troops in sight. Shi Ge was conducted by a young woman wearing a dress into the dining room—too brightly lit for someone accustomed to rationing and power cuts. The garden outside was also hung with lights on trees and walls. The President, sitting at one end of the long dining table, on which there was much polished silver and glass, made a sign with his hand. His white hair under the bright lights made him look distinguished and serene. His deep-set eyes looked shrewd.

An orderly drew up a high-backed chair for Shi Ge and the table was soon covered with Russian dishes. Apart from an interpreter sitting between them, they were alone. The President raised a glass of vodka and made a motion of touching glasses with Shi Ge, who after reciprocating emptied his. The strong liquor, flowed pleasurably down his throat. For no reason he suddenly thought of winter evenings in Xianren Village on the brick bed and of the high plateau of yellow earth, where the wind used to whistle past his ears. The President looked with approval at Shi Ge and also drained his glass.

The sight of all this food made Shi Ge's stomach flutter. He had been hungry for so long that seeing so many dishes was like being in another world. He finished four dishes in silence, pretending not to notice the President's look. It ought not to be too difficult to come to an understanding with a President who remembers that a man needs to eat. He noticed some Chinese Maotai liquor on the table, filled his glass and raised it to the President, who also filled his. They made a motion of clinking glasses then emptied them.

'Chinese refugees have created a lot of trouble for your country,' said Shi Ge. 'I have long wanted, on behalf of the Chinese Government, to present our apologies.'

'The wording of that needs some correction, ' said the President impassively. 'It is not *trouble* your refugees have caused, but disaster. I don't think you have come here to apologize: at least I can see no sign of that from the conduct of your government.'

'Apologies cannot always be expressed by actions. At a time when the Chinese people is on the brink of extinction, some things cannot be avoided however much we apologize. What has already happened cannot be changed.'

'Cannot be changed?' said the President. 'That is too early to say. Do you think Russia is paralysed in the face of base and underhand methods?' The President's anger seemed to have been at boiling point for some time, but his training made him restrain himself immediately. He took several strides around the room, his hands behind his back, then drank two more glasses of liquor as if it were water.

'The world will not know about our meeting,' he said. 'Both of us would deny it anyway. So let us be frank. I can tell you that I am waiting for Winter—the winter that destroyed Napoleon's armies and Hitler's and can kill half of your refugees by cold alone, since they have neither food nor clothing.'

'You may be disappointed,' Shi Ge replied. 'Chinese have suffered for hundreds of years and you can have no idea of their powers of resistance. Even if half of them die of cold and starvation, there will still be two hundred million left.'

'There is also a possibility of using chemical and biological weapons,' the President interjected.

'You were not able to get the refugees into your trap in Manzhouli not long ago and they are now scattered over several million square miles. You can only use such weapons if you are prepared to wipe out half the population of Russia at the same time. No one denies that Russia has had glorious victories in the past. But the trouble you are now in has no comparison with anything in your history, neither with Ghengis Khan, Napoleon nor Hitler. They disappeared like stones in the deep pool of Russia. But a few hundred million Chinese refugees are like an uncharted ocean and it is Russia that will sink.'

'For almost a hundred years your country has been trying to increase the Russian population of Siberia.' Shi Ge said. 'Why are they trying to get back to European Russia now? Because they don't want to be surrounded by Chinese. The refugees, for their part, do not want to leave and will not take a step beyond the Urals. Unless you do something, Russia will split into two: the European part consisting of a few regions of the Eastern European plain west of the Urals and Siberia to the east. When the Soviet Union collapsed, you lost several million square miles. The loss of Siberia will be another five million square miles.'

'Is this the way you Chinese are planning to conquer the world?' said the President with savage sarcasm.

Shi Ge sighed.

'The Chinese have no wish to conquer anyone: only to survive.'

The President toyed with his glass for a moment.

'I remember a young research student I had once, who compared China to an ulcerated leg. In order to save itself, he said humanity would have to steel itself to cut off that leg; that is to say, to expel China from the world. He proposed a protracted blockade of China by the world's military forces to prevent anyone from leaving, so that the collapse and obliteration of China would be contained within China itself, like a watertight compartment on a leaking ship: sacrifice a part for the whole, and save the ship; isolate a disintegrating China until it presents no danger to the world. I think this is the only hope for humanity. Your national anthem contains the words "form a new Great Wall with our blood and flesh". Each time I think of the idea, I imagine a Great Wall built of dead bodies.'

'You know the world would not do it.'

'Of course. Consequently humanity is going to destroy itself. How can you imagine that we will lightly abandon the Russian Far East? Peter the Great, Potemkin and Muriev drew the map of this great empire with the blood of our ancestors. It was not I, but the army who set the Manzhouli trap: they take no notice now whether I approve or not. Fascism and racial hatred are growing in my country. If, as you say, Russia cannot kill all the Chinese refugees and has no means of stopping them, the army may well make a desperate strike westward, to gain more territory, or glory, or psychological compensation. A world war would be the consequence. The destruction of mankind would begin and the disaster and horror will have started in China, with you Mr Prime Minister.'

'I came here to suggest a way of avoiding such a situation,' said Shi Ge.

'Is that so?' The President smiled frostily.

'You made no mention of the United States; but I think you are aware as I am that the US is pleased about the flow of refugees into Siberia, because the possibility of Russia re-emerging on the world scene as a great power is now no more threatening than a bubble. The break-up of the USSR was a bitter defeat for Russia, that does not mean that she will not recover. The Russian army has been utterly routed more than once. Yet Russia has been able to rouse the people and turn defeat into victory. It is unthinkable that Russia with all her advantages and the character of her people will sink to the level of a second-rate country. Russia will always be a threat to US ambitions to dominate the world. If you allow the refugees to drown Russia, the very foundations will be destroyed for a long period, perhaps several centuries. It is naturally in the interests of the US, at no cost to herself, to "sit and watch the fire from the other bank of the river", as we say in China, and reap the benefits. Is that no so?'

The President was silent.

'No politician really believes all that nonsense about "the family of nations". Shi Ge went on. 'The watchword of capitalism may be "fair competition"; but the nature of capitalism does not allow it to be put into practice. Has the US given Russia a fair deal? What western capitalism fears most is Russian and Eastern European development and competition. They hope you will remain a market and source of raw materials, even if you become capitalist democracies like them.'

'Your Excellency knows better than I that the west's policy of containment has hampered your country's development and damaged your interests. So why not respond in kind? For a country to become strong its rivals must be weakened.'

'What is your precise suggestion?' The President did not appear pleased with Shi Ge's preamble.

'To drag in the USA.'

The President stroked his chin doubtfully.

'The fundamental principle of Russian-US relations has always been parity,' Shi Ge explained. 'This should continue; but not only parity in weaponry, there should be parity in difficulties, problems and adversity as well. To be more specific: the United States should have at least as many Chinese refugees as you. If this kind of parity is achieved, the USA will soon stop gloating and sit down at the table and work out a way of solving this international problem.'

'What you are saying is that we should not try to get out of our difficulties alone but share them with the US?'

'It's the only thing you can do, at least in the short term. To exhaust yourself trying to deal with the problem can only weaken your country and make it vulnerable to attack, which would be worse. You share a common frontier with China and it is relatively easy for refugees to cross it. If you do not divert them to the USA, you will have to bear the burden alone. You cannot feed or control the two hundred million starving people in the part of China you have occupied and they will inevitably find a way of crossing into Siberia. There are still 400 million in the interior of China and the coastal regions, and they may well be forced northwards by famine. If I were in your place, I would regard the situation as desperate.'

The President said nothing but his eyes narrowed.

'At present,' Shi Ge went on, 'I can be sure of re-settling perhaps 300 million of those left in China. The remaining 300 million must leave if they are to survive. If they are transported to the United States that means that 300 million less will enter Russia.'

'We have an ancient proverb; "misfortune stems from happiness: happiness precedes misfortune". In the long run, the trouble we have inflicted on your country may turn out to your advantage. If 300 million refugees go to North America it will create space in China, so once the pressure of population is relieved and the environment has recovered, most of the Chinese in Siberia, who are not acclimatized or used to the primitive conditions there, will return to China. The ocean protects the USA from immigrants: but it is also a natural barrier which makes it more difficult for them to return home. As long as Chinese refugees in the USA can subsist there, they will not leave. So "parity" will begin to swing in your favour and Russia can take an historic opportunity to become great. So in absolute terms Chinese refugees have caused you to suffer, but in relative terms they will have made you stronger.'

The President had already drunk three glasses of wine and his eyes were becoming increasingly brighter.

'You are referring, in effect, to the question of transporting 300 million refugees over the Pacific?'

'That's right. Quite a big operation. . . .'

'Tell me your plan.'

'At present,' Shi Ge replied, 'we have 20 million tonnes of private shipping, five million tonnes of navy ships and six million tonnes of old ships that we have recently bought. Add to that eleven million tonnes of shipping provided by Japan and ten million tonnes in Taiwan and Hong Kong: a total of 52 million tonnes, enough to carry sixty million refugees to North America in the space of a few days. If there is no trouble landing, the ships can be back on the coast of China in thirty days. Our fuel oil and food supplies are now entirely exhausted and we have no means of taking a second consignment. Therefore, we hope that Russia will be able to provide fuel and food; secondly, a round trip will take 50 days. If we rely only on the 52 million tonnes of shipping we have available—taking into account a ten percent loss per trip, for damage and accidents—it is going to take at least six months or more to take all 300 million refugees to North America. It is absolutely impossible for us to feed the refugees while they are awaiting transport. Famine will force most of them to make for Russia because they can do so on foot. If they continue to cross the frontier and disperse, they will finally become uncontrollable and there will be no means of directing them elsewhere. The only way of avoiding that is if you participate with your shipping.'

'That is too much to ask,' said the President, knitting his brows as if in pain.

'It is,' Shi Ge said emphatically. 'But if you are not willing to pay this price the result will be the collapse of your country and the decline of the Russian people.'

'How much shipping?'

'Your ships have not been refitted and we can only calculate on the basis of one person per tonne. You have 60 million tonnes of large merchant ships. How many people they can carry is for you to say. As for fuel, the Japan and Hong Kong ships, made their own arrangements. You only need to provide the fuel for our ships, and grain: a minimum of twenty thousand tons.'

There was a long silence.

Finally the President said, 'If one of our ships starts landing Chinese refugees in the United States, it would be tantamount to a declaration of war.'

'That was not the case with Japan. The Japanese killed two birds with one stone: diverted refugees away from Japan and at the same time caused chaos for their main economic competitor. They declared that all the ships had been hijacked by the barbaric Chinese. If Chinese refugees could cross the sea to Japan to seize Japanese ships, why not Russian ships which are just next door? China will take all the blame.'

The President was nervously cutting into small pieces a fish fried in butter. 'Send a team to Moscow.'

It was enough. Shi Ge concealed his satisfaction and raised his glass in gratitude. But the President had not finished.

'Since we are, in the future, to be citizens of the same country, let me say that we are merely coming to the assistance of our fellow countrymen.'

Shi Ge's glass stopped in mid-air. 'Excuse me. I don't understand.'

'Don't you think that in reality Russia and China are inevitably moving towards amalgamation?' The President said with a significant smile. 'Your people started by "spontaneously" using our territory as if it were their own. Since we have no choice but to accept this fact, and that it would be both unreasonable and unacceptable to expect us to cede Siberia, the most equitable solution would be to unite our two countries into one.'

'Do you mean that Russia will swallow China?'

'It would be better to say that China will annex Russia. But it is of little importance how the combination will come about. The result will be a new country with both the largest territory and the biggest population in the world. The Chinese refugees who have migrated to nearly every country will eventually become a force that will enable the new country to dominate the world. The United States will be a pygmy in comparison. The presence of 300 million Chinese in the US will guarantee that it will eventually join us.'

'As far as I am concerned, this is not the time to indulge in chauvinistic fantasies,' Shi Ge said with a bitter smile.

'But for me, it is necessary to envisage this kind of future if Russia is to be saved from obliteration,' the President replied calmly and firmly.

It was more than just 'envisaging', Shi Ge thought to himself. The Russian occupation of part of North China was already a fact. The President might officially be on an 'inspection tour', but he was inspecting occupied territory. Later he might force China to suggest that the two countries amalgamate. Russia would take this as a justification for the occupation of the rest of China. Shi Ge could not help feeling that many things had been left unsaid. But he had no time to worry about that now: it was more important to save the lives of millions of people.

There was suddenly a commotion outside. The glass door of the dining room was violently pushed open, blowing over the vase of flowers on the table. The Lieutenant General strode in holding in his hand a small mud-covered box and spoke at some length to the President in Russian, occasionally looking at Shi Ge with great suspicion. He was accompanied by a soldier, who did not enter the room, but kept his rifle aimed at Shi Ge's head, through the barely opened door.

'The General informs me,' said the President, 'that his men have tracked down a strange radio signal that comes from a transmitter under your car. He is therefore doubtful about your identity and your motive in coming here and has asked me to leave here. He has developed a desire to arrest you.'

'I understand his point of view,' Shi Ge said looking at the small box. The feeling that he was watching a film came to him often these days; his surroundings seemed to be a stage set and the actors might at any moment break into laughter and remove their make-up.

'Can you explain?' the Lieutenant General asked him in Chinese.

'I assume this is some kind of espionage equipment used for listening in or following someone.' The little knowledge he had of such things came from occasionally reading thrillers. 'I don't believe the mud on it was put there by your men. . .'

The Lieutenant General shrugged at these superfluous remarks.

'If it was being used against you, I would have installed it just before coming here and there would not be so much mud on it. If it has been fixed under my car for a long time, then I am the victim. So why get excited?'

The President laughed candidly.

The Lieutenant General remained very formal. 'This apparatus is neither for listening or following. It emits a continuous secret coded signal to all Chinese satellite ground-stations within a certain distance, which is then transmitted and can be received anywhere in the world. What is the content of the message? Who is to receive it, and for what purpose? As long as you cannot answer these questions I find it difficult to believe that you are "a victim".'

'Is that so? said Shi Ge thoughtfully. 'If that's the case. . . This must have something to do with Wang Feng.'

He suddenly felt cold. He did not know anything, but if Wang Feng was concerned it was certainly not a trivial matter.

12

To the West – Beijing – Los Angeles – The Far East of Russia – Beijing

ௐ

To the West

The outline of the mountains was faintly visible in the bright starlight. The evening wind carried a smell of the soil of a foreign land and unfamiliar vegetation. Xing Tuo-yu brought up the last load of dry wood to the top of the hill, from which he had a wide view of the mountains around. He was sweating heavily and sat down on a stone. Eight-103, whose responsibility it was to keep the fire burning, was sweating more than anyone. All five members of the Eight-103 level were already there, having carried up enough wood to keep the fire burning for several hours.

A voice came from the radio: 'China' calling 'Northwest'. Eight-103 turned the volume up.

'China' spoke to the refugees' leaders in a secret language, used for centuries by secret societies and bandits, that everyone on the Special Training Brigade had been taught. Also for reasons of security, all members of the Brigade had code-names based on names of places. The codes for commanders of the seven great refugee 'armies' were the names of the seven great regions of China: lower-ranking leaders were named after provinces, cities or counties.

Xing Tuo-yu had been a deputy commander of the Special Training Brigade at the Green University and was also leader of an 'army' of over fifty million refugees. His code-name was 'Northwest'. One of his subordinates, 'Yinchuan', was in command of the 'Ningxia' division' and his code-name was that of the provincial capital of Ningxia province.

Numerical code-names were used for all the leaders in the Multi-Level Election System. The first figure referred to the level to which a leader had been elected. Xing Tuo-yu for instance had been progressively elected from a lower level to the highest, Level Nine in this particular 'army' of refugees, and commanded the vanguard for all the refugees destined for Europe. His code name was therefore Nine-01. All those elected above level Eight were almost invariably members of the Special Training Brigade, because of their exceptional ability, training and spirit of self-sacrifice.

The code-names based on place-names had been allocated from above, whereas the numerical ones were imposed from below. The two coding systems facilitated the smooth direction of the migration by 'China', and was the basis for the adoption of the Multi-Level Election System by the refugees. Now that 'China' had signed off, the place-name codes were abandoned, leaving only those relating to the Multi-Level Election System.

The message from 'China' was that thirty five million refugees would start arriving in northern Slovenia the same evening and join up with the vanguard of almost eleven million commanded by 'Northwest' (Xing Tuo-yu). The following day they were to begin crossing the frontiers of the European Community. More refugees would follow.

Xing Tuo-yu and the vanguard had been waiting on the border between Slovenia and Austria for three days. Until now every frontier crossing organized by him had been done with the secret cooperation of the government of the country concerned. The next one would be a genuine violation of the frontier. The refugees would then be divided into three large contingents destined for Western, Central and Eastern Europe respectively, later to be distributed evenly throughout the various European countries.

'China' repeated the numbers of refugees to go to each country, which had been decided in Beijing after careful research. Once the numbers were reached this stage of the migration would be complete. Finally 'China' announced that owing to the lack of electricity, regular broadcasting would now stop, perhaps permanently. From now on there would be no need for a centralized command and the refugees must organize themselves by means of the Multi-level Election System. It was therefore time to say goodbye to everyone, in case there should be no other opportunity. 'But, though we must part, my thoughts will always be with you.' These were the last words of 'China'. It was also the first time since the broadcasting started that he had not spoken in code.

The radio station broadcast a few Chinese songs and no one listening could restrain his tears. Xing Tuo-yu gazed at the dark blue night horizon, and saw the moon, thin as a shaving, creep up behind the meandering ridge of a mountain in the distance. The lowland and valleys below were bathed in a silvery light. The huddled shapes of thousands of refugees, sleeping on the roads, in dry riverbeds, in ravines were just visible, as if the land had been covered by a sea of dead bodies.

Xing Tuo-yu was profoundly moved by the fact that these wretched, unfortunate people had found in the Multi-level Election System their own framework of organization and mutual support. He had once been bitterly opposed to the idea. At Taibaishan he had finally voted in favour mainly because of Chen Pan; but also because he disliked Ouyang so much. Although he had not stayed there long, the smooth operation and advantages of the system had greatly impressed him. During the disturbances in Beijing the night after the US-Russian nuclear attack, the rising he had led was his last step along the road of 'red revolution'. Once more the bullets of the special troops had shed his blood and that of his comrades. The inescapable collapse of China had blocked all roads to reform, so when he eventually escaped the clutches of death, he left his bed and enthusiastically enrolled at the Green University.

The radio became silent. He almost felt the generator in Beijing shudder to a halt as the last drop of fuel was used up, and imagined Shi Ge's thin hair and his bowed head in the darkness that followed. The mission of 'China' was at an end. China itself had completely disintegrated. No one knew, apart from the leaders of the seven great armies of refugees, that 'China' was Shi Ge. Xing Tuo-yu's total conversation with Shi Ge amounted to hardly more than the few words they had exchanged when he had interrogated the 'spy from the Central Committee' in the headquarters of the People's Front. Now he had a genuine feeling of loss. Shi Ge appeared mild and commonplace but was an indomitable, courageous man of immense stature. It must have been the will of heaven that the destiny of China should be in his hands and that the Chinese people should not die out.

Xing Tuo-yu often wondered whether the disaster of June Fourth would have happened if China had adopted the Multi-Level Election System, whether China would have taken another course. At least the rabble-rousing demagogues of Tiananmen Square would not have got the upper hand and the popular movement would not have allowed incompetent individuals to become leaders. There was a far better basis for mutual understanding among the amorphous mass of refugees, Xing Tuo-yu reflected, than in the crowds demonstrating on Tiananmen Square. After talking amongst themselves for a while, the refugees could form small groups and start putting the Multi-Level Election System into practice. The first elections might not be very satisfactory; an unsuitable person might be elected and have to be recalled and new elections held; but a better mutual understanding between the electors would develop and the system perfected. Xing was convinced that there was no better way of organizing the chaotic multitude of refugees.

The demonstrations in Tiananmen Square in 1989 were marked by the spirit of traditional popular protest accompanied by modern slogans about democracy. The result was that anyone who could monopolize the loudspeaker and talk longest became a leader that the crowd could only influence by either clapping or hissing. The cheapest way of getting applause was by cynical competition to see who could be the most extreme. The voice of reason was hissed off the stage. Xing Tuo-yu had been moved to tears when some people took an oath to burn themselves alive for the cause, until he noticed that they took to their heels faster than anyone at the first sound of a gunshot.

There were soon three other fires visible on hill tops some distance away and soon a fifth, due South, signalled the beginning of the meeting. At each fire—they were all in Slovenia—there was a Level Nine leader, including Xing Tuo-yu, each of them in charge of ten million refugees. Information was given by fire signal that the last few groups to arrive had already elected a Level Ten leader, code-name 'Qinghai', or Ten-01 in the Multi-Level Election code.

At the special training course everyone had been taught the technique of fire signalling which, in the absence of radio transceivers was more effective than semaphore or drum signals. The Level Eight leaders who were with Xing Tuo-yu took off their tattered jackets and trousers and attached them together to form two screens, one on either side of the fire. The signalling was done by the four men raising or lowering these screens, which could be seen from any direction, according to Xing Tuo-yu's instructions. In the light of the fire the four naked men making irregular and exaggerated movements looked very strange.

'Qinghai' had been a division leader under 'Northwest' and had been elected to Level Ten to replace Xing Tuo-yu who was then at the frontier with the vanguard. He now signalled his suggestion that Xing Tuo-yu should take up his previous position.

Xing Tuo-yu was annoyed at this suggestion, which to him smacked of the false modesty of the old days; he was about to object, but decided to consult the colleagues who had elected him first. Nine-04 immediately signalled that he was opposed to 'Qinghai's' suggestion on the grounds that it was unwise to change the top leadership at such short notice. Moreover Qinghai had shown himself as good a commander as Xing Tuo-yu. The others signalled their agreement with this. Xing Tuo-yu thought of quoting Shi Ge on the subject, but it would have been too complicated to explain by signals and a waste of time. So he merely replied that he agreed with the others.

He had been wondering whether they would think him resentful and suddenly remembered the day at the Green University when four students, a number of researchers, teachers and seven departmental directors had elected Shi Ge as President of the University. Shi Ge said that he was happy to be elected, but the day he was recalled he would be even happier. He explained that it was very natural that he be elected President, being founder of the University as well as Prime Minister. Electing someone, Shi Ge had said was not nearly so problematic as recalling an elected person. If one day his election was revoked that would show the true superiority of the Multi-Level Election System and he would be proud, he said, to be its inventor. Xing Tuo-yu's unhesitating rejection of a proposal to promote him was also evidence of the same superiority.

The main purpose of the meeting was to decide the distribution of the migrants in different directions—to decide their fate in fact; whether they would become French or Polish for instance. Such a question was not something that could be decided by the refugees themselves, or even by a few hundred of their representatives. Since fire signalling was not a suitable way of having a detailed discussion, the Level Nine meeting was very short and to the point; specific proposals were voted without debate, and passed or rejected by a majority vote.

The eastern routes would be the most difficult and arduous: one of them led to the coldest part of North Europe, others to Eastern Europe and the poorest part of Russia, still marked by the heritage of Stalinism where the danger of starvation, violence and death was greater than elsewhere.

The commander of the Eastern Route vanguard, Nine-03, expressed his anxiety that his group of refugees, whose role was to make the initial break-through at each frontier for those behind, would not want to press on to the next frontier. Refugees are not soldiers; they obey instructions only in order to survive. On reaching a country where there was a possibility of settling, it might be difficult to get them to move on. The meeting decided that once a frontier was breached, the vanguard would enter and remain in the country in question until they had recovered their strength; the next group to arrive would then become the advance guard and break through the next frontier, and so on.

It was an important principle of the Multi-Level Election System that elected leaders at each level collectively exercised 'legislative' power over those they elected as 'executive' leaders at the level above. This was far more flexible, and expeditious than the usual separation of legislative and executive powers, yet still retained the function of restraint. Xing Tuo-yu, in addition to his specific leadership roles in Level Nine, for instance, had a certain legislative power over those elected to Level Ten. To the five leaders of Level Eight who elected him to the position of Nine-01, he was the administrative head of that

Level who carried out decisions made by them. As soon as the meeting came to an end, the Level Eight leaders ran back to their units, to make arrangements with the leaders of Level Seven.

The white dawn sky was already spreading over the eastern horizon. Xing Tuo-yu stayed alone on the hilltop. He was not by nature easily moved or worried yet recently he had often found himself daydreaming. The disintegration of China and the ruination of her people had not given him a corresponding feeling of shock and sadness—perhaps because it was so close at hand and there was so little time—but rather a feeling of dazed surprise, disbelief and listlessness. Each nightfall when there was no sound of people, he imagined he saw far away what looked like a question mark in the form of a white tree, from which came the sound of a long desolate wail of graveside mourning, always the same tune, accompanied by the fluttering in the sky of a piece of paper money.

The Austrian frontier to the north was lit with bright white lights. A row of tanks and armoured cars lined up darkly like a steel rampart protecting the frontier. European troops had almost all been sent to the frontier of the European Community on the Slovenian border. The yellow flood flowing from the east had sent Europe into almost apocalyptic hysteria. Facing the deadly weapons aimed at them the Chinese refugees slept on the ground, some of them no more than ten yards from the tanks.

It grew lighter. Birds began to sing in the trees. Xing Tuo-yu recalled Chen Pan at Taibaishan analysing his hostility to the Green movement. It was not merely because of his belief in 'red revolution', she said: deep down he longed for blood and fire and heroic action. The Green movement was pacifist and insipid. He had rejected Chen Pan's 'diagnosis' at the time, but now felt there was some truth in it. He had once dreamt of being a great general, like Caesar or Napoleon: now he too commanded 'troops'—ten million, six hundred thousand of them—the biggest army in history. But there was no martial music, or romantic heroism and no medals. Only mass starvation, disease and death. There were yellow, ashen-faced people everywhere, the ground their beds, their blankets the sky. Yet this miserable army was sweeping across the world.

As dawn approached, the colour of the sky gradually changed from something like blue black to dark red, then to a more and more beautiful bright red. He would liked to have waited on the summit until the rays of the sun rose rapidly up to where he sat. But he knew he must join the mass of people who were resisting the cold air of morning by the collective heat of their bodies.

Xing Tuo-yu followed a small path through the grass down the mountain. As he negotiated a narrow passage between fallen rocks he suddenly felt a pair of large, hairy hands seize him by the throat from behind. He instinctively kicked backwards to no effect. Then several Europeans appeared in front, all in the tattered clothing of refugees. Less than a hundred metres away there were millions of his fellow countrymen, but he could not shout with the man's hands round his neck. A big man in front expertly punched him in the belly and he felt his internal organs propelled violently upwards before all went black.

When he regained consciousness—very quickly he thought—it was already daylight. It took him a long time to focus his eyes on the red horizon and a big man in a white overcoat. He was lying on a sofa, watched by several pairs of eyes.

'I am most sorry,' said a voice a long way away in very bad Chinese. Xing Tuo-yu had never learned a foreign language and did not understand what the grey-haired General was saying. But at the training course he had learned to recognize the flags of European nations and knew he was in the hands of the German army.

'What do you want with me?' he asked, interrupting the interpreter and sitting up painfully. It was obvious from the general's cold and indifferent apology that they were worried that he had been unconscious for so long. They had not expected that he would be so weak: the blow he had received had not been particularly hard.

'I admire your parachuting technique,' the General said. 'However we must not beat about the bush. We have asked you here only in the hope that you will dissuade these Chinese refugees from crossing the frontier into Europe.'

An officer gave him a glass of wine, but Xing Tuo-yu pointed to the remains of breakfast on the table.

'Why do you think I can do that?' Xing Tuo-yu asked with his mouth full of bread.

The General said nothing and merely pointed to the 'Nine' on Xing Tuo-yu's armband. Food had stimulated Xing Tuo-yu's traumatized stomach and he was now having painful contractions.

'You are wasting your time.'

'We can give you anything you want,' said the General, 'and I mean anything. You only have to ask.'

'Personally I have no control over this matter.'

'All of you who have armbands above Level Four, we can make into respectable European citizens. . .provide homes, money, work and property. . .'

Xing Tuo-yu, trying to stop his spasms, drank a glass of wine. 'You think that higher or lower levels make any difference?' he said.

'According to our intelligence Nine is at present the highest.'

Xing Tuo-yu laughed. 'Mathematics won't help you understand our structure. The higher the level, the more things are decided by others; the more we obey, the less we are obeyed. You have captured one of the smallest fish. If you catch the biggest and agree to their conditions, you are likely to succeed: but they are all those *below* Level Four. They are all the refugees—exactly the people you don't want.'

'You are juggling with words.'

'My stomach hurts like hell and I have no desire to play games. You don't know much about the Multi-Level Election System. I'll have to give you some simple information, then you can test it. Even if you tortured me into doing what you want, I would immediately be dismissed by my subordinates and become someone of absolutely no use to you.'

'Immediately? I don't believe you. We have had democracy for centuries and even we cannot do such things so rapidly. So I don't see how rabble like. . .'

Xing Tuo-yu interrupted him. 'That only shows your democracy has not made much progress in all that time. In your terms, my "subordinates" at Level Eight are in fact my superiors. There are only five of them and for them to dismiss me only takes a few minutes. None of them are inferior to me in intelligence. If I had direct control of the ten million refugees under my command, I could trick them into taking the wrong direction; but I could not do that with those five colleagues of mine, even if you were to bring them here and give each of them a punch in the belly, because there are twenty eight Level Seven leaders below, who have power to replace them. I could tell you everything about our organizational structure, without holding anything back, without the slightest hope that you would get your way. Because in the Multi-Level Election System, short of buying over everyone without exception, you could never destroy it.'

'I dislike your self-assurance.'

"I can well believe it.' Xing Tuo-yu looked at his watch. 'Nevertheless a new Level Nine has just been elected to replace me.'

'But they don't even know that you've been taken prisoner!' The General seemed in danger of losing his patience.

'The reason for my absence is irrelevant. The new Level Nine has been elected because there is work to be done. That looks like a watchtower over there and the fellow probably has binoculars. If you will allow me to use them perhaps I can prove my point.'

The General fixed him momentarily, then said, 'Very well.'

The watchtower was quite high and overlooked a considerable

expanse of territory. Through the high-powered German binoculars, it was possible to distinguish people's faces very clearly, but only someone familiar with the structure of the organization would find what he was looking for in the sea of people. When Xing Tuo-yu focused the binoculars he almost laughed.

He handed him the binoculars and invited the General to take a look. They were focused on a young man who was giving instructions to people standing near him, and pointing this way and that, so that his arm was frequently out of the picture, but when it was not, his Nine-01 armband was clearly visible. As Xing Tuo-yu had hoped and expected, if anything happened to him, 'Yingchuan' formerly Eight-103, had been promoted to replace him.

The general looked sombrely at him for some time. 'Have you Chinese no sense of shame?, invading people's countries like parasites?'

Xing Tuo-yu would normally not have tolerated this insult. Now he merely stopped smiling. One of the refugees' rules was that they must exercise restraint in the face of insults, provocation and even physical assault. In no circumstance were they to disturb people's lives, nor could they force anyone to respect them. They hoped to put down roots in the gardens of others, so politeness was the only suitable attitude. Apology and self-control only would attract sympathy.

"I want to ask you a question,' Xing Tuo-yu asked the General mildly. 'It is said that for millions of years, there were no humans on earth and no nations. The globe was a single entity, "in the hands of God", some people would say. But now, after thousands of years of human history, some places in the world are packed with people, others are almost empty. Who gave races, or peoples the right to divide up the world, and behave as if this division is something "ordained by heaven"?'

'Humanity needs order if it is to survive. The sovereignty of nations, created by mankind as it progressed, is the most important kind of order.'

'In my opinion, the sovereignty of nations is the source of human disasters. Think back, what instigator of war has ever done without it? Sovereignty is inseparable from violence. States are created by unprincipled occupation. The boundaries are drawn by war and armies. Three hundred years ago Europe "discovered" a new continent. Was the "sovereignty" of the "Indians" respected? Your history is one of killing and plunder: all *we* want is to survive. Is your expansion or migration at an end? *Your* order has become eternal: does that mean that the migration of others is shameless?'

'Don't forget,' said the general, 'the past is already history. We are living here and now.'

'As far as the future is concerned, today is also history.'

The General glared at Xing Tuo-yu and clenched his fists. Xing Tuo-yu realized that the Multi-Level Election System had somehow changed his own character. Human violence is mainly caused by pressure and tension, but in the Multi-Level Election System, it is unnecessary to put immense burdens of responsibility on the shoulders of individuals, because the system gives them the feeling—and reality—of extremely dependable support. This makes them calm, self-confident and gives them an instinctive ability to deal with exceptional situations.

The changing situation at the frontier brought the debate to an end and made everyone look outside.

After dawn the refugees began assembling on the Slovenian side of the frontier. There was a wall of young men, standing shoulder to shoulder, holding back the rest of the refugees.

The wall opened like a gate and a group of old people came out. Advancing slowly they spread out left and right in a single line. Xing Tuo-yu recognized a ninety-year-old man in the middle. When the migration started, he was proud and sturdy and, as far as walking was concerned, a match for men thirty years younger than he. Later his stubborn nephew had pushed him all the way on a bicycle. The old man himself apologetically mumbling that he had not long to live, was holding up the others and still sharing their food. Now he walked very slowly and painfully, but held up his head proudly.

Loudspeakers at the frontier kept repeating a warning in Chinese that there were landmines everywhere in the land ahead. The troops had placed several million mines and other devices along the frontier, mainly to frighten the refugees and stop their advance. They were all visible and painted in bright colours, and there were warning notices everywhere. Real or make-believe the message was clear: Come any closer and you will be blown to pieces!

The old people's hair fluttered in the wind like white flames, giving them an aspect of holiness. None of them understood the warnings and continued to move forward as if the mines did not exist. The first explosion made everyone jump. Then a whole series of mines went off, balls of fire shot out of the ground and seemed to engulf the figures of the old people. The smoke dispersed but there was still no sign of them, they seemed to have flown away. The only trace of their presence was a piece of clothing fluttering on a burning stake; it soon caught fire and was carried away on the wind.

There was absolute silence. Xing Tuo-yu felt a profound sadness. Yet, he thought, if one day I become senile, this is the death I would choose, the least distressing, and bringing perfect contentment. The sight of the shocked and astounded Germans soldiers made him feel proud for the first time in the presence of foreigners, of his fellow countrymen. A people that had degenerated, whose freedom and liberty had been taken from them, who had survived tyranny, had been twisted by corruption, greed and disappointed hopes; had lost the sense of what is right, their own integrity and the respect of the world. Yet, at the time of the greatest difficulty and suffering, when the level of material life was at rock bottom there was no place for greed. The equal sharing which was an essential part of the Multi-Level Election System, was not only the sole means of survival, but also the basis for the revival of virtue, morality, self-sacrifice and love. Perhaps the disaster that had struck the Chinese people might prove to be their salvation.

The well-trained German troops at the frontier had thrown themselves to the ground just before the first explosions. But they had hardly stood up when they had to take cover again. A second line of old people were advancing along the ground cleared by the first, and the remaining mines were exploding. Those still alive walked slowly past the troops. Wave upon wave of refugees became a flood, silently and peacefully moving forward, through the frontier into Europe opened by the blood and flesh of the vanguard. The soldiers waited for the order to fire.

The officers' eyes were all on the General, whose face changed from a metallic grey to purple. Suddenly he turned to Xing Tuo-yu, took hold of his collar and shouted furiously at him. Xing Tuo-yu put up no resistance and calmly observed the red face and fierce distorted mouth.

'What's he saying?' he asked raising his eyebrows when the General finally let go of him.

'He's asking where the Chinese army is,' the interpreter said. 'And why do you use sheep to invade our countries? He says, this is a despicable and unfair kind of warfare. We are capable of wiping out as many genuine troops as you've got. . . . This is an insult to the honour of the German Army!'

The General soon calmed down and with his hands behind his back, looked gloomily at the refugees flooding through the frontier. He turned to a Major. 'Can you open fire on them?'

The Major looked as if he had just swallowed a very bitter medicine. He shook his head.

'I have the reputation of an expert on defence,' said the general bitterly. 'But I've never heard of this kind of warfare before. I am faced with a sea of sheep, not a cruel and violent enemy. I've been waiting all my life for a war and thought I was a match for any enemy. It looks as if I have wasted my life.'

The refugees began crossing the frontier en masse; the wall of tanks was overrun, as if it were no more than an earth bank. From the lookout tower the tanks were invisible, just a bulge under a sea of people, like a river flowing incessantly over a reef.

Xing Tuo-yu felt that the scene before his eyes had a mysterious resemblance to a dream of his youth. The enormous crowds of ragged and dirty refugees were no different from the armies of a Caesar or Napoleon: they too were victorious. The millions of old people, children, women carrying babies, all trudging the yellow earth, would one day spread all over the world.

'Goodbye.' He saluted the General in the Chinese military manner. He had developed a certain sympathy and respect for him—the same feeling he had in his youth for the brave but defeated Generals in storybooks.

Beijing

The sudden rain came through the holes in the roof, as if several taps had been turned on overhead. Long-kou had been trembling with hunger before, now, he was shaking all over. He had to keep wringing out his clothes. If the floor of the three-wheeled van had not also been full of holes it would have filled up like a wash-basin. His heart tightened with a tingling sensation: it was nearly two months now and still difficult to believe that he only had one leg. The fact that he was the only member of the special training course to be left in China was proof enough that it was true. He ought to have been at the head of tens of thousands of refugees 'hijacking' ships in Japan to take them to the United States. The plane flying him to take up his post had run out of fuel. The forced landing had been successful, except that he had lost a leg. Now he was waiting in a rainstorm for a hungry devil who might never turn up. He looked at his watch for the tenth time, and as he cursed there was a clap of thunder.

He had been the youngest member of the training course and was just twenty-four. When he went with his crutch and tearfully asked Shi Ge for some work worthy of his training, he was asked to join a team investigating the transmitter that had been found under Wang Feng's car. Shi Ge gave him a fuel ration for the three-wheeled vehicle that would at least make him more mobile.

The transmitter was now in his pocket. He had been the last to join the team. The other members were all old hands at solving such problems and did not think much of this amateur. But now he was the only one who refused to be defeated by the puzzle; the team hardly existed now. He shared their frustration, but they thought that the problem could be easily solved by prising Wang Feng's jaws open. They did not understand that such methods would not work with Wang Feng. His haughty manner made every interrogator feel that it was he himself who was being questioned and no one could get a word out of him. Experts at interrogation considered that only torture would break his will; it had always worked in the past. But without permission, torturing Wang Feng was impossible. Shi Ge would not hear of it and reprimanded Long-kou for even suggesting it. Such methods were a disgrace to China and mankind and should never be used, he said. So cipher experts were assembled and people from state security, who spent a lot of time with no result. The code would not be broken and everyone either resigned or simply left.

Before joining the Green University Long-kou had been an electronics engineer. His training led him to concentrate first of all on the transmitter itself. As Shi Ge said, it had been transmitting for so long that any danger must be past so there could be little risk in letting it continue to transmit. To stop it might make something go wrong, and it was far too risky to take it to pieces. There was no name of the manufacturer, no hint on the outside as to the wiring system. Long-kou deduced from the workmanship and material that it had been made in a Chinese research institute. However there had been several thousand such institutes and to examine them one by one would be like finding a needle in the sea. In any case most of them had been destroyed. The personnel, if they had not joined the migration abroad, had probably gone to the Green Party survival bases. Long-kou had his own plan. Since the object was so mysterious, it could not have been created by an ordinary laboratory. Wang Feng had been head of the National Defence Committee and the transmitter was most likely to have been made in the Engineering Department. The field was large; nearly a hundred separate research and construction units. On examining Wang Feng's dossier, he noted that he liked to keep a close watch on the activities of certain units and their research, therefore an institute in Beijing was most likely. For the last few days Long-kou had been going to and fro between five institutes that researched and produced electronic communications equipment.

They were all empty, deserted and partially destroyed. Long-kou's strong card, he felt, was that the policy of Shi Ge's government was to provide food for specialists who remained in China. The people who remained in Beijing were very few but this policy enabled many highly qualified scientific and technical personnel to stay. If their homes had not been looted or burned, they were probably living in their old accommodation, usually belonging to the organization that employed them. So he hoped that a search in the vicinity would bear fruit.

It was more difficult than he had expected. Some of the apartments were very dispersed and far from the institutes, difficult to find and nine out of ten were empty. He might spend hours going up and down stairs without seeing anyone, until his armpit and hand were bleeding from constantly using his crutch. Often people would not open their doors: Who was going to trust someone who came asking about some sort of scientific apparatus?

Then he had a good idea. He was, after all, working for Shi Ge, and drew his rations from Zhongnanhai. He stormed into the distribution centre and demanded immediate allocation of the two days' rations owing to him, plus two extra days during which he had eaten wild plants. This came to four large compressed 'biscuits'. He also hired a loudspeaker, which he connected to his car battery, and went to broadcast outside the areas where there were a lot of institutes and accommodation for their personnel. He repeated several times: 'anyone here who recognizes this transmitter and can give information about it will receive four days' rations. Immediate payment!'

This was an excellent idea. He did not need to rush around any more. Once he had broadcast his message, ghostly emaciated figures emerged from the sinister, deserted apartment blocks. They were all so thin that a breath of wind might have blown them away. They surrounded him with expressionless faces; only their spectacles suggested that they were intellectuals; but they did not recognize the transmitter. The compressed meal biscuits Long-kou held up in the air, interested them much more. There were excited cries of 'They're real! They're real!' Sometimes Long-kou even felt in danger. If these starving people suddenly pounced on him, even though they were a bunch of enfeebled intellectuals, with only one leg, he would not been able to put up much resistance. Whenever he felt threatened, he would stuff the cakes into his shirt and pull out a pistol. Not very good manners of course, but he felt no remorse until he had driven away fast.

The building facing him was hazy in the heavy rain. Veins of lightning crossed the sky. Perhaps this time. . . . He cursed and prayed, looked at his watch, at the sky and at the building in front of him. Forty minutes earlier a man carrying half a basketful of edible wild plants had stopped next to his three-wheeler.

'Can I have a look at that thing of yours?'

Long-kou put back in his pocket the piece of biscuit he was about to eat and lazily produced the transmitter.

'Open the lid,' the man said. So he knew there was a lid!.

When it was open the man merely glanced at it. 'Give me the biscuit.'

'You recognize it? Long-kou shouted.

'I was in charge of researching and making the receiver, so of course I recognize it.'

Long-kou was very excited. 'What was the purpose of the receiver and where is it? What's the code? Can you break it?'

At each question the man shook his head. 'How should I know? I was no more than a tool.' He did not take his eyes off the three biscuits. Long-kou wrapped them up again.

'Whether you recognize it or not, it will be absolutely useless unless you can tell us everything.'

The man swallowed, he was a little worried and immediately began to concentrate.

'When I was working on it, I first built the receiver and installed a special decoder that instantaneously decoded messages from the transmitter. If this is still transmitting maybe it will be possible to find something on the prototype receiver that will break the code.

'You're right!' Long-kou tapped on the lid of the transmitter. 'Where is the prototype?"

'It could be still in the workshop.'

'Get in.'

'Give me the biscuits first,'

Long-kou looked sideways at him. 'You don't trust me?' The man gave a wry smile. 'If I go with you, it will take half the day or more, and perhaps my daughter will starve to death in that time.' Long-kou gave him two of the four biscuits.

'I'll give you the others when we've finished.'

The rain suddenly stopped again, and the sunlight immediately broke through the clouds. Long-kou looked at the man as they stood together in the doorway of the building. He was not a cheat, just afraid of getting wet. Merely crossing the road several times made him shiver. The door to the store-room of the research institute had already been broken into; but what was inside, being inedible, was mostly untouched. Both the men were weak with hunger and each time they shifted a crate they had to take a moment to recover. Thank heaven! The prototype receiver was finally found on a bottom shelf.

But in getting it to work the man hesitated a lot, as if he was not very familiar with the design. It was difficult to believe that it was he who had created it. Long-kou said nothing. He was well-qualified in electronics but could understand nothing. Finally a light suddenly came on and the printer began to work. A tape emerged and Long-kou pounced on it. . . .It was in Chinese characters! The code was broken.

His joy was short-lived; he could read all the characters and understand the meaning, but what was the message? It was simply a continuous list of family members of 127 people. Why did this have to be transmitted by such a sophisticated apparatus, that could transmit a message to the whole world through all the satellite ground stations? Was this how Wang Feng, the super powerful man who looked on everything with disdain, had had spent his last hour as a free man? Shi Ge himself must deal with this, together with Russian Intelligence. Or should he solve it himself by working and running about day and night?

The other man took absolutely no interest in the tape and did not even look at it. He merely sat at one side, puffed and mopped his brow.

'To tell you the truth, I only design aerials and am not very familiar with the apparatus itself. Aerials are easy. If someone asked for an aerial that can receive signals 527 metres under the sea. . .' Once more his eyes fell on the biscuits.

Underwater! 500 metres. . . .127 men. That means a submarine, Long-kou said to himself.

Los Angeles

The Governor of California thought he was witnessing the end of the world. He had driven almost four hundred miles down the coast from Sacramento and it was like a nightmare voyage through hell. The golden sand usually crowded with tourists was covered with bloated corpses of drowned Chinese. The rotting bodies had attracted clouds of flies that covered them as if with black shrouds. The cyclone over the Pacific had just blown itself out. In the clear sky, a mass of dead bodies could be seen floating on the surface of the sea. Carnivorous fish up from the deep waters were seething and thrashing among them. According to satellite observations at least a hundred ships carrying Chinese refugees had been sunk during the hurricane.

Although California had suffered great damage, there was an atmosphere of celebration. People raised their glasses and thanked God in his wisdom, praying that the wind and the waves would continue and drown all the Chinese refugees.

Only ten days earlier public opinion would have been totally different. The Governor had often thought that democracy is a terrible system when it comes to dealing with disasters. Autocracy is far more effective.

The man responsible for sending only one ship to start with, knew what he was doing. The effect that this ship had on public opinion made him profoundly gloomy. In spite of the fact that every day the TV showed clear satellite pictures of *thousands* of ships making their way towards the coast of the United States, people only saw the single one that was in front of their eyes. Curiosity, a natural partner of consumerism, was far stronger than anxiety. Thousands of reporters swarmed around the refugees, who were given free publicity by the television stations. Americans are simple and straightforward people who like theatre and also like to demonstrate their Christian charity. Watching television, they can see all the details, but are not too close, which is more conducive to sympathy.

The Governor himself had first seen the ship on television. When *China the Beautiful* (the name was rather distressing) appeared off San Francisco, the decks were covered with *shugua*, as if on flat fields. There were a few scarecrows to keep the seabirds off, but no one was in sight. In contrast with this peaceful 'farmland', the obstructive activities of the US navy seemed to annoy people. It was out of the question to open fire or to ram the ship, so if it had not politely anchored outside the port, they would have been unable to prevent it from approaching the shore. Its mission was undoubtedly to arouse sympathy and influence public opinion.

The refugees' leader who conducted visitors round the ship spoke perfect American English. Pointedly he recalled the history of America as a beacon for the suffering people of the world and praised the principles of George Washington, Jefferson and Lincoln. The ocean winds had blown to the shores of America the ancestors of so many Americans from distant lands and he was confident, he said, that the Americans of today would not greet the homeless Chinese with warships and shells. As he spoke, large numbers of refugees emerged from the cabins and hold, formed into teams to work among the plastic tubing in which the *shugua* was growing. The Governor could imagine only too well the sentiments this scene would evoke when people saw it on television. All the refugees were naked, and their almost transparent bodies looked as if made of layers of cellophane. They moved as if sleepwalking. They were so thin that it looked as if the slightest wind might blow them away. All visitors were surprised that none of the refugees—men, women and children—had any hair. It was heart-rending to see them all lined up. The leader explained to the press that in order to maintain a basic minimum of health the refugees had to take it in turns to come on deck for fresh air, but only for half an hour a day. Their clothes and hair had all been necessary for the production of the nutrient fluid for growing *shugua*, because nothing else suitable could be found at sea. Everyone on the ship now had only a tattered gown made from pieces of rag, worn especially for visits from the press.

The Governor could see there was an element of stage-management in this, but the misery was real.

The visitors and press were shown the cabins and hold, where the conditions were miserable and shocking. On layer upon layer of bunks consisting only of bare boards, people were lying shoulder to shoulder. In the photographers' floodlights the bare heads looked like floats fixed to the borders of fishing nets.

All the bodies were making the same movements: first they filled their lungs with air, then drew in their bellies. The sound of all these people breathing deeply resembled an intermittent windstorm. A brash know-all among the pressmen explained that they were doing *qigong* exercises to relieve the pangs of hunger. While talking he went over to a fat congressman and said to the TV camera following him that this kind of *qigong* can reduce food intake and solve the problem of obesity. It should be welcomed by the American people, because it can make them healthy and good-looking, and the food saved would help feed the Chinese refugees. They were certainly not fat!

What made the Governor feel gloomy was that this kind of show at first caused a sensation in the US. There were meetings, people signed petitions and relief organizations were set up. He knew his countrymen well. They liked to think of themselves as saviours of the world, and their enthusiastic compassion for the dramas of human existence tended to make them close their eyes to consequences. Then there are the women's groups, religious pressure groups, actors and actresses, who all like to call attention to themselves.

The Governor firmly believed that government and politicians, who are extremely clear about the consequences, can do nothing in situations like this, because they are tied hand and foot by democracy. Since their political destiny is in the hands of ignorant and short-sighted electors, their own level of intelligence is reduced to that of the electors, and even at a decisive moment their reaction is weak and dilatory.

Three days after the arrival of *China the Beautiful,* at the moment when the wave of blind sympathy caused by mindless publicity reached its height, a large fleet of refugee ships arrived. In the prevailing climate it would have been impossible to drive them away by force, so all entries to ports were blockaded and guarded. The refugee ships made no attempt to enter; instead innumerable life-boats were lowered, and lashed together to form landing stages. By this means the refugees casually broke through the US Navy blockade and walked ashore. The disembarkation points were then surrounded by troops to prevent the refugees from going further into the country.

The Chinese refugees who landed were very respectful of authority, and in fact it was the US relief organizations who caused trouble by continually trying to break through the barriers to deliver food, clothing and medicine to the refugees.

In the space of three days thirty-eight such landing stages were used between Santiago and the port of Prince Rupert in Canada, and a yellow flood of people poured into North America. As soon as they were empty the ships immediately set sail for China to take on more refugees; each successive fleet was bigger than the last and the flow of refugees along the landing stages was continuous.

Another ridiculous feature of democracy, in the Governor's opinion, is that people seem to have no definite views of their own. In the space of a few days the excitement, their pledges, promises and feelings can all melt away and turn to something totally different.

The first to change were the three states on the West coast: California, Oregon and Washington, where the inflow of refugees had been greatest. The tourist industry in these states collapsed, hotels closed and people fled. International conferences and conventions moved elsewhere. The entertainment industry was hard hit—even Disneyland, which had not closed during the earthquakes. Unemployment soared, business slumped. But Chinese refugees continued to arrive in even greater numbers. The government, caught between humanitarian concern and the interests of the country, failed to find a reasonable practical solution. It passively accepted all who landed and obtained food supplies from state emergency reserves while increasing *shugua* production and the manufacture of the necessary equipment.

There had to be effective measures to prevent the spread of infectious diseases and avoid the introduction of bacteria carried by the refugees into the US. This was standard procedure for the reception of refugees. The problem now was that there were unprecedentedly large numbers of them. An internal tumour the size of an egg can sometimes be dealt with, but one the size of an ox is a different matter altogether. Other methods are called for.

Then 'Lice Extermination Squads' began to appear all over the West Coast, financed by businessmen and manned by the unemployed. They proclaimed that 'the Chinese have destroyed their own country and have no right to exist. Now they want to live like parasites in other countries. They must be wiped out like lice. That is what we are going to do, since the US army won't.'

The racist element in this development was strong. The Governor of California was black and well knew what racial discrimination is like. Yet most of those in the squads were black, Hispanics, Cubans and Filipinos. They seemed to hate the Chinese refugees and regard them as the dregs of humanity. There were even many American Chinese who were hostile towards their unfortunate countrymen. They neither joined the squads, nor condemned the killing.

As a result US troops and police, who had been brought in to prevent refugees from landing, spent all their time stopping the bloodshed: they became protectors of the refugees in fact. No one is supposed to be above the law in a democratic country and murder is illegal, no matter who the victim is. This was the main reason why the US military found itself in an embarrassing situation. The Chinese refugees were modest, courteous and disciplined; to deal with the 'exterminators' was very difficult and often necessitated armed intervention. Several refugee camps were attacked and occupied by the squads; the governor was appalled and revolted by the merciless slaughter that went on for several days. Refugees fled in all directions and the army was unable to control them. Completely ignorant of the language and the country, the majority were caught and killed by the extermination squads, often hanged on trees or on road signs.

There were some people who spoke up in defence of the refugees but most people merely felt sorry for them and contributed money. Those who had once joined in demonstrations on their behalf were now silent. They were not in favour of the killer squads, but their silence was not a condemnation. There was no blood on their hands.

The actions of the extermination squads did serve to mobilize mainly intellectuals, religious, charitable and human rights groups, well-educated young people who had been active in the original relief and money-raising groups. Now they united in what the media called the 'relief squads', in direct opposition to the Lice Extermination Squads, and protected and brought relief to the refugees. Their motivation was purely ethical and humanitarian. There were also people who sought a life of drama; the conflict provided them with a stage on which they could play the part of sublime idealists, in a lonely world that rarely provides such opportunities.

Of course there were also radicals ready to make political capital out of the crisis, especially university students full of vigour and vitality, who went into action almost as fast as the Lice Extermination Squads. They braved the furious seas to go to the aid of the refugees and clashed with the extermination squads, trying to protect their landing. They helped defend the refugee camps against attack, established refugee protection stations, which provided food, lodging and armed protection. They also tried organizing 'self-reliance' groups among the refugees, and because of this, came into conflict with the owners of land and property.

The Governor was nearing Los Angeles. The sides of the road were bordered with huge hoardings covered with advertisements. He noticed that a large hoarding with an advertisement showing a woman's behind and a pair of high-heeled shoes which he had seen the last time he passed, had now been replaced by a very different, ancient-looking picture. It was a blown-up copy of a print dating from 1895 based on a drawing by the German Emperor Wilhelm II. Long forgotten, it now had topical interest and was often reproduced and commented on. It showed the Archangel Michael, standing on a cliff, flaming sword in hand. Behind him were six ladies in armour, representing the European powers. With outstretched hand, the Archangel is showing the ladies how their fine lands, with towering castles and spires, are already burning. In the clouds and smoke, a phlegmatic and Buddha-like figure, representing the Yellow races, is riding cross-legged, palms together on a dragon's back, in an attitude of calm contemplation, dispersing the flames of burning cities and the storm clouds approaching from the horizon.

In the Governor's mind the term Yellow Peril had always conjured up a picture of soldiers of the yellow races mounted on small Mongolian horses, shooting arrows from the saddle. He understood now why the artist had presented the Yellow Peril as a Buddha. That was exactly the impression the refugees gave, yielding as water, but more easy to subdue and destroy than the armoured horsemen of Genghis Khan.

The Governor and the convoy of cars entered the city limits of Los Angeles. There was hardly any traffic and no sign of life in the streets; all the windows were closed and barred from the inside. Cars had been turned over and lay in the streets, their tyres in the air. Some of them had been burned. A cloud of black smoke hung over the city, buildings were on fire. Occasionally the silence was broken by gunfire.

Since the night before last, the 'relief squads' protecting refugee survivors of the tornado trying to get ashore, had been at war with the 'extermination squads' all over the city. The army and police, as well as the refugees, had become involved, resulting in a chaotic and dangerous situation. The Governor had been obliged to postpone his visit to the White House and had rushed to Los Angeles. It was already a civil war. He was apprehensive and extremely alarmed by the conflict between the American people themselves. Two days ago a congressman on television had even made reference to the age of Lincoln and the American Civil War. The Governor had considered this unnecessarily alarmist, but now he had visions of the millions of firearms in private hands being used by Americans against other Americans. Fighting between the rival squads was at present confined to the West Coast, but if it spread? The Governor's blood ran cold. That would be the end of the USA.

The Governor agreed with the President that this was Russia's intention. Russian had not only contributed thirty million tonnes of shipping to carry the refugees, providing food and fuel, but had also used extreme pressure to prevent the international community from interfering and had several times used its veto in the UN's Security Council to block the United State's proposals.

Refugees not only from North China had been shipped from the Russian Far East ports. Those already in Siberia had been persuaded to exchange their primitive way of life there for the dream of paradise in the USA and had embarked en masse. Russia was only too anxious to dump the lot of them in the United States. If they were not stopped the country would be buried alive, starting with California.

The Governor was well aware that the squads could not really solve anything. Mass slaughter was unacceptable these days, but no government could afford to uphold moral principles in all circumstances. The intransigence of the relief squads was partly responsible for the increasing violence of the extermination squads. If everyone would only cool down a little, people would realize that the US could not accept an unlimited number of refugees. It was now urgent to stop the flow of refugees at source, which would at least prevent the one hundred to three hundred million who were now awaiting transport from entering the USA. Every day lost, the Governor reminded the President more than once on the telephone, would multiply the difficulties many times over.

He had already suggested a US blockade of the Russian ports in the Far East. It would have been wise to do this under the flag of the United Nations, but there was no chance of that: Russia would certainly use her veto in the Security Council. Russian strategy was to play for time, by saying one thing and doing another, while shifting all the blame on to the impotent government of Shi Ge. To postpone the decision for one day meant decreasing the pressure on Russia. The matter was of the utmost urgency. Without the necessary legality provided by United Nations involvement, to start a war with Russia was dangerous. But there was no other choice: a war in Asia was better than civil war in the US. The Governor's view was that the attack on Russia should be limited and localized. Russia was unlikely to wage a full-scale war for the sake of the refugees. It should be done immediately, because Russia was weaker than the US: but if the flood of refugees continued that would change. Moreover, a limited conflict with Russia would distract the attention of the trouble-makers in California.

The President had seemed to appreciate the Governor's advice and asked him to come to Washington. He intended to cut short his stay in Los Angeles and then fly to Washington.

‘Stop here,’ he told the driver. He had noticed at a crossroads that down a side-street, there was a crowd of people in shirts printed with a skull—the logo of the Lice Extermination Squads. They were surrounding ten or more terrified refugees, squatting on the ground, whom they were sprinkling with gasoline. One of the killers was lighting a torch.

‘Stop!’ shouted the Governor, jumping out of the car. In the same instant, the refugees were enveloped in flames and ran screaming in all directions. There was a smell of burning skin and flesh, women’s hair flamed and children became balls of fire. A man with his clothes on fire suddenly rushed up to the killer who had lit the gasoline and took him in his arms. The other killers fled for their lives.

The Governor was transfixed. In despair he raised his long arms. He was surrounded by people on fire and had no idea what to do. Through the flames he saw one of the killers turn and open fire. He felt something like a burning worm enter his chest. A stain of blood on his spotless white shirt was expanding like a dream. He wanted to shout, ‘I am the Governor. .’ but he could no longer hear his voice. The sky and the earth turned. He saw another human torch fall with him, perfectly synchronized.

The Far East of Russia

It is dawn. The sea looks like grey silk, undulating softly. There are no ships in sight. The Sea of Japan is surrounded by the Korean peninsula, Japan, the island of Sakhalin and the coast of the Russian Far East with its ports between Vladivostok and Nikolaevsk. Apart from the south, access is via a few narrow straits, that are now mined. The huge warships and aircraft-carriers of the US Pacific Fleet have blocked all the entrances. The Chinese refugees do not know this: word has been passed that they only have to get to the Russian ports and they will be taken to the USA. So day and night they are hurrying towards the coast by road and river. Trains are running again from Harbin and elsewhere to the Russian ports and back non-stop, as efficiently as if they were being operated by professionals. The refugees who arrived first embarked immediately and every day, between three and five million refugees have been leaving the Russian ports, which are closer to the USA than the South China ports, so the journey is three to six days shorter. The ships are stuck in port, no ships can enter the Japan Sea, but more and more refugees arrive at the Russian ports every day.

The US had sent warships to prevent any ships of the Russian navy from reaching the Russian Far East. At the same time, in a conciliatory manner, the US government explained the very difficult situation in the US and suggested direct talks with Russia and an international settlement. The Russians replied the matter could no longer be solved by negotiation. The situation in Russia was desperate and had led her to open up a route on her own territory by which the refugees could make for the USA. The purpose was to release the refugees in Russia and save the country from a terrible disaster. What had not been foreseen, the Russian Foreign Minister explained, was that twice as many refugees in North China had surged through Russia to the ports, than had already left for the US. The ports were now blocked; but that had not discouraged the refugees, who were still arriving in even greater numbers. If the crisis in Russia continued to deteriorate, the government would have no alternative but to break the US blockade by military means.

It is dawn. The Sea of Japan looks like grey silk, there are hardly any waves.

Five thousand gas-turbine missiles, followed by five thousand fighter aircraft, like a flight of pigeons, thunder across the dawn sky. Not long afterwards, the sun rises and the expanse of grey silk becomes azure. Five American bases in Japan and Korea are destroyed. The US fleet blockading the Sea of Japan is wiped out, the minefields are destroyed by heavy bombing.

The Sea of Japan becomes calm and beautiful again. Innumerable Russian ships carrying refugees put to sea and rapidly reach full speed.

Beijing

As Shi Ge had expected, the discussion with Lu Shi-jia was unproductive. Ouyang Zhong-hua himself did not put in an appearance and had asked Lu Shi-jia to stand in for him. Shi Ge was invited to drink tea with sugar in it and eat some cakes made of white flour: not things that were available anywhere else in China.

Lu Shi-jia apologized, with apparent sincerity, yet everything the Green Party possessed, in one way or another, had been provided by Shi Ge, whose stomach would not stop rumbling after eating only a sweet biscuit. The Green Party's gratitude was clearly limited. Shi Ge could not guess how much material and food the Green Party had accumulated. When international aid had been abundant, he had personally signed an order enabling Ouyang and the hundred or so bases controlled by the Green Party to receive continuous supplies. Each base was like a colony of ants whose sole activity was to bring food into the nest. If a substantial quantity of supplies were to be found anywhere in China, it was in the hands of the Green Party.

The office in Beijing was itself proof of this prosperity. It had been opened at a time when all organizations in China were collapsing, and had not stopped expanding since. It had become the most powerful body in the capital and even the Premier had to go cap in hand to the door. The office occupied the whole of the courtyard that once housed the Foreign Affairs Society. The gate and surrounding wall were guarded by Green Guards armed to the teeth, and from dawn to dusk, crowds lined up around the gate to register and fill in forms.

The most important function of the office staff was to select people for admission into the bases. Shi Ge was astonished to see the old bureaucratic procedure still being used, which showed that the Green Party not only had a substantial network, but was making every effort to see that it functioned efficiently. The contrast with the surrounding chaos could not fail to make an impression. The government was incapable of restoring communications and information exchange was non-existent. The equipment and production machinery was there, but not electricity. The petroleum industry, it goes without saying, was no longer producing a drop of oil. In the last few days, the few hydroelectric plants in the Beijing area had all stopped. When food supplies from abroad dried up, the workers instantly dispersed. Although Shi Ge was still Premier, his only means of transport was a bicycle. There were no newspapers, radio or television, The world was minute, consisting only of what one could see and hear. Time had taken a great leap backwards to the days when there were only tribes and no need for governments or premiers.

Lu Shi-jia saw him out and watched as he mounted his bicycle. 'You are always welcome on one of our bases,' he remarked. His eyes could not conceal his conviction that to take refuge in a base was the only way to stay alive.

Shi Ge had thought of keeping the government structure in existence. The migration had been like a flood, and once the dam had been breached the government no longer had any role to play. But there were still three to four hundred million people left in China. They must survive in order to reconstruct the country: a government was still necessary to carry out this mission. He had once thought that the Green Party survival bases could take on the functions of government. After all Ouyang had used his position in the Government as head of the National Environmental Protection Bureau to set them up. The bases could not absorb three to four hundred million people but they could become centres of assembly and organization. They could provide an extended network, a kind of substitute government, so that China could continue to have the form of a nation state. They would be able to extend the Multi-Level Election System and plan the production of *shugua*. They could work for the revival of China. This would make it possible for the areas abandoned by the mass migration to survive and reconstruct.

However it was very clear from the conversation Shi Ge had today with Lu Shi-jia that Ouyang Zhong-hua had no intention of allowing the government to have any role in the survival bases. They would belong not to the government but to the Green Party or to him personally. He had made it clear, through Lu Shi-jia, that he had no intention of allowing the government to share the resources or network of the bases or to tolerate any government interference.

It was understandable. Shi Ge wanted to create a social system and finally establish a national government based on the Multi-Level Election System, to replace the present government. Ouyang had created a one-party administration of the bases, which was entirely contrary to the principles of the Multi-Level Election System. Naturally, Shi Ge would not be allowed to interfere.

He rode slowly on. He did not know what to do, or where he would to go. He felt a little like a spring that has been stretched to a dangerous point, broken loose and bounced away. With one hand he turned his portable radio so that the photoelectric cells faced the sun. Foreign broadcasts were now the only source of news and all were reporting US losses in the Sea of Japan. Analysts were anxiously trying to guess how the US would respond. The conflict was rapidly escalating into all-out war. Shi Ge had no guilty feelings about the US losses, although he knew than an investigation would reveal the role he had played. But he had been and was still surrounded by death on such a scale that he was unmoved, even by the prospect of a generalized war. All he hoped for was that the refugees would waste no time in embarking and getting out of the death trap of the Sea of Japan before the US counter-attacked.

There were very few people left in Beijing. Foreigners had long since been flown home. In the heat of the sun, the imposing embassies like empty mausoleums cast silent shadows. Flowers had begun to grow between the railings, already mottled with rust, and were overflowing the pavement where no one walked. The lines of the poet Du Fu suddenly came into his mind like a dagger: 'The state is destroyed, the mountains and rivers remain; in the city the spring grass grows deep.'

In the principal streets there were groups of people on bicycles or on foot leaving the city. Some of them, in search of a safe future, were making for the Green Party survival bases. They had only to recognize the principles and leadership of the Green Party to be admitted. This gave them a life-long guarantee of survival, no matter how hard life might become for others.

Most of those leaving were former government personnel. When it was decided to reduce the size of the government they had volunteered to go and live in the rural areas, to get agricultural production started again. They were mainly young men and women from the Green Association and the Green University, who carried with them *shugua* production equipment and were intent on spreading the idea and practice of the Multi-Level Election System. Shi Ge felt proud and moved by these pale, thin young people, full of idealism, who were going to a world of chaos and desolation, where they would rely on their own insignificant powers of resistance to face the future and its unknown terrors. They made him think of the educated young people in the not very distant past, who had gone to the mountains and villages to share and improve the hard lives of the peasants. If there was a future for mankind, it would surely depend on the heroism and idealism of such young people, even if their idealism might sometimes seem immature and even absurd. Shi Ge had more sympathy with such idealism than with cold realism, brilliant strategy and subtle calculation.

An item of news on the radio caught his attention: Huang Shi-ke had shot himself in his Presidential office in Nanjing. According to the United Press report his Minister of Finance Liu Ya-ji, had allegedly been killed by the Russians with the connivance of the Beijing government. He had been hailed as a martyr in Nanjing and been given an imposing funeral. The truth however was that the Minister of Finance was not dead: he had vanished, together with ninety million US$ of aid funds given to Huang Shi-ke's government by the United States. The money had now disappeared down the black hole of international banking and had become private property. Huang Shi-ke, aware of the damage this disgraceful incident would do to the reputation of his government, had decided that it would be best 'to knock out the sore tooth and swallow it', hence the stage-managed 'martyrdom' of the Minister of Finance. No one had expected that the truth would come out only two days later, as a result of quarrels within Huang Shi-ke's government

Shi Ge did not believe that Huang Shi-ke's suicide was purely a matter of honour: he was not thin-skinned to that extent. Only a complete despair and disappointed hope could push him to this point. Shi Ge knew that any number of people had taken their own lives because of the tragedy and disaster that had struck China. But Huang Shi-ke had only just achieved high office and was one of those ambitious men who believe that 'no one but I can do it'. He must have experienced an unbearable loss of confidence.

The anxiety Shi Ge felt about the Green Party gradually dissipated and in a spirit of self-mockery he recalled his own 'suicide'. He had been sitting on the bank of the Yangzi River trying to work out a complicated theoretical problem concerned with wages. He had been lost in thought, gazing at the water for several hours, without getting any closer to a solution.

First a woman from the river navigation signal office nearby came and observed him for some time before going away. She came back shortly afterwards with a policeman who pestered him, would not let him go, but kept talking in an inexplicable manner, saying encouraging things and apparently trying to calm him. Then a deputy director and two teachers from the college he was attending arrived, very flustered. They said the college had received a phone call saying that a student with the college badge was about to throw himself into the river.

Ever since then, when he was trying to work everything out, from top to bottom, to perfection, he always had a picture in his mind of a young would-be suicide, silently gazing at the river. Later, as an official, he became increasingly convinced that the highest achievement in politics is to 'govern by non-action'. No one, no power or technology that works from above downwards, can adequately administer an increasingly complicated and changing world. The attempts of those with power to adjust the system, is like trying to push a vehicle with brakes but no engine. This is true of what has been honoured for so many years with the name 'reform'.

Shi Ge hated power: it was not safe to play with, and imposed an intolerable burden of fear and exhaustion on whoever possessed it. His 'suicide' was perhaps the initial inspiration of the Multi-Level Election System. He had been powerful, but had never used it for the benefit of any power-hungry individual. His highest ideal was to obliterate the kind of power that used to be associated with dazzling crowns and hard thrones; to transform it by means of the Multi-Level Election System into something as formless as air—belonging to everyone. This was the 'non-action' action of the Taoist philosophers: not relying on one man's individual actions but on the energy of the system itself, directed from below, not from above.

Why should he worry about his personal powerlessness? The non-cooperation of the Green Party was not a decisive setback. By now there were enough cells that had been nourished by Multi-Level Election System: if they had sufficient vitality they would multiply like cells—from the bottom up—and develop into a whole social system. If in that period of growth, he went on holding the baby's bottle, it would be like his 'suicide'.

He realized he was going in the opposite direction to Zhongnanhai and found himself in front of the gate of a factory that used to make internal combustion engines and later became the biggest producer of *shugua* production equipment in the country. He had visited it several times. It was very hot, silent and deserted. A fog of melancholy invaded his mind. He knew that it was the memory of Chen Pan that had brought him here again. The last time he had come on an inspection visit, she had been technical director in charge of the production of portable *shugua* equipment. He had seen her but they had not spoken much and had not seen her since.

Shi Ge was surprised to see a small car emerge from the depths of the factory site. When he hesitantly stretched out a hand to stop it, the car braked in front of him. He stopped wondering who might still have access to petrol at this time. It was Lu Shi-jia , who got out of his car with a slightly embarrassed smile. Shi Ge swallowed his enquiry about Chen Pan's whereabouts.

'She is not here.' Lu Shi-jia did not say who, but they both understood. So Lu Shi-jia was not only Ouyang's spokesman but also ran errands for him; he had obviously come looking for Chen Pan. Shi Ge felt like a thief caught in the act of trying to appear as a honest man.

'I'll take you home,' said Lu Shi-jia, perhaps to fill an awkward silence.

'No need. I have nothing in particular to do. . .' Shi Ge said politely. The car drove quickly away, leaving an unfamiliar smell of petrol.

If man's inner nucleus is the heart, Shi Ge pondered, then that of the heart is nothingness. He narrowed his eyes in the bright sunlight. He had never achieved nothingness and had never lost it. He gloomily mounted his bicycle and pedalled off. Profound exhaustion seized him like a monstrous octopus, and he fell off several times. He wanted to sleep where he fell. He thought he had long since strangled his desire to sleep. But as soon as the rope was loosened, as soon as he stopped making the effort, it needed ten times more will-power to control it again. Pain brought him an instant of clarity and he struggled to his feet, afraid that once he fell asleep he would not wake up for many, many months.

There were no guards at the gate of Zhongnanhai. Ten days ago he had given the personnel permission to come and go as their wished, so that they could search for food. This had been the only place in the city where there were still some insects, fish and edible plants. Now even the earthworms had been dug up.

There were holes three foot deep everywhere with the earth piled up alongside. Rare flowers and shrubs and ancient trees had been stripped and felled. What was left of the government was confined to a small courtyard in the Northeast corner of Zhongnanhai. Most of the other buildings were in ruins and looked like something out of a dream. Even the duty officer slept like a dead man at the gate.

In a daze Shi Ge opened the door to his room. The bed in the corner of the room looked extremely rickety. He did not want to go anywhere: the carpet in front of the door seemed to be pulling him down. There was a sound, a cry. His heart thumped. For some reason he felt that it had something to do with him—was part of him even. He looked round and saw, squeezed between the wall and the door an inflatable baby doll. It had fallen and only the head was visible. Two large eyes were fixed on him. The slightly pouting mouth seemed to protest at being squeezed. Shasha!

He leapt out of the abyss of exhaustion. It was no dream. Shasha had been standing in the doorway waiting for him and had been squeezed behind the door when he opened it in a daze. He took him up and as he did so, the pressure of his hand made Shasha give voice to a series of sounds like a spoiled child. The small arm was holding a piece of paper stuck to his chest and seemed to be giving it to Shi Ge.

I have joined a work brigade going south and am leaving at once. I have waited for you for nearly two hours. It looks as if fate is still manipulating me. I no longer think about whether we will ever meet again. I must make my own decision. I am leaving Shasha with his father (at least with the one who has agreed to be his father). Don't say I am laying down a burden.......ai! I wanted to joke but I cannot stop my tears. Not because I cannot bear to leave the child, I am leaving him for you. More than that, I think that I am leaving a part of myself with you. (How I wish it was all of me!) I know why you have kept your distance from me, and I don't want to explain that incident. Things called fate can neither be explained nor changed. I only want to say: what I said in court at the very end is the truth and has never changed and cannot change. I still do not know whether you heard my words. If you did not I repeat them: I love you. 13h.17

Shi Ge looked at his watch—13h.28. Then he picked up Shasha and rushed out. He was not sure which direction to take, but she could not have gone far in ten minutes. He must run for dear life and catch up with her.

Only after running four or five hundred metres did he remember his bicycle. He could not bear the thought of going back for it and continued in the direction of the Xinhua Gate of Zhongnanhai. That was probably the way she had taken; but not the way he had just returned home, unfortunately. He took a short cut by a small path between hedges and jumped down on to the road leading to the Xinhua Gate. Before he could steady himself, he felt a rush of wind and the force of a blow. He found himself and another person rolling head over heels into a hole dug by someone looking for edible roots. He got to his feet, his face all scratched; Shasha was unhurt but lying under the branches, complaining each time they moved. It was Long-kou who had bumped into them in his electric pick-up. His crutch was under a pile of batteries.

Shi Ge had no time to worry about Long-kou and started to run. Long-kou caught him by the trouser leg.

'I know the secret of the transmitter. . .!'

'We'll talk about that later,' Shi Ge replied, shaking him off.

Shi Ge was running. Long-kou shouted after him. 'Wang Feng has a submarine with nuclear missiles.'

'He sent a list of the crew's families killed. . .by US missiles. . .' Shi Ge was within sight of the Xinhua Gate. Long-kou's voice sounded far away. 'The submarine was not destroyed.'

Shi Ge stopped as if he had run into a wall and was seeing stars. The gate shrank into a blood-red spot. He lost all feeling of reality, leaving only a jumble of images. The shock of Long-kou's words shattered all logic and memory.

There was no positive proof but Long-kou had found a retired submarine commander who had seen at once that those named in Wang Feng's list of the dead were families of among the best engineers and missile experts of the navy. The order transferring these men had come from the highest level; since then they seemed to have disappeared from submarine command. The conclusion Long-kou had reached was pure assumption, but Shi Ge did not doubt for an instant that it was correct. It was typical of Wang Feng.

He and Long-kou took batteries from vehicles that had been abandoned for lack of petrol and put them in the three-wheeler. Most of the batteries were low, so they loaded more than they needed and when one ran out exchanged it for another. After a few dozen kilometres they were all flat and they had to search for more.

When they arrived at the detention centre for state prisoners the sun was already low in the sky. Shi Ge had signed a decree releasing all prisoners, so that they could fend for themselves. Wang Feng was not included because the question of the secret transmitter had not been cleared up. The prison staff had all vanished and the keys to the cells were in the middle of the office table. Shi Ge himself had been a prisoner here, so everything was very familiar. Long-kou, who had been driving, had a cramp in his hand and could not hold his crutch, so Shi Ge gave one arm to him and carried Shasha with the other.

The high window in Wang Feng's cell made it feel like being in a well. He looked as if he had nothing to eat or drink for some time; his plain grey uniform was dirty and his beard had grown. But he still stood erect and arrogant.

Shi Ge abruptly asked him whether there was still a nuclear submarine carrying missiles. Wang Feng never moved an eyebrow. His lack of reaction to this sudden question gave him away, clearer than words. His height allowed him to look down on Shi Ge.

'Everything to do with the submarine is a state secret: what right have *you* to ask?' He looked away and his eyes became cruel and full of scorn. Shi Ge knew that this man would not shrink from destroying the world: but he lacked the courage to give the order himself and be called the greatest criminal in history. Perhaps it was the self-love of the high born that had led him to use the despicable and cowardly trick of inciting the crew to revenge in the depths of the sea, by sending them nothing but a list of their dead

'Had you no pity for the crew?' Shi Ge asked. 'Their loved ones died a cruel death. Yet you wanted to send them to hell in your place.'

Wang Feng gave him a poisonous look. 'You! You are a pitiful circus dwarf!' Indeed, compared with Wang Feng he was indeed a dwarf. But why 'circus'?

Shi Ge restrained Long-kou and told Wang Feng,'You are free to go.'

Shi Ge did not lock the door of the cell behind him. In a mirror in the corridor he saw blood on his face and Shasha's cocked eyebrow and sidelong glance. Long-kou carrying a pistol, jerked along beside him on his crutch. When they all got into the three-wheeler and sped down the hill, Shi Ge did indeed think for a moment that he must be in some circus act.

All sorts of solutions flashed through his mind. But there was no electricity, no fuel, no information network and no signboard marked 'international communication'. The scorching sun made him feel dizzy. Only the Russian Headquarters at Zhangjiakou was in contact with the rest of the world. How many batteries would it take to get this vehicle there so that the Russian army could warn the Americans? The US was the most likely target since the families of the submarine's crew had all been killed in the US nuclear attack on the Naval Base. Perhaps Russia would not be sorry if the US was subject to a nuclear attack. But of course they would want to make sure there was no misunderstanding about where the attack came from. . . Even in the heat of the sun his blood turned cold at the thought: a misunderstanding. Why had the submarine remained so long inactive? Was it waiting for a misunderstanding? Now was the opportunity. There was not a moment to lose. 'Turn the car! Head for Zhangjiakou!' he shouted into Long-kou's ear.

Long-kou seemed not to have heard, but drove into the big compound and gave a piercing whistle. Five or six emaciated men wearing spectacles appeared. Shi Ge watched him unload some dried fish and share it among them. Only then did he realize Long-kou had insisted on taking all the fish out of the lake before Zhongnanhai was opened to those searching for food. He had assembled all the technicians in Beijing who had been working on the transmitter and fed them on fish, in case he might need them again. When Shi Ge heard what he had in mind he warmly embraced him. The transmitter was clearly the only way of communicating with the submarine. The list of the dead was not an order but a hint. If the transmitter could send out a clear order that would cancel the hint, it would have the force of an order restraining the crew from inflicting nuclear revenge on the US.

The problem was how to send the order. Without a complete grasp of the code it was impossible to use the transmitter directly. But as long as an order used only words contained in the list of dead, it would be possible to use the prototype receiver that Long-kou had found and search until they found the keys on the transmitter corresponding to the words they chose.

The procedure was very difficult and complicated, so in order to save trouble Shi Ge selected only seven words: YOU-ARE-FORBIDDEN-TO-USE-NUCLEAR-MISSILES. Each of these were words used in the list of dead. Fortunately the research institute had all the instruments that made this possible, but it was necessary to find more batteries to run them or painfully turn a model of a sea-wave generator by hand. Slowly the receiver began to print out the Chinese characters. The specialists stood around it like surgeons round an operating table, laboriously tracing each extremely complicated and simple signal.

When the codes of the seven words had all been found and entered, they immediately began to be transmitted in a recurring cycle. The designer of the transmitter had included this facility: the subsequent cycle wiped out the previous one so that it would not be retained in the transmitter. Long-kou used an electromagnetic wave finder to show Shi Ge that the satellite ground station in the northern suburb of Beijing was sending the coded message into space. The station was on a solar electrical circuit and could therefore operate continuously and automatically.

The light this evening was very strange, the sky seemed to be full of blood-red spots. The indistinctly visible world seemed to have been dyed red. Shi Ge had never seen the moon so red, like an open wound, still and silent, bleeding profusely. Terrifying.

13

In the Pacific Ocean – The Puskin Moon Station – In the Taihang Mountains: a vagabond's story – Shenjianong Nature Reserve – Beijing: Zhongnanhai – The World of Mankind – The Dog Pens – The Wilderness

In the Pacific Ocean

A transparent flexible plastic tube, as thin as a pencil stretched from the sea-bed to the surface, where it secreted a gluey metallic substance, that became strong and pliable on contact with the seawater and formed a net almost invisible to the naked eye. It could not be damaged by waves or fish, or detected by passing ships or a Mexican patrol boat. If it was broken by a ship's screw or other sharp object under the surface, the plastic tube would secret the metallic substance until the net was repaired.

The net lay on the surface covering an area of up to one hundred square metres. Its purpose was not to catch fish but radio waves, which were carried by the metallic thread through the plastic tube into the submarine below, whatever its depth.

At this moment the air was alive with radio signals as if the whole world was shouting, and already could be heard in the submarine. There were even rumours of a submarine covered by some kind of parasitic mollusc.

The BBC was transmitting the report of a foreign correspondent:

> I was at the top of a two hundred metre high TV tower here in Vladivostok filming the scene of the Chinese refugees embarking and witnessed the most extraordinary sight. Every dock, quay and pier in the port has been crowded with ships; every space in sight covered with Chinese refugees. Suddenly, at high tide, the level of the sea went down at a great speed and I could see a huge expanse of the seabed laid bare. Marine animals that did not have time to escape tried to hide and a rare white shark was caught between two rocks. Ships in shallow water suddenly found themselves lying on the bottom and people on board were sliding down the decks. The big ships at the deep-sea docks broke their moorings and crashed together with a sound of thunder.

I was possibly the only person high enough to see that the sea had been sucked back by a crest of water on the horizon. This phenomenon, usually caused by an earthquake under the sea, last occurred, I believe, off the coast of Chile in about 1960 and affected the whole Pacific, causing the loss of several thousand lives.

The hungry refugees already on board ships slid down to the bare seabed and gathered shellfish and ate them raw. Refugees on land rushed to join them.

After an interval, a wave almost 45 metres high came thundering in, drowning everyone on the sea-bed. There was no possibility of escape. Hundreds of ships were lifted up and hurled one against another killing innumerable refugees and others. A ship of about 250,000 tons was thrown into the street, knocking down big buildings as if they were made of matchsticks and ended up in the public park. Unexploded US mines were swept ashore, many in the city centre and exploded, causing much damage

The second wave, about ten metres high, was far less destructive.

I could see half of Vladivostok under water and devastation all around. Nothing is left of the docks along the bay; shipyards, warehouses, cranes and all port facilities have been destroyed. The biggest Russian port has been reduced to nothing. The prosperous main street has been turned into a watery ruin; seaweed hangs everywhere. Buildings near the railway station were on fire. I saw a turtle, still alive, stranded on top of a monument.

It is not known exactly how the US produced this seismic wave. Japan and Korea were both affected, but the wave was no more than a few metres high and the damage far less than in Russia. To be able to control the direction of the wave in the Sea of Japan is proof of remarkable technical skill.

Russia has not given details of the damage; but according to our information, the two most important ports and transit centres used for Chinese refugees, Vladivostok and Nahodka, were almost entirely destroyed. Russia has reported at least 200,000 dead. The number of refugees who lost their lives is unknown, but it must run into millions. The Russian Far East fleet has been almost totally destroyed and at least ten million tons of shipping on the coastline. Sovietskaya Gavan and the Amur river port of Nikolaevsk are the only remaining continental Russian ports in the Far East, and both are in remote areas. At one blow the Russian capacity to transport Chinese refugees has been reduced by four fifths. The threat to the USA has been almost entirely removed.

Ding Da-hai listened carefully. He now wore head-phones even when sleeping. This is it! This was what he had been waiting for.

What would the Russians do now? There might be a gradual escalation, but it was unlikely. But the decisive result of this action was that it was now impossible for Russia to transfer the burden of refugees on to the US. The ports were all destroyed and millions of refugees would inevitably make their way to Siberia, even more than had left. The United States would win without firing another shot. Ding Da-hai had thought the Russians ought to use nuclear weapons against the US. But Russia was no match for the US, even weakened as she was by her own problems. He would have to strike the first blow himself. The Americans will naturally assume that Russia is the culprit. Who else was capable of launching a surprise nuclear attack?

This is why the submarine had been lying so long like a rock at the bottom of the sea. He was aware of the dangers involved: perhaps he should not expect anything other than his own destruction. If only he had two submarines, he would be able to act sooner. He did not want to take his revenge by attacking one old enemy and let another escape punishment. Therefore, after much thought he determined to kill two eagles with one arrow

He switched off the radio receiver, hung up his head-phones and after closing his eyes for a few seconds, very carefully pressed the signal for battle-stations.

He felt the submarine move slightly: the energy released by the sudden movement of 127 men relieved at last from deadening boredom. He could imagine everyone jumping out of bed, out of chairs, crowding round the spiral stairs and running each to his station.

He shaved carefully, put on a new uniform and attached the epaulettes of a Senior Captain, his present from Wang Feng. Not since his wedding had he taken such care about his appearance. By the time he stood in front of the camera in the control room the whole crew were at their stations watching the video screens.

He always thought that he had no more feelings than a stone, yet his heart was thumping. The lenses of the camera were like the black eyes of his crew. For a moment he felt that his boiling blood was evaporating; his mind was blank and empty.

'You. . .' he seemed to get stuck, and there was a long silence. Senior officers in the control room with him began to feel uneasy. 'You do not have access to the radio. . .so you cannot know what has happened in the last few months. It would be difficult for me to explain everything. There are some things that do not concern you. Those that do, the most important things are on the command receiver.'

Ding Da-hai slowly adjusted the video camera and turned to the Communications Officer. 'Please go to my cabin and switch on the receiver.' In a moment all the video screens showed the officer standing beside the receiver and a long strip of paper sliding out on to the chart table.

'Please read it.' The crew had never before heard the Captain given an order in such a mild voice. He then turned away from the screen and wished he could block his ears, he would rather have a hot wire burn through his eardrums than listen to that list of the dead again.

The Communications Officer read out: 'you are forbidden to use nuclear weapons you are forbidden to use nuclear weapons you. . . . .'

Ding Da-hai shook his head. He must be dreaming. . . He abruptly raised his head to look at the screen and could see the officer's lips clearly enunciating the words: 'you are forbidden to use nuclear weapons.'

The senior officers kept looking first at the screen then at Ding Da-hai and back. They looked as if they were trying not to smile, listening to a receiver that had gone mad.

'What the devil?' Ding Da-hai thundered. There was silence. The Communications Officer, stunned, stopped reading on the word 'you'. Normally Ding Da-hai would want to strangle anyone speaking so loudly.

He strode to his cabin and ran his eyes over the length of paper: there was nothing but those seven words, and no space between them. Where did this message come from? Everything around him seemed unreal and floating. Perhaps he had even begun to sway, because the communications officer put out a hand to steady him. Then his mind cleared. He brushed the officer's hand away and closed down the video. The crew had seen enough of his agitation.

'Leave me.'

He closed his cabin door. He must have imagined it. He bit the tip of his tongue—an ancient test: the words on the tape were unmistakable. Like those nightmares when he was in prison in America and woke up suddenly covered with sweat. God forbid! Not that! At such times he could find no boundary between dream and reality. He pulled up his sleeve. The scar on his left arm made by his son's fishhook was still there. He could feel the swelling and hardness. He handled his navigation logbook and irreversible mug. The cloth wallet containing his watch was black and hard with his own dried blood. That was no dream. The watch was still signalling that a message had been sent; vibrating faintly. The batteries must be almost flat.

There was no question that the wavelength had been changed: how or why, he did not know. He did not believe that Wang Feng had changed it: he never contradicted himself and it was not his style to send a message like that. In any case Ding Da-hai did not intend to obey the order. There was no question about that: there was no one, no power in the world that could prevent him from taking the next step. Ever since the list of the dead had arrived he himself had become an armed missile: the firing programmes could not be changed, nor the targets. What could he do? Explain to the crew? That would take days. Just tell them their families are all dead? Would they believe it? He could not even prove that the list of dead had ever existed. They were not likely to believe that the message had simply consisted of a list of names. But if they had seen the list they would probably understand that it meant permission to take their revenge. At the very least it did not forbid them to do so. Now there was only an order that no missiles should be fired. The training and discipline members of the crew had received about nuclear missile launching procedures would make it impossible for Ding Da-hai to convince or force them to obey him. It was going to be difficult to kill two eagles at once.

He took his son's fishing rod from its place on the wall, and half closing one eye stretched it out as if over the sea and saw in his mind's eye a big white fish swim past, its skin a multicoloured dream in the refracted light of the sun.

A self-destruct firing—that was the only way. He rubbed his spectacles for some time. The crisis of confusion in his mind settled down. When he left his cabin, he was calm and determined.

The crew were still at action stations, talking anxiously among themselves. His arrival made them feel more at ease.

'There is a problem with the receiver,' he said, again polishing his spectacles. 'It seems to have gone mad and driven me crazy too.' Some of the crew smiled discreetly—they had not heard him joke before. The Communications Officer raised his eyebrows and gave him an angry look.

'The first part of the message has evidently got lost. It was certainly an order to go through Number Two Practice firing procedure, though it's obvious we wouldn't fire the missiles. Someone was probably worried we might forget.' Normally when he gave an order, it was so short that no one had time to even glance at him. This time most of the crew smiled. The officers found the explanation odd, but couldn't think why.

Number Two Practice involved going through the whole firing procedure from beginning to end without actually firing the missiles. The submarine rose extremely slowly towards the surface, taking sixteen minutes to rise from 290 to 25 metres. During this time Ding Da-hai was extremely calm.

Every night he had to hold in his hand the small metal box hanging round his neck—it felt burning hot—and open it again and again, before he could go to sleep. This time he did not only look at it. He took out the small semi-transparent circuit card, which turned off the safety mechanism of the twenty missiles and started the firing procedure. As he replaced it in position, his hand was absolutely steady.

The submarine gradually approached the surface. It was the first time it had surfaced in daytime since leaving the naval base.

'Heavens above!' exclaimed the sonar officer, pointing a finger at the video screen with an expression of horror on his face. There were several video cameras set into the pressure hull at different points. For the purpose of the present exercise, they were all directed upwards towards the surface. As the submarine rose, the screen became brighter. Everyone was used to diffused light coming through the water, but this time the surface of the sea was grey and opaque like the sky of some indistinct world. A sky in which clouds were floating, clouds—clouds in human shape with arms and legs, floating, rocked by the waves as they were flying. As the submarine rose to the standard depth for firing, the human forms swept past endlessly, so many that they were touching and cutting out all but patches of daylight. It was as if the whole Pacific was covered and it seemed that the submarine would never get out from under this terrible roof. In the control room every face was frozen to stone with horror.

No one who had not witnessed this scene could possible imagine it. If Ding Da-hai had not heard reports on the radio, he would have wondered whether this was a hallucination and the submarine was floating into the sea of hell. He opened and closed the intercom time again and finally decided to explain nothing. The bodies were all of Chinese who had been drowned in the tornado or killed in the slaughter on the coast of California. If they were not consumed by fire, they might be carried by ocean currents, home to where they came from. His throat tightened at the thought of going home.

The submarine steadied and the twenty missile ports underwater opened simultaneously. He gave orders to float just below the surface of the sea. The regulation depth for Number Two Practice was twenty five metres. No one questioned the order. Perhaps some were too shocked to notice. For what he wanted to do it was best to be as near the surface as possible, as long as there was no danger of giving away the submarine's position.

He made the changes he wanted in the firing procedure, making sure that no trace of them would be appear on other video screens. Not that anyone one would understand their significance. None of them would ever know that there was a procedure for self-destruct.

It was something he had worked out himself in the slow hours of waiting on the sea-bed—a double-edged sword. Missiles are normally expelled from the submarine by compressed air one by one before the rocket engines are ignited. There is insufficient compressed air to launch them all at once. There also has to be about three seconds after each launch for the submarine to re-stabilize. A minimum of nine minutes, thirty seconds is usually sufficient to launch twenty missiles. But if a submarine is threatened with immediate destruction, it is possible to launch the missiles simultaneously: by igniting the rocket engines *inside* the missile tubes. They all fire together and the strength of the recoil sends the submarine straight to the bottom of the sea.

Ding Da-hai had no regrets about the submarine: better to destroy it himself than allow the enemy to do so once the missiles had all been fired. A homeless submarine had no reason to survive. This solution had always been in his mind, but only as a last resort. His own life was no loss, but it was his duty to protect the lives of the crew and he was about to kill them. By using the pretext of 'another firing drill' he could allow the crew to complete all preparations, then it was only a question of hitting the button and firing the missiles. If he fired only one—the normal procedure—the crew would be unharmed. The exercise would be stopped and everyone would be furious at having been tricked. Only if the firing was simultaneous would they have no time to react before the submarine sank to the bottom; by then the twenty missiles would already be beyond recall.

If there had been time to explain, the crew would perhaps understand and consent to die with him. Their loved ones were already in another world so why remain in this one? He had no reason to blame himself. Once in the nether world, he would assemble them and ask their forgiveness.

The submarine was close to the surface, the periscope almost out of the water. The sky was clear, the seagulls dazzling white. In the bright sunlight the sea should have been pristine and sparkling. Instead it was covered with dead bodies. The submarine seemed to act like a magnet, that made more and more of them gather round it. Perhaps their souls were using what was left of their bodies to hide it from enemy eyes. . . .

A huge face bloated by immersion, was pressed up against the glass of one of the video camera ports. The sight made Ding Da-hai's hair stand on end. He saw the body of a woman float past; one breast had been eaten by fish. . .

He thought of his wife. He had only been able to remain four months on the bottom of the sea without going mad: because, day and night, apart from a short sleep, he spent all his time in front of the computer working on procedure: twenty missiles, forty nuclear warheads, forty targets. Like forty stars, flickering in the night the only light in his dark soul; positioning, target-seeking and finally the autodestruct firing. The amount of work involved was astronomical and it became an essential part of his life—like oxygen.

Now that his life was about to end in an explosion, he found some consolation in the fact that he had assembled a small apparatus, a floating radio-beacon like those used in life-rafts The submarine was going to be destroyed, but the beacon would float on the surface and send out non-stop, a pre-arranged message. He installed a timer and set the beacon to begin emitting on the surface of the sea shortly after the missiles were on their way: time enough to see the end of a nuclear war.

He did not want there to be a mystery forever as to who had fired the forty nuclear warheads: the message to be repeated by the beacon informed Russia, the United States and the world that China had settled accounts for the 205 missiles she had received. Chinese always pay their debts!

It was time. The preparations were complete, the arming programme faultlessly installed. He pressed the firing key with his finger: the last time he would touch anything. The past, the present and the future were all going to be fused together. In the stillness, he heard the drawn-out call of his mother from the entrance of the village. He heard the sound of his own bare feet walking on the sand. He longed to feel the sea on his naked body once again, the welcoming, cool and luminous sea, the blue, generous sea where he would soon be.

There were more and more dead bodies floating on the surface of the sea, packed together as if in an embrace of death. They suddenly rose into the air, and as if by their combined strength, pulled the twenty missiles out of the water, before being fused together by the white-hot flames from the rocket engines. Perhaps all those Chinese did not want to become part of America. That was the direction the missiles were taking.

Between nine and thirteen minutes later, at twenty times the speed of sound they re-entered the atmosphere, Each missile had two automatic target-seeking warheads, each with a different target, and each with an explosive force of 1.2 megatons.

The Pushkin Moon Station

The long nights are quiet on the Moon. In the slanting rays of the sun, the flat grey plains look mysterious and desolate. Wherever you look, you have a feeling of rootlessness. Only the earth, looming over the lunar horizon, now dark, now bright, warms the heart and gives a steady, dependable, peace of mind.

'That's home,' Andrei said to himself every day when he had finished work, looking through the window at the earth, drinking coffee and listening to something by Tchaikovsky.

It was the best moment of the day. The earth was beautiful and so big—four times the size of the moon, reflecting light into the little cabin so far from home. He never tired of looking at it.

His two colleagues were looking at the earth on the video screen. One of them was from the Volga Delta and the other from India. The side of the earth facing the moon gradually darkened. There were no clouds. Andrei gazed at Moscow. In his mind's eye he could see Katy and her beautiful neck as she looked up at the moon.

Moscow's orders were that the lights in the moon station should remain on day and night. But Andrei and his colleagues ignored this rule every evening when they gazed at the earth, because the reflection on the glass in the window interfered with the view. If Moscow complained that they couldn't see the station clearly, they merely switched off the sound and left only an angry, but silent man glaring on the screen.

The screen itself they never switched off, though the view was always the same: the boring control centre, the same face seen day in and day out—not to mention the constant scolding. The screen was their lifeline and gave them a sense of safety. Only it could haul them back home from this dead rock.

Andrei often dreamed that this lifeline was cut off and he was flying uncontrollably in outer space. When he woke up, drenched with sweat and saw the slight flickering of the screen and those faces watching over him day after day, he was sometimes moved to secret tears. Now, perhaps as a reaction, he glanced quickly at the screen, just in time to see the command centre disintegrate. The face of the director crashed into the lens like a runaway locomotive. All in a fleeting instant—so fast that he was not sure anything had happened. Then nothing. The screen was blank.

Andrei switched on the sound. Nothing.

He heard the panic-stricken shouts of his companion. On the screen of the telescope, the beautiful earth was still there; the northern part of the continent, his home, the wide rich lands of Russia, across which hundreds, even thousands of lights appeared, as if whole constellations of stars had fallen, stars that grew brighter, and expanded like flowers of fire opening. Unimaginably beautiful and soul-stirring and enough to stop the heart and freeze the blood.

The biggest flower of fire opened where Moscow was.

In the Taihang Mountains: a vagabond's story.

There's a lot of strange things going on these days, and as they say, it's not strange to see strange things. But last night I heard someone laughing, and when I think of it, the roots of my hair tingle.

The wind was something awful last night, and blowing hot, as if it was coming from somewhere that was burning. Even the half-moon wanted to get out of the way if you ask me. I couldn't sleep, so I went off to a deserted village, to find something to eat. I wandered around for a long time and found nothing. All of a sudden I saw this man lying in a yard, dead I thought. In the light of the moon I could make out a pile of something near his head that might be food, but when I felt it with my hand, it was only a pile of little batteries.

I get the shock of my life when the man said 'Help me please.'

'I can't carry you,' I said straight out. These days it's hard enough looking after yourself, let alone others.

'I don't need carrying. . .just help me with my radio,' he said. He had to gasp for breath all the time. I could tell he was an official from some city or other.'

'I can't find a battery that will work, and my hearing's not so good.'

Then I noticed that he had a radio in his hand. That was strange. Here's a man at death's door, crawling around a village not looking for food but old batteries. I put the earplug in my ear, but the battery was just about useless and I could hardly hear. How a man dying of starvation could hear anything is a mystery to me. It was some foreign language so I couldn't understand. The man said there was a Taiwan radio station that spoke in Chinese and told me to turn the knob and in the end I did hear Chinese. But the radio made a lot of noise and I couldn't make out much but I repeated it close to his ear. I don't remember the words but it was about nuclear missiles. Sometimes it was a man speaking, sometimes a woman. They said Russia had dropped forty of those things on America, all on big cities and the country was in a terrible state. America then did a counter-attack (I think that's what they called it). I don't know how many missiles that was, perhaps a thousand, to knock out Russia so she couldn't hit back. But they didn't know that Russia had missiles on board ships at sea, so they couldn't destroy them all. As I figure it, it was like a dog fight. If one gets bitten bad, it will do anything to kill the other one. Now both countries are completely ruined. The radio said that now everyone is throwing missiles at each other and people are burning in the fires.

That's what I heard until the radio stopped working. The batteries were finished. The man didn't want to hear any more. I looked at his face and got a shock. He was laughing! Not out aloud at first, but he seemed really happy. His eyes were like two balls of coal glowing red in the moonlight. The more he laughed the louder it became and ended by hurting my ears. Does that sound like a starving man? At first it didn't scare me. He was half dead after all. But I didn't expect him to stagger to his feet. Then I dropped the radio and ran for my life. Once I got out of the yard I turned to look. He was very tall, and was standing facing the moon, his neck stretched out like a wolf, and I could still hear him laughing when I was far from the village. Scary. I was shaking with fear half the night, and the wind was so hot, my mouth was on fire and I couldn't sleep. In the morning the sky was green. I've lived a long time but I've never seen anything like that before. I don't know why but I couldn't get that man out of my mind. When the sun came up I took a club and went to look.

He was dead, his head on one side against the pig trough. He had the radio in his hand. There was no sound, but I swear he was still smiling. I went round and looked at his face. Sure enough, he was smiling happily. Face to face with the King of Hell, what did he have to smile about?

The sun looks strange today, as if it's been smeared with mud.

Shennongjia Nature Reserve

The sky was a pale green colour, gradually becoming yellow, as it does in North China when there is a dust-storm. Though there was not a breath of wind, a low fog kept forming and dispersing. The rays of the sun slowly became diffused and yellow like the sky. About midday the sun reappeared as a red ball overhead and was like that throughout the day. At dawn and at sunset above the pale yellow horizon, the sky was a little brighter. Finally the red ball vanished, leaving an even black sky with a few short, threads of light. On clouded-over days in summer, it might be almost as dark, but the sky was layered, in motion and living: and when there were black clouds overhead, they were living black clouds. The black sky now was at a high altitude and below was the vast and unnatural desolation of death.

It was the hottest season of the year yet the hills were covered with snow. The sky was black and the snow white: the world was upside down. The white was not pure white but dark blue or green, even black if you looked carefully, with radioactive dust, melted rubber, the smoke and ashes of the cities and no doubt the burned remains of bodies, all fused together to make up each 'snow flake'. The air temperature fell day-by-day even by the minute. The mercury in thermometers almost disappeared.

Until morning, when she saw the snow, Chen Pan did not believe it, but nuclear winter was already here. It had snowed: it must be winter. After the nuclear attack, it had been said that it had not been on a scale large enough to cause nuclear winter. Yet nuclear winter had not only occurred, but had done so far more rapidly than anyone could have predicted.

Under the thin, soft layer of 'snow' there was muddy water. The sound of the horses' hooves was pleasant to hear. They were very hot and sweating and white steam came from their nostrils; but the signs of nuclear winter did not seem to frighten them very much. Her health was gradually returning and Chen Pan felt relaxed, as if she had escaped from a nightmare. She rode well, holding the reins first with one hand then the other, so that she could warm each of them in turn under her cape.

Her two bodyguards rode on either side of her, speaking little but looking after her conscientiously. Her bodyguards had been changed several times during the journey and all had been equally attentive. She felt very grateful: without them she might not have survived.

They never saw anyone, though to judge by the footprints, many people must have come along this road. At a crossroads one of the bodyguards pulled up his horse. Chen Pan always thought of him as Dandao (broadsword), though she did not call him that, because the most noticeable thing about him was that he carried a hand-made sword forged by some rural artisan. He had used it yesterday to scare off some starving people who had tried to steal their horses. He now jumped down and examined the footprints before choosing the road, then placed some stones on the road in the form of a triangle.

On a tree that had been stripped of its bark by starving people a notice had been nailed up, one of many similar ones they had seen on their journey. It was written in a mixture of archaic Chinese, English and computer jargon. Directions to the nearest Green Party reception station were followed by a statement:

Only those capable of reading this notice should go to the reception station to be examined. Those accepted will be welcome in the Green Party's survival base where they will be protected from the effects of nuclear winter. Space is limited and the examination will be exacting. Those not able to understand the notice should not proceed to the reception station.

Such notices made a very bad impression on Chen Pan. The former Green Association Nature Reserves, with their ideal of 'beauty' now belonged to the Green Party and had become cold, insensitive, callous, elitist and forbidding. The necessity of providing the physical conditions for survival inevitably meant that idealism would lose some of its importance. But Chen Pan attributed such a fundamental change to Ouyang Zhong-hua's godlike pretensions. It was certainly he who had set the standards for selection. She did not meet them and would be eliminated.

When she had been carried into a Green Party reception station near the Yellow River in a semi-conscious state, she heard her companions say several times that she had a perfect command of the three languages. But the man in charge had haughtily replied that understanding the announcement was only part of the requirements. The survival base was not a hospital, a welfare institution or a retirement home; the sick or disabled, children and those over fifty-five were not admitted. Those who remained were again sifted according to level of competence in a particular speciality. The appeals of her companions were like wind past his ears. However, as soon as he heard her name, he jumped to his feet and she became instantly a top priority and was sent with two bodyguards to Shennongjia.

There were 'post-stations' along the way, as in former centuries, where food, lodging and medicine were available and horses could be changed, so although they had travelled fast she felt better and was soon able to ride.

She learned later that each reception station had been provided with her name and photograph, so she was treated as an honoured guest everywhere. She was pleased, but felt a little uncomfortable as well. If she had not been unconscious when the journey started, she would certainly not have parted from her companions, but would have gone on foot like everyone else, to one of those bases where there was no special treatment for the privileged.

After crossing another mountain pass, Dandao produced a bamboo pipe and blew a piercing whistle. After a short interval a tree was raised in the air on a nearby hill, and they galloped towards it.

It was impossible not to admire Ouyang's genius for organization. In the present state of the country, a network of this kind was essential in order to maintain communications and the transport of people and goods. All was done with secret signals, bedraggled old horses, rustic swords, carrier pigeons and grass capes—as in the popular adventure stories about old times—but they formed the sole nervous system of a moribund country.

Chen Pan often tried to understand why it is that mankind has developed the knowledge and ingenuity to create this freakish sky, to turn nature upside down and create winter in the middle of a hot summer. Yet mankind itself is in a wretched and pitiful state.

Human intelligence has reached an extraordinary level, but mankind is stupid enough to waste incalculable wealth, time and labour developing nuclear weapons that are either totally useless or, if they are used, will destroy the world. A poet wrote: 'Civilized man strides over the face of the earth leaving behind him barbarity and desolation.' The progress of humanity over the ages is like an insignificant 'O' drawn in the sands of time.

Chen Pan thought of the man with slightly hunched shoulders and bright little eyes, who looked like a wild cat about to pounce. He was now wearing a yellow robe, embroidered with dragons and an appropriate headdress and was claiming to be 'Emperor of Heaven'. Three hundred thousand well-organized refugees at the end of their tether had no sooner seen him raise his little finger than they instantly abandoned the Multi-Level Election System, threw themselves at his feet and presented him with the *shugua* equipment the government had given them. The description the 'Emperor' gave of the end of the world and the darkening of the sky was far easier for them to understand, and more convincing, than any rigmarole about nuclear winter they heard from those intellectuals in the *shugua* teams. He used terms that they and their ancestors had been familiar with for centuries. Though the end of the world was at hand, the Emperor of Heaven could arrange for them to be re-incarnated, but if they did not submit to him, they would be punished for eternity in the eighteenth level of hell.

The 'Emperor' had appropriated the whole wardrobe of a theatre and dressed up his numerous retinue in the costumes of imperial military and civil officials. Over a hundred thousand refugees, under the influence of some strange form of *qigong* were seized with uncontrollable hysteria, rushing everywhere in frenzy, shouting, having convulsions and making all sorts of ferocious gestures. The Emperor's followers increased like an avalanche and innumerable starving people died in this state with smiling faces,

Chen Pan was horrified. These were people who, thanks to the Multi-Level Election System, had begun to learn how to control their own destiny. Now, out of ignorance and fear, they had again put themselves in the hands of an idol in order to escape from reality through madness and self-intoxication. She hated herself and even hated reason. Why did superstition triumph over reason? Why did reason make people even more vulnerable to despair? It was hunger and despair that had made her ill.

Some of Chen Pan's companions had recognized the 'Emperor' as Zhou Chi, the man who had been exposed on television not long ago. When they told this to the refugees and denounced the man as a known charlatan, a mountebank and a thoroughly evil man, his supporters attacked them and Zhou Chi had sent a gang of ruthless killers after them. They escaped, carrying Chen Pan, who was unconscious by that time.

On reaching the top of a hill, Chen Pan felt a twinge of terror: the hills and valleys below there thick with people in drab grey-brown clothing all carrying hoes, forks, other farm tools and sticks. If it had not been for a tree that indicated that the base was close, Chen Pan and her bodyguards might have blundered into this menacing crowd.

The Shennongjia base was already in sight: a stockade strategically placed between a precipice and a deep surrounding ravine and accessible only through a few mountain passes. The stockade gates that guarded the passes were all tightly closed and thousands of people were gathered outside.

One of the guides who had now joined them—a former geology teacher—explained to Chen Pan that in order to ward off famine, the base had employed these peasants to grow crops on about seventeen thousand acres of land in return for food and armed protection. The crops had been growing well until they were entirely destroyed by the nuclear winter and the sudden fall in temperature: a fall of five or seven degrees centigrade would have been enough at this time of year. But it had fallen twenty degrees, which might mean crop failure worldwide. Chen Pan dared not think about the future.

Once they had passed the 'signal tree', Dandao lowered it by means of a rope and pulley and went down a narrow winding path on the hillside that led to a passageway, just wide enough for a horse. When they had almost reached the Shennongjia base, they heard shouting and laughter and the sound of a woman screaming. The path grew wider and they found themselves in a space as large as a football field, with buildings, fortifications, sheds and stables around it.

Their attention was immediately drawn to a sheer rock face in which the entrance to the base had been cut, fifteen or twenty metres up. The only access was by means of a large basket, which was now being raised by a pulley. Two men in the basket were holding a young woman outside it; she was screaming in terror the higher the basket rose. The two men then pulled up her clothes, leaving her almost naked.

'She's pissing herself!' some of the men below shouted, slapping each other excitedly and pushing each other under the stream of urine.

The basket reached the top, levelled out and disappeared into the tunnel.

'What's going on?' Chen Pan demanded angrily. Dandao and the geologist frowned but did not answer. The armed men standing around watching were all wearing the armbands of the Green Guard. One of them said, 'Fuck me if those two have not got themselves another one!' giving Chen Pan a mean and dirty look.

'Mind your manners!' the geologist said severely. 'This is Ouyang's guest.'

'The boss's guest?' Most of the men lost their nerve at this point, but not the one who had spoken. 'The boss won't allow us to meet girls in town or invite village girls here. If that's not deliberately oppressing us! You town people just look after your own comfort.'

'Who was that girl?' Chen Pan demanded.

'Girl? That was Big Ox—our captain's honoured guest. And she won't be a girl for much longer,' he said, making an obscene gesture.

Chen Pan got into the basket, followed by Dandao and the geologist. 'Pull us up!' Once the stockade gate was locked and barred this was the only way in and out of the base.

'Why are there people like this here?' Chen Pan asked, 'They were aggressive enough in the reception station, but were at least civilized. But these men are nothing but hoodlums.' Dandao who had been a mountaineer, looked sombre but said nothing.

'Maybe, but they can do certain things that no one else can do.'

'What things?'

'Beating people up...' The geologist said bitterly. 'I'm serious. Without these brutes, it would have been impossible to get the tilling and planting done, for instance.'

The basket had reached the tunnel and was lowered on to its platform. There were two strong men working the pulley system, pedalling a makeshift contraption using a bicycle.

A little further into the tunnel, the same two men were pawing and kissing the girl who was screaming and begging for mercy.

Chen Pan ran over to them. 'Leave her alone, you brutes.' They froze for an instant and the girl broke loose, threw herself at Chen Pan's feet and clasped her legs. Her hair was dishevelled and her face dirty, but she was young and good-looking.

'Don't' be afraid,' said Chen Pan lifting her to her feet. 'Come with me, then I'll take you home.'

'Take her home! It took us days to find one who looked OK.' The two men, unsure of Chen Pan's status, dared do no more than complain. 'What are we going to tell our Captain?'

'Tell that Big Ox or Big Ass of yours to go and find Ouyang Zhonghua.'

Ouyang's name and the looks on the faces of Chen Pan and her companions were enough to silence the two Green Guards—for the time being—but their expressions said: we'll see about that.

The tunnel was level and wide, and after about a hundred yards, changed direction and reached the stockade, the entrance to which was half way up the side of a mountain. Below was a huge expanse of flat land on which hundreds of simple shacks had been put up; the mountain slopes themselves were honeycombed with cave dwellings: there was enough room for the population of a small town. Otherwise every inch of land had been planted with crops and vegetables, now all withered and yellow. All the plastic tubing in which *shugua* had been grown was now empty; the plants had all died in the sudden cold of nuclear winter.

Chen Pan noticed that in one area, there were a lot of people who looked like intellectuals, either engaged in light manual work, or using their spare time to work out mathematical problems or chemical formulas, writing with charcoal on flat stones, since there was no paper. Others were analysing soil samples using makeshift equipment.

A notice about a discussion meeting seemed to be attracting much attention. The subject for discussion, Chen Pan found out later, was this: 'Man has always demanded too many rights for himself and given too little attention to his duties to others and to nature. This is the main reason for the disaster that has struck humanity. Future humanity must give precedence to duties rather than rights. Charters and constitutions regarding rights are not enough. The purpose of the discussion is to draft a charter of duties.'

This was an idea of Ouyang's. Chen Pan had once thought that it was a good one; now it made her feel uncomfortable. The people at the reception centres selecting people for the survival bases were doing their duty. But all those who had been rejected at the 'selection stations', what was their duty? Or that of this young woman beside her, or her family and millions of other peasants?

The young woman was still far from calm, but from her confused account Chen Pan learned that the base had taken in a hundred thousand local peasants to work on the land for 750 grams of *shugua* a day, under the strict surveillance of the Green Guard. But with the coming of nuclear winter all crops failed and the peasants had become a useless burden on the community. The *shugua* distribution centre, the agronomists and the Green Guard had all been moved out of the stockade and the peasants had simply been abandoned and told to go and fend for themselves. Where should they go? The stockade was the only place in the world where they could stay alive. The seed and *shugua* had all been removed, yet everyone said that inside the base there was enough food to last for years. Her father and brothers were outside among the silent mass of people. Their only chance of survival was in the stockade, but all the gates were closed to them

Ouyang lived in a solitary shack that was easy to find: there was an ancient tree with gnarled roots outside the door. His small white horse was gnawing at the moss on the tree trunk and there was a thick carpet of dried leaves everywhere. The geologist went to find Ouyang, while Chen Pan made the young woman lie down in the shack, then went outside. After picking up a handful of dried leaves, she suddenly became lost in thought. . .

'I'm going to look at the *shugua*,' she told 'Dandao', but refused his company. 'Stay here and look after the poor girl.'

In her brain a tiny spark had suddenly become a bright flame. It was so simple. There were masses of wood and other combustible material that could be collected. The *shugua* would grow if the nutritional fluid was heated! The fluid was absorbed through the trailers that were highly sensitive to cold. The *shugua* having no leaves cannot get chemical energy from photosynthesis, but increasing the temperature of the fluid by even a little might produce a dramatic result.

The agronomists in charge of *shugua* production, knowing that Chen Pan was the inventor, immediately began experiments along the lines she suggested. They slightly raised the temperature of the nutrient fluid in a vat, changed the way the fluid was delivered to the plants, and lagged the tubing so that the fluid reached all the plants at more or less the same temperature. Once the temperature was constant, planting was started again.

The agronomists were pleased with the results and Chen Pan suggested that all *shugua* production should switch over to this system. Work on this started at once. The sooner *shugua* could be made to ripen the more lives would be saved. Chen Pan no longer thought about taking the young woman home, but of allowing the masses of starving peasants to return to the stockade to help with *shugua* production. But she was told that since the matter concerned the whole base, only Ouyang could make the decision. No longer used to such over-cautious attitudes, she could not resists saying ironically, 'It seems your Green Party is not very different from the Communist Party.'

The geologist searched the whole stockade without finding Ouyang. Chen Pan was impatient and went herself to look for him. After humming and hawing, the geologist went with her and, only when they reached a place where there was no one around, told her that Ouyang was in the 'dog pen'.

'The dog pens? Then why didn't you go and get him?' Taken by surprise she raised her voice.

After looking left and right the geologist whispered 'He doesn't let anyone in there.'

'Why not?'

The geologist hesitated. He knew about Chen Pan's past relationship with Ouyang and did not want to put a foot wrong.

When she insisted he replied, 'He hasn't said anything but he doesn't want anyone to know that he goes there.'

'What's in there?'

'Dogs.'

'He's breeding dogs?'

'Yes. He gets wild dogs from outside and breeds them. That's the only source of meat in the base. We only get a little every few days, but given the number of people in the base there must be a lot of dogs in there. That's all anyone knows.

'It's a good idea. Why not let people see?'

'He's probably afraid they will get bitten.'

'What does he do there?'

'I don't know.'

'Or why he stays there so long?'

The geologists shrugged.

'He stays as long as this each time he goes in?'

'Only the last few days.' The geologist hesitated again, there was something strange about his expression. 'Sometimes. . . . he stays more than half the day.'

It was nuclear winter, perhaps the end of the world. Even that did not cut short his visits. She wondered what secret was hidden there: it was a bit like a horror story. She continued questioning the geologist and learned that only one or two electricians and biologists had been allowed in; but they refused to say anything about it. It was clear that the geologist knew no more.

The dog pens were in a gorge in the southwest corner on the stockade far from habitations. The entrance to the gorge was protected by a strong log fence or palisade. From far inside there came the sound of many barking dogs, of all sizes, judging from the sound. There must have been several thousand.

As they approached, the geologist became more and more uneasy: he had never been so close before.

On one end of a rope hanging down inside the palisade from somewhere out of sight, there were several large pieces of rusty metal, such as broken ploughshares. The other end of the rope, outside the palisade, served as a bell-pull, which made the ploughshares clang together and resound in the depths of the gorge. This brought out a hunchback who approached with a tense look on his face. His small shiny eyes like those of a hedgehog peered through the palisade. He looked extremely well-fed—a strange phenomenon in a country that was starving. His first gesture was to shake his small black fist. When he saw Chen Pan, his expression immediately became lecherous. He had no key and looked as if he would not have opened the gate anyway. Chen Pan picked up a dried leaf from the ground, wrote her name on it and told him to give it to Ouyang Zhong-hua. She had to repeat herself several times before he understood. As he shuffled away he kept stopping to look back at her.

Chen Pan wiped her finger with disgust; it had chanced to touch his hand when he took the leaf. It was sticky and slightly red. The geologist covered his nose and remarked that he had heard that there was strange creature in charge of the dog pens who was either deformed or a half-wit.

They were not allowed to enter through the palisade and had to go round to a special gate at the back of the dog pens. There was something strange about the way some of the dogs were barking. Sometimes they seemed to be mad with rage; then suddenly they would all stop barking then, after several seconds starting barking again all at once, even more frantically than before. Chen Pan and the geologist looked at each other uneasily. When the barking had stopped, another sound far less loud, but much more sinister and frightening, could be heard, a strangulated whine full of terror, hatred and humiliation. A sound that seemed to terrorize the other dogs in the pen and made them howl. Chen Pan suddenly felt cold.

Ouyang Zhong-hua strode quickly out of the gorge, holding Chen Pan's leaf in his hand as if it were a flower, his face radiant. He was thinner. He had been clean-shaven before, but now had a thick beard and a new kind of charm. The keys to the gate were in his hand. He opened lock after lock and let them in, then immediately re-locked them.

He courteously thanked the geologist, who understood that his presence was no longer required; but Chen Pan asked him to tell Ouyang about the experimental heating of the *shugua* nutrient. Ouyang was pleased and called it 'a great achievement', adding 'We must devote more effort to growing *shugua* and make the technology known. It will help to get agricultural production started again.'

When the geologist hurried away Ouyang looked affectionately at Chen Pan, opened his arms wide and waited for her to embrace him as before.

'You've got dog hairs all over you,' Chen Pan said lightly, glad of a means of escape.

His tight-fitting canvas overall was indeed covered with hairs and smelled bad. She was now troubled by another thought: The dogs had stopped barking when Ouyang had come out of the dog pen but not suddenly as before. What on earth had he been doing? She looked back towards the gorge and noticed the hunchback peering at her from behind the palisade gate. Ouyang evaded her questions by making jokes, which was convenient for Chen Pan since it stopped him from becoming too affectionate. She did not want to hurt him intentionally; but she was determined that there would never be a return to their former intimacy. It was a decision dictated not only by reason, but by her feelings as well.

When she had heard that she was being sent to Shennongjia, she had no thought of avoiding him: proof that she no longer doubted her ability to control her emotions. There was now a distance between them and Ouyang was sensitive enough to realized that things had changed. His self-respect would make him avoid a rebuff.

She had fallen in love with Ouyang Zhong-hua because he was an exceptional man. So was Shi Ge—and he would surely go down in history as a great man. But chance had played an important role in his greatness. He could easily have remained an ordinary man, his talent and qualities buried in an ordinary life. Ouyang could not be ordinary no matter what century or country he was born in. He was naturally great and was destined to leave his mark on history.

Shi Ge accepted fate. Ouyang wanted destiny to obey him: that is why she had worshipped him. But a mature woman was bound to discover that worship is not the same as love.

She loved Shi Ge, not because he was a greater man, but because he was an ordinary man and would be an ordinary husband and father; yet his warmth and tolerance were out of the ordinary. Any woman loving Ouyang would have to give herself to him. Loving Shi Ge meant holding him in her hands and heart. Perhaps because of this combination of greatness and ordinariness, Shi Ge could use his almost absolute power in a way that warmed the heart. Ouyang's greatness lacked that simplicity, finding expression in rigidity and high-handed behaviour

Ouyang Zhong-hua listened without interruption to Chen Pan's fervent appeal to help the tens of thousands of peasants outside; but his patience was nothing but politeness. He did not reflect for a moment. 'I would like to but it is impossible.'

'You can't stand there and watch them die!' She did not want to quarrel with him but could not contain her indignation.

'Stand and watch?' he replied with a smile. 'I am now doing everything I can to save them. The survival bases I founded have taken in fourteen million people and continue to give refuge to several tens of thousands a day. Those people were doomed to die, and I saved them didn't I?'

'But there are still countless millions. . . .'

'To rescue all is to rescue none, including those already rescued.'

'But these people are here, at your door.'

'Since we cannot save them all, we have to choose.'

'By grading them, you mean?'

Ouyang knitted his brows like someone who has toothache.

'You can say that, yes. To die insisting on equality is ridiculous. The purpose of the survival bases was to save a civilized China, not a race of animals.'

'That's the attitude of a slave-owner. Some people deserve to live, others to die. But it's not for you to choose, but God.'

'God?' Ouyang's expression was one of utter disdain. Chen knew that look very well. It did not appear often but when it did, it expressed his inner self. 'God is allowing mankind to exterminate itself. What role do you play in his selection? Can you fight or kill? If you are given human flesh will you eat it? If the choice is left to God, the survivors in China will be semi-animals covered with hair, knowing only food and sex, roaming over the bones of civilized man. At least in this I can do better than God.'

Chen Pan was speechless and walked in silence over dead leaves that rustled under foot. She did not know what to say. It was the end.

From the direction of the east gate of the stockade came increasingly loud shouting and commotion; then suddenly what sounded like cannon shots, accompanied by cheers of encouragement. Inside the stockade chaos reigned. Ouyang as usual remained calm, and sent Chen Pan to his shack and advised her to rest. Then he went towards the gate of the stockade.

The sun, one could imagine, was not very far from the horizon, hidden by the smoke and fog. The stockade gate, indistinct in the distance, might have been the gate of hell. The door of Ouyang's shack was wide open and the white horse, head down, was still near the ancient tree. Dandao lay on the ground, his face covered with blood. His sword was broken, the remaining half was stuck into the ground. The girl was not in the shack.

Chen Pan shouted and Dandao opened his eyes: one was punctured and lacerated. His mouth was full of congealed blood and not being able to speak, he pointed in the direction of the stockade gate. Seconds later Chen Pan was astride Ouyang's immaculate white horse. This is like galloping in hell, she thought. The hooves made hardly any sound, the horse's head scarcely moved. It was as if there were no air, temperature, distance or time. Only unreal forms in the even semi-darkness and a feeling of total unreality.

Ouyang was striding in front towards the high gate of the stockade, made of stout tree trunks, held in position by ten slanting crossbars. Stone walls filled the gaps on either side between the gate and the cliffs. As the white horse galloped past him, Chen Pan could see Ouyang's mouth open in surprise but, as if in a vacuum, she did not hear his shout. The horse raced up the slope and stopped not far from the cliff.

Outside the gate the mass of peasants, previously silent, had been transformed into a flood tide of thousands upon thousands of roaring, howling people maddened by hunger and desperation and the thought of all the food stored in the base. About a hundred of them were using a long tree-trunk as a battering ram, pounding again and again at the gate. The walls on either side of it shook and stones fell from the cliffs. Flaming torches thrown by the crowd traced curves in the air and fell at the foot of the gate, setting it on fire.

To save ammunition, the Green Guards on the wall and the cliffs were firing arrows, throwing stones and using various other ancient methods of defence. The mass of people was so packed together that every missile found a target. The peasants seemed to have lost the instinct to run away from danger. If one of those manning the battering ram was hit, he was immediately replaced, even if it meant trampling on the wounded man.

Flames crept up the log gate and a column of smoke rose high in the air. The crowd was encouraged and began to sound triumphant: a few more blows of the battering ram and the gate would burst open.

Then there was a sound of rapid fire from an assault rifle. The peasants nearest the gate fell like leaves in a storm. The huge battering ram fell to the ground, crushing those who had escaped the firing. Others fled in terror, fearing the rifle-fire, not death.

Big Ox stood laughing on the wall, firing his rifle with one hand and carrying a naked young woman under his arm as if she were a sack of flour. She was limp, perhaps unconscious.

'Kill! Kill! Kill them all!' Big Ox shouted and raised the girl above his head. 'The Ox has had himself a virgin! You young ones can have a look. She's been wounded in action. . .' It was the same girl. Big Ox almost dancing with joy, parted her legs.

The Green Guards hooted and sniggered, and began firing their rifles at the crowd.

"Kill! The more you kill, the more Big Ox will reward you. Let them taste this!' He thrust the barrel of his rifle into the girl's vagina.

Chen Pan looked round frantically, and in vain, for a knife she could plunge into the heart of that loathsome brute. Instead she found herself on the rampart hammering his thick body with her fists, which was no more effective than punching a mountain. The coarse leather face of Big Ox turned towards her and he laughed obscenely.

Strong arms seized her from behind and moved her away from him. It was Ouyang. She felt weak at the knees and wanted to hold on to him.

'Big Ox. Get out. Get out of the base!' Ouyang shouted 'I don't want to see you ever again. You are worse than any animal.'

Chen Pan had never seen him so angry. She felt almost proud to have loved him.

Big Ox's face became distorted with rage. '*Me* get out!' He suddenly raised his rifle. 'Me or you? I've been thinking of getting rid of you for a long time. Me an animal? I fuck your ancestors. You're just a ball of shit from a camel's arse. You've read a couple of books so you think you can boss me around. I'll show you who's boss! You city shit-balls can all get out.'

The Green Guards made a show of taking up their rifles: they were all for Big Ox taking control of the base. Fifty per cent of the inhabitants were 'city shit-balls'; once they were gone there would be enough food to support the others for years. They had the guns, so why should others be in charge of everything? They were waiting for Ouyang to answer. If he was tough they would get tougher and Big Ox would take action—if he gave in he would be finished.

Ouyang Zhong-hua looked Big Ox straight in the eyes as if he had not seen the rifles and suddenly laughed. 'Big Ox,' he said in a neutral, matter-of-fact tone of someone indifferent to danger and conscious of his power, like a bandit chief. 'Have you forgotten your Master? When he entrusted you to me, what did he warn you about? He said "women will be a source of trouble". That was why he was afraid for you. I cursed you just now because I remembered what he had said. If it had been someone else I would not have been so angry. Are you going to dishonour yourself and shame your Master for the sake of a woman?'

Chen Pan froze with fear and apprehension as Ouyang spoke, yet his words were well chosen. Big Ox looked like an animal caught in a pitfall. He stammered incoherently, then suddenly howled like an animal, swung the naked young woman on to her feet and fired a burst from his rifle point blank at her. Then he stepped over her dead body as if it were a piece of scrap paper and swaggered off.

Chen Pan threw herself forward like a mad woman, but Ouyang Zhong-hua put his arms round her and turned her, struggling, in the opposite direction. Everything had happened so quickly that some people must have thought that Ouyang had not seen Big Ox kill the girl and was carrying Chen Pan away, perhaps because the city woman had gone mad. Crying, she tried to free herself from his arms, in which she had once felt rapture.

The smell of blood was in her breath. The sky was very black and the snow of nuclear winter had begun to fall again. Ouyang whispered urgently in her ear: 'Don't shout whatever you do. He's capable of killing you.' He was trembling and she felt the drum-beat of his heart.

Once away from the crowd, he released her. The curious white horse stood motionless, looking towards the sky.

'Believe me,' Ouyang said. 'I will wipe out Big Ox.' She no longer felt him tremble, though they were only an inch apart. He seemed strong and self-assured. 'I will make him pay—in blood.'

She looked at him in agony and he gently wiped her tears.

'This was not my fault. The world. . .'

There was a crash and a shout of triumph that echoed round the hills. The battering ram pounding against the burning gate had suddenly created an exploding ball of fire. Once more the peasants began to attack the stockade. Ouyang looked towards the wall. The Green Guards who were supposed to be defending the stockade were merely watching. Some were drinking and chewing dog meat, some were even lying down.

'You go back quickly,' Ouyang told Chen Pan and ran to the wall. She followed.

The burning gate had begun to split under the blows of the battering ram, sparks flew in all directions.

Ouyang Zhong-hua pulled up a junior officer of the Green Guard, who was lying down, his head covered, very scared.

'Why are you not fighting back instead of doing nothing?'

'The boys say. . . .' He was trembling. 'They want to see the boss open fire first.'

'The bastards!' There was fear in Ouyang's voice for the first time.

Someone said, 'If you kill one we'll deal with the others.'

The Green guards stood still, all holding their rifles, and coldly watched Ouyang. The gate was leaning and would fall at any moment.

'Don't you want to live?' Ouyang said, pointing to the scene below. 'If they break in, no one will be spared. Don't imagine that because you are armed. . . . There are no magic weapons. Think carefully.'

No answer. No one thought. He was facing a group of near animals that he had created himself. He looked at them in fear, weakening. Suddenly he found Chen Pan. 'Why are you following me?'

She gave him a stony look but did not answer. His lips quivered and he went white. Even the fall of the great gate did not rouse him.

'Total destruction is cruel and painful,' he said, asking for forgiveness. She continued to stare at him silently.

'Take her away,' he shouted to the guards. She went struggling between two burly men. The gate was falling apart. She saw Ouyang, giving himself no time for fear, take an automatic rifle from the junior officer.

'Ouyang!' Chen Pan shouted. 'Let me see you kill someone. Let me see you as a butcher. Show me your Green principles and noble ideas of beauty!'

There was an ear-piercing volley of fire from the wall, a dagger in her heart. Automatic rifles were firing from the wall, with the fury of a storm. Chen Pan saw only blackness in front of her. The whole universe was nothing but a deep black sky.

Beijing: Zhongnanhai

Shi Ge opened his eyes. . . No, it would be more accurate to say that they were already open, or had not been closed. Yet he had seen nothing, his mind was a blank. Now he opened the eyes of his mind.

He was sitting in a large wide old-style armchair. Someone had thrown a pair of blankets and a curtain over him. Outside the window, against the distant black sky, leafless trees were faintly visible. When those trees began to lose their leaves because of the nuclear winter, he had called all the remaining members and employees together and announced the dissolution of the government. He had been sitting here since then like a statue. Perhaps resting: he was extremely tired; not one brain cell was working. Perhaps he was in shock or dazed by the end of mankind and at a loss what to do. The future did not exist. Perhaps it was because he had no strength to do anything except disappear into the emptiness.

Now he no longer had such feelings. It was as if he had awoken in the land of the dead. Why worry about the former world? He threw off the blankets, and as he did so, a shopping bag fell to the floor. He opened it and saw a dozen dried fish staring at him. He recognized the bag: Long-kou carried it everywhere with him. Now that the end had come, he had left it here. He stood up and looked around. No one. He shouted and there was only silence. Since the nuclear attack, it had become cold and quieter day by day. Today the silence seemed frozen solid; no shout could penetrate it but only return to his ears, hard and stiff, and painfully resonant.

He looked at himself in the mirror. Then slowly raised his hand and touched his hair in disbelief; it was still soft and thin as before, but had become white, before it had been black, hardly more than grey at the worst, now it was entirely white, white as snow and pitifully sparse. He felt he was looking at some indistinct shape behind him, but he did not turn round: if there was something, it was the spirit of death, behind his back, wantonly laughing and dancing, and would not allow anyone to see. Shi Ge was untroubled. He had long since been purged of the fear of decrepitude and death. There is no reason to feel resentful about death; there are so many different substances that live in perpetual darkness, as you will. The only difference in your case is that by chance such substances combined to make a life and allowed you to open your eyes and see light. You should be grateful for the favour and enjoy every minute; it is free of charge. For someone who has lived for fifty or more years you have had more than your share of advantages and good luck. You should be perfectly content to return to the womb of death. To have enjoyed undeserved fortune and then feel indignant when you have to pay the bill is ingratitude and upsetting yourself unnecessarily.

In the centre of the hall there was a pile of ashes, where the temporary employees had lit a fire to keep warm after the beginning of nuclear winter. The last of the fuel they had been using was half a case of highly secret archives of the Central Committee. When he had first seen such documents being used as fuel in the kitchens, he had lost his temper. He discovered that Mao Zedong's personal papers had all been shared out, who knows when, but only because the leather bindings could be boiled and eaten. Now he burned the last pile of archives himself and used the heat of the fire to charge the solar battery of his radio so he could listen to news of the world.

Neither Russia nor the US completely collapsed after the nuclear war between them. Government structure and administration were functioning and the conventional armed forces were mostly undamaged. This was especially true of the United States where preparations for war had long been complete and functioned effectively. The US remained the most powerful country in the world and was no longer obsessed by Russia. Instead the duties of the military took them to Australia and Latin America—with whom they had no quarrel—where they set about occupying all the grain growing and livestock producing areas of the Southern hemisphere. Russia invaded Europe and occupied Africa and South Asia.

Both the US and Russia, on coming to their senses after the nuclear engagement, realized that the greatest threat was not the other, but nuclear winter. The only way to survive it was to get hold of the food supplies of other countries, as quickly as possible, and as much as possible, in order to get agricultural production going in their own, and lay hands on land in the Southern hemisphere, where crops ripen six months earlier than in the north. The victims of this plan had no time to make preparations against the lightning attack and were rapidly occupied. The Russian army took a severe beating at the hands of Europe, and then attacked Frankfurt, Lyon, Liverpool, Milan and Barcelona with nuclear missiles. This was the end of European resistance. Although Europe had the means to make a strong nuclear counter-attack, who would want to cross swords with a country with so little respect for human life that it had recently fired several hundred nuclear missiles and also been hit by a similar number?

The world was changing at the speed of a hurricane. Human society that had evolved over a period of thousands of years was disintegrating into dust. Would there come a time when there would be no sound of a human voice under this sky, only the indifferent radiation of the distant universe?

The fire burned strongly. The heat made him tremble and he felt that blood was flowing again through his veins. Behind all the written comments and signatures of Chairmen and General Secretaries of the Communist Party, behind the hand-written comments on lists of appointments or dismissals, records of secret decisions or open letters, behind every word, every page, there was a history of innumerable plots, vicissitudes and bitter struggles that never saw the light of day. All these papers were now curling up in the flames, becoming black and disappearing. More than ever before, he suddenly felt the desperate mediocrity and boredom of all that hustle and bustle.

His name had appeared on some of those papers and he had genuinely believed that he was creating the future, for eternity. Now the future had turned into black smoke, before disappearing without a trace.

The light on his solar battery lit up and he switched off his radio. He felt hungry and put a dried fish into the cinders. His life was now nothing but smoke. He finally realized that the last moments of his life were for himself. Hunger had acted like a call to arms or the stirring of life. His new life would not be as Prime Minister, or a figure in history or someone who as soon as he opened his eyes wanted to take everything into some sort of container in his chest. The world could do as it liked: it was no longer his business. What surged up in his resurrected life was an utter rejection of any obligation or desire. He must go and find Chen Pan and never again leave her.

He ate the fish, head, bones and all. He was warm now. All the archives were burned into a pile of ashes. The flames became constantly smaller, then vanished. He began to put a few things together for his journey, the blankets, a mountaineering rope, and the dried fish. All these he stuffed into his pack, together with the survival kit he had bought at the Green Exhibition.

At the time he had vaguely thought that this day might come. Now everything else had become vague and indistinct. After he had closed his pack, he opened it again and put in the radio. He had not intended to take it, but when the sun appeared again, he would want to know what had become of the world, even if he was not going to interfere with anything again. But having watched this soul-stirring drama all his life, he ought to see how it would end.

Shasha was still lying quietly in the armchair. He was cold all over. While he was being wrapped up, his cry sounded trusting and tender in the dead desolation. Shi Ge kissed his mischievous face and said, 'We're going to look for ma-ma.' He sat Shasha on the schoolboy satchel he had made for him in prison awaiting execution. Chen Pan's farewell letter was in it. Finally he tied his shoes carefully, knowing that he was going to walk a long way, but as a child he had already learned to walk long distances.

The sound of his solitary footsteps echoed as he made his way through the Forbidden City. There was no other sign of life. Beijing had become a ghost city. He made his way up the tower of the Tianan Gate. For no particular reason, just to take a last look at what had been the centre of China.

An enormous portrait used to hang from the tower. The frame had been ripped away and the canvas lay crumpled on the ground below. From close to, the face could not be seen clearly, but from above he could recognize the eyes—eyes that had looked at him day and night all his life, from everywhere. On the dusty canvas the eyes looked indifferently upwards like dried-up wells. As he passed he did not tread on the huge face, like an expanse of yellow earth, not because it was taboo, but because he had never wanted to tread on anyone's face. Mao Zedong's revolution was destroyed: he had been a destructive genius. But if humanity now struck out along a new road, he would count as a genius who promoted the progress of humanity. Perhaps the destiny of this generation of suffering humanity was to replace the greatest possible misery with the greatest possible change and bring about the greatest transition in the history of mankind.

The image of Gui-zhi falling dead in the dust came back to him once more, like a film in slow motion. Why was it that when the helicopter was already high up, the red hole between her breasts was always so close? What destiny could wipe away such tragic and beautiful blood?

As far as the eye could see there were buildings of concrete and steel, built by the labour of men, towering in dead solitude. The streets stretched into the distance. The huge city was dead: the streets and conduits were all empty, the electric cables were all cold, no vehicles moved, every apartment was deserted—all covered by the shroud of the sky.

He shouldered his bag and took Shasha on his other arm. He did not know where to go but it was not important. He would not stop, but go on until he reached the end of the earth. In this life everything else was finished, except to find Shasha's mother.

The World of Mankind

By the time that Ding Da-hai's transmitter started sending out his message the US and Russia had fired 2,911 nuclear missiles at each other, equal to nearly 1.8 kilotons. The message was repeated for 57 minutes before the transmitter was destroyed by a conventional missile from somewhere. The US and Russia broke off negotiations, each accusing the other of provoking nuclear war. It was impossible for the US to admit that the most destructive, tragic and expensive war in history had started because someone had blundered. Russia was not willing to reveal the truth because a 'mistake' cannot excuse the actions that follow. The holy banner of patriotic resistance was a better excuse for Russia to invade other countries and take what was needed to survive nuclear winter.

Europe intelligently surrendered in order to preserve the lives of its people. A few excitable small countries which had been invaded by the US or Russia, unhesitatingly counter-attacked with nuclear weapons. A number of old grudges were remembered in the end-of-the world madness and nuclear weapons were used, by Iraq against Israel, and Pakistan against India. The world naturally did not care about a few extra nuclear explosions; the chaos and the flames of war were everywhere.

Agricultural production throughout the world was destroyed by nuclear winter. The seasons were all out of joint and livestock died when pastures stopped growing. Marine products were severely reduced because of the rise in temperature of the sea and rivers. Even when nuclear warfare came to an end, its long-term influence on the climate remained. The amount of ozone in the upper atmosphere decreased, the changes in the distribution of rainfall, the water and plant cover in turn altered the reflective capacity of the earth, heat tolerance and vaporization rates, which in turn influenced the growth rate of land and marine life. The food chain was disrupted world-wide. The full extent of the consequences are not yet known. But even without taking the long-term into account, it was clear that the effect on human society was not far from total destruction.

World-wide collapse began with the occupation of other countries by Russian and US forces. The troops did not understand the universal nature of the conflict and were violently thrown on to the battlefield of a war that had already started. With the coming of nuclear winter, the truth was written on every inch of the sky. Mutiny and desertion soon reached uncontrollable proportions. It started with a few troops who hijacked aircraft or ships to take them home to see if their loved ones were alive or dead; soon whole divisions and regiments were demanding to be repatriated or else handled the matter themselves.

The occupation had not been efficiently organized and rapidly became uncontrollably chaotic. Resistance in the occupied territories was increasingly fierce. So the self-repatriation of the armies of occupation became a flood.

In the absence of order and government, all sorts of organizations and phenomena appeared. Nazi-style groups re-emerged in Europe and in Latin America; saviours of various kinds in Islamic countries; underworld figures came out into the open and became important local bosses.

On the North China plain a *qigong* master declared himself emperor of the Zhou Dynasty, with more than ten million subjects.

Order and discipline ceased to exist. Popular hatred of the invaders grew, robbery and looting spread, armed bands burned, raped and killed. Smoke particles and dust in the upper atmosphere led to cyclones that caused great damage. People in the northern parts fled blindly southwards to escape the falling temperature.

Japan was a notable exception to the widespread collapse of states, and profiting from the weakness of Russia invaded the Russian Far East and Siberia. Years of painstaking preparation made it possible to expand the new Japanese possessions with great rapidity: in next to no time they became ten times larger that Japan itself. The Black Dragon Society, until now always more or less a secret organization, became a powerful force and publicly announced that this 'gift from Heaven' was a golden opportunity for Japan to dominate the world. For over a century a crisis mentality had existed in Japan; for many years large stocks of the basic necessities of life had been assembled and hidden underground or under the sea. As an island nation Japan had the best-equipped fishing industry in the world: when agriculture and stock raising was destroyed, the immense resources of the sea could almost feed her population. Japan had also developed a superior variety of *shugua* seed and had greatly expanded production. As a nation the Japanese are frugal, patient and disciplined, and have a strong spirit of self-sacrifice and cohesion. What better qualifications for a new superpower?

The most significant new form of social organization was the Successive Multi-Level Election System, not only because the majority of those who had adopted this system were Chinese refugees, the most numerous and widely distributed of all the migrants; but also because it was probably the only way to organize rapidly a heterogeneous, highly mobile and fragmented mass of people. More important still, were the nature and characteristics of the system itself.

To avoid all perishing together in a ruined world, people were obliged to coordinate their activities, help and respect others, and act with fairness and impartiality. Communication between groups of refugees had to be easy so that reaction to a changing situation or an emergency would be swift. The Multi-Level Election System was capable of meeting these requirements, as if it had been invented precisely for this age of disaster. The Chinese refugees introduced the Multi-Level Election System into different countries at a time when their need for such a system was greatest.

That the System spread to the four corners of the world was also partly due to the fact that the Chinese refugees remained relatively calm when the whole of mankind was in a state of panic on account of the nuclear winter. They were indifferent to death as if they had already experienced it. They had been the first to suffer a massive nuclear attack, widespread destruction and the collapse of the state and the economy. They had lost everything. Hunger had been a daily experience, almost part of their physiology. Their ability to bear hardship was the result of a thousand years of poverty and disaster, and they had an astonishing ability to survive in the most adverse environment. People in the West, who had been accustomed to the luxuries of modern life, better protected from the vagaries of nature and distant from the suffering in the outside world, appeared by contrast weak and pitiful in the face of disaster.

The Chinese refugees had been 'uninvited guests' and now had a duty to help their hosts. The organized teams of refugees rapidly absorbed groups of people of other countries, colour, nationality and race, and as the teams grew, they divided and multiplied. The search for the means of survival also obliged the teams to continue to migrate: this also made the Multi-Level Election System more widely known.

People of different race, culture and historical background joined together in order to survive and new ideas germinated. For instance, a group of former linguists worked out a system that enabled people speaking different languages to communicate with each other to some extent; and in doing so brought about a certain synthesis between languages that made communication progressively easier and less limited. There was an obvious need for such a system and it spread rapidly.

The linguists were delighted to discover signs that sooner or later a new world language might develop that combined elements and characteristics of different languages. This was something they had long dreamed of, but in the ordered world their efforts had been disappointing. Now that sovereignty and frontiers had gone, they became optimistic.

Sociologists who had advocated small societies and economies, discovered that their ideals had suddenly come much closer to realization. States, political parties, armies, great cities—most of these had been wiped out. Banks, capital, monopolies and large markets had all disappeared. Money had lost its function. Humanity divided into small, self-managed communities. Collectivism became the norm.

Although people were still struggling for survival from starvation and death, they came closer than at any other time to the kinds of society that mankind has always dreamed of. The social relations and forms of production that had been the aim of ecologists for years began to develop. Relations between people and with nature concerned people more than materialism. Although it was a matter of necessity rather than choice, the use of technology became more closely linked with respect for the environment. Hydraulic and wind power became the main sources of energy. Windmills were constructed on a large scale, especially wind turbines adjustable to the angle and speed of the wind. Large-scale mines, blast-furnaces, rolling mills and factories had all stopped production; but commodities in storage were more than sufficient, especially when 'old-fashioned' standards of economy, careful budgeting and reduction of waste were practised. The rubbish dumps of the world also contained much that could be used or recycled.

The world's fixed assets and materials were sufficient for humanity for more than a hundred years. Once humanity was forced to abandon the demand for ceaseless improvement and change, it was found that the life of most articles can be considerably extended and there is less demand for raw materials. Most of people's money, labour and attention had been expended on the acquisition of unnecessary goods.

The production of *shugua* had fortunately spread fast: from Iceland to Chile, from Egypt to Sri Lanka, and beyond. Developed countries which had urgently produced *shugua* equipment to help relieve starvation in China, now needed their production capacity to feed their own population. The competition between private companies in various countries stimulated research and many improvements had been made, including the use of abandoned buildings to grow *shugua*.

Civilization was being destroyed. People were dying in large numbers. Yet courage survived and gradually increased. Would human society die out completely? Or go backwards a thousand years? When will a new point of equilibrium appear? Or would collapse continue to the end? Is there any possibility of a turn of the tide? Or even new life growing from the body of the rotting carcass of the old society? We cannot answer these questions.

The Dog Pens

Ouyang Zhong-hua rarely went to the innermost part of the gorge. Although the dog pen was entirely his own idea and he was well aware what went on there, he had no desire to see for himself. It was now essential for him to make sure the gate was properly closed. He had often reminded the hunchback but did not really trust him.

The partition served rather like a safety bulkhead in a ship. If anything untoward happened in the dog pen, the gate in the partition wall could be immediately closed. Ouyang had just ordered all personnel out of the dog pen and that the gate be locked.

The log fence on either side of it was very high, so that even the most athletic dog could not jump further than half way up; but the numerous newborn puppies could squeeze in and out between the logs.

When the dog pen was started, five hundred wild dogs had been rounded up in four different localities. No one knew how many there were now. With their high-protein diet, the rate of reproduction was very high and the butchers were kept busy day and night. There can have been few other enterprises in this ruined world that were so flourishing. Every enclosure was packed full, and the dogs were so plump they could hardly walk. On his inspection round, Ouyang discovered that the food trap of one of the enclosures was not closed. If the dogs had not been so fat they would certainly have got out and gone in search of food. Ouyang felt a little disgusted at this thought. They would have searched for the kind of food they were used to and he reckoned they would not be choosy about whether it was living or dead. He closed the trap and noticed some half-grown dogs gnawing at what he knew without looking was a human head. . .

He suppressed his instinctive disgust. The nutrient fluid for the *shugua*, consisting of processed excreta, that the dog pen supplied, had to be carefully inspected. If people found such things in it, it would cause a rumpus. They could obviously do nothing about what they had already eaten, but did they never suspect? Ouyang asked himself. Dogs have to eat something after all. It was strange that no one ever asked. But a dog was better to eat than a human—that was common knowledge.

There was a cart-full of dead bodies blocking the gate. Ouyang was annoyed. How many times had he given instructions to bring only the amount needed. If not they had to be taken back. With carts in front of it, he could not check whether the gate was properly closed or not. But on reflection, it was perhaps not a bad idea: if there was a cart full of dead bodies in front, if dogs broke loose they would be less inclined to go to eat live ones. But still he would have to squeeze round it; he did not want to admit to himself that he had been held up by a cartload of dead bodies.

The bodies were of all shapes and sizes, some whole, some partially dismembered. All were naked (that was the rule) and piled up in the cart as they had been found. He was careful not to bump into a clenched fist that protruded, holding a lump of soil for some unknown reason. Because of the nuclear winter, the temperature was very low, so there was not much smell.

Ouyang had got the idea of raising dogs for food on his way to Taibaishan, when he saw a group of people eating dogs that had been feeding on dead humans. He had discussed it with no one. Even now, apart from those working in the dog pens, no one else knew what went on there. This new 'food chain' had appeared spontaneously, but people would have been horrified to discover that it had now become an industry run by humans. Only the most courageous rationalists recognized the value of using dead humans. No other sources of protein existed, while the number of dead bodies increased daily. To allow them to rot away or be scavenged by wild dogs would be showing little respect for human life. Dead bodies had no life, so to use them indirectly to maintain the living was to endow them with new life.

As someone with a historical mission, Ouyang Zhong-hua felt he was entitled to go beyond generally accepted concepts and think purely in terms of the food chain. To turn dead people into food for dogs to feed humans is not very different from using them to improve the soil in order to produce grain. It was merely one link less in the food chain and took less time.

The palisade and the gate were both made of small tree trunks. Inside the dog pen some workers were warming themselves at a fire, most of them scratching their lice and eating dog meat. Some of them were pulling faces and making grotesque gestures; one was walking on all fours imitating a dog. Many of them were deformed and mentally deficient and their appetites were astonishing; they rarely stopped eating when they were not working and were allowed as much dog meat as they wanted. No one in the whole base was better nourished. This was the main reason why they worked hard and were afraid of being fired. Ouyang was convinced that normal people were psychologically incapable of doing the work they did. He had already had the measure of more intelligent workers, who had never had to handle corpses or feed dogs and who felt sick at the smell of boiling dog-meat. Only these handicapped people could do this work without turning a hair. Their corporal deformities and psychology had given them a power of resistance to abnormalities that normal people lack. At this moment they were calmly sitting, eating beside a pile of dead bodies, indifferent to the hideous sight and smell of putrefaction. Marauders had been constantly attacking the base recently and they were plenty of bodies to be found close at hand. Even clearing up outside the stockade provided more than enough.

The gate of the partition wall was closed and tightly secured with ropes so that dogs could not push it open; the hunchback had carried out his orders properly. It was a little strange that the knot had been tied on the *inside* of the gate, through which he had ordered all the workers to leave. Had the hunchback stuck his hand through the log fence to tie the knot? It was difficult for normal people to understand the logic of these people.

He returned to the front part of the gorge, where the dormitories for the abattoir and dog pen workers were. To one side there was a narrow gorge, not very long, which led to a cavern with an area of a few hundred square metres. Two dog pens, each surrounded by thick, high earth walls filled the whole cavern, leaving only a small empty space between them. As soon as Ouyang's footsteps resounded in the silence of the cavern, a number of fierce dogs began to bark. He was always prepared for this, but the sudden sound invariably startled him. The dogs here were specially selected: all very large and fiercer than wolves. As he approached the dogs jumped up at the iron gate, biting the bars and making a lot of noise. They were hungry to the point of fury, Ouyang thought with satisfaction.

Each dog was wearing an unusual form of muzzle, made of leather and metal, with an upper and lower part, joined by a fine metal hinge attached to the dog's collar. Ouyang had a short truncheon hanging from his belt and as soon as he took it in his hand the dogs immediately backed off. It was an electro-shock police truncheon that had been adapted so that it could also open or close all the muzzles simultaneously by remote control. He could stop them barking by closing the muzzles, but now that they were trained, it was enough to show them the truncheon.

Ouyang pulled a rope and a mechanical trap in the iron door fell with a crash. The dogs all rushed into the empty enclosure, as they had been conditioned to do. But on this occasion there were no dead bodies to eat. Ouyang closed their muzzles. He would never dare enter the dog pens when they were open, let alone put a leash on a huge black Tibetan mastiff. He sometimes wondered what would happen if the remote control mechanism failed to work. The specialists who designed and made the muzzles guaranteed their efficacy, but he had nevertheless kept a wind generator working day and night recharging all the batteries. Everything seemed normal today. The electric truncheon was working perfectly., Apart from the Tibetan mastiff, the others dogs went when he ordered them, into the dog pen behind the iron-barred gate; after closing it he hung a straw mat over it, so that the dogs could not be seen from the outside.

He put the Tibetan mastiff in the empty dog pen behind the other earth wall. The mastiff could be clearly seen through the gate of wooden bars. Ouyang went up onto the earth wall by a wooden ladder. The wall was wide enough for a handcart to be pushed along when it was time to feed the dogs. He brought the end of the rope that controlled the iron gate on the other side up on to the wall. He intended to attach it to the hand-cart which was kept, covered with a mat, under an overhanging rock; but thought better of it and attached it to a wedge that he hammered into the rock.

Now he had only to wait. He got closer to the fire and was soon asleep. He dreamed of a volcano, out of which came wine, not lava. He sat cross-legged on the ground, his head in the clouds. The volcano was the size of a flagon, and each time the cup in his hand was empty he tilted the flagon and filled it up to the top. This continued until a clanging sound dispersed the clouds.

They had come! He opened his eyes. The rope was being pulled tight and the pieces of iron struck one against the other. A confused sound of shouting could be heard coming from the entrance to the gorge. His heart sank: there were more men there than he expected, many more. He could hear that they were in an aggressive mood.

He slowed his pace and quickly estimated the number of the shapes he could make out on the other side of the palisade that barred the entrance to the gorge. At least thirty if not more, and they were all armed. He had expected five or six. He couldn't handle so many. . . Nor could he back out. . . He felt his brain become very hot, though his face remained as usual.

Now they were beating on the palisade gate with the butts of their rifles, shouting and cursing as usual. When he approached the gate, he saw Big Ox in the middle. They were all leaders of the Green Guard, every one of them very dangerous.

He pretended he did not want to open the gate and let them in, playing for time. He was in two minds: he was a dead man if he failed but if he missed this opportunity it would be almost as bad. If everything worked out as planned the Green Guard would immediately cease to be a threat. In fact there was nothing to consider. Whether there were five or thirty he could not stop them from entering the dog pen. They had all been excited by the rumour that 'there's a dog in there that fucks a woman', and would not give up until they had seen it with their own eyes. He would have to go ahead.

'Open the door, you fucking windbag!' Big Ox shouted, 'What do you do, hiding in there all day? You're the lucky one. Why don't you let us have a look? It's not fair.'

He had to pretend to look guilty and seem reluctant to admit there was 'a dog in there that fucks a woman'. Otherwise they might get suspicious. Big Ox was stupid but some of the others were not. He invented excuses, contradicted himself on purpose; but did not give them the key,

'If you don't open the gate we'll break it down!' Big Ox roared. The others now felt brave enough to join in, cursing and threatening. A squad leader poked the barrel of his gun through the fence right opposite Ouyang's eye. Even a man like this dared to insult him! Since the day he had clashed with Big Ox, he was less and less respected by the Green Guard and the day was not far away when they would kill him.

He pretended to be frightened. In fact he was genuinely afraid: never before had he faced such naked violence. He realized that he was not as brave as he thought. He was not only frightened. He felt the instinctive desire to run away or beg for mercy. But such reactions do not normally show: he may not have been brave but at least he had will power and self respect. There was no need to conceal his fear now because he had already planned to pretend to be very frightened and then become ingratiating. He smiled tensely. 'I was waiting until the training was complete before asking you, brothers. But since you can't wait I invite you to come in.'

The gun-barrel was removed from the vicinity of his eye. 'None of your fucking smooth talk. If we hadn't got wind of it you'd have kept it for yourself.' The squad leader relieved himself of a noseful of snot. 'He's having a go himself!' There was a roar of obscene laughter.

'Hey Ouyang! What's it like fucking a dog?'

Without saying a word Ouyang opened the gate, let in this group of devils with green headbands and closed it again. It was Ouyang himself who had decided that the Green Guards should be distinguished by green headbands. Now he hated the sight of them. After his quarrel with Big Ox, the Green Guards had become completely uncontrollable and had terrorized the whole base. More than seventy women in the base had been raped and at least two hundred people beaten up.

When they saw Ouyang lead an eighteen or nineteen year-old girl out of a simple shack, their eyes lit up and their voices became shrill and impatient. Big Ox's nostrils quivered with excitement and he thrust his bear-like hand between her legs. Ouyang saw that she was trembling with fear and terrified speechless. She had crossed her arms tightly over her breasts. Before Ouyang took her to the shack, he had sworn to protect her; now he could only say with a smiling face to Big Ox that it would be better to wait until after the show. . .

She was a village girl and could not guess what the 'show' could be. Not long ago she had looked little different from a corpse, but now had a well-rounded figure. Ouyang had chanced to see the hunchback returning to the base carrying a young woman's body, which he reverently put in the shack. Ouyang knew that the workers in the abattoir all abused female corpses, except when outside the base in search of 'supplies'. The hunchback soon found that she was still breathing. Ouyang immediately confiscated her and put a lock on the gate where she alone was confined. His intention had been to save her from rape but he gradually came to regard her as a decoy.

Big Ox had torn the young woman's trousers and the sight of her buttocks as she climbed up the ladder was greeted with wolf-like howls from the Green Guards. Excellent, thought Ouyang to himself. Now they will not notice the mat-covered gate behind them, nor hear any sound of movement there. All would be well as long as they believed that there was only an earth wall behind and in front nothing but a demonstration of 'a black dog fucking a woman'.

Big Ox was in the middle facing the wooden gate and would have the best view; the others were pushing and shoving. The unsatisfied ones demanded to get up on the wall. Ouyang groaned inwardly; he had not thought of this possibility. If they insisted everything would be ruined. Before he could think of an answer someone said that up there they would only get a view of the dog's arse, whereas down below they would be able to see everything. So the idea was abandoned; they left their rifles behind and squeezed forward between the legs of the others.

Even better! Ouyang said to himself. He followed the girl up the ladder on to the top of the broad earthen wall. She was trembling and unsteady on her legs. There was little he could do but help her up. His heart was beating like a drum and his nerves were taut to breaking point. There were 150 dogs—149 not counting the Tibetan mastiff. Could every man take on five dogs? Five Eskimo dogs could handle a polar bear it was said, but polar bears don't have rifles. . . If even a few got away there would be terrible slaughter.

The Tibetan mastiff was very excited, especially when he saw someone on the earth wall—normally a sign that he was about to be fed. Big Ox asked what was the contraption on the dog's head, and Ouyang told him it was to prevent the mastiff from biting the girl, who was almost hysterical with fear on hearing this. Ouyang took her in his arms to comfort her and at the same time removed her clothes. He looked down at the thirty green banded heads below. The men were waiting impatiently for him to send the girl down to the mastiff in the enclosure below.

Ouyang Zhong-hua himself had got someone to start the rumour about the coming performance and make sure it reached the ears of Big Ox. He was sure that he would come here immediately he heard it, perhaps with five or six of the other main leaders. But the plan has misfired: many others had heard the rumour too.

The girl was now naked, her young skin pimpled by the bitter cold of nuclear winter. Her teeth were chattering and she was shivering. One hand hiding her sex, the other her breasts. Her tear-filled eyes, like those of a small dying animal, looked appealingly at Ouyang. She had trusted and relied on him. He had saved her life and looked after her and had been more courteous than she could ever have imagined. He had not even touched her. Now he had stripped her of her clothes himself and on one side there was a terrifying mastiff and on the other a crowd of animals in human form. What was he going to do with her? She had no idea of the rumour that she was Ouyang's plaything and that he had trained a dog to fuck her every day while he watched; or that Ouyang himself had invented this story himself. Now, without a thought for her feelings, he was showing her naked to the Green Guards.

He pulled the ladder up and lowered it on the other side of the earth wall, as if he was about to send her down into the enclosure where the mastiff was. In fact, he did this to prevent the Green Guards from coming up. Every movement had been carefully thought out beforehand.

The guards were getting more and more impatient. Big Ox even fired a few shots from his automatic rifle over Ouyang's head. Keep calm at all costs. Ouyang clenched his teeth, took out the truncheon hidden in his clothing, pulled hard on the rope attached to the bolt on the iron-barred gate, and simultaneously opened the dogs' muzzles by remote control.

The gate fell open with a crash, raising a cloud of yellow dust, like a smokescreen. The dogs burst out like water through a flood-gate, muzzles all open, white teeth showing, and threw themselves in a turbid wave straight at the stupefied Green Guards, before they had time to see what was happening. There was a deafening sound of terrible screaming and blood appeared from under the wave of dogs. Ouyang could see, between the thrashing bodies and struggling limbs, broken bones and throats that had been bitten through, and blood spreading like patches of colour on wet paper. Ouyang covered the girl's eyes with his hand. In her terror, she had forgotten she was naked and pressed up against him, trembling.

It was done. His fears had been unnecessary. In the eyes of men, the Green Guards were predatory devils: for the dogs, they were fresh meat. A hundred and forty nine dogs were more than enough: half of them had not even got near their prey. Dogs were being used as soldiers for the first time. They could gobble up anything... ten times more effective than he had expected. The smell of fresh blood had roused the dogs to a frenzy.

Ouyang held the young woman tightly. He was horrified and relieved in equal measure. A victory! A total victory that belonged to him alone. It was not true that intelligence cannot not defeat brute force, that civilization is no match for barbarism? This was a victory of man over beasts.

Suddenly he heard a shot. A muffled shot, and close by.

It came from under the dogs and their victims. It was not an accidental shot, because it was followed by a continuous burst at maximum speed from an automatic rifle in a steady hand.

The pile of frenzied dogs gradually diminished and Big Ox stood like an iron tower among the dead men and dogs. His head and face were covered with blood, most of it had dripped down on him from above. When the dogs charged, Big Ox had been knocked down and buried under some of his men: he had been firing at them. He stood for a moment cursing Ouyang obscenely and threatening him with terrible vengeance, fucking eighteen generations of his ancestors and promising to wring his neck.

Just before Big Ox turned and fired at him, Ouyang had thrown himself to the ground. A bullet only grazed his collar.

The dogs forced Big Ox back against the wall; he had been badly bitten on the shoulder but he continued to fire at them—regardless of his own men in the way. Those who were still capable of trying to fight off the dogs, and the dogs themselves, had all been wounded. Perhaps there were still some men underneath who had not yet been attacked by dogs, but Big Ox's bullets were more lethal, and soon the ground in front of him was covered with the bodies of dogs and men. Few of the men could move, and the dogs continuing to attack were shot by Big Ox in increasing numbers.

The canine army which he had taken so much trouble to train seemed about to be wiped out. If this bloodthirsty animal should turn on him, even without a gun, Ouyang had no faith in being able to fight him for more than two rounds. At this moment he felt small and useless and entirely without energy. He and Big Ox were two different species. He could only hope that the automatic. . . At that very moment, the firing suddenly stopped. Thank God! The ammunition was finished. It was the sole chance of turning defeat into victory. Six or seven large dogs immediately jumped on Big Ox, and plunged their teeth into his flesh. Big Ox screamed enough to shake the mountain and, with one foot after the other, kicked away two huge dogs with such force that they landed more dead than alive. He fell, but as he did so, broke the back of another dog with the butt of his rifle. His huge body rapidly turned over and over on the ground, knocking dogs out of the way. But the attacks continued from all sides, until he was again buried underneath a wave of dogs. His body was no longer visible or any movement. Victory! Ouyang almost shouted aloud. Too soon. There was another burst of rifle-fire under the tangle of dogs and Big Ox was on his feet again. He was covered with blood, his clothes were torn to shreds and he had been bitten all over, in some places so badly that bone was visible; but he still showed no sign of weakening, and was firing even more furiously, shouting and cursing even louder.

Ouyang, seeing the number of dogs rapidly decreasing, was seized with fear and horror. Big Ox stooped to pick up the rifle of a dead guard but did not stop firing. There was no hope now that he would run out of ammunition. Once this savage animal had killed all the dogs it would be Ouyang's turn. He wondered what to do: run away or fight it out? There was no way of escape and little hope of fighting someone strong enough to hold out against 149 savage dogs. Even if those that were still alive never stopped attacking him. Ouyang had absolutely no desire to fight, he felt like a sponge crushed out of shape by terror. Never in his life had he been so frightened and helpless.

At this moment, the naked girl he had thrown to the ground when the dogs attacked, still lying half under him, gave a sudden cry of extreme terror. Turning his head Ouyang saw the Tibetan mastiff climbing the ladder he had not long ago lowered into the dog pen. The mastiff, excited by the smell of blood had realized that the only way to find something to eat was by going up the ladder. It was not used to such things and its progress was slow. It was thirsty for blood and its red tongue was quivering.

Ouyang's first instinct was to push the ladder over backwards, with the mastiff on it. Then an idea flashed through his mind how to make use of the mastiff. The remote control in the truncheon was regulated so that if any dog with its muzzle open came within 1.5 metres of the truncheon, the muzzle would automatically close. Therefore he had no need to be afraid of the mastiff: it could be allowed to come up the ladder. As he expected, as soon as the animal's front paws touched the top step of the ladder, the muzzle closed and the red tongue was no longer to be seen. Ouyang was a little afraid this might make him stop and even jump off the ladder, so he seized hold of a paw and hauled the mastiff bodily onto the top of the earth wall.

The girl was even more terrified at the sight, and tried to get away. Ouyang needed two hands to hold the mastiff and only the pressure of his body prevented her from moving and the mastiff walked over her.

Big Ox was backed up against the wall while this was going on, and saw nothing. There were now far fewer dogs and he had more freedom of movement. He was forcing the remaining dogs to retreat and was slowly moving forward himself.

Ouyang used all his strength to push the mastiff along the top of the wall in the direction of Big Ox. The mastiff leapt several metres through the air on to Big Ox's back. Its muzzle automatically opened 1.5m away from the remote control. The mastiff's jaws closed on Big Ox's jugular.

Big Ox fell on his back and tried to roll over but the mastiff would not let go. The powerful jaws severed the jugular then pierced the cerebellum. The other dogs joined in and Big Ox died screaming.

For a long time Ouyang dared not believe his eyes, almost expecting to hear another burst of fire and see the devil emerge from under the pile of dead dogs. He had seemed impossible to kill, even more impossible to subdue. Yet now there was a tearing sound of meat being torn off, of bones being crunched by the dogs. Even a pig or a cow in a slaughterhouse did not suffer such indignity; but this barbarous nightmare in his mind, convinced him that this stupid and great brute being quickly torn to pieces, had been destroyed by him! The victory was his! Once more he was master of himself and the world. There was an explosion of wild joy in his mind.

'You're safe,' he shouted to the young woman lying unconscious from shock and horror. He took her in his arms, shook her and kissed her wildly. 'You're safe. We've won!' He determined to train another army of dogs. He would be a match for anyone. No one would dare betray him or challenge him again. As he kissed her pale lips and his hand rapidly caressed her smooth bare skin as far as her sex, a sharp desire rose instantly from his lower spine, and took possession of his brain. Amid the rising stench of blood and the sound of the dogs eating human flesh, with a violence he had never felt before, Ouyang raped the unconscious girl, and experienced an orgasm that almost left him in shock.

The tide ebbed towards the horizon, as fast as it had come up; his body was damp with cold sweat like a shaded beach; exposed to the limitless emptiness, it rapidly shrank. Gasping for breath he raised his head. The cliff opposite looked like a gloomy painted stage backdrop. The cart by the wall was shaking. Below the wall there seemed to be a pit full of red meat. The ground was red. The dead men and the dead dogs were red and the dogs still fighting over the dead. . . He quickly fastened his trousers and dressed the young woman as best he could: there was red between her thighs. The image of Big Ox raising another girl above his head became superimposed on everything else—also red and violent as a whiplash on his brain.

The young woman moaned and was beginning to regain consciousness. Ouyang became very agitated, afraid she would open her eyes. He looked around hastily. The handcart was still shaking. Surely not an earthquake. . . He threw the end of a rope towards it. The straw matting over the cart moved and a man got out. Ouyang was so shocked that everything went black. It took him only a second or two to calm himself. It was the hunchback.

'What are you doing here?'

The hunchback was very frightened. He must have seen everything that had happened. He was trembling as if performing a strange dance, which explained the shaking of the cart.

The smooth face screwed up in a grimace and there was extreme terror in his eyes, as if he were facing a man-eating monster. As soon as Ouyang took a step towards him, he screamed hysterically, turned and ran.

Ouyang cried out but it was too late. The hunchback stumbled over the shaft of the hand-cart, lost his balance and plunged head-first into the dog-pen. Only ten dogs were left alive: they were almost replete but still wanted to kill. They mercilessly pounced on the poor man. By the time Ouyang picked up the truncheon in his hand and closed the muzzles the dogs had already bitten him severely. He managed to stand up, his face half-torn away, and ran away screaming, his short legs sinking into the gory mess underfoot. The dogs continued to jump at him even though their muzzles were closed. He was again caught by the dogs. His demented screaming continued, blood gushed from his mouth and he had no eyes. Watching him, Ouyang thought he understood why the hunchback had hidden in cart. He was the most lecherous of the workers in the dog pen and both sly and cunning. When Ouyang had spoken to someone about starting the rumour he had seen the hunchback eavesdropping. He had hidden in the handcart to watch.

He watched the hunchback struggling and finally used his truncheon to open the muzzles. The dogs all pounced, the hunchback stopped moving and soon only the curve of his back was visible, like an island, above the gore.

Ouyang was stupefied, and slowly turned his head. The young woman at his feet was looking fixedly at him with neither fear nor hatred, only relief and tenderness. She shyly lowered her eyes and pressed her head against his leg

This action brought tears to his eyes. Did she know that he had raped her? That he had let the dogs kill the hunchback because he did not want a living witness to his lapse into animal behaviour. If she too knew all this, was he capable of throwing her into the dog pen as well? He could not stop his tears. When the girl silently put her arms round his leg, apparently to comfort him, he sobbed openly. He raised his head and wept, looking at the long stretch of sky above the gorge. His shoulders shook and he covered his face with his hands, the tears dripped between his fingers. Had he really become an animal, a demon that could make the hunchback mad with fear? Did the blood and flesh around him everywhere signify a man's victory over wild beasts, or a victory of wild beasts over other wild beasts?

He heard again the devastating sound of Chen Pan crying, as he did every day and every night. She had left the Base, alone, swearing never to see him again and refusing the survival he offered her. Since then he had lost his faith in the pursuit of Beauty, in his Green ideals and the world of spiritual man. He thought only of the transformation of mankind by force, imposed by an exceptional man, with absolute power. . .

The Wilderness

She lay naked on the ground watching the leisurely fall of the snowflakes, like a combination of hardly discernible musical notes. She did not feel the cold, perhaps because the fire was not entirely burnt out, or perhaps because her body no longer felt anything.

The primal chaos when earth was first separated from heaven spread evenly over the wilderness. Clouds of fog wandered everywhere like herds of dinosaur in distant times.

In this world humans seemed to exist no longer. The globe was revolving backwards, back to the bleak desolation of the Cretaceous Period.

She had sworn to save the destitute people abandoned by Ouyang, and now she was hurrying through the wilderness. She had taught them how to make *shugua* grow in the nuclear winter. She had shouted until she was hoarse at the people scurrying through the darkness like ghosts. If her heart had been combustible, she would gladly have given it to provide them with a little warmth and light. They had lit fires, in the dark wilderness and clustered round them. Not to heat nutrient fluid for the *shugua*, but human arms or legs: the smoke was that of roasting human flesh. Without needing to be taught, they knew just as well as the most savage beasts, how to bite the necks of their own species. Thousands of years of evolution had given them the ability to judge that human flesh is easier to obtain and more nourishing than such things as *shugua*. But they were different from wild beasts in understanding that roasted meat is better than raw, perhaps with a little salt.

When her clothes were torn off by hands that had retrogressed and become claws, again she hoped that their owners were hungry, and death would be quick. But the men's bellies were already well rounded. All they wanted was to use her body to let out the heat generated by the meat they had eaten. They took it in turns to howl with pleasure on her body. They had fought savagely for precedence. Women were getting scarce now and perhaps would die out altogether.

When she regained consciousness, the male animals had all gone. She lay calmly on the fine straw mat. She could no longer move and had lost all feeling of pain. Her soul was at ease. While being gang-raped her greatest fear was of contact with the men's' bloody mouths, smeared with fat and shreds of meat. Her fear was superfluous. No mouth came near her. Kissing is something that humans do, not those who have reverted to animal behaviour. The rape itself did not bother her too much. To be raped by animals was not a matter of choice, nor a very serious matter.

She looked up. A gap had appeared in the black sky, very faint and only visible when looked at for a long time; yet it was an intimation in the dead sky of a slight chance of survival, a gleam of hope. Through the gap, an infinite distance away, the limit of the universe could perhaps be seen.

Her soul flew up, threading through the crack towards the sky beyond the sky. She slowly closed her eyes and everything receded into the darkness and disappeared, leaving only her heartbeat, both clear and distant, like footsteps a thousand miles away, gradually approaching her.

Epilogue

ca

The Earth

A man is walking alone on the earth.

There is a pack over one shoulder and he is carrying an inflated baby doll on his arm. He walks steadily, neither quickly nor slowly. You can see at once that he is used to walking long distances. He has already crossed countless mountains and rivers and will cross as many again.

Yet he stops suddenly and does not want to go on.

A warm ray of sunlight mysteriously shines on the barren ground at his feet. The destitute land seems suddenly full of longing. He feels that he has arrived, but does not know where, or why. If he has not arrived, why had he walked on and then stopped several times?

He puts down his pack and the baby, takes off his shirt and begins to scratch the earth.

He sees the white bones of a skeleton nearby. On the way here, even stopping for a short time, he always avoided skeletons. He does not move away and does not mind at all that the skeleton is near him. More surprising, he even considers it beautiful. It is all he can do not to keep turning to look.

He loosens the soil on a very small patch, because he has very few seeds, seeds he found, one by one, in the dead earth along the way. He rubs the soil until it is very fine and greedily absorbs the heat of the sun. He finds a fragment of ancient coloured pottery half hidden in the ground. What is left of the design looks like the eye of an ancestor.

He sows the seeds one by one. There is a slight breeze. Hearing the voice of the baby, he turns his head.

Perhaps blown by the wind, or for some other reason, the baby is lying across the white rib cage of the skeleton. Perhaps it is the wind too that causes the baby to make endearing sounds and stretch out his arms as if wanting to be hugged.

The man notices on the ground below the rib cage, where the heart would have been, that a first tender green shoot has grown in the wilderness.

THE END

www.ingramcontent.com/pod-product-compliance
Lightning Source LLC
Chambersburg PA
CBHW060528310726
48982CB00002B/464

* 9 7 8 1 9 0 5 2 4 6 5 0 2 *